THE LAST WIZARD
OF ENERI CLARE

APRIL LEONIE LINDEVALD

BALBOA
PRESS
A DIVISION OF HAY HOUSE

Balboa Press books may be ordered through booksellers or by contacting:

Balboa Press
A Division of Hay House
1663 Liberty Drive
Bloomington, IN 47403
www.balboapress.com
1 (877) 407-4847

Because of the dynamic nature of the Internet, any web addresses or links contained in this book may have changed since publication and may no longer be valid. The views expressed in this work are solely those of the author and do not necessarily reflect the views of the publisher, and the publisher hereby disclaims any responsibility for them.

The author of this book does not dispense medical advice or prescribe the use of any technique as a form of treatment for physical, emotional, or medical problems without the advice of a physician, either directly or indirectly. The intent of the author is only to offer information of a general nature to help you in your quest for emotional and spiritual well-being. In the event you use any of the information in this book for yourself, which is your constitutional right, the author and the publisher assume no responsibility for your actions.

Any people depicted in stock imagery provided by Thinkstock are models, and such images are being used for illustrative purposes only. Certain stock imagery © Thinkstock.

Print information available on the last page.

ISBN: 978-1-5043-5446-2 (sc)
ISBN: 978-1-5043-5448-6 (hc)
ISBN: 978-1-5043-5447-9 (e)

Library of Congress Control Number: 2016905489

Balboa Press rev. date: 06/13/2016

ACKNOWLEDGMENTS

WITHOUT THE UNSHAKEABLE FAITH AND continual encouragement of so many people, this book might never have seen the light of day. My heartfelt thanks go to Suzanne Cardinal, who urged me to write, and even took me along with her to the Santa Barbara Writer's Workshop, where my eyes were opened to many wonders. I am grateful to Rachel Cobb Chamness, Tyler Lee, Marge D'Ottavio, and Shameakha Flood, who read the beginning chapters, and enthusiastically begged for more. Special thanks go to Ethan Lindevald and Robert Haining, who made valuable suggestions to improve the content, and to Judy Turek, who edited and critiqued the original manuscript with an eagle eye and a gentle insistence on making every page the best it could be. I am also indebted to dear friends, such as Michael Palmer, Marie Dodd, Doug Wright, Elizabeth Morgan, Gwen Johnston, Mary Fernandez, Jewell Aull, Shari Ahlers, the Goddess Circle, Ian Lindevald, and Cindy Cooper, Dave, Doreen, and Michael Levesque, and many other family and friends who kept up a steady stream of encouragement. I owe a debt, as well, to every English teacher I ever had who fostered in me a love of language, and told me I had talent. Many thanks must go to Sunrise House in Montauk, the perfect venue for a writer's retreat in the dead of winter – where the ocean's rhythm, a roaring fire, a hearty breakfast, and an absence of distraction cannot help but conspire to foster inspiration.

I wish to acknowledge Stewart, who made it into the story as a representative of the many canine companions who have deigned to share their lives with me, to the Tvrdik family who loaned me their name, and to all the characters you will meet in these pages, who took up residence in my head and would not be silenced until I had taken down their story.

Most of all, I dedicate this work to my parents, Ernst Paul and Lorraine Lindevald, who valued reading and education over all things, bought us books when there was barely money for food, and instilled in us a lifetime love of reading and story. They also encouraged me at every turn to follow my dreams and never to doubt what was possible with a little determination. And, to my wonderful husband, Brian J. Abrams, who never flags in his loving support and gives me the freedom to spend time on those pursuits that bring me joy.

CONTENTS

PROLOGUE

Out on the harbor, dawn was only just beginning to paint the horizon, but the woman stood on deck with her companion, leaning on a rail, and allowing her mind to roam where it would. They were taking the early ferry back to the city after a weekend with family. The woman was not a person who saw the dawn often, but they had places to be this day, and tasks to do, so they had made an early start. The city was still sleeping, for the most part, and looked lovely and peaceful at this distance. The first morning rays glinted off of its steel and glass, making the buildings look bejeweled, enchanted. She was enjoying these moments of calm before the day would begin in earnest. A chill breeze whipped off the water, sharp and invigorating. She shivered a bit, and sighed with contentment.

As the sky lightened, the woman caught sight of a dark shape floating in the water, not far from the ferry's trajectory. "George," she said, pointing, and her utterance tore the fragile fabric of peace that had surrounded them, "do you see something out there?"

"Hmmm…" George craned his neck and squinted in the direction she was waving. "Yes, there is something out there – some sort of little boat, really small. Not even a motor boat. And there's a woman – no, a man standing in it."

"He doesn't seem to be in any trouble, does he? He's not waving at us, or trying to be rescued. He's not fishing. Wonder what he's doing out there so early?"

"In his pajamas, too. And not a youngster, either – look at all that white hair."

They laughed. "You know, George," she said, "in this city you could see just about anything, and no one would think it the slightest bit strange."

"Amen to that. So long, old man. Hope you find what you are looking for on this fine day."

The woman nodded, watching the strange figure in the little dinghy recede as the ferry continued on towards its destination….

ONE

THE NIGHT IT ALL BEGAN

HER LAUGHTER RANG OUT LIKE lovely little tuned bells. "Benjin! Benjin, stop it," she whispered.

"I can't help myself – you are so irresistible, and I…I am drunk with anticipation." Sounds of a scuffle came from behind the screen that divided her cubicle from the rest of the dormitory, and then the musical laughter again. Her voice was clear despite the screen. "Benjin, you have to stop now. You'll wake him."

"Who? The old man? He's on the other side of the house. No danger there."

"Not him. You know…Tvrdik. He'll hear us, and he might try to follow."

In the darkness behind the thin partition, a pale-haired, gawky youth was indeed wide awake in his bed, hearing every word, not daring to stir or breathe.

"Small surprise," the deeper voice sneered. "He follows you around everywhere like a lost puppy."

"Benjin, don't be cruel. We're supposed to be his friends."

"All right, I'm sorry…but that one is such a sap. He gets on my nerves. He's too sensitive, and I don't like the way he is so attached to you."

Behind the partition, ice-blue eyes winced in silent pain.

"He's just a little young, is all."

"He's seventeen, just a year younger than we are."

7

"I didn't mean in years. I meant…how he is. Shy. You never give him a chance, Benjin. He can be sweet…"

"Now you're the sap, my dear. In any case, he's the Master's little pet. Everything by the book. Anything old Xaarus says. He would never approve of what we are about to do."

"Which is why I said we should be careful not to wake him; it would be hard to explain. He might even fetch Xaarus and try to stop us."

The pale youth twitched, and his ears pricked now to catch their exchange. *What was it they were about to do*, he thought, *and why would I not approve?* His throat went dry, and gooseflesh covered his arms as he sensed danger. It was bad enough to find out like this that Benjin and Ailianne were…together. His sixth sense was telling him something else was afoot that was far more upsetting. *What should I do? Should I stand up and confront them now, and demand to know what they are planning?* But then he would have to admit he'd been eavesdropping on their entire conversation. *That would be awkward. Should I run and get the Master? And be branded forever as a snitch, a spoilsport, the Master's pet?* He held his tongue, and strained to hear more. They were still talking in hushed tones, amid sounds of what were perhaps items being packed into a carrysack

"I have the book," Benjin said. "Is everything else there?"

"Yes, yes. I checked three times," the girl hissed. "Only hurry! The moon will be setting soon, and we will miss our mark."

"You sound nervous, girl. Are you having second thoughts? You aren't afraid, are you?" He spoke this last with a faint air of derision, a challenge in his voice.

"No…no, really. I'm just excited, and eager to have done with it."

"You won't be sorry, my queen. You are far too good for this dull existence. In a few hours, you will feel a power coursing through your veins that the old man hasn't even dreamed of. We will be fulfilling our greater destiny, you and I. Think of it! Masters of time, and life, and death – powerful beyond imagination – immortal! We will have anything we wish for – fame, riches, youth, and beauty that won't fade. And we will be together forever. Ailianne, you're trembling."

The laughter again, but this time with an edge of uncertainty, which was only perceptible to someone who knew her well.

"I...I am excited, trembling with passion. Oh, Benjin, kiss me again. Steel my nerves, fire my resolve. Tell me again how good it will be..."

Now it was the pale youth who was trembling, but in terror. Desperate to keep silent, he struggled to push down the wave of horror and dread that overtook him. Certain they would hear his shuddering breaths, he shoved his fist into his mouth and squeezed his eyes closed. *What should I do? What in heaven's name are they playing with?* They were not yet adults, ill-equipped to handle the dark and dangerous forces they were attempting to unleash. Xaarus had often cautioned them against exploring the old magic without guidance. Hadn't they been listening? How could they both be so foolish, so rebellious when there was so much at stake? Overwhelmed with fear for his classmates, but deeply wounded at their snubs, Tvrdik was paralyzed with confusion.

"Let's go. It's almost time." The girl's voice sounded further away. He heard footsteps; a door opened and closed quietly. Still frozen, and uncertain what course to take, he sat another moment praying fervently that Benjin and Ailianne had stumbled onto something they did not understand and would fail to activate. They would slink back to bed in a few hours, half embarrassed, half amused, and in the morning the whole incident would be a dim, unpleasant memory, better unspoken and soon forgotten. Perhaps they only wanted to sneak off to lie together anyway, the specter of danger lending more passion to their tryst. Of course, that was what this was all about. An icy pang stopped Tvrdik's heart for a moment, and he moaned in agony. Six years he had worshipped Ailianne. In her classic beauty and grace, her keen mind and remarkable talent, he saw all that he idealized in the fair sex. She was kind to him, as a sister. But he had hoped for, longed for so much more. Well, tonight had wiped away any doubts he might have had about which way her affections tended. *Fine,* he thought, wounded. *If it was to be like that, the two of them could have each other. In fact, they deserved each other, and they deserved whatever fate they were courting for themselves.* Why should he care a whit if they insisted on being so blind and stupid? Oh gods! What was he doing? How could he even *think* such spiteful thoughts when the two of them could be in real danger? They had been his schoolmates, his only friends all these years. They had never done anything to harm him on purpose, and now...what if something terrible happened? He could never live with himself. He had to go after them and stop them. He had to try.

The tall, gangly youth leapt from his cot, pulled on a tunic and leggings, fumbled to adjust a pair of wire-rimmed spectacles on his pale face, slipped on his boots and bounded to the door, careful to close it behind him. Checking to make sure he was not being watched, he padded down the path to Xaarus' front gate, clenching his teeth as he attempted to swing it open and shut without the usual loud creak. Once on the main path, he paused and looked both ways. He cursed himself for allowing his friends such a head start. *Which way had they gone?* There was no sign of them on the road in either direction. If he understood them correctly, they were planning some sort of sorcerer's ritual, but there were several places they might have chosen for that. He did not think they would have headed back toward the palace, where there was every chance they would be detected or detained. *The other way then…but where?*

Tvrdik ventured a few steps and stopped, scratching his blonde head and combing through the lessons in his mind for anything in his apprentice wizard's training that might help now. Precious minutes ticked by. The moon was on the horizon, about to disappear. *Think!* With a fumbling incantation and a sharp gesture of his right hand, he threw before him a handful of glowing dust which settled itself on the energetic wake his schoolmates had left in their hasty escape, showing their trajectory in clear trails of light. It was well after midnight, and they had been so confident that they were alone that they had not even bothered to make themselves invisible or cover their tracks. Tvrdik sighed in relief and hurried down the path, following the shining flinders that pointed out the way Benjin and Ailianne had gone. He was so intent on his quarry that he did not notice another figure, cloaked and almost invisible against the night sky, gliding along behind him and shadowing his every move.

Tvrdik was almost running now, feeling a sense of urgency he could not name or comprehend. Down the riverwalk he ran, past all the familiar landmarks, then up a hidden side path that led away from the river and into the woods. He thought he knew where he was going now, a small clearing among the tall trees where they had all gone to practice invocations at dawn, and to learn the secrets of the faerie realm in the pristine wood. Sure enough, there was already a fire burning in the clearing when he came upon it. They had drawn a circle on the ground, lit the fire in the center, and surrounded it with an assortment of odd objects and some sort of unfamiliar runes drawn in charcoal about the mossy perimeter.

Ailianne and Benjin stood within the circle. She held up a wooden goblet containing some liquid, and her companion read incantations aloud in some foreign-sounding tongue, from a huge, ancient-looking book. The hair stood up on the back of Tvrdik's neck. He threw himself behind a large tree where he hoped his presence would not be detected. He need not have worried. They were so far immersed in their rituals that they never would have noticed an observer – or two – standing in the wood.

The moon had set, but the flames illuminated the scene clearly. Terrified, Tvrdik watched the scene in helpless fascination, wondering whether to call out to them, or jump out and rush forward, arms waving like a madman. He stood still. Switching to the common language now, Benjin held the book high and intoned, "Lord of the darkness, of the formless void, of the chaos before there was life, of the nothingness wherein all power, all potential, and all the impetus for creation and destruction, hear us! Keepers of the Ancient Magic, the old ways, the first and eldest, we bid you acknowledge us now, we who come to you as willing servants. Our hearts and minds we offer you, in exchange for your secrets. We have mingled our life-blood in this cup, which we pour out to you as a worthy tribute and sacrifice." Ailianne emptied the contents of her goblet onto the flame, which hissed and jumped and turned colors. Only then did Tvrdik notice the fresh, raw cuts on both of their arms, still oozing red.

"Fill us with your primal power," Benjin continued, "your knowledge of the infinite, as we call forth your essence in this place so that we may pay homage to the Old Ones. Come forth from your sleep....NOW!" Benjin began reciting the foreign words again in a sort of mantra, over and over, the same unfamiliar phrase. But already a wind was whipping up in the clearing, rustling leaves and branches, tossing Ailianne's long golden hair back from her face and feeding the flames. The great book's pages rifled and flipped about. For a moment, Ailianne looked confused, as Benjin continued his recitation unfazed. In seconds, the wind had intensified, accompanied by a deep rushing sound that drowned out the young man's endless droning. And then, without warning, something rose up in the center of the circle, something that was there, and not there, like a dark mass rearing up from the earth; a tear in the fabric of the air. Black, formless – a widening, bottomless space devoid of light, or hope, or joy. Tvrdik thought he heard laughter again, but not the little tuned bells he knew and loved so well. This was a laughter that froze him to the bone and turned his legs to quivering jelly.

Somewhere in the expanding dark patch appeared two hungry red eyes – eyes with no sense of soul behind them. Benjin had stopped chanting. His strong, young body began to shake. The power he had so carelessly invited to possess him was streaming into the fragile container of his physical form and overwhelming it. Ailianne was by his side in an instant.

"Drop the book, Benjin. This is all wrong. You cannot control it…let it go." she shouted over the roar of rushing air and booming laughter that surrounded them.

"I can't!" he responded, looking more surprised than anything, "It won't free my hands."

Alarmed, she grabbed at the other end of the book with her own hands to wrench it from his grasp. But, at her touch, sparks flew from the tome, and her hands became fixed to its cover. Trapped, the two of them stood together in the circle, facing each other, the ancient volume between them holding them fast. Hair and clothing blew about furiously, and the rushing noise rose to deafening levels. The fragile mortal frames of the two young students convulsed violently, as raw power they could not contain coursed through them. Ailianne cried out. This was too much for Tvrdik, who leapt from his hiding place and ran toward the circle, shouting, "Ailianne. Ailianne!"

"Stay back!" she ordered, recognizing his voice, "I cannot hold it." She turned her face toward him and their eyes locked. In those beloved eyes, which had always been bright and beautiful to him, he now saw agony and abject terror. His own eyes widened, recognizing the depths of fear and despair in her lovely face. It was to be his last memory of her, seared into his soul for all time, for as he lunged forward to drag her out of the circle, some force knocked him off his feet and a commanding voice rang out, "No! Do not touch them."

Tvrdik collapsed on the ground. A flash of light more brilliant than a dozen suns blinded him for an instant, and he lay there with his hands over his face. When he could once again open his eyes, he saw Xaarus, his Master, standing nearby like an avenging angel, tall and imposing, brows drawn together in concentration, sharp eyes darting fiery purpose over his crooked nose. His staff was raised high in the air, a stream of light pouring from its tip straight at the dark mass in the circle. The old man was shouting out spells and incantations, his voice almost eclipsed by the roaring sound that filled the wood. His face was set in grim determination, power and light exploding from every part of him, pushing back the hostile blackness, and trying to surround its hapless victims with some sort of shield.

Tvrdik closed his eyes again in exhaustion and relief. Xaarus was here. Everything would be alright. There was another flash, several soul-wrenching screams, the sound of an explosion, and then, silence – a silence rendered more profound by contrast to what had preceded it. Breathless moments passed. At last, the pale, thin youth opened his eyes and let them focus on the Master wizard, standing stock still before him. "Master," the boy ventured, his voice breaking, "Master, I followed them, but I did not try to stop them. I should have stopped them. Thank the gods you are here."

"No, Tvrdik," came the whispered answer through the stillness, "I have come too late."

As the meaning of those words washed over his frayed consciousness, Tvrdik turned his head toward what had been the circle. In the light of Xaarus' glowing staff, he saw. There was no fire, no book, no goblet, no carry-sack, no objects placed around the edges. There was no sign of Benjin or Ailianne. Just a patch of scorched ground, and wisps of smoke still twisting and drifting up toward the starry sky. The ice-blue eyes stared in disbelief, then turned back to Xaarus, who stood rigid, staff in hand, a stricken look on his ashen face. Tvrdik had never seen his Master with such an anguished expression…the look of defeat.

"We have failed them, boy," the old wizard said. "They are gone."

T W O

TWELVE YEARS LATER

THIS PART OF THE ANCIENT forest was so remote, so untouched, so close to the heart of the Great Woods, that tree fairies and water sprites still played openly in the changing light. They were rarely seen in the inhabited lands, edged out by civilization and harassed by the curious and the cruel alike. But here was deep quiet and security. Here an intruder rarely stepped, and the little naïve nymphs delighted in their daily games without even the thought of being alert or cautious. Only one of them noticed the tall stranger, hooded and cloaked, approaching the waterfall with silent tread. Her name was Ondine, and she was by nature more curious than most – more aware, it seemed, of a greater landscape beyond the confines of her tiny world, and of the dramas that might play out there.

She paused in her pirouette and regarded the man. Old he seemed, like the trees she knew or the stone shelf on which her waterfall splashed. Old, but strong, like those things. The part of his face she could see was lined, she couldn't tell from laughter or care, or maybe both. As he approached, he tossed back his hood, and she noted the full mane of pure white hair, the slightly beaky nose, and eyes as deep as the pools below in which she made her home. Dark eyes, into which one could fall and be lost…. She shrank back in terror as he leaned into the streaming water inches from where she hovered, sure she would be discovered. And yet, she could smell no aroma of malevolence about him, no cruelty or darkness. Only a deep sadness that hung all around him, and perhaps …yes…a whiff of urgency. Ondine darted behind a nearby leaf as the man splashed his face with sweet, cool water, and filled his large hands with its goodness to quench his thirst.

He ran those hands over his face and hair, as if smoothing away disturbing thoughts, and then, replacing the hood, backed away from the falls and picked up a gnarled walking stick. Ondine could not take her eyes off of the stranger as he strode away between the ancient trees. Just before he turned the corner following the cliff face, she started, as he momentarily winked out of existence completely! The little nymph gasped, blinked…but no. There he was after all, heading around the bend. Ondine furrowed her tiny brow. She must have imagined it. But how, when she had not even shifted her gaze for an instant? All around her the rush of the water, the music of birdsong, and the laughter of her sister naiads combined in a natural symphony. The sunlight filtered down in warm patches that described a perfect, lovely spring day. And Ondine shivered as she sensed to the depths of her core that nothing would ever be the same again.

There was no mistaking that waterfall. It was exactly as it had been described to him – idyllic, powerful, and sonorous in its rush over the rock face, three times the height of a tall man, and broad. Swollen now with early spring thaws, it formed a sparkling curtain over the cliff-side on its journey to the wide pools below, and eventually into the stream that carried its waters away to far-off realms. Surrounded by supple young birches and scented flowering vines, it passed the day in a sort of filtered green haze, interrupted by rainbows, where patchy sunlight shone through droplets bouncing off the rocks below. Only a few moments in this place, and the rhythmic falling waters, the colorful lights and sweet fragrances, the warm sun on one's face would wash away burdens, soothe tired muscles, and lull troubled dreams to sleep. "Perfect," the old man muttered to no one in particular, "the perfect place to escape, or to hide."

He splashed his face with the welcome coolness, and drank his fill of the sweet water before picking up his walking stick and continuing on his way. It could not be far now. His source had said to follow the cliff's edge around behind the falls, and then to bear right through a stand of tall oaks until you came to a giant old tree with three trunks joined as one. From its shelter, he had been told, you could see the little clearing, and the cottage would be there. The old man found his instructions to be quite clear, and only a few moments later, he was peering around from behind the great triple oak at a small hermit's dwelling so in harmony with its woodland surroundings that it was scarcely distinguishable from its environment. It was round in design, constructed of stones and logs which were well-matched, and mud-chinked. There was smoke puffing from a hole in the woven branch roof, suggesting a hearth of sorts, and a woodpile stacked in neat bundles before what looked like the vine-covered front door. Several homemade buckets of various sizes stood about the forecourt, some empty, some upended as sitting places, and others filled with water. There was an assortment of flat stones that looked as if they might have been used for table and chairs, mortar, pestle and drying surfaces. Beyond the cottage spread a small rectangular garden, walled about with sticks and stones, and showing first shoots of what might be potatoes, leeks, squash, beans, peppers and various herbs. Everything looked neat and tidy. *Cozy,* the cloaked visitor observed, and then, *resourceful.*

He pulled back behind the tree as vines parted and the cottager appeared in his doorway, engrossed in his chores. He was wearing soft ankle boots, extremely worn, and a long, rather threadbare tunic that reached below his knees, belted about the waist with a length of thick vine. Some sort of leggings, ingeniously patched with pieces of ancient blanket, closed the gap between the torn robes and disintegrating shoes. From this distance, his head seemed enormous, if you counted the huge bush of pale, uncombed hair, and the straw-colored beard, untrimmed and weedy. The hermit's age was impossible to determine. He was tall and dreadfully thin, but moved with surprising grace and strength, attending to his tasks with the energy of a younger man. But his shoulders seemed stooped, pressed down by some terrible weight, and his face was almost totally obscured by the cloud of white hair that surrounded and covered it. And was it the white of advancing years, or a pale gold such as denizens of northern climes boasted? *No,* thought the old man, peering out from behind his tree. *This cannot be the man I seek. It is not possible. I have come all this way and wasted precious time for nothing.* But at that precise moment, the cottager, checking the sun's progress across the sky, turned his face up and squarely toward the concealed visitor, revealing piercing blue eyes behind wire-rimmed spectacles. That face was unmistakable. The man in the cloak thrust the back of his hand up against his mouth to muffle the involuntary sound that escaped him. In a few heartbeats, his control was restored, but as he continued to watch the threadbare hermit in front of his hand-crafted little house, silent tears overflowed his dark eyes and slid down both sides of his nose.

———— ⬥ ————

The sun was already well along on its homeward journey when the weary hermit strode out of the woods into his forecourt, carrying a bark sling full of dried kindling collected from the forest floor. The woods were always generous to him in their yielding of a thousand needful things, and he remembered to thank the trees for their bounty as he approached his simple dwelling. So wrapped in this meditation was he that he almost failed to notice the visitor sitting on an overturned bucket beside the woodpile, until he nearly tripped over him. Startled, the hermit dropped his load of sticks and then scrambled to retrieve a few before seeming to remember that some sort of greeting was in order. He could not recall a visitor ever passing through these parts in the entire time he had been living there, and this one had appeared in a most unorthodox manner.

The stranger sat, cloaked and hooded, very still and straight-backed, two hands resting atop a gnarled walking stick. The hermit reached out a calloused hand. "Sir," he sputtered in a voice cracking from long disuse, "please pardon my confusion. It is so seldom that my home is graced with visitors out here, and you took me by surprise." His words and syntax gave him away. This was no simple woodsman. The intruder neither spoke nor moved. The cottager tried again. "Is there something I can do for you, sir? Are you lost? Is there someone or something you seek that I may help you to? Or perhaps you desire some rest after a long journey. Food? A stopping place for the night? Speak up. My home is humble, but such as I have I am happy to share." No response. The hermit threw up his hands, "Oh, where are my manners? You must be thirsty from the trail. Let me get you some cool water…it is quite sweet here…" He bustled about inefficiently trying to find a cup and a ladle. The visitor rose in one slow movement, leaning on his cane, and stood tall and erect, a somewhat intimidating sight. The hermit froze, blinked several times behind his spectacles, then took a step backward, almost toppling himself over a stone in the yard. A commanding voice emerged from somewhere within the black hood, "I have need of the services of a wizard. I was told that a very good one lives here, in this place, and I have made a very long and difficult journey to find him."

The hermit let the wooden cup he had just found fall from his hand. He stood very still for a moment, pulled his spectacles from his face and mopped his brow with his other sleeve. Staring at his shoes, he replied at last, "I am sorry to tell you, you were misled. There are no wizards in these parts, nor, to my knowledge, any at all in the world anymore. They say the last of them vanished over twelve years ago and has never been seen since. I regret you have come so far for naught. But you must share a meal with me and rest awhile before you head for home."

"It is a matter of great urgency. I will not be put off lightly," the stranger spoke again. "Would gold, perhaps, help my cause?"

The hermit frowned, "Sir, I do not test you, nor do I want your money. I only tell you truthfully that there are no wizards here, and I cannot tell you where you might find one."

"Tvrdik," the stranger's tone became tender, familiar. He reached up with one hand and pulled back the black hood from his face. In his other hand, the walking stick he carried began to grow, thicken, elongate, until it was a sturdy, seven foot staff. He spoke again, "Tvrdik, do you not know me? I confess I scarcely recognize you…"

The hermit's mouth fell open with a sharp intake of breath. His eyes were blinking as if to erase some unbidden mirage that refused to vanish. His lips tried to form words and failed. Then slowly, he sank to his threadbare knees before the tall figure. "Master," was the only word he could utter aloud, "Oh, Master…"and he buried his face in his hands.

"Tvrdik, Tvrdik, it is I who should be on my knees to you, though I confess at my age, I do not think it a very wise course. *I* was the one who left *you*, at a very crucial time in your young life, and now look in what a state I find you! Can you ever forgive me, son?"

Tvrdik did not raise his eyes. He was shaking bodily. "How can you ask me that, Master? 'A wizard's ways are inscrutable,' you always said. It is not for me to question, to forgive or not to forgive."

The older man crossed the distance between them, and hooked his left hand under Tvrdik's arm to raise him to his feet. "What nonsense! Did I teach you that? Feh. Honestly, if I were you, I would be more than a little disgruntled. Would it help if I told you that I never, ever intended to leave you alone here, nor have I ever for a single moment stopped trying to get back to you these entire twelve years?"

"Master?"

"Come, come, you are a man now. My name is Xaarus."

"Yes, Master...Xaarus. But then, why did you disappear? What happened? Where have you been all this time? And why are you here now?"

"Slow down, boy. That is a story of classic proportion, and I promise to tell it to you. But for now, it seems to be getting darker. I do find myself a bit weary, and would welcome a chair by the fire and some of that food you offered."

Tvrdik seemed to come to life. "Of course! Come in, come in, and welcome. Let me see what there is to offer..." And he took the arm of his old teacher and escorted him through the vine-covered entry into the little stone house.

THREE

REUNIONS AND TALES TO TELL

INSIDE, THE COTTAGE SEEMED MORE spacious than it looked from without: a square-ish, single room, furnished simply with a few homemade wooden benches, a small table, a straw pallet in one corner with a few threadbare blankets, some makeshift shelves with a few supplies and a number of dog-eared old books. Tvrdik had built the place with great care, perhaps even a little magic, but the early spring nights could turn chill, and Xaarus was very glad of the fire. He sat, eyes closed, absorbing the welcome warmth and considering how to plead his case, as Tvrdik bustled about the space, preparing some sort of meal for them and apologizing for the rudeness of just about everything in the process. Xaarus smiled. It was good to know that at the heart of things, not much had really changed between them. But just how deep did the young man's wounds go?

They managed to avoid any meaningful conversation until they had polished off large bowls of hearty soup made from last season's potatoes and leeks, some rustic brown bread and hard cheese, and warm cider. Well satisfied, Xaarus leaned back and sighed. "I was worried about your well-being here, Tvrdik, but you seem to manage well enough for yourself. This house is sturdy and comfortable, and you've learned to grow food for yourself. How did you manage the bread and cheese?"

Tvrdik took the compliment with humility. "Every now and then I make the trek to the nearest village and trade for a few things I need: flour, sugar, cheese, cider, occasionally tools, books when I can find any." At the mention of books, the young man unconsciously fingered his spectacles, re-adjusting them on the bridge of his nose. Xaarus flashed back to a memory of grinding those lenses himself when it had become clear that the boy's eyes were weak. Helpful appliances like glasses were not common in the kingdom then, but there were advantages to being a wizard, and having access to the knowledge of many times and places. Xaarus was pleased to see they still seemed to be useful to his young pupil. Drifting back to the present moment, he realized Tvrdik was still talking. "Sometimes I do odd jobs or bring herbs to sell. Or I mix a few potions for the sick and injured. I have done a bit of simple healing now and then. I suppose you would be happy to know I retained something of your teaching from the old days. At any rate, the people know me and are kind enough. Mostly, they leave me alone."

"As you prefer it?"

"As I prefer it."

A pregnant silence hung in the air between them, heavy with tales untold and explanations withheld. Tvrdik, as the junior member, decided to break the ice. He stood and snatched up a stick to stir the fire, his back to Xaarus as he spoke.

"After Ailianne and Benjin were…were…after they died, I nearly lost my mind with grief. I felt so lost and helpless. The shock of it was…well… horrible. The only thing I could think of to do was to throw myself into my studies, to work harder. I think…I think I foolishly must have believed there was some way I could bring them back if I learned enough. I was young and shallow. I never considered what you must have been going through as well. You seemed to me pre-occupied and distant. I felt very alone. And then, barely a month later, you just vanished! I was bewildered. At first I thought you must be ill, or engrossed in some important project or another. I waited for you to return, but heard nothing from you. As the weeks passed, I began to be alarmed, and went looking for you. I searched your rooms, your workshop, your favorite teaching places, even the palace itself. There was no sign you had even been to any of them in ages. I screwed up my courage and asked around. No one had seen you; no one spoken to you. No one could think of anything you had said or done or written to predict this sudden absence. Soon after, I think the king, in great alarm, ordered a kingdom-wide search, and everyone was talking about your disappearance in hushed tones and wondering if you had come to harm. But by then, I had reached another conclusion."

Tvrdik paused to put down his makeshift poker and sat on a free bench, his gaze on some far-off time and place. "I had become convinced that you were testing me somehow – that I was supposed to find you, or that you would contact me in some cryptic riddle or another that I would have to unravel to discover where you were hiding. I pored over my books, my notes – went over everything you had ever told me in my head a thousand times. I tried to fit in with the castle folk, but you had kept us so isolated that I did not really know anyone, and they didn't know what to make of me. I couldn't go back to my home; there would be no welcome there for me any longer. As the months dragged on and there was still no word of you, I think I started to vanish myself, bit by bit. One day, I threw a few things in a bag and just walked away. And kept walking. I had no destination, no purpose in mind. I don't even really have any clear memories of that time...how I survived, who I met, places I passed through...it's all a blur. I lived inside my head and replayed the events of the year before, again and again, wondering if somehow it had been all my fault, and if this purgatory of a life were my punishment. I just kept putting one foot in front of the other and sinking further into despair, even madness. I guess I began to avoid the company of people, or they began to avoid me. I cannot tell. But at some point I wandered into these woods. I walked far and wide through the forests, barely keeping myself alive, and hardly noticing my surroundings. It is a miracle I did not end up a meal for some bear or pack of wolves in those days.

"One day, I chanced upon that waterfall you must have passed just around the bend up there, and I stopped. It was so beautiful, so soothing, so perfect.... I just stood there staring at it for hours, drinking in the sound, the cool spray on my face, the rainbows and diamonds of light, the scent of honeysuckle. It was spring then too, I remember – a time of new beginnings and awakenings. It all seemed so idyllic, that for the first time I began to relax and let the heavy burdens and inner demons I had carried so far fall away and dissolve in those deep pools below. For the first time in months, I began to feel peace."

Tvrdik stole a glance at Xaarus, who sat with eyes closed and head bowed, then continued his narrative, "I took off my clothes and clambered up the rocks, to the top. I found a flat stone to stand on and stood listening to the roar below. I raised my arms high, closed my eyes, and leapt into the falls. I was certain I would be drowned in the turbulent waters or dashed on the rocks, but it seemed a brief inconvenience to be suffered so that I could either join my lost friends, or else simply cease to be. I am not proud of this, mind you, but at the time I was so lost that it seemed logical – an obvious solution, a good way to stop the pain, and a fine place to end my miserable, brief life."

There was a long pause, as the young man relived for a moment all the feelings he was recounting in such detail. Twelve years had not dulled their sharpness a bit. After a few minutes had passed, Tvrdik seemed to return to the present. "I woke up cold and hungry, lying sprawled on the far bank of the pool, sore but unharmed. I had no idea how I had survived the ordeal, or how I had come to be out of the water. Nor how long I had been lying there unconscious. But I took it as a sign that whatever gods there were meant for me to live after all. And if I was going to live, I thought, then I had better be about the business of it.

"The rest is not so interesting. It seemed as good a place as any to set down roots. I found this clearing, and set about building shelter. It took me the better part of a year, but as you say, it is comfortable and suits me. Plenty of water for bathing and drinking. The woods have been most generous to me, and fortune as well. I have learned to do a good many things that before I would not have imagined myself attempting. I make it a policy not to harm the creatures that live here or to disturb anything more than necessary. It is peaceful and remote, and the chores of survival keep me busy. For the most part, people leave me alone and I get by. It has been a good life for the last eleven years."

"Has it?" Xaarus finally responded to the heartbreaking narrative he had just heard.

Tvrdik shrugged, moving to clear the plates. "My needs are few. It is a beautiful, quiet place. I am content."

"And do you never feel called, or driven, to a higher purpose? Do you never dream of fulfilling a bigger destiny?"

The young man frowned. "I thought once that I was part of something grand and important. Now it all seems a distant dream, an illusion. I am no one of importance. My absence has gone unnoticed, and will not in the slightest affect the great tapestry of history."

Now it was Xaarus' turn to frown. "And are you never lonely here, away from your own kind?"

Tvrdik met the old man's gaze evenly, and answered in quiet tones, "Who is there left of my kind? I am alone, if I say it or not. And what did relationships ever bring me in any case but pain and despair?"

Xaaarus leaned toward him and spoke low, "You loved her?"

"I...how could I know that? I was young; we were friends. She was the brightest star in my heavens then, so luminous I dared not even reach. And we were all of a kind then, all glorying in finding each other and our power. And you were there..." Tvrdik trailed off, looking at the floor. Then, in a small voice, lips stretched taut and thin, he finished his thought, "It is better to be comfortable with one's own company, and not to invite such suffering into one's life again."

"Tvrdik," Xaarus began, choosing his words with care, "what happened to Benjin and Ailianne was a terrible tragedy. But you must know they brought it on themselves. I say this not to speak ill of our departed comrades, but so that you might know for certain that you had no part whatever in what happened."

"I might have tried to stop them."

"I do not think you would have succeeded. You remember, as your teacher, how many times did I warn you of the dangers of dabbling in arts you did not understand or had not yet mastered? Did I never caution you about dark sorceries that promised much, but came with a high price?"

"You told us often, Master."

"And if they refused to listen to me, what makes you think they would have taken counsel from you? Tvrdik, when you knew what they were about, why did you not go with them on that night?"

The pale young man's face twisted in torment. "I was afraid!" he blurted out, wrenching his spectacles from his face. Then, in a hoarse whisper, "I was afraid."

"And good for you that you were, my son. There are many things in this universe of which we should be afraid, and chief among them is ignorance, especially combined with haste, and lust. Did you also wish for the powers they thought to conjure?"

24

Tvrdik's hands were holding his head as if it were about to explode. "No! No – I did not understand why they were doing what they were, why it was so important to them. I did not know how they could wish to defy you. I only wanted to learn everything I could. I wanted to be able to help people…"

"There it is." Xaarus sighed, "You were always my best pupil, son."

The younger man looked up, startled. "I? Your best pupil? How can you say that? Ailianne and Benjin were so bright, so quick. I was slow and plodding, always behind them by leagues – a dullard by comparison. You mock me."

"Do not mistake me. All of you were gifted, a joy to teach and the pride of my days back then. But you were all different. Those two were always ambitious and clever, always questioning and wanting more. But they never cultivated patience; they never learned to listen deeply. And they missed the very heart of what our profession is about. That, my son, was where you far outstripped them. You took the time to understand the 'whys' behind 'hows,' and made them a part of yourself."

Tvrdik shook his golden head. "I do not understand…"

"You will one day. You are a gifted and talented wizard, more powerful than you could ever imagine. But your gifts are tempered with an innate wisdom, and a great deal of compassion."

"I am no wizard at all."

"My son, your classmates were young and foolish. They chased after power and wealth, and it led them to lay their hands on something they could not handle. They paid the ultimate price. But they also did not consider the probable consequences to you, or to me, or others they might have injured in the process. Perhaps with time, and maturity, they might have changed, become the kind of people worthy of the gifts they had inherited and the knowledge given them. We will never know now. But it is also possible that the poor judgment they displayed that night was a serious flaw that might have been part of their nature always. You, Tvrdik, do not share that flaw."

Tvrdik raised a hand in a gesture of impatience, "Have you come here now, after all this time, to torture me with ghosts and painful memories I thought I had laid to rest long ago?"

Xaarus' eyebrows arched. "Why, I've come to complete your education. There is so much that I have yet to teach you."

There was a long silence. At last, the young man spoke. "That book was closed years ago. I have locked it away and the key is lost forever."

"Not lost, Tvrdik. I can help you find yourself again…"

"I and myself are quite content to be just what we are, and have been for twelve years, thank you very much. All the rest is just a page from a past I barely remember."

"Tvrdik, you must listen to me. Time is passing and there is great need. There is work for you out in the world."

"I know nothing of the world. Leave it to the king and the court, and all those who play important roles."

"The king and queen are dead – perished at sea in a terrible accident. Their only child, the rightful heir to the Crown, is but an infant, and there are those who would wrest the throne from him for their own dark purposes. There is a regent and a good council at Theriole to handle affairs of state, but they are besieged on all sides. They will soon be preparing for war. Tvrdik, the world you walked out of was peaceful and prosperous, but the storm clouds are fast gathering. The kingdom badly needs help…"

"Then you must give it, old man, for I have none to offer. I am neither warrior, nor courtier, nor scholar. After all these years, why do you come to me with this story? I, who know nothing but digging stones, chopping wood, and carrying water? You are a great mage – the Court Wizard ! You left them to face these dire circumstances years ago. Why do you not go to them now and put things in order? Why are you wasting valuable time in this place with a hermit?"

Xaarus rose from his makeshift chair, his tall frame slightly bent beneath the low ceiling, and paced away from the hearth. "Tvrdik, listen to me. My time is very short. I will not be here to join forces with those who are working to save the kingdom. Trust me, I would give a great deal to be able to offer assistance to those good folk, but it is simply not possible. And the stakes are much higher than you could even imagine."

"What are you saying?'

"I promised to tell you where I had been these long years, and why I left you alone." Xaarus issued a long sigh. "I think it is my turn to tell you a story. I pray you will believe it. When Benjin and Ailianne perished, I was as distraught as you. Perhaps moreso, if that is possible. As their teacher and mentor, I was responsible for them. I had cared for them and had high hopes for them. And how do you think it made me feel to know that I could not even keep them safe from their own folly? Like you, I thought there might be a way to undo what was done – to pluck them back from the edge of disaster. I was desperate to find it. What you did not know was that I had already been studying and experimenting in time travel. My son, on higher planes than ours, there is no such thing as time, as we know it. In theory, one should be able to transcend the bondage of linear time, and then control at what point one might re-enter the time-line. I had been researching the subject for years, and had made some promising breakthroughs on a minor level. But after the tragedy, I became obsessed with the idea that if I could just leap back before the accident, I could use every means at my disposal to prevent it from ever happening, saving Benjin and Ailianne from themselves.

"I was arrogant enough to believe I was close to success, but I knew there was a limited window within which my powers would be effective. With each passing day, we moved further from the event, and from the possibility of reversing it. If you found me distant and unresponsive in those days, I deeply regret it. In fact, had I been wise enough to pay attention to your needs at the time, things might have happened in a very different way....but, never mind. All is in the hands of a Higher Force anyway, and as you will see, there is a larger plan in play. At any rate, I was consumed with the desire to succeed in my quest – forgot sleep and food, friends, teaching, and recreation. I lost perspective, and in my desperation and haste, I fell prey to the very errors in judgment that had been the undoing of my pupils. I rushed my work forward with neither wisdom nor caution, and then, one night, just a month after Benjin and Ailianne's disappearance, I attempted the leap.

"I had made a foolish error in calculations, and somehow, instead of moving a short distance into the past, I found myself catapulted far, far into the future. And, of course, as you might guess, the doorway I had created disintegrated behind me, beyond recall. When I came to my senses, I realized the grave consequences of my pride and rashness. I was trapped in a strange time and place, without my books or my equipment, without friend or sustenance. I thought of those I had left behind without a word of explanation, you foremost among them. And I must tell you, Tvrdik, no man could have condemned himself more harshly or suffered more remorse than I at what I had done. From your perspective, I realized, I had just disappeared. And I was trapped – no way to return or even to get a message to you."

Tvrdik had been following the tale with rapt attention and growing amazement. "But, Master," he breathed, "however did you survive?"

Xaarus allowed a little crooked smile. "By my wits, boy, much as you have done. Men are still men, even in the future, and I am not without resources. I keep a low profile and support myself in various ways, as I may, and I observe. But you must believe me that almost from my arrival there, all my intention and skill, and every scrap of intellect I could muster has been bent on finding my way back to you to make amends for my error. Twelve years I have worked without respite to bend time to my will, so that I might come home..."

"But, if you are here now, it must mean that you have triumphed. Master, this is a feat of great wonder!"

"I have not triumphed," Xaarus replied bitterly, "I have failed."

"But..."

"Only by bending every ounce of skill, energy, and power at my disposal toward my intent, have I been able to temporarily stretch the timeline back like a bowstring. But you cannot conceive the effort required to remain intact, physical and present in this moment. In fact there are instances even now when I lose my concentration and am pulled back to the future, where I am still chained..."

As if to demonstrate his point, suddenly Xaarus flickered and vanished from sight. Wide-eyed, Tvrdik leapt to his feet. But in a moment the older man reappeared, tottered, and would have sunk to the floor if he hadn't been caught by his former student and lowered onto the nearest bench.

"My apologies – I confess I am growing a little weary after the journey, and the hour is late."

"Perhaps it would be better if you rested now and we continued this conversation tomorrow?"

"No! No. I have found my focus again, and there is still so much more I need to tell you tonight. At any rate, you can see my dilemma. I have calculated that, giving all I have to this venture, I should be able to remain in this time just long enough to accomplish my goals, but only this once. After I am pulled back to my future position for good, it could take years to accumulate the strength and power needed to try again. Unless of course, I find the key I seek to unlock my prison and return here once and for all. I fear I may still be far from that hope, though. I have already spent some of the precious days I have here seeking you in this remote place, and I cannot know with any certainty when my visit will end."

"But, hold on. Do you mean to say that you were able to choose this place, this moment in which to appear?"

"Of course. Years of study have enabled me to aim more accurately at a given time frame. I at least had that benefit this time."

"But if you knew you could only do this one time, why did you not go back to a time before the accident, as you originally intended? Why not stop all of this from happening to begin with?"

Xaarus was hoping to be asked that question, "Because, in the interim, I have discovered a far more important mission demanding our attention."

Tvrdik threw up his hands in exasperation, "What could be more important than having a second chance to put everything to right? To give Ailianne and Benjin back their lives and free yourself to come back where you belong?"

"Changing the future."

"Say again?"

"Tvrdik, we may have one chance to change the course of history for good."

The hoot of a very distant owl could be heard in the silence that followed. Tvrdik stared at his master, speechless for a moment, and then found his voice. "Is that wise?"

"If you had been there with me, son, lived among the people, you would not have to ask that question."

Xaarus motioned for his student to sit, and leaned in close to him, "Tvrdik, the future is a gray and grim place, filled with fear and violence, divisions and inequities. We see all of those things in our own world of course, but in the time to come they have grown to such overwhelming proportions that they are nearly irreversible. There is no balance, no light, no magic anywhere. The people hate, exploit, and enslave one another; war breaks out everywhere, often over greed and lies and folly. It is only a matter of time before they all wipe each other out. To make matters worse, they have treated their lands selfishly and without wisdom. Only a small remnant of the ancient forests still stand, and the seas are all poisoned. Many creatures have perished; all the naiads and dryads have long gone away. There are no dragons, no unicorns, no talking beasts, and most certainly no wizards. It is a time of great hopelessness and joylessness. Oh, folk still laugh and sing, form friendships, fall in love and bring babes into the world. But these things seem as flickering candles in a very dark room. The downward spiral has begun, and in that time, I fear, cannot be reversed."

"From your description, Master, I…I am greatly relieved not to have to exist in such a world. And more than ever, I am disturbed at your own misfortune in finding yourself there. But what does any of this have to do with here and now? And with the reason you have come to find me?"

Xaarus leaned even closer. "My recent explorations in time theory have taken me into the matrix of possibilities more than once – the field of chaos where causality, probability, and free will meet to summon forth our physical experience. And after some searching and pulling at the threads of time, I have found a parallel reality – an alternate story, if you wish, one which is as radiant and joyful as my current prison is grim. It is not so far-off or unlikely that it cannot be retrieved, but is fading, almost by the minute, as human choices and errors tick by. I have tracked its strands backward over the warp and woof of history, through crossroads and missed opportunities. And I have discovered, through some grand stroke of irony, lo and behold, they originate here and now. Here is the intersection of roads. This is the moment, my son, when we are gifted with one last dazzling possibility of changing the very fabric of the future, and all the lives it touches, for the better."

Tvrdik was silent for a moment, the enormity of that last pronouncement filtering into his consciousness. When he spoke, it was barely audible. "And just what exactly do 'we' have to do in order to accomplish this incredible task?"

"That, my boy, if you will allow me, I was hoping to divulge to you over the next few weeks that we are together. The hour is late for me to go into detail, but suffice it to say it will require a great many dangerous and unorthodox choices. Those who sign on must have enormous faith, courage, and resourcefulness. There may be heavy sacrifices as well, but the rewards that stand to be gained are immeasurable."

"You speak as if there were a number of folk already committed to this scheme, whatever it is. I must ask again why you have come to me?"

"I have as yet told no one else my fantastical story, and shared with no one else my hopes. Success will depend on the concerted efforts of those at the Palace of Theriole, along with a wide array of supporting players. But they will not win the day, Tvrdik, without the help of a gifted mage. I regret I cannot be here in the critical moments. My job this time will be to pass the torch. The real work ahead will fall to you."

Another long silence, while Tvrdik stood, head down, wrestling with his very soul. He looked up to meet the elder wizard's eyes. "Surely there is someone else you can seek out – another, more powerful wizard – somewhere in all the world?"

Xaarus regarded him with compassion, and his voice was soft, "My dear boy, when we began our studies together all those years ago, it was the proudest moment of my life, but also one of the most anxious. Long before that, I had watched my own teachers and the few colleagues I had known, age and pass into oblivion. Our kind ages differently from ordinary men, but we are not immortal. We wrestle time, face disease, accident, and violence like any other. Finding myself alone, I set forth to scour the countryside, searching, searching for anyone, especially for young people, with something of the spark – some talent and potential. I questioned thousands of families from castle to humblest cot, tracked down rumors, followed every lead and every tale, tested hundreds of candidates. And when I finally brought the three of you together to form our little school, I had such high hopes for you all. You were so bright and eager and talented, all of you. You were my insurance against the future in precarious times. You were my hope and my legacy. You will begin to understand now why the loss of Benjin and Ailianne affected me so profoundly. It was a greater blow in many ways than you could have known then. Tvrdik, I …I could be wrong…I pray I overlooked something, someone, somewhere in my search. But as far as I know, you are the last wizard in the world. There is no other to whom I may pass my knowledge or plead my cause. It is a heavy responsibility, I know, but it is for you alone to either put on the mantle destiny has assigned you – or to allow a great and ancient tradition of service to fade and die. The choice is yours."

Tvrdik was stunned. "I am the last?"

"It is not certain, but I think so. Tvrdik, come outside with me."

The young hermit looked up, startled, then snatched one of the threadbare blankets up from his corner pallet and threw it around the old wizard's shoulders as they edged through the low doorway out into the clear, chill night. Xaarus shrugged into the extra wrap with gratitude, as he strode into the center of the clearing, stopped and stood gazing up at the sky, his protégé right behind him. It was an uncharacteristically clear night for early spring. There was no breath of wind, and the invisible new moon left the cloudless sky dark and clear, sprinkled liberally with tiny bright lights in an explosion of glitter. Familiar pictures began to form themselves from some of the most prominent among them, and stood out from the sky-scape in three-dimensional relief. On a night like this, you could almost follow the subtle movements of these night-time wanderers as you watched, or hear the music they were said to sing on their journey. Xaarus pointed up.

"What do you see, boy?"

Tvrdik shivered, "Boundless sky…stars…the ancient constellations by which the wise may navigate, divine the weather, the seasons, the whims of providence and fortune…"

"The old books tell a story of the race of wizards being star-seeded."

"Star….seeded?"

"What if I told you that each of those bright lights is a distant sun, and that under many of those suns are worlds upon worlds like ours, peopled by civilizations of every kind, like ours, and not like…"

Tvrdik's mouth fell open in awe. He could not reply, but felt the tingle of truth resonate throughout every corner of his being. Xaarus went on.

"It is written that long ago, travelers from a great race of wisdom and power far exceeding that of men, sojourned to this place and found it good. They lingered in the pleasant woods and valleys, enjoying the warm sun, sweet waters, and peaceful peoples of whom they grew to be quite fond. Like gods they were to the local tribes, and taught them many useful skills. Some of them partnered with the native folk and begat children, who were firmly of this world, but had inherited something of the qualities of their star-fathers and star-mothers. The visitors wished to bless their adopted home with something of themselves, so that when they died or returned home, there would be those who could serve and help men as visionaries, creators, guides, and guardians. It is said that the original half-bloods were radiant beings, and very powerful. Over millennia, the bloodlines have been diluted, scattered, and hidden. But the gift of those star-people has always survived somehow in our race of wizards. We, who have found ourselves to be inexplicably different from our fellows, who have discovered hidden talents and unusual powers, who find ourselves drawn to the old texts and ancient wisdom, we are descended from those visitors from the stars. And it is bred into our bones to learn and grow, to create, to discover, to exercise power, and above all, to serve.

"Unless I mistake myself, or unless we succeed in changing the shape of what is to come, that noble line ends here. Can you turn your back on such a heritage? The life you were born to?"

Tvrdik stood very still, eyes fixed on the constellations, numb with cold or with revelations too profound to take in all at once. In a few brief hours, the life he had crafted for himself stone by stone over the course of twelve long years, had been pulled out from beneath his feet, and had crumbled to dust. Tomorrow seemed impossibly distant, foreign, inconcievable. Somewhere deep within his chest, he felt an enormous crack, so loud he was sure Xaarus and the whole world must have heard it. A sturdy wall around his heart had broken clean down the center, and something huge, warm and alive rushed through, filling him up from toe to crown with power like that of his beloved waterfall. Bone, flesh, and sinew began to vibrate with the energy coursing through him. He was the waterfall, tumbling and racing and pushing ahead on its journey. But now he was expanding joyfully – limitless, his feet rooted deep in the heart of the earth, and his head among the stars, looking out on eons of creation working itself out in time, and outside of time. All around him the scene was decked in marvelous colors, and everything was singing, dancing a stately dance that went on eternally, in perfect order. He smiled.

A flash of light shocked him back into his slim body and limited mind. Tvrdik lowered his head from its upward gaze and hugged himself tightly, as if to assure himself that he was still real and alive. He found, to his surprise, that his face was wet with tears, and for the first time in his life, he knew who he was.

He turned to face Xaarus, who waited beside him for an answer, and saw him as if for the first time. There was the face he remembered of his beloved teacher, mentor, and surrogate father. It was older, lined with pain and weariness, imperfect and vulnerable. But the eyes were eternal, wise, compassionate. Fires in them were apt to flare up in visions of great moment. Yet, there were lights in them that were personal too, shining just for him – for Tvrdik. They looked at him now with recognition, love, pride…and hope. He breathed deeply, as a great icy wall in his chest thawed and melted. He put his arm around the old man's shoulders and turned him toward the vine-covered door.

"Come inside," Tvrdik said, "It is cold and we must rest. You take my pallet; it is rude but not too uncomfortable. I will lay a blanket for myself by the hearth. Get some sleep. Tomorrow we have a lifetime of lessons to cover and a whole world to save."

FOUR

FOND FAREWELLS AND FIRST MEETINGS

Tvrdik sat on his favorite flat stone, so near the waterfall it was almost under the thundering stream. Normally, in that position, a body would be soaking wet in just a few moments. But he had erected a sort of protective, invisible shield around himself which deflected the water away. It was one of a thousand simple, useful tricks he had recently learned. If there had been anyone there to notice him, they would have been at pains to recognize this young lad as the same hermit of a few short weeks ago. He had bathed, washed his clothing in the pools below, and used his sharpest knife to shave his face clean and trim the tangle of pale gold hair to a manageable shoulder-length. Tvrdik was preparing to re-enter the world from which he had retreated years ago, and he was more than a little anxious. He sat in this cherished place that had always brought him comfort and peace, and tried to summon the courage to say goodbye.

As his mind wandered ahead and back in time, the pointer finger of his right hand was absently levitating small stones from the stream's bank, and letting them fall with a resounding *sploosh*. With every *sploosh*, a shower of spray leapt up to catch the warm afternoon sun in an explosion of tiny rainbows. The general effect was like a little symphony of sound and color, running continuously for the better part of an hour. The activity was more than play, however. Xaarus had insisted on continuous practice for Tvrdik, who hadn't the luxury of time to hone and master his magical skills. Tvrdik had gotten used to taking every opportunity to apply his new abilities until they became second nature, and he could summon them almost in his sleep. Despite his earlier, humble self-assessment, he had proved a quick study, and quite talented. But two short weeks was hardly enough time for anyone to absorb the entire catechism of wizard lore. Two weeks! That was all they had had for training before Xaarus, as predicted, had vanished into the future.

Tvrdik had thrown himself heart and soul into his education, studying and practicing long hours as he strove to memorize countless complex formulae. When Xaarus had finally outlined the details of his grand plan, however, the younger wizard had come close to throwing up his hands and walking out again. For a moment, he had wondered if his old master had gone mad with age and care. It all seemed so impossible, so counter to all of nature, so naïve, that he could not imagine this plan ever accomplishing much of anything except to get all of its proponents killed. And yet, the more he learned, the more he studied and considered what Xaarus laid out for him, the more he understood its beauty, its inevitability, and, ultimately, its truth. Soon, he could feel its rightness in the depths of his heart, and began to develop a passionate belief in what the old wizard was trying to achieve.

Redoubling his efforts to learn as much as possible in the time he had with Master Xaarus, Tvrdik had begun to neglect simple essentials like food, sleep, chores, exercise. Even the fire on the hearth almost went out one day from lack of attention. It was after that unfortunate incident that Xaarus had come up with his remarkable shortcut which carried with it a wonderful extra bonus. Xaarus guessed that, because of their long relationship as master and student, he might be able to use that seed of familiarity to create a bond between their minds which would link them indelibly in consciousness. His first intention was to give his student a sort of window into his mind, allowing Tvrdik to pluck whole concepts, rituals, deeper understandings, and entire packages of information, straight from the old wizard's thoughts. There were still the matters of process, practice, and integration, but the trick worked to make learning swifter and more efficient. As the two mages became accustomed to, and more adept at using this unusual telepathic link, Xaarus posed the possibility that they might be able to keep it at least partially open through time and space, so that they could stay in some contact after he had returned to the future.

"I'm sure it would work," he exclaimed, "but mind you, I would only be present in your head. You would see and hear me because of our unique connection, but no one else would. And I couldn't *do* anything physical – cast any spells or the like…it would take a great deal of energy to keep the lines open over that distance, too, so I would not be overseeing your every move. I could, however, be there for you at greatest need, to give guidance and support you."

The idea was more than agreeable to Tvrdik, who was already feeling a bit overwhelmed, and still nursing so many doubts about his own quality.

"You must know how much faith I have in your ability to succeed, my son. You do not need me at every turn in the road. You are courageous, strong, bright, creative, resourceful, gifted, and above all, I know your heart. It will always lead you down the right path." Xaarus spoke during one of their simple meals toward the end of their time together. He could sense, that, though Tvrdik was growing by leaps and bounds, the young man was still in need of a boost to his self-esteem.

"I wish I shared your confidence, Master," Tvrdik mumbled, pushing at his food without interest, and blushing. Then he looked up and met the elder man's steady gaze, "How will I ever convince anyone at the palace that this is the way they should go? They will think it preposterous, and label me a madman. If we are not all joined in purpose, we have no chance."

Xaarus shrugged, "You will do what you need to do to win them over one by one. Use your intelligence, your charm, your wit – use the power of the truth. It can be an amazing tool to wash away resistance."

The young wizard shook his head and went back to staring at his plate. The Master saw that something else was called for. Moments passed while he considered, then…

"There is someone there whom you must seek out. She, of all the court, is destined to be your most powerful ally. She will truly listen to your tale, and she is given the authority to make things happen."

"Tell me….who is she?"

"Her name is Jorelial Rey, of an old and proud family, and now temporary guardian of the infant king."

Tvrdik frowned, "I partly remember her…the dragon girl. She was not much more than a child when I left."

"And not much younger than you, boy. She is young, but already saddled with grave responsibilities, and up to the challenge, I think…"

"A bit full of herself, if I recall correctly. Always riding around on that dragon, above everyone else…"

Xaarus' tone turned harsh. "Do not judge anyone whose path you have not shared. She walks a solitary road, very different from others of her own age, growing up motherless, being prepared to inherit a position she never wished for, but which she must shoulder. And her best friend and constant companion is a creature whose enormity and fierceness isolates her from her peers. Why, she is not so very different from you."

"I-I did not realize…I will take your counsel to heart."

"It is most certain she is your link, comfortable as she is with both the trappings of power and the magical world. And she *is* beloved of a dragon – a rare bond indeed."

Another pause. Tvrdik frowned again. "But how will I ever get to speak with someone of that rank? Look at me, Master. I have no money, no suitable clothes, no family or reputation to recommend me."

Xaarus pondered for a moment, then pointed to a small stone on the ground nearby. "Fetch me that stone, will you? There's a lad. It's going to take every last bit of strength I have to do this, but I believe it will hold…" The old wizard palmed the rock, closed his eyes and furrowed his brow, muttering some sort of incantation. When he opened is hand, a glittering, golden object sat where the stone had been. He smiled as he handed it to his student, "I used to carry these coins in former days as a kind of calling card. I think she might remember that. If I have any influence or credibility left at court after all these years, it might give you an opening."

Tvrdik took the coin and examined it. On one side was a profile of the familiar face before him: long hair, sharp, but kindly features, prominent nose. On the opposite face was simply etched a large "X." The young wizard pocketed this small gift, but pressed it in his hand within the folds of cloth, endowing it with all his hopes.

As the second week of training unfolded, Xaarus began to have more of those vanishing episodes, like they had experienced on their first evening together. Each time, it seemed to take more of the master's energy to come back, and he would need more rest to regain his strength on his return. Tvrdik fussed and worried over him, trying to make him comfortable in the rude hut, and offering whatever assistance and nurture he could. But Xaarus would always insist on getting back to work after only a brief rest. Gradually, Tvrdik could see in the older man's face the toll their schedule was taking, and something about his teacher began to seem frail and brittle, at times almost luminous.

At noon on the fifteenth day of their reunion, taking a break from study, sitting out in the gentle sun, the two men were talking, and Tvrdik thought his master looked oddly transparent. Still, they continued. "Set your intention always for what you wish to create, Tvrdik, and stand behind it with all your passion and belief and power. In that way, you will always draw the circumstances you wish for. Allow no room for doubt, and you will be successful, and safe…"

"I do not ask for safety, Master. I believe in this cause. I know some of the dangers I will face, and I am not afraid to die."

Xaarus laughed, and seemed to un-form with the laughter. The last words that passed his lips were, "My dear Tvrdik, you are not *supposed* to *die*; you are *supposed* to *win!*" And he was gone, dispersed on the four winds. Tvrdik sat gaping in awe and dread at the empty space before him. All afternoon he sat there motionless, waiting, hoping against hope that the old wizard would reappear just one more time. By midmorning of the next day, it became apparent that Xaarus would not be coming back. Slowly, deliberately, Tvrdik rose and began to put his house in order.

With careful deliberation, he selected a few treasured possessions and essential items which would be needed for travel: food, water, a bedroll, firestones, tools, notes, a few books, several medicinal herbs, and an assortment of other useful items. He packed them in several small pouches and one large carry-sack, then piled everything else he owned or had made neatly inside the little cottage. It was then that he had bathed, laundered his threadbare clothes, and dried them at the hearth, and taken up his best knife to trim his wild hair and to shave the unruly whiskers from his face. The knife came along. The fire had to be extinguished and tamped down, dirt spread over the last glowing coals. Then he stood in the little makeshift doorway and looked around the place. So much of his young life had been poured into this place, so much of his heart. But memories of despair and grief lived in the walls as well. He doubted he would ever see the humble little cottage again, but wanted everything to be in order just in case, or perhaps to serve some passing traveler in need. He placed the palm of his right hand on one of the stones in the nearest wall, bowed his head, and sent a message of thanks. Then he turned, without looking back, and strode out of the clearing to spend a few moments with his beloved waterfall.

Sitting now at its edge, playing with stone and light and water, the young man tried to inhale and hold within the feelings of peace and security that always came over him in the water's presence. He would need them in the days to come. He pulled off his spectacles to wipe them clean, but fumbled and almost dropped them on the rocks below. Quick reflexes saved the day, and he let out a sigh of relief. Of all the possessions he had managed to preserve with exacting care over these long years of isolation, his glasses were the most valuable. He needed them without doubt, and they would not be easy to replace. He could conjure a pair; any apprentice wizard could transmute matter from one form to another, but those creations rarely kept their shape for very long, and no one yet could just materialize real items out of thin air. Some things were just better done the old-fashioned way. Gingerly, he placed the wire arms back on his ears and settled the bridge on his nose, giving it a little pat, as if to say, *close call, old friend, but all's well now.* Then he uncoiled his long legs, stood up, yawned, stretched, and dissolved the magical barrier that had been keeping him dry. Putting his hand in the spray, he intoned, "Ancient, magical place, you have been my companion, my strength, and my inspiration for twelve years. The time has come for me to leave your serenity and rejoin my fellows in the world. I offer you my thanks and blessing, a wish that you will continue undisturbed in your perfection, and that I might revisit you someday, and once again enjoy your unique gifts." Tvrdik removed his hand from the stream, shook the water from it, and with much reluctance, turned to go.

"Excuse me."

It was a small, unfamiliar, musical trill, enough to stop him mid-step, but not enough to convince him that he had actually heard anything. It must have been the warble of a passing bird, or the song of the water on the polished stone. He took another step.

"Excuse me, Lovely Man…"

40

There it was again – a tiny voice speaking unmistakable words. Eyebrows raised in curiosity, Tvrdik turned back to the cataract slowly… and found himself face to face with a little blue girl. At least, that is what she most resembled. She hung suspended in the waterfall, somehow resisting its downward force, naked and blue. Or green. Or blue-green. Her hair was a profusion of frothy curls which were not quite distinguishable from the water's foam, and her features had an otherworldly caste that seemed ageless and somehow charming: a very wide, thin-lipped mouth, a little button of a nose, and disproportionately large eyes that were long and narrow and slanted up at the outside edges with a trace of mischief. She stood, or floated, before him, no bigger than the length of his face. But some of the details of her shape were less defined, blending in and out of the moving water. Eyes wide in wonder, Tvrdik queried, "What…*who* are you?"

"I am Ondine. I am naiad…water fairy. My sisters and I live here, in this waterfall."

An incredulous smile crept across the wizard's face. "Water fairy? I didn't realize there were any of you left. I *knew* this place was special. Well, Ondine, a pleasure to meet you face to face. I am called Tvrdik." He gave a slight nod of his head in gentlemanly greeting. She wrinkled up her whole face in distaste.

"Teh-vur-dik" she scowled, "That is strange name. What sort of name is that?"

He shrugged, "Well, it is *my* name…"

I will call you 'Lovely Man'. I always call you this…"

He was startled. "You know me?"

"Yes, yes, of course. You are Lovely Man who comes here many seasons ago. I watch you come and go here often."

"Well, why haven't you ever introduced yourself before, Ondine? I would have so loved to have gotten to know you better before it was time for me to go."

She tilted her little head, "My sisters and I, we do as we like here. Not bother anyone – wish for no one to bother us. Ways of men strange to us, good for us to learn. We stay close, safe – watch."

Tvrdik blushed, "Well, I hope I have been a good representative of my race. In any case," he reassured, "none of you have anything to fear from me." He leaned in conspiratorially, "I will keep your secret, I promise. And I am most honored that at last you chose to come out and say hello. It has been a great privilege for me to make your acquaintance, but now, I must be on my way. Be well, Ondine." He smiled, and then turned to walk away. A cold splash hit him in the back of the head. "Owww! Why did you do that?"

"Excuse me, Lovely Man, you are leaving this place? Going away?" She was frowning now.

"Um, yes. I have work to do in a place far from here, so I must make my farewell…"

"You do not come back?"

"I wish I could say. Right now it seems I might be away for a good long time. But, if I am ever again in the neighborhood, you can trust that I will surely come to call." He was struggling to comprehend what she might be getting at.

"Lovely Man, you will take me with you."

"Excuse me?" Tvrdik had in no way anticipated this. "And please don't call me that. Look, Ondine, why would I want to do that? You are perfectly happy here. Believe me, I wish I was staying too."

"My sisters happy here. I am weary of all play. I think big things happen now in the world outside – want to see and learn. I go with you."

"Oh, I see – an adventurous spirit. Very commendable. But I am going on a mission where there may be grave danger, and there is no way I can look after a little creature like you…"

Her face grew stormy, and she did something like stamping her foot, only underwater. Immediately, the pools became roiled, turbulent. Water bubbled up over the rock where Tvrdik stood, soaking his boots and feet. "Hey!" he yelped, dancing in place.

"Can take care of self, thank you," she seemed to control her temper with effort, and the water receded. "I watch you many seasons. You are mage, I think. I know old magic, too. Can help…help you do mission."

For a moment, Tvrdik considered this, thinking she could be an asset at that. But he dismissed the fleeting thought right away. It was just too uncertain ahead, too dangerous. "I'm sorry little naiad. It's simply out of the question. I promise to come back and tell you all about it when I have finished. Farewell." Again he turned to go. This time his entire back was slapped with a very large wave. Dripping and aggravated, he slowly turned back. But before he could chide her, she shouted at him in her piping little voice.

"Lovely Man, you owe me. I save your life. I claim my debt now. You take me with you." She screwed up her face in a pout and thrust it straight at him, eye to eye.

Tvrdik blinked first, "What in heaven's name are you talking about?"

"Long time ago, when you first come here, I watch you. You stop at our waterfall, spend long time here. You like our waters. You think to come swim here with us. I see you – I think you are very lovely man (Tvrdik winced); maybe not so bright not to think of rough waters below, hard rocks. I make waters come up high to catch you, lay you softly down on grass." She blushed a sort of purplish shade, "I am happy you are not hurt in water here."

Tvrdik squatted down on the flat rock, silent, as the answers to his own personal mystery were revealed at last. He kept his head lowered as the truth of what had happened those long years ago washed over him. He saw no reason to explain to this little elfin being how her version of the story was not quite the way things had gone. But it seemed he *did* owe her his life. He looked up at her, one blonde eyebrow raised behind the spectacles. "Well. It seems we *do* have a situation here. I remember that day well. I never knew how I came to that bank in safety. It appears I do owe you a debt – and my deepest gratitude."

She nodded to him with a rather self-satisfied expression. He continued.

"But, how can I ever hope to repay your kindness now? Even if I thought it wise to let you come along – and mind you, I'm not saying I do – how could it be possible? Unless I forget my fairy lore, you cannot survive out of water."

"You take me *in* water," she insisted. "For travel I only need small amount – you can carry." It was obvious she had thought this through.

"Ondine, I am sent on a difficult quest which could take us far from here. Perhaps we might not get back to this place ever again. There is danger everywhere. I might not survive to come back."

"This is important?"

"Oh, very important. Vital, in fact."

"I will come. Help you with important task. Save you again if danger comes near, Lovely Man."

Tvrdik looked at the feisty little fairy, and his heart warmed with appreciation. Somebody was on his side already. That *had* to be a good omen.

"So, you are quite set on this course? There is nothing else I can say to dissuade you? Nothing else I can do to repay you?"

"I say farewell already to my sisters. I come with you."

"To be honest, it would please me well to have some company on the road. And, as you mentioned, I do owe you. Wait here."

She did, but poised and vigilant in case of some trickery. Tvrdik stepped into the woods a few paces and glanced around for inspiration. He found a sizeable piece of birch bark, flexible and intact, rolled it into a thick tube, and sealed the edges with sap and a bit of magic. He affixed some sturdy leaves over one end of the tube, and cast a spell that the whole contraption would not leak. Stepping back to the waterfall, he filled his makeshift cylinder with water, and offered it to her.

"This should do until we come to the first village, and can trade for something more suitable. Let me know if it is too close or uncomfortable."

She leapt in and smiled up at him. "Good," she nodded with enthusiasm, "I am not heavy for you?"

"No, no," he replied, "but what should we do about sealing it so it doesn't spill on the way? Hmmm." He waved his hand over the open end of the bark cylinder, and sealed it shut with an energy field. Almost at once, the homemade container began to jump and vibrate. He dissolved the seal, and Ondine popped up, gasping.

"Need…air…too, Lovely Man." she scowled at him.

"Oh, sorry! I didn't realize. You are the first naiad I have ever carried. And, if we are to travel together, *please* don't call me that." He whispered the intention for his magical seal to be porous to oxygen, but not water, and waved his hand over the open end again. This time he was met with a smiling face peering up from inside the container. Tvrdik cast about for a sturdy length of vine, cut a piece with his good knife, and affixed it to the birch bark tube. He slung the finished product across his body and around his neck, backed away from the magical falls, arranged his other pouches and carry-sack, picked up his wooden walking stick, and started down the road to meet his destiny. But, miraculously, not alone.

FIVE

AT THE PALACE OF THERIOLE

JORELIAL REY STRODE THROUGH THE bustling inner courtyard of the palace, on her way to the formal Hall of Audience. She forced her eyes to stay trained on the goal ahead, invisible blinders shutting out everything vying for her attention on the left and on the right. Her lips were set in a grim, determined expression, and she led with the top of her head, as if she could push her way through the crowded corridors with sheer mental energy. This was her least favorite part of the day in what had become the least favorite year in her young life. Having been in council meetings all morning, and having spent the entire afternoon attending to one essential, impossible task after another, she still had at least one audience to survive before dinner. Any chance of sweet privacy was hours away under the best conditions, but she clung to the slim filament of hope that there would be time later to spend with Tashroth.

They had been together as far back as her memory could conceive, since her father had set the great green dragon as guard over the tiny infant when her mother had died. Tashroth was protector, counselor, confidante, playmate, steed, and friend to the young heir to the house of Rey. Their unusual bond was the stuff of legend in field and village. More than one hopeful suitor had been frightened off by the piercing regard of a dragon eye, or the proximity of a giant clawed foot. Tashroth himself was of an ancient and noble lineage. Among his own kind he might have been a great leader, even a king. But he had preferred a life among men, and was devoted to Rel, his beloved charge.

45

She thought of him now: magnificent, tall, graceful, vast wings folded neatly, or stretched in flight, his pine-green scales shimmering and shifting with opalescent lights. And from his huge, luminous eyes shone his spirit, his extraordinary compassion, and age-old wisdom. In moments of extreme anger or ecstasy, a dragon's eyes could flash like twin torches. But all she ever saw in his regard was unconditional love and understanding, with perhaps a trace of pride.

Tash would be off now hunting, or sunning himself by the river. He never felt comfortable for long hemmed in by the palace walls, and she never felt quite herself while he was out of sight. And the recent days and weeks of scant time together probably contributed to her impatient mood as she crossed the courtyard now, where a hundred waiting petitioners would be calling out for her attention, tugging at her sleeves, wanting a piece of her. She felt for them all, she really did. Some of them had been waiting for days, and had legitimate issues and complaints she would have to deal with at some point. But she was only one person carrying a disproportionate load, and these were perilous times. Things had to be prioritized, or nothing would ever get done. If they only knew how much she longed just to climb up on Tashroth's back and disappear into the mountains. But a Rey must shoulder his or her responsibilities, and always put the good of the kingdom first. She had been drilled in this principle since she took her very first steps.

To complete the ultra-delightful character of this particular day, the appointment she was rushing now to keep was with Lord Drogue, probably her least favorite noble in the entire catalogue. Oh, he was always polite enough to her, almost drippingly so. But there was something slimy about the man that she just did not like. Well, she had been expecting him to demand a hearing for a while now. Might as well get it over with.

"Yes, Steward, I'll get to it as soon as I can. Send me your recommendations…"

"Lady Rey, the ambassadors from the Lake Regions beg your ear…"

"Thank you…they are already on my calendar for tomorrow…"

"My lady, I beg a moment of your time…"

"My lady, we simply *must* go over the budget…"

"…the menu…"

"…the Harbormaster needs…"

She had learned not to even check her stride as she fielded the barrage of requests and demands. Never make eye contact and never slow down – she had learned from bitter experience that each of these well-meaning petitioners would happily take an hour or two of her already over-programmed day to address their own peculiar issues, if given half the chance. However did the king and queen cope, it always seemed with such grace and generosity? Ah, but there had been two of them, and the realm had been at peace, humming along without much disruption. Things were very different now. It had been barely three months since both the beloved king and his bride had been drowned during a terrible storm at sea, on their way to visit a neighboring kingdom. The entire nation was still in shock. This king, and his father before him, had kept peace and prosperity, justice and opportunity alive for two generations, and almost no one could remember the shadows of want and war that touched earlier times. King Darian and Darian II were revered by all, and it would have been natural to assume many more years of good governance from the latter, as he had not yet reached his fortieth birthday when tragedy struck. To make matters worse, his lovely queen, warm and gracious to all her subjects, had long failed to produce an heir, until only recently. Four-year-old Darian III, the delightful, precocious apple of his parents' eye, was now an orphan, bereft, confused, and the responsibility of Jorelial Rey.

Rel had inherited that position from her father, Gareth Rey, a wise and wonderful man who had also been taken from them a little over a year ago, after a brief but devastating illness. For centuries, the Rey family had been powerful counselors and advisors to kings, and had shouldered the responsibility of keeping monarch after monarch safe, honest, and ethically on track. Jorelial's forebears were intelligent, fair-minded masters of diplomacy: courageous in battle, creative in peacetime, and content to be support to the Crown, rather than being ambitious of its privilege. It was a lineage of pride and pressure, and Gareth had been the priceless jewel in his family's crest. Jorelial missed her father so on days like today, both because she knew he would have been much better equipped to handle all of the chaos of recent events, and because he was her father, whom she adored. Not having produced a male child who would inherit the Rey tradition and legacy, Gareth had reared Jorelial with equanimity as his successor. He taught her history and statecraft, made sure she was capable in the physical arts and sciences, and shaped her to understand the twists and turns inherent in human behavior. He always insisted she strive for excellence in every discipline she set her hand to. Gareth recognized in his eldest daughter the qualities of a true leader, but it was certain he had thought there would be plenty of time to develop and nurture those qualities.

He had been wrong, and with the passing of the crown to an infant, young Jorelial had found herself not only an advisor to kings, but the default government herself. So far, it was a temporary arrangement. Someone had had to step in and organize a state funeral, arrange care for a royal infant, comfort a grieving nation, and insure that all the many details of bureaucracy would continue running smoothly. Anyone else even remotely fit for the job was either too ancient, too compartmentalized, or too partisan. There was a council body in place to debate decisions of importance and tend to the myriad details of running a kingdom. It consisted of several aged ministers – well-meaning, but more concerned with their departmental details than the bigger picture – and regional representatives, who could not all be trusted not to have personal designs on an unstable throne. It made sense for a Rey, even a young Rey, of a family time-honored for wise counsel and even-handedness, to preside over the whole mess for the moment.

Very soon, the expanded gathering of council members and regional representatives would convene formally to anoint Darian III as legitimate heir to the throne. At that time, they would also elect a permanent regent who would rule in his stead, with the ministers' help, until he reached his majority. This regent would not only be acting government for the entire kingdom, but would be largely responsible for the proper education and training of the young king, as he grew into his inheritance. Jorelial Rey considered the regent's position to be about as attractive as a prison sentence, and dreaded the idea that she might be considered for the long-term. But her father had raised her to believe in the worth of duty and destiny, twin charioteers of the noble life, and she would give her best to whatever they brought her. A great comfort and help to her in these weighty matters was Tashroth. In his long experience, deep wisdom, and objectivity, she often found reliable guidance when the humans around failed her. Tashroth knew how to lead her to her best thought without telling her what to do. If it had not been for his magnificent presence in her life, Jorelial Rey would have felt unprepared to handle all that had fallen to her.

"Lady Rey, the blueprints for the memorial…"

"Rel! Rel, wait. Wait a minute. Wait up…"

There it was – the one voice in the crowd that she could never ignore: Delphine. Jorelial Rey stopped in mid-stride, shook her head, smiled, and turned to greet her little sister.

"Rel, where have you been? I've been trying to steal a moment with you for days, and I always seem to just miss you, or catch you running by."

"So sorry, Delphine. You can't imagine what it has been like these last few days. I barely get to eat or sleep. You know I'd have come to find you if I could have…"

"I know, Rel. I feel for you, and I don't want to add to your burdens, but this is important."

Jorelial looked at the earnest green eyes, the porcelain skin framed by long rivulets of hair the color of flame, and her heart melted as always.

"Sorry. What can I do for you, Sweet Pea?" she said, using her old pet name for her sister.

Delphine glanced around in horror and embarrassment, "Shhh! Please don't call me that here, in front of everyone. Can we step over behind those columns for a bit, out of the way?"

Jorelial let herself be led aside to a quiet corner, suddenly not caring if she was late for Lord Drogue's audience. Delphine hesitated and turned pink in a way that always made Rel laugh. "Well, what is it? Out with it. You're making me fall off schedule." She chuckled, feeling lighter just to be in Delphine's presence.

"I'm sorry, Rel, but it's just that I need to ask you…beg you… if you could just find a few minutes today to see Mark. He's been waiting for days and days. He even got himself on a list, but he keeps getting bumped by more impressive dignitaries. At this rate, he's afraid he'll never get in to see you."

Rel looked blank, "Mark. Mark… Mark the bard? Is that what this is about? Oh, Delphie, you are just too easy. I won't be able to take you seriously at all if you let every pitiful young tradesman with an agenda persuade you to take his part."

"But, Rel, that's not…"

"I know you mean well, but I am dealing with matters of grave consequence here, and I can barely keep my head above water…"

"No, Rel, listen to me! It's not what you think…" Delphine looked devastated.

"Look, if it makes you happier, dearest, you go and tell your little friend Mark that he is by all means hired for the coronation, and that we'll go over the program closer in, OK?"

Tears formed in the corner of the younger girl's eyes, and she stamped her foot. "Ooooh, Rel, you can be so infuriating! Of course I wouldn't bother you with such trivia now. This is something of a …a more… personal nature…"

Rel looked puzzled, "What on earth are you talking about?"

"Sister, where have you been for the last six months that you don't know? He wants to…well, *you* know…he wants to ask you for my…my hand."

"Your hand?"

Delphine near exploded in frustration, "To marry me, Rel. We need your permission to get married."

As the meaning of these words found its way into Jorelial's stunned brain, her eyes widened and her breath stopped. When she was finally able to form words, they sounded considerably like shouting. "Married! Get married? Where have I been indeed? What are you thinking? You're only 16."

"Seventeen, Rel, and lower your voice, please. I thought you knew – almost everyone else does. We've been seeing each other for a year. He would have asked sooner, but then everything happened and it seemed a bad time to bring it up. So we waited and waited, but, Rel, it's never going to be a good time. Can't you just talk to him?"

"Delphine, he's older than you. *And* he's a travelling minstrel. He doesn't even have roots or a home. He's not of noble birth – not that that should be the only criteria – but Father would *never* have approved."

"Father isn't here. You are, Rel, and you know me. I am not foolish and impulsive, am I?" Delphine's face was red, but her lovely chin was lifted and her eyes stared into her sister's unflinchingly. Jorelial found herself speechless, her sensible arguments beginning to evaporate beneath that gaze. She never could deny Delphine anything. But, then, it was true, the girl had never been flighty or fickle. She stared into her sister's green eyes, trying to read their depths. The younger girl moved closer, and laid her flaming head on Jorelial's shoulder, dropping her voice to an intimate whisper, "Rel, he's a wonderful man – kind and smart and funny, and so very talented. And he has plans for us. You always liked him…"

"I hardly know him! Gods, Delphine, it's not that I don't trust your judgment, but you are still so young, and it's been such a trying year for us all. Are you sure you know your own mind?"

"Rel, we know we belong together. We don't want to wait forever. Who knows what challenges tomorrow might bring?"

Well, she had a point there. It was hard to imagine any future at this point that would be carefree and secure and predictable. Jorelial Rey felt herself softening. She grasped her sister by the shoulders and turned her so they were face to face once more, "You really love him that much, Sweet Pea?" The expression on Delphine's face told her all she needed to know. She scratched her head. "Well, alright. I need time to think – it's still a bit of a shock, you know – but I suppose I can talk to him. No guarantees, mind you, but I'll see how he strikes me. To tell the truth, I could use a timely interruption to get rid of awful Lord Drogue. I'm late for him now. Hmmmm. Go and find Mark and tell him to come to the Hall of Audience in about half an hour. I will be most grateful for the interruption, and he may have his interview."

Delphine jumped up and down in childlike glee, the smile on her face as pure and absolute as the sunlight slanting into the courtyard. She threw her arms around her sister and squeezed the air right out of her lungs. "Oh, thank you! Thank you, dearest. I knew I could count on you. You'll love him as much as I do, you'll see. Thank you, Rel."

Jorelial couldn't help her own broad smile, even while trying to be firm. "Half an hour, then, and no guarantees." That's how Delphine was, she thought, as the younger girl danced back into the crowd: effervescent, persuasive, downright contagious. She shook her head, wondering how to handle this newest wrinkle, and started back toward the Hall of Audience at the other end of the courtyard.

Delphine had been the child of her father's second marriage, strongly urged upon him by King Darian himself. Her mother had been the daughter of a foreign prince seeking beneficial alliances. She had been very beautiful, in an otherworldly sort of way, and Gareth had loved her well, despite the age difference. She might have loved him in her own way too, but she was always somewhat frail and shy, subject to bouts of depression or nervous anxiety. She was homesick most of the time, and seemed oddly unsuited to the social obligations that a wife of such an important courtier incurred. She never seemed to make any real friends at court, spending much of her time closeted alone in her chambers. Gareth had thought that being with child would give her a new sense of purpose and connection to him, and a new level of maturity. But the pregnancy was difficult. She was miserable and resentful of all it brought with it, and seemed horrified at the prospect of being responsible for raising a child. When Delphine was delivered in a long and troubled labor, the babe was taken to a wet-nurse for care, while her mother lay in bed for weeks, pale and listless, ostensibly recovering from the ordeal. One day she just disappeared, stolen away back to her homeland and family, leaving behind a suckling babe and a note with a single word on it: "Sorry." Gareth was heartbroken, but not entirely surprised. He turned his affections on his baby daughter, who had inherited her mother's translucent beauty, but not her frailty or temperament.

A doting father and a competent nanny made sure the child had all her basic needs met. But it was Jorelial, a full ten years older, who stepped into a mother's role, having fallen in love with the tiny babe on first glimpsing the wide, innocent, green eyes. And now that there was only the two of them, Jorelial still felt the impulse to protect her younger sister as a tiger guards its young. She wanted Delphine to be happy, but it would be difficult learning to let go and allow the young woman to make her own choices – and her own mistakes – in a world of so many dangers and false friends. Rel sighed to think she would not be able to protect her much longer. But that would not stop her from giving this 'Mark' a thorough grilling today.

Arriving at the Hall of Audience, she shifted her thoughts to immediate matters, as she came upon Lord Drogue already pacing the room. She decided that gracious diplomacy was her best approach.

"My sincere apologies for keeping you waiting, Lord Drogue. Vital affairs of state detained me. No disrespect was intended. My attention is now all yours. How may I serve you?"

Drogue stopped in mid-stride, turned to face her, bowed, and smiled. He was impeccably and expensively dressed all in black, which was not altogether inappropriate, as the official royal mourning period had only just ended. Jorelial recalled that black was Drogue's usual preferred color in any case. He was well-groomed and somewhat too liberally scented, but nevertheless a respected man of wealth and property, keen intelligence, and perfect manners. Jorelial could not put her finger on exactly why she disliked him so. Descended from one of the oldest noble families in the realm, Drogue might be considered a handsome man. Tall and trim, with a regal bearing, his high cheekbones and chiseled features spoke of pedigree, and his black hair and mustache, black eyes under perfectly curved brows, and the pale skin of privilege attracted many a longing glance from the eligible maids of the kingdom. Was it her imagination, though, or did the elegant face lose its charm under closer scrutiny? Eyes a bit closer together than aesthetics might wish, and rimmed with dark circles; lines around the mouth, demarcating a haughty, sour expression rarely interrupted by true laughter; fingers that refused to be still, but always seemed to be grasping, roaming, reaching for more. Perhaps it was his remarkable lack of humor and warmth, or the uneasy feeling that he was never quite saying exactly what he really meant that put her on her guard. But none of those qualities were crimes, and she had no concrete reason to treat him rudely. Still, her father had taught her to heed her gut impressions, so it seemed prudent to be cautious, at least. Besides, Tashroth had no use for the man, and a dragon's instincts should never be dismissed. Drogue addressed her, his voice cultured, and his words chosen with care.

"My esteemed Lady Rey, no offense taken, as I am aware of the great responsibilities resting on your slim shoulders. It is precisely that about which I have come to speak with you. Perhaps it is I who may serve you."

"Oh? Go on, please." She eschewed the grand throne on its raised dais, and instead took a seat at a long conference table on the floor, and motioned for Drogue to sit as well. He did.

"Lady Rey, while others of your tender years are out enjoying the pleasures of youth and the lovely spring sunshine, I have perceived you are here at Theriole day and night in musty chambers, meeting with dull old ministers, poring over documents, and attending to the multitude of endless details involved in running a kingdom. Your father, a great man, and such a tragic loss for all of us (she nodded at this homage), has trained you well to step into his very large shoes, and we are all fortunate to be the beneficiaries of his foresight and your devotion to duty..."

"Perhaps you could come a little more quickly to your point, sir, though your kind words are noted. Time is precious, as you are aware. Are you about to question my ability to carry out those duties?"

Drogue started backward with a theatrical gesture, his hands flying to his breast, "No, no – of course, not a bit! Rather, I question the appropriateness of placing so great a burden on so young, and, might I say, lovely, a personage. Forgive my concern, my lady, but you are pale and weary, and are grown serious. You do not laugh and caper like the other youth of the court, and it is well past time for you to be considering an appropriate union..."

Jorelial was struggling to maintain her composure, but at this last she cleared her throat. The man was one word away from overstepping the bounds of propriety. If she hadn't been amused at his blatant strategizing, she might have been incensed. Drogue responded to her prompt.

"My sincere apologies if I overreach, my lady, but I have ever been your admirer, and only speak in thought for your well-being."

"Your concern for my health and happiness are heart-warming to me, my lord, but I assure you it is my choice to step up to the task fate has assigned me. The times are not usual, and therefore demand unusual commitment."

He seized the opening she had thrown him, "Exactly! Exactly, my lady. The times are not usual. In fact, perilous. In times such as these, it is essential that men of quality, experience, courage, and vision come forward to take the helm and guide the ship to safe harbor."

"An unfortunate analogy, Lord Drogue, considering the source of our recent woes."

"My apologies again, but the image holds." He rose from the chair and began to pace the floor, agitated. "The entire kingdom of Eneri Clare founders, my lady, on stormy seas. Our king is taken untimely from us, and we are left rudderless under the rule of a mere child. After years of easy living, we barely have an army to protect ourselves from foreign princes, and the lords of the alliance squabble amongst themselves for control of trivialities…"

"Sir, we are at peace with all of our neighbors. Long-honored treaties protect our mutual interests – why manufacture enemies where none exist?"

Drogue turned back to her with a canny expression, "Your faith is commendable, but experience teaches a man to plan for the unexpected. In our current state of vulnerability, we are a tempting prize for some ambitious state to pick off or annex. It is only prudent to imagine these likelihoods and prepare for them."

Jorelial was uncomfortable with his assessment of foreign policy, but entertained a moment of doubt that he might indeed know what he was talking about. Drogue went on with his well-rehearsed points, still pacing.

"A firm hand is needed on the economy, and on the merchants and farmers of this land, who too often shirk their financial and physical obligations to the Crown. And most certainly, the lords must be reigned in and united in purpose under a strong, central leader, by force if necessary. You have done an admirable job of keeping things running in this brief interim, but, Lady Rey, I seriously question if you have the stomach or the experience to tackle such difficult problems." He had become carried away in his narrative, and revealed a little too much of his inner mind. One glance at her face stopped him in both his speech and his stride. With great deliberateness, projecting her best illusion of stature, Jorelial Rey rose from her seat and turned to face the speechless man.

"Lord Drogue, I have listened with rapt attention to your *opinions*, and will take all that you have said under serious consideration. Is there something right now that I can do for you?" Drogue hesitated, and seemed to make a tactical decision.

"Well, to be blunt, yes. I have come here to ask for your support next week when the Grand Council meets to select a permanent regent. I plan to put myself forward as the best qualified candidate, and with your backing, Lady Rey, I believe the members will be swayed in my favor."

"You believe my voice will carry such weight in the deliberations?"

"But, of course, my lady. You are well respected in all circles. Allow me to plead my case to you here and now. The position of regent is a decades-long commitment, and will require a great deal of dedication and self-sacrifice. I am no stranger to this court, and have always been a lover and supporter of our king and his royal house. I am of noble birth, a man of property and means, with no reason to seek access to the royal coffers. I am a seasoned warrior, having learned the craft in overseas conflicts in my youth. I am a practiced statesman, in fact, a man of great experience in all arenas pertaining to governing. I have always been reckoned a strong leader of men, and I have a vision for this kingdom, to keep it secure, wealthy, orderly, and powerful in the world. You know I speak the truth of my credentials."

"Indeed, sir, you paint a compelling picture." She was revealing nothing of her inner reaction to his speech. It seemed to occur to him that he might have forgotten something.

"And of course, in exchange for your vote, I would want you to continue in the vital advisory capacity your family has traditionally held, and would value your input most highly."

Kind of him, she thought, but smiled and said, "Lord Drogue, you have presented your case most excellently..."

"Then I may count on your support?"

"Sir, you must give me time to consider. As I am, 'young and inexperienced,' I would not wish to leap to any decision of import in haste."

"I would not leave this room without your promise..."

"You have my promise to consider the matter. It is the Council, in the end, who will decide, I have no doubt, wisely. Before this interview, it had not occurred to me to throw my personal support behind any one candidate, nor am I convinced that it would influence the members in any case. I appreciate your taking the time today to present to me your unique qualifications, and I am heartened to see that we are both, above all, committed to the welfare of the kingdom, its citizens, and its rightful heir. And now, I believe, I have another appointment to keep...good day, Lord Drogue."

Unaccustomed to not getting his way, Lord Drogue stood with his mouth open in disbelief.

"Thank you, sir. Good day." Jorelial Rey repeated, and motioned for the doorman, who kept watch over the room's only entrance, to approach. She was never so relieved that she had instructed Delphine to send Mark about this time, and prayed that the young man was indeed just outside waiting for his audience. She had been truthful that it had not occurred to her to support any one candidate for the position of regent, but if anything had become clear to her during the course of this interview, it was that she would most assuredly *not* be voting for Lord Drogue. Everything about him – his manner, his ideas – seemed to run contrary to her most cherished beliefs. He was a petty tyrant in the making, and she prayed that someone else would emerge as the clear frontrunner by next week, so that she would not have to deal with his nonsense at all.

The doorman came up beside her with a little bow, "My lady?" She spoke to him in a low voice. "Can you tell me if the bard Mark is outside awaiting an audience?"

"He is indeed, my lady."

"Will you please ask him to come right in," then in a more public tone, "and please escort our good friend Lord Drogue back to the courtyard. Thank you."

Drogue found himself confronted by the doorman, and, out of options, began crossing the floor toward the oversized door. "You will consider what we have discussed?" he called back, "I will expect an answer…"

"Of course, sir. You shall have it soon."

"I do protest this summary dismissal. There was more that might have been said."

"Apologies, sir, but I do have quite a full schedule today. I believe I have the gist of you. Please do stay to dinner if you are so inclined." This last was spoken as he vanished over the doorframe, shaking his head. *And don't let the door hit you on your way out,* she added to herself. *Good riddance!* She hurried to the dais and the big throne from which the king usually greeted state visitors. Settling herself on the thick red cushion, she thought, with a wicked grin, that she would really give Mark the full treatment, and see how he handled himself.

She had barely taken her seat when the door opened again, and a tall young man, dressed in colorful leggings and tunic, stepped in. Feathered hat in hand, hesitant, he cast an awed glance over the furnishings in the enormous room. Jorelial put a hand up to her mouth to stifle a giggle. He had obviously picked out his best performance outfit, and while she had seen him behave with great self-possession in the Great Hall while plying his trade, a high-level audience without a harp in his hand was another matter altogether. Noting his vulnerable expression, she relented a bit.

"Mark! Please come in, and welcome. I owe you a debt of gratitude for delivering me, just now, from the shameless self-promoting of my last visitor. Thank you. I understand as well from my dear sister that you have been waiting many days for a chance to speak with me on a matter of some importance?" She was not about to let on that she knew his mission. She wanted to see just how he would attempt to win his prize. "My apologies, sir; my time has not been my own for some while now, and a thousand details of statecraft battle for my attention every day. There always seem to be more issues than hours. I appreciate your patience, and hope that you will not hold the delays against me. Come up, come closer where I don't have to shout…there, that's better." The man was nervous, fraying the edges of his best hat with his fingers as he stood there, knowing this to be the audition of his life. But there was a sweetness and an open quality to him which Jorelial noticed, particularly in contrast to the guarded, calculated manner of Lord Drogue. No wonder Delphine was drawn to him.

"My Lady Rey," he began, in a strong, trained baritone that only trembled a little, "Thank you for seeing me now, when I know you have so many other matters to attend to. And if my timing was of service to you, I am doubly glad."

A good beginning, she thought. He raised his face for the first time to meet her sharp, probing gaze. His eyes were soft and kind and brown. Taking courage from the silence, he went on, "If I have been insistent in requesting a moment of your precious time, my excuse can only be the deep devotion I bear your sister, Delphine. Over the past year, I have been fortunate enough to come to know her and her quality, and the desire to have her always by my side fuels my boldness. It is not her loveliness alone that has snared my heart and made it her servant forever. It is her inquisitive mind, her generous heart, the sunshine that radiates from her being wherever she goes – these all enchant me completely whenever I am in her presence. To me, she is like a lovely song that is so perfect by every standard that one begs to hear it over and over again, never tiring of the repetition, but only growing fonder in familiarity. I cannot imagine a life ahead without that song in my heart always, without Delphine in my arms. We are destined for one another, of that I am certain." With that he dropped to one knee, hat in hand, brown eyes lowered. "You hold the key to our future, Lady Jorelial Rey. Here and now, I humbly ask your permission to take Delphine as my cherished bride."

Jorelial was impressed with his effusive request, and even more with how he seemed to believe every word. But then, he was a bard by trade; how could she be sure? She leaned forward in the great chair, eyes narrowed, as if that could help her see more clearly into his heart, "Well spoken, sir. I confess I have sounded my sister on the subject, and to be frank, she seems to be of the same mind as you. But she is very young to be bound in a lifelong commitment. You are attractive and accomplished, sir. How do we know she does not suffer from a schoolgirl's crush, which she will outgrow in time?"

A shadow crossed his face, but passed swiftly, leaving behind a most determined expression. "Lady, you of all people should know your sister is a maid of uncommon wisdom, far greater than her years would suggest, and is not given to rash decisions or hasty judgments. I would beg you to take seriously her professed desires in this matter, if you value her happiness."

"Well parried!" Jorelial sprang from the chair, and stepped off the dais, circling the young man, who was still on one knee. "There is almost nothing on this earth dearer to me than the happiness of my sister. Besides Tashroth, Delphine is the most precious treasure in my world. But I am entrusted with the task of looking out for her welfare, beyond her desires alone. You must realize that it would be...unusual...for the daughter of a high-ranking courtier to be betrothed to a landless artisan, regardless of his skill. And you are a minstrel, making his fortune on the road, travelling from village to town across the kingdom, most likely barely earning enough for your own keep. What sort of life do you think that would be for a high-born maid as delicate and noble as Delphine? And how far would your affections carry you in times of scarcity?"

He was prepared for this question. "Lady, I am a harper out of love, not need. Before Delphine graced my life, music was ever my greatest joy, and source of nourishment. My parents hold a small estate in the hills outside the city limits. I will one day inherit this property, along with a modest sum. With these, and some savings I have been putting away, it has long been my hope to found there a school of the harpers' art. There is not yet anything of that sort in these parts. Lady, are you aware that your sister has an extraordinarily beautiful singing voice and a natural talent for music? Not to mention an easy manner with folk of all ages. I can imagine no fitter helpmate in transforming my dreams to reality. We had hoped this would be an enterprise which would meet with your approval."

Jorelial had not seen this coming. A school, eh? What a remarkable idea. She had to give this fellow credit – he had certainly thought the whole thing through. That would solve the problems of roots and income, even a purpose and passion for her baby sister. She was beginning to like Mark. Stepping to his side, she gently cupped a hand under his elbow, indicating that he should rise. "A most noble enterprise, and one which I could support with a glad heart. I think our Father might have been excited by the idea as well, had he lived."

Standing, he was more than a full head taller than her, but she met his hopeful gaze full on, and for the first time in the interview, spoke to him as herself – no masks, no courtly ornaments, no manipulation.

"Look, Mark, you seem to be a fine fellow, honest and decent, sincere in the love you bear my sister. I can see why Delphine is charmed by you. I know you to be excellent in your craft, and am heartened to hear you speak of bigger plans. You obviously have a practical side, and have considered many options. I like you – what I know of you. I must admit I have been preoccupied with bigger events these last months, and haven't been paying attention to my own household. The whole idea of my baby sister getting married is something of a surprise – no, more of a *shock* to me, and I have to get used to it. I suppose it would be wonderful to have a happy event on the horizon for a change, something to look forward to? That would be refreshing. It has been a very long time since anyone laughed or sang or danced."

She was pacing again in front of him, fingers drumming on her palms as she spoke. Mark's face relaxed as her meaning began to settle over him, his wide mouth twitching by degrees into a radiant grin, his breaths deepening audibly in relief and joy. Rel faced him again, "I don't know that I am ready yet to give my unqualified consent, or tell you to choose a date. At the moment we are all somewhat overwhelmed with the Grand Council election and the Coronation just ahead. But I would like to hear more." She took his arm and led him toward the table and chairs, "Sit with me a few moments, and tell me about where you come from, your family and home, and this school you envision..." She planted Mark in a chair, but before she could sit down herself, she heard the door to the chamber creak open, and looked up to see the doorman hesitating on the threshold.

"Something wrong?" Jorelial called across the room. The doorman had been a trusted palace employee for decades, knew protocols, and followed them with impeccable care, except in very extreme circumstances.

"My lady," he called back, "I regret the intrusion, but may I speak to you a moment?" He sounded uncomfortable. Rel's brows drew together as she excused herself and strode toward him. He met her half way, and spoke for her ears alone, "Lady, I am sorry, but there is a man outside who is most insistent that he *must* see you and only you, *today*, on a matter of utmost urgency."

"Warlowe, everybody wants to see me right away over a million matters of utmost urgency. I still have more to do here, and I am sure dinner is about to be served. I really ought to make an appearance tonight. You'll just have to send him away."

"He won't go away, Mistress. I've tried. He insists you will *want* to see him."

Jorelial was perplexed. "Well, who is he?"

"I don't know, Mistress, he won't say."

"Well, then, what does he look like?" The pitch of her voice was beginning to rise in frustration.

"That's the thing, Mistress – the man is dressed in rags like a beggar, with packs and sacks draped all over him as if he had travelled a great distance with all his worldly possessions. He talks like a stranger, and yet, something about him seems vaguely familiar. I feel I should know him, but I can't quite place it. And he seems so earnest..."

Jorelial hesitated. Warlowe should know better than to interrupt an official audience for some beggar, when there was already a long list of petitioners waiting their turns for her attention. But she trusted his judgment, and could not dismiss his intuitions. She looked at him and cocked an eyebrow.

"Mistress, there is just something about him, and he *will not* be turned away."

She sighed, paused, shook her head, and began to usher him back to the door, "It simply is not a good day for this. Take him to the steward, and see if you can't get him on the list somewhere in the best possible position, and then find out if he needs something to eat. We can't deny the man hospitality, but I'm afraid that's the best I can do tonight."

Warlowe seemed almost disappointed. "Yes, Lady Rey," he replied, bowing slightly, and crossed back to the door, disappearing behind its heavy oak paneling. Rel turned back to Mark, who was still sitting at the table, trying to look casual. "Now, where were we?" she asked.

SIX

OVER THE THRESHOLD

Tvrdik stood in a remote corner of the palace courtyard, gratefully munching on the generous portion of bread and cheese he had been given at the steward's command. The sun had just about disappeared below the horizon, and within the walled yard, shadows lengthened across the cobblestones. It was quiet now, almost emptied of the usual crowd of hopefuls daily vying for official attention. An occasional servant scurried by on an errand, and a few lords conversed in low voices in dim corners, punctuating their points of view with gesticulating hands. A lovely young girl sat opposite him on a low bench, twirling a hank of long, bright red hair in her nervous fingers, and, at intervals, jumping up to look toward the Hall of Audience. After a moment she would pace for a bit and find her seat again. She did not seem to notice the pale, weary, ragged young man in glasses, chewing a sandwich and talking to himself.

It hadn't taken him long to arrive at the palace, from his waterfall in the deep woods. Eight days, to be precise. It seemed ironic that all those years, he had never really been so far from home, or from what he had once called home. For this journey, the mage and the naiad had travelled to the nearest village where Tvrdik was known, and traded some simple healing work and kitchen magic for a few provisions and a sturdier water skin in which Ondine could travel. Every few days he stopped again, wherever he could work for food or ask directions. But though he was often offered shelter as well, Tvrdik always chose to camp alone in some remote place under the stars by a stream or a lake. There, Ondine could spend the evening out in the open, and he could practice the wizarding skills which were still new to him, without fear of being noticed. Ondine would spend hours watching the young mage levitate, transmute, transform, dis-apperate and apperate any number of items, occasionally jumping up and down in the water, clapping her hands in glee at his accomplishments. Just as often, she would be giggling at his near-misses. Her favorite trick was the one where he'd turn himself into a big white owl, his spirit beast, and fly all around the campsite. The transformations were always thrilling, but the landings, where he would attempt to morph back into his natural human form – not so good. He was a diligent and tireless student, though, and she delighted in his rehearsals. Where he dealt with other humans, he kept her hidden in the wine skin, for fear that she would end up as a carnival sideshow somewhere. But in the lengthening spring evenings, and on some of the long empty roads they travelled, he would uncork the container, and they would talk. She taught him all about the life of a water sprite – probably more than any human ever knew on the subject – and he filled her in on the mission he was about to undertake, and of Xaarus' plan. Tvrdik left out the details of his past, his flight to the woods, and his state of mind when she first saw him at the waterfall. Somehow, he did not want to seem smaller in her eyes, and was convinced the real story would disappoint her. Truth be told, he was enjoying her effervescent company, a new phenomenon after twelve solitary years. Why, he had actually laughed at her antics, on several occasions!

One evening, camping by the riverside, far from any village, they found themselves hungry, and staring at the last of their meager provisions. Tvrdik chewed on a bit of hard crust, deflated. But Ondine splashed down into the river, shook the drops from her curls in a cascade of spray, held up a finger, and disappeared into the deep. In a moment, Tvrdik heard what sounded like a very loud and raucous song being sung under water. Before he could wonder at its source, two large fish leapt from the river and beached themselves at his feet. A tiny blue face appeared next, grinning at him from the water. With amazement and gratitude, Tvrdik blessed the fish, conjured a fire, and roasted them to a turn. Often, afterwards, he teased her that her singing had been so horrible that it sent the fish flying up from their watery lairs, just to escape the torment.

Now, at last, they had arrived at their destination, and found themselves locked out. Here they were, standing in the palace courtyard, the sun sinking, the day ending, and a chill breeze beginning to ruffle Tvrdik's pale hair, and he did not have a clue as to what to do next. Of course, he had gotten himself put on some list for an audience with the Lady Rey, but it was a very long list, and who knew when the actual meeting would materialize. It could be weeks, or months even, and his business could not wait that long. *Hmmph*, he thought with bitter reflection, *a list for a simple audience? Still full of herself, if you ask me, despite Xaarus sticking up for her.* XAARUS! He stopped mid-chew, struck by the lightning bolt thought of the bond he and his Master had forged in order to make their lessons more efficient. Xaarus had said he felt it might work to keep the lines of communication open even across time and space, but only sparingly, only in Tvrdik's mind, and only in the hour of greatest need. Tvrdik had not tested the theory yet, not wishing to abuse such a privilege. But if this was not greatest need, he could think of none. If he could not even get in the door for an interview, they were stopped in their tracks. He felt certain that Xaarus would know what to do.

Swallowing, he closed his eyes and poured all his intention into conjuring his memories of the older wizard. Holding these pictures in his thoughts, he focused on reaching out for Xaarus' mind. It should feel familiar – the path had been well-worn in the final week of his training – but it was so far away now, it felt like a very long stretch into a vast unknown space. Tvrdik's face began to sweat as he poured a little more energy into isolating his teacher's unique energy. Then, with the scent of sage and old wax, there stood the older wizard before him, a bit translucent, perhaps, but very recognizable. Not wanting to waste precious moments with his master, Tvrdik seized the opportunity to present his dilemma. Meanwhile, peering over the rim of the wooden tankard in which she was temporarily housed, Ondine watched in fascination as her 'Lovely Man' seemed to be conversing most passionately with the air.

"Master, I am here at Theriole, but the lady will not see me. It is as you said here: chaotic, much fear and grief everywhere, uncertainty and confusion. The Lady Rey is in such demand that she will only receive petitioners who have registered on a list weeks in advance. We do not have the luxury of time or patience, nor am I sure she will see me looking like a threadbare beggar in any case. I tried to be as firm as courtesy would permit, but I do not think breaking the door in would be well-regarded. What do I do?"

Xaarus' image flickered, but remained, the old wizard seeming to be considering this new information. Now his mouth moved, but the familiar voice seemed to come from a place inside of Tvrdik's brain, as if from a great distance, while at the same time as close as his own heartbeat. It was a strange sensation, but Tvrdik could only freeze mid-breath, listening for the response his mentor might give. *Use the coin,* he heard, and shook his head blankly. *The coin I gave you – my calling card. I daresay she will remember it. That should get you inside.* Like a sunrise inside his head, Tvrdik recalled the small gold piece he had been carrying around in his pouch. Reaching a hand now inside the small one reserved for important personal items, he felt within until his fingers closed around the cool, flat circle, and he pulled it out, releasing his breath in relief to find it still there.

Good, that's it! Xaarus' image continued, *Once you meet her, you must convince her of your sincerity, and the truth of what you have to tell her. As for the first, be honest if she questions you. Hold nothing back. If you have opportunity to meet the dragon, submit without question. Tashroth will be able to read your heart, and could prove a valuable ally. For the latter, relate to her all we have discussed, and stress what I have told you about the coming war. Mention the name of Lord Drogue; it will resonate with her today, I think. I must go. I cannot hold the link. All my faith rests in you, my boy. You will succeed if you only believe it.…* And he was gone.

Tvrdik sank to the ground, his back propped against a stone wall. Holding their communication link open for only a few moments was exhausting. But he had gotten what he needed and more. Somehow, even the shadow of Xaarus made him feel powerful, energized, hopeful. He leaned his head back against the wall and closed his eyes. As soon as his strength returned a bit, he would go approach the doorman again, coin in hand.

A cold splash full in the face startled him awake. Ondine was staring at him, an expression in her wide eyes somewhere between curiosity and bewilderment. "Lovely Man, you sick?" she asked innocently, and then with a sharper tone, "Or maybe brain-addled?"

Tvrdik laughed out loud, "No, no, I'm fine," he reassured, "I was asking for help from my Master, but no one else can see him…" She leaned backward like he might be contagious. Tvrdik laughed again. "It's a long story – I'll try to explain later. Sorry to say I need you back in your little house, Ondine. We have more work to do this evening." He held the water skin out to her, and shaking her curls with exasperation, she disappeared inside. The sun had dipped low and the courtyard was fully in shadow now. Tvrdik noticed the young girl still sitting rather dejectedly on her bench, as he gathered the rest of his possessions. No time now to find out her story. Perhaps another day. He stuffed the last morsel of cheese in his mouth, tossed the gold coin in the air, caught it as it tumbled down, and started back toward the giant doors of the Hall of Audience.

Not five minutes later, the enormous door swung open again in the Hall of Audience, and Jorelial Rey, still in conversation with Mark, found herself again summoned to private conference with her doorkeeper. His eyes were as round as saucers as he addressed her, "Pardon again my intrusion, Lady…"

Annoyed at the turn the day had taken, Jorelial was not her best self as she snapped, "What is it this time?"

Warlowe stammered, "My lady, that man I spoke of earlier…"

"I thought I said…"

"He gave me this, and bade me present it to you by way of introduction." The doorman handed her the small metallic object. Jorelial took one look at it, turned it over in her hand, and gasped, "Holy cat-tails and dragon's bones, Warlowe! Did he say where he got this?"

"No, Mistress. Just said he thought it would interest you, and repeated that he had urgent business to discuss with you on behalf of the original owner, at your earliest convenience." Warlowe blinked.

"At my earliest convenience, indeed…" Rel swore under her breath as she spun about. "Mark, I am afraid we will have to continue our discussion at a future time. Something has come up – you understand?"

Mark rose at once and attempted a little formal bow, almost unbalancing himself, "At your pleasure, lady, and I hope to call you 'sister' very soon." She stared after him, deep in thought, as he disappeared through the large doors, and then turned back to Warlowe. "I apologize for my ill temper; it has been an excruciatingly long and trying day. You did exactly the right thing. Give me two minutes and then show him in, please. Oh, and could you please find the steward and tell him not to wait dinner for me? And if you happen to see Tashroth hanging about out there, could you tell him for me that I will join him on the north tower as soon as I can? Thank you, Warlowe." She touched his arm in genuine appreciation. He bowed to her and stepped outside, raising a single eyebrow on the way out in response to the suggestion that he speak to a dragon.

Jorelial looked at the coin in her hand one more time, then strode over to the formal throne on the dais. It would be important to start this particular interview from a position of authority. The door creaked open again, and Warlowe reappeared, ushering in a stranger. As the man crossed the long room, she had a moment to take his full measure. He was tall and lean, dressed in some sort of odd rustic clothing that was patched and threadbare. He carried a collection of packs slung over both shoulders and on his back. His age was difficult to assess, as one moment he looked quite young, and then, in another light, lines of care appeared on his face that made him seem much older. Around his head was an aureole of hair so pale as to be nearly white, while his piercing blue eyes peered out from behind gold-rimmed spectacles that seemed to give him a perpetually surprised look. Facing this man, Jorelial felt a powerful impulse both to laugh and to cry. Instead, she tried to look stern. The man approached, made a perfunctory bow, and spoke first. "Jorelial Rey, I hope you will forgive my forwardness, but I am sent here on a mission of grave importance."

She narrowed her eyes at him and brandished the coin, "Where did you get this?"

"From him whose image appears upon it."

"That is not possible, for he is long dead."

"You are mistaken, as I have spoken with him this very evening, and he asked to be commended to you."

"If you have spoken with him, then you must take me to him, that I might plead for his return, since there has never been a time that this realm needed his good guidance more."

"That, I regret, cannot be, as he is not in a place we may come to."

"But you just said you spoke to him this very evening."

"I did."

"You speak in riddles, sir. Is it your intention to confuse me, or try my temper?"

"No, Jorelial Rey. It is my intention to tell you nothing but the truth, and if you will hear me out, all will be made plain."

There was a pause. She found it interesting that he called her by name without any of the respectful titles that everyone else used. She tried a new tactic.

"Who *are* you?"

"I am Tvrdik."

"That's an odd name. What kind of a name is that?"

He shrugged, "It is my name."

Another pause. How to come to the meat of the matter with this odd stranger? And what had he to do with Xaarus? At that moment, the man shrugged and took a step to shift all his packs about and redistribute their weight. Jorelial realized he must be weary of them. She stood. "Sir, will you lay down your burdens for the moment, and then try to start from the beginning?"

Grateful, Tvrdik divested himself of all his parcels and packs, laying them in a careful pile on the floor. Only a single water skin he kept close to his chest, a detail that did not escape Lady Rey's trained eye. He seemed at first uncertain as to how to begin, and then made a decision.

"Jorelial Rey, if you search the recesses of your memory, you might find that you know me, or at least have met me before. Long ago, I lived near this palace, and was an eager student of Master Wizard Xaarus. There were three of us apprenticed to him at the time. Perhaps I did not stand out to you from among the group. But I remember you, coming and going on the great green dragon. You were barely fifteen when I last saw you, I would guess, and something of a lone wolf. No disrespect intended..." He paused as she came down the stairs and walked right up to him, circling once, and then staring directly into his face while he held very still...

"Tvrdik!" she shouted, making him flinch, "The Wizard School. Of course...I *do* remember you. Not that we'd ever really spoken to each other back then, mind you, but I do remember the three of you hanging around Xaarus all the time. The hair...the glasses...why, you were only a teenager yourself when I last saw you." The flooding back of memories seemed to re-energize her, wipe away the aura of suspicion and weariness that had clung to her a moment before. "You know my father was very close to Xaarus; they were often together. And you three seemed always to be sort of slouching around in the background, waiting for something, or following him off somewhere in a little train." A chuckle escaped her at the recollection.

Tvrdik's throat tightened, and he could feel his ears getting hot. "Xaarus was a very great teacher," he stammered, "we all felt so fortunate to be learning from him...we would have followed him into the depths of the underworld..."

But Jorelial Rey was lost in her own memories. Her face changed. "And then, suddenly you were all gone. All of you. Overnight, it seemed. No more wizards. What happened?" The blond man closed his eyes at that, and sighed in a way that nearly broke her heart. Clearly, this was not going to be an easy or brief story to relate. She made a snap decision. "Tvrdik, come sit down here at this table. If I am at last to hear the resolution of the greatest mystery in the entire history of our kingdom, we ought to make ourselves comfortable and do it right. Warlowe!" She sprang back toward the door, summoning the doorman once again, as Tvrdik sank into a chair. Warlowe was there in an instant, fearing some problem with the stranger.

"Here, my lady. Is anything wrong?"

She clapped him on the back. "All is well, friend – you were right. This is Tvrdik, one of the original students in Master Xaarus' Wizard School. We are just getting re-acquainted. Could you arrange for rooms for him at the palace, and send over a carafe of wine and something to eat, please? We may be here a while, and I am positively famished." Warlowe, startled, stood stock still, staring first at one, then the other. Tvrdik gave a little wave. Speechless, the doorman bowed and disappeared behind the large oak doors. Jorelial, feeling newly invigorated and truly curious, strode back to sit at the conference table. Looking Tvrdik in the eye, she said, "All right, then...go on. I'm all ears."

SEVEN

THE HEART OF THE MATTER

THEY SAT THERE TOGETHER AT the conference table for the better part of two hours, sipping wine and picking at a variety of pastries, fruits, and more cheese. Tvrdik told her as much as he thought prudent, about the terrible thing that Benjin and Ailianne did that had cost them their lives, about how a distraught Xaarus tried to go back in time to prevent the awful event from occurring, but ended up instead trapped in a dismal future. He recounted the story of his own retreat to the ancient woods, and of Xaarus' recent appearance there on his doorstep in order to enlist his aid on a special mission. He explained how Xaarus had been pulled back in to the future, but that he could be communicated with through a special bond that had been forged between the two wizard's minds, and how this had helped him gain access to her that very evening. He left out many of the details of his own history, and did not think it yet wise to introduce Ondine, who at the moment was sleeping quite soundly in her water skin, close to his chest. But about everything else, he was as truthful and as thorough as possible. Perhaps the wine helped his story to flow more easily, but, then, so did a rapt and attentive audience, asking pertinent questions and devouring every word. It had been a very long time since Tvrdik had had a meaningful conversation with another mature human being, excluding his two weeks with Xaarus. And those seemed like more of a dream now.

71

"So, let me get this right," Jorelial queried, munching a grape, and waving a stem of them in her hand, "when you have these long-distance conversations with Xaarus, no one can see or hear him except you?"

"Correct."

"He is only present in your mind?"

"Yes."

"Shame. I should have liked to talk to him again. You know, this is the strangest story I have ever heard. It's pretty unbelievable, I have to say. How do I know you didn't make the whole thing up?"

"I can't think why I would do that. And besides, you have the coin."

She opened her other hand and examined the familiar old face again, "I suppose you will be wanting this back?"

"I might have need of it sometime," he apologized. She flipped it up and caught it as it tumbled back down, spinning in mid-air. Warm with wine and feeling nostalgic, she said, "When I was a very small girl, Xaarus used to come and visit my father and me. He would announce every visit with one of these coins, and then later on, after dinner, he would play games with me, pulling the coin from behind my ear, or finding it in my pocket where it hadn't been before…simple sleight of hand, nothing really worthy of his skill. But I adored him, and cherished those visits. And I think that was the last time I remember laughing with complete and utter abandon…"

Tvrdik was silent, but was thinking that he knew just what she meant. Jorelial was still talking, "Seeing this coin tonight brought back a flood of memories. It really took me by surprise. It was, in fact, the one thing that could have turned me from my purpose, and gotten my attention tonight."

"There is your proof. Xaarus said it would work."

"So, am I also to learn what this 'special mission' of yours is? Is it something I can help you with?" She chased the sentence with a rather over-large piece of sweet cake, and crumbs fell all over the table.

Abruptly sober, Tvrdik sat up very straight, and looked her right in the eyes. "Jorelial Rey, I was sent here to find you, to warn you."

She swallowed, "To warn me of what?"

"That you, the boy king you protect, and indeed the entire realm are in grave danger."

"Well, it has been an awful year, and everything is in chaos now. But we have good people all doing their best to right things. I'm sure eventually we will pull it together."

Tvrdik's mouth was dry as he forged on with his difficult message, "No, you will not. Xaarus has combed over the timelines of history in exacting detail, and he sent me with word of your most probable future. There is more trouble ahead."

"Tell me," she replied.

"Do you know someone by the name of Drogue?"

Jorelial turned white, and the hairs on the back of her neck stood up. "Lord Drogue. He is one of the more powerful nobles at court, from a very old family. I spoke with him today; he is ambitious to be named regent, but he will never get the job if I have anything to say about it."

"You will be named regent. There is no doubt of that in any timeline. It is correct."

"Wait a moment; I am not even sure if I want to be considered…"

"You *will* be named, and you will do it because you feel called to duty. Lord Drogue will not accept the situation. He will wage war against you and the infant king, and will try to wrest the throne from you by force."

Jorelial leapt up, overturning her chair and a wine cup, "That miserable traitor! We will crush him." she shouted.

"No, you will not." Tvrdik kept his voice calm and even, his eyes fixed on the tabletop, and his hands splayed out on the surface before him. Only the white knuckles showed his own tension at being the unwanted messenger. "Drogue is a ruthless, determined man, and he will rally and equip a large army. This realm is not prepared to meet him on his terms. You will lose. Drogue will take the throne and become the tyrant you feared he would. But worse is to come. Xaarus told me that, starting with Drogue's ascent, the timeline moves irrevocably toward the grim future in which he now resides. Balances shift, likelihoods tip, millennia pass, and human beings become fearful and soulless. There are no wizards, no magic, no talking beasts, no nature sprites, and people question if they ever existed at all. The dragons and unicorns are harried and hunted mercilessly until the last survivors simply depart for other, safer dimensions. Wars wrack the world: nation against nation and factions within nations fighting over petty differences and scarce resources. The ancient forests are all cut down and burned. The air and waters are poisoned with noxious fumes so that they are no longer fit support for the birds and fish and sea creatures. The scenario I bring you is dark, indeed…"

"Stop, I will hear no more!" Jorelial Rey was standing stock still with her hands over her face. When she finally dropped them to look at him, her features were drawn and ashen, "And all of this is to be laid upon me? All of this is my fault? Not only do I lose a kingdom, allow the end of an entire royal dynasty, and cause countless deaths in a fruitless war, but I am to be held accountable for the miseries of the future as well? And, now, I suppose, I am to thank you and Xaarus for going to all this special trouble to come and apprise me of my nightmarish destiny? *This* is your mission? Tell me, what satisfaction can you possibly glean from seeing me crumble helplessly before you in agony? Why would you *do* such a thing?" She was shaking violently and deadly pale.

Tvrdik winced, but kept his voice low and soothing, "There is another timeline. Another possible future. It is this that I was sent to lay before you. There is still time to set it in motion, but it will take courage, resourcefulness, faith…"

"Tell me now, in this other future, do we win?"

He gave her a curt nod, "One possible road leads to victory, the restoration of order to Eneri Clare, and the beginning of a new path into the far distant future where all good and worthy things are preserved."

"Tvrdik, what must I do?"

"You must remain true to your ideals."

"What sort of an answer is that? I am always true to my ideals…"

"You believe that violence is abhorrent, that war is futile and wasteful, and that taking life is wrong."

"Well, yes, but I'm not the one starting the war."

"But you must at all costs avoid being seduced into fighting it on his terms. You must find a way to fight this war with your own weapons: intelligence, truth, faith, creativity, magic. And…and you must strive not to shed blood on either side." There was a silence as the Lady Regent took in what the ragged stranger had just said. She stared at him, eyes wide.

"Drogue's forces will be fully armed, and equipped…"

"And ruthless…correct."

"And you are suggesting that I meet him with the forces of this kingdom unarmed and unwilling to harm anyone?"

"Exactly."

"But this isn't principle, or ideals, it's suicide! Tvrdik, I am responsible for the welfare of my people. I can't just send them out unprotected. And how would that stop Drogue from taking what he wants anyway?"

"We must protect them in new and different ways. Xaarus searched exhaustively and he found that the fork in the road is here and now. Someone must set an example of a way to triumph over Darkness, not with more Darkness, but with Light. He believed that someone might be you. You cannot win by fighting Drogue's way, and even if you could, you lose anyway, because you become what you despise in your enemy. And on and on into the future until there is no more Light, no hope – only fear, self-interest, and violence. Violence, even in the cause of good, only begets more violence. It can never preserve Light."

She stood frozen, horrified, staring at him, her voice a hoarse whisper, "You are insane. This can never work."

For the first time in his long litany, he raised his eyes from the table, those ice-blue, piercing, searching eyes, and met hers, "Oh, so we were mistaken? You *do* believe that might makes right, and that truth, compassion, resourcefulness, and intellect have no true power in the real world?"

"I didn't *say* that!"

He was up in a flash, beside her now, holding her eyes and urging his case with his entire being, "Then put them to the test. Invoke their power. Believe in them."

"Tvrdik, be reasonable. What exactly are we supposed to fight with?"

"With the certainty that we fight for what is right. With ideas, and of course, with a little magic."

She let out a wail, "I have no magic!"

He stood firm and kept his voice even, "You do now. Xaarus sent me here to help you. I am committed to doing everything in my power to see this succeed. Someone *has* to make a stand for a new way. Xaarus was sure it would be you. If we put our heads together, we can do this." He held her gaze and tried to sound more confident than he actually felt.

She searched his face, and whispered, "Can we win?"

He shrugged and dropped his eyes, "There are no guarantees. In one timeline, we make our stand, and fail, which might do the trick for the far future, but might not be so pleasant for all of us in the present. But, in the one Xaarus is counting on, we take it all, on our own terms."

"We?"

"I told you, if you decide to do this, I am here to help you, come what may. Right to the end. We'll need a lot of support from other quarters as well, of course…"

"Yes, and there it is. Even if you could convince *me* of the merits of this harebrained scheme, how would I ever sell the idea to the rest of the Council, the army, the ministers and generals? They will all think that I have been out in the sun too long."

"One step at a time, Jorelial Rey, one step at a time. I know all of this is a lot to digest, and time is short. But sleep on it, and see what your heart tells you. I have faith that you will know what to do." He sounded remarkably like her father in that moment, and it startled her. She paused, trying to comprehend all that had passed between them.

"I do not know what to do. I am overwhelmed. But I do know someone who will help me to find the truth in all of this. I will speak to Tashroth tonight and see what he thinks. He is ancient and wise, and always sees things much more clearly than I do on my own. I beg you, stay close in the chambers which I will give you. Rest, and speak to no one else about any of this. If Tashroth will consent to see you tomorrow, I will send for you. You will have our answer by sundown."

Tvrdik took a step back and bowed his head in respectful assent. He then moved to collect his packs and possessions. Jorelial Rey stopped him with a surprisingly childlike tone, "Tvrdik? Can you really do magic?"

He frowned. "I *am* a wizard, still learning my craft, but capable enough…"

"Show me something…anything. Help me to believe."

He understood her need, and smiled. Wrinkling his brow a moment in concentration, he spun around once, and suddenly stood before her in robes of velvet and cloth of gold, elegant and expensive. A fashionable poof of a hat was perched on his golden locks.

"Better?" He raised his pale eyebrows and peered at her with his intense blue eyes behind their spectacles. Jorelial Rey began to laugh. And laugh. She laughed so hard, it seemed she might not be able to stop. His face fell.

"What? What is so funny?" he demanded.

Finally catching her breath, she gasped, "Oh, Tvrdik, if you could do that, why did you come to me for an official audience in rags and patches? Did it not occur to you that your chances might have been better dressed like a proper courtier?"

She watched as his face mirrored a parade of emotions, seeming to consider her rebuke, and at first revealing that such a precaution had never crossed his mind. But at last, an odd expression of clarity came into his features as he turned his gaze back to her, eye to eye, and the corners of his mouth turned up ever so slightly, "Jorelial Rey, this is nothing but illusion. Illusion has its uses, as you will soon see. But I came before you as I am. I wished to present myself to you honestly, in truth, as you have every right to expect from me. How could I ask you to believe anything I told you if I started out with a falsehood? Do you understand?"

She nodded, the laughter fading from her eyes as respect began to dawn in them. There was more to this lanky, pale, myopic dreamer than one would imagine. He had walked in uninvited and thrown what was left of her ordered life into chaos, but somehow she felt oddly safe in his presence.

She clapped a summons, "Warlowe!" The doorman appeared. "Warlowe, please take Tvrdik to the rooms you have arranged for him. Treat him like an honored guest. Make sure he has everything he needs – a bath, new clothing, food, whatever he asks of you. But tell no one that he is in the palace or that you know anything of his existence for the moment. It is to be a close secret for now, and thank you."

"Yes, my lady, as you say."

She turned her attention back to the young mage, "Tomorrow I will send for you. Be patient."

"Thank you for seeing me, Jorelial Rey."

She smiled crookedly, "It seems to have been my destiny."

Jorelial Rey's sumptuous apartments in the palace were empty that night, as often they were, while she spent the night with Tashroth on the roof. Tash liked to curl up on the largest crenellated turret and, especially on these warm spring evenings, Rel would fold herself into his left foreleg, falling asleep against his beating heart. After a long day handling the continuous demands of running a kingdom, it was often the only time she had to spend with the dragon. And she never felt fully herself, being parted from him for long. He too would grow restless and cranky if many days went by without her company. Their bonds were deep and enduring. And tonight, as Rel's thoughts spun dizzily with all the information she had been handed, and sleep seemed a distant, elusive dream, there was nowhere she would rather have been than beside her trusted protector and companion. She lay propped against his flank, his massive head curved around to meet hers, and together they watched the stars overhead. Patches of fast-moving cloud scudded over the constellations here and there, but did not linger in any one place for long.

"See, there is the Warrior Prince, and there the Archer!" she pointed as she spoke. "Even in our lore of the stars we honor those who have triumphed in battle. Our civic statues, our bardic ballads, our heroes of history – nearly all warriors."

"We dragons pay homage to the brave and skilled as well, and those who perish in defense of a friend, or a cause that is worthy."

"I have been trained, Tash, in strategy, weapons, and the art of combat, and I am reasonably good in any contest of skill. I can't say I've ever had much stomach for applying any of it against a real flesh and blood adversary, though. The thought is horrifying to me."

"You have grown up in a time of peace, little one, and have had the luxury of choosing non-violence. Some evils come along that must be stopped at any cost."

"I would not hand the likes of Drogue this kingdom for any price," she agreed, "and I am not afraid to do whatever it takes to stop him. But Tvrdik says we rely on the old default position of armed conflict without even questioning if there could be another way."

"He has a point there, little one. While we may be asked to defend ourselves and what we love, how we do it is always a choice. It is expedient to choose what has always served, instead of reaching to create something new. I am intrigued."

"It is a powerful argument that the message came from Xaarus, if I am to believe the story is true. My father respected Xaarus over any other man. I feel sure he would have taken this seriously if it truly came from the Court Wizard."

"Xaarus is revered among my folk as well. His wisdom is legendary. At least, it was…"

"How do I know I can believe this stranger who shows up without warning, telling such a wild story? I mean, I do recognize Tvrdik, and my intuition is to trust him. He seems so genuine. But what if he is just a madman, or part of some malevolent plot? He could have killed Xaarus himself, or be in league with Drogue for all I really know."

"Ask him to come to me tomorrow, and I will weigh his heart. I will know if there is madness or falsehood in him. I will certainly uncover any deception."

"Thank you, dearest. I knew I could count on you. But, oh, Tash, if it *is* all true, do you realize what we are in for? Our lives will be turned upside down. I don't know how I will ever sell this bloodless battle idea to anyone on the Council, or to the generals, and then, what if we fail? It's too awful to even imagine."

"One thing at a time, beloved. If it is written for you to do this, all things will then conspire to assist you. But first, we find out."

"Why me? I never wished for all this responsibility. Why can't I just climb on your back, and fly off far away, just the two of us? We could be happy, and leave the kingdom to its own devices."

A deep rumble in Tashroth's throat signified his amusement with her plan, "As attractive a notion as that might be, when destiny lays a task at your doorstep, you cannot outrun it or hide from it for long. It will always find you. If this work belongs to you, you know you will embrace it, and do your best to accomplish what is needed. This is who you are, and who you were brought up to be."

"It's Tvrdik's mission." she pouted.

"Think, girl. He has no authority to gather or sway anyone at court, or to rally support for a new idea. He knows no one, and no one knows him as yet. That is why Xaarus sent him to you. Look around…if not you, who can make such a thing happen?"

"It doesn't seem fair."

Tashroth chuckled again, knowing her moods so well, "You had the marks of greatness on your forehead from the moment of your birth, child. I have always known that. We have only been waiting for the circumstances which would put it to the proof. It may be that time is now. But remember, you are not alone in this. You will never be alone. There will be many who will rally to your standard …and I will always be with you."

Finally sleepy, Jorelial Rey turned on her side, and snuggled into Tashroth's warm scales.

"And that, Tash, is the rock to which I gratefully cling in any storm."

Her eyes closed in exhaustion. It would be a while longer before the dragon also slept.

EIGHT

TASTE OF LUXURY

Tvrdik was distracted from the events of the evening by the comforts of the room he had been assigned in the palace. It had been twelve years since he had even seen a featherbed, much less slept in one, and the soft coverlets brought tears to his eyes. He freed Ondine from her confinement, and set her in the pottery washbasin that sat on a large wooden chest. But he had to warn her to duck and hide at the arrival of two palace servants, hand-picked for their loyalty and ability to keep their counsel, who asked if they could draw him a hot bath. Speechless with delight, he nodded, and they were off about their tasks before you could say "scrub-brush."

Soaking in the hot, scented water was one of the most luxurious experiences he had ever had, as he felt the cares of the past weeks drift away, along with the tension and aches in his muscles. When he was fully immersed, and the servants had disappeared, he reached over and tipped Ondine into the tub for a brief splash about. Of course it was a bit embarrassing to be naked in a tub with a small blue girl who insisted on calling him, "Lovely Man." But he drew up his knees for awhile and let her frolic in half the bath. She certainly appreciated the extra space for a change, but was appalled at the temperature, and kept calling it, "nasty, dead water." Tvrdik realized how much she must miss the lively diversity of a natural stream or lake.

"I think we will be in this place for some time, and I suspect I will be on my own for much of tomorrow. I will take you down to the river in

81

the morning and find a special spot to release you. I promise to come find you there every day and fill you in on whatever is new. We will have some waiting to do now, and then the real work of drumming up support will start. No reason you should stay cooped up in that old water skin."

"Very good," she replied. "I will explore. Try to find more like myself in waters by palace. Maybe cousin naiads still live near here. Will give you good reports." She made a little salute.

Tvrdik smiled. "Sounds like a fine idea. We can use all the help you can rally." He offered a single finger to her tiny hand, and they shook on their agreement. "Do you know, if I am lucky tomorrow, I might just get to meet a real dragon close up. Do you want to come along?" Ondine leapt backward, sending droplets everywhere.

"Dragon? No, no! See shadow of dragon fly over home sometimes. Very big. Frighten me. You go, Lovely Man. See dragon and tell Ondine story, yes?"

"I'll tell you all about it, and maybe you can meet him yourself later." Tvrdik then took the time to fill her in on everything that had happened in the last few hours, putting into words all his hope and intuition that Lady Jorelial Rey would indeed be won over to their cause.

"So, for now we wait. But, in luxury at least. I surely appreciate the bed and the bath – it has been a very long time."

She giggled and shook her curls, spraying his face, "Silly man. Better to be outside in sweet air, green things all around. No good in small box – no sky, dead water." She made a rude sound, and did a graceful somersault in the water. Tvrdik laughed despite himself.

"I'm sorry. This 'small box' is a real treat for me. Tomorrow we will take care of you." He raised a hand in oath, "I swear, first thing." Footfalls in the hallway interrupted their heart-to-heart, and he had barely enough time to scoop her back into the washbasin with a *ploop*. "Stay there," he cautioned, "I think I can make you seem invisible." A thought, a quick flick of the hand and some muttered syllables, and then he stretched out again, trying to look casual. The palace servants knocked and entered bearing a soft nightshirt, and a set of clothes for the morning, plain, but elegant. Leggings and a long vest in a deep stormy blue, and a long tunic in a pale shade to match his eyes. He touched the fabric and marveled at its quality. A plain belt and new matching boots were also provided – the kind that were more for comfort and show than hard wear. Oh, he was really going to feel like a courtier in this outfit. A quick glance told him that someone had a good eye, as it looked like everything would fit well enough. He did not dare ask what had happened to his old garments – probably gone beyond retrieval, even burned. They had served him well for so very long, he sent them a grateful blessing in his mind and let them go. That episode of his life was over. He had already stepped into a new world.

And now, cleaner than he'd been in ages, dried, and wearing his cozy nightshirt, he sat down on one corner of the bed, and watched the servants clear away the bath equipment. He had to bite his lip as the invisible Ondine (Tvrdik could see through his own magic) amused herself with bouncing in and out of the washbasin, making grotesque faces at them as they worked, oblivious to her presence right beside them. Someone appeared with a steaming cup of fragrant tea, asked if there were anything else he required, and when he assured them he couldn't think of a thing, withdrew, shut the massive door, and left him alone. With a quick gesture, he lifted the invisibility charm and watched Ondine leap into the air in a pirouette, landing back in her basin with nary a splash. She blew him a kiss and settled down for the night.

The young mage let himself fall backward onto the bed, and stared at the ceiling. The overstuffed mattress felt wonderful against his back and weary limbs. He had not expected to be treated with such royal hospitality. When they entertained guests here, they were serious about it. And when Lady Rey gave an order…

His thoughts snagged on Jorelial Rey, and their first encounter. He was ashamed to admit that he'd been wrong about her, just as Xaarus had said. Far from spoiled or egotistical, she seemed instead just an exceptionally capable girl overburdened with far more responsibility than she'd ever bargained for. She was doing her best to hold things together with as much grace and integrity as she could muster. She had remembered him. Under different circumstances, they might have grown to be friends. Perhaps, when all this unpleasantness was behind them, they still could be? Tvrdik realized with a dull shock that indeed he *had* been lonely for quite a long time, and was excited by the prospect of finding a kindred spirit. As quickly as that notion flared up in his consciousness, however, it went cold. What on earth was he thinking? This was a woman who was running the entire kingdom of Eneri Clare – as far above him as the stars in the heavens circled above the trees. Only a few short hours ago, he had not even been allowed to set foot in the same room with her. *Come out of the clouds, Tvrdik,* he thought to himself, *you were sent here to give her the facts, and Xaarus' guidance, and then to serve her in whatever way she needs.* Tvrdik took off his precious glasses, and laid them with care on the chest. "And that I will do." he continued out loud, to no one in particular.

On hands and knees, he crawled up to the center of the big, inviting bed, and weary beyond thought, collapsed into its downy embrace. From a high window drifted the relentless, regular sound of surf battering the gray cliffs below, teaching his breath a slower, deeper rhythm. A cool breeze from without teased his nostrils with a strange aromatic blend of lilacs and salty brine. Just before he dropped into a sound sleep, a dream of glowing dragons' eyes piercing his soul like twin coals, furrowed his brow for a moment, and then released him into oblivion.

NINE

DAY OF DISCOVERIES

Tvrdik could easily have stayed in bed all the next day, but morning came early at Theriole, and before he even realized he had fallen asleep, someone was knocking at the door to ask if he wanted breakfast. The young man sat up in bed, pulled the covers up around him, reached for his glasses, and shouted, "Come in." A different servant from the night before entered the room with a large tray of enticing foods, and set it on a small wooden table at the opposite end of the room. The scent of fresh warm bread beckoned. It took all of Tvrdik's skills of persuasion to convince the servant that he was fully capable of washing and dressing himself, and in the end, he had to promise to call if he needed anything at all. Alone once more, he got out of bed, checked on Ondine – who was humming, while doing the backstroke in the wash basin, – located the small alcove where he could take care of his morning ablutions, and changed into the outfit that had been left for him. Catching his own reflection in the polished glass on one wall, the young mage was startled to see a man he did not recognize. Tvrdik lingered a moment and frowned at himself, sizing up the picture he presented. He had to admit the fit, cut, and color of the clothing suited him quite well. Realizing that he was famished, he sat down at the little table to explore what delights they had sent up for breakfast. There were ripe berries, and warm bread with churned butter, fragrant hot tea, and some sort of sweet custardy pastry, which he did not recognize, but which he decided was now his favorite food. Tvrdik ate with gusto, savoring every flavor and texture with a new awareness, feeling alive and awake in a somehow fresh way.

Over breakfast, he chatted with Ondine about things of little consequence, sharing a few memories that had surfaced of life at the palace in his youth. Ondine rarely partook of human food; it wasn't her preferred fare most of the time. But, aware that she hadn't been out in a natural setting for a few days, and protective of her well-being, he insisted she take a little fruit and a taste of the custard, which elicited another of her charming pirouettes in the air, followed by a noisy splashdown.

Just as they were finishing up, there came another knock on the door. Ondine ducked, and the same servant who had awakened him stood there with a written note from Lady Jorelial Rey. Tvrdik unfolded and read it: *Stuck in important meetings all day. Meet me on the roof of the north tower at the sixteenth hour. Ask Warlowe for directions. Tashroth wants to meet you. Keep a low profile until then. Jorelial Rey.* Tvrdik thanked the lad, who promptly set about clearing the breakfast things. *Well, here it is,* he thought to himself. Both the audience he was hoping for, and a liberty pass for the rest of the day, delivered with perfect timing, just as he had been deciding what to do next. *Most considerate of her.* Now, he was free to sally forth and reacquaint himself with the grounds.

As soon as the young servant had received thanks and exited for the final time, Tvrdik sprang up and addressed Ondine. "Well, what do you say? Are you ready to go exploring? The day looks pleasant…...Hmmmm?" For answer she kicked up her heels, did several somersaults and flashed him her most winning smile. It seemed alright to leave most of his travel gear in the room; it could always be sent for if something changed. So he slung two water skins over his shoulder, one to actually drink from, and one loaded with an exuberant naiad. He opened the door of the room, stepped out into the hall, looked around, closed the door behind himself, and ventured out at an unhurried pace.

It took them a while to find their way out of the palace. Things were not too busy for the moment – at least, in his wing. Servants would hurry by at intervals on some mission or another, but no one seemed to pay any attention to the mysterious stranger in blue strolling through the halls. He was starting out in unfamiliar territory and made a few wrong turns along the way, until he happened upon the grand staircase that he knew ended at the Main Hall and the front door. Once he was in an area that he remembered from his youth, he recognized that very little had changed in twelve years, and his feet began to find their own way down the stairs and into the vestibule. Here, scattered groups of lords, merchants, and landowners congregated in low conversation. But these seemed too preoccupied with their own affairs to notice him. He quickly slipped over the threshold and out into the sun-drenched day.

He made his way through the palace gardens, which were vast and already filled with a profusion of stimulating colors and scents. Nobody he passed questioned that a young courtier should be out for an early morning stroll on the landscaped grounds.

The palace, christened Theriole by its original builders, was built on a small hill at the confluence of the river Maygrew and the sea. On the ocean side there were short cliffs and a panoramic view. Here on the backside, the land sloped gently down to the delta and a well-travelled riverwalk. Further upstream was the capitol city, Therin. It was little more than a fair-sized town supporting an array of shops, crafts, and services. Fertile delta and riverfront fields surrounding and radiating outward from Therin supported its residents with all manner of food and raw materials. Off to the west, rolling hills gave way to low ancient mountains and bluffs. Sheep and goat herders abounded in the hills, and there were some mining operations as well. Deep old forests spread off to the North, becoming less civilized and more impenetrable as one traveled further into them. This is where Tvrdik had found his refuge so many years ago, away from the bustling crowds of the capital and court.

From anywhere in the town, and far into the farmlands, one could see Theriole, turrets standing watch over a contented and prosperous society, and the sight inspired confidence, and a feeling of security. But, as Tvrdik stood and looked back at the magnificent building, he realized its design had been planned more for aesthetic and emotional effect than for strategic defense. He shook his head, wondering if he could make the whole thing invisible in a crisis... then decided that was a question for another day. He made his way down the slope on the winding path, lined with flowering shrubs and occasional sculptures, toward the riverwalk. Some of what he saw was new and unfamiliar. But his feet seemed to know the way of their own accord, though he was not conscious of a destination. It did not take long to discover the reason: there on the left, overgrown and almost invisible from the path, stood Xaarus' old cottage, where Tvrdik had lived and studied and worked for six years of his young life.

Always preferring to live a little apart from the palace proper, Xaarus had built a spacious country house, which contained his chambers, his library, his workshop and laboratories, as well as a later extension which provided a classroom and dormitories for the school. Everyone had called it "The Cottage," not so much for its size as for its quaint character. On the grounds was an extensive herb garden, which provided every sort of vegetation used for food, seasonings, and potions. Tvrdik recalled many hours of backbreaking labor planting seedlings, harvesting, and weeding in that garden. Now it had gone to seed, and was covered in tough leaves, vines, and grasses. The house itself seemed still sturdy, but in disrepair. It was badly in need of re-thatching and a good whitewash, and there were bird and rodent nests in the eaves and gutters, and possible leaks in the roof.

Tvrdik stood still, silent, overwhelmed by memory and an emotion that he could not put a name to. As a small boy he had not been close with his parents and brothers, who were fearful and suspicious of his emerging talents. So when Xaarus tracked him down at the tender age of twelve, and took him to live at The Cottage with the other two students, it was the first real family he had experienced. Xaarus had not only been teacher and mentor, but surrogate father and mother to the youngsters. When Tvrdik's genetically weak eyes worsened from hours of study by candlelight, Xaarus made sure the boy was fitted with glasses, though such a device was not common in that country. When any of them struggled through the night with fever and cough, Xaarus would sit beside them and apply wet poultices and healing herbs. The Master worked them hard, but he made them feel like they belonged somewhere and were cared for. Tvrdik found himself remembering all of these things in a sudden flood of nostalgia, scenes he had submerged or forgotten for years.

He now felt doubly committed to accomplishing the task that Xaarus had set before him, and he was more determined than ever to succeed in enlisting the help of Jorelial Rey. Part of him wanted to have a closer look, go inside. But a movement at his chest reminded him that he had promises to keep.

Now that he knew where he was, he remembered a spot by the river where he had spent time as a boy whenever he needed solitude to study or practice. As he recalled it, behind Xaarus' house there was a kink in the river, so that it slowed and broadened, growing mossy and dense. But at this secret spot further upstream, water burbled over rocks at the banks' edge, and willow trees drooped over a large, smooth, outcropping of rock large enough to sit on, or to lie dreaming. Berry bushes surrounded the space, yielding rich fruit in late summer, and all manner of birds, fish, and frogs visited. Few courtiers ventured so far afield on their constitutionals, and he had come to regard it as his own special place back then. It would indeed be the perfect spot to release Ondine into friendly waters, and from which to make regular contact with her in privacy. Hoping against hope that the place would be as he remembered it, he quickened his pace along a somewhat neglected path, pushing aside stray branches and stepping over clumps of coarse grass. The way there was etched into his memory as deeply as his own name, and though in general the entire area seemed a bit wilder than he recalled, no real obstacles appeared to confuse or deter him. One last bend of the road, a push through the shrubbery, and the river lay sparkling before him, rushing over its stone-strewn bed. The flat rock was still there, a little smaller than it used to be – but that was probably a matter of a child's perspective changing with maturity. The willows hung undisturbed, denser than before; the bushes shivered in a light river breeze, and a frog's odd bellow punctuated the rhythmic accompaniment of running water at regular intervals. It was a lovely, lonely spot, reminiscent of the waterfall, and Tvrdik understood now why he had been drawn to both places in his moments of flight from the world. Ondine would love it here. Unslinging the water skin from his shoulder, he opened it and peered into its mouth. "Ondine?" he called. A curly blue head popped out of the opening and looked all around, taking in every feature of the place at a glance. And then a wide smile spread over her violet-freckled face. She laughed, sprang out of the container and landed noisily in the Maygrew.

"Hey!" Tvrdik called, "No thanks? No goodbyes? What do you think of this place anyway?"

"Good place, Lovely Man. Very happy with new home. You leave me here now. I will go hear what river has to tell me. Also search for nymph companions. Maybe some here."

"Well, it was always a very magical spot to me, but I never saw any…"

At that, she laughed so that her tiny body shook, "You are funny, Lovely Man! You only see *me* because I want you to. We hide well. If there are naiads here, I find them."

Tvrdik squatted down on the flat rock, watching her swim and frolic with wondrous grace. He cocked one eyebrow, "I'll miss you…" He was beginning to feel almost abandoned.

She laughed again and called back, "You come tomorrow, high sun. I will be here – tell you news. Yes?"

"All right. Enjoy yourself. I'll see you then if I have any power over it." He closed his eyes and turned his face up to the willow-filtered sun, sighing in the stillness. A moment later his reverie was destroyed by a very wet kiss planted smack on his cheek and he opened his eyes to see Ondine suspended in the air right before his eyes. With a little wave, she reversed herself, dove deep into the water and disappeared. Tvrdik sat down on the rock and waited a minute, two, five… but she was gone, off about her business. Retracing his steps on the path back toward the palace, the wizard's shoulders sagged a bit as he found himself once more alone. It had been oddly pleasant to be watching out for someone else's welfare. But the little naiad had been confined far too long in tiny spaces and had borne the inconvenience with patience. Better she should be out in the open again, where she could live as she was accustomed. He hoped they would be in frequent contact.

As he passed The Cottage again, his steps slowed, and then stopped, as he stared at the overgrown yard, the stained walls and sad, slumping pillars. He struggled once more with the impulse to go nearer, perhaps try the lock and look inside. A part of him was very keen on exploring what was there, but his feet remained frozen to the spot. Sighing, he decided that this, too, was work for another day, and he continued down the riverwalk. He had not gone twenty paces when he had the distinct feeling of being followed. He paused, turned, scanned the empty road behind him, continued on, but could not shake the sensation that something or someone was shadowing his every move. Tvrdik slowed again, and casually glanced around in every direction. Nothing. Frowning, he continued on his way. He had only just begun to relax again when he heard a bright tenor voice behind him call, "Excuse me sir, may I speak wi' ye? I was wonderin', are ye a wizard?"

Tvrdik whirled to confront the voice – and was surprised to have to adjust his gaze about three feet downward. The party addressing him was, in fact, a wolfhound, nobly built, perhaps 100 pounds, sporting various shades of charcoal and fog. He stood at attention, tail raised, head high, eyes partially obscured by thick drooping brows, head cocked to one side as he awaited the answer to his odd question.

Tvrdik was startled. Talking beasts were often rumored, but increasingly less likely to be encountered, especially in or around the cities. He had only known a few in his lifetime. Something about this canine looked familiar.

The beast cleared his throat and tried again, "I wondered if perhaps ye might be a wizard?"

"Who are you and why on earth would you ask such a question?"

"I am Stewart. I live nearby, and am known in these parts. I mean ye no harm, sir, and quite frankly, I ask because ye… well… ye *smell* like a wizard."

"Oh? And have you had occasion before now to actually scent one?" Tvrdik countered, dodging the question.

The dog hung his head, "Well, not exactly, but ye see there was once a very fine wizard who lived in that house ye just passed. My grandsire, Angus, served him as friend and helper for years. He raised my dad and all of us pups on stories of the old wizard's life and ways. He described everything in such detail – all the sights and smells, words, and deeds he remembered, and adventure after adventure until they were second nature to us. That particular wizard vanished many years ago, and my grandsire is gone now, peace to his soul. But I've spent my life hoping to meet one myself. I've made a study of the subject, and I feel confident that I could recognize one, should he come along…," the dog raised his eyebrows in a hopeful expression.

At that moment, Tvrdik remembered Angus, the distinguished and loyal wolfhound who was Xaarus' constant companion. After Xaarus disappeared, no one knew what became of the dog either. The young mage made a decision and motioned Stewart closer, speaking to him conspiratorially, "Well, to tell the truth, I also served the wizard who lived in that house as student and apprentice. I remember your grandsire Angus well, for I lived there myself for several years."

"Why, then ye *are*...," the dog's tail began to wag.

Tvrdik laid a finger to his lips, "Shhhhh! Yes, I am, but I hope you can keep a secret. The lady Jorelial Rey would not like it to be widely known just yet that there is a wizard at Theriole again."

Stewart stiffened. "Sir, my family have never been accused of idle gossip or tale-tellin'. Ye may rely on my discretion."

"Good. I felt sure I could," the young mage replied with a bit of an amused twinkle, "I am here to accomplish certain things and if everyone knew of my presence, there would be far too many distractions."

"I quite understand. Still, I am gratified to meet ye in the flesh, sir."

"And I am delighted to make your acquaintance as well, Stewart. I confess I have not encountered too many of the talking beasts in my travels, aside from your grandsire and a horse or two. Are there many of you hereabouts?"

Stewart sat in the middle of the path and regarded him, head tipped to one side. "Well, now I must beg yer discretion as well, good sir, for there are quite a few of us in these parts. But for various reasons, we tend also to keep our heads low." He continued in whispered tones, "There are many humans about who are not honorable in behavior or intention."

"I understand. What sorts of creatures make up your fellowship, if I might ask?"

"You may. We are quite diverse. Dogs, cats, mice, rats, birds, horses of course, mules, squirrels and raccoons, foxes and wolves, even a turtle..."

"Well met, then, friend. I may in future have need of your services in a matter of great importance. How may I find you again when I know more? Who is your master?"

Stewart bristled, "Sir, I have no master! I am my own dog."

"I meant no offense. I only wish to know how to contact you again in the future. And I was under the impression that most canines preferred to mingle their fortunes with humans, trading their good counsel and companionship for hearth and food."

The dog relaxed once more, "And so they do, no offense taken. I come from an old and proud family. I fend for myself well enough and I have not yet found a man I thought worthy to be called *master*."

"Bravely said," responded Tvrdik, reaching out his right hand. "Come, let us part friends. I shall look forward to meeting you again on this path." Stewart placed a paw firmly in the wizard's outstretched hand.

"I can be found nearby most any time, and I should be glad to observe at close range the work of a genuine wizard, or to be of any service I may. I fear my grandsire would haunt me if I failed to offer. What is your name sir?"

"I am called Tvrdik." He shook the paw and released it.

"That's a very odd name." The dog cocked his head again, "What sort of a name is that anyway?"

Tvrdik shrugged, "It is *my* name."

It did not take the young mage very long to regain the palace grounds and gardens, and when he got there, he was surprised to find himself humming. It had been an interesting morning, and he was already beginning to feel less of a stranger here. As he crossed into the fragrant gardens, wondering how best to pass the time until the sixteenth hour, he saw a young woman sitting alone on a bench surrounded by statuary and flowering shrubs. She was leaning back on her hands, her face, eyes closed, turned up to the sun. He paused and stared at her, thinking he knew that face, the rivulets of red hair, the slim grace of her... why, it was the girl from the courtyard the night before, when he had been waiting for his interview! She had been there as well, pacing and looking anxious, waiting for someone or something. He had been too preoccupied then to interfere. Perhaps, feeling as expansive as he did now, it would be a friendly gesture to approach her. He strolled over to the seated girl, looked down at the serene face, and cleared his throat. Green eyes fluttered open in surprise.

"Pardon me, m'lady. I hope you do not think me too forward, but I recognize you from last night in the courtyard. We were both waiting outside the Hall of Audience. You seemed at the time to be in some distress, and occupied as I was with my own affairs, I neglected to offer my services. That was ungracious of me. I thought perhaps to remedy that oversight now?"

She smiled, an open, dazzling smile. "Sir, you did no wrong. In fact, I was waiting to see Lady Jorelial Rey, and there was nothing you might have done to ease the passing of the minutes, I was that impatient."

Tvrdik's face fell. "Lady Rey? But indeed, then, you did not have your turn, for I was also awaiting an audience with her, and was next to be seen."

The girl shook her head. "In fact, it was my betrothed in conference with her as you waited, and I was only impatient for his return with her answer. You see, he went to ask for my hand in marriage."

"Marriage! You seem young for a step of such gravity..." Tvrdik was amazed at how quickly this style of courtly banter came back to his tongue after so many years of near muteness. The words seemed to flow from his lips with more ease than when he was eighteen. Perhaps he had picked something up from the many books he had read during his time as a hermit, as there had certainly not been any opportunity for practice with actual people. The girl was meanwhile unfazed by his comment, but kept her smile and her warm, friendly manner.

"You must not confuse the greenness of my years with the steadiness of my heart, sir. It is set on this course and glad of it."

"Then fortunate is the man who receives such unshakable devotion from so fresh and lovely a source. I congratulate you both, assuming the news was good?"

She shrugged, "Good enough for now. My Lady Regent seems to be favorably inclined towards our suit, but has not yet said yes, or no, with any certainty, nor allowed us to set a date to move forward with our plans. To be fair, she also must address plans for the election of a permanent regent and for a coronation in the upcoming weeks. We must be patient that she will remember us when these weighty matters are passed."

"I see. But I am surprised you must wait upon her pleasure. Do the powers of an interim regent extend so far into the personal affairs of her subjects now?"

The girl threw back her head and laughed a merry, expansive laugh. "Why yes, they do, sir, when the interim regent happens to be my older sister, and only living relation."

Tvrdik was taken aback. He took off his glasses and squinted at her, "Your sister? Why, surely you could not be .... Delphine?" A cloud crossed her face for a moment. Tvrdik realized his mistake too late.

"Do you know me, sir? Should I know you?"

"Umm....uh...why no, not at all. It is just that I used to live near here as a youth, and spent a great deal of time at court with my family. When I was last here you were a tiny child of four or five, the apple of your father's eye. I can hardly believe so many years have passed, and that you are so well... well grown." Okay, that was fairly dunderheaded. But she seemed to accept it without question. *It is*, he reflected, *after all, only a slight bending of the truth.* She rose from the bench, regaining her smile and touching his arm.

"Well, let me take this opportunity, then, to welcome you home, and wish you joy of your stay, even if these are confusing times. Did my sister treat you with proper courtesy?"

"Oh yes," he nodded, adjusting his glasses back on the bridge of his nose. "I owe her a debt of gratitude. In fact, I will be seeing her again later today." The cloud was back – another mistake, but she recovered almost at once.

"My," she said, her smile a tiny bit less broad, "you must have important business indeed. We have always been close, my sister and I, but I rarely see her myself these days, except to wave at her as she runs by." Delphine's tone changed then, and she spoke with less formality, "I *so* feel for her. She is not a person who seeks power. I am sure she is not enjoying herself in the slightest. In fact, I worry that she is not taking care of herself amidst all the comings and goings."

Tvrdik heard the sincerity in her voice and really liked the girl, "I shall say I saw you and that you send warm regards," he offered.

The smile came back. On impulse, she took him by the arm. "You are most kind. Have you had lunch yet? Come along. If I can find Mark - that's my fiancé - you must join us at table. He is a very gifted poet and harper, perhaps around your own age. He would like to meet you, I am sure of it."

"And I him," the young wizard replied, allowing her to escort him toward the palace. And truly, he did look forward to a nice, unpressured meal with other young folk with whom he might have something in common. He would have to be careful, though, with what he said and how much he revealed about who he was. It seemed a shame that deception would siphon some of the delight out of making new friends, but it couldn't be helped.

Mark proved easily found, and the three of them sat down in the refectory to a delicious meal. Tvrdik, finding himself hungry, tucked into a heaping plate of savory goodies, while listening to Mark and Delphine chatter away about their hopes and dreams, how they met and grew close, and their plans for a school. They were a charming, intelligent couple, and their enthusiasm was contagious. Tvrdik found the idea for a school especially intriguing, wondering if there might even be a place for him, perhaps teaching, or in the library. In the presence of these two, the future looked so exciting that he wished with all his heart for everything he knew about the coming travails to prove false, so that he could just come back to court and begin a normal life with friends and honest labor and the comforts of a home. At this moment he couldn't really remember why he had stayed away so long. And now, it broke his heart to think that the future Mark and Delphine imagined might never come to pass. The idea was unthinkable. He would simply have to succeed.

For his part, he told them some innocent fiction about growing up in Theriole as the son of a foreign ambassador who had been recalled to his homeland when Tvrdik was eighteen. And now, he had returned on business of state, concerning the coronation, or trade agreements, or water rights, or some such. Mark and Delphine were so open and a-political that they accepted everything he said at face value, and did not ask the kind of revealing questions a more savvy companion might have. In any case, he kept directing the conversation back to them and their plans, in which he had a genuine interest. When they parted company, Tvrdik was smiling so hard he thought his face would crack. The whole experience was a new one for him. Even his relationship with Ailianne and Benjin had been based more on the circumstance of being isolated together than on mutual choice. And they had all been so serious and focused, even competitive, during the years they spent together.

Musing thus, he happened to hear the bells of the tower announcing the hour. *Dragonsbreath!* He had not realized how much time had passed in amiable conversation. *I have just enough time to prepare for my interview, and to find my way there.* Concentrating on recalling the pattern he had walked that morning, he headed back to his room. Only a few wrong turns and switchbacks later, he managed to locate the chambers he had been assigned, washed, tidied himself, and gathered a few things he might need. Then, it was down to the Main Hall again, this time without any errors, across the courtyard to find Warlowe at his post and ask directions to the north tower. Back across the courtyard, and through almost the entire length of the complex, Tvrdik hurried to the oversized corner turret, no one stopping him to inquire after his business, or even glancing his way. He supposed he might have made himself invisible, but there seemed no need. It was normal for courtiers to be travelling through the castle delivering messages, or en route to meetings. The young mage blended right into the castle's bustling activity.

Once at the tower, there were several stories of curving stone stairs spiraling up and up, as far as he could see. The north tower was especially tall, so when Tvrdik at last arrived at the trap-door which would allow him access to the roof, he was out of breath, and it was approaching the sixteenth hour. He lingered there a moment at the top of the stairs to calm himself, collect his thoughts, and straighten his clothing, then pushed the trap open and climbed through...and almost bumped straight into the enormous nose of a green dragon, who was regarding him with intense curiosity. Tvrdik's heart skipped a beat as he clambered out of the stairwell, let the trap door shut, and fell immediately to one knee. He had never in his life been this close to a real dragon, but there wasn't time to hesitate now. He began his composed address:

"Mighty Tashroth, esteemed Lord of Green Dragons, I am honored that you have consented to hear my cause. I come at your summons...how may I serve you?"

The dragon's voice was so deep it made the young wizard's bones vibrate like harp strings, and yet, it was musical at the same time, "The Lady Rey is unavoidably detained, but it is fit that we should meet and talk, mage, for so you style yourself."

Tvrdik's entire body was shaking, but he pushed ahead with his speech, "My Master, Xaarus, sends you warm greetings, long overdue, and commends himself to you."

"If, in truth, you come from him, then those greetings are received with joy and heartily returned. Xaarus was ever a true friend to dragons, and a great wizard."

"I beg you, then, not to speak of him in the past tense, for Xaarus is alive and well, and it is at his urging and on his business that I come here to you."

"So you have said, and such has been related to me. But your story is, shall we say...unusual? Even fanciful. The truth of it I mean to determine here and now. You may have heard that we dragons have ways of penetrating the heart to know the quality of a man. Do I have your permission to proceed?"

Tvrdik had been expecting this, though the prospect, now that he was face to face with Tashroth, terrified him. He mustered his courage and raised his eyes to meet the dragon's gaze, "Search me, great Dragon Lord, for I swear to you on my life that I have presented to Lady Jorelial Rey nothing but the truth as I know it."

Tashroth grinned and stared back at him, "Truly it IS your life that may be forfeit if you have dissembled and mean to do harm. Very well. Stand and submit."

Tvrdik rose and opened his arms wide and low, closed his eyes, and lifted his chin, exposing himself to any probing the dragon might decide to employ. He was still trembling, but he was confident that nothing but honesty and openness would be found in him. Even with his eyes shut, he could still see the great luminous eyes of the dragon boring into his soul. They began to glow, more and more brightly. For what seemed an eternity, the breath was crushed from his lungs. A searing, flame-like pain passed through every fiber of his being, lingering in his heart, and then his head. He had no air to cry out, and though his legs felt as if they had dissolved, he was held upright in the dragon's gaze. There was no past or future, but only this one eternal moment of raw nerves and pressure. *Oh, gods, make it stop!* he heard himself think, as if from a great distance, but the awful pain seemed to go on and on.... And then, with an abrupt and ungentle release, it was over. Gasping in long, desperate breaths, he fell to his hands and knees, head spinning. One by one he recovered his senses, the rhythm of his breathing, his strength. Tashroth was silent as the young man straightened stiffly, rested on his haunches, hands on his thighs to steady himself. Tvrdik reached up to straighten his glasses, and raised his head to meet the dragon's eye. The deep, lilting voice spoke again, and it seemed to echo through all of his being. "I find no falsehood in you. Your heart is unusually open, but extremely wounded. Those with broken hearts can often be turned to darkness. Tell me your tale."

Tvrdik had no power to withhold anything from that relentless gaze. His voice felt disembodied and unnatural when he responded. "I...I was young and impressionable when my fellow students ventured into forbidden sorceries that claimed their lives. Soon after, Xaarus disappeared without explanation. They were the only real family I had ever known, and I felt abandoned and alone, grieving and lost. I fell into despair and nearly took my own life. Instead, I hid in the ancient forest and shunned company for the last twelve years. Look deeper, and you will see that the burden I carry is sadness, and not malice or rage. It has been a difficult wound to heal, though I am fixed on doing so..." Tears were slipping down his cheeks behind his spectacles.

"And what did you learn in your exile?" Tvrdik had not really thought about it, but it seemed a reasonable question.

"I learned...I learned that solitude and self-reliance can be wonderful teachers." He paused to reflect. "That nature is a powerful teacher as well, and that hard work and simplicity are an elixir to the spirit."

"And what have you learned since?" Another surprising question. He considered.

"It has only been a short time, but I think - I think I am beginning to learn that the best teacher of all is relationship. Eventually, we must all learn who we are through our interactions with those whose lives intersect with our own." Tashroth's eyes seemed to soften a bit.

"Are you a good wizard?"

"I have studied hard. I have some skill. I know I can help. I can always be better." Things were just coming out of his mouth now, and he had no idea if they were the right things, or utterly wrong. It was the interview of his life, and his mouth just seemed to have a mind of its own. He had no idea if it was propelling him toward acceptance or death.

"And what do you want from life? Your dreams, deepest desires. Power? Wealth? Fame, perhaps?"

"Oh, no! I have seen those things bring as much misfortune as joy on those they favor. I only want to live in peace, perhaps to do some good – leave the world a little better than I found it. I have always wanted to use whatever gifts I might have to help and to heal," he paused and felt shame. "My colleagues often laughed at me. They saw me as weak and silly to harbor such small ambition. But I cannot change who I am."

"What is your name?" strange that Tashroth should wait so long in the conversation to ask.

"I am Tvrdik." There was a low, rumbling sound in the dragon's throat that was impossible to interpret.

Then, "It is an interesting...an *unusual* name. It suits you well, young mage. What are those things of wire and glass on your face? I am not familiar with these ornaments, and am intrigued."

Tvrdik laughed despite himself. "Oh, these are not ornaments. I'm afraid I was born with an inherent weakness of the eyes, made worse in my youth by countless hours of reading and studying old texts by candlelight. I'm afraid I need these spectacles to see clearly."

"It is my opinion, young mage, that you already see more clearly than most. Come, sit beside me here. You will find stools there beside the battlements. I feel Jorelial near to us – she will join us soon." Tvrdik blinked and hesitated, let out his breath, which he had not known he was holding. Apparently he had passed the test. He struggled to stand, unfolding his aching joints, which were objecting to kneeling so long on stone. He made a small bow to the dragon, whose eye still followed his every move, and crossed to where the promised stools stood. Gratefully, he pulled one out and sank onto its solid wooden support, feeling drained. But before another word could be spoken, the trap-door crashed open and Lady Jorelial Rey climbed out, already apologizing.

"Please forgive me. As usual, I was near drowned in a sea of petitioners, budget meetings, and decisions about every detail of the upcoming Grand Council and coronation. It was impossible to sneak away until just this moment. I trust you found your way here alright?"

Tvrdik rose and bowed, "Lady Rey."

The petite young woman rolled her eyes and strode over, pulling out another stool to sit on, "This is *my* sanctuary, here. *Please* don't call me that. I can't bear it another moment. My name is Jorelial." She dropped down heavily on the stool. Tvrdik reached out a hand in playful mock greeting.

"Ah, yes, Jorelial Rey. Thank you. Good to make your acquaintance. Mine is Tvrdik." Catching on to his light-hearted gesture, she grasped the proffered hand and shook it once.

"How do you do, Teh-vur-dik? Gods, I hope I got it right. How will I ever get used to that name?" She dropped his hand. Tvrdik shrugged, and sat.

"It is my name." he mumbled. They regarded each other in silence. Tashroth broke into the awkward pause.

"The young wizard and I have been having a very interesting little chat…"

"More like an inquisition," Tvrdik quipped, leaning in with a conspiratorial gesture, but Jorelial was just registering the dragon's words.

"Young wizard? Uh-oh! That means…"

Tashroth nodded his great head, "All true. The young man is entirely trustworthy."

Her head fell into her hands for a moment, "I thought as much – I *felt* as much." She glanced toward Tvrdik, "I would have been disappointed to find you out a villain, but do you realize what this means?" She did not wait for a response, "It means we can expect everything to happen just the way you described, and we shall have to go forward with this impossible plan of yours!" She grabbed his hands, still stumbling over his name, "Tvrdik, tell me…the future is not written in stone. Is it not possible that things could work out a different way? That Drogue might think better of his decision, and refrain from challenging the election? That someone else might still be declared regent? That we could all go on in peace and some kind of order?"

Tashroth remarked, "There are many timelines and many possible futures, after all…"

Tvrdik squirmed at her touch, "I…I suppose anything is possible, but…"

She dropped his hands, jumped up, and began to pace back and forth across the circular roof, "You don't sound at all convinced or convincing."

"Look," he countered, "from where Xaarus stands, figuring backward, we are already embarked on *his* timeline, the one that ends up so badly. Of course, he could be mistaken, or things could take a different turn, but the likeliest events are those that I have presented to you. Yes, it is all so frightening for those of us here on this side of history. But the circumstances also present us with an amazing opportunity to change things – for the better! We can make a real difference for ourselves, and for the future. If we put our heads together, we will surely succeed."

Jorelial stopped and ran a hand through her dark hair, "I suppose you are right. There is no escaping it. How will we ever convince the council members that we are all in mortal danger, but that we are going to mount a defense without weapons? It is simply too much to expect them to go along with that. They will think I have gone mad, and will clap me in irons, or confine me in a madhouse, and then where will we be? We shall have to be very careful how we proceed."

Tvrdik moved over to her side, "We will come up with a list of strategies that are powerful, and we will frame our arguments to be compelling. The name of Xaarus will carry some weight with them, and they will be pleased to have magic on their side once more…"

Tashroth's deep voice completed the sentence, "…and in the end, little one, they will put their faith in you. You have never let them down yet. They will trust you." Jorelial Rey stood still with a finger in her mouth, chewing at the nail, glancing about as if she were looking for some secret escape route off of the roof. Finally, her shoulders dropped, her breath rushed out in a gusty sigh, her hands fell to her side and she turned her face up to the great green dragon beside her.

"Tash?"

"I see no other choice, little one."

There was a pause, and then Jorelial Rey turned and stared Tvrdik right in the eye. "Alright, we're in. If things fall out the way you described, and that's a big 'if', Tashroth and I will be your champions, and, by the gods, we will make this happen."

Tvrdik returned her gaze with unwavering intensity, "And you can count on me to be *your* champion, and we *will* triumph!" This time, she was the one to offer a hand, and he took it, both of them knowing that in that moment, they were forging a bargain that would change the very fabric of the world. Tashroth roared, adding his assent to the contract. They had chosen their course.

Jorelial Rey resumed her pacing, "A few more points I need to discuss with you. Right now, we can do nothing but wait. There is no enemy. Drogue has yet to tip his hand. Today is Friday. One week from this day is the Grand Council, where a full-time, permanent regent will be selected. There are several likely candidates, including myself and Lord Drogue. If anything is to happen, it will begin there, at that meeting. Tvrdik, I'm going to need you to be around at that meeting – to be an extra set of eyes and ears for me, observing and recording what you think is going on, and what Drogue is up to. Afterwards, we can compare notes and see if a clear picture emerges."

"Willingly, my lady."

"You're the only one I can trust to do this, as Tash can't fit in the chambers, and makes the council uncomfortable at any rate. But, I think it's premature to introduce you to the council as Xaarus' lost student, and maybe the last wizard. I'd rather save that for later. Is there some way you could be there without being detected?"

"I can make myself seem invisible, or arrive as an owl, a wren, or a mouse, so that you will know where I am should you need me."

"We can decide later, but thank you. That will be a relief. There is one more thing…"

"Yes?"

"Well, I've been thinking about it a lot, and, you see, I had the idea… but you'll have to tell me if it is insensitive of me to suggest…I wasn't quite sure how you would feel about it…"

"Go on."

"Well, I think having you wander around Theriole before we reveal your identity could arouse suspicions. Plus it confines your activities. I was thinking maybe you could move into Xaarus' old cottage. No one has touched or tampered with it since he disappeared. Mind you, it's been sitting untended for twelve years. I'm not sure how habitable it is just now, but we could remedy that. You'd have space, freedom to come and go, and access to Xaarus' library and equipment. And it's just far enough away that you wouldn't have to be too cautious about what you were doing. I could even come to see you there, and not be distracted or discovered. Now, if it's too emotional for you, I'll understand…"

"Yes."

"Excuse me?"

Yes, it's a wonderful idea. You are right on all counts. I'll take it." Tvrdik had been standing with his mouth open listening to the unexpected offer, and trying to determine how he did feel about it. But as she spoke, it came to him how perfectly 'right' it was. The library, the laboratory, the equipment – all could be invaluable. And he would have a place to practice in privacy, and be closer to Ondine. He leapt at the chance.

Tashroth swung his head around low to look the young wizard directly in the eye, and with uncharacteristic compassion, said, "Are you *sure* there are not too many ghosts there for you?"

Tvrdik was moved by his kindness, but very confident of his response. "No, no, it's alright. The books, the labs…she's right…I will need them. Fixing the place up will give me something to do until we know if we are correct, and it will be like coming home. To tell the truth, I am not much of a courtier sort anyway. I feel more than a little uncomfortable rattling around the palace with little to do. Thank you, Jorelial Rey. I am grateful that you would consider this."

She was visibly pleased that he liked her suggestion, "Right, then. Tomorrow, I will send Warlowe with a purse and some letters of credit to local merchants we trust, so you can get yourself clothing, provisions and raw materials for the house. Will you need help to put it back in shape?"

"I am no stranger to physical labor. No one should see some of the secrets of that house anyway. I will do the work myself."

"By all means, ask for whatever you need. I will arrange for it personally. And feel free to stay at the palace as long as it takes to make that house livable."

"You are most generous, my lady."

"No one goes out that far much anymore, so I think we are safe for a few weeks. But if anyone notices the activity, I will just say I thought it was about time I leased the old place to a cottager." The sun was beginning to sink low in the sky, and the air was cooling. Jorelial Rey looked around and continued, "Now that all of that is settled, I must get back downstairs. I want to make sure we both get something to eat, and then spend some time with the king before his bedtime. He will be forgetting what I even look like now, let alone that I am supposed to be his guardian."

Tashroth reassured, "Your sister, Delphine, has been spending a good deal of time with him. He is well, and they play together…"

"Oh!" cried Tvrdik, remembering, "I met your sister today, and her intended."

"My sister? I hope you did not tell her anything. You were supposed to keep a low profile."

"It was purely coincidental, but I told her I had grown up in the palace as an ambassador's child, had been recalled to my country, and was back to negotiate trade deals. I'm sure she believed me. She and Mark rather adopted me. They are charming and delightful people and I quite enjoyed their company. I do not think any harm was done. She only expressed her sadness that the two of you rarely spend time together anymore, and her concern for your welfare, with so many burdens on your shoulders."

"And she doesn't know the half of it now, does she." Jorelial sighed, "I'm sorry I snapped at you. I am very protective of Delphine."

"No apologies necessary. I understand your concerns, and did not mean to overstep my bounds."

"Tash, thank you, thank you for everything, dearest. I will be back tonight. Wait for me. Tvrdik, walk with me to the kitchens, will you? I am famished, and I'll bet you are too. Oh, and Tvrdik?" she grinned with a spark of mischief, "My compliments to your tailor." He frowned in confusion, and she laughed, "The clothes. They suit you well, and are a vast improvement over last night's choice."

He shot her a crooked smile, "They are at that. I think the color brings out my eyes, or had you noticed?" he teased as they disappeared down the stairs and the trap-door banged shut. The great green dragon stared after them both for a moment, an odd expression on his face, then lifted his huge wings and sailed off in search of his own supper.

TEN

THE CAMP AND THE COTTAGE

AT THE OTHER END OF Theriole, far from the riverwalk and the gardens, grassy fields extended out from the grey stone walls into the valley, almost as far as the eye could see. There, it was customary for visiting lords and dignitaries who could not be accommodated within, to set up tent camps. Some would be relegated there by virtue of their small importance in the political hierarchy, and others, with large retinues of family, servants, soldiers, and horses, preferred the freedom and space afforded by the outdoors. Often the lords themselves, along with their immediate families, would be invited to dine in the Great Hall with their peers, taking the opportunity to socialize, network, and enjoy the hospitality of their hosts, the monarchs of Eneri Clare. Some of the encampments were quite luxurious in their own right. Colorful silk tents sported bright pennants that bore the crests of the occupants' houses. They were comfortable, well-appointed, and well-provisioned, and of course, near enough to the palace to request anything they might lack. In another few days, there would be tents covering the lawns from the palace walls away out to the visible horizon, as delegations arrived for the great Grand Council meeting. On this night, there were still but a handful of motley tent clusters, early arrivals in the vanguard of the flock of expected pilgrims.

This night, beneath a full moon, beside a dancing campfire, under the sign of the black raven, back-winging, with claws fully extended, Lord Drogue stood. Thin lips pressed together and brow creased in concentration, he peered down by the light of several torches held for him by servants.

On his left arm rested an ancient, musty volume, pages crumbling around the edges. It was open to a leaf that displayed a number of graphic and disturbing illustrations, hand-drawn by a meticulous artist from the dim past. There were captions written under every picture in some unfamiliar, disused language. Drogue kept glancing at the page, and then shifting his glance to the ground, squinting as if searching for some correspondence.

"Bring those blasted torches closer," he snapped, "I can't make out anything there." The servants scrambled to obey. A stray thread hanging from the nobleman's sleeve began to smoke. "Not *that* close, you nitwit!" he exploded, tamping down the potential flame against his hip and scowling at the cowering, confused torchbearer.

At his feet, the fires revealed the partially eviscerated remains of three creatures: a chicken, a hare, and a small goat. Their broken forms lay in a pool of blood that still sent up little columns of steam in the chill evening air. Drogue reached down with his free hand and shifted some of the small organs back and forth with a pointed finger – heart, lungs, liver – first the chicken, then the hare, and the goat.

"More light, there! That's it. Argh. It's hopeless. I can't see anything of use here." He threw his bloody hand up in frustration, and motioned with a nod for someone to take the book from his arm. Someone else handed him a napkin, and, without any acknowledgement, he took it and began wiping the offal from his right hand. "I am *exceedingly* disappointed. They should have been clear as our mountain streams. Gargan!"

The beefy brute who claimed that name, as well as allegiance to Drogue, answered in a hoarse bass, "Yes, my lord?"

"You've done a dismal job with the knife. I told you the cuts had to be precise. Some of these organs were shredded before I even had the chance to look."

Gargan shrugged, used to being the object of his lord's vented spleen. "My lord, it was no simple matter to get the beasts to hold still whilst I was stickin' 'em." He grinned a gap-toothed grin, while a few of the men in the group laughed outright at his joke.

But Drogue was still staring, unsmiling, at the carnage by his feet, jaw working while he considered his options. "This is simply not acceptable. I *must* know what the omens are for my election as regent."

"Yes, my lord."

"Make no mistake; I will claim the title. It belongs to no other. But if the auguries do not that way tend, I must know *now,* so that I may find a way to tip the scales...." He sighed and closed his eyes, seeming to change tracks for a moment. No one moved. They all knew better. "Clean up that mess." Drogue commanded, coming to life. He turned his back, gesturing to the poor butchered creatures with a derisive flip of his hand. "Those are worse than useless. Everything there is too small to see. How can I be expected to read the signs correctly?"

"My lord?" Gargan was not sure if a response was expected.

"Never mind. Someone fetch my manservant. Where can he have gotten to? Declan?"

Several servants ran to retrieve the missing Declan, aware that the peevish tone they were now hearing from their master was rarely followed by anything pleasant. In a moment, a gray-haired, wiry figure appeared, shuffling toward the golden periphery of the campfires.

"Here I am, master," soothed Declan, "I was just after arrangin' your bed for you." He smiled and his wizened face broke into hundreds of tiny creases. "'Tis getting' to be fair late, milord. Come to bed. I have prepared and warmed it, just as you like..."

"Declan, have you prepared my bath?"

The old man stopped, a look of surprise on his pale features. "Why, milord, the lateness of the hour...I did not think..."

"No one asked you to think, old man. I have been immersed in a foul business here and wish to bathe before I retire. Does that meet with your approval?" Drogue's eyes glinted with mirthless amusement at the obvious discomfort of his menial, but Declan sighed, familiar with his lord's moods.

"My apologies, but it will take just a little while to arrange. I will send for some help from the palace. You understand, lord, that I am not as young as I once was. It is difficult for me to carry the full buckets from the fire. And you know how you like your bath, sire, hot and steaming." The servant smiled warmly, as if placating a small child. Gargan and some of the others in Drogue's retinue shuffled a few steps off, backs turned, stifling giggles at the interchange. Drogue did not seem to notice. His attention was all on his manservant, who asked, "Would my lord wish to enjoy a nice mug of spiced wine while he waits?"

"Declan, how long have you been in service to me?"

"Why, my lord, I have been at your side, man and boy, since you were but a little babe, and your father before you."

"Yes, yes, and you have always done well by us, loyal and dependable."

"Thank you, my lord."

"I am sorry that with all the weighty affairs of state that claim my attention of late, I have not noticed how the burdens of age have crept upon you."

"My lord, I do not complain. I only tell you the fact of it."

"Yes, yes. I was thinking it must be difficult now to discharge all the laborious duties I often require of you."

"Well, my lord, as they say, the spirit is always willing, but the flesh…" the man spread his hands out before him and shrugged.

"Say no more. I have been remiss not to be aware of this before. Being my manservant is really a younger man's post. How would you like to serve me now, in a different, less taxing capacity?"

The old man's eyes opened wide with excitement and gratitude. "My lord, you are indeed good to me. How can I thank you for your kindness? Whatever I may do to please…"

Drogue turned and casually picked up the still bloody knife from the stump on which it had been laid. Casually, he used the soiled napkin which he still held in his left hand to wipe the blade clean, his eyes focused on the task while he continued to address his servant.

"Good, Declan. I am most gratified by your answer. No more carrying and fetching heavy bags and buckets, saddles and bedclothes. I have something special in mind for you. Something which would serve me well, be of vital importance, even, and also give you the rest your weary bones require…"

Gargan had turned back to the conversation, no longer amused, the hair on his arms and neck rising. Declan approached Drogue with eager anticipation. He bowed stiffly in deference and urged, "My good lord, I am always here, at your service…"

Drogue smiled with warmth at the man who had catered to his every whim, and made him comfortable for decades. He put his left hand on Declan's shoulder, said, "Thank you, old friend," and plunged the sharp knife up to the hilt in the old man's ribs.

Declan dropped without a sound, his eyes still glowing with appreciation and the smile frozen on his lips. The restless fire illuminated his odd expression with an eerie flicker. There were several audible gasps from the other side of the campfire. Drogue snapped his fingers.

"Gargan, to your work. Open him up, and mind you, be neat about it this time. You there, bring the book. Hold those torches steady. Now we shall see clearly what the omens have to tell us…."

No one moved. One of the logs in the fire popped and crackled in the silence. Drogue looked up at the horrified faces around him.

"What? He was a good man, but he was old. Here is a way he can serve my need as he wished, and he will have his rest. Now, move, or we will lose our advantage."

Gargan and the others did not need additional prompting. At once, the area was alive with frantic activity. Drogue stepped back to give his men room. Once again he wiped his knife clean, sheathed it in his belt, and dropped the telltale cloth in the fire, where it fizzled and turned slowly black.

"You there!" he called to one of his guards, "Go and round up some of the servants – wake them if you have to – and tell them I will require a bath. And make sure it is hot and steamy. Now, where is that book?"

After another night's sound sleep on the luxurious featherbed, Tvrdik woke early next morning feeling rested, refreshed, and with a renewed sense of purpose. Jorelial Rey, true to her word, sent Warlowe around while the young mage was enjoying the hearty breakfast delivered to his chambers. The faithful doorkeeper handed over a fat purse of gold coins, and an assortment of letters of credit to many of the merchants who plied their trades just outside of the palace walls. There were recommended clothing stores, masons, food stalls, blacksmiths, wood and tool merchants, seed and gardening supplies – she had left nothing out. Nevertheless, Warlowe also bore assurances that anything else could be quickly arranged if he but informed them of his need. Warlowe then offered his own personal assistance with the project of restoring Xaarus' old house. Tvrdik smiled, and laid a hand on the man's shoulder.

"An attractive offer, my friend, truly. But I think I should begin alone. I'm not even sure of the extent of the damages yet, and you have your duties here. I think I can find my way around alright. I might call upon you later, if I may."

Warlowe nodded, as Tvrdik removed his hand from the veteran doorkeeper's shoulder, and extended it. Warlowe did not hesitate to clasp it warmly before disappearing down the hall. Tvrdik was beginning to feel like he had friends.

During the morning hours, he busied himself at various merchant's stalls, purchasing boots and clothing better suited to manual labor, basic provisions, whitewash, brushes, tools, and some wood. All of these were to be delivered later to the site of the old Cottage; he had not yet assessed the full extent of what was needed there, but he calculated that these items would at least be sufficient to make a start on some of the outside repairs. If any of the shopkeepers raised an eyebrow, or made sociable conversation about the delivery address, he took Jorelial Rey's lead and affirmed that he was helping the Lady Regent restore the old place for future leasing. The official letters of credit from the Lady herself lent some credibility to his story, and Tvrdik knew the rumor mill would be grinding out speculations a-plenty that afternoon about who might be moving into Xaarus' old house. A few of the folks he met did make wistful little comments about the good times when Xaarus had been at Theriole, and what a terrible shame his absence had been. A few even ventured their pet theories as to what had happened, or where it was said the Master Wizard was keeping himself nowadays. One story was more outrageous than the next, and yet none more outrageous than the truth, Tvrdik thought. At any rate, he was gratified that among the townsfolk his old master was still fondly remembered and keenly missed.

As the sun climbed higher, satisfied that he had begun to set wheels in motion, Tvrdik bought himself a sandwich, and hastened to the little secret spot on the riverbank where he had promised to meet Ondine. It was shaping up to be another lovely spring day – bright sun pouring all over the green world, white cloud ships sailing at a leisurely clip across an azure sky, and a slight cooling breeze off the water. As he hoped, the place was deserted – or more accurately, undiscovered – and he stretched out on the flat rock to wait, enjoying the various scents and sounds, and munching his sandwich with gusto. He was about to address the last bite, when a gentle splash from the Maygrew caught him full in the face, announcing the arrival of his little blue friend. He frowned as he found himself pulling off his glasses to dry them on his vest, but then smiled despite himself. Even a short day's separation from her had made him miss the antics he had grown accustomed to on the road.

"Lovely Man! Yoohoo, I am here." warbled the tiny nymph. "Having a most excellent time, and find good news for you too."

"What? Have you found others like you? Have you met the other naiads?"

"No, Lovely Man…not find any more like me in river. I search more… maybe find some soon. But I meet many creatures who live here…one turtle who speaks like human."

Tvrdik recalled his conversation with Stewart the dog, "Oh, yes, I believe I have heard of him…"

"This turtle, very polite, distinguished soul. Tells me upriver a ways, beyond village, is secret wood where unicorns live. Very good thing to know…I go and watch there, I see them watering. Turtle tells a true thing…five, six, seven, more maybe, very good unicorns…"

"Unicorns!" Tvrdik gasped, "I haven't seen one of those anywhere in so very long – almost since childhood. I know there are still some in the ancient forests, but they do not let themselves be approached. This is indeed a wondrous piece of information, and I would dearly love to see them, but I am not sure that I understand how that will help our cause?"

"Silly man, do you know nothing about creatures?" she rebuked. "Unicorns are lovers of peace, very offended by any violence. Hide from men all the time because they think all men do harm. Unicorns will like your plan…will like you, too. Maybe believe you can change things like you say…maybe want to help. Unicorns very good, very powerful allies. Have big magic, and can talk to all the wood creatures for you." Ondine was clearly excited about sharing her discovery. In only twenty-four hours, she already had assembled a wealth of information.

"Did you speak to them?"

"No, no. Not yet. Wait for time you say…when to go. I know unicorns – can speak to them OK."

112

"Well, that is good news, indeed, my friend. We will wait to trouble them with our ideas until we know better what we are doing, but it seems we are gaining new potential supporters every day. Well done, Ondine, well done!" She shot out of the water in glee at his compliments and did a swan dive back in. Tvrdik continued, "I have a surprise for you too, my girl…" She hovered close, eyes wide with excitement.

"Yes, Lovely Man?"

He rolled his eyes at the appellation, but went on, "There is a house up the road very close to this place. It was where I used to live many years ago. The Regent would like me to fix it up and move in there for the time being. I'd say, with luck, inside a week I should be all moved in and will be right in the neighborhood. I can come and see you often, and you can catch me up on all the news. That is, if you still like this place as a sort of a home base?"

"Oh, yes, very good place. I am so happy here."

"Do you have all you need? Are you comfortable?"

"Everything good. Thank you for asking. But you do not need to come every day…maybe you can find me when you wish. We make special signal I will hear, come then to meet you?"

Tvrdik considered. He would be very occupied in the next few weeks, and doubtless the nymph had more exploring to undertake. "Hmmm. How's this?" He picked up a small stone and tossed it into the water with a muffled *ploop*, then whistled a crooked little tune. Ondine laughed.

"You *are* silly. I will know you are waiting. Good signal. How was dragon?"

Tvrdik's eyebrows shot up, "Oh, very scary! And very wonderful. All in all, though, I think you made the right decision not to be there. But the Regent and her dragon have consented to join our cause. The first important event that might set things in motion is a big council meeting next week. A lot could happen there. She wants me to be present at the meeting in disguise. She doesn't want anyone to know yet that there is a wizard at court."

"So, you are secret, like me." Ondine cocked her head charmingly to one side.

"Well, for the moment, yes. But very soon, I shall invite them down here to meet you, my dear. I promise. First opportunity. They will love

113

you, and you will get to see your dragon close-up after all." Ondine made a little sound of alarm, and darted deeper into the rushing river for a moment, then gingerly resurfaced, a question on her face. It was Tvrdik who laughed now.

"Not today, dearest. You're safe, for a while at least. I'll let you know."

Their eyes met in companionable silence for a moment, and then the young mage sighed, "All right. I won't keep you any longer. Go and have fun. Bring me back more news, and I will come and find you in a few days to check in. If you need me, I suppose you could also show up at The Cottage just downriver and call. I think I will hear you, but take care there is no one else around if you do."

"Good, Lovely Man. I search and spy. I come and visit you soon. I am so happy to see you today."

"Be well, love. Take good care of yourself." She did a full somersault in the air, came down with the usual splash, waved once and was suddenly gone. Tvrdik looked after her for a few minutes, half a smile tugging at his lips. Then he lay back on the flat rock and let the sun warm his face while he drifted for a bit, dreaming of unicorns and talking turtles.

It might have been fifteen minutes, or several hours that he lay there enjoying the sun and breeze playing over his face, with the peaceful sounds of moving waters, rustling leaves and birdsong refreshing his soul. But by the time he did rise, it was afternoon, and Tvrdik knew it was time to face the old house and whatever ghosts lingered there. As he rounded the bend and it came into view, the state of it slammed into him like a blunted arrow, and rendered him breathless. Once he regained his composure enough to turn into the familiar yard through the opening where the remains of a gate hung useless, however, it struck him that much was remarkably well-preserved after twelve long years of neglect. The fence would need attention, both structural and cosmetic, and the grounds, overgrown with shrubbery and coarse weeds, needed clearing. The gardens, of course, were a tangle of dense vegetation. But, where they were not entirely choked off by uninvited plants, it seemed as if some of the food and medicinal crops had self-perpetuated, and were attempting to grow and produce on their own. Fortunately, weeding and landscaping were activities at which he was quite adept, having lived for so long in a place where the forest eternally attempted to reclaim its own.

Tvrdik paced the perimeter of the entire building, paying careful attention to every detail, and making mental notes about what would have to be done in order to make the place habitable again. There were a few rotting beams that needed to be replaced or shored up, a stone here and there out of place, the roof obviously needed re-thatching, and all the walls would benefit from several coats of whitewash. Someone had taken the trouble to board up all the windows, and he surmised underneath there might be broken panes. And that was just the outside. And yet, all the basics were there, still sturdy, somehow enduring. He suspected that Xaarus had perhaps added a little magic to the mortar of this house, rendering it somewhat impervious to the elements and the effects of time, which might have flattened a less well-protected structure.

He was reminded yet again that this had been a wizard's home when he steeled himself to go inside and found he could not open the door. Aging as it was, it was solid oak and sturdy, and locked fast shut. Old Xaarus was not about to yield his secrets lightly. Tvrdik tried the muscular approach, running at it and crashing into it repeatedly until he was bruised and felt silly. He tried prying it open with a stick, but the stick broke, and none of the tools he had just purchased seemed to find a leverage point. The young mage scratched his head, thinking that if his old master had locked the door with spells, they would be powerful, but everyday magic (not having anticipated a long absence, as it were). Tvrdik tried a generic spell to override any magical lock-outs, but of course it failed. He tried using passwords: names, phrases, words that might carry some meaning, with no success. If he were ever going to get inside, he would either have to be cleverer, or remember better. He had, after all, lived in this house for years, but so much time had passed, and they had almost always been with Xaarus when going in or out. In those days of peace and bustling activity before the accident, doors were often left wide open, everyone's thoughts untainted by worry and suspicion. Of course, he could summon Xaarus in his head, but it seemed a feeble excuse for such an extreme measure, and felt a little like failure. No, he wished to master this challenge by his own wits.

Tvrdik stood silent, breathed deeply, closed his eyes, and willed himself to travel back to those days when this had been his home. He saw in his mind's eye his younger self and his two classmates following their master about everywhere, trying to absorb the bits of wisdom and instruction which were given out as a running commentary. He tried to listen, to recall anything that Xaarus had said to them that might be a clue. He saw them all standing before the door, Benjin and Ailianne sharing some private joke, his younger self aching to be included in their horseplay, none of them paying much attention to their teacher's ongoing monologue. Somewhere, from the depths of his unconscious, Xaarus' words echoed, *Never neglect to be grateful for those beings and objects in life which serve you well. Bless them and say thank you. Enter your home always with blessings and depart from it with thanks....* Tvrdik had internalized this advice, and had been faithful to it even in his humble woodland retreat. It had always seemed a good and reverent practice to him. But now, opening his eyes back in the present, he wondered if there was something more concrete there. "Bless this house," he muttered, and the door sprang open. He stepped back and shook his head in an effort to return from the uncomfortable emotional landscape of his past, half expecting some foul stench or a cloud of dust to assault his senses. But all that greeted him was stillness, and the odor of slightly stale air. He took a deep breath and crossed the threshold.

Outside, bright sunshine still flooded the yard, but with the windows boarded up, scant light penetrated the interior of the house. Not wanting to walk straight into anything dangerous or disgusting, Tvrdik paused a moment to allow his eyes to adjust. Then, leaving the door open to admit whatever light might follow him in, he stepped deeper into what felt like a dream of his past. It occurred to him that if he was to style himself a wizard, he should probably start thinking like a wizard, using every tool at his disposal. Concentrating for only a moment, he sent up a soft glow-ball which hovered over his head and illuminated the space with a gentle, warm light. In this new light, details began to emerge. Here was the sitting room, with its comfortable chairs, small table, broad hearth, throw rugs and shelves lined with books. Looking around, Tvrdik began to suspect Xaarus of protecting everything in his home with a smattering of magic. Things were unnaturally still, yes, and covered with a visible layer of dust. But after twelve years, nothing was out of place, and there were far fewer signs of wear and degradation than one would expect. Spiders had set up residence in a few high corners, but they were mostly neat and out of the way. There was evidence that rodents might have visited for awhile early on, but everything edible or spoilable had long since been consumed or fallen to dust, and the rats and mice had abandoned the empty larder for greener pastures.

Room after room revealed the same story – things almost eerily untouched, as if left out for the morning, frozen in a moment that seemed an eternity ago. Room after room Tvrdik passed through, the glow-light preceding him, lighting up familiar passageways and spaces, all just as he had last seen them. His conscious mind was busy tallying up the work that needed to be done, relieved at the lack of serious damage. At the same time, a deeper part of his psyche was encountering a veritable parade of memories, and, as Tashroth had warned, 'ghosts' of his former life. There was the kitchen, its oversized hearth and counters lined with pots and bowls and utensils, pantry shelves that had always been crammed with foodstuffs, medicinal herbs, tinctures, salves and ointments. Next, a small refectory, where they had gathered around the long wooden table for meals, or at other times, to study, write and debate the theories, philosophies and methodologies Xaarus had presented to them.

Heading into the school annex, he crossed the room they used as a main classroom, with its large teaching slateboard on one wall, and workstations around the sides where they had done laboratory and practical work. Beyond was the dormitory, a spacious room where they had all slept at first, but which had been partitioned off into separate, more private cubicles as they had gotten older. There were bathing facilities off to the side, simple but functional. Stepping into his old cubicle, Tvrdik gazed at his old sleeping pallet, desk, shelves of books and small collection of possessions as if they belonged to someone else he had once known a hundred years ago. There was the triangle-shaped bit of glass he had spent joyful hours with, turning sunbeams into rainbows, the favorite quill pen he had fashioned himself from the fallen feather of a hawk, a dust-covered lesson book, where he had jotted down every word of wisdom that had fallen from Xaarus' lips. Seeing these once-treasured items sent a stab of nameless pain through his being, but he did not reach out a hand to touch them. Likewise, something kept him from stepping into the spaces that had belonged to his schoolmates. It still seemed a violation of sorts to invade their small, private sanctuaries. Tvrdik stood still in the middle of the dormitory for a few minutes, blinking behind his glasses, uncertain of his feelings. Then, he turned and walked back through the annex, the kitchen and the parlor to the other end of the house, the older section, containing Xaarus' private apartments. Rarely did he remember setting foot in this inner sanctum. Rarely were any of them invited to cross into Xaarus' private world, where the Master retreated at the end of each day to pursue his own interests. Here were Xaarus' own bedchamber and bathing area, his extensive private library, and his laboratory. Somehow, now that he was taking possession of the house, and knew he would need every resource that Xaarus had amassed in order to fight the coming darkness, Tvrdik didn't feel quite as reluctant to intrude here as he might have. Entering the bedchamber, he cast an objective eye over the simple, but comfortable appointments. Everything was covered in dust, and it was obvious that the drapes and wall-hangings, as well as the bedclothes and probably the rugs, mattresses, and cloth-covered chairs would all have to be replaced. A simple cleaning would likely take care of the rest.

Conscious that space in the palace would be at a premium as the lords began to arrive for the Council Meeting, the young mage resolved to begin in the bedroom so that he could at least sleep here as soon as possible. Moving into the adjoining library, he gasped at the vast assemblage of books, parchments and scrolls of all shapes, sizes, ages, languages and subject matters that lined the walls floor to ceiling. Scanning the titles of those nearest him, he realized the priceless treasures he had inherited, and imagined spending many happy, constructive hours here attending to his own further education. A comfortable chair and a separate hearth invited the visitor most warmly to stay and partake of the wisdom collected in that room. Tvrdik sighed and longed for leisure to enjoy such bounty. It might be some time before that dream was realized. But, meanwhile, there was sure to be some immediately helpful information among the volumes surrounding him. He would do his best to locate everything that could be useful for the current situation.

One final door led to Xaarus' master workshop - his laboratory. It seemed a surprisingly vast room, considering how modest The Cottage appeared from the outside. Tvrdik's eye took in the tables piled with beakers, test tubes, glass pipettes and flasks; the shelves of liquids, powders, tinctures, oils, salves, drying herbs, preserved and floating objects or bits of who knows what in jars. There were detailed anatomical and cosmological charts, drawings and maps on all the walls, and mechanical models ranged about the room. Heavens, was there no subject of inquiry in which Xaarus had not dabbled? There was one special corner piled high with parchments and scrolls, various schedules and graphs, and a host of timepieces of all sorts from all over the globe. Some sort of magnetic or generating equipment seemed to be tossed into the mix nearby, all arranged as if the master would return presently after having a sandwich. No doubt, these were the elements of Xaarus' last great project; it was likely that he had vanished from that particular corner twelve long years ago. Tvrdik shivered to think of it, considering also that there was probably no one on earth who could begin to comprehend the neat rows of calculations and formulae laid out before him, and no hope of anyone ever reversing the process to bring Xaarus back. He sighed. It was certainly a task far beyond his own limited brain, at least for the foreseeable future.

For a moment, the glow-ball danced away from him, and in its pulsing light, his eye caught something else in another corner, something that captured his full attention. The young mage edged over to where the light pointed, and found himself standing before three tall, sturdy, beautifully crafted wizard's staffs, each carved from a different sort of wood, and each crowned with a different color crystal. He reached out a trembling hand and ran it along the nearest, which was tall and sturdy, of knotted black walnut, and tipped with obsidian. The parchment wrapped around the center had a word scrawled across it – no, a name. He willed the glow-ball closer, and bent his head to read, "Benjin." Startled, he pulled back, eyebrows knitted together. Xaarus must have been making these staffs of office for his students when the accident occurred. To win one was a rare and much desired accomplishment. A wizard's staff had to be made by hand, crafted with care of specially selected materials, by one who understood such things. Properly matched with the recipient, it became like a living thing: a flexible extension of one's powers, a partner for a lifetime or for many, and a visible sign of prestige which afforded one respect and privilege among townsfolk and cottagers alike. Tvrdik had never dreamed that they all had been so close to being thus gifted, thus honored by their teacher. What they had missed!

He barely touched the next one as it stood there, slim and supple, of pale birch topped with a clear quartz crystal. It was light and graceful like its intended owner. He did not have to read the parchment to know for whom it had been intended – Ailianne. But that meant the third staff... Tvrdik hesitated a moment, and then purposefully reached out his right hand to grasp it. Tall and strong, of solid oak, it was more gnarled than the others, and seemed to bend in odd, unexpected ways until it found its way up to the faceted violet amethyst fixed at the tip. It seemed to fit his hand, and himself, perfectly, and felt lighter than expected. In a flash he already felt as if he had carried it all of his life, and would feel naked without it. He was thinking of Xaarus at that moment with such awe and gratitude that he was almost not surprised to see the master's image floating before him, and hear the old wizard's voice clearly in his head.

"I was going to give it to you for your nineteenth birthday. I had completed them all and was only waiting for the right moment to present them. I am glad you have it now – it was always intended to be yours. You have certainly earned it these last few weeks. Go ahead – hold it... lift it... point it. How does it feel?"

"Oh, Master, like nothing I ever imagined! Like a part of my soul manifested – a way to reach further, faster, deeper, more powerfully – like I was born to wield it."

Xaarus' image was grinning with delight, "I thought I had done a rather good job on that one. But, then, the raw materials presented themselves somewhat magically as well. That entire branch was torn by lightning from its mother oak deep in the wood not so far from that waterfall of yours. Legend had it that the old tree sheltered a fairy ring. And the amethyst was given to me in trade by a miner in exchange for an elixir that cured his little boy of a rather severe croup. He was most grateful and a bit mystified, as he said a strange feeling came over him when he first pulled it from the earth, and he knew it to be the proper payment. But you and I do not raise an eyebrow at such omens, do we boy. I knew it was meant for you – you are twice the healer I will ever be.

"Master, you do me far too much honor. My skills have barely been tried."

"Nonsense, each of us has our peculiar strengths. And besides, I have knowledge of your future, remember?"

"Then tell me, Master, so far you have been right about everything, but despite my faith in you, and in our cause, at times I feel terribly inadequate to the tasks laid out for me. Are we destined to succeed in this venture then?"

"I cannot tell you that, my friend, for you stand in a place in history where every road you choose at every crossing changes the outcome. I can only say that I am very proud and gratified by what you have accomplished thus far. And I mean everything. Tvrdik the man is, as I had hoped, every bit of what Tvrdik the boy promised, and more. You will see."

Tvrdik bowed his head, inwardly grateful for, but uncomfortable with, such praise, even if no one else could hear it. But as Xaarus' image began to fade, he came to attention.

"Master – the house?"

"Take it! Use it. Everything you find here is yours to assist you. I will always be very close to you here. I will do what I can to help and guide you. Keep all your senses tuned, boy, and your eyes open..." This last was like an echo from a great distance, and he was gone again, leaving Tvrdik to question if the encounter had been real at all.

But, in his right hand was something extremely real, and very substantial. Once again he bowed his head, leaning the top of the staff against his forehead, while he gripped it with both hands. For a long moment he stood there like that, silent and still, the glow-ball hovering over him like a blessing, energy surging up from the earth through the oaken branch and through the man, mingling where they touched and binding them powerfully together. When he finally stood erect and walked out of the room, staff in hand, he felt for the first time in every fiber of his being that he was indeed a wizard.

ELEVEN

DELPHINE AGAIN

As he stepped back into the gardens, Tvrdik realized by the sun's position and his awakening hunger that the best of the day was behind him. Having assessed the entire project, he felt he would be better off beginning the real work in the morning, after a night's rest. He was reluctant to relinquish his newly discovered staff, since it already felt like a part of his anatomy. But he could not risk it being seen at Theriole. So, leaning it just inside the front door, he conjured a little assistance arranging and putting away all the items which had been delivered to the grounds from the market. Then he physically locked the front door and reset its magical password, adding a bit of his own sorcery to hide the tools and building materials, neatly stacked in the yard, from any would-be pilferer. Heading back up the riverwalk to Theriole, he turned back once, reflecting on all he had seen and experienced in the house that afternoon, and on the memories beginning to surface as a result. He would have to keep these thoughts to himself, closely guarding his true identity for the moment. Soon enough, he mused, soon enough it would all be a matter of public knowledge; he had best enjoy his anonymity while he could. Meanwhile, tomorrow promised to be a very full day.

The sun dipped lower as he approached the palace. He was considering the possibility of trying to wheedle some dinner out of the kitchen staff, when he noticed, on the same bench as the day before, a lone figure with auburn hair. It was most certainly Delphine, in her accustomed spot, but as he drew nearer, he noticed her swollen eyes and red nose.

"My lady!" he called out, and waved, giving her a chance to arrange herself. Tvrdik frowned, wondering whatever could have brought such an effervescent soul to tears. He took his time on the path, discreetly watching as she wiped her eyes and nose with a delicate handkerchief, smoothed back her hair, and arranged her skirts in an attempt to look nonchalant.

"Well met once again, Lady Delphine. I was out for an afternoon stroll and lost track of the time. Do you suppose I am still in time to scare up a bite to eat?" And now he was by her side and she was smiling up at him.

"Why, Tvrdik! What a pleasant surprise to see you. I was just about to go in to supper myself. You must come along and tell me all about what you've been up to today." Her broad smile looked so out of place on that swollen, blotchy face that it broke his heart. Tvrdik was aware that to a girl of seventeen, he might appear positively ancient, a member of another generation who could not possibly understand the way things were. And yet, she had been so open and warm yesterday, and in a way, they were both misfits. He could well imagine how a girl of her high position might find herself without many *true* friends in whom to confide. He made a sudden decision, sat down on the bench beside her, and leaned in close.

"Supper will wait a little longer if there is something on your mind that needs airing. In my own country I have some reputation as a good listener, and look...broad shoulders as well...hmmm?" The smile faded from her face as she stared at him, speechless, and then, in a heartbeat, she had collapsed in sobs on his breast. A little surprised, he made an awkward attempt to fold his arms around her, comforting. "There, there, what's this?" he cooed, "You are a beautiful, intelligent, noble young woman who is very much in love with a wonderful young man who adores her. It is springtime and the gardens are lovely. What could be so terrible that will not pass?"

She tried to collect herself, and straightened up on the bench, "Oh, Tvrdik, I am so sorry. Here we have only just met one another, and what a foolish goose you must think me. I – I don't know what came over me. But somehow, I do feel you are someone to be trusted."

He made a sign at his mouth, "Not a word to anyone. And no judgment here. Trust me when I say I have had my share of moments like this." The girl smiled despite herself, even laughed a bit, and her face lit up beneath her tears like sunshine vying with a passing shower. Tvrdik continued,

"There. That's more like the Delphine I remember from yesterday. Now, is there anything I can do to fix whatever it is that has upset you so?" he queried, gently taking her handkerchief and dabbing at her cheeks.

"I doubt it. It's my *sister* (the word was spoken as if it tasted awful in her pretty mouth). Sometimes she just *infuriates* me. Ugghhh!" This last was a visceral explosion of pent-up frustration that went beyond language. "I can't stay mad at her…she's my best friend, and I *adore* her. I know how difficult things are for her right now, but why must she torment me so?"

"What happened?"

"She invited me to lunch with her today, and I was overjoyed, partly at the prospect of spending some real time with her at last, and partly as I was expecting some further news about the wedding…"

"Did she bring it up?"

"Did she bring it up? I'll say. She told me it was out of the question. I was stunned. I thought Mark had impressed her – that she even *liked* him. I mean, who could not like Mark, I ask you? I thought that we had made a good case for our plans…our hopes and dreams…I thought that she cared about my happiness. But all she said was, 'Delphine, it's just out of the question right now; you will have to put it out of your mind for the moment.' Out of my mind? She's *driving* me out of my mind." Delphine was becoming increasingly agitated as she relived the unfortunate encounter, and hot tears were beginning to appear again.

Tvrdik interjected, "Did she say why?"

"When I asked her for a reason, she couldn't give me one, exactly. She kept saying that she had new information about things coming up that she couldn't speak of, but that starting anything new right now, like a life together, was a bad idea, and I should just trust her on this and obey. I asked her if she had a problem with Mark, or with me, and she kept saying, no, she liked Mark well enough, but that I was just going to have to believe her that she was making this decision for my own good. Can you imagine?"

Tvrdik straightened – he knew what all this was about. "And what did you say to her?"

"I told her she didn't know anything about what was for my good anymore, that I was no longer a child she could control. She told me I was acting childishly and should therefore be treated as a child, and that she had far more serious matters to deal with than her sister's hurt feelings at not getting her own way. And then we had a horrible fight, and I'm sure both of us said things we didn't mean. I stormed out of there and have been sitting here ever since trying to figure out what to do. Oh, Tvrdik, why doesn't she understand how important this is to me? Why does she insist on hurting me like this? Why can't she be happy for me? Am I really asking so very much?" Tvrdik's mouth moved but nothing came out. The girl's voice drooped, "Do you think it could be that she is jealous of me? That she doesn't want me to marry first? I would never have believed something so vile about my own sister. And besides, all of her life she has had Tashroth – she's never been alone, and now she would begrudge me the companion I so long for?"

Tvrdik, blushing, shook his head, "I – I don't think that's it at all," he stammered.

Delphine's face snapped back toward him, and her eyes met his square on, "What then? Why is she doing this to me?"

Tvrdik paused a long moment. He knew exactly what was going through Jorelial Rey's mind, as it had already gone through his own. But he felt for this young woman, so earnest, so hurt that the one person she relied upon had seemed to dismiss her. How much could he say? How could he help without going too far? He grasped the distraught, disheveled girl by her shoulders, and looked her straight in the eye.

"Delphine, listen to me. I am truly sorry that you are feeling ill-used right now, but you do not know all the facts."

"What do you mean? Tell me."

Tvrdik sighed, "Well, as I am here on something of a diplomatic mission, I actually know something of the circumstances to which the Lady Rey is referring. I am not at liberty to divulge the details, but I can tell you that your sister is afraid that this kingdom might be going to war soon, and the world will become a very dangerous place."

Delphine's face clouded, "A war? That's ridiculous. There has not been any such thing as a war here in living memory. We have no enemies."

"A child holds the throne and there are those who might see that as an opportunity to take what is not theirs. It would be wonderful if I am proven wrong, but if I am not, your sister cannot let that happen. Much chaos and unhappiness may lie ahead for everyone. I can only guess that she feels it is unwise for you to begin your new life now, when so much is uncertain."

Delphine's face changed as her perspective shifted, "Why, if all that is true, then why won't she be honest with me? Poor Rel. What a horrible burden to be carrying and the silly goose won't even talk to me about her fears and suspicions…"

"I'm sure she doesn't want to spoil these days of your youth with so much heaviness…"

Delphine jumped up off the bench, "Well, if that was her aim, she's done a fair job of missing the target, hasn't she? My days are spoiled already as long as she denies me happiness, and then lets me think she is just being a witch about it for no good reason…she's wrong, you know."

"Pardon?"

"She's looking at this all wrong. If the future looks so grim, all the more reason for us all to chase the sparks of happiness and love as we find them, to value the connections that make us whole, to focus on the truest parts of life that will always endure. She never did get that, about people and relationships." Delphine threw up her hands in a gesture of dismissal, and began to pace, mostly talking to herself now. Tvrdik sat on the bench alone, his mouth fallen open in wonder at the wisdom that was pouring out from this almost-child, who moments before had been sobbing, inconsolable, into his vest. The girl went on, a tone of confidence entering her voice, "Someone is going to have to sit her down and make her see how she is looking at this all wrong. And that it isn't healthy for her to keep trying to carry all of these burdens and responsibilities alone.…"

Tvrdik cleared his throat loudly. The maiden stopped in her tracks and turned to him, looking surprised to find him still sitting there on the bench.

"Um, Delphine? If you go and tell the Lady Rey – your sister – that you know all about the war, and that you want to make some suggestions – and mind you, I quite agree that they might be good ones – but, you see, she is going to want to know exactly where you got that information. And it might not go so well for *me* if she finds out that it was *I* who told you."

Delphine cocked her head at him for a moment while a range of expressions played across her face. For a heartbeat, she resembled Ondine so much it was almost eerie. Then, without warning, she flew to the bench and threw her arms around him in a spontaneous and rather thorough embrace.

"Oh, Tvrdik, you dear, dear man! You have been such an angel. I really do understand everything so much better now. Thank you, thank you, thank you. And don't worry at all. Rel will never know what we spoke of here; I would never get you into trouble. I just knew when I first met you that you would be lucky for us all. Come on. Let's go and see if we can find something good to eat. I'm famished." She took him by the hand and pulled him to his feet, then off down the road toward the giant front doors of Theriole. Tvrdik couldn't think of a thing to say. Perhaps it was hunger, or weariness, but his brain seemed to be spinning, and the only distinct impression he could pin down was that life with this woman would be, most definitely, an adventure.

———— ❂ ————

Had Delphine even attempted at that moment to find her sister and set things to right, she would not have found her in the palace. Jorelial Rey had finally snapped, and was even then clinging to Tashroth's broad shoulders, en route to a favorite retreat of theirs in the mountains. The pristine lake that filled an old crater was only accessible by air, and was the perfect regenerative spot to hide from anyone and everyone who might be searching for the Lady Regent, wanting a 'moment of her time.' Jorelial knew she would not be disturbed here. She also knew she could not justify disappearing for long at such a critical moment. But the endless parade of petitioners, the weight of the knowledge she carried, and the unpleasant episode with her beloved sister had combined to fray her last nerve, and she wisely realized she would be of no use to anyone without a brief period of solitude and regeneration.

The air was bracing in this mountain retreat. The sharp scent of evergreens purged every muddled thought and untangled all the knots of confusion. A profound silence that seemed almost primordial wrapped itself around the crater, but on deeper examination revealed a tapestry of natural music pieced together from birdsong, the creak of swaying trees, the distinctive calls of frogs and locusts searching for companionship. While Tashroth hunted for his supper, Jorelial swam in the icy waters, then dried herself on the stony shore, under a low, but still warm sun. As dusk fell, they sat in easy silence for awhile by the lake's edge, a roaring campfire that Tashroth had breathed into existence upon kindling Jorelial had gathered, taking the chill out of the air. She had brought along bread and cheese and dried fruit, and sat idly chewing and staring off at the distant fading sunset. Finally, as if the conversation had already been flowing for ages, "Tash, I hated to leave Delphine in such a state. I know I lost my temper, but did I make the wrong decision? Was I too hard on her?"

The deep, organ-toned voice rolled, "You know that I try not to tell you how to think, or what to do, little one, but tell me why you deny her?"

Jorelial raised her eyebrows, a bit surprised. "Well, I have nothing against this Mark fellow. He seems to have a good head on his shoulders, and I believe he really cares for her. But she is so young. I'm not sure she truly knows her own heart. And the future is so uncertain now. We don't know where we'll be in a year, or five. We could be at war, or, heaven forbid, we could lose control of the kingdom. They could be parted, or destitute, or worse. I just don't want her heart broken, and I can protect her better if I can keep her here with me. Surely it isn't too much to ask them to wait and see if the relationship will weather the coming storm. A girl like her will have so many opportunities in the future – gods willing there *is* a future for all of us."

"And how would *you* have responded to someone who sought to part us from one another ten years ago? I seem to recall those who claimed that it was not appropriate for a fine young lady of marriageable age to be spending all her free time with a savage beast, hmmm?"

"Well, we never listened to those old biddies, dearest. We have always been together, and we always will be. No one could force us apart. What? Oh, come on, don't look at me like that; it's entirely different. You have been my companion since I was born, and we weren't facing such chaos in the world back then."

"Would the world situation have mattered to you then, or anything but what your heart told you? Jorelial Rey… (whenever he whispered her whole name intimately like that, Jorelial's bones nearly melted), wise or foolish, right or wrong, the heart has its own compass that guides us to the source of its fulfillment. Thought may see obstacles, and differences, but the heart's compass points true north, and will not be swayed by reason or argument. Your sister may be young, but you know she is constant when her desire fixes on something. You have seen this over and over; you have laughed at it, and cursed over it. You might call her stubborn. Or you might say she follows where her heart's guidance leads. Is that a thing to be despised or envied? Who can tell?"

"Are you saying I should let her marry the bard? Put aside any misgivings and my better judgment?"

"I am saying she is likely to pursue her heart's desire, with or without your consent, and if you wish to keep her in your life, you would best not try to restrain her, or put more obstacles in her path. What she longs for is for you to rejoice with her in her newfound happiness."

"You think she would defy me? I can't imagine such a thing. But it certainly is not my intention to force her hand, or to push her away. I am miserable without Delphine. Look at me now. I couldn't bear our being estranged for long. I'm only trying to be a good guardian to her, trying to think what our father might have done. I can't help feeling responsible."

"Dearest, on this plane, you cannot stop the hands of time. She is growing up and finding her own path. You can no longer keep her in innocence, or protect her from experience. You can only love her, and be her refuge if she is ever knocked down."

"That is what you did for me, isn't it, Tash?"

"It is what I try to do every day."

"Was it hard, to let go, I mean? To let me fall on my face sometimes?" The fire flickered and almost went out, under a gusty dragon sigh.

"Yes…and no. You are headstrong and curious, little one, and often flirt with danger. But it is *your* journey, and you must make your own way. While I breathe, I will be beside you on that journey, but I trust you, and know you will always find the way to what is right."

"You are wise, Tashroth, so much wiser than I, and I am a little ashamed at what I have done. I only want Delphine to be happy, and maybe I have not trusted her enough. I do think she is a remarkable soul, and perhaps there is a thing or two I could learn from her. I will think this through again, and I will put things right with her as soon as we return."

"Whatever you say, little one," the dragon agreed, wryly. Jorelial cocked her head.

"As if you aren't the slightest bit aware of how persuasive you are, you big green goon…"

"I? Why, I was under the impression we were merely conversing on a problem. As I said, I would never presume to tell you what to do…"

"Oh, no, never!" Rel laughed, feeling lighter already. Then, more seriously, "Tash, as long as I have breath, you know I will be beside you on the journey as well. You know that nothing and nobody will ever take me away from you. You are my heart, my wisdom, and my strength."

There was a long beat of silence, as if the dragon needed to frame his next sentence most carefully, "Jorelial Rey, someday a man may come into your life who will be a fit partner for you. A helpmate, a lover, a friend, a father for your children…"

"I do not care about any of those things. I already have all I need."

"Listen to me. You think you do now, but there are experiences you need to have in this lifetime, and you must open to them or a part of you dies."

"Tash, there was a time I wanted those things, but my life is very full now – more than I even want it to be – and I doubt there is anyone out there who would be willing or able to link his life to my crazy existence in that way. And there is no one out there who could ever take your place. That is certain."

"Dearest, it is the same for me, but I am not suggesting anyone will come along and make you choose between us. I *am* saying that a great heart has room for many loves, and you must allow yourself to look for the one who can love you so generously and deeply, that he loves all you are, and all you bring with you. You will know him easily, because he will never make you choose."

"Sounds a bit like a fantasy lover to me," she yawned, her eyes growing heavy, "but if you say so, I will try to allow the possibility…someday. Tash, what about you? Are you lonely for a mate of your own kind?"

Another thoughtful pause, in which Jorelial might have dozed off, but she thought she heard his response clearly, a moment later.

"I am content, my dear. If something more is to be, I, too, am open to whatever gifts destiny has in store for me. Rest assured, you will never be displaced from my dragon's heart, Jorelial Rey."

She closed her eyes and leaned back. The fire was flickering low, but Tashroth's chest was warm. They would have to fly back at dawn, back to responsibilities and demands. But this time was precious and sacred.

Night noises filled the air, evidence of the ongoing drama of survival taking place in the shadows around them. But Jorelial Rey was not worried about danger, teeth or claws, sting or venomous tongue. She slept soundly, secure in the knowledge that there were indeed some advantages to being loved by a dragon.

Anyone crossing the courtyard would not have noticed the trio of figures at the corner, shrouded in cloaks and loitering behind the columns. Not that there would be anyone crossing the courtyard at this hour of the night. Dark clouds scudded across a gibbous moon, and somewhere far off, a wolf sent up his plaintive, lonely howl. The small, wiry man with the pockmarked face pulled his cloak closer, despite the pleasant warmth of the midnight air.

"E's overdue! I ain't waitin' any longer. Someone's bound to see us out 'ere and start askin' questions."

"Keep your shirt on, Brubaker. Not a soul about. He'll be here," replied a rather lumpy man with unruly curls.

The third figure, tall and sour-looking, hissed at them, "Won't be a picnic for any of us if you two don't quit yer squawkin'. Don't you know these walls are like a canyon? You'll be heard clear across the yard. Shut yer traps."

The curly-headed man held up a hand, "There! That shadow just moved. See, there? It's coming towards us. That's Gargan alright. I'd know him anywhere – big man."

"Hush," said the wiry figure, "wait until yer sure."

"I tell you, I know him."

"Quiet. Whoever it is has heard us now. You'd better hope it's him, alright."

The hulking form was indeed upon them, emerging without a sound from the shadows and mist, nearly invisible in its dark cloak. A deep voice addressed the odd trio.

"It's a good thing that everyone in Theriole's asleep now, or the whole of Eneri Clare'd know what it is we're about. What are you nimwits up to, making such a racket?"

"Told you."

"Ah, ye did no such thing…"

"Quiet!" Gargan commanded, and the others slunk back like wild dogs acknowledging their pack leader.

"Brubaker, look alive." Gargan continued, and tossed a grapefruit-sized sack, which the wiry man caught with a quick, dull jingle. "It's all there. Euligian gold coins, just as you requested. You won't have any trouble passing them off in the market." The wiry man nodded and tucked the purse under his cloak, a half-smile tugging at his thin lips.

Next, Gargan pulled out a rolled piece of parchment, sealed with a wax insignia. He held it out to the curly-haired man. "Land," he stated simply, "two hundred acres, woods and good upper pastureland. A small mine or two. A sturdy house and a couple of outbuildings. Agreed?"

The stout man reached, but hesitated, "Mine? Recorded and deeded? No questions or problems?"

Gargan handed him the scroll and sniffed, "Everything official. What do you take him for?"

"But how? Where?"

"The previous owner had…an unfortunate accident."

The curly-haired man twitched, but hastened to fold his new treasure safely under his cloak. "Lord Drogue is most generous," he muttered, hanging his head.

The sour-faced figure stepped forward boldly, "And my reward?" he probed. Gargan reached under his cloak one more time, and pulled out some sort of metal medallion on a long, colorful loop of ribbon.

"Congratulations, *Squire* Colrick. Your new title comes with a fairly decent manor house, and the governance of a small, but prosperous fiefdom, subject to His Lordship, of course."

The new Squire inclined his head toward Gargan. "Of course," he replied, pocketing the proof of his title, and bowing extravagantly, "Please convey my deep gratitude to His Lordship."

Gargan spoke almost on top of the man's sentence, "Alright, then, is everyone satisfied, just as we agreed?" There were assurances all around, and then Brubaker chimed in once more.

"Lord Drogue honors us with 'is most liberal gifts – more than I could ever say for that twit as sat last on Clare's throne – but what *exactly* will 'e be wantin' from us in return? What will 'e expect us to *do* at the council meetin'?" The others shook their heads and murmured exclamations of agreement.

Gargan smiled, "Oh, quite simple, gents. He just wants you to support his run for regent is all. Talk him up to your friends and families, put his name forward for nomination, vote for him when the time comes, of course. Show some excitement if he should get up to speak. And maybe a bit of noise for anybody that's fool enough to oppose him, see? Not so much of a task, really, for so generous a bribe, eh? Oh, and he'll expect you all to follow his lead, should he choose any other course there at the meeting, and support him with action if need be…"

The curly-haired man's brow furrowed, "Well, that's going a bit far, now, isn't it? I agreed to put his name up for regent, but I never said as I would give up my good reputation and follow the man into whatever hell he chooses…" The others laughed – all except Gargan, who grabbed the man's shirt and yanked him close.

"You've taken the land, sir. You have your deed. Lord Drogue owns you now. I would consider very careful-like how you reward my lord's generosity. Because, I will tell you plain, he does not like to be disappointed. Are we clear?"

The stout man's eyes were wide, and he wheezed a bit as he nodded vigorously in reply. Gargan released him, and the man's hand flew up to his throat protectively.

"Good. Very good. Do him proud, gentlemen. Pleasure doing business with you. Now I am going to tippy-toe back the way I came. Count ten – assuming that isn't too high a number for any of you – and then back to your camps in each other's company like you've been out to enjoy an ale with friends. Understood?" He was answered with a chorus of 'ayes' and a great deal of nodding. And then he was gone, a shadow among shadows once more, leaving his associates open-mouthed, but speechless, where they stood.

Jorelial Rey flew back to Theriole on Tashroth at first light, determined to find her sister before anything else distracted her. She intended to have a long talk with her, and apologize for being so rigid in her handling of the situation. But, there was already a crisis waiting for her upon her arrival, involving two regional lords coming in for the Council Meeting, bickering over which should have the rights to pitch tents closest to the palace. Jorelial sighed, splashed some water on her face, rolled up her sleeves, and launched into some rather inspired diplomatic machinations. Delphine, as usual, would have to wait. Jorelial trusted that her sister would forgive her the delay, but made a mental note not to let too much time pass before re-visiting the girl's concerns. Predictably, with the Council Meeting just days away, hours flew by with one situation after another requiring her immediate attention. Embroiled in so many vital decisions, conflicts and plans, she forgot to do anything about mending fences.

Delphine, for her part, made several attempts both the evening before and at various intervals throughout the day to find Jorelial, or to intercept her between meetings, but without success. She was concerned and frustrated that their last ugly encounter was still hanging in the air between them without resolution, and torn between sympathy for her sister's overwhelming schedule, and hurt that their relationship once again rated last priority. Failing in her quest to right things, she resigned herself at last to running into Rel whenever providence allowed. Then she went off to spend time with little King Darian, who adored her company, and with Mark, whose advice she freely sought on what they should do next.

Meanwhile, Tvrdik was up and out so early that morning that he might have noticed Tashroth's shadow as the great beast soared back to the roof of Theriole. Perhaps he might have, had he been a little more awake and alert to the outside world. But the day promised to be fair once again, and he was determined to put a good day's work in on The Cottage and have something measureable to show by the end of the day. He had dressed in his sturdy boots and coarse work clothes, and was making mental lists of the day's projects in his head at the moment Jorelial and the green dragon swooped silently over his head. The whole day was his to dispose of as he wished – no appointments, no deadlines, no interruptions expected – and he felt invigorated to be once more tackling something physical and finite. It was the kind of project he was more than familiar with: one that showed real results very quickly. It was barely light when he arrived at the house and stood looking at it, hands on hips, formulating his plan. Then he bowed his head, uttered a blessing on the work he was about to undertake, spit on both palms, rubbed them together, and strode to the door. He unlocked both the physical and magical locks, stepped within to pick up a crowbar. Emerging again with tools in hand and a healthy dose of determination, he began to make his way around the building, prying the wooden boards off of the windows, letting light and air into the stuffy, dark, long disused rooms. The transformation had begun.

T W E L V E

IN THE COTTAGE

IT WAS NOON WHEN THE dog came by to see what all the commotion was about, and what he saw must have thrilled the young wolfhound who had spent his brief life dreaming of wizards. Tvrdik was nowhere to be seen on the grounds, but two scrub-brushes were independently dipping themselves in a sudsy bucket, and applying themselves to the walls and mouldings of The Cottage. Four broad paintbrushes followed close behind, spreading fresh whitewash from another bucket, quite evenly and thoroughly – one might even say cheerfully – all over the house's exterior. The place was already beginning to look brighter. No one else was anywhere in sight in either direction on the riverwalk. Stewart stood stock still at the gate, staring at the flying brushes in their orderly dance. He shook his head, woofed an enthusiastic greeting – and then sprang backwards in alarm as, all at once, the brushes fell lifeless from their endeavors, making a loud *sploosh* in their buckets. A pale head popped up from among bundles of straw thatch on the roof, peering down through spectacles that reflected the sun's rays.

"Who's there?" the head on the roof shouted, sounding a little nervous.

"It is I, sir, come to see what all the activity at The Cottage signified. Stewart, sir…ye remember, we met on the road the other day?"

The voice from the roof seemed to relax a bit, and the head, followed by a torso, lifted from its bundles to become more visible. "Oh, Stewart! Of course, and welcome. Are you alone, friend?"

"Quite so, sir."

"In that case, please come in, through the gate there. I'll be right down." Stewart started into the yard, his attention never wavering from the man on the roof, who...was no longer there. In his place an enormous white owl rose out of the thatching, circled once, and came swooping into the front courtyard, headed right for the spot where the big dog stood. Startled, the poor beast sidestepped just in time to miss colliding with the owl on its clumsy landing trajectory. And then, (perhaps he had blinked), a tall, dirt-smudged young man in work clothes and tousled hair stood before him, brushing himself off, and testing various joints to see if they still worked. He seemed to be already talking, a bit winded, but with good cheer.

"Stewart. Welcome. So glad you stopped by. Sorry about that near collision; I never can seem to get the landings right. Oh, and about my less-than-enthusiastic greeting, apologies too. It wouldn't do to let just anyone passing by see magical doings yet; rumors would fly. I'm set back from the road enough to be safe from the casual traveler, but you took me by surprise. I was afraid my secret had been discovered." He reached out a hand, which the dog sniffed by way of greeting.

"No apologies necessary, good sir. *I* should apologize for arrivin' unannounced. But what indeed are ye up to here? No one has even gone in there in over a decade."

"Aha!" Tvrdik shook a finger at the dog, "Well, we will remedy *that* soon enough. I have been commissioned by my Lady Regent to reopen and make repairs on Xaarus' old house, such that it should be rendered habitable, and then I am to move in myself."

Stewart waggled his tail. "Why, that is wonderful news. Hearty congratulations, sir. I hear it is a fine and spacious home. But what a lot of work it will be to restore, no?"

Tvrdik scratched his head, "Well, it's not as bad as you might imagine, but there's still a long way to go before I can give up my room in the palace and sleep here. I started off this morning doing each task by hand, and then it struck me, of what use is being a wizard if you can't cheat a bit once in awhile, eh? I spelled some of the tools and brushes to go ahead and take care of a few of the more routine, repetitious tasks..."

"And a fine job of it they were doin', to my mind, sir," the dog interjected, "while ye, yerself were on the roof?"

"Why, yes. I was repairing and replacing the old thatching up there. There are quite a few thin spots, and perhaps some leaks as well. That I need to do myself, by hand. Which reminds me…" He waved a hand and in an instant, all the brushes rose up and resumed their chores. Stewart's eyes were round as saucers under their charcoal brows, "Gorrrrrr!" he exclaimed, "That's fantastic."

"I'm supposed to keep in practice anyway," Tvrdik sighed.

"Say, would ye mind if I, well, if I hung around here for awhile today? Perhaps I can be of some assistance?"

"Not at all. Your company would be most welcome, and I'm sure you could be useful at that, if you don't mind. For one thing, would you let me know if you spot anyone on the path who might notice these shenanigans? As I said, it is efficient, but I wouldn't want any gossip getting out just yet…"

"Will do sir, and anythin' else ye need, you just call fer me." The big dog came to attention and dipped his head once in salute.

Tvrdik smiled, "Many thanks, friend. Well, it's back up to the roof for me…quite a few hours of light left and a good deal to accomplish before this day is out."

"Aye."

And the young man vanished once again, leaving Stewart gaping at the large white owl with oddly rimmed eyes, winging its way to the top of the building.

For the remainder of that day, and the next four, Tvrdik worked hard on cleaning, repairing, and restoring the home of his youth. Each day he was up at dawn, and out to The Cottage as soon as he could dress and pocket some bread and cheese. He concentrated first on infrastructure, then on Xaarus' personal apartments, so that they could be in shape for him to occupy as soon as possible. Despite the constant influx of visitors, dignitaries, and lords arriving for the council meeting on Friday, no one seemed to be pressuring him to vacate his luxurious suite at Theriole. This was a very good thing, as it was taking longer than anticipated to bring the house up to livable condition, even with the help of magic. He wasn't spending many hours at the palace, but after a full day of physical labor, he truly appreciated the featherbed. Warlowe looked in on him each evening to see if there was anything else he needed, and to take a progress report, while the palace servants made sure there were wonderful meals, clean linens and clothes, and plenty of hot water for washing. Those evenings, before bed, he kept to himself, reading some of Xaarus' intriguing books, picking up new knowledge and lore, and practicing his techniques.

Back at The Cottage, Stewart seemed to have taken up a loose residency on the grounds, drawn by curiosity, respect, and a natural friendly nature. He made himself quite useful, fetching and carrying things, offering opinions, and telling amusing stories, mostly about his grandsire and Xaarus. Tvrdik enjoyed his company, and found himself growing attached to the curious wolfhound, looking forward to meeting him each day at the gate. Sharing the work of rebuilding made it seem easier, and chatting with a personable companion turned a day of labor into an enjoyable project.

At Theriole that week, the Lady Rey seemed to be functioning in high gear every moment, as the details of welcoming and housing so many visiting dignitaries, planning entertainment and menus for their comfort, and smoothing the feathers of those who had complaints about one thing and another fell upon her slight shoulders. After her brief, restorative escape, she felt better able to cope with it all, and handled herself with grace and easy diplomacy. During the few slower moments, she was thinking of the meeting itself, of what she might say and do and what might happen there. She was also keeping a weather eye out for her little sister, regretting that they had last parted on a sour note, and wanting to be sure all was forgiven. But they never seemed to cross paths, and, oddly, no one seemed to have seen her – or Mark either, for that matter. Since there was no time to go searching, Rel had to give up and trust that opportunity would be provided at the right time. Nights, which were starting later and later, she spent on the roof with Tashroth, in the clear, comfortable spring air, fragrant with early blooms. They sat up long into the quiet hours talking of what the day had brought, and what was to come. From this she took strength and courage for the next day's demands. Even Tashroth, as solid and wise and unflappable as he usually was, seemed somewhat agitated with the overcrowding of the palace, and the anticipation of the big event. Sometimes, it was Jorelial who calmed him, bringing his thoughts back to the present moment, and keeping a sense of humor about every aspect of their situation.

On Thursday, as things were beginning to shape up at the house, and Tvrdik was contemplating whether he should move in that evening or wait another day, he had two surprises. Just after noon, as he and Stewart were clearing some underbrush from around the main entrance and gate, a strange little melody drifted through the air to his ear. He stood up where he was, very still, and listened. There it was again – someone whistling a tune, followed by what sounded like a splash. At the moment he remembered who might be responsible, a voice called out, "Lovely Man…Lovely Man! Are you here?" A grin spread across the young mage's face from ear to ear as he dropped his tools and raced to the back of The Cottage, where the river flowed by. Ondine had found the place to come and visit him at home, and was turning cartwheels in the air as he rounded the corner.

"Welcome dearest. How good it is to see you! Found the place alright, I see?"

Tvrdik found a little break in the tall grasses that lined the riverbank, and half slid down to the lapping waters where Ondine was frolicking, Stewart bouncing along behind him. When his toes were nearly in the water, he squatted down to be closer to her level, took her tiny hand and drew it to his lips in a welcoming kiss. The little sprite giggled, blushed a deep purple, and finished with a back flip into the slow, somewhat murky waters. Tvrdik continued, "Ondine, I want you to meet a new friend: this is Stewart the dog. His grandsire knew my teacher, Xaarus, and he has been helping me with the repairs on this place."

Stewart stood erect and cocked his head once politely, tail waving behind, "Pleased to make yer acquaintance, missy, though I can't say as I've ever encountered such as ye before." Stewart's eyes were gleaming with delight. By now he had come to expect that anywhere Tvrdik was, exciting adventures were sure to follow.

"I do not know 'dog' either, but you are most courteous. Happy to meet new friend of Lovely Man." She flashed a pretty smile, and twirled in the water, showering the dog as he stood there. Stewart responded with a full body shake that tossed the droplets right back at her, and at everything else in range, including poor Tvrdik. Ondine was delighted to find a kindred spirit in Stewart, and bobbed about in the river with laughter. Tvrdik was smiling so hard his face ached.

"I've missed you, girl. I've been so busy with this place that I never realized days were passing. Can you forgive me for leaving you on your own so long?"

"No worries, Lovely Man. Ondine busy too. Look, I also bring new friends." She gestured with her head, and for the first time everyone's attention went to the four timid little souls who floated just upstream of Ondine, their eyes bulging and their mouths open at the scene they had just witnessed. "Come, come!" Ondine beckoned sharply, "Come, cousins. This is my Lovely Man and his dogfriend, Stewart. Here are cousins I find after long searching…" The cousins hung back, clearly terrified. "They are shy. Lovely Man, say hello."

Tvrdik stretched out a hand toward the small sprites, but they sprang backward. He took a good look at them. Cousins of Ondine they might be, but distant at that, the years of hiding from men and swimming in less than pure waters having taken their toll. Where Ondine was bright blue and seemed to sparkle, these little creatures were an odd shade of greenish grey, dull, without light. Where she was slender, they seemed positively frail. And where she was playful and sociable, they seemed afraid of their own shadows. Still, it was a coup that Ondine had routed out evidence of a community of water sprites still living among men, and perhaps, with a little tender, loving care, even these could blossom, and regain something of their cousin's spark. The young mage summoned his kindest smile and most non-threatening tone of voice, "Wonderful to meet all of you. I will be living here soon, and hope you will not be strangers."

"This your house now?" Ondine interjected, glancing with curiosity at the house and the grounds.

"As soon as I can clean and fix it up, I can move in, and you can hang around here anytime you want. I can even put in a pond, or a fountain, if you like?" Ondine raised one eyebrow. "No, really. A little fountain for you to visit would not be so difficult…" Tvrdik sat down on the river bank, feeling weary, but content. Stewart was stretched along beside him, his sharp eyes fixed on Ondine. The local sprites seemed to calm down a bit as they found themselves no longer in the spotlight, but kept mostly to themselves. Still, they remained close by, and seemed to be listening to the conversation. Ondine floated in the slow, mossy water and related to her friends on shore how she had gone exploring up and down the river searching for her own kind. Two days ago, she thought she caught a glimpse of something: a familiar silhouette, a furtive movement. But it had taken the better part of a day to track the shy creatures, root them out of their hiding place, and convince them that she was only a country cousin come to visit, and meant them no harm. It took even more persuasion to get them to accompany her on her visit this noon. But in the end, curiosity had won over nerves, as none of them had ever had much contact with humans before. Ondine had made a persuasive case that a real wizard would be something worth seeing. Tvrdik heard the cue in that sentence that he ought to make good on that promise, and started his trick of levitating pebbles high in the air with one finger, and letting them splash into the river, careful of course not to hit anyone.

A small, delighted commotion erupted among the visitors, who seemed to be squealing and conversing among themselves in some otherworldly language. Tvrdik flashed them a charming smile, and made the next pebble do a loop-di-loop in the air before its descent. Ondine giggled and paused in her narrative, watching the reaction of her little charges. Stewart's tail thumped the ground. Feeling encouraged by his audience, and in a somewhat creative mood, the wizard levitated some twigs and grasses over the river and formed them into the shape of a sailing ship, suspended in the air. Then he pulsed a finger and set the whole thing ablaze with green flame as it made its way across the sky, the ashes falling harmlessly into the water as the picture faded. A chorus of *ooos* greeted the feat, and Ondine clapped with enthusiasm. A few more such pyrotechnic displays in various shapes and colors, along with some rings and heart-shapes summoned from the smoke, and he had their rapt attention, enchanted expressions on upturned faces. It was all play and silliness, of course, but who doesn't have a child within that loves such magical performances? And Tvrdik, for all he had spent twelve years in near solitude, had an innate knack for making friends. It might have had something to do with his openness and utter lack of guile, or perhaps his wizard's intuition made him sensitive to what was needed in each new encounter. But, at any rate, he knew how to listen and respond with a compassionate and generous heart. Whoever met him seemed to let down their guard and warm to him quickly.

So, when Ondine went on her way that afternoon with her charges, she was shepherding happy souls, who were absolutely besotted with the pale young wizard, and were promising to visit again soon, and to assist him in whatever he should need. Ondine had committed to staying with the little naiads awhile to teach them a few of her own 'tricks' from the land of the ancient forests, and to trade stories and ancestries. But she hung back a moment to tell Tvrdik that she had also been in conversation with the unicorns. Just an introduction so far – you had to go slow and easy with unicorns – but it was progress in the right direction. Then she winked at him and blew him a kiss, and was gone beneath the shining surface of the water.

Her sudden absence echoed in the warm spring air, leaving a void that made him feel lonelier than before she had arrived. But then, a voice beside him broke the heavy silence, "Well, sir, *that* was most extraordinary." Stewart said.

"Indeed it was," replied Tvrdik, with gratitude for the stalwart wolfhound's company. He reached out and put a hand on Stewart's shoulder, and after a brief pause in companionable silence, both staring off downriver, lost in their respective thoughts, they rose at the selfsame moment and went back to work.

Hours later, when the sun was edging toward the horizon, casting long shadows in the yard, and Tvrdik was considering at least one more night at the palace, while he swept out the sitting room of twelve years of dust and debris, the second surprise arrived. An even longer shadow seemed to fall across the world, nearly blotting out the sun, and a sudden whoosh of wind over the freshly thatched roof startled the dog and the mage, causing them to run to the doorway to see what the commotion was. It was the roar of a dragon's wings whipping up the air – a great green dragon who circled low and skidded to a landing on the riverbank just behind the house. Tashroth and his rider had waited for this quiet time of day to approach from the side opposite the road to avoid rousing any suspicion at their presence. Since they were giving it out that the Lady Regent was contracting repairs on Xaarus' old cottage anyway, it would be natural for her to drop in and monitor the project's progress. But she was in no mood to field questions or requests from the curious or the needy tonight, and so some precautions seemed wise. No one was out and about walking the river road at this hour, so Jorelial Rey threw a cursory glance about, and judged it safe to dismount. Tvrdik and Stewart had raced around to the river side of The Cottage for the second time that day, and greeted their guests' arrival with proper low bows.

"Jorelial Rey," Tvrdik intoned, as she dropped down on the riverbank, "and my lord Tashroth. Be welcome here." Tashroth gave an acknowledging nod as he rearranged himself into a more comfortable, and, he hoped, less conspicuous position on a strip of riverbank barely able to contain him. Jorelial Rey made a curt little bow in answer to their formal courtesies, and then strode over and grasped Tvrdik's hand in both of hers in a warm greeting. He could feel, nevertheless, her agitation, just beneath the veneer of cultivated grace.

"Tvrdik, it is good to see you again. I hope you don't mind this unheralded and unorthodox visit. We wanted to see how the house was coming, but didn't want to attract any attention. I hope we haven't startled you, or arrived at a bad time?"

"Not at all, my lady. You know you are always most welcome. Come, let me show you around. Things are still a bit rough, but coming along..."

"But who is this?" she stopped in her tracks, noticing Stewart.

Tvrdik backtracked, "Oh, pardon me – this is my good friend Stewart, who has been a great help to me over the past several days."

Stewart took his cue, "My Lady Regent, 'tis an honor to make yer acquaintance. Call on me if I may ever be of service."

Jorelial lifted an eyebrow to hear the dog speak. Apparently, she had encountered few talking beasts besides dragons in her short years, but she continued without hesitation, "I thank you with all my heart, and am happy to meet you as well. I am always grateful for faithful friends I may count on."

"Health and long life to the infant king; so say I," Stewart averred with enthusiasm.

"Amen to that!" Rel countered, and then, almost under her breath, "Indeed, amen to that."

Tvrdik ventured to put a hand on her shoulder, happy for the additional company, and excited about showing off what they had thus far accomplished, "Come along. I hope you will be pleased at our progress..." There was still light enough to take a turn around the exterior of the building, pointing out the new roofing, the brightly whitewashed walls, the uncovered windows with new panes installed, the orderly, weeded gardens and the neat flowerbeds up against the foundation, the repaired front gate, swept walk, and solid front door. Rel was impressed, if not amazed.

"This is remarkable, for only a few days work. However did you get so much done?"

"Well, Stewart has been invaluable, but to tell the truth, I did cheat a bit."

"Cheat?" She wrinkled her brow. He leaned in close to her ear and whispered, "Magic."

"Oh." she raised her eyebrows in surprise, and then, without warning, he winked, which made her smile for the first time in days.

"It's beautiful," she told him sincerely, "Almost as I remember it."

"I'm afraid the inside still has a way to go, but I've been concentrating on the kitchen and private apartments." Jorelial nodded as they stepped inside. Just within the arched doorway, Tvrdik paused for just a moment of indecision, and then reached out toward the foyer wall and retrieved his magical staff. Rel stepped back, startled. Tvrdik set it between them, "What do you think? Xaarus had it put away all finished with my name on it. You can't imagine how good it feels in my hand."

"Does it work?"

For answer, Tvrdik gripped the staff, closed his eyes and concentrated. In a twinkling, big, cold snowflakes fell on Jorelial's hair, nose, and eyelids; fell in quantity, fell from out of nowhere. She swatted at her clothes, at the air around her, dancing in place on the floor where white flakes were accumulating.

"OK, OK, make it stop! Make it stop," she shouted. And as fast as it had begun, the snow disappeared at once, leaving them both breathless and giggling. "Impressive," she remarked, between bursts of laughter, and, staff at his side, Tvrdik ushered her into the house.

"Weather is the easiest," he confessed, "I'm still experimenting on lots of other things…"

Rel jumped back, smiling, ""Well, promise me you won't do any more experimenting on me today, alright?"

"If you insist," he pouted in mock disappointment, and she gave him a cuff across the shoulder in mock annoyance. Suddenly they both stopped midstep, and their eyes met, both realizing that they had been 'playing' – a thing neither of them had any experience in at all. Something unspoken passed between them, the silent sharing of how good it felt to let go of the burdens of past and future, and just enjoy the moment, to be young and lighthearted and feeling immortal. It was only a second's connection, but unmistakably real. And then, the young mage turned away and muttered, "This way…" and it was over.

The sitting room they entered looked almost inviting – still in need of paint and decoration, and perhaps new chairs – but it was swept and clean, cobwebs long gone, the hearth already emptied and stacked with new wood and kindling. Tvrdik explained how he had closed off the teaching annex and left it for another time. It was such a large area, not essential for his current needs, and besides, it was, for him, so filled with memories. Rel nodded, understanding.

The kitchen was beginning to shape up. A small stock of new or refurbished pots of gleaming copper, along with a few utensils and basic provisions had been laid in against the mage's eventual move into the place. "You can see how liberal I have been in spending your money," Tvrdik ventured, with a sheepish grin.

The lady smiled, "I can see it is going to be a wise investment."

As they continued on through doorways, Rel gasped with wonder at the amazing library, and the workshop/laboratory, which Tvrdik had cleaned and tidied, but left for the most part unchanged.

"I don't remember ever being invited in here," she remarked, her eyes travelling over the shelves and shelves of books and scrolls and equipment. "The breadth and depth of his knowledge was astounding."

"*Is* astounding," Tvrdik corrected. "I am still counting on seeing him back among these tomes and projects in the near future. Xaarus appeared to me and told me to help myself to anything here that might be useful, but I'm afraid these rooms will always feel like his personal property, which I am privileged to borrow. I daren't move or reorganize anything he was working on for fear of spoiling some long-awaited and deeply significant result."

Rel looked him square in the face, "I feel his presence here too, but soon you will be doing your own important work, and you will need to put aside your reverence and use everything at your disposal. In that way, you also honor him as teacher and master."

Tvrdik peered at her over his glasses; how and where had that insight come from, as well as the surprising level of confidence in him? He dropped his gaze, whispering, "It is too soon."

She touched his arm. "Time is a luxury we do not have." There was a long silence. Tvrdik turned and ducked through the last door.

"...and this would be the master bedroom, no pun intended. I could stay here now if necessary, but it really needs a new mattress and a coat of paint, some repairs on these old floor tiles..."

"Of course, you should be comfortable. You have done so much in only a brief time, and I am in no hurry to shoo you from Theriole. Please do not hesitate to use our resources to get what you need: new furniture, a mattress, hangings, equipment.... I am serious. That is, at least, one thing I can provide. How you have improved this place already, all by yourself, is nothing short of miraculous. I want to help in whatever way I can."

As they turned to leave the room, Tvrdik caught sight of his reflection in Xaarus' big glass hanging on the far wall. He stopped short to see the pale, disheveled young man in dirty homespun, hair tangled and sticking out at odd angles, smudges of dirt and grease on his face. Horrified, he reached up a calloused, dirty hand to smooth his hair. "Gods, my apologies! We have been at work all day, and your visit took us by surprise. Why didn't you tell me?"

She caught his arm and pulled it down, "There is no shame in honest labor, and, just as you say, we did not give you any warning that we were coming. Please..." She was coaxing him away from the mirror and met his eyes with great seriousness. "Tvrdik, there is another reason I am here just now...the Grand Council meets tomorrow."

"His eyes grew wide, "I had forgotten."

"Is there somewhere we can sit a few moments and talk?"

He led her back through doors and corridors into the sitting room, where there were two big chairs (a bit threadbare, perhaps, but not uncomfortable), and a small table by the hearth. "Come into my 'Hall of Audience,'" he teased, smiling in recollection of their first meeting. "Can I offer you a seat?" He batted at one of the old chairs and a cloud of dust engulfed them.

Rel laughed. "That will do for now." She waved away the flinders and sat. Tvrdik glanced in turn through several windows on opposite sides of the house. Stewart, sensing the import of this visit, had posted himself just outside the front door, guarding the entrance like a stone lion, and Tashroth was doing much the same on the riverbank in the rear. Both seemed to have their heads cocked and ears pricked to pick up any stray conversation that might float by. Now it was Tvrdik's turn to laugh.

"Our guardians seem to have things well in hand out there. I think we can speak in safety." The light was fading by now and a chill breeze picked up outside. The temperature in the stone house had dropped noticeably in the past half hour. Rel shivered where she sat. Tvrdik waved a hand at the hearth. "Fire," he said, and without delay, the stacked wood burst into a cozy blaze. Another motion lit the lamps in the room. Then he pointed to the kitchen door and moved a finger. "Tea," he spoke, and a bright copper kettle floated out to the hearth stone, while through the kitchen doorway they caught a glimpse of two mugs, spoons, a little earthen teapot, a teaball stuffed with dried leaves and a small pot of honey all assembling themselves on a tarnished silver tray. It started to float in their direction on its own, but Tvrdik pointed at it one more time and said, "biscuits," and it moved back to the kitchen, re-emerging moments later piled with some sweet pastries he had purchased. As the tray floated out from the kitchen again, and set itself down on the little table, and the copper kettle hung itself from a hook over the cheerful fire, Rel laughed in delight and clapped her hands.

"Your hospitality is impeccable. I rather like hanging around with a wizard."

Tvrdik made a little bow, "It has its advantages. This should take just a few minutes. I hope it will warm you up a bit. Honey?"

"Excuse me?"

"In your tea…" They giggled at the old joke, while he spooned some into her mug, and poured the hot water from the kettle into the little teapot to steep. Then he took a seat, more dust exploding around him, causing another rash of giggles. But the gravity of the conversation to come sobered them in an instant. Tvrdik leaned forward toward the Lady Regent. "Now, then, tomorrow…?"

She sighed, "Yes, tomorrow…" She took a small corner of biscuit, and chewed thoughtfully, swallowing before going on. "The day has finally come when we will see if things head down the road you have predicted. Delegates and regional lords have been arriving all week. The open fields around the palace are overrun with campsites, and the inns in the town are full. As temporary regent, I must preside. Tashroth, who often acts as my extra eyes and ears, and helps lead me to my best judgment, cannot be in the room because of his size, and the inhibiting effect he has on some people. Tvrdik, I repeat my request for you to be there. I need you to observe, to watch and listen, keep me honest in my memory of what happens there, and to pick up on anything I might miss. A word, a glance, body language, even a hunch – whatever information you gather will be useful, as I will be in the thick of things, and am likely to miss a great deal. You have no official right to attend, nor do I think it prudent yet to present you formally as Xaarus' student and heir. You will have to be there in secret. Yet I think for you to be invisible would not do. For my own peace of mind, I want to know where you are." Tvrdik rose and poured the tea.

"I can come as an owl and perch on a rafter, or become a cat or a mouse; no one would question such a creature in a big, drafty, stone room. I could remain quite unobtrusive, while you would always know where I was if you needed me."

"She stirred the contents of her mug, "Can you perceive…see, hear, comprehend in the same way in those forms?"

The mage made a dismissive gesture, "Oh, yes. It is but simple illusion we clothe ourselves in, but I am always present. You can count on me to catch a great deal as it goes by, and I have a very good memory." He took a biscuit and a sip of tea.

"Tvrdik, it will be a long day. There will be a formal welcome, followed by reports from all the Ministers and the heads of the Guilds. We try to encourage brevity, but such events do not happen very often, and some of these personages are quite in love with the sound of their own voices."

"Xaarus trained me well for stamina and concentration, my lady; I am sure I can handle it."

She sipped at her tea. "Mmmmm. Lunch and refreshments will be brought in to the Council Chamber so as not to disrupt the flow of things, or lose half the participants partway through. You won't get a real break all day."

"I understand."

"There will be a discussion of the recent state funeral, proposals on a date for the king's coronation, and a vote deciding that. Only then will come nominations for the post of permanent regent. Several of the lords present will likely put themselves or their friends forward for the job in long, elaborate speeches, and there will be debate. Finally, there will be a vote, and we hope, a clear decision, and then…the fireworks."

"Are you speaking literally, as in entertainment, or figuratively, as in Drogue stirring up trouble?"

"Tvrdik, you know what I mean. We have been waiting all this time for Lord Drogue to show his hand. I don't wish for trouble to find us, but if you are right, tomorrow will be the day it comes calling." He could hear the agitation rising in her voice, and could feel her about to jump out of her seat and begin pacing the floor. He reached over and laid a hand on her arm.

"Jorelial Rey, you were born and raised to this. You will weather it with grace and wisdom as always, and you will know what to say and do. I will be there, watching and listening. I will make sure I am always within view, and if you have need of me for something more tangible, you have only to say the word, and I can be a wizard again in a moment."

She shook her head, "You will have to keep a low profile and resist the temptation to reveal yourself, no matter how outrageous the things you hear. It might be difficult…" She had not yet met his gaze. Now, he squeezed her arm, so that she looked up to find his reassuring, ice-blue eyes.

"So, are you trying to persuade me to say yes, or to run away screaming? I was the one who brought you the unwelcome news of what you might be facing, and I have already promised that I will be here by your side to face whatever comes. I welcome this opportunity to actually be useful. So, tomorrow, we begin. Don't worry, I can do this. I will not abandon or embarrass you." She paused, held in his intense regard. Then, with a hint of a smile, and a long sigh, returned to her tea.

"I never meant to suggest that you would. I only wanted you to know what you would be in for. Last chance to escape…." He smiled and shook his head. She continued, "Tashroth will be waiting for us on the roof. Whatever happens, we can slip away when it is all over and meet him there for his input. We can compare notes up there and fill him in on everything important."

"Sounds good. What time, and where?"

"Not the Hall of Audience, where you came to see me. This is in the Great Hall – a much larger room with pikes and banners and long tables and a platform up front for speakers. You will sleep tonight at Theriole, and in the morning, I will send you a hearty breakfast. Warlowe will come then to escort you to the hall. You can find a safe place out of sight to… to change, as soon as you know where you are going. If you miss the early speeches, it won't matter, but remember, I shall be looking for you."

"I shall strive to be there early. It will do me good to have a lesson or two in statecraft – a subject in which I am woefully deficient." That should have been a cue for another laugh, but somehow, neither of them could quite muster one.

She set down her empty teacup, "Mmmm, this was good. Thank you so much."

"The tea? I'm glad you enjoyed it. Thank you for my house, and I hope you will be a frequent visitor here."

"It's getting late. I must be getting back." She rose and started toward the doorway, then turned back, "Oh, one more thing, Tvrdik. I recall you said that you had made a friend of my sister, Delphine. I was wondering if you had seen or spoken with her in the last few days? We argued when we were together last, and I have been hoping to find her and set things right. But, she is nowhere to be found."

"You have not spoken to her since then? That was the last I saw of her too, soon after your encounter. She was upset…told me of the argument. I did what I could to soothe her, and pointed out that she might give you a little extra understanding just now, as you had many weighty things on your mind."

"Thank you."

"But when I left her, she seemed eager to find you and make up. That never happened?"

"I am sometimes impossible to access, with all that is going on. Our argument upset me so much that I escaped with Tashroth to the mountains for a day. When I returned, there was more than the usual pile-up of situations demanding my attention. As soon as I could, I sent for her, I asked after her, and went looking for her several times, but no one seems to have seen her lately, or knows where she might have gone. It weighs on me that we have not yet forgiven each other. We are very close, and I do worry about her."

"Hmmm. It *is* odd that your paths haven't crossed, and that she didn't respond to your summons. Perhaps I am partly to blame, as I encouraged her to give you a little space during these stressful weeks. She is probably just staying close in her room, or off with Mark somewhere…"

"Well, *that* doesn't make me feel less anxious…"

"Working on music together, is all I meant…"

"I hope you are right, then. I would dearly have liked some time with her, but it's not something I can do much about now for at least another day." She sighed, "I will try to think good thoughts, and make a renewed effort to speak with her after the Council is over."

"I am certain she is fine, and harbors you no ill will. But, if I see her before you do, I will speak with her, alright?"

Rel glanced out the window. "It's awfully dark now – too dark to walk back on your own. Come on, I'll give you a lift back to Theriole."

"What? On a dragon?" Tvrdik's stomach jumped into his mouth in a wave of panic, "Oh, I don't know…"

"Don't be afraid – he won't bite, and there's plenty of room."

"I – I've never – well – *flown* before. I might fall off. Don't worry about me. I am happy to walk…"

"Nonsense. You'll be back in a flash. It's very safe…he's quite careful. You'll see." Tvrdik's face turned a shade closer to Tashroth's color even just thinking about the offer, but it seemed the Lady Regent would not take no for an answer. So he reluctantly brought the tea things into the kitchen, cleaned up and put them away, then stepped outside to speak with Stewart.

"Stewart, my friend, I thank you for your assistance and your good company all week. I am called back to the palace tonight…most likely will be back the day after tomorrow. Would you like to come along?"

Stewart shook his head, "Thank you, no. I'm rather beginning to feel at home here, if ye don't mind. I'll be fine."

"Would you like me to leave the place open so you can come and go as you please?"

"I'm happy enough on the grounds, sir. I don't think I'll be needin' to go inside."

Tvrdik leaned close and whispered, "Well, if you *should* need to go in, just say, 'bless this house' out loud, and the door will spring open," and he winked at the dog. Stewart fairly beamed. "Thank ye very much, sir. I'll take good care of it, sir, ye'll see."

"I have no doubts, friend. Be well." Stepping inside again for a moment, Tvrdik put out the fire with a wave of his hand, banked the embers, doused the torches, and glanced about for anything left untidy. He reluctantly leaned his beloved staff against the wall of the foyer once again, and stepped out of The Cottage. "Bless this house," he murmured as he passed over the threshold, and never looked back as the door clicked shut. With a wave to Stewart in the dusky shadows, he followed Jorelial Rey around back to where Tashroth stood poised by the river's edge, reading his rider's thoughts, and eager to be away. Climbing up on a bent front leg, and grasping a leathery neck ridge, Rel sprang lightly into her accustomed seat just in front of the great beast's shoulders. Then she turned back and offered a hand to Tvrdik, intending to pull him up behind. Tashroth turned his head and regarded them, never complaining at the prospect of carrying a second passenger. But the mage hesitated, paler than usual, if that were even possible.

"Come on – I'll give you a boost." Jorelial Rey shouted down. Tvrdik swallowed hard, clambered ungracefully up onto Tashroth's forearm, and reached up. Almost before he could blink, he felt his own forearm being gripped, and he was sailing up to a perch between vertebrae just behind the Lady Regent. Breathless and terrified, he clung to the neck ridge in front of him with white knuckles as the great wings rose and beat the air. In a heartbeat, they were up and away, rising far over the treetops and leaning precariously, as the dragon banked to turn back toward Theriole's shadowy bulk on the horizon. When he could bring himself to open his eyes and draw breath, the trembling Tvrdik had to admit that the view from up there was indeed rare.

THIRTEEN

THE GRAND COUNCIL

Morning arrived all too quickly at the bustling palace; kitchen folk and chambermaids were at their chores before dawn, stable hands scurried to find room for the crowd of horses arriving. Neither Tvrdik nor Jorelial Rey believed they had slept a wink (save for the occasional brief, fitful nightmare), before the sun's first rays called them from their beds. Rel raced down from her rooftop perch at Tashroth's side and entered her rooms. She bathed, picked half-heartedly at some fruit and warm pastries, combed and braided her long, dark hair, and dressed. Despite the fact that this was a State occasion, or perhaps because of it, she refused to wear the flowing elegant gown expected of a court lady. This was one moment where she did not wish to feel sabotaged by her clothing. Instead, she chose straight black britches and a tailored, high-collared jacket of fine raw silk, in a rich purple color, ornamented with appliqué of gold braid and amethyst. Though she was slight, the effect of such an outfit was striking. Belted with the ceremonial sword of her office, she looked and moved like a young prince, secure in his authority. It was a look she cultivated on purpose, which served her to great advantage.

Tvrdik rose, washed himself of all the grime from the past few days' labor, and put on the original blue outfit he had first been gifted with at the palace, freshly laundered. This was in case he was seen in the halls before or after his transformation, so that he would be taken for a courtier from some entourage or another, and left alone to go about his business. He shaved and neatly combed his hair, and sat down with a hearty appetite to the hot, delicious breakfast sent up to him. Then he sat on the edge of his bed in silence, closed his eyes, and focused, gathering all his strength, power, and skill, centering and calming himself, and setting clear intentions for the day. He fingered the coin in his pocket for a moment and debated summoning Xaarus for some words of advice before the big event, but decided it would be wasteful to squander that privilege until a more desperate time – or at least until after they saw what the Council Meeting would bring. At last, feeling prepared and connected, he rose just in time to meet Warlowe in the hallway and be conducted to the Great Hall.

When Jorelial Rey entered the vast, ancient room, she paused just inside the doorway and cast an eye over the noisy gathering already in progress. There were lords greeting one another with hearty claps on the back, family pictures, and jokes; delegates and guild leaders arguing vigorously, hands gesticulating to punctuate their assertions; ministers chasing after the trays of morning refreshments, carried about the room by attractive young men and women. There were lords and ministers poring over maps and documents unrolled at corners of the grand table, and those who were bunching closely together to discuss secret strategies, or the latest gossip at court. And, there was Lord Drogue himself, perfectly groomed and impeccably dressed in his accustomed black silk, standing apart from the crowd in a shadowy corner. He was surrounded by several lesser lords she imagined might be supporters. But she noticed that he was not so much conversing with them as watching the activities in the rest of the room with an intent expression. There was a small consort of musicians in one alcove – a tabor, harp, and flute – her idea, to begin the day with a pleasant, upbeat atmosphere. She peered at them, noticing Mark was not among them. They were playing their hearts out, but were barely audible as anything other than background against the dull roar of so much conversation. For a moment, her senses assaulted by the chaos all around her, it was all she could do to force herself not to turn on her heel from such a scene and run in the other direction as far as her legs would take her. And then, somehow, miraculously, above all that great din, she heard a sound that caught her attention – one that anyone else might have missed – like a soft cooing, or a gentle *hoot*. Without moving, she lifted her eyes to the ceiling, and there, perched on a cross rafter not so very high above them all was a white owl, peering down at her, from eyes that appeared oddly rimmed, as if with spectacles. It looked straight at her, cooing once more, and fluttered its wings once, edging back and forth along the rafter perch. Jorelial Rey's face broke into a smile then, and lowering her gaze to the tall chair at the very head of the table, she squared her shoulders and strode into the room to take her place there.

She stood beside the chair for a moment, and, as various groups in the room began to notice her presence there, the noise began to die down. The serving personnel retreated, and someone motioned for the musicians to cease playing. They wrapped up a sprightly little jig they had just begun, packed up their instruments, and disappeared out a side door. The ministers with documents rolled them up and stood quietly waiting. Guests began to sort themselves out and find their assigned places. Finally the palace steward crossed to the front of the room, resplendent in colorful attire and a feathered hat, and carrying a huge, official baton almost the size of a wizard's staff. He positioned himself just beside the still figure of Jorelial Rey, rapped the baton three times loudly on the wooden floor, and called out in a formal, cultivated voice, "Hear ye, hear ye, one and all! The Grand Council Meeting of Eneri Clare, in the spring of the sixteenth year of the reign of our beloved late King Darian the second is now called to order. Presiding is Lady Jorelial Rey, eldest surviving member of the distinguished family Rey, and acting regent for His Young Majesty, Darian the third. If my lords and ladies will please take your seats, the Lady Rey will open with a formal welcome."

Tvrdik, as an owl, was taking mental notes on everyone and everything he saw, as promised. Bargarelle, the palace steward, a short, rather pudgy man with a perpetually harried look, and a sheaf of papers clutched under one arm, was nevertheless reputed to be a genius at running the massive machine that was Theriole. He had assembled a crackerjack staff to which he delegated the execution of his orders, in every department. But, without his skill, his incredible memory for detail, impeccable sense of order, and tireless effort, the very center of government would grind to a halt. In addition, he was absolutely devoted to the Rey family, was very protective of Jorelial (despite his frequent overt frustrations at her sometimes unorthodox and disorganized behavior), and insisted on acting as her personal secretary as well – a task which had put a tremendous extra strain on his time of late. Just now, however, he appeared to be enjoying the honor and attention of acting as Master of Ceremonies.

Tvrdik watched as the company took their seats and a hush descended on the room. Jorelial Rey stood very still – straight-backed, chin lifted, eyes roaming over the assembled faces and meeting the gazes of friend and skeptic alike. *How magnificent she looks,* he thought. *How confident and beautiful and strong.* And, having been privy to her private moments of doubt, he felt a rush of pride at being so soon a confidante of someone he now could see was a major player on the stage of his world. After that came a wave of humility at how unworthy he felt of such an honor. For a moment he was the gangly, awkward teenager once again watching the privileged girl take off on her dragon – watching, it seemed, from a great distance. But then she was opening her arms in a gesture of inclusion, and he was back in the present, admiring her skill and aplomb.

Her trained, rich voice rang through the chamber, "Esteemed guests: my lords and ladies, ministers, delegates, guild leaders, Master Mayor – friends all – a most hearty welcome to Theriole. I pray your journeys have been easy and our hospitality sufficient (someone called out, 'Hear, hear!'). You are assembled in this place today because you are all leaders in your respective arenas. You are the heart and soul of our beloved kingdom of Eneri Clare, the engine that keeps it moving into the future. *Oh, she is good,* thought Tvrdik. *Begin with a bit of flattery.*

The Lady Regent went on, "We are met here today so that together we might address matters of great import; matters the like of which this kingdom has never seen, and on which the future turns. I look around, and I see new faces to welcome, and familiar faces of good old friends, almost family. Many of you knew my beloved father – a truly great man taken from our midst well before his time… (she paused for effect, and many more voices shouted out words of affirmation. Tvrdik cooed and ruffled his wings). But all of you, all of *us* here now will be making history. I thank each of you for putting aside his own business, and making it a priority to be part of this day.

"The last time many of us embraced one another was not so long ago, at the funeral of our dear monarch and his bride, silenced in their prime by a cruel twist of fate. We face the possibility that their passing could bring to a close the reign of a dynasty that has served Eneri Clare well for generations. This royal family has kept us in peace and prosperity, rendered justice with fairness to citizens of every station, and made our kingdom a model of good government for so long that most of us do not remember war, poverty, or discontent except as the stuff of legends and history books. (Another pause…some shifting in seats). With one stroke of bad fortune they are gone, and we are cast adrift on a sea of fear and uncertainty. (*A bit dramatic, perhaps, but effective,* Tvrdik thought). But need we be thus alarmed and confused as to what the future holds?" She was pacing back and forth now, a habit of hers that Tvrdik knew well by now. "I say, no! No, brothers, we are still whole, for our royal tree has left us a sapling, healthy and straight, true son and heir of Darian and Marisa. Young he may be, and unseasoned, but already he favors his father, and in every aspect shines forth the promise of becoming a worthy successor to his forbears. I promise when you know this boy, you will love him as I do. And you will rest confident that he will grow, given time and good guidance, to rule, as his forbears did, with honor and wisdom.

"Good friends, it is my contention that, in gratitude for the peace and prosperity we have all enjoyed these long years, it is now our sacred duty as loyal subjects of this young king, and good stewards of his kingdom, to care for it, protect it, improve it where we can, grow and nurture it and return it to him at his majority in the condition his father left it, or better." Her eyes were now fastened on Drogue, who darkly returned her gaze across the table, a frozen smile on his handsome face. She went on, "It is our responsibility as well to raise and educate, to guard and guide this young man, and to draw out of the raw materials of his nature the true portrait of the monarch he will no doubt become. It behooves us here and now to show patience, faith, good judgment, and loyalty in supporting his true claim, thereby insuring the uninterrupted continuity of Eneri Clare's royal line.

"This day, we will each have opportunity to speak our minds and hearts. We will share with one another our reports on how the kingdom fares on all fronts. We will offer creative ideas on how to correct its flaws and celebrate its triumphs. We will decide whether and when to crown a king, and then we will put our heads together to choose someone who will stand at the helm of this ship until the day our king can steer on his own… (*And here comes the big finish,* Tvrdik observed, fascinated)…

someone you deem wise enough, fair enough, firm enough, seasoned enough, and humble enough to sail boldly, but stay clear of storms; to rely on the counsel and expertise of all those who keep the vessel afloat, and to step aside willingly when the true captain comes on board. Whoever will inherit the job will find that it is a daunting, challenging, overwhelming, exhilarating, and ultimately rewarding task, not to be entered into lightly. But they will not have to undertake this burden alone, being buoyed up by the magnificent expertise of a brilliant Finance Minister (Tvrdik noted which attendees gave nods of acknowledgement as they were recognized), a veteran Commander in Chief, and an incomparable Minister of Justice. You have already met our remarkable Palace Steward, and there are a host of other players behind the scenes whose excellence and competence keep everything running smoothly. Whoever you choose will have the great blessing of this fine team to assist, guide, counsel, and on occasion, correct. I, personally, am ever in their debt and hope that together we have been able to deliver to you a State well-preserved during these last months.

"Today, I am here presiding on behalf of my dear father, a man whose quality most of you know, and of my family Rey. For centuries, the Reys have been first and foremost protectors, counselors and friends to the Crown. In my father's absence, you can count on me to diligently discharge those duties as far as I am humanly able. I thank you for the confidence you have thus far showed in me in these trying times, and pray that I have earned it. My final obligation as interim regent is to insure that this Council does its job well, and that we all go home feeling we have worked together to insure the future for ourselves, our neighbors, our children, and for all of Eneri Clare. I begin by exhorting each one of you to leave petty differences, self-interest, greed, and intolerance outside of those doors there, and to reach deep inside yourselves for the very best of who you are, and what you believe to be for the highest good of all concerned. In that way, you show yourselves the great men and women that you are all reputed to be, and you do honor to your own family names and to the memory of our late, beloved king. Thank You."

It was a fine speech, touching on all key points and stirring emotions, and quite masterfully delivered. Tvrdik screwed his owl head almost clear around in awe of Jorelial Rey's persuasive powers. If the ovation she received was any indication of her success, he was not alone in his opinion.

There were cheers and clapping as she came to her rousing finish, and many present sprang to their feet with a new respect on their faces. Lord Drogue did not. He sat in silence, reclined in his seat, smiling and tapping his applause lightly on the table top. Was the Lady Rey angling for the job of regent? Tvrdik knew that she would rather it go to almost anyone else. But there was no denying the strong impression she had made, and the mage/owl could almost feel the seed of an idea sprouting in many of the minds of those present. He could almost hear the gears and wheels turning in their heads. And it was yet early. She would be chosen, he was certain, and a good thing too. She had already proved herself capable, and he couldn't imagine anyone doing a better job.

The morning labored on, speech after speech, some well-crafted and enervating, some pedestrian. Tvrdik kept careful track of who was who, and committed to memory his impressions of each. At one point he had to work hard to stop himself laughing out loud (and how would *that* have sounded coming from an owl?) to see how comically stereotypical the ministers appeared. Master Verger, the Minister of Finance, was a smallish, soft man with vaguely rodent-like features and a perpetual squint, he guessed from poring over figures all day. Tvrdik made a mental note to speak to him later about the miracle of spectacles. Perhaps they could invest together in a local cottage industry. The Commander in Chief, General Boone, was a simple, plain-spoken sort with graying, close-cropped hair, barrel chest, muscled arms and short, thick neck. One would not be likely to mistake this very pragmatic - looking character for a poet. The Minister of Justice, a man named Alanquist, was tall and lanky, with sharp features, a slightly hooked nose, and an expression that revealed him as a complete stranger to laughter. His head seemed overly large in proportion to the rest of him, as if his body were merely a vehicle to carry his oversized brain.

Colorful as they were, Tvrdik could find nothing to dislike in any of them. They all seemed devoted to duty and the Crown, and each seemed supremely competent, even ingenious, at his discipline. Besides, they all reported good news during Jorelial's tenure as regent: revenues were up, trade agreements forged or renewed, budget balanced, capital projects begun, treaties shored up or newly negotiated, crime relatively low, highways safe for travel, some innovative public works programs on the drawing board. Despite the kingdom's recent tragedy and resulting uncertainty, times were still good for most of the citizenry. There seemed to be a sense that what had happened had somehow drawn all of Eneri Clare together in solidarity, transcending the smaller issues that at times divide disparate peoples. In addition, an outpouring of support and sympathy from neighboring nations who were shocked at the terrible news, insured peaceful borders and friendly allies for the foreseeable future. It wasn't that the precipitous loss of the royal couple was in any way a good thing – rather it was that with the proper handling of the situation, good could indeed come out of grave misfortune.

Hours passed, and the speeches and reports went on. The Lord Mayor was a jovial and somewhat theatrical sort. He had been a local businessman – an owner of several popular taverns. His ruddy complexion and ample girth suggested that he also partook of the wares that were his stock and trade. He spoke in a robust baritone, encouraging everyone present to make sure and allow time for spending their coin on goods and services in the nearby capitol city of Therin before heading back to the provinces they called home. This got a hearty laugh, though the young wizard was certain the man had hopes that many of the visitors would take him up on his suggestion.

The Farmers' Guild expected a banner year for crops and livestock, assuming the lovely spring weather they had enjoyed thus far eventually succumbed to rain. The Merchants' and Crafters' Guilds all had equally positive news to share. Tvrdik found himself musing that the disciplines of Arts, Culture, and Education, as well as Wizardry (understandably) seemed woefully under-represented at this conference, if they were even mentioned at all. He thought of Mark and Delphine, their innovative plans, and the exciting conversation they had had on their first meeting. They had the right idea, he decided, and prayed that they would all live to see a future where the three of them could throw their lot in together and manifest their dream of a school.

Throughout the morning, whenever a speaker would wander into some longwinded extemporizing, Tvrdik would turn his attention to Lord Drogue, sitting stone-still, leaning far back in his chair with his feet rather disrespectfully propped on the table before him, one elbow resting on the arm of his great wooden chair, and the fingers of that hand curled in front of his mouth. His attention seemed riveted, but it was obvious that the cold flames dancing in his eyes had nothing whatever to do with crop reports or budget manifests. Hour after hour he sat without moving a muscle except for those fingers in front of his face. Tvrdik had never even met the man, but something felt wrong about him. A cold shiver ran through Tvrdik's tiny bird bones, and for a moment, he felt with a certainty he could not explain that the man practiced some sort of sorcery himself, and not a kind that Xaarus approved of. Indeed, he could be weaving some sort of unholy spell at this very moment – some manipulation or mind control on a weaker cohort perhaps. With a flash of righteous indignation, Tvrdik threw out as much psychic shielding around Drogue as he thought he could safely generate without being detected. This had an immediate effect. Drogue broke concentration and shifted position, ever so slightly, glancing all about as if at an annoying insect. *Aha!* Tvrdik thought, ruffling his feathers excitedly, *got him*. Still, the thought that their adversary might also have some magic at his disposal was most disturbing, and sharpened his resolve to stay alert for anything unexpected. Two or three regional lords caught his attention as well among all those assembled. Their manner seemed somehow sullen, their body language pointing *away* from the various speakers instead of toward the proceedings. Their eyes darted to Drogue frequently as if they were watching him for some cue, or for instructions. Tvrdik made a mental note to find out from Lady Rey and Tashroth who these might be, and if they had reason for discontent, so that they could be closely watched.

As the reports drew to a close, and it neared the time when midday refreshments would be served, a motion was made and a vote taken to certify once and for all the Council's intention to crown the infant prince 'king' as soon as possible. Jorelial Rey had been eager to nail down a public declaration that the leadership's clear intent was for the boy to assume the throne, along with assurances that no other plan was on the table. The motion passed unanimously, as she had hoped. After her rousing speech that morning, invoking patriotism, loyalty, and sacred duty, no one would dare contest the succession publicly. Debate consisted of a few brief, florid words of affirmation from various delegates eager to position themselves as loyal subjects. After a bit more wrangling, a formal coronation was planned for just one week and a day hence, in order to make it official as soon as possible. Thinking practically, those from far off who wished to participate in the ceremony would not need to make a second expensive and arduous journey this season. They might, however, just have time to send for family members, gifts, or supplies as needed. Of course, Jorelial had already consulted at great length with Steward Bargarelle, who considered the palace resources could be stretched another week to accommodate all the visitors, without severe strain. It seemed a fair and considerate solution, and as far as the Lady Rey was concerned, the sooner the better. Now, with only one important item of business left on the agenda, it was time to break for lunch.

Heaping platters of baked goods, cheeses, fruits, and hot and cold vegetable casseroles were brought in, along with pitchers of clear water and cider. The musicians resumed their earlier places and broke into a lively dance tune. Everything had been prepared, summoned, and posted just outside the Great Hall doors, only awaiting a cue. At the right moment, it all appeared as if by magic before the eyes of the impressed participants, who were grateful for the chance to move about, stretch their legs and whet their whistles. In a few moments, the entire room was plunged into a delighted chaos of new greetings, animated conversations, and self-indulgence.

Letting out her breath in a long sigh, and searching for a quick exit from the noise, the bustle, and the confused aromas, Jorelial Rey chewed around the edges of her fingernails and told herself that up till now the entire event had been smooth and successful. Her speech had been well-received, and all her priorities had been accomplished thus far without opposition. Most of the reports shared had been full of good news. People seemed genuinely happy with the palace's hospitality. So far, a good day.

She palmed an egg and watercress sandwich off of a passing tray and squeezed out through a small side door into a little-used courtyard which was empty at the moment. Finding herself surrounded in relative silence and warm, bright sunshine, a fountain burbling away only meters away, she leaned backward against the door to prevent anyone following her out. Jorelial Rey let the tension fall slowly from her muscles as she bit into her sandwich. It was a good feeling to have gotten this far, but she was aware that the most difficult part was yet to come. The odd thing was that if Tvrdik had never arrived to predict his gloomy scenario, she might have felt elated now, so close to anticipated freedom. She might have assumed the positive momentum of the day would carry forward to the unanimous choice of some worthy, seasoned lord as regent, and that would be that. Armed with Xaarus' information, though, it was difficult to cling to the hope that things could play out as easily as that.

A fluttering above her head caught her attention as a large white bird squeezed itself through a high window propped open to allow some fresh spring air into the Great Hall. The owl hovered in mid-air for a moment, blinking, and then landed heavily on her shoulder. With a gesture calculated to look like he was picking at her ear, the bird leaned in close and whispered, "So far, so good...I am taking careful notes. You were magnificent out there, my lady. You had the whole room at your command." The bird was bobbing oddly now and sidestepping back and forth along her shoulder. Trying not to turn her head, but concentrating on what was left of her sandwich, Jorelial Rey giggled despite herself, "Cut it out! You shouldn't be making me laugh, today of all days."

"I was in earnest, but why not laugh, in any case? Laughter has a wonderful restorative power, and at this moment, you look as if you need some restoring. Truly, you *were* magnificent out there. Drogue, by the way, is into some sort of nasty sorcery. I suspected it, but I am certain now. I think he might be using it to control some of the other lords' thoughts, in order to garner support for his bid. There are two or three I don't like the look of. I'll describe them later. I would judge the whole morning a smashing success, though. I can feel the positive energy building in the room. I even learned a lot from all of those reports."

"So, you still think that he is going to go ahead and spoil the whole thing?"

"Oh, yes. He's been building up to it all day."

"Drat. You know I have no desire to be regent any longer. I would rather almost anybody else would take this millstone from around my neck – except Drogue! We simply cannot let him take the helm. He will destroy the kingdom."

"Agreed. Don't worry. Most of the others would never trust him in that position. They will not be persuaded by rhetoric, nor by sorcery. They will choose the best person for the job; I have an uncanny sense about that. The rest is up to destiny."

A deep, inarticulate, primal growl seemed to issue from the depths of her being, expressing all the conflicted feelings that battled within her heart. Then, "Tvrdik, how can I leave this quiet little courtyard with its sunshine, its birdsong, and its peaceful fountain, and go back into that room? How do you suggest I make myself walk into that uncertain future?" There was a long pause, but no answers. Jorelial Rey absently took another bite from her sandwich.

"Would you save me some of that? I'm starving."

"Tvrdik!"

"Well, it's not like I can be seen picking my favorite morsels off of the trays in there." She laid the rest of the sandwich on the ground in front of them.

"Here. Take it. I have to get back in there. Luncheon is supposed to last an hour, but it would not do for me to be absent the entire time. I am supposed to be the hostess. If you are willing, I'd appreciate you back at your post when the proceedings resume." She turned on her heel.

"Jorelial Rey."

"Ummhh?"

The little owl sidled gently along her shoulder, closer to her ear, and leaned its warm downy weight against her head and neck. The feeling was oddly comforting. "How did I leave my little cottage in the ancient wood that I had built with my own two hands, and lived in contentedly for over a decade? How did I turn my back on my beautiful waterfall, and the birds and trees who knew and nurtured me, in order to return to a world that had last represented grief and pain and confusion to me? I honestly don't know. I guess one day I just decided that it was time I became what I was born to be...," and in a whisper so soft she almost missed it, "...and I have not regretted it for a moment since." Tvrdik felt the girl's shoulders slowly release with a deep, shuddering sigh.

"You'd better eat. The best part of the show is about to start." A little shrug dislodged the bird from her shoulder, and with a few flaps he descended to the sandwich remains on the cobblestone. Jorelial Rey took the door handle in her hand, but then turned back, with a smile that dazzled him like a sunrise revealing home after a long night's journey. "Thank you," she said, and she was gone.

FOURTEEN

THE WHEEL TURNS

It took some time to get everyone settled back in their seats and ready for business again, but even when the official proceedings began, things got off to a slow start. It seems there were not many in the room who wished to put themselves, or even their neighbors, forward for consideration as regent. There were quite a few folk who were not interested in such a demanding occupation. This became evident when the first few lords who rose to recommend some distinguished friend were answered by the proposed candidate with a polite, but firm, "Thank you for the honor, but I could not possibly…," "Responsibilities on my estate…," or, "I have elderly parents and a new baby to care for…." The dance was warm and gracious, but not terribly constructive.

Jorelial Rey felt that she should keep a low profile during this part of the process, neither appearing too eager to embrace the position, nor to run from it – indeed, not to remind anyone of her existence at all for the moment. Her father, of course, would have been the obvious choice, had he been alive. And therein lay the tragedy of the situation; his absence created a void without an obvious remedy. Jorelial was still hoping the cream would rise to the top. Someone stood, cleared his throat, and proposed that the reins of government be turned over to Defense Minister Boone: the army's Commander and Chief, a seasoned veteran of foreign wars, an experienced High Council member already in residence at the palace, and a man whose integrity could not be impugned. Jorelial Rey winced. Boone was brilliant at what he now did. It was something he understood to the depths of his being. She felt him to be of vital import in the future training of the young king, but regent? She was convinced that the myriad details, the pace, the sheer volume of tasks involved in the job might come close to overwhelming him, and would take him away from his true calling, where he was genuinely needed.

To his credit, this good-hearted, plain-spoken man stood up, bowed to the friend who had suggested him, stroked his chin and addressed the group, "My old friend Julian does me great honor. Earlier in the week, I actually thought about putting myself forward for consideration. You all know I would give my best for this king. You could do worse than to choose a tough old brick like myself, who knows a thing or two about the world. And there is that within me that reaches for excellence, which would enjoy the honor, the privilege, the notoriety, and yes, the raw power inherent in this position. But… (he paused and sighed) I am not the right man for the job (there was an audible groan of disappointment from the assembly). I am a simple man who knows one thing, and does it very well. I am in the position I hold now because it is the very top of my field, I know what I am doing, and I can make a real contribution. But I am not a man of vision, nor of much imagination. The world spins ever faster, changing and evolving, and we must be led by those who keep pace with it, or even run ahead of it. Our young king will be of the next generation of rulers, and we must give him a regent who will nurture in him a hunger to reach for the stars – not one who will hold him back with old ways. We can give him the wisdom of our experience and the counsel of our maturity. But the person who rules in his name must be prepared to take risks, to see possibilities we have not yet imagined, and to model for Darian, as he grows, these traits of a great leader. That is why I am content to stay where I am, at the new regent's pleasure, and be the best support I can be for them both. I am moved, more than I can express, at all of your high opinions of my character, but I am afraid I must decline.

"I think, from our conversations, that I may also speak on behalf of my fellow High Ministers, that they feel the same way as I do, (there were curt, but meaningful nods from both the Ministers of Finance and Justice), and I urge you to look deeper into our midst to find the person who will be our best hope in this difficult time of transition. I thank you all."

Boone sat. At that moment, Jorelial Rey wished she could run up and hug the man, who had so clearly and honestly assessed his own abilities against the necessary qualifications for the position in question. Boone was a man she had always respected, but found difficult to read and hard to connect with. She felt she had never understood or appreciated him as deeply as she did right now, and silently vowed to let him know that at the first opportunity. Likewise the other Cabinet Ministers, who had obviously discussed this eventuality, and laid aside their own personal ambitions in order to be of best service. These were men she could admire, and emulate – men her father had trusted, and whose quality she was just beginning to recognize.

But, all of this still did not solve the problem at hand, and in the uncomfortable silence following Boone's speech, chairs creaked, whispers echoed, and an air of anxiey began to creep over the assembled participants. Jorelial Rey could stand it no more. She rose to her feet, and in her most powerful formal voice, spoke out, "My lords, worthy all, this is becoming embarrassing. Is there no one present who will step up as candidate for this most important of callings, nor knows of someone fit for the task?"

As the last words she uttered spun out into the hall, she heard an odd flurry of wings and a frantic cooing from somewhere in the rafters. She glanced up and took its meaning; Tvrdik was signaling her from the floor – Lord Drogue was about to make his move. Her eyes dropped to his and met them, halfway down the great table, blazing and intense. She watched him pull his limbs from their casual position on the table, and gather himself to rise. There was something vaguely reminiscent in that move of the way a snake coils itself tighter while holding your gaze, in preparation for its venomous strike. But before he could complete the intended gesture, someone pre-empted him – someone at her elbow was already speaking. The fire in Drogue's eyes banked for a moment, and released her, as he sank back in his chair. Heart pounding, she turned to see who had rescued her. It was Corbin Maygrew, one of her father's oldest friends, and the current head of a family so old, powerful, and respected that the River Maygrew was actually named for them. Corbin was a big, robust man of middle years with a round, friendly face; ruddy, prominent cheeks; thick reddish-brown hair and beard, streaked with gray; blue eyes always dancing with humor, mischief, and intelligence, but often softening to deep kindness and compassion. He had been a frequent and welcome visitor to their home while she was growing up. She had always looked forward to seeing him. He often had a sweet, or a little game reserved for the children, and was always able to make her beloved father laugh, even when they were discussing weighty matters. In short, a man of prominence, wisdom, and goodness. Corbin Maygrew – of course! Why ever had she not thought of him before? The perfect choice. But he had already begun his address…

"…embarrassing it is, but only because we all know our own strengths and limitations, and await the word of the one person among us who is truly fit for this task. My good friend Boone has eloquently expressed so many of my own thoughts and feelings on the subject, and in his remarks on the need for vision, imagination, energy, and innovation in our new regent, I take him to be in agreement with me that the best person for this position is none other than she who has already done such a fine job of discharging it. And that is none other than you, yourself, Jorelial Rey!"

She was completely taken aback by this unexpected vote of confidence from one she considered her better. But as she spluttered ungracefully in response, her speechlessness was covered by a growing chorus of "Hear, hear!" from the Hall, and pounding on the table. Maygrew lifted his hands for quiet.

"What say you, Jorelial Rey? Will you step up and answer the call?" He spoke for the crowd, theatrically, but his eyes twinkled at close range for her, challenge and expectation shining from them. Somehow she found her voice.

"My esteemed Lord Maygrew, I am flattered by your confidence in me. But…but…I have not sought this election. I am content to be released from my duties in favor of a more appropriate candidate…"

He interrupted, "Who could *be* more appropriate? You have already shown your worth in these months of ruling so admirably. And it is precisely *because* you do not seek the election that I am comfortable nominating you. Many of us might be drawn to this position for all that it offers – wealth, status, power, glamour…. But a good regent only holds the throne in trust for the true king, and hands it over to him without reservation at the proper time. How many of us could honestly say we could easily relinquish the perks of royalty? But you, my dear, you find no attraction in any of it, and would gladly be quit of the whole mess. Service and duty are your only motivations, and the desire to continue to do what all your family has done for generations: to protect and support the ᴋing. That is enough for me. Lady Jorelial Rey, you are truly your father's daughter, and I hereby throw the weight of my vote behind you for regent."

More noise from the floor, mostly approbation and relief. A landslide was beginning to build. Tvrdik, from his perch, was both thrilled and horrified at the same time. It was all happening so fast. Jorelial now gestured for quiet.

"My lords all, you do me great honor, but, as has been noted before, I am young, inexperienced in the ways of the world. A great man of proven quality and maturity, a man of wisdom, intellect, statecraft, and diplomacy stands right before you as a superior choice. Lord Maygrew, permit me to defer to your greater years and to nominate you, the head of one of the oldest and most respected families in our kingdom, as a perfect candidate." Her voice was clear and sincere, but held a bit of a strident quality born of desperation. Slowly, a silence fell in the room – a silence of confusion – no doubt few there had ever witnessed an important competition where the prime candidates were trying with all their might to give the wreaths of triumph to each other.

But Maygrew was the veteran player. In the silence, his jovial, rich voice rang out, "Ah, that is where you are mistaken, my dear. Your very youth argues for you in this case. The infant king is but four years old. The regent we choose this day is in for a lifetime's commitment. That's almost two decades; an entire generation. This is not a position we offer, it is a lifework. By the time the young monarch has reached his majority, I shall be a doddering old fool, of little use to him in the transition of power and hopelessly mired in old traditions. And frankly, I should prefer to spend my twilight years relaxing in comfort in my own home, covered in grandchildren." There was laughter from the floor. "Yes, you are young, but already grown into an impressive leader. I have watched you since your childhood, and have been amazed by you. Fearless enough to ride mighty Tashroth, and bold enough to stride into this room, unfazed, the first female to preside over Council in all the history of this land; wise enough not to be seduced by glamour and power, and humble enough to lean on those who are expert in their disciplines for guidance. You are well-trained in history, statecraft, diplomacy, economics, and the arts of war and peace; steeped in the values of courtesy, protocol and tradition, but an independent thinker, more valuing justice, fairness, kindness, and honesty. You are a Rey, through and through, as your father before you. You will do this job to the best of your ability for as long as you must, simply because you have been prepared for it your entire young life, and because your kingdom has need of you. Frankly, I agree with Minister Boone that for this land to thrive, and move into the future, the person at the helm must have courage and vision and energy and a freshness of perspective, along with a willingness to try novel ideas, and take risks. Ministers and counselors can always reach out a steadying hand, but a spark of passion and enthusiasm must light the way. I believe you have all it takes to lead us forward until Darian's ascendancy, and to assure a smooth transition when the time comes."

People were jumping to their feet, pounding the table shouting phrases of approval. Tvrdik was mesmerized watching the scene unfold below him. Few delegates looked uncertain in their support, swept up as they were in the emotion of the moment. Maygrew had played the crowd as if it were his own personal instrument, appealing to all of their most idealistic impulses. He was a virtual artist with words, an inspiration to watch. And yet, Tvrdik had to admit, everything he had said had been true, and made perfect sense. And now that he had whipped the room up into a frenzy, he was about to go for the finish. He was shouting over the din, Jorelial open-mouthed beside him, and his beefy arm settled protectively about her slight, purple-clad shoulders, "What say, friends? Do we have our regent? Shall we elect her by unanimous acclamation then and be done with it, or is there still one among you who wishes to contest the point?"

Maygrew's first mistake. Drogue took his cue without hesitation this time, and rose from his seat. His tall, black figure seemed to cast a larger than possible shadow, which chilled the fervor of everyone on whom it fell. He stood where he was – still, quiet, waiting, confronting his adversaries eye to eye across the vast room, until everyone present noticed him, and a hush fell once again over the assembled delegates. "I contest." He spoke in a cultured, slightly nasal tone that, nevertheless, carried clearly to every ear in the room. Then, without haste, or any hint of agitation, he began his own suit.

"Most of you know me. I am Lord Drogue, of the mountain regions. My family is also a very old and respected family, as distinguished as the royal family, or the Reys, or the Maygrews. You might remember my father, Lord Harrow Drogue, who was quite well thought of in every corner of this kingdom." There were some assenting nods and murmurings. *Apparently,* Tvrdik mused, *Drogue's father was a decent man. There's an apple that somehow fell an awfully long way from the tree.* "My…love…for Eneri Clare is so intense, so over-arching, that I find myself unable to stand idly by and allow what seems to be happening here. Heaven knows I am not ambitious for myself – in my own fiefdom, I am called 'Prince.' I am Master of enough lands, power, and riches to last several lifetimes. I have no ulterior motive save my sense of duty, and a sincere desire to preserve the good of this nation." Tvrdik gagged, and imagined anyone or anything that touched Drogue sliding helplessly down the oily aura in which he was wrapping himself; it was almost visible. The owl/mage cautiously flew to a beam nearer the speaker.

"My…esteemed and…distinguished peer, Lord Maygrew, urges many interesting points in favor of the Lady Regent's sudden election. Lady Rey is indeed a fine and accomplished young woman, and has done a superb job of keeping the kingdom unharmed in this interim period. But, is it really fair of us to ask her to make further sacrifices for Eneri Clare? Lord Maygrew, you speak of spending happy hours with your grandchildren. And yet, you would saddle the Lady Rey with responsibility for the royal heir, and for the welfare of the entire land all the years of his minority. What of entertaining suitors and the joys of raising her own family, insuring the Rey bloodline might continue with strong new scions? The delights of maidenhood and motherhood, these are the careers for which our dear sister is infinitely better equipped, and likely more inclined to pursue, truth be told."

That remark drew a wave of muted exclamations from the floor, some shocked, some sympathetic, and others downright disgusted. Tvrdik watched Jorelial's face turn an odd shade of aubergine. If owls had eyebrows, they would have been raised high in alarm. The man was presuming to tell Jorelial Rey in front of the entire court what her personal and professional ambitions should be. The owl/mage braced himself for a spirited retort, but instead saw her jaw muscles ripple and her lips turn pale as she kept her feelings about Drogue's remarks under tight control. The Grand Council was no place for a free-for-all, and Drogue had the floor.

The mountain lord continued. "And while Lady Rey is a bright and capable girl, no doubt having learned a thing or two at the feet of her father, the fact remains that she is but a girl. I fear it falls to me to point out that the future of this kingdom has been entrusted to all of you assembled here, and you are about to hand it over, in your idealism, to a four year old babe and an unseasoned young woman. Oh, my dear lords, where is your reason, your wit, your sound, sensible judgment? I am no longer a callow youth; I have seen the world. Many of you here have rarely ventured beyond your own estates, and have never taken it upon yourselves to explore what lies beyond our very comfortable borders. I have had the opportunity to travel abroad, and have encountered much to harden my heart. I learned war-craft, fighting in foreign conflicts. I have witnessed lands decimated by plague and privation, where crime and cruelty were everyday occurrences. I have met powerful men who were ruthless and untrustworthy, and having dealt with men of all sorts, I have learned that we are really all the same – opportunists all, just under the skin."

Someone called out, "Sit down, Drogue! Must we listen to this?" There was a brief surge of commentary from the floor, but a firm rap on the tiles from the Steward's baton, and a heart-stopping glare from Drogue himself silenced the crowd. He went on.

"The plain fact is that we are now *vulnerable*. Our king and queen are perished, along with their most trusted advisor. We reel in crisis. What will our neighbors be thinking when they see how unguarded we are, and ready for the picking? Do not let their sympathetic smiles and paper treaties fool you – there is no ruler on earth who would not look at a lovely ripe fruit sitting under his nose unprotected, and would not desire it for his own. You are too trusting and too complacent, my lords. The years of peace have made you soft. What will you do when the foreigners come streaming over our borders to burn our estates, take our sons as slaves, and our daughters, sisters, and wives to ravage?"

Delegates began to shout outright, and the noise level of the room rose to something just short of cacophony. Drogue seemed to take energy from the chaos, stirring up outrage, shouting over the din, underlining his points with staccato jabs of his bony finger. "I tell you, lords, I am afraid.

As you should be afraid. So much talk we have heard today of loyalty to a family, of vision, innovation, new ideas… Well, none of that will be worth a fig if we do not first have a care for ourselves and our families. We must put self-preservation first and foremost on our agenda." He paused to let his dark vision settle over them, for the Steward to bang his great baton on the floor, and the noise to die down. Then he smiled, without warmth.

"This is a time in Eneri Clare for older, stronger, more capable hands to take the wheel. If there is no other here today who understands what is at stake, who can take decisive action, who is willing to step forward to protect our land from threats within and abroad (*You yourself are the only real threat here*, thought Tvrdik, furious), then I humbly offer myself as candidate for regent, setting aside my own personal happiness and freedom in order to serve, as your leader and protector."

There was a single bold cry of, "Hear, hear!" from someone at the table, a round man with curly hair. But it died quickly when few joined in. An uncomfortable silence blanketed the room as Lord Drogue bowed low and resumed his seat. *Fear*, Tvrdik fumed, *he's using fear to control people; stirring up phantom dangers with half-truths and imaginings that have no basis in reality. He's even trying to convince everyone to question their earlier good instincts. How many of them will allow him to superimpose this false picture onto their psyches? How many will succumb to these despicable tactics?* It irked him to stand by and listen to such an evil rant without being able to counter it in any way.

Jorelial Rey was pale and silent, uncertain how best to dispel the poison in Drogue's monologue, and quite aware of the tradition that at Council, in the Great Hall, anyone was permitted to speak his mind, no matter how ugly its contents might be. Lord Maygrew, looking more like a defending lion now than a jocular uncle, his arm still circling Jorelial's shoulder, broke the spell, his voice taut. "Right, then. Two strong candidates are proposed. The sun is sinking. Let us put it to a vote. Discussion?" No one uttered a sound. "Good. You all should know how this is done, but for you first-timers, each of you has been provided with a collection of colored wooden chips, the kind used in gaming. We will make the green chips for Lady Jorelial Rey, and the red for Lord Drogue, who has so unselfishly volunteered his services. We will all file in orderly fashion to the front of the room where our good steward holds a covered box with a slit in the top. He will be guarded at all times, so that tampering will not be possible. Drop in the chip representing your selection, and the results will be counted by an objective party agreed to by both candidates. Stand well back from the box to give your fellows a bit of privacy, please, and keep your own choice close as well. Lord Drogue, will you suggest someone to tally?"

A moment passed. Drogue raised an eyebrow, "I trust our esteemed Minister of Justice would serve?" he ventured.

"Lady Rey, is that acceptable?"

"Of course," she nodded.

At a signal from Bargarelle, the musicians returned to play some solemn background as the long line shuffled up to the box, each delegate making a final choice. During those agonizing minutes, no conversation was permitted. But, as the box was taken to be counted by Master Alanquist, everyone stretched and relaxed, gathering in small groups to discuss the day's events. Whatever the result, they had all done their duty, and were already anticipating the banquet prepared for the evening's finish. Tvrdik kept one bird's eye on Jorelial Rey, who sat in her big chair ashen- faced, while Maygrew, her champion, stood several paces off, silent and supportive. The owl/mage's other eye was fixed on Drogue, who had gone back to his original relaxed posture in his chair, equally isolated from interaction with anyone else. Around these two islands of stillness, the noisy bustle of a weary crowd eager to be quit of its responsibilities grew and circulated. There were, of course, those few who were deeply concerned about the vote. Tvrdik could see them assembled in corners, brows furrowed, talking among themselves in low whispers. He tried to memorize their faces for later need. The three lords who seemed to be in league with Drogue huddled together a few paces from him, faces solemn, eyes on the mountain lord, who ignored them.

When Bargarelle entered with the results, things had relaxed so that he almost wasn't noticed. With a sense of great purpose he marched to the front of the room and rapped his heavy staff of office on the floor, shouting, "Order, order!" until he had everyone's attention. He then continued, formally, "After three careful counts by our impartial representative, Lord Alanquist, the final tally is…Lord Drogue, twenty-three; Lady Jorelial Rey, one hundred two. Lady Rey is elected permanent regent to the king, beginning at once, and lasting until his twenty-first birthday, or the death of either party, whichever occurs first."

Tvrdik heard an audible gasp from Drogue. (*Amazing,* the mage mused, *he actually believed that he would be victorious.*)

"Papers will presently be drawn up and signed vesting royal authority in the regent elect, and symbols of the office will be conferred upon her person by Council at the Royal Coronation, to be held one week from tomorrow, Saturday, at two hours past mid-day. We wish to thank Lord Drogue for his willingness to serve, all the delegates for their participation in this momentous event, and we salute Lady Rey in her new capacity. This Council is formally adjourned. A banquet will be served for your comfort and pleasure in this same room in one hour. If you will be pleased to vacate the Hall until that time to allow us to lay the tables..." He lowered his voice and, with a broad smile, extended a hand to the new regent, "and may I add my sincerest personal congratulations, Lady Rey. I am relieved and delighted at this result."

It was done. There was no escaping it. She was regent, just as Xaarus had predicted. But now that the uncertainty was over and there was no turning back, her breeding took over and she stood taller, allowing a gracious smile and her genuine warmth to break through. She took Bargarelle's outstretched hand and clasped it firmly, "Without you, my right hand, I do not know what I would do." He flushed, basking in her praise. She looked around, coming to life at last, "Do you think you could get them to listen to a few more words, from me?" In response, the Steward began banging his baton again, shouting, "Order!" Groups had already begun to head toward the main doors as the musicians played, but most turned back to attend to this last summons. The music halted mid-song, and an expectant hush descended on the crowd. "Our Lady Regent would like a word..."

Jorelial Rey, newly-elected permanent regent to the king, and, effectively, ruler of all of Eneri Clare, took her place at the podium for the first time, looking every inch a leader of men. Tvrdik was again breathless at the instant transformation. Her voice rang out across the long room, "I have no wish to detain you all from your well-deserved refreshment; I will see many of you later at the banquet, and will thank you then in person for the confidence you have placed in me this day. For now, I will just say to all of you that I am humbled and overwhelmed at your faith in me, and I promise I will not fail you. I will strive to hold the throne as a sacred trust for our beloved Darian, and to keep his kingdom safe, just, wealthy, and at peace with our neighbors until the day of his ascendancy. Until that time, I rely on our High Ministers for their sage counsel, and I invite all of you present to feel free always to speak your minds. Tell me of your concerns, and know that you will always find a willing and concerned ear here. Do not be strangers in this place, where you are always welcome. Friends, I thank you, and send you with a full heart to your revels..."

"NOOOO!" It was a visceral, unearthly wail that seemed to issue from Lord Drogue, who had been sitting like a statue in his assigned place since the election results had been announced, his fists clenched and his gaze fixed on some inner landscape. But now, it was indeed as if something within had snapped, and all pretense of grace or propriety melted away. Instead of smolderingly handsome, his face now appeared frighteningly deranged, the features twisted in rage at the perceived injustice of his rejection. His voice cut through the room like the shriek of a wounded beast, "This is wrong. It cannot happen. The throne is mine. It was always meant to be mine. You fools...*fools*! You have trusted your future to a child in diapers, and a spoiled girl. It is folly of the highest order. You will all live to regret the mistakes of this day. The time will come when the strong will triumph, make no mistake. You will not get away with this travesty."

Tvrdik, who had watched Drogue working up to this for some minutes, now flew in haste to the Lady Regent's shoulder and perched there, flapping his great white wings to steady himself. Such a move would have turned quite a few heads had they not already been turned in shock and horror toward Lord Drogue. "Let me *do* something," he whispered frantically in her ear, "let me take him down *now*...he's clearly insane."

Jorelial shook her head, "No, you can't. We can't. It won't change anything."

Lord Maygrew, oblivious to their brief interchange, stepped forward, "What are you saying, Drogue? Are you threatening to override the will of the Grand Council by force? If so, it is treason, sir – I could have you arrested on the spot. Guards."

"Wait, no!" Jorelial called, "Lord Drogue, I am sorry you are displeased with the election's results. I shall do everything in my power to try and change your opinion of me. But for the moment, it seems I am made regent. It is our policy, our time-honored tradition, that in this room, council members are free to express their honest opinions, even if they are unpopular ones. I cannot arrest you for expressing your disappointment. However, draw your sword or threaten us at your peril. I beg you now to regain your composure, and put aside any rancor between us. You are our honored guest, and we invite you to enjoy our hospitality."

Tvrdik marveled at her poise, generosity, and good sense, not to mention how easily she seemed to drift into using the royal 'we' in formal speech. There was a moment when it seemed as though not a soul drew breath, awaiting what might happen next. And then Drogue snarled, looking much like a rabid dog, and made his reply, "Do not attempt to silence me with honeyed words. You are too late for that. You have taken what is rightfully mine, and I warn you, I *swear* that you will not hold it long, Lady Jorelial Rey." He spit out her name syllable by syllable, as if committing it to memory for some future evil incantation. A chill ran through her, Tvrdik's claws digging into her shoulder muscle.

Maygrew gestured to the door, his rich baritone ringing out for everyone to hear, "Leave this place, sir. You shall not be harmed or detained, as the Lady Rey wishes, but neither shall you stand here before me with impunity, and make threats and insults against our monarch and his chosen regent. Go now, while I still have some control over my temper, and do not show your face here again."

"Or else what?" Was Drogue actually laughing? Time slowed as he turned to survey the room, taking in the appalled expressions on every face. Then, in a soft and chilling voice that every ear nevertheless heard, "I promise each and every one of you, you will regret this day's ill-begotten work. You have not heard the last of me." He turned on his heel, and strode from the room. Not a soul stirred, not a sound was heard, but the echo of retreating heels on marble floors. Then, in that emotion- charged pause, one by one, three other lords turned to the door and stalked out after Drogue. Yes, they were the same that Tvrdik had noticed earlier as sullen or suspicious. Not good at all.

Again, with remarkable poise, the Lady Regent quickly took it upon herself to diffuse the tension, "Let him go, friends. We are confident he will cool down and come to his senses. These are stressful times. Please go now and find your families, and return in an hour for a good hot meal and a little entertainment. I can't promise you as exciting a show as we have just had, but it will at least be worth returning for." That quip, and her veneer of easy grace, generated a ripple of laughter all around, and started people moving out the main doors once again. As the hall emptied from one direction, serving men and women began scurrying in at side doors, racing to set up for the massive party. Jorelial Rey blew out her breath, releasing the tension in her shoulders. Corbin Maygrew stepped over and laid a hand on her free arm in a comforting gesture, then almost as an afterthought, raised an eyebrow at the white owl still perched at her other ear. "I'll explain later," she told her recent champion. Bargarelle, the Steward, a few paces off and white-faced, was standing stock still, leaning on his official staff, and staring at her with an expression midway between horror and worship on his face. Tvrdik preened his feathers with his beak, thinking, *Oh, Xaarus, it was all as you said. Everything, exactly as you told me. It has most certainly begun.*

FIFTEEN

MISSING PIECES

As the rest of the guests shuffled out of the Hall, and preparations for the banquet went into high gear, Jorelial Rey turned to face the man who had, in all practicality, set her on the throne. "Lord Maygrew, I don't know whether to bless or curse you for what you have done this day. I – I don't know if I am worthy of the trust you place in me, or if I am any of the things you promised them I could be."

He smiled, "Rel – or should I call you my Lady Regent? There is no doubt in my mind that you are the one for the job. Half of those lords out there are oblivious to anything that goes on in the kingdom outside of their own little corners. Another quarter are too aged, too infirm, or too otherwise occupied to want such a huge responsibility. At least your High Ministers are intelligent enough to know in what capacity they can best serve the kingdom. And the rest of us? Well, I'd like to think there are still men of quality in this land, and I'd like to count myself among them, but I could never finesse things with the kind of grace you showed tonight, the kind of devotion to our laws and traditions, and the quick thinking with which you handled that idiot. And *that* was your only real competition? Gods defend us from those who lust after power for its own sake and have no idea what it really entails! Now, your father – *there* was a man of quality – he would have been the man to do this alright, no contest. And he took great care with you, Rel; I watched him teach you everything he knew, and you've always taken to it like a cart-horse to the harness."

"Hmm. Perhaps not the most fortunate analogy, now that I am feeling a little like I have just been weighted indefinitely with a yoke of heavy responsibility. You know, I always thought my father was disappointed that I wasn't the son he so wanted…"

"My girl, did you not know how proud he was of you? He was always boasting about you: how quickly you learned, how you tamed that dragon, how talented you were with sword and rapier…he always saw greatness in you. I'm sure it was the very reason he was so hard on you."

"I never…thank you for sharing that with me, Lord Maygrew. You can't imagine how much it means…"

"Ach, but you are a grown woman now, and ready to take your own place in the world. Certainly you have more to learn about ruling a kingdom, but you'll grow into it, I have no doubt. Your head's in the right place, that's certain."

"I do not think we can dismiss Drogue so lightly. I believe he is serious in his threats. We might have a bumpy road ahead of us…"

"Don't worry. I will be right behind you all the way no matter what lies ahead on the road. And there are many more I can name who would be at your service in an instant as well."

"I will hold you to that promise with a good will, sir, and again, many thanks for all you have said and done on my behalf. I am in your debt. But if you will excuse me now, I must take a few minutes to attend to Tashroth. He awaits news…"

"Of course. I will see you later, no doubt, at the festivities. My Auria will be pleased to see you again. Where did that owl come from, anyway? Darnedest thing I've ever seen."

"Oh, him? Something of a pet…he must have gotten out of his cage and followed me here. Ow!" she yelped involuntarily as Tvrdik's claws dug further into her shoulder.

"You'd better teach him some discipline, my lady. You don't always know where you stand with wild things. I shall take my leave of you, until tonight." He bowed, and kissed her hand, "Long live Lady Jorelial Rey, and rule well."

"And fortune smile on you and yours, Lord Maygrew." She nodded to him and he strode across the floor.

As soon as he was out of sight, Rel took off in the other direction, heading toward a side exit, a large white owl still attached to her shoulder. "What did you do that for?" she asked in a peevish whisper.

"'Something of a pet…teach him some discipline?' How did you expect me to react?" the bird snapped in her ear.

"Well, I had to say something. Should I have introduced you as 'my good old friend Tvrdik, the friendly neighborhood wizard?' And just after the man put his own neck on the line to convince everyone that I was fit to rule an entire kingdom? Why did you fly down onto my shoulder, anyway? Now *that* was unobtrusive."

"I was afraid you might be in danger. I didn't know what Drogue might do."

"I had things in hand, thank you very much…"

"Pardon, mum?" queried a serving maid, who was setting up tables, and had stopped to stare at her as if she had two heads, which of course, at the moment, she did. "Pardon, were you addressing me, my lady?"

"Oh, no…so sorry. Just practicing my speech for tonight – it's always better if it's memorized. You know how it is….well, maybe not. You can just go about your business there, thanks. I'm fine. Sorry to interrupt you…." The owl hooted. Rel frowned. "You hush," she said, as they hurried through a door into a deserted corridor. Scanning the passageway and seeing no one nearby, she dislodged the bird from her shoulder and looked it straight in its circle-rimmed eye, "Would you mind changing back now?"

The broad white wings rose and flapped powerfully. For a moment there was an owl suspended before her in mid-air – and then the tall, lanky young man in blue was standing there adjusting his spectacles. Her eyes grew wide in amazement at the transformation, but one look at the familiar, lost-looking face, and her angry mood melted.

"I'm sorry I was cross with you. I do appreciate your sitting up there all day long, and I know you were only trying to protect me…"

But Tvrdik's mind was already fastened onto something else. He was regarding her with wide-eyed amazement. "Jorelial Rey…you *are* regent! You rule the entire kingdom – you've done it. You managed to walk into a room filled with old school lords and officials, skeptical and set in their ways, and somehow inspire them to choose *you* to run the whole thing."

Uncertain of his point, she squirmed, "I had a lot of help. I didn't really do anything special…"

"Yes, but they could not have been persuaded if they did not like what they saw. They are convinced that you are the best person for the position."

"Nobody else would take the drat job…except Drogue."

"Nobody else thought they could improve on what you were already doing. Do you realize what an accomplishment this is? Jorelial Rey, you have made history!"

"Do *you* realize that I am now trapped for the next twenty years? *And* that everything Xaarus predicted is happening just as you said it would? Now we are bound to go to war with Drogue. Hundreds of years this kingdom rolls along in peace and contentment; they hand it to *me*, and in five minutes I have enemies."

"It must be in your stars to be a catalyst…"

"A what?"

"A catalyst. It's an alchemical term for something that causes other elements to react. It means someone whose very presence stirs things up – brings about change…"

"Look who's talking. Seems to me *you* started the ball rolling. And if things really have to change, why can't they just go ahead and do it without me."

Tvrdik looked at her small, anxious, very vulnerable face then, and did an odd thing. He took a step back, sank down onto one knee and bowed his head.

"My Lady Regent, I honor you, and I herewith swear myself into your service for as long as you have need of me, and in any way that I may be of assistance. Please accept this humble wizard's fealty, and command him as you will."

Rel stood frozen in surprise and horror, watching this unexpected display, and then she smacked him hard across the shoulder, and said, "Oh, get up off the floor – you look ridiculous. Come on. I don't have a lot of time, and we need to find Tashroth."

Tvrdik blinked and scrambled to his feet. They hurried through corridors and across courtyards to the north tower where they knew the dragon awaited them. Up and up the circular staircase they climbed until they were breathless and their hearts were pounding. At length, they reached the summit and Rel threw open the trap-door to the roof, clambering out. Without a word, she ran to the familiar space between the great beast's front limbs and threw herself upon his broad chest, head against his beating heart. Tvrdik followed out onto the roof, but hung back in the shadows, allowing them their private moment. Tashroth lowered his head to hers and nuzzled her gently. His voice rumbled across the space even in this intimate moment, "What news, little one? I have seen riders leaving the compound not long ago, and then the palace guard in hot pursuit. Is it as we expected?"

"Oh, Tash. Everything is unfolding exactly as Xaarus predicted. We are over the edge now and falling into an abyss I cannot see the bottom of." She remained standing in his comforting embrace, eyes closed, cheek pressed to scale. Tvrdik stepped forward and filled in the details.

"The Council was a resounding success. The kingdom is reported to be in remarkably good condition, and it is agreed that Darian will be crowned king, with all due ceremony, one week from tomorrow. Lady Jorelial Rey was put forward as a candidate for regent by… Lord Corbin Maygrew, I believe he was called. She was voted into the permanent position by a rather large majority. That is, until the king turns twenty-one. She really had no serious competition. Oh, except for Lord Drogue, who nominated himself, went berserk when he lost the election, threatened the entire assembly and Jorelial personally, and stormed out in a huff. Three other sour-faced lords followed along behind him. Lord Maygrew told them to vacate the premises and not to show their faces at Theriole again. The new Lady Regent was brilliant at managing to calm everyone else down after all the drama, and the servants are even now setting up the room for the closing banquet, which all the guests await with happy anticipation."

Rel straightened up and blinked, "My, you certainly have a flare for reducing a very long and complicated day into a tidy little summary."

"It's a gift." Tvrdik smiled his crooked smile, "Did I leave anything important out?"

"Lord Maygrew is a good man," Tashroth weighed in, "and honest. I am not surprised he stood for you. He was a good friend to your father. Who were the other lords that followed Drogue? Do you know them, and what forces they command?"

"I know no names," Tvrdik answered, "but I can describe them, and would know them if I saw them again."

"I think I know at least two of them," Rel added. "They are neighbors of Drogue's who I know have nursed petty grudges against the Crown for years. Doubtless they have also been listening to Drogue's poison of late. The third we can inquire after."

"My congratulations, little one," the dragon cooed. "You will rule well. I expect great things of you."

Rel knitted her brows into a deep frown, "I wish so many people didn't expect quite so much of me."

"You are all you need to be, dearest," the dragon replied, "and you are not alone."

"I know," she relaxed a bit and began pacing the roof, "I am not afraid of Drogue. What weighs on me now is that since Xaarus has been right so far, I think we can expect him to be correct about everything else. Which means our next steps will be the hardest, because they are the most illogical. Despite our long-cherished peace, the kingdom will know how to handle a war, and will prepare to defend itself. But convincing my generals that they must not raise a finger against their adversaries – now, that will be a mighty challenging task."

Tashroth uttered a short chuckle, "Then it has fallen to the right person. You will make them see. It is your destiny."

Tvrdik chimed in, "You should have heard her address today. She had them on their feet within the first few minutes. I do believe she could persuade the moon down out of its sphere." Tashroth chuckled again, and Rel sighed.

"Well, thank you both for those compliments, and your confidence, gentlemen, but I am not even sure how I am going to proceed from here, or how to plead our case."

"One day at a time, little one. It will become clear to you as events unfold. Lord Drogue may have tipped his hand, but he has yet to make a threatening move."

Tvrdik added, "Perhaps it is time I came to life as well. I could help you explain how we know what we know, as outlandish a story as it seems."

"Yes, we must plan how and when we will do that, and to whom. The sooner, the better. Although," she seemed to be thinking aloud, "perhaps it will be best not to confuse things before the Coronation. I do not wish to cast a pall over it. Can you last another week in anonymity?"

"Whatever you think is best. I shall continue my work on The Cottage and move myself in there, and then I can begin to craft some ideas for strategies. And, by the way, I never said we were not to raise a finger in defense against Drogue's forces – I myself intend to raise several. It is the intent of what we do with them that ultimately matters. I am certainly not advocating that we present ourselves as sitting ducks. There is a big difference in perception."

"I will bear that in mind as I attempt to explain the distinction to the Army." Her comment came out tinged with just a touch of irony.

"Lord Tashroth," Tvrdik added, "I forgot to mention that Drogue is also versed in some sort of sorcery, and not a good sort either. I believe he fancies himself some kind of dark spell-master."

"How accomplished do you estimate he is?"

"To the best of my knowledge, he would have to have gotten all his information from books, which would somewhat limit his true mastery of it. He did not succeed very well today with what he was attempting, and I was able to block him almost at once, but he did not know I was there, of course, and wasn't expecting any resistance. I only think we should be forewarned and take this additional danger seriously, lest he catch us off our guard."

"Well done, mage. I will make inquiries of my brother dragons, and see if there is word of his activities in that area. We dragons count ourselves as guardians of a sort for the old magic, so I daresay any stirring in the ancient matrix would not have gone unnoticed."

Rel had been listening to them, partly distracted by her own thoughts, but she gave herself a shake, and stood taller, "I must return to the banquet, Tash. I would far rather be here with you tonight, but as hostess, and Regent Elect, I will be missed if I do not make an appearance."

"Go, dearest. Find some part of your triumph this day to celebrate. It is a magnificent thing. Rest easy that you are supported in every way. I am proud of you."

"If I can, I will come to you, very late." She smiled, soothed by his presence.

"I will be here." The dragon promised. "Mage?"

"Yes, my lord?"

"My gratitude. You have done well. Keep her under your eye as you can, will you?"

"Yes, sir. Count on it." and Tvrdik, still none too comfortable being addressed by a dragon, nevertheless turned away smiling.

He followed Jorelial, who had already disappeared through the trap door, and closed it behind them. Down the long staircase they wound, floor after floor, the Lady Regent conscious that she was already overdue at her own festivities. But as they left the tower and headed into the darkening courtyard, they were greeted by a very agitated Warlowe.

"What is it, Warlowe? I am on my way to the banquet now, if you were sent to find me..."

"My lady, I was sent to *intercept* you. You must come with me right away to the Hall of Audience. There is something within that you will wish to see."

"Warlowe, with all due respect, I am already late for a banquet in *my honor*. Anything else can surely wait until tomorrow..." She was about to push past him, but the poor man, obviously uncomfortable, blocked her way, and tried again to deliver his message without saying too much. Tvrdik edged up closer to hear him.

"My lady, this cannot wait. It concerns your – your sister."

"Delphine?" Rel turned white. "Is she alright? Where has she been? I've been worried sick about her."

"She is fine, my lady," Warlowe reassured, "but you will want to see this for yourself. Right this way...."

Without turning back, or hesitating even a beat, she shouted, "Come with me," to Tvrdik, and the three of them set out across the courtyard at a run, to the familiar Hall of Audience, where they were greeted by a most bizarre scene. A number of palace guardsmen in full regalia were attempting to hold back a distraught and disheveled Delphine, in homespun britches and a tunic, from Mark, who was being detained somewhat more roughly by other guards. A number of carry-sacks and stuffed bags were strewn across the floor.

"What is this?" boomed Jorelial Rey, in her most authoritative voice, as she entered the room, "Release her."

"Rel!" cried Delphine, and broke through the line of startled guards to fling her arms around her sister's neck. "Thank the gods you are here. Tell them to let him go – they'll hurt him." A quick glance around told her that Mark had no intention of going anywhere, so she raised a commanding hand. The guards immediately loosed their hold on the hapless bard, but stood at attention, pikes in position to stop him if he should try to escape.

"Now, someone explain to me what is the meaning of all this? Why is my sister being forcibly detained in her own home?"

The Captain of the Guard stepped forward then and saluted her, every inch a professional.

"My Lady Regent, General Boone sent a portion of the guard out tonight as a precaution, to follow Lord Drogue and his company off of Theriole's grounds. Our instructions were to make sure they broke camp and left without causing any trouble or attempting to return to the palace. While we were out on patrol, my lady, we came across these two, in travelling cloaks, and with all of this luggage, obviously planning to sneak off of the grounds together. Naturally we thought you would wish them apprehended in their flight and brought to you."

"That's not true!" shouted Mark, in as assertive a voice as anyone had ever heard the gentle musician use, setting off another wave of threatening motions among his guards. Rel raised a hand again to calm them. "It's not true." continued Mark. "We weren't trying to sneak off the palace grounds at all. We were attempting to sneak back *onto* the palace grounds. We've been gone for nearly four days. Our timing was off, is all. We'd have made it back undetected if we hadn't forgotten there would be so much extra security with the Grand Council and all."

His words hit Jorelial like a blunt stone, and there followed an awkward silence where everyone's eyes travelled from player to player in this little unfolding drama. Finally, Jorelial Rey, as the person ultimately in charge, summoned the captain to approach nearer, and in a low voice, addressed him.

"Captain, I think I see what is going on here. You did well to bring them in. I am most grateful for your vigilance." Thinking she recognized the young officer, she placed a hand at his shoulder blade and urged the man a little aside. "I know you sir, don't I? Your father worked in service to mine, if I do not mistake. Your name is …Virian, yes? Did we not only last year celebrate your wedding?"

The Captain relaxed a little and smiled, delighted at the Lady Regent's personal reference. "My lady, it was two years ago last week. You do my family great honor to recall."

"And how is your lovely wife, Virian? The Lady…"

"Anira, my lady. You are too kind. She is well, very well. We are expecting our first child within the month."

Jorelial Rey leaned in closer, "How wonderful! Please accept my heartfelt congratulations. So, Captain Virian, you are no stranger to the exquisite joys of *family*. The joys and (she sighed and cast a glance back at Delphine, who was now arguing with another guard over her carry-sack) the heartaches inherent in those bonds which touch us like no other force on earth." The Captain raised his eyebrows, shifting his stance as the Lady Rey continued, "I wish you every blessing on your new family, Captain. As for mine…" she lowered her voice and gestured toward Delphine with her head, "I think I can probably take it from here. You and your company will see a small expression of my gratitude in your next pay – that is a promise. But for now, I believe you all have a more dangerous quarry to track, yes?"

The Captain came to attention. "Yes, Ma'am. Thank you Ma'am. Company, fall in…" Virian made bold to offer her a little wink, and turned on his heel, "March!" And with that, the handsome young man led his charges out the great doors and into the night, leaving the Lady Regent alone in the big room with her younger sister, Mark, and Tvrdik. Warlowe quietly excused himself to his customary position on the other side of the doors as they thudded shut.

"Sit," she commanded the two youths, and they both set themselves down wearily at the great table. "Now, one of you explain to me what happened, and where you've been for the last four days. I've been searching everywhere for you, and have been nearly sick with worry."

Mark replied first, "Really? Delphine swore we'd never be missed, as you had no time for her right now."

"Ouch! Delphine, what an unkind thing to say, although I suppose I deserve it. Listen, I was so upset and confused after our argument that I flew off with Tashroth to the mountains for a day to cool off. When I got back, there was an awful lot of state business and last minute arranging for me to attend to, but I kept searching for you whenever I could. I wanted to apologize…"

"*You* wanted to apologize?"

"Well, yes…among other things, I thought I might have been a little insensitive with you. But you were nowhere to be found. No one had seen you. I was starting to panic…you know I am never happy when we are at odds. But the Council Meeting was demanding all my attention by then, and I had to assume we would patch things up after. Where were you?"

Delphine's eyes were fixed on the floor, "After we argued, I couldn't seem to find you either, so we decided to go off to Mark's family estate in the mountains. We were going to – to - well, to elope."

"Elope? After the discussion we had, you were going to defy me? Mark, I must say, this is not the best way to impress me with your good sense."

"She talked me into it," the poor minstrel hedged. "I had grave reservations, and I told her we should wait, but she was so sure, and I just can't seem to deny her anything she wants." He hung his head in misery. Rel frowned and turned back to Delphine, calmer now and genuinely trying to understand.

"Why in heaven's name would you do such a thing to me, Delphine, after all we've been to each other? What were you thinking?"

Delphine was crying now. "I don't know…I was so upset when you just out of the blue closed discussion, and then Tvrdik told me how you had so many worries and weighty affairs on your mind, and fears for the future… (Rel shot the mage a stern look, while he rolled his eyes heavenward and turned away, hands behind his back, a picture of innocence.) I…I thought I was just giving you one more tough decision to make on top of everything else, because you always feel you have to protect me. I figured that if we just went ahead and did it, and came back married, and you didn't have to worry about making any decisions, you would be relieved and just get used to the idea in time. I…I hoped you would accept it and come to love Mark as I do, and then we'd all be happy…it just seemed like the right thing to do at the time." The two sisters just stared at each other for a moment, Delphine still shaking and sobbing. And then, quietly, Rel spoke.

"You really thought this was a good idea? And you couldn't see how it would hurt me?"

"You never noticed how hurt I was that all you seemed to want to do was keep me away from my happiness."

"You want to be married as much as that?"

"Oh, Rel, he is my soul! Every day that we are apart is torture for me."

Mark chimed in, "Nothing happened, if that's what you are worried about, my lady. We couldn't – I couldn't go through with it after all."

"Why not? Have you changed your mind about her?"

"Gods, no! I love your sister more than life. I want her to be my bride more with each passing day. But when we got to my parents' home, and my little sister greeted us with such excitement – she's only thirteen now, but growing up so fast – and I got to thinking if someday she just ran off with a boy I barely knew, and never gave me the chance to sing at her wedding, or to share in celebrating their happiness, I'd probably never forgive them. It just seemed so wrong. That wasn't how I wanted to start off our relationship, my lady, yours and mine. That was never my intention. So I screwed up my courage and told Delphine we weren't going to do it this way, and that we were going home. She wasn't happy, but I made her go. We thought we could just sneak back in with everything going on at the palace, and just reappear before any real harm was done. We were wrong."

"Young man, you have just risen to new heights in my estimation. I want to thank you for that – for your wisdom and thoughtfulness, and for delivering my sister home to me safe and sound." Her tone changed, "But the two of you have no idea how you caused me to worry, how much *real* danger you were in out there wandering around unguarded in the mountains."

Mark looked confused, "My lady, I know that region like the back of my hand. It is my homeland, and I know my way around. I would never have jeopardized Delphine's safety in any way."

Rel shook her head, "You see? Sometimes you just don't have all the facts. This afternoon, I was elected by the Grand Council to be full-time, permanent regent to His Majesty."

"Oh, Rel, congratulations! I am so happy for you." Delphine jumped up and rushed forward intending to embrace Rel again, but the Lady Regent stopped her with a gesture.

"Save your congratulations; it is at the very best a mixed blessing. Lord Drogue was a candidate for the same position and lost to me. He swore up and down that he would take what was his by force if necessary, and be avenged on me personally in the bargain. Lord Maygrew threw him out. Three other mountain lords followed in protest. That's why the palace guard is out in force – to make sure they all crossed the borders without wreaking any havoc. And wouldn't Drogue have been delighted if a juicy plum like you should fall into his hands – one he could use against me to great effect. Oh, Delphine, the thought is unbearable! If anything ever happened to you, I don't know what I would do." Tvrdik, who had stayed silent all this time, letting the family drama play itself out, made a move toward Jorelial, and gingerly laid a hand on her shoulder. She did not shake it off. Mark's face had become pinched and positively green, imagining what could have occurred.

"My lady, I am so sorry. I swear I did not know..."

"I am no monster to keep you two apart from sheer meanness. I have nothing against you, Mark. Indeed, I respect your gifts, your steadiness, and your ideas for the future. I believe you love Delphine the way you say you do, but will it be enough? If we are not officially at war now, we soon will be. The future is uncertain – I cannot keep you safe, or insure your financial security, or even your position. Times are tricky. What kind of circumstance is that in which to start a new life together? You could end up separated from each other, losing everything."

Delphine, tears still glistening in her eyes, but a kind of serenity shining on her face, took both of her sister's hands in her own and spoke with warmth and passion. "It is the best possible time to start a new life, Rel. If the future is uncertain, the present is all we have. One must cling to love and joy in dark times wherever one finds them. I don't want to postpone our happiness one moment longer, do you understand? And you, too, need reasons to rejoice in these challenging days. Rejoice with me. Please?" They stood locked in each other's gaze for a beat.

"Delphine, you are not royalty, but you are the daughter of one of the highest ministers at court – a counselor to kings. And you are sister to the Lady Regent. You are entitled to engagement announcements far and wide, celebratory balls, gifts from all of our peers, and the fairy tale wedding of your dreams. If we do this precipitously, you will be sacrificing all of that."

Mark looked stricken, taking in Rel's point. But Delphine remained radiant, "None of those things mean anything to me." She took Mark's hand in her own, "I have all I need right here." The young man smiled, but tears shimmered on the edges of his eyelids.

Rel turned back to him, pointedly, "You visited with your family? You introduced her to them? And do they approve of this match?"

"They thought an angel had dropped into their home from the sky, and that I must be the luckiest man alive," he looked down at Delphine, "and I am."

There was a long pause while Jorelial Rey stood silent, contemplating, arms folded. After what seemed an eternity, she sighed heavily, threw her hands in the air, and pronounced, "Well, it looks like we will be planning a wedding as well as a coronation."

"Oh, Rel, thank you, thank you!" Delphine flung herself at her sister and embraced her with such force that they nearly both toppled to the ground. Jorelial hugged her back, awkwardly, and then broke free.

"All right. I am *ridiculously* late for this banquet now, but I suppose that could play in my favor. Mark, would you say goodnight to your intended and escort me over there? I want you to point out some of the artists in your circle anyway. I'd like to get to know their names. I will send someone later on for the bags. Tvrdik, would you take Delphine to the kitchen for something to eat – you must both be famished – and then see she gets back to her rooms? May I impose on you one more time this day, my friend?"

"No imposition, my lady – a delight." was Tvrdik's reply. "How I love happy endings!" He smiled and offered his arm to Delphine. As the two couples exited into the night, the red-haired girl queried of her escort, "Why are you not invited to the banquet?"

"It's a long story," the mage replied, and Jorelial Rey turned back to catch his eye for a moment with a meaningful nod, then hurried away with Mark on her arm.

"Besides," Tvrdik continued, "big, crowded parties like that are not really my style."

"Oh, I can quite understand that," Delphine replied, "I never liked them much myself. Tvrdik?"

"Hmmmm?" She stopped them in the courtyard and looked him in the eye, "In our tradition, at a wedding, it is custom for the bride to be given to her partner at the ceremony by two close family members, representing male and female role models – god and goddess. My parents are not here. My sister will of course take her part as goddess, but, well, would it be too forward of me to ask you to consider standing by me at the ceremony on the other side? It would mean a great deal to me…"

A host of emotions played over Tvrdik's face, "Delphine, I am greatly honored to be asked, but we have only just met. Surely an old friend of your family, or one of the lords or ministers you've known your whole life would be a more appropriate choice?"

"No, there is no one I would rather ask. I know it has only been a week or so, but I felt drawn to you from the moment we first spoke, and I know I can trust you. Somehow I am certain you will be lucky for all of us."

Tvrdik's face fell as he realized the irony of her remark about trust. He hesitated, hung his head, then met her eyes, "Delphine, I can think of no sweeter task than to be a part of your wedding. Your faith in me and your friendship warms my heart. But, you spoke of trust, and I cannot permit you to go on believing in me when I have not been entirely honest with you."

Her brow furrowed, "How so?"

"I am not who or what I told you I was. If you have time now, I should like to tell you everything while we share a bite. It is likely that after you know, you will think twice about your offer, and indeed about whether you still consider me fit company at all."

Delphine grasped his hand and led him toward the kitchens, "Don't be silly – it can't be as bad as all that. Come, tell me your story…I have all night."

And so, the two of them found a warm corner out of the way of the busy kitchen staff, and away from prying ears. They heaped a plate each of sweet and savory foods, and he shared his tale with her; who he really was and how he had grown up around Theriole, and the tragedy that had resulted in his self-enforced exile in the forest. She sat with rapt attention and wide eyes while he told of Xaarus' sudden reappearance and his own recruitment to a mission. He told of his completed education, of Xaarus' instruction to find Jorelial Rey; shared with her the story of his journey back to court with Ondine, and all about his first meeting with the Lady Regent on that fateful recent night, and with the dragon Tashroth the following day. He spoke of the days he had spent repairing and restoring

Xaarus' old cottage, and the nights reading, studying, and practicing for the conflict ahead. He told her what had happened that day at the council meeting, and what they expected they would encounter in the coming weeks. In Delphine's trusting gaze, he felt it impossible to hold back, and it felt good, so good, to unburden himself of all the small deceits and misdirections with which he had begun their friendship.

As the story came to an end, he avoided her eyes, expecting her to be hurt and angry at the lies he had told. Instead the girl threw her arms around his neck and wept openly, exclaiming, "Oh, Tvrdik, you poor, dear man! Welcome home at last. How hard it all must have been for you. You will never be alone again – we will make sure of it. And thank you for all you are doing for my sister. She needs someone to stand by her, and support her, and listen to her, and help her connect with her best self. Not ministers and advisors; I mean a real friend. She has so few friends. And as far as your plan goes, Mark and I are solidly against using violence to solve things. We fancy ourselves to be creators at heart, not destroyers, and I know he will be excited about this idea you propose, quite as much as I am. I never really knew Xaarus – at least I was so young that I barely remember him. But I know you, and if you say this is what must be done, I believe you. We will all help. Consider us allies in your quest. And please, please, *do* consent to give me away at my wedding…" She sidled up to him with a coy expression, "I shall be the only girl in the realm with a real wizard at my ceremony." She giggled, then whispered to him, "I should dearly love to see some real magic…"

"All at the right time, my dear, all at the right time…"

"And to meet a real water sprite."

"That too. But even you sister doesn't know about Ondine yet."

"Ooooo! I love secrets." She beamed.

Tvrdik frowned, "Then you are not angry that I lied to you about my coming here?"

"You were not at liberty to tell the truth then, and actually, I'm not at all sure I would have believed you. How could I be angry? Tvrdik?"

"Hmmmm?"

"It's not your words that I trust so easily, but your eyes. They are sad, you know, and a little lost, but kind. I know you would never hurt me."

He looked at her once again, amazed at the simplicity and depth of Delphine's insight, and the breadth of her heart, and then he hugged her tightly, drinking in the goodness of unconditional love like a man dying of thirst. "I would be honored to help give you away, dear Delphine, and may you ever find your bliss and your heart's desire in this union."

Plates empty now and confessions complete, they realized their extreme weariness. He walked her to her chambers in the palace, and just before bidding her goodnight, Tvrdik reached into thin air and presented her with a little bouquet of spring flowers. She gasped in delight, and hugged him again, "Thank you, my dear wizard," she whispered, and slipped inside. Somehow, the wizard found his way back to his own room, his head reeling with images of all that had transpired that day. Bone tired, and only half aware of what he was doing, he washed and changed and fell into the soft bed, replaying those images in confused bits and pieces in his dreams.

Lord Drogue stood quite still, hands clasped behind his back, gazing up at a large portrait of a man with a fierce expression. The figure on the painting was slight, with long, black hair, a beard, and pronounced eyebrows knitted over intense eyes that stared out at the viewer. He was dressed in clothing long out of fashion, holding a very large antique sword in his left hand, the point facing straight up, but poised for action. Behind him, the artist had filled in a lush outdoor scene, but the sky was stormy, and the tops of trees bent low in a wind one could only deduce from its ravages. Drogue was alone in the hall where his ancestry was recorded in portraiture. Massive gilt-edged frames lined the walls on every side, but it was this image that had all of his attention. The mountain prince spoke aloud, though his only audience was a crowd of painted ghosts from the past.

"How many times have I heard the story, great, great-grandfather? How much a sacred part of our lore it has become: a tale of two noble youths, equal in gifts, and bonded heart to heart. How they played and grew together, studied and sparred together, achieved great things and garnered accolades, side by side. And when the alien hordes came to take Eneri Clare, they united the provinces and beat back the assault together. Each of them performed admirably in battle, each did his part to send the invaders packing. Both were wounded in brave struggle. And yet, when the dust settled, and peace returned to a unified land, only one of them was named king. The other was relegated to a remote, undeveloped land, where the labors of wresting fields, estates, and precious metals from the reluctant earth sapped his strength, and ended his life before it had run a fair course. Why was that, great, great-grandfather? Why did the golden house of Darian assume the crown, while the house of Drogue was made to wring every drop of its wealth from the hard earth? Hmmm? Did they quarrel, those boys? Was it over a woman? Power? Some ephemeral ideology perhaps, on which they could not agree? You do not yield your secrets to me, my esteemed forebear, but I smell the rotten aroma of betrayal. Darian wanted to rule. Kings do not share, and just like that, enduring friendship becomes irrelevant."

"Well, you may rest easy in your grave now, great, great grandfather. Our time is coming. The house of Drogue will take its turn at the helm, and I will be the one who sets it there at long last. One hundred years is quite long enough for the line of a false friend to reign. I am about to avenge the indignity you suffered, and take the crown in your revered name. Everything is in place. I have planted the seeds over time, and it will not be long before the fruits of my labors are ripe for harvest. I gave them the opportunity to cede the kingdom peacefully to my superior skills, but they refuse to see the truth. No matter. I will take what has always been ours, more roughly now, and it will not be as pleasant for them. They have made their choice. Ah, grandsire, how satisfying it will be for you to see your descendant take possession of what you were denied so many seasons ago. Perhaps, from wherever you sit now, you will bless the labors of this devoted servant who is the arm and engineer of your triumphant restoration."

Drogue bowed low with a slight flourish, then straightened and turned away from the portrait, making his way to the door with silent, swift footsteps. He had almost left the room, when he halted, stood still for a moment, as if contemplating his options, then retraced his steps until he found himself before the very last portrait in the room. He lingered, head bowed, for an uncomfortable interval, then slowly raised his eyes to meet those of the portrait's subject.

This painting was different from all of the others in the gallery, in that it portrayed two subjects, an older man with his arm around the shoulders of a youth. The older man was dressed all in bright cloth of gold, and he could have been a twin of the current mountain prince, save for a more muscular frame, and eyes that were set a bit further apart in his countenance, a phenomenon that made him look somehow kinder than Lord Drogue. There was sadness in those eyes, underscored, as they were, with a hint of shadow, and the arm that rested on the shoulders of the painted youth gave the impression both of ownership and of protection. It was a masterful painter, now forgotten, who had been able to capture so much subtext with mere cloth and color.

The young man in the painting did not bear a close resemblance to Lord Drogue, or to any of the other portraits on the walls. He was tall and well filled out, with broad shoulders, and wavy brown hair that framed an open, friendly face with a genuine smile. Richly dressed, with a touch more lace and ornament than that displayed by his elder, one might assume he favored his mother more truly in both face and temperament.

Lord Drogue smiled, but the gesture did not touch his eyes. "Yes, Father, I could not leave without paying my respects to you, and to my dear brother, Abendor. I trust you might have overheard my intention to take the throne? Doubtless you can scarce believe a 'worthless, ill-conceived mistake' such as you always called me, could ever pull off such a stunning achievement. Ah, but you always did underestimate me, father. For you, it was always Abendor. Abendor this, and Abendor that; Abendor the golden child, the light in your eye – a light that was snuffed out once he was gone. Poor Abendor. You never did believe me about the accident, father, did you. But seriously, did you think I was such a monster as to wish harm on my own brother? Hmm? Did you? And if your worst fears were proven true, what did I ever get out of it, eh? Certainly not the transfer of your affection, or any attention from you whatever excepting your contempt. Well, perhaps now, you will turn that noble head in my direction and take notice. You will see your son, your misbegotten, second son, ascend the throne of all of Eneri Clare, a throne he captured with his own wit and strong arm. And, you will perhaps beg my forgiveness for never thinking that I was worthy of your respect. We will see who is worthy in the end, old man. We will see who holds all the aces..." Drogue glared at the portrait one moment more with narrowed eyes, then turned on his heel and strode from the gallery, leading with the top of his head like a bull about to gore and toss aside some frustrating obstacle in his path. Generations of Drogues stared after him, moved by neither his promises, nor his taunts.

SIXTEEN

CELEBRATIONS

Over the course of the next week, Theriole, its grounds, and indeed the entire city of Therin were abuzz with public preparations for a Coronation – an event which usually took place only once or twice in a lifetime. There was work for every soul who sought it. Gold and silver were changing hands in a steady stream in all the shops, and a spring-like excitement lifted everyone's mood from under the shadow of autumn's catastrophes. The rains finally came in earnest during the first part of the week, which wrought havoc at the tented campsites of all the visiting lords and ladies, but could not dampen the enthusiasm with which everyone prepared for the coming event. Life was good. Order would be restored. A king would be crowned and his regent set in place.

The economy boomed as clothing, foodstuffs, and decorations had to be crafted and purchased, entertainments rehearsed, and halls scrubbed sparkling for the gala festivities. A week was not nearly enough time to prepare for such an enormous affair. But, Jorelial Rey, and her steward Bargarelle had been putting the pieces in place for months, in anticipation. Lord Drogue's petulant tirade was all but forgotten in the atmosphere of hope and delight which buoyed the entire kingdom, and most who even remembered it wrote the incident off as idle ramblings from a disgruntled border lord, or perhaps a touch of indigestion.

Quiet preparations were also going forward for Mark and Delphine's wedding, which, partly for expedience and partly out of some perverse sense of humor, was to take place in a lovely, obscure corner of the palace gardens on the very morning of Coronation day. It was to be an intimate, private affair among the flowers and statuary; just the happy couple, Rel and Tvrdik, Mark's family, and Nyree – Mark's teacher and head of the harpers' guild. She was one of the most seasoned and respected bards in all the kingdom, and despite her white hair and failing eyesight, she still had a voice of such unearthly beauty that it stopped people in midstride. No one knew exactly how old she was, and there were rumors that she was half elf, or fairy – rumors she would neither confirm nor deny. Listening to her, one was easily convinced that they were true. Nyree rarely ventured far from her home these days, but she had always been rather fond of Mark, and he prevailed upon her to come and officiate at the ceremony as his special gift to his bride. Delphine would have loved to have included the young king Darian in her wedding party as well, since they had always shared a special bond. But with his Coronation just hours away, and legitimate security concerns, his attendance was judged to be an unwise move. Delphine was disappointed, but made the sacrifice for everyone's peace of mind. Tvrdik managed to wrangle Stewart an invitation, a gesture which thrilled the big dog almost into a frenzy. Tashroth, too, would be able to stand nearby on a clear stretch of lawn, and oversee the proceedings.

Jorelial Rey had at first been furious to learn that Tvrdik had divulged all of his secrets to her sister on the night of the Grand Council. But Delphine swore on everything she held dear that no one except Mark would hear a word from her lips, until Rel deemed it wise to reveal Tvrdik's true identity in public, and the Lady Regent calmed down. In fact, it was a relief to have someone close to her know what was going on, someone she could talk to freely without keeping key points concealed. And she was delighted that Delphine had invited Tvrdik to be a part of her wedding ceremony. He had been privy, in his brief time there, to all the drama leading up to the occasion; it only seemed fair that he should also share in the happy conclusion.

After the Grand Council, Tvrdik had gone back to work on The Cottage, redoubling his efforts to get himself moved in by week's end, as Mark's family would be taking his rooms at the palace. On rainy days, he worked indoors: cleaning, scrubbing, arranging, and decorating the rooms in which he expected to be living and working. He took Lady Rey at her word, and revisited the market one day to order curtains, hangings, kitchen necessaries, and a new feather mattress for the bedroom (he had grown rather accustomed to the one in his palace chamber). He wasn't by nature extravagant, but she had said he should be comfortable, and he realized he was outfitting this house for the foreseeable future. Two new soft chairs followed for the sitting room (as he would likely be entertaining visitors there), as well as a new chair for the library, and several throw rugs for the floor. Paint and brushes came back with him as well, and he set about making the bedroom and sitting room inviting. Stewart was there almost all the time now, keeping him company, and assisting where possible. The dog seemed to have decided he had a personal stake in this project. And, though no words were exchanged on the subject, Tvrdik would have been most happy to have Stewart just move in. Whenever the weather cleared, the mage spent his time outdoors in the garden attempting to salvage what useful vegetation still grew there. He weeded and dug and cut back and moved things until he was fairly sure the herb garden and some of the root crops would thrive. Anything else that was already flowering, he left alone for sheer delight. It was all exhausting physical labor, but he was accustomed to hard work, and tackled the challenges with fervor, buoyed by the prospect of settling into a place of his own.

Delphine came by one afternoon at midweek, and dragged him off to the market again to help her shop for wedding things. It turned out that she actually did want his help in selecting accessories, but that the main item on the agenda was fitting him for a new suit of clothing appropriate to his role in the ceremony. Tvrdik was a little squeamish about the cost of the fashions the young bride preferred, but in the end, he let her dress him, reasoning that for this one occasion, everything should be as close to perfect as possible in her eyes. They settled on a tailored, long silk jacket in a rich cobalt blue, with buttons of gold and gold-threaded embroidery across the breast and down the sleeves. Matching leggings and dyed soft boots completed the picture, which was, he had to admit, very complimentary to his frame and coloring. Delphine was having the time of her life, and was positively glowing, Tvrdik noticed. Her mood was contagious – she had him laughing and exchanging stories throughout the afternoon as if they had been friends for ages. She also took the time to explain in detail exactly what would be expected of him at the traditional joining ceremony in his capacity as surrogate father, and she walked him through the simple rituals involved.

Later that day, between rehearsals for the Coronation music, Mark joined them to help move all of the mage's things into the freshly refurbished home, and Tvrdik invited the young couple and Stewart to stay for tea. What a delight to be able to actually offer hospitality to his new friends! They ended up staying into the evening in serious discussion of Xaarus' plan for defending the kingdom against Lord Drogue, should things come to that. Mark revealed himself as a serious, principled young man who embraced the idea of bloodless, creative warfare right away. He contributed many good ideas of his own, and promised to work on enlisting the whole company of harpers as allies in the project as soon as the word was given.

After Mark and Delphine had finally departed for the palace on that warm, starry evening, Tvrdik stood at the gate and reflected that it had only been a few short weeks since his arrival as a stranger in rags, alone, unknown, and carrying a great burden. Already he was settling into his own home, dressing like royalty, spending happy times with good friends and sharing his burden with partners who were eager to help. He sighed and looked up at a clear night sky liberally sprinkled with bright, pulsing lights. Then the young mage closed his eyes, a prayer of gratitude overflowing his heart. Returning inside, he doused the lamps and retired for the first time to his own bed in Xaarus' old bedroom, in the house he was slowly making his own. He slept peacefully, without dreams.

The next day was Friday, and with both ceremonies looming, Tvrdik decided to take a rare day for rest and regeneration. There was always more work to do, but most of it could wait now. What was essential for his simple needs was in place, and even beginning to seem cozy. Stewart excused himself to take care of some personal business. So, after fixing himself breakfast and cleaning up after, the young wizard found himself with time on his hands. He wandered into the library, which had been his master's pride and joy, and let his eyes wander over all the titles at eye level. Many he recognized from his studies so long ago. A few were in foreign tongues, or had titles so long and technical that he mentally put them aside for another day. One volume stood out, catching his eye several times as he scanned the shelves. It was called, *The Qualities and Uses of Colored Vibrational Energy – a Comprehensive Guide*. Well, that sounded as dry as the rest, but it was as if some unseen hand was insisting that he notice that particular tome. So he pulled it out of its place, blew off the dust, and sat down in his new comfortable chair by the cold library hearth, adjusted his glasses and opened the front cover. The book was quite old, written by hand in a graceful looping script. Something about its feel drew him in instantly. Almost an afterthought, he flicked a finger and created a hovering glow right above his chair…though it was high morning the book-lined library walls did not allow for sufficient windows, and he had long ago learned a hard lesson about reading in dim light. He called for sweet tea to prepare and deliver itself to him where he sat, and settled into his study in earnest.

Several hours, chapters, and cups of tea later, he emerged from the ancient, fragile pages feeling like he had just stumbled into a great treasure trove of important information. But his brain was saturated and he needed a breath of air and a change of scenery. He unfolded stiff limbs from the chair, turned off his magical reading light, laid the book on the seat with care, and sent the tea things back to the kitchen to sort themselves out (there were indeed some perks to being even a novice wizard). Stewart had not returned, but the day remained bright and pleasant, fresh after all the rain. He let himself out, and peered down the road toward Theriole. But he could imagine how everyone in the palace would be overwhelmed with tasks and preparations for the events of the following day. There would be a great deal of bustling about and frantic activity in nearly every corner. He decided that he might be more in the way than helpful, and let his feet wander in the other direction, to the little secret sanctuary on the riverbank where he had liberated Ondine.

Warm in the bright sun after the exertion of walking, he took off his shirt and boots, folded them and placed them on a boulder. He sat down in his accustomed place on the sun-baked flat rock, his bare feet dangling in the cool, rushing waters. Dappled sunshine filtered through leafy branches, tracing shifting patterns on his chest and legs. He set his hands down on the bare rock behind, leaned back and turned his face, eyes closed, up to the shining sky. Sounds of all sorts tumbled into his ears: birdsong, insects buzzing very close, rustling leaves and creaking branches tossed by a breeze, rushing water in rhythmic flow. He loosed the reigns of his mind awhile, after having spent the morning in deep concentration, and allowed it to drift where it would. But today, it went nowhere in particular, choosing instead to revel in observation, in vacant openness. Tvrdik enjoyed staying busy, but now and then it felt good just to be alive and aware, present in the moment, immersed in nature, no past or future, no hopes or dreams or plans, no problems needing to be solved, no anxieties or fears, guilt or grief. Just sensory input and the leisure to enjoy it. He did not know how long he remained in that position, sun on his face and earth's music in his ears, when another tune imposed itself on the subtle symphony – something familiar and pointed – a whistle, an awkward, charming melody. Tvrdik sat straight up, opened his eyes and blinked at the sight of a smiling blue face suspended only inches from his own. Then it vanished, plunged into the waters below, startling him with the usual shower of droplets and causing him to cry out in good-natured protest.

"Ondine, you wicked little imp! What am I going to do with you?" Laughing out loud, he shook the water from his arms and wiped his face. "It is always a delight to see you, dear friend. Come closer...I have the whole afternoon, and I would love to hear all about what you have been up to." As they chatted, an idea dawned in his mind, one that seemed finer with each revisiting. "Ondine..." he interrupted a story she was telling, "How would you like to go to a wedding?"

Saturday dawned clear and fair, the horizon adorned in pink and orange streamers as the sun lifted its head over the rim of the world. It was a perfect backdrop for a wedding, Jorelial Rey thought, wondering if her sister had special cosmic contacts with the weather gods, as well as with all the merchants in the village who had offered so many complimentary items for the occasion. Delphine had a way of charming the trees to change color at her request. Well, she deserved a magical memory of this day, anyway, and Rel was happy that even nature was conspiring to contribute her most perfect arrangements. The Lady Regent, like all of the wedding party, had already been up for hours, bathing, dressing, adorning herself, and preparing for the ceremony and the rest of the day. It was going to be long and demanding, but the sweetness of its opening would hopefully set the tone for all that followed. The corner of garden Delphine had chosen was a meditation area almost entirely closed off by tall rhododendron bushes, just beginning to bloom. There was a circular cobblestone expanse, approached by paved walkways from east and west. In the center stood a large, ornate fountain surmounted with six stone swans, and curved benches all around the edges. Flower beds surrounded the cobbled area, scenting the air and delighting the eye with a profusion of color. For this occasion, petals had also been strewn over the stone walks and around the fountain, and delicate windchimes were hung in branches, adding their random, crystalline tones to the orchestra of birdsong at dawn, and the burbling rhythms of the fountain. Every sense was uplifted by something lovely served up by nature or craft. All was perfection.

As the sun's rays first appeared over the pink-golden horizon, Nyree began to strum her harp, deep-toned and rich, and to sing the traditional opening chants appropriate to a joining. Her ethereal voice made the familiar tunes sound like heavenly music:

The journey of a lifetime is your own.
The roads you travel you must choose alone,
Until the day your soul's desire is known; you want to share it.
And all at once you're reaching out a hand,
And turning down a path you hadn't planned,
But when the winter comes, you know you'll stand, together bear it.
Walk with me through dark and light,
My desire and my delight.
In your eyes my heart takes flight;
I'm safe, I'm home.
Be my teacher and my friend,
Now in youth, and at the end…
From this day our dreams we blend, under the dome…of heaven.

As Nyree's enchanting voice wound around bush and tree and into the ethers, Stewart, and Mark's sister Nelrose took their places on opposite sides of the fountain. Mark was next to proceed, slowly, ceremonially, down the western cobblestone walk, flanked by his beaming parents. They were simple but sweet-looking folk who were immensely proud of Mark's accomplishments, and now delighted in his chosen bride. Joining their family to the illustrious Rey line might be a daunting prospect for these humble folk, were it not for their deep belief in their son. Mark cut quite a figure in his emerald silk jacket, his brown curls falling to his shoulders and soft brown eyes shining in anticipation. His mother, more than a full head shorter than her boy, held his hand with both of hers, and seemed perpetually on the verge of weeping. They entered the space and approached the groom's assigned position in front of the fountain, Mom giving him a final squeeze and Dad, a manly handshake, and then both backed off to join Nelrose on the sidelines. When Nyree began the third verse of her song, it was time for the bride to make her entrance. Jorelial Rey and Tvrdik escorted her along the eastern walkway, one on each side. Delphine was radiant in a simple silk shift of pale spring green, ornamented and belted only with fresh flowers plaited into ropes. Her wavy auburn tresses framed her lovely face and cascaded down her back, crowned with a delicate circlet of fragrant flowers. Her intense green eyes were only for Mark as she made the most of this long, slow walk that would take her out of her childhood and into a new life of shared adventures.

At her right shoulder was Tvrdik, tall and handsome in his long cobalt jacket, his hair like white gold. On the left, representing the energy of the goddess bringing her sister forward, Jorelial Rey had broken her own tradition and worn a gown. It was a rich shade of deep red, accented with black lace at bodice and sleeves, form-fitting until the full, floor-length skirt billowed out beneath the hips and swirled around her ankles. She had gathered her long, dark hair in two braids, hanging in front of her shoulders, and a single substantial ruby hung upon her forehead from a ribbon pinned into her hair. This was an unusual look for the Lady Regent, but an extremely flattering one which showed off her feminine side.

Tvrdik was glowing with the joyful gravity of the moment, and with the great honor that had been bestowed upon him by Delphine. He stood very straight, and tried to play his part in a manner worthy of her confidence in him. He could not help musing, however, seeing these two sisters side by side, on how very different they were in almost every aspect: Jorelial slight and dark, an aura of strength, but also nervous energy about her, and a hint of something private, held in reserve. Delphine, on the other hand, was soft and shapely, even in the bloom of first youth, fair and graceful, quintessentially feminine, and utterly open in her expression, her eyes, her heart. Both of them exhibited the keen intelligence they had obviously inherited from their father – you could see it in the eyes, and on the brow.

And he already knew that both of them had good hearts, even if they were revealed in different ways. As they approached the fountain where they would deliver Delphine to her groom, Tvrdik caught a glimpse of the way she and Mark were gazing at one another, oblivious to almost everything except their feelings for each other. He felt a rush of joy for these two who so obviously belonged together, but also an unwelcome pang of envy, wondering if the same happiness would ever materialize for him.

At the same time, Rel was playing scenes from their childhood in her head, recalling laughter, tears, moments of closeness and of sharing: holding the babe for the first time, and being followed everywhere by the toddler; nursing her through illness and teaching her things; whispering silly secrets in the dark and giggling until they were weak and gaspingfor air; scolding her, and pushing her away during that brief time when it was so very inconvenient to have a little sister always underfoot; and their closer friendship of late as young women feeling their way into the world. Ten years was a large gap in age between them, but then not so huge, especially as Delphine was always precociously wise. Rel shook her head in disbelief that she was now about to hand her beloved sister over to the man she would be joining her life with forever. It had come so soon, unexpected, and while Rel was happy for her sister's good fortune, she felt keenly the loss of a relationship that could never really be the same again. Lost in these thoughts, she was almost startled when Tvrdik took her by the hand and led her gently back to stand with Stewart on their side of the circle.

The opening song had come to a close, and Nyree let her harp hang at her back. The famous bard stood facing the excited couple, flanked on both sides by family and friends. In her trained ceremonial voice, uncompromised by age, Nyree began the wedding.

"Friends, we are here together gathered, in the presence of air, water, fire, and earth, at the rising of the sun and the dawn of a new day, under the canopy of blue sky, and firmly standing on the green turf that is our support, to witness the sacred joining of these two precious lives. We are here to partake of their overflowing joy at finding one another, and to witness their commitment to journey together from this day forth. We are here to promise our support to this union, and to these individuals, in good times and in challenging ones, knowing that not even the best matched couple thrives without the nurturing of family and the strength of community. And, we are here to gift them with our sincerest wishes for their continued health, prosperity, safety, happiness, and love throughout their lives together. Mark and Delphine, is it your wish and your intention that you go forward in life joined as one, beginning in this hour?"

Together they responded, "It is."

Nyree turned to where the guests stood, feeling their energies despite her sightless eyes, "Is there anyone present who objects for any reason to the fulfillment of this sacred union?"

No one spoke.

"Then, let us now freely and with goodwill call forth the gods, goddesses, guardians, guides, nature spirits, and cosmic bodies to lend us their aid in magically knitting together the Path of Destiny for these two, Delphine and Mark..."

The ceremony went forward, with all of its symbolic gestures – rings were exchanged, hands bound together with a silver cord, wine was sipped from the same ancient chalice by both bride and groom, and the remainder poured over their joined hands. When the time came for the couple to profess their love and publicly declare their intentions, everyone was in for a wonderful surprise: Mark and Delphine had written their vows as a song, which they now sang in canon, with their strong, young, exceptional voices. Mark began, with Delphine answering back the same words and melody a fraction after. Later, they reversed the pattern, so as to symbolize equality in their relationship:

Heart of my heart, and soul that sees my soul,
What here we start, forever be my goal.
What once was part is now becoming whole –
You give yourself to me so sweetly.
From this day forth, you'll never be alone.
I'll help you carry every heavy stone.
This day I pledge to know and to be known...
To love and to be loved, completely.
I'll teach you faith, and hope, and joy,
I'll bring you laughter and sweet song.
And there is naught on earth that ever could destroy
The promise made this day that by my side is where you e'er belong,
Heart of my heart, and soul that sees my soul.

As the last notes of their duet drifted off into the garden, Mark's mother was weeping without shame, and there were others in the company who were not far from it. These two young people with their innocent, trusting vision of their future together had lifted and inspired every person present, and had wakened hope in the hearts of those for whom the future held uncertainty and darkness. Tvrdik and Jorelial exchanged a knowing glance – it was absolutely imperative that they succeed in creating a tomorrow that was safe and bright for this couple, and for all others like them. The Drogues of the world must not be allowed to triumph.

Nyree chanted final blessings, and pronounced the bride and groom eternally joined under the eye of heaven. Stewart's tail batted the air. "At this time," the bard continued, "it is customary for family and friends to come forward and present gifts of love to the happy couple if it is so desired."

Mark's parents exchanged a look, and stepped forward, his father pulling some sort of folded paper from a leather wallet he wore at his side. When he spoke, one noted the rich baritone of his voice which Mark had inherited, "We are not wealthy folk, son, but we do well enough. Land is our most valuable asset, and land is our gift to you and your bride. We know you will not pass your life with sheep and goats as we have, but we believe in your dream, son, and therefore we present the deed to the lower pasture, twenty acres, on which to build a home and your school, together with your beautiful Delphine. It will take time, we know, and we will help all we can. It is there for you when you want it." He walked forward and handed the paper to Delphine. Mark, clearly surprised by this generous gesture, was speechless. He hugged his parents, each in turn, and Delphine followed to thank them warmly. Nelrose, pretty in her mauve dress, next stepped up with a bundle she had earlier laid aside in the bushes, "It is a warm quilt for your bed, stuffed with clean new wool. Each panel has pictures of things special to you both: a harp, flowers, the mountains, and a green dragon....I– I made it myself. I've been working on it all year, hoping a wedding would come."

Delphine let Mark accept the package, and took both of the girl's hands in her own, "What a beautiful and thoughtful gift, dear Nelrose. We will treasure it always. Please know you will always be welcome wherever we are at any time. I have been blessed in my life with one amazing sister – older, to help and guide me. Now I am gifted with another, younger, and I hope I may be as good a friend to you as Rel has always been to me." Nelrose turned the same color as her gown, while Mark kissed her tenderly on the forehead and thanked her, admiring her handiwork.

Stewart stepped up next, "What I bring ye is trust – a gift not lightly bestowed. For humans of heart and integrity, such as yerselves, I do not hesitate to reveal my true nature. And what is more, I pledge the watchful eyes, the assistance, and the protection of all the talkin' beasts in the realm. We shall be near ye to assure yer well-being when ye least expect it. Call on us when ye are in need. So it has been agreed, and so swear I."

It was Mark's turn to respond in awe, "A rare and generous gift indeed, sir, and one we will do all in our power to deserve. Trust us never to betray your secret into the wrong hands, or abuse the confidence you have placed in us. Call on us as well, if we can ever be of service to you or your friends, and please relay our deepest gratitude."

"Hmmmm." thought Jorelial, "the boy does have a gift for poetry." And then she realized it was her turn to present a gift. Smiling, she approached Delphine, "My dearest sister, our father left both of us well provided for, and in any case, you know that whatever I have is yours. While I live, you will never want for anything you need, and I will help you with anything you desire to the best of my ability. That was always a given. So, I thought and thought on something more – well – *personal* to give you, from my heart, on this special day. And it came to me that maybe with all the chaos around the Council Meeting and the Coronation, and planning the wedding so hastily, that maybe you haven't had a chance to work out a wedding trip. You know, a retreat? Some time *alone* together, away from the goings on at Theriole? Well, Tashroth and I have a favorite place that we go whenever I want to escape, to relax and regenerate. It's a crater lake in the mountains surrounded by soft sand and forest. It's beautiful and pristine, and safe and comfortable this time of year. And there's not a chance anyone will show up to bother you as I'm pretty sure you can only get there by dragonback. So, tonight, after the festivities have wound down, and you can both get away from your formal obligations, Tashroth has consented to take you both there and help you set up camp. I've packed a small tent and food, and anything else I thought you might need – he can carry it all along with you. The ride itself is part of our gift,

Tashroth's and mine. It's so wonderful to be wheeling around the sky on his back. Anyway, he'll leave you alone and check in on you every so often just to make sure all is well, and in case you need anything. When you want to come home, you just signal him, alright?"

She was speaking very quickly, nervously, hoping they would consider this as wonderful an offering as she meant it to be. Jorelial fidgeted, awaiting their response. The couple exchanged a look, and then Delphine said, "But, Rel, this will never do. That's *your* place… your special, secret place….and …and Tashroth too! It's…it's too much."

"That's the whole point, though, isn't it, to share something that's really mine with those I love the most? Please say yes. Tash wants to give you something, too. And you'll love it there, I promise." Delphine and Mark glanced at each other again, and simultaneously succumbed to wide, delighted grins, "Well, then, if you're serious, yes! Oh, yes. It's the most wonderful, thoughtful idea ever, Rel. Thank you, thank you so much." Delphine was hugging her sister and nearly bouncing with excitement. A shadow passing overhead caused them all to look up, just in time to see Tashroth's oversized face swinging in over the rhododendrons. He had curled himself on the lawns just beyond for the entire ceremony and now looked in to pay his respects to the bridal party. The deep, musical voice rang out, "A hearty congratulations to you, little sister, Mark. You make quite a handsome couple. I wish you every happiness."

Mark's mother was clinging to her husband in terror as if she were about to faint (likely the reason Tashroth had chosen to monitor the proceedings in secret up to this point), but young Nelrose lit up in absolute glee. "Can I touch him?" she asked Rel in an awed whisper. Jorelial nodded to her and showed her a place behind the ear that Tash enjoyed a good scratch now and then. *The girl has taste, and spunk to boot*, the Royal Regent thought, as she regarded Mark's fearless sister with a new respect.

Nyree's white head turned toward the commotion, "Ah, Lord Tashroth! How good it is to be in your presence once again. It has been far too long."

Tash acknowledged her with a special, gentle nuzzle, "Nyree, I would fly from across the sea to hear your rare voice one more time. The ceremony was, as always, memorably beautiful."

"My thanks, old friend," she bowed her head to him and added, "but the young people made quite a lovely contribution themselves, yes?"

"Impressive." Tash agreed, and Mark turned red at the compliment. Delphine jumped in, "Is it true, Tash?"

"What, little one?"

"Is it true you have offered to fly Mark and me away tonight? It's very out of the ordinary..."

"It will be my pleasure, little sister, to carry you both on your wedding day. I am at your service. Call on me when you are ready."

Mark spoke up, "Mighty Lord Dragon, I thank you for this generous gift..."

Tash chuckled, "We all wanted this night to be *memorable...* " Nelrose turned to her parents, enchanted, "Mamma, I want a dragon for *my* wedding!"

Mark's mother nearly *did* faint at that pronouncement, and Tashroth laughed outright, good-naturedly delighted by the youngster's fascination, "Come and find me when the time comes, little one."

Tvrdik was regarding Jorelial Rey from across the circle, watching her relax and laugh with the rest. He liked her this way, her guard down, all burdens of leadership set down for the moment, her personality allowed to just shine through with a dazzling brilliance. He felt inexplicably proud of her, guessing that it had taken a lot of soul-searching for her to give up her special secret retreat, her exclusive claim on the dragon. A worthy gift. As he stood there, musing thus, he realized that all eyes had turned toward him. Of course. He was the last of the wedding party not to have presented a gift. Almost as if it were choreographed, everyone present looked away again. He realized they did not wish to make him feel uncomfortable, assuming there was no way he could have any gift to present. Ah, but he was prepared. He stepped forward as the others had, and cleared his throat.

"Ummm, Delphine, it was barely two weeks ago when I arrived in this place, not a cent to my name, my few possessions on my back, and knowing no one. Right away, you offered me your trust, your smile, your friendship. You shared with me your deepest feelings, your fears and joys – shared Mark with me as well. And now, you have invited me to participate in this most significant moment in your lives, and made me feel like family. I do not know how I ever came to deserve any of this, but I am most grateful. I have nothing that belongs to me that I may give you as a gift. Still, I do not come here empty-handed..."

"Tvrdik, you don't have to...we never meant to...for you to feel obligated...."

"No, no, I *want* to give you something special in return for all your kindness. My gift to you is the fulfillment of a wish you expressed to me several days ago. But its purpose is to show you that, after all, the world you live in is a very magical and beautiful place. That even in times when all seems dark and hopeless and oh, so uninspired, there is always a magical adventure awaiting you, magical possibilities hiding just beneath the surface of things, if you only just look for them and believe. Will you remember that for me?" As he spoke, his voice began to take on a tone of authority not usual for him, and he was almost glowing with a strange, internal radiance. Even Tashroth was still, attending to the young wizard. Delphine wrinkled her brow in question, "Why, yes, I will, but what...?"

He held up a hand to interrupt her and she fell silent, glancing up at her new husband for an answer. Mark shrugged, and nodded. Tvrdik strode up to the burbling swan fountain, and held out his right hand as if presenting something, or someone.

"Ladies and gentlemen, I should like at this time to introduce you to a very dear friend of mine: an authentic naiad – that's 'water sprite' to the uninitiated – whose home is in a pristine waterfall in the heart of the ancient forest. She travelled all the way here with me from the wood in order to better know the world outside her small neighborhood. Friends, may I present the lady Ondine? You can come out now..." There was a moment of awkward silence, all eyes on the fountain, which flowed on undisturbed by anything unexpected for what seemed an eternity. Tvrdik shifted, cleared his throat once more, and stared at the waters, brows knitted. Then, in a heartbeat, a small blue, glistening ball of energy exploded from the basin, shot up into the air, hung there a moment and fell back down with a gigantic *kerplunk*, spraying everyone within a five foot radius of the fountain. A curly blue head poked out of the water, "Hello, lovely people. Happy joining day to you."

Delphine threw back her head and howled in unadulterated delight, clapping her hands and jumping up and down like a small child. For a second Tvrdik noted again just how similar the young girl and the water sprite were in so many aspects. Ondine leapt and spun and somersaulted in exuberant greeting, splashing everyone yet again. And then Tvrdik went down the line and introduced her to everyone individually, paying special attention to the bride and groom, the Lady Regent, and her dragon.

"Well, well," Tash purred, "I have not seen your kind in many a year. How delightful to meet you in person, Ondine!"

Ondine froze in the basin, staring wide-eyed at the huge dragon's head addressing her, a look of uncertainty on her small face. Then she shot up and planted a wet kiss right on the big beast's snout, "Hello, dragon! First time I meet dragon so close – not scary. Dragon sweet. Lovely Man, you not tell us dragon is sweet...why you not tell us?" Tvrdik's mouth opened, but he could think of no reply. Ondine turned her attention to the Lady Regent, who was staring at her with head tilted to one side and brows arched quizzically. "And Lady Juh-reh-lee-uhl." Ondine struggled with the name she had heard. "Pleased to meet you too. Hear much about you from my friend. Want to see you myself." Jorelial Rey cleared her throat and extended a hand toward Ondine's. Gently she grasped the tiny fingers, and did something like a formal handshake.

"I am astonished to meet in person such a wondrous creature, Mademoiselle Ondine. We would like to welcome you to our fair city and express our sincere pleasure at your visit. If there is anything we can do to make your stay more comfortable, please do not hesitate to ask. We are honored." Ondine gave her a pretty little bow and thanked her, stating she was enjoying herself 'plenty well' thus far. Then the nymph turned her attention to Nyree, "Oh, so lovely singing, beautiful lady. I like music, sing too. Someday, maybe we sing together, yes?" Nyree was smiling ear to ear.

"My, my, Mark, I had no idea when I consented to come to your wedding that I would be surprised by your interesting assortment of friends."

"Neither did I," interjected the groom sheepishly.

Nyree went on, "My dear little naiad, you make an old woman very happy with such a compliment. I shall be ever so glad to make music with you any time you wish." At that, Ondine rose up in the air and did one of her amazing pirouettes, causing everyone to gasp in delight and dissolve into laughter.

Delphine could barely catch her breath, "Oh, Tvrdik, this is truly too much. You are amazing. Thank you, thank you for this wonderful gift. I will cherish it in my heart and memory always, just as you say. It *is* a magical world, and I am blessed to have such remarkable friends. I hardly know what to say." She threw her arms spontaneously around the pale wizard in an enthusiastic embrace, and then stepped back to let her grateful regard fall on each who was present there, in turn. Nyree, always the wise woman, was the one to respond, "Child, they are all here because they love you, and you have earned that yourself by the way you have treated them. Remember the love you give will always come back to you a hundredfold. Never be afraid to love. It is always the appropriate response." Delphine squeezed the old bard's hand in acknowledgement, then turned to Ondine, "Thank you for coming to my wedding, Ondine. I shall visit you soon, and I hope we shall grow to be great friends."

"Oh yes, surely we shall. I bless your marriage now with a little bit of the old magic; we naiads are of water – we know water magic. Water flows, is powerful, deep, filled with shifting moods, but also healing, life-giving, thirst-quenching. I give you all these qualities for all your days together. Then you will never be bored, or dull, or rigid, and you will be life, and refreshment, and healing to one another. Now it is so."

Mark nodded to her with appreciation, and Delphine bowed her head, eyes closed. In the pause that followed, the Lady Regent snatched her opportunity to shift the mood, "Well, this was nice. Who's for some breakfast? I'm famished, and I'll bet it's still early enough for us to have the kitchen all to ourselves. And there may yet be time for a nap before the Coronation gets underway."

Tvrdik walked over to Stewart to trade greetings and commend him on his gesture. Tashroth courteously took his leave of the wedding party, then stopped to connect briefly with Jorelial. Delphine and Mark finally found a moment to seal their union with a long and meaningful kiss. Stewart trotted away on his own while Tvrdik made a point of greeting Mark's parents with a warm welcome and compliments on their son. Nelrose, beaming, stole an opportunity to stroke the dragon's lovely opalescent scales one more time before he withdrew his head from the arena. After a moment, they all saw him rise in the air and wing off into the blue distance. Then, as Mark and Delphine each attached themselves to one of Nyree's arms and escorted her down the cobblestone walkway toward Theriole, closely followed by Mark's entire family, Jorelial Rey lingered a moment to watch Tvrdik carefully gather Ondine up into a small basin he had hidden behind the benches. The little nymph was twittering and splashing in the bowl and the young mage was all smiles. Rel strolled over.

"Well done, my magical friend. You are ever full of surprises."

"I try. Well done, yourself. That was quite thoughtful and generous of you."

"I can do thoughtful and generous…sometimes." They laughed. "Coming to breakfast?"

"I'll just return Ondine to her favorite spot in the river, and join you all in a bit, shall I?"

"Good. Don't be long. Delphine would want you there. Ummm… Tvrdik, you know I can't invite you officially to the Coronation. It's a closed affair, by invitation only, being in a relatively small space, and people would wonder who you were…"

"I understand."

"I was wondering if I could, well, impose on you one more time, to, uh, to …do your bird routine? I know it's asking a lot. I'm sure you have better things to do with your afternoon…"

"I hope this doesn't offend you, Lady, but I was already planning on it. You never know what might happen at a crowded event like that. We can't be too cautious; an extra pair of eyes and ears might be useful."

She was grinning, "You really are too much, do you know that? Well, I can only say thank you, and I promise it won't be long before you can emerge from anonymity for good."

"All at the proper time. You have enough on your mind just now. By the way, you look lovely. That color and that style suit you well." He was appraising her appreciatively. She blushed.

"Not bad yourself. Quite the festive jacket!" Now it was his turn to blush and lower his eyes.

"Delphine picked it out."

"She has good taste." There was a brief, awkward silence, which Tvrdik broke.

"You should go. They will all be looking for you."

"Yes. See you. Don't be long." She turned and hurried to catch up with the others as fast as her gown would allow, leaving the wizard shaking his head, still smiling, gazing after her retreating figure.

After returning Ondine to her special river sanctuary, and thanking her for her contribution to Delphine's wedding, ("Oh, thank you, Lovely Man. I had such a very good time – love meeting all the new friends, hear beautiful music. You come take me to more special things anytime."), Tvrdik strolled back to the palace through the empty gardens at a leisurely pace. The day was promising to be warm with a clear, fair sky. *A perfect day,* he thought. He went straight to the kitchens, where he joined the others in a hearty breakfast already in progress. They hastened to set out a chair for him and made him feel welcome. The day would be long and full – no one knew when they would next find opportunity to eat. So they feasted on eggs and bread and fruit and fresh butter, warm milk and cider. To Tvrdik's delight, they even dug up some of the little custardy pastries he had developed a taste for on his first morning at the palace. He confessed that they were fast becoming his favorite treat, and they gave him two. They all lingered long at the table, eating and laughing and sharing stories in warm, easy fellowship. Mark and Delphine told the story of how they met, and talked with exuberance about their plans for a school, Nyree paying close attention, and showing more than a passing interest in their original ideas. Jorelial Rey described in great detail her favorite features of the retreat spot at the crater lake. This time the bride and groom were listening with rapt attention, excited about their upcoming escape to the beautiful place. Tvrdik was asked to tell all about his adventures in transporting Ondine from the ancient forest to Theriole, and he did have a few humorous moments to relate that kept everyone entertained. Nelrose kept asking Rel where she could get her own dragon, and the Lady Regent kept finding ways to obliquely avoid the subject, an accomplishment that earned her no end of devotion from Mark's mother. All in all, it was a morning of good fellowship and happy camaraderie that no one wanted to end, but as the last bit of bread disappeared, someone checked the hour, and they all reluctantly realized it was time to address the next of the day's obligations.

As they all parted for different destinations, everyone wished Mark and Delphine great happiness and thanked them for a lovely ceremony. The two sisters embraced long and tenderly and Rel shook Mark's hand. Then Tvrdik motioned quietly to the Regent, "I'll be there if you need me." She nodded and headed back to her rooms. The rest of the palace was already abuzz by now, as its inhabitants all rose to bathe, dress, and adorn themselves for the social and political event of their lifetimes. Servants bustled about in every direction carrying food, clothing, hot water, fresh towels, floral arrangements, cleaning tools, and hearth equipment. Making her way through the halls was like an obstacle course, but she managed to arrive in her rooms in one piece. Unfortunately, Bargarelle was already there awaiting her decisions on a hundred and one last-minute details that apparently no one else could handle. With a sigh, she set to work. If she had truly hoped for the afore-mentioned nap, it became a pipedream as the hours ticked by. She did finally get half an hour in a chair with eyes closed, and a chance to wash her face and re-braid her hair. And then it was time to make her way to the chapel.

SEVENTEEN

A NEW KING AND A CLIPPED WING

THERIOLE WAS NOT A SINGLE edifice, but a large, sprawling complex of buildings and additions which had sprung up over centuries around the original keep, as the inhabitants' needs had shifted from defense to a thousand civil functions. At one corner of this miniature city stood a very old chapel, or spiritual sanctuary, where the residents could celebrate their connection to a higher power, however they perceived it. There were many local flavors of spiritual practice scattered throughout the kingdom, and the builders wisely sought to bring together common elements in this sacred space, without making any of its citizenry feel uncomfortable or unwelcome. Eneri Clare boasted a tradition of tolerance which continued right up to the present time. It was in this chapel, then, that the coronation would take place, so as to invoke the blessing of Divine Providence, whatever the populace currently conceived it to be. The space was not large, only seating several hundred, which was why only the highest echelon of lords, ministers, ambassadors, dignitaries, civic leaders and their spouses could be accommodated for the actual ceremony. These few could then witness and attest to the fact that all the usual ceremonies and conventions were duly observed. The general populace could then welcome the new king outside on the palace steps, while feasting and secular celebration could later continue in many venues, both inside and outside of Theriole.

The chapel was beautifully decorated with breathtaking murals, carvings, stained glass, and statuary whose aim was to guide one's thoughts to otherworldly pursuits. It was always open to anyone who wished to engage in personal contemplation or prayer, except when being used for such formal, official occasions as weddings, funerals, celebrations of holidays, festivals, changes of season, commemorations, and of course, the occasional crowning. Senior bards conducted all solemn ceremonies, but as a coronation could be a long and demanding ritual, Nyree had declined the honor of performing it herself. She was quite comfortable attending as an honored guest, leaving the duties of her guild to her second, a fortyish veteran named Morelle. Morelle had been in the game a long time, had a pleasant enough tenor voice, and was more than competent on the harp. However, his true specialty was history, lore, and the preservation of traditional and ceremonial chant, a fact which made him uniquely qualified to preside at an occasion as ancient and ritual-bound as this one. There would be a small musical ensemble in the room to play during processional, recessional, and transitional moments in the service, but most of the actual chanting in the body of the ceremony was unaccompanied. Morelle had assisted fourteen years earlier when the young king's father had been crowned, and therefore was not only familiar with what was required in scholarly terms, but also by experience.

It was a perfect day, weather-wise – dry and sunny, but not terribly hot. The room was filled to capacity with the wealthy and influential of the kingdom, all dressed in their finest garments and ornaments. Everything moved along without a single unwelcome surprise. The musicians played while Jorelial Rey walked down the center aisle, leading her infant charge. They were followed by the High Ministers, Morelle, and Lord Maygrew. Each of these took pre-determined places at the front of the room before the eager onlookers. Chants were sung invoking the assistance and wisdom of the powers of the Universe, and special attention was paid to calling forth the symbolic divinities embodying Justice, Wisdom, Prosperity, Harmony, and Peace. There was a long section listing the young king's lineage, reinforcing his bloodline and birthright to the throne in front of all present. There were a series of questions of intention for the candidate, which the Lady Regent was allowed to answer in the child's stead, since he was so very young. There was a recited statement by the gathered witnesses, offering support and fealty to the rightful monarch. Then came the conferring of symbols of office – the Scepter of Power and the Yoke of Responsibility (which was really a very large pendant), as well as the ring with the royal seal. Sacred, fragrant oil was used to anoint the boy's yellow head, officially beginning his reign. Last of all came the crown (a child-sized replica was used for this occasion), a plain band of finest gold surmounted with the seven stars of Clare (also appearing on the kingdom's flag), each one set with a different precious gem cut to a brilliant sparkle. As Morelle set it on the new king's brow, the musicians played a stately, but joyful melody, and cheers erupted from the assembled crowd.

Given the length and complexity of the ceremony, one might have expected young Darian to have become restless and impatient. But he bore up well through it, standing quietly tall, and still as he could manage, paying careful attention to every detail. He seemed to have a self-possession and a grace well beyond his tender years.

As the room began to settle, Darian turned to face his subjects and lifted a hand, indicating that he wished to speak. Jorelial Rey's eyebrows arched in surprise, but she stood back and let the boy take charge.

"Now that I am king," he began in a piping, child's voice, and the room became hushed, "my first decree will be to make it a crime for wind and waves to overwhelm any traveler." There was a very audible intake of breath from most everyone in the room, as they grasped the poignancy of that pronouncement. "As your king, I decree that all children shall have warm clothes, and places to live, and food, and places to play. And that everyone be kind to one another." People in the crowd glanced around at one another, or lowered their heads, moved by the child's naïve wisdom. "Those are my wishes and my dreams. But for now, I rely on my Lady Regent, and the ministers, and Lady Delphine, and all my tutors, who are helping me to learn a great deal, so that I might become a good king, and make my father and mother proud of me." Darian gave a curt nod, indicating that he had completed his speech. The crown slipped to one side, and his pudgy hands flew up to make sure it did not fall. "Whoa!" he shouted, and a ripple of laughter ran through the noble assemblage, followed by applause, and sounds of approval.

Jorelial Rey, an involuntary grin on her face, and moisture in her eyes, reached down to conduct the little boy to a seat, whispering encouragements to him as the crowd's approbation continued. Darian, his little feet swinging back and forth beneath the seat of his rather stately chair, and all his attention now on tracing the ancient inscriptions embossed on the pendant around his neck, had spoken his mind without any coaching, and had won the hearts of his most powerful subjects. It was early in the game to know for sure, but he certainly seemed to have the makings of a fine king.

It would have been grand to end on such a high note, but the rituals were not yet over. It was now the Lady Regent's turn to answer questions of intent, to receive the promise of the masses and symbols of office. She too received a Scepter of Power and a Yoke of Responsibility, also a ring with the royal crest for her own frequent use. After Morelle offered a brief dissertation on the duties and privileges of regency, and Jorelial Rey stepped forward to publicly swear that she would faithfully discharge said duties, she was officially installed. Kneeling, she received her own circlet of silver with a single purple star, pressed upon her head. Another burst of music and cheering greeted her as she rose. Prayers were then offered for the new king and his Lady Regent, for good counsel and divine guidance, and for their wisdom and responsiveness to the needs of their people. Finally, a cry from Morelle of, "Long live the King and well may he rule!" was echoed first by the ministers, Lord Maygrew and Jorelial Rey herself, and then was taken up by the entire company assembled. The musicians began a cheerful little catch and the event was complete.

As King Darian the third and his appointed regent made their way back down the center aisle, this time stopping to make eye contact with or grasp the hands of many well-wishers on both sides, Jorelial Rey sighed in relief that this piece, at least, was finally accomplished; the rightful king was installed in his office with reliable support put in place until his majority. Now, anyone who stood against him was officially committing treason, a daunting deterrent for most would-be usurpers. It had been an emotional, memorable ceremony, the attendees seemed happy and enthusiastic, and would of course be feted for the remainder of the day. By any estimation, there should be a peaceful pause now to rest and regroup before the next crisis. Jorelial took the king's hand and smiled down on him, feeling that, for that moment at least, all was well with the world.

It was time for the customary greeting of the citizenry by the newly crowned king, from the palace steps. For hours, a huge crowd had been gathering in the forecourt and across the lawns, anticipating a glimpse of Darian III and a chance to cheer his ascendancy. There were villagers and farmers, shopkeepers, crafts-men and -women, artists, fishermen and sheepherders, weavers and cooks. There were women with newborn infants hoping for a benediction, and families who brought their elderly for a look at a royal countenance. The atmosphere was festive and collegial, as they all waited for the climactic event. Later on there would be feasting for all, provided by the royal coffers, and fireworks were promised, along with mead and dancing far into the night. The people were joyful, and filled with holiday spirit, greeting each other and wishing good fortune aloud to friend and stranger alike. Palace guards were posted all up and down the great stone staircase, and at intervals throughout the crowd. Their presence was as much symbolic as precautionary, but they nevertheless kept a vigilant eye out for drunkards, malcontents, and the usual altercation that might crop up in the crowded courtyard.

True to his word, Tvrdik, in his owl guise, was perched up on a stone scroll which protruded from the lintel above the main doors. From there, with his sharper owl's vision, he could peruse the crowd, and had a pretty good view of the steps as well. He heard the great oak doors creak open, and looked down to see Steward Bargarelle and Lord Maygrew emerge onto the slate stoop, closely followed by the High Ministers of Defense, Justice, and Finance, as well as the Lord Mayor of Therin and several other influential lords. Four ceremonial guardsmen flanked the knot of dignitaries, who stood about looking self-satisfied. At last, the Lady Jorelial Rey appeared, along with the young king, his golden curls adorned with the small jeweled circlet of gold, which glinted in the sun. He let go of Rel's hand and reached for his nanny, who had followed the notables out on the landing, and now took the extended hand firmly. But otherwise, Tvrdik thought, Darian seemed to be handling the long day's demands and the noisy crowd better than one might expect of a four-year old. Jorelial, in her striking red dress, and the sunny-headed king stood dead center of the group on the stairs, waving to the crowd, easy to pick out at any distance.

As soon as the child king appeared, a deafening cheer went up from the crowd, and continued to roar for minutes without diminishing. Folks waved hands and handkerchiefs, held up babes in arms, and whistled and stomped their approval. Jorelial looked bright and poised as she waved to the crowd. On inspiration, Lord Maygrew lifted the little boy to his broad shoulder, which elicited a fresh wave of shouting from the masses, as many more of them caught a glimpse of their monarch. Sensing the spirit of the moment, Darian began waving his tiny hand in the air at his subjects, a gesture that instantly endeared him to young and old alike. It was a brave and glorious moment, perfect in every respect.

Tvrdik gazed down with satisfaction at the idyllic scene on the steps beneath him. The next moment, an odd feeling shifted his attention. He would never know how, in the midst of all that noise, and in a veritable sea of waving arms, he caught the one motion that seemed out of place. It was far to the rear of the crowd, a small gesture that his owl eyes zoomed in on, a shape that did not seem to belong. And yet, for frantic seconds he could not put a name to it. His heart pounded as he strained to make out more. All motion slowed out of time; he was frozen in that eternal moment of question. And then he saw it all – the whole picture snapped into clean focus – the hooded man, bow held out before him and right arm drawn back at cheek level, a high-pitched *twang,* and the deadly arrow speeding over everyone's heads, aimed straight at the heart of Jorelial Rey! There she stood, smiling and waving, oblivious to the mortal danger that bore down upon her with terrible accuracy. Swift as thought, the owl/mage raised his wings and leapt from his perch. Extending his claws, he plummeted to the center of the scene below, beating his wings directly in the Lady's face, and then shoving his powerful clawed feet against her shoulder with all his might. Startled by the white tornado descending upon her, the Lady Regent instinctively ducked, and raised her hands in a protective gesture over her face. Then, caught off balance, she took the full force of the owl's attacking claws and fell to her hands and knees on the stone floor. There were gasps and screams as those around her saw her go down. But before anyone could move, they were confronted by the vision of a large white owl, wings extended. The great bird hung suspended for a moment in midair, and then careened backward in a tumble of feathers, as an arrow pierced its left wing.

In that split second of chaos, Lord Maygrew lowered the king to the ground and his nanny whisked him into her skirts. The guardsmen on the steps sprang forward to surround their leaders. The lords and ministers huddled in a tense knot, instinctively drawing together in front of the child to whom they had just sworn allegiance. The guards on the field dashed into the crowd, searching for the source of the offending projectile. The sounds of joyful celebration transformed into shouts, wails, and terrified cries. Rumors ran like flames through the courtyard. Families frantically tried to find each other, while many ran for cover, fearing some foreign attack was upon them all. Guards were pushing through the frightened mob in all directions. And then, above all the din, sounded a blood-curdling scream and the growls of some ferocious beast. A clearing opened near the center of the crowd, quickly widening as townsfolk scrambled to put space between themselves and the struggle happening there. The guards arrived to find a trembling, emaciated man in torn clothing, lying on the ground, bow by his side, pinned by a giant wolfhound, teeth bared and snarling. The man had his hands raised in front of his face, and was screaming and whimpering, begging for his life. A captain of the guard gestured for two of his men to take the bedraggled figure into custody, and he was dragged off into the palace, the huge dog following along behind, his stern brown eyes fixed on the captive.

Meanwhile, on the steps, barely a moment after the fateful arrow struck, the great white owl had vanished. Crumpled on the ground where it had been a moment earlier was a pale young man in a cobalt blue jacket, one arm of which was pierced through by a wicked shaft. Jorelial Rey first looked to assure herself that the king was safe, then rolled over and was just getting to her knees when she saw him.

"Tvrdik? Tvrdik!" she screamed, but there was no answer. Crawling to his side, she struggled to turn him over, and lifted his head and shoulders onto her lap. Her left hand came away covered in bright blood as she tried to cushion his head while avoiding jostling the awful dart. "Tvrdik, can you speak?" she asked him, then shouted, "Someone send for a healer."

Tvrdik raised his head to survey the damage to his arm, and seeing the arrow sticking out at a rakish angle and a bloody stain spreading, he winced and fell back with a groan of pain. Jorelial shook him a little, "Tvrdik, hang on. They are going for a healer now. Say something!"

He winced again, then croaked, "Delphine will never forgive me."

Jorelial started, "What are you talking about?"

"The jacket. It isn't even paid for yet, and I'm afraid I've gone and spoiled it already." He tried to smile, but it came out more of a twisted grimace.

"Oh, you ridiculous man," the Lady Regent scolded. "Forget the jacket – and what did I tell you about swooping in to rescue me?"

"Sorry," he groaned, "It seemed a good idea at the time..."

"Just rest here, don't move," she soothed.

"Don't worry, I'm not going anywhere. Awwwwfff..." Tvrdik couldn't help moaning as his shock gave way to searing pain.

"Where is that healer?" Rel shouted impatiently to no one in particular, but as she looked up, she saw the faces of Lord Corbin Maygrew, General Boone, and Bargarelle, their eyes wide, staring at her and her limp charge. She realized that, despite all the confusion on the stoop, they must have seen the mage's precipitous transformation. She swallowed, and met Maygrew's eyes. One brow raised, he broke the silence,

"Jorelial Rey, do you know something about this...this remarkable occurrence?"

She sighed, "I was going to introduce you as soon as the moment was right, but it seems the moment has been thrust upon us. Gentlemen, I would like you all to meet Tvrdik, apprentice to Master Wizard Xaarus. He has returned here after years abroad in order to offer his service. Friends, you may be looking at the last true wizard in the world, and I believe he has just saved my life." Nobody said a word for what seemed an eternity.

The first to venture into that uncomfortable pause this time was Tvrdik, who, with his signature crooked smile, managed to rasp, "Very pleased to make all of your acquaintances, I'm sure."

Maygrew blinked, then seemed to visibly pull himself together, "Guards, come and take this man within. Gently, now – watch that arm." As soon as they shifted him, pain shot through the downed mage, and he cried out.

"Careful." the Lady Regent commanded, "Take him to my own chambers; they are the nearest. Someone tell the healer to meet me there." They were already angling him through the great doors when he cried out again.

"What is it?" she asked.

"My spectacles. Do you see them?" he was quite agitated.

She felt around on the ground and found them, unharmed. She rose to her feet and placed them in his good hand, curling his fingers around the wire frames, "Here they are, just fine. Rest easy…"

"I…I'm lost without them…" he mumbled, but let himself be carried without protest, pain and loss of blood beginning to crowd out all other sensations. At that moment, Delphine tumbled through the crowded doorway, closely followed by Mark. She grasped her sister's arm, "Gods, Rel, what has happened? I just passed Tvrdik and he was bleeding and grey as ash! I couldn't even get close enough to speak with him."

In a low voice, but with barely contained rage, the Lady Regent filled her sister in, "Someone tried to kill me just now – no doubt a message from Lord Drogue. Tvrdik put himself in the line of fire." At Delphine's expression, she hastened to add, "He was injured, but I think he will be alright. They apprehended the man; we will question him later and get to the bottom of this. The king is safe. I am fine, don't worry. Delphine, could I impose on you to follow Darian and his nanny back to the nursery, and try to take his mind off all of this unpleasantness? Take Mark with you – you two are so good with him. I think we are all safe for now, but I don't want to take any chances. Once he is calm, he needs to at least put in an appearance at the royal banquet. I may be delayed myself; can I trust you to get him there if I can't?"

"Of course, Rel. Whatever we can do to help," Mark nodded, as his new bride went on, "Thank the gods you are alright." Delphine gave her sister a quick, but firm hug to punctuate the sentiment, and turned back toward little Darian, who was looking confused in his nanny's skirts.

"Wait a moment," the Lady Regent gestured for her sister to wait, and cast an eye over the milling crowd still scattered across the forecourt and lawns. Some had dispersed, some had run for home already, but the majority was still there, disoriented and uncertain in the deepening twilight. Not the best way to end this momentous day.

"Lord Maygrew, would you boost him to your shoulder again, do you mind?"

Taking her meaning, the big man approached and lifted the little golden boy high once more – a gesture that made the little boy laugh with delight. Jorelial Rey turned to face her audience, and projected her voice with as much authority as she could muster, "Citizens, subjects, and friends,

I beg you raise your eyes and see truly that your King and his appointed regent are unharmed. While we are most grateful for your concern on our behalf, we wish for you to go on and enjoy the festivities prepared for your pleasure. Spread the word – the crisis is averted, all is well. We must not let the actions of one traitor spoil the joy we all feel today. Our thanks to you all for your support." She smiled widely and waved again at the masses, standing tall and feigning more confidence than she felt. It helped that the little boy was also smiling, enjoying his human 'horsey ride' on Lord Maygrew's shoulder, the traumas of just a few moments ago completely forgotten. One could feel a collective sigh of relief pass through the entire assemblage, and gradually, arms around one another's shoulders, in groups of two or three or ten, the citizenry began to disperse, headed for the places where food and fireworks had been promised.

"Well done," Lord Maygrew commended, handing off a sleepy young king to Delphine, who immediately disappeared into the palace with the boy, his nanny, and Mark. "So, that owl was no owl from the beginning, eh? I might have known. We owe him a great deal, that young man. You were right. I should have taken Drogue far more seriously."

"This must have been his doing. I have information I have been keeping to myself thus far. It is time I included all of you and explained everything."

"About the wizard?"

"Yes, the wizard and Drogue and a great deal more. But I think we all have enough on our plates for tonight. Will you all come to the Hall of Audience tomorrow at, say, two o'clock, and meet with me concerning these matters?"

"With a willing heart, Lady," Lord Maygrew replied, and there were nods and general agreement all around. Boone stepped up to her side, "My lady, we will want to question the man who committed this treachery right away. We'll need some confirmation of who is truly behind this cowardly act of aggression."

"See what you can do. No torture. I must go now and attend to my wounded champion...I will come to you presently myself and hear the man's story, if he is talking. Lord Maygrew, it appears I may be detained once again getting to the official banquet. I will try to make a belated entrance, but can I rely on you meanwhile to greet the guests, see that everyone feels recognized and entertained? I've already recruited Delphine to escort little Darian around the room. I would be so grateful if you could consent to handle the dignitaries…"

"Consider it done," he replied, with a steadying hand on her shoulder. And with that, the lords and ministers all retreated into the palace, and hurried off to their various tasks. Jorelial Rey, however, stood still on the stairs, as a giant darkness fell over the palace lawns, and a hair-raising sound scattered what remained of the public in every direction. Tashroth had smelled trouble, and was trumpeting to her. A powerful rushing wind lifted her clothing and blew loose strands of her hair about her face as the dragon pumped its great green wings in preparation for landing. Most of the populace knew well the stories of Jorelial Rey, dragon rider, or had seen the odd pair wheeling overhead at some unexpected moment. The locals knew well not to fear Tashroth or doubt his intentions. Still, most of them had never been this close to a full-grown dragon, nor did they wish to be, especially one in such an agitated state. Tashroth set down with precision on the already trampled sod just in front of the palace steps, and his eyes were glowing with an unearthly fire. Rel ran out to meet him.

"It's alright," she cried, "I'm fine." He swung his great head back and forth several times and bellowed once again. Rel sped straight to his heart and placed her warm hands on his chest where he could feel her presence. Gradually, the dragon calmed himself, subdued by her purring reassurances, and swung his head down beside her to hear what had happened.

"Someone in the crowd fired off an arrow in my direction this afternoon. Somehow the guards missed it, and I was inches away from being a corpse this evening. No doubt Lord Drogue's work; with me out of the way, he may have thought to try again for the regent's spot. Not that he could ever again be seriously considered for any position except mayor of the lunatic asylum, after this. Next time he will probably go straight for the king, or for the both of us."

"It is a great torment to me that I cannot be everywhere you are to protect you, especially now."

"Tash, I'm a big girl – you *do* protect me on so many levels, but the facts are, there are many places you cannot go. I have to learn to look out for myself a little better, that's all. This one caught me off guard, but that won't happen again."

"How did you escape harm, dear one?"

"Remember, there was someone else whom you commissioned to be your eyes and ears wherever you could not be, Tash. Tvrdik took the arrow for me."

A deep rumble emerged from Tashroth's throat followed by a hiss. The dragon was clearly disturbed by this news.

Rel stroked his scales, "It's OK, Tash. It hit him in the shoulder. It's bad, but he'll recover. I know, I know, we owe him a great debt. He pushed me out of the way. He might have been killed, and then where would we be? He must have taken what you said very seriously."

"We are fortunate that he did. He has earned my heart's gratitude, and I shall send him what healing energy I can."

"It's become more complicated, though, Tash. Tvrdik took the arrow as an owl, his disguise while he spies for me. But the shock changed him back to a wizard right there in full view. The lords and ministers saw it all, and I had to tell them our secret. Now, tomorrow, I must fill them in on the whole story and plead Tvrdik's case. I was hoping for a little more time; I'm not ready for this."

"We do not always get to choose our moments, little one. Circumstances have propelled all of us into the very center of the storm. It would seem that now is the time to act. Lord Drogue has made that abundantly clear. Do not fear, dearest, your passion will persuade them all, and I will support you in whatever you decide to do. The opinion of a dragon may count for something still."

"I should think so!" she lingered for a moment, her cheek nestled against his warm scales, drawing in comfort and strength. Then she sighed, "Tash, I must go and check on Tvrdik. I don't know if Mark and Delphine will still want your services tonight, but I would encourage them to go and enjoy the time they have together. Would you still be willing to go with them? It would be an enormous favor to me..."

"You are sure you are safe? I am reluctant to leave you..."

"The danger is past for now. I am fine. There's really nothing else you could do tonight anyway. If they will go, please, will you do this for me?"

"I am yours to command dear one, as you see fit. Only take good care, and if you need me for any reason, summon me, and I will return in a heartbeat."

"I know Tash, I know. I am sorry to have given you such a fright. Wait for me on the roof. It might be hours yet before we know what else this night may bring."

"I await your pleasure." He touched her gently with his dragon's snout, and as she backed up and signaled to him, he lifted his great wings, rose from the muddy lawns, and circled once overhead before flying out of sight. She stood, staring after him, and then, remembering somewhere else she needed to be, she turned and strode back to the big oak doors, taking the stairs in twos. On the landing, servants were already scrubbing the bloodstains from the slate where Tvrdik had fallen.

EIGHTEEN

THE VIGIL

JORELIAL REY'S SUITE OF ROOMS at Theriole was conveniently near, though she seldom used them, preferring to spend her few leisure moments on the north tower with Tashroth. Those rooms that were often empty were now bustling with activity. The Palace Physician had arrived, along with several assistants, and house servants were dashing back and forth for hot water, cloths, blankets, and various other items. Warlowe had personally stepped in to direct traffic as soon as he had heard what happened. His face was white and pinched as he met her in the anteroom, and related to her what had transpired in the last half hour. They had laid Tvrdik in her own bed and covered him with warm blankets. But when the physician had arrived to assess the situation, the initial shock was beginning to wear off, and the patient had squirmed and cried out in pain, unable to hold still for the examination. As a student of Xaarus, it was probable that the young mage knew more about tending to a wound like this than all the palace doctors wrapped up in one, but he was in no shape at the moment to be making suggestions or arguing.

It was evident that the arrow would have to be removed, and there was no way anyone could endure that process while awake and alert. So they made him swallow a draught of some foul-tasting herbal tincture to calm him and dull the pain. Weak and miserable, he had gone right to sleep. The arrow had gone in just under the collarbone, beside his left shoulder, fortunately just missing his heart, lungs, and the bones in the area. But it was a thick shaft, and had pierced muscle and tendons, and possibly nicked

233

a fairly significant blood vessel, as evidenced by the copious bleeding that seemed to be impossible to staunch. The assistants had cut away his clothing, including the beautiful blue wedding jacket, now hopelessly stained anyway. They cleaned the site as best as they could, and then used heavy shears to cut the arrow just at the spot where it protruded from his shoulder. The feathered tail fell away, and they were able to pull the shaft out through the rear wound, continuing in the direction it had entered, but taking care not to dislodge splinters in his arm. Once the arrow was out, there was a fresh eruption of bleeding, which the healers had a devil of a time stopping. They applied poultice after poultice, infused with herbs designed to thicken the blood and ward off festering at the site, but for a while, the cloths soaked through in only a few moments. Just as the Lady Regent arrived, they were taking a chance that things had slowed sufficiently so that they could properly bandage the shoulder and immobilize it. Beyond that, there was not much more they could do besides controlling the pain, nourishing the body, and allowing the patient's natural healing abilities to take over. Then it would just be a waiting game to see if there would be any infection, or permanent impairment.

Jorelial Rey took all of this in with growing apprehension, but as Warlowe finished his update and led her into the bedchamber, nothing could have prepared her for the sight of the gentle, likable young man she had recently come to know, lying so drawn and still in her bed. Her attention was so focused on his grey face that she almost tripped over a large, furry shape at the foot of the bed. She looked down to see Stewart, distressed and panting. Warlowe remarked, "He followed us in here and won't leave. We tried to shoo him off, but he would not be lured or chased."

Her eyes met the great dog's in a knowing exchange, and she replied, "I have seen them together and believe they are acquainted. It is obvious the dog is concerned. Let him stay." The wolfhound looked up at her in gratitude, acknowledging her kindness and respect for his secret, then sighed, closed his eyes and laid his big head down on his paws. Warlowe went on, "My lady, perhaps you do not know that this is the same courageous beast who routed out and tackled your assailant before the guards had even gotten near."

The Lady Regent's eyebrows lifted, "Really? I had not heard of it. We must see him rewarded for his loyalty and bravery." Stewart raised his head again and seemed to angle it toward her in a sort of nod, then gathered himself up and trotted around to the side of the bed where the physicians were not working, and where Tvrdik's good hand hung down. There, he set about licking the young man's fingers – a poignant gesture, unaware as the patient was of these ministrations.

The Palace Physician addressed them now in a low voice, "This young man was in some ways very lucky, but we are not out of the woods yet. We think we got the arrow out clean, but he has lost a great deal of blood, and there is always the chance of fever and infection. He will need rest, and fluids – as much as you can get him to swallow – and someone should keep an eye on that bandage; change it every few hours. I will come around in the morning to check on him again. There's not much else we can do but wait and see. Keep him warm. If he wakes, he will be in pain. I have left more of that sleeping draught…he really should not be moved again if possible. Do you have any objection to his staying here a while longer, my lady?"

"No, no. He can remain right here, and I will make sure he is looked after as you say. It is small payment for saving my life. Thank you for your efforts, sir…you may take your leave."

The healer made a peremptory bow, gathered his equipment, signaled his assistants, and retreated through the outer door. Rel, Warlowe, Stewart, and one of the serving women who had been assigned as a sort of nurse, were left alone with the patient. While Warlowe and the nurse busied themselves straightening up, removing trash, soiled clothing, and towels, and stocking in supplies for the vigil ahead, Jorelial took the opportunity to approach the bed. She sat down in a big, comfortable easy chair that had been moved near to the patient's head. An end table stood beside her, holding a basin of cool water and a clean cloth. She dunked the cloth in the basin, wrung it out and gently wiped his brow with it, as she had done years ago when little Delphine had taken a fever. She smoothed the pale golden hair away from his even paler face, feeling a confused mix of emotions, a jumble of thoughts crowding in on her weary mind.

Only weeks earlier she had not even met this man, or known of his existence. A part of her wished things might return to what seemed like a simpler time before his arrival. He had so quickly turned her world upside down, and things were likely to get much worse before they got better.

And yet, it wasn't fair to blame Tvrdik for their current circumstances, which would have played themselves out in any case. Tvrdik had only been the unwelcome messenger. He had come to offer knowledge, to offer solutions – to offer himself. Her eyes traced the still features, seeing them animated, in her mind's eye, as she remembered them at various moments in their time together. In truth, she reflected, this young man had been nothing but kind, warm, funny, honest, and reliable. Ultimately, he had been willing to sacrifice his own safety, even his life, for her. How many people in her world – friends, peers, courtiers, ministers – how many could she truly say that about? Even her beloved sister had sneaked off behind her back, in an appalling lapse of judgment. If she was truthful with herself, her father and Tashroth had been the only beings in the world in whom she put her absolute trust. She had no other real friends. In the brief time since he had come into her life, Tvrdik had treated her like a friend, and she had been grateful for it, had even begun to take it for granted.

Replacing the cloth in its basin, Jorelial Rey rose, leaned close to the still face on her pillow, and whispered, "I have been telling everyone you will recover. You had *better* recover, you foolish, brave, ridiculous, dear man. Because, I will tell you one thing: I am *not* going forward with any of these insane plans on my own. And besides, I have grown rather used to you being around. So don't even *think* of bailing out on me now, because it is simply out of the question. Do you hear me? *Out* of the question." Tvrdik moved fitfully for a moment, but did not wake. When he settled back again, she could almost swear there was a hint of a crooked smile on the dry lips. A sound in the doorway caught her attention. Delphine had come to find her.

"Come in, Sweetpea. What's the news out there?"

Delphine approached and her brow wrinkled at the sight of Tvrdik in the big bed. "Umm…Lord Maygrew is doing a wonderful job circulating with the king among the banquet guests. Everyone was buzzing about the excitement on the steps, but Maygrew is brilliant at diffusing people's fears and speculations. He had them all redirected to the food, the fireworks, the ceremony, and the latest gossip and politics. Before long they had forgotten anything disturbing had happened at all. I wasn't needed any longer. The guests seem well satisfied, and Darian will be trundled off to bed soon. There are guards assigned to his person at all times now – General Boone's doing. They will stand outside his room all night. I think you can rest easy that all is under control. How is he doing?" She nodded toward the patient.

"He's sleeping now. They've done all they can for tonight. Time will tell. Delphy? I still have to go and confront the man who attacked us, and I probably should make some kind of appearance at the festivities, even briefly, just to reassure everyone. Could you...would you be willing to stay here with him – sit with him while I go and take care of those things? I hate to take you away from Mark on your wedding night, but Tvrdik really shouldn't be left alone, and I don't think I will be too long..."

It's fine, Rel. Mark is busy playing at the banquet anyway, and won't be free for hours. I'm all yours."

Jorelial arched her eyebrows, and let out a single laugh, "Well! Welcome to life as a musician's wife. Still, I do appreciate your help. I'll be as quick as I can."

Delphine put a hand on her sister's shoulder, "Take your time. Tvrdik is my friend, and besides, he saved my sister's life. Happy to take my turn here." Rel watched as Delphine took her place in the chair, leaned in, and affectionately stroked Tvrdik's hair with her delicate hand. *Nurturing seems so easy and natural for Delphine,* the Lady Regent reflected. Stewart chose that moment to spring onto the bed and curl up in a vacant corner, lending his own energy and body warmth to the mage's thin frame.

Knowing she was leaving her rescuer in good hands – and paws – Jorelial Rey hurried out of the room, out of her apartments, and through the maze of hallways that led to General Boone's offices. Presuming that the suspect would have been taken there, she swept up to the Defense Minister's door, and was gratified to hear voices on the other side. She knocked to get the attention of those within, and called out, "General, it's Jorelial Rey. May I come in?"

The door swung open to reveal a weary, grizzled face, "Of course, my lady. We have been expecting your arrival." He motioned her to a chair near his own. Seated across the room on a hard wooden stool, flanked by armed guards and quivering miserably, sat a slight, dirty man, poorly dressed in worn and shredded clothing. He did not raise his eyes from the floor. Somehow, Jorelial Rey did not think he looked so much dangerous as pitiful. But Boone was taking no chances, and had him restrained.

"Have you discovered anything so far?" Rel asked the General.

"Only that he is indeed guilty of this reprehensible act, but was put up to it and paid by someone else."

"May I question him, or am I interrupting something in progress?"

"Be my guest, my lady; perhaps you will get more out of him than sniveling and whimpering." Boone gestured with his big hand that she should approach the suspect and proceed. She paused a moment with brows knitted, looked the man over, and decided on a straightforward approach.

"What is your name, sir?" The man remained silent and motionless for a beat, and the General barked out, "The Lady Regent is addressing you, man! You *will* answer." The man jumped as if he had been physically struck, and mumbled a barely audible, "Praeger, my lady."

"Praeger, then," she continued "do you know why you are being held here?" The man nodded slowly up and down. "Praeger, there are eye-witnesses who claim to have seen you with a bow. They say it was, without doubt, you who released that arrow which came so near to striking my person. Do you deny that this is so?"

Without raising his gaze from the floor, the man shook his head from side to side. No denial, then.

"Praeger, do you have any reason to want me dead?" Praeger looked up and met her eyes. His own were tortured.

"I – no, my lady – not for myself, anyway, only *he* says it must be done…"

"Who said? Did someone recruit you to try and kill me? Who was it, Praeger?"

"I – I don't know his name, Lady. A highborn lord, he was. Expensive clothes; black hair and brows. He says the young king'd fallen under the influence of an evil witch, and that with her sorcery, she'd charmed all the palace folk into settin' her up as regent for keeps. He says it were a dark day for every good citizen, and that the king must be saved from her wicked control, or terrible things'd happen. He tells me he's lookin' for a brave soul to rid the land of this canker once and fer all."

Lady Rey, while taken aback by the horribly false characterization Drogue's twisted mind had invented, wanted to understand more.

"And, how came you to this highborn man you did not know, Praeger?" Somehow she sensed that her repeated use of his given name was cutting him to the quick, wearing him down, as if she was seeing into his soul. He was trembling uncontrollably again.

"Two men. They come to my door and they shove their way in. They was ugly, ma'am – sinister, if ye know what I mean. My wife, she were terrible afeared o' them. But they smiled and spake as they were there to do us a great favor. Says they'd heard we'd fallen on hard times, and asks if I might be willin' to do their master a service for a price. I didna like their looks, ma'am, I swear it, but we needed money so badly, and they didna seem the sort to take kindly to not getting' their way, if ye take my meanin', ma'am. So I – I says I might be interested. They blindfold me right there, and push me out o' the house. We was on horseback, seemed a fair many hours, and then, I were standin' in this big room, all fashioned o' raw timbers, an' I am starin' right at this highborn lord, sittin' in a big chair, som'at like a throne it were. He smiles at me, and speaks o' how he has to stay hid because o' politics an' bad forces in the palace and some such, but he swears he just wants to save our little king from the Shadow. I tell you truly, ma'am, I didna have a good feeling about him from the start. All that secrecy, and the thugs that do his biddin', and the smilin'…. He never stopped smilin', but it just didna seem true, you understand, my lady? I was dead afraid of him an' his men, knowin' they knew where my family was…." Praeger coughed. Jorelial Rey could see that his lips were dry and cracked, and motioned for the guards to bring him water. The man gulped down a healthy swallow, water pouring down from the corners of his mouth onto his shirt and the floor. He looked up at her with a flicker of gratitude in his eyes, and went on, "They offered me silver. So much silver, I could hardly believe my eyes, an' I couldna turn 'em down. For all I knew, he might've been right about those at the palace; how could I know such things?" He hung his head, "Once they had my word on't, I were bound to go through with the act, terrible as that seems, my lady."

"Why did you need the money, Praeger? Have you no honest business?"

He straightened slightly at the implication in that question, "I am a fletcher, my lady, a maker of bows, arrows and crossbows. If I might say it myself, I am right good at my craft, and had a good business too – a fine business until…until…" The man began to weep openly at that, his nose running unchecked and tears streaming in rivulets down his grimy face, "It's my little girl, ma'am. My little girl's been sick for such a long time. We've tried everythin' to help 'er, the missus an' me, she being our only babe, an' the apple of 'er mum's eye. We've taken 'er to healers an' apothecaries and wise women – sold everythin' we had for medicines and treatments and spell removals, but nothin' seems to help. My wife an' I, we've been that desperate to save her, our little jewel, and in just the past year we have spent all our savin's, and all the money I had for supplies, and my business has fallen by the wayside." He wailed uncontrollably now, and she could barely make out what he was saying, "We have lost everythin' now, and her so sick and like to die anyway. I just couldna pass up another chance to save her, Lady. It was just one shot, and he said I were doin' my country a great service. I wanted to believe it were heaven sent and all would be alright, but I'm no killer, I. A deer, or a goose, maybe, once in awhile, for my family, but I never willfully killed anybody in my life. Oh, gods, help me, I've done a terrible thing! But it was all for my Lynette, my little angel…and now they will have no father, no husband to keep them from the beggar's life." Praeger's head drooped forward, and he wept noisily.

Jorelial Rey hadn't planned to feel sympathy for the attacker who had nearly succeeded in ending her brief life. But the man's story moved her deeply. Watching him dissolve in sobs of anguish before her eyes, it certainly rang true. And she already knew what Drogue was capable of – using another's misfortune to his own nasty advantage seemed completely in character. She took a few moments to consider her options and their probable consequences, pacing the floor of Boone's office, as was her usual habit while thinking. Then she made a swift decision. She reached into the girdle of her dress and pulled out a small purse of gold coins she carried for emergencies. Before General Boone could ask her what she was up to, she had flung it into the little man's lap, where it landed with a jingle. Praeger looked up, startled, "My lady?" while Boone simultaneously queried, "Lady Rey, what are you doing?"

She motioned for a guard to loose the man's bonds, while she addressed the prisoner with authority. "That is for your daughter. Send this very hour for your family. I will send riders to fetch them to Theriole, where you will all be housed under our personal protection for the time being, in case Lord Drogue, or his thugs, should seek to mete out punishment for your 'failure'. I shall send my personal physician to look over your little girl and see if anything can be done for her. After a suitable interval, we will help you set your shop back on its feet, here in the capitol, where it should attract good custom. All of that, in exchange for your personal pledge here and now, that you will do no more harm intentionally, in your lifetime, and that you will swear fealty to King Darian and his rightfully appointed Regent. Oh, and there is one other person to whom you owe a debt. The man who saved my life lies even now in my quarters, gravely injured at your hands. When he recovers, and we must all pray fervently that he will, you will go before him and apologize, and offer your service to him in any capacity and for any duration he may see fit to ask of you as payment for his injury, suffering, and lost time. He is a fair man, and I trust will ask of you only what is just. Do you agree to these terms?"

Boone was purple, and interrupted her, "My lady, what are you doing? As head of security, I am afraid I cannot allow you to let this criminal go free…"

"General, while I appreciate your concern, I have pronounced my judgment in accordance with my conscience, and what I consider to be the highest good in this situation. Your support…"

"But, my lady, this is unheard of! This man tried to kill you. What if next time he succeeds, or comes after the king? The penalty for treason is death, or at least imprisonment…"

Jorelial Rey looked squarely at the prisoner, and very pointedly said, "Oh, I don't think we will see any more trouble from this quarter, will we, Master Praeger?" The man had been sitting in shock, mouth and eyes wide open, barely comprehending the generous offer before him, or the twist his fortunes seemed to have taken in a few moments time. He sat speechless for a beat, staring up at Jorelial Rey, and then, realizing that a response was required, he spluttered, "Oh, no, my lady, no indeed. I have no stomach to hurt anybody or anythin' ever again. You have no reason to be afeard o' me."

"Do you then accept my terms, as I have lined them out for you?" Another pause while the man wrapped his mind around all that she was offering. Then he threw himself on the ground, grabbing her ankles and kissing her feet, weeping and exclaiming, "Oh, my lady, you are no witch, but an angel – an angel o' compassion you are. Yes, yes, I accept with all my heart! I swear never to seek to harm a soul, and that my arm an' skills, my mind an' heart will ever be at the service of the rightful King Darian, and his lovely Regent, the Lady Rey. An' I will atone for whatever harm I've done to that injured young man as my arrow pierced. I promise it all on my daughter's life." The guards had stiffened in readiness when the man catapulted out of his seat, but relaxed once they realized what was going on. Jorelial Rey was not entirely comfortable with all the groveling, but thought it salutary for the man to suffer *some* mortification for his terrible error in judgment. Responding to his last profound oath, she responded, "Amen, and let us hope it is a long and happy life you swear on; we shall do everything in our power to insure it."

"Oh, my lady, thank ye, thank ye. I am yer man forever. The gods be kind to ye, and to our good King Darian. Thank ye, thank ye."

With some difficulty, she managed to extricate herself from his grip, and restore the man to his seat. "Prove me wise, Master Praeger, and I will be satisfied," she said, and then, "I must go. General Boone, please insure that the terms of my offer are carried out to the letter, immediately." And adding, in a low voice, for his ears only, "While your expert counsel is invaluable to me, General, I would appreciate it if you did not publicly contradict my direct orders in the future. You'll have to trust a little that I know what I am doing."

Boone scratched his head and shook it, incredulous, "My apologies, Lady Rey, I stand corrected. Only looking out for your safety, you understand?"

"Of course I do. No harm done."

The General walked her to the door, Praeger laughing and crying in the background.

"You know," Boone mused, "I was sure you were making a grave error, but I have to give you credit – I do believe that man who nearly killed you only hours ago would gladly die for you now."

She gave him a wry smile, "Well, let's hope he never has to, nor anyone else for that matter. Thank you, General. Your support is much appreciated. And now, I fear, I must show my face at the banquet, at least briefly, to reassure our citizens. I wish you good rest. Until tomorrow."

"Until then, my lady." He bowed, a glimmer of respect in his eyes. She turned and strode off toward the Great Hall, feeling proud of herself and gratified to have won Boone over in the end. That was no small achievement, especially having stood up to him the way she did. She did not know where she had found the grit to do that. But apparently, it had been the right way to show her competence. At the first bend in the corridor, she noticed that Boone had sent a guard to shadow her movements, and was frankly glad of it.

For the next few hours, though she had been up since before dawn, and was bone tired, Jorelial Rey managed to circulate among the various coronation guests – lords, ladies, delegates, ambassadors, and dignitaries – with grace, charm, courtly wit, and as close to genuine warmth as she could muster. These people had come from all over the kingdom to support and celebrate the crowning of a new king, and it was a very real part of her duties as regent to come to know all of them, and show them hospitality. She managed to give each visiting family a moment of personal attention, which they might recall favorably when they were back at home in their own castles and provinces. She tried to make each guest feel special, and valued. She listened to their concerns, promised to look into things, allayed any fears they might have about the dramas of the day, and managed to reassure the entire company that all was well and truly under control. It was almost midnight when the last of the guests finally took their leave, and Lord Maygrew sidled up to her and whispered, "Your diplomatic skills are most impressive, and your instincts and stamina nothing short of miraculous, but you must be exhausted. I think you have done your duty twice over. Go and get some rest. After today's events, I am grateful we are both here to bid each other a good night. I look forward to our meeting tomorrow." He squeezed her shoulder and went off to retire for the night.

Sagging, as the last of her poised façade fell away, Jorelial Rey stood in the center of the floor, blinking, unable to take another step. A strong arm across her shoulders urged her toward the door. She looked up – it was Mark, harp in one hand, and supporting her weight with the other. "Come on," he chirped cheerfully, "What a day it has been! Let's go find that wife of mine and call it a night, eh? Where to, sis?"

Tired as she was, and grateful for his timely assistance, she didn't even mind the informality, "Ummmm…I left her at Tvrdik's bedside in my chambers. We didn't want him to be left alone tonight."

"All-righty, then, you lead the way, and I'll keep you from falling over." The two of them made their weary way back to her suite, and entered without any announcement. They found Stewart and Tvrdik in much the same positions in which she had left them, and Delphine was dozing in the chair, holding his hand in hers. She looked cherubic in the soft candlelight, and Mark halted to regard her there, disarmed. He put his finger to his lips in a hushing gesture, then tiptoed up to his new bride and kissed her on the forehead. Delphine was startled awake, but when she saw the grinning face of her groom hovering over her, she smiled, rose, and buried her face in his chest, as his arms wrapped round her. After giving them a moment, Jorelial asked, "How is Tvrdik? Any change?"

Delphine lifted her face long enough to respond, "He's been sleeping almost the whole time you were gone. He opened his eyes once, saw my face and muttered something about how sorry he was about the coat. Then he drifted off again. Can you imagine him worrying about the silly coat at a time like this?"

"Yes, I can." Jorelial answered, rolling her eyes up to the heavens.

I sent Warlowe and the nurse away. It was getting late, and I didn't think there was anything else they could do."

"That's fine. I'm glad you did."

"I'm a little worried that his face seemed to be getting warmer this last hour, but maybe it was my imagination…"

"I can take it from here. Thank you for covering these last few hours. I was able to attend to a lot of important tasks."

Mark chuckled, "I watched her playing 'royal host' at the banquet, and was amazed."

Rel shrugged, "Not my favorite part of the job, but all those visitors deserved a little personal attention. Listen, it's late, I know, but Tashroth is still standing by to take you two away to the lake. You've both been wonderful, but everything is under control now. You should go."

They exchanged a look between them, and then turned back to her. Delphine spoke for both of them, "No, Rel, we don't want to leave you after the day you've had. Thanks, but it is not important."

"It most certainly *is* important. Today is your wedding day – once in a lifetime. The opportunity to get away might not come again anytime soon. You said yourself, no one can do anything else here tonight, and it would make me feel so much better if I thought that at least you two were happy somewhere. Please? Tash will take you to our very favorite place.

No one will disturb you there. I've packed everything you will need for a few days – I hope I haven't forgotten anything. He'll help you get set up, and flame a campfire for you. Then he'll let you have some privacy, and look in on you now and again to make sure you don't need anything else. You two can relax, away from all of this drama, and then signal him when you want to come home. If I *really* need you, I can always send him with a message to fetch you." The couple still hesitated, glancing from Tvrdik's still form, to Jorelial, to each other's uncertain faces. Rel continued to urge them, "It's so peaceful and beautiful there. You can swim, or walk, or just lie around and enjoy the view. Please go."

This time Mark was the one who spoke, "What if we all tried to get some sleep now, and then, if everything still seems stable in the morning, we'll go, first thing. Sound good?"

There was a pause, as Rel considered. Delphine added, "Rel, we are grateful for this wonderful gift, but I think we will all feel clearer about everything in the morning."

Jorelial Rey sighed, and nodded, "Alright. Get some sleep. I hope to send you off with a good heart early tomorrow. Just one thing – do you think you could manage a little detour up to the north tower and let Tashroth know? He's been waiting for word, and I don't think I should leave our patient alone…"

Mark's eyebrows arched in alarm, but Delphine elbowed him and smiled at her sister, "Consider it done. And, dear sister, you are also in need of some sleep. Shall we call someone to take over here?"

"No, no, I'm here now and wide awake. He's sleeping – I'll get help later."

Delphine kissed her sister, and Mark gave her an awkward hug, and they let themselves out, leaving her alone with the sleeping wizard and the oversized dog. She glanced sidelong at her patient. He seemed so peaceful for the moment that she dared to slip into the adjoining room, stripped off the confining gown she had been wearing all day, washed, put on loose britches and a plain tunic with soft boots, and unbound and brushed her long, dark hair. Somewhat refreshed, and now, at least, comfortable, she tiptoed back into the bedchamber to check on her charge. Stewart was now on the floor at the foot of the bed, but sound asleep. Quietly, Rel crept up to the big soft chair by Tvrdik's head, but as she leaned in to check on him by the dim light, she noticed a less peaceful expression, and beads of sweat collecting on his face. So, Delphine had not been imagining it; there *was* fever. Likely the wound had become infected, despite their best efforts. She wasn't sure how serious that could be, but knew it was not what they had hoped for. She pulled the patient's blankets up under his chin, and wrung out a damp cloth by the bedside to cool his brow again.

As she was dabbing at his face, the eyelids fluttered and came open, "Water, please," the patient croaked. "Please may I have a sip of water?" Rel put down the cloth, and found a wooden cup and a pitcher on the bedside table. She sat beside him and supported his head as he swallowed a long draught. As she settled his damp head back against the pillows, his eyes seemed finally to focus on her face.

"Jorelial Rey," he said with some surprise. "How are you?"

"How am I?" she countered, somewhat amused. "I am well, sir. You saved me, remember? The question is, how are you?"

He shifted and winced, "Hard to say. What time is it? How long have I been out?"

"Only a few hours. It is something after midnight now, and everyone else has finally turned in. Stewart is here – won't leave your side. The doctor will be back in the morning."

Tvrdik yawned, "I'm so tired…"

"You've lost a great deal of blood. They had a terrible time trying to get that wound to stop bleeding. In fact, that reminds me, I am supposed to change your bandage. Since you're awake, this is as good a time as any. Do you mind?"

"Don't you have better things to do? Like sleeping, perhaps?"

"Be quiet and let me take care of you." She folded back the blankets and carefully unpinned the end of his dressing. Gently she unwound and lifted the layers of cloth, revealing the inner pad they held in place. It was not soaked in blood, a good sign. With renewed hope she lifted it from the wound, but what was underneath had turned an angry red, the skin puffy, with little spider webs of red veins spreading out from the puncture. Something beside blood was oozing stickily from that wound, something yellow and viscous.

Her face must have given it away, as Tvrdik raised his head with brows knitted and asked, "What is it? What do you see?"

She recovered quickly, "Oh, the bleeding has stopped – a very encouraging sign. For a while there, it looked like it was never going to stop." She tried a smile. It fell flat.

"Jorelial Rey, I am a healer. I know something about wounds. How bad does it look?"

Her shoulders and face fell, "Red, hot, oozing, some red lines creeping down your arm."

Tvrdik nodded and let out a little burst of air, like a sigh of encountering an inevitable annoyance. "It must have gotten infected, deep within the wound where the arrow was lodged. There are things at Xaarus' place, and certain herbs in his garden which might help. Do you have a pen and paper here, so I can describe them for you and note where to look?"

"Tvrdik, it's the middle of the night. I won't be able to send anyone for them until sun-up anyway – why don't you just rest now and tell me later?"

He fretted and shifted in the bed, shaking his head, "If this goes the way I think it could, I might not be able to think clearly enough to do this later. Best I tell you now while I remember…"

Alarmed at the implications of that sentence, she ran to fetch paper and pen from her writing desk in the adjoining room, and sat beside him, dutifully writing down his description of some tinctures in Xaarus' pantry at The Cottage, as well as several plants in one corner of the garden whose leaves had medicinal properties. He gave instructions as well for how to apply them once they were in hand.

"As soon as it is light, I will send Stewart with someone to find these," she promised, "but what can I do to help you now?" He was sweating again and beginning to look uncomfortable.

"Well, do you have any spirits nearby?"

"Spirits?" she was startled.

"No, no, I mean strong drink…" she thought she almost detected the ghost of a laugh.

"Oh. Not something I keep in my bedroom as a rule…" her eyebrows arched ironically and her head cocked to one side.

Tvrdik's pale mouth twitched a bit on one side, "Sorry," he whispered, "didn't mean to imply…"

"However," Jorelial Rey interrupted him, "there might be something in the cabinet, leftover from entertaining dignitaries…hold on." She slipped into the drawing room, and he heard sounds of shuffling, scraping, banging, a hushed curse or two accompanying the noise. At last she re-emerged, holding a crystal decanter two thirds filled with some golden elixir. "Brandy," she announced. "We are in luck."

"Good." He sighed, and then coughed.

"What do I do with it?" she asked, concerned.

"Find another of those pads, and soak it with the liquor – that's it – now squeeze it into the wound – as much as you can – more – oh gods!" She pulled back as he cried out in pain, the golden liquid touching torn flesh. "It's alright," he assured her, "hurts like the devil, but that means you're doing it right. Now soak it again and dab it on the wound, and around the whole area. There. That's right, yes." His voice was hoarse and tense, but his instructions were patient and clear. Finally, he had her place the brandy-soaked cloth right on the wound, and apply clean dressing cloths and bandages. She rearranged the blankets, trying to warm him. He smiled his lop-sided smile, "I'm so sorry it was you having to do all that, but thanks. I think it's the best we can do for the moment, and it should help."

"Well, I'm not sorry to be here…I think I owe you at least that much. Tvrdik?"

"Hmmm?"

"It's not that I don't appreciate being alive, you know, but you really can't go around putting your life in danger for me or anyone else. You are far too valuable to be playing the hero. Think about it. You may be the only true wizard left in the kingdom, in the world even. And if something were to happen to you, any hope we have of carrying out Xaarus' wishes vanishes with you. Without your skills, we are reduced to fighting with the old ways, and you say those are doomed to fail."

"There wasn't exactly time to think it through on this occasion. I was acting on instinct. I didn't intend to be the victim myself, believe me. I was just a hair too slow. I'm glad I at least managed to get you out of the way in time. Wouldn't have helped our cause very much for *you* to be out of commission, either, you know." She glared at him, and he surrendered. "Alright, alright, point taken. I promise to be more careful in the future. There. Are you satisfied? And if you ever hear me holler, 'down in front!,' move first and ask questions later, yes?"

"Tvrdik," she leaned in close and spoke very softly, "the Ministers all saw you change form. They want an explanation. I could delay telling them your reason for showing up at Theriole, I suppose, but I think I am going to fill them in on everything tomorrow. We know now that nothing is beyond Lord Drogue, and we should all be united in purpose. It will be so much easier for all of us, once everyone knows about you."

The patient shifted in his bed and sighed, "Well, as long as we are discovered anyway, I think it is a wise idea. I'll be there to back you up. Wake me when it is time to go."

She scowled, "Don't be ridiculous. You can't go anywhere."

"I'll be fine by tomorrow. You were never meant to reveal the whole story to the skeptics by yourself. I would never do that to you. I might have to sit down, but come and get me when it's time. Maybe a little sooner, so I can wash up…I must look a sight."

It was clear that he was in total denial about what he would and would not be able to accomplish the next day, so she smiled and patted his good shoulder. "Alright. We'll see." He closed his eyes, and minutes ticked by. She wasn't sure if he had fallen back to sleep. "Tvrdik?"

"Hmmm?"

"Couldn't you just…well…wave your hand, and magic yourself all better?"

A soft sound came from the prone figure that might have been a chuckle, "I wish it worked like that, but no. I have to take my lumps like everybody else."

"Oh."

Another long silence, and then he moved restlessly and winced again. Rel remembered the potion. "I'm so sorry. You must be in a great deal of pain. The physician left some more of that sleeping draught he gave you earlier. I'll get you some to help you relax."

"Ugh! That foul stuff? Please, no. It tastes awful and I don't like being so groggy. I think I'll be alright without it; I'm so tired." He paused, then, "Is there any of the brandy left? Perhaps a little of that, instead?"

"Sounds like an excellent idea. In fact, I think I'll join you; it's been a very long day." She went back to the cabinet in the other room and found some glasses, pouring generous helpings of the liquor for each of them. She sat in the big easy chair beside him and helped him swallow a mouthful at a time, between sipping at her own. It seemed to relax him in moments. When they had finished what was in their glasses, she put them aside, rearranged his pillows, and he sighed deeply, letting his head sink gratefully into their welcome embrace.

"Tvrdik?"

"Hmmm?"

"Did I remember to say thank you?"

He did not answer.

"Tvrdik?"

The only answer was the regular breathing of one who has been overcome by deep, dreamless sleep. Exhausted beyond reason, and feeling a little of the brandy's warmth, Jorelial Rey curled her legs beneath her in the big armchair, laid her head down on the arm, and dozed off herself.

Things did not remain peaceful for long. Only a few hours later, she was roused by a loud cry, "Ailianne! Ailianne!" Disoriented for a moment, and wondering who was shouting and who Ailianne was, she returned from the land of dreams to see her patient covered in perspiration, thrashing about in her bed, and calling out for some mysterious stranger. Rel called his name and shook him, but whatever nightmare Tvrdik was caught in at the moment, she could not waken him. The fever had taken hold and he was delirious. She felt his forehead and drew back in alarm at its extreme heat. Glancing about the room, she saw Stewart, standing poised for action, a look of consternation on his fur-covered face. Jorelial Rey had little experience in caretaking, but she had nursed Delphine through several of the normal childhood illnesses, some of them rather serious. She chewed her nails, trying to remember anything useful she might have picked up from those days.

"Stewart," she called, "Grab that extra blanket over there. We still have to keep him warm." Stewart sprang into action, dragging the blanket over with his teeth. Between the two of them, they managed to spread it over their tossing patient. Rel faced the eager dog, who was waiting for more instructions. "Stewart, do you think you could find the kitchens in this palace?"

"M'lady, never underestimate a wolfhound's finely tuned nose. Of course I can."

"I hate to ask this of you, but it is very possible that at this hour, someone might already be there, lighting fires, and preparing for the morning meal. If you can find someone awake, would you…could you… be willing to relay a message?"

"I am that concerned, Lady, that I would. I would do near anything for him. What is the message?"

"First, tell them to send someone to wake up Warlowe, my doorman. Say they should tell him the Lady Rey has need of his services, alright? Then, ask them if there is any ice left over from last night's feast. Tashroth flew some in from the mountains, and I am hoping it is not yet all melted. Tell them to break up as much as they can in small pieces and send whatever they can here as soon as possible. Can you do that for me?"

"Lady, I am on the way." And the good hound bounded out the door she held open for him and disappeared down the dark corridor. Back in the bedchamber, Tvrdik was beginning to shiver, though his skin was fiery to the touch. She used the cloth with clean water to try and cool his brow, and talked to him in soft, reassuring tones, in the hopes of calming his distress. But he kept squirming, moaning in pain, and calling out bits of incomprehensible information. Frequently he called out for the mysterious 'Ailianne'. Then, several times, it was, "Master, where are you? Master, don't go…" and similar heartbreaking cries. Then something about, "…the stars, so many stars – the people from the stars…" which made absolutely no sense. Frightened as she was at his deteriorated state, she could not suppress a wry little grin when the next thing out of his mouth was, "No more, please. Dragon's eyes – too much. Turn off the Dragon's eyes!" She suspected that might be a reference to his original interview with Tash.

Her lone ministrations were doing very little to restore him to peaceful rest, however, and it seemed an eternity before Stewart returned to the rooms, accompanied by a servant holding a basin of chipped ice. "Warlowe is on his way, ma'am," Stewart offered, causing the servant to nearly drop her bowl. They tore cloths and wrapped ice in them, placing some on the wounded area and some on his brow. Now and then she tried to lay a chip or two on his tongue to help prevent dehydration, as he was sweating profusely. Warlowe arrived at last, and sizing up the situation, suggested that they attempt to shift the patient so that they could change the soaking wet bedclothes. This proved a complicated maneuver, but in the end they accomplished it after a fashion, and Tvrdik did seem a little more comfortable.

That being done, Warlowe, realizing that Stewart was indeed a talking dog, introduced himself without making an issue of any earlier deception, a gesture for which Jorelial Rey was deeply grateful. They changed the bandage again, using up the rest of the brandy, and noticing that the wound looked dreadful. All the while, Tvrdik continued to mumble things, and to cry out, and seemed to be in a great deal of pain. From time to time he opened up his eyes, but did not appear to recognize who any of them were. Terrified, and at wit's end, Rel asked, "What hour is it?"

Stewart ran to an outer room and checked the window. "M'lady, I dinna ken where the night has gone to, but it is dawn; the sky is just beginning to brighten, and the birdies are already up."

She nodded and reached for the paper on which she had written down Tvrdik's instructions. "Earlier, when he was more lucid, Tvrdik suspected something like this could happen, and told me of several powerful remedies back at Xaarus' Cottage that he was sure would help. Some are in bottles, others fresh in the front garden. Stewart, you know the place, how to get in, where things are; Warlowe can help you gather the items and carry them back here. I couldn't send you out there in the dead of night, but go now – be thorough and be quick – we might be fighting for his life."

Warlowe took the paper and studied it to make sure it was clear, "My lady, we will be as fast as we can be, but I think it might also be time to wake the Palace Physician. You have done all you can alone."

"Agreed. He promised to return in the morning. I would characterize this as a crisis worthy of hastening his steps a bit." She caught the servant's eye, "Would you be so good as to go and rouse the healer, and send him here quickly? If he grumbles, blame it on me, and say you were ordered..." The servant nodded, wide-eyed, and disappeared through the door. Stewart and Warlowe departed right behind her, waving back at Rel in reassurance.

Left alone again with Tvrdik, she sighed and sat in the chair, applying ice and cool cloths to his face, trying to slip ice chips into his mouth, and feeling helpless. He was shivering now at intervals, teeth chattering. His color was an odd grey-green, and his eyes were dark smudges burnt into his face. She didn't think his spare frame, weakened by blood loss, could take much more of this. And yet, he was young and strong, had survived alone in the woods all those years without the benefit of the simplest comforts. Perhaps she was underestimating his resilience and tenacity of will. Despite herself, she smiled, thinking that Tvrdik was a person it was easy to underestimate, and that he had already proved full of surprises.

These thoughts heartened her somewhat as she awaited the physician's arrival for what seemed like an eternity. When he finally came, a bit rumpled and cross after being rousted from bed so early, he took one look at the situation and apologized for not being there sooner. He praised her efforts thus far, impressed by her resourcefulness in tackling the fever. Then he shook his head and looked grim, stating that he had seen circumstances like this on many occasions, and that there was not much more anyone could do at this point but wait and pray. He un-bandaged and examined the wound area, making a sound with his tongue that indicated that his worst fears had been realized. "The infection probably started deep inside where we could not clean properly, and has spread already. It is no wonder it has hit him so hard. When did the delirium start?"

Rel thought. "I was just talking to him a little after midnight. He was weak and uncomfortable, and his face was beginning to be hot. I think it turned for the worse maybe two or three hours later. I dozed, and was awakened by his cries. I couldn't even rouse him."

The doctor did a quick calculation in his head, "We should know very soon which way this is going. The ice probably helped to keep his body temperature below lethal levels. Still, you should be prepared for the worst."

"I refuse to accept that possibility, sir. There must be something else we can try?" She was beginning to feel desperate. The man sighed and shook his head, but then he took a long swab with a soft, gauzy end out of his bag, rolled it in some sort of copper colored salve with a strong odor, and inserted it deep into the suppurating wound, twisting it. This elicited such a shriek of pain that Rel's eyes welled up and she backed away.

"Sorry," the healer explained. "I knew that would be difficult, but we needed to try to get to the internal tissue." He laid the pad gently back over the wound, but did not replace the bandage for the moment. Shortly thereafter, Stewart and Warlowe dashed in with a basket of items from

Xaarus' house and garden. Winded, they almost knocked the physician over in their enthusiasm.

"Here we are," Warlowe panted. "The gods grant that we have the right medicines." He held up a bottle of brownish liquid, and a bigger blue bottle. "According to the paper, this one is to swallow, this other one must be poured or dabbed on the wound, and these leaves should also be crushed between fingers and packed onto the affected area. Stewart glanced at the physician, and then barked once in agreement, standing tall with legs planted and tail swishing back and forth. Rel leapt to her feet and reached for the first bottle, but the healer intervened.

"Hold on a moment! What do you think you are doing with those?" he exclaimed indignantly.

"Apologies, sir, but the patient is something of a healer himself, and earlier told me to send for these items which can combat fever and infection," Rel tried to explain politely, even though her patience after the last twenty-four hours had grown thin.

"Well, you can just give them over here. I have treated kings and courtiers; I think I know what I am doing better than some upstart folk apothecary." He was working himself into a dither of righteous indignation.

Rel held the basket out of his reach, drew herself up to her full height and addressed the petulant man in her most commanding tone. "Sir, while I respect your knowledge and gifts, and very much appreciate your efforts so far, I am afraid you will have to indulge me on this small point. You have already informed me that there is little else you can do, and I want this man alive. Therefore, I am willing to try any options that may present themselves. These certainly cannot make matters any worse than they already are, and there is a chance they might actually help."

The wounded healer retreated, bowing with a sullen expression. "As you wish, my lady." He watched from a distance as the others fumbled with the tinctures, potions and leaves, according to Tvrdik's own instructions. Softened some by their obvious and desperate dedication, he stepped back in to show them how to properly crush the leaves, re-apply the bandages correctly and fasten them securely. He then announced that he had a few other patients to attend to, and that he would like to be excused to make rounds and return in an hour or two to check on Tvrdik's progress.

"If there is a sudden turn for the worse, I will be in the palace, and you can send for me," he offered. Attempting to mend fences, Jorelial Rey replied that she understood, thanked him again, and gave him his leave. Now there really was nothing left to do but wait. While the servants, who had slipped quietly in, bustled about, fetching fresh water and cloths, piling up clean blankets and taking away damp ones, Tvrdik's three angels sank down wearily, Jorelial Rey in the big easy chair near his head, Stewart on the floor at the foot of the bed, and Warlowe in a straight chair on the other side of the room. They were spent and worried, and spoke not a word aloud during the vigil that followed, though many a meaningful glance was exchanged. Rel held the young wizard's hand, and periodically wiped his brow with the cool, damp cloth. At one point, a kind servant pressed a cup of warm tea into her hand, but she did not recall drinking it. Warlowe dozed on and off in his uncomfortable chair, and Stewart was the soul of canine faithfulness, head on paws, eyes fixed on his friend. The only sounds in the room were the creak of the bed when Tvrdik tossed and turned, and the fevered moaning and mumbling they had grown used to, punctuated on occasion by some loud and incomprehensible exclamation. They had no sense of how long things went on in this manner; an hour or two, perhaps longer. Suddenly, Stewart lifted his head, ears erect, and whispered, "Listen. D'ye all hear that?"

"What?" replied Jorelial Rey, who had been drifting.

"Just listen…" They all held their breath a moment, trying to focus, and slowly, gradually perceived what the dog had first noticed: the blessed, miraculous sound of silence. No creaking, thrashing, moaning, mumbling, or crying out. Seconds went by, and then minutes, and nothing interrupted that glorious vacuum. And then came the sweetest sound any of them had ever heard – the sound of snoring! Loud, rhythmic, blatant snoring. All three of them jumped up, cheering and laughing in relief, and fell upon one another with embraces and hearty claps on the back.

They all raced to Tvrdik's side, and Rel laid her hand on his forehead.

"Maybe it's just wishful thinking, but it feels to me like his skin is cooler to the touch."

Warlowe also checked, "No, you are right, and he's sleeping comfortably for the first time in hours.'

Stewart chimed in, "I think we're past the worst of it, M'lady. The crisis is over."

"Good old Xaarus," she mused, "and thank you both for your trust and quick action. Likely it made all the difference." Warlowe led her gently away from the bed, "My lady, you have been up with him all night and there are important tasks ahead for you this day. Now that he has turned a corner, we can take it from here. Why don't you go into the drawing room and try to get a few hours of rest? I daresay you are overdue."

She looked at him with gratitude, then back to their patient, his chest rising and falling in regular rhythms, "You're both sure?"

Stewart replied, "Go on, M'lady. The healer will return soon and give an official verdict, and we'll stay with him until then."

"Alright. I *am* fading." She grabbed a blanket off of the fresh pile that had been brought in, and dragged it into the adjoining room. Casting about for a comfortable place to fall, she pulled all the stuffed cushions from the chairs in the room onto the floor in a formless heap, wrapped herself in the blanket, and lowered herself into the soft mass, curling up like a small child on its mother's lap. Half a moment of rearranging pillows under her head and hips and she was already gone into oblivion.

NINETEEN

SECRETS REVEALED

JORELIAL REY WAS AWAKENED BY a sharp tugging at one of her sleeves, and an oddly accented voice at her ear, "My rady, wake ub! Cub an' see, my rady."

It was Stewart, her sleeve in his mouth as he attempted to address her. He seemed agitated. She blinked and tried to prop her achy frame on the pile of cushions she had slept on. It did not happen without a few choice words at the stiffness in her muscles. But the dog was impatient and insistent.

"What is it, Stewart? Something gone wrong?"

"No, no, m'lady, all's well." He had dropped the sleeve as she sat up, and sounded more like himself.

"How long have I been out?" she questioned, still trying to focus.

"Just three hours, mum; we hated to wake you, but it is almost high noon, and there is a sight just beyond that will warm yer heart. Aye, that it will. Come with me."

She scrambled to her feet, stretching out her limbs, and smoothed her hands over her sleep-swollen face and hopelessly wrinkled clothing. "Dragonsbreath," she muttered, and then stumbled after the bounding dog, back into the bedroom. There, sitting up in bed, and being spoon-fed broth by a servant, was Tvrdik. His face was haggard, but there was color in his cheeks as he sipped the hot liquid. Hearing them come in, he turned and nodded to her, then broke into a sheepish grin. "I was a little hungry...."

Jorelial Rey shrieked in delight, and Stewart let out a howl, the two of them dancing around the room. At that moment, the big hound could not resist licking her face in his exuberance, even though she was the Lady Regent of all of Eneri Clare. Tvrdik frowned, "Did I miss something?"

Rel came to his side, a broad smile lighting her face, "Yes, almost everything. We thought you were a goner, but here you are having breakfast. It's just too wonderful. Here, let me do that – go and get some well-deserved rest." She took the steaming bowl and spoon from the servant, who curtsied and made her exit. Rel sat down by the patient and offered him another spoonful, as Stewart filled her in.

"The doctor has already come and gone and pronounced him officially on the mend. Ye should have seen the way he scratched his head, and the mystified look on his face when he saw how improved our patient was. I think he will be givin' ye his apologies, missy, and that for certain. Master Warlowe has already gone to his post, the two young folk stopped in to visit, and are, by now gone off on their weddin' trip, and if ye don' mind, I'll be takin' my leave of ye also. There are a few things out in the world that I should be attendin' to."

"Go on, Master Stewart, with my blessing and my profound thanks. I don't know that I could have gotten through this night without your support. You will be hearing from me."

Tvrdik waved his good hand, "Farewell, friend. I am in your debt. Take good care, and I hope to see you soon at the house…"

"Och, I'll be comin' 'round here to check on ye before that, long as it's alright with you, m'lady?" She nodded and smiled, and the wolfhound made her a graceful bow, trotting off through the door of her apartments, which the serving girl had left partly ajar.

Jorelial Rey got up and crossed to shut the door tightly behind him, then came back and settled herself in the big chair at Tvrdik's side. He took another spoonful of soup, and frowned again, "Everyone is making such a fuss."

Rel rolled her eyes, "You have no idea. Your wound was badly infected, and the fever took you. You were miserable and delirious all night, and we thought we had lost you. The palace healer near threw up his hands, but I sent Warlowe and Stewart at first light for the things you suggested from

Xaarus' cottage. We used those, and anything else we could think of, but we didn't know if any of it would turn the tide. And look, here you are!"

"Well, not quite ready to run a race yet, but far from dying."

"You can't imagine how relieved I am to hear that."

"Were you here all night then? I am sorry…"

"It's alright. I suppose I owe you something for saving my life, and besides, if you think I am about to face Lord Drogue any time soon without my secret ace, you are mistaken."

Tvrdik's eyes drifted down. "Oh." he said, a little dejectedly. Realizing how impersonal she must have just sounded, Rel went on. "I see, however, that your sense of humor has tragically passed away during the night…" When he looked up at that, she gave him a cheerful wink, which elicited a brighter expression. He pushed away the spoon.

"I think I've had enough for now. Could I have a bit of water? And do you see my eyeglasses lying about anywhere? I am lost without them."

Ah, she thought, *he's asking for his glasses. He must be better indeed.* She stood, put the soup bowl down on a table, and gave the room a quick once over.

"There they are, on the bureau." She strode over to retrieve them, found a clean cloth to wipe off the lenses, and presented them to him. "All in one piece, nary a scratch."

Tvrdik held them in his hands for a moment and muttered, "Bless these, and the assistance they give to me." Then he slid them onto his face, adjusting the wire over the bridge of his nose.

"Oh, my!" he exclaimed, "That's much better. I feel more myself now. Oh! You look terrible." The words escaped his mouth before thought could catch them. "I – I mean, you must have had a difficult night…"

Jorelial Rey raised an eyebrow, "You try getting up before dawn, participating in a wedding *and* a coronation, narrowly escaping death by being hurled to the stone stoop, reassuring the citizens, interviewing the perpetrator, greeting guests at a banquet, and then sitting up all night with a friend you think you've probably killed, and then see if you look as fresh and lovely as a lily. And, by the way, you aren't likely to win any beauty contests this morning yourself either." She glared at him with an exaggerated angry face, but it made her look so ridiculous, that they both burst into laughter. Jorelial filled two of the wooden cups with cool water from a fresh pitcher the servants had brought, and handed one to Tvrdik. She urged him to lean forward, and rearranged his pillows into a more cozy, supportive nest. After draining the cup, he settled back on them with a sigh. She refilled it and gave it to him again, picking up the other for herself. For several minutes they sat in companionable silence, sipping water. And then, with feigned nonchalance, Jorelial Rey asked, "Who is Ailianne?"

"Pardon?" Tvrdik started, and almost spilled his cup.

"Ailianne. You kept calling out that name all night. Just wondered. Perhaps it is someone I may send for?"

There was a long pause, Tvrdik staring into the wooden cup, and then, in a low voice, measuring his words, he answered, "Ailianne was one of the other students in Xaarus' school. The only female. We grew up together."

"You were in love with her?" Rel prodded. Another long pause.

"I think I would have said so then. We were so young, how could I have truly known? She was very beautiful, and bright, and talented. And the only girl I ever had contact with at all. She was always kind to me, as a schoolmate, even a friend, I suppose. But, beyond that, I don't think she ever knew I existed. There never was anything between us."

"You could have tried to remedy that…"

"I – I never had the chance. Ailianne was too curious, too hungry for power. Her mistakes cost her her life. She has been gone a very long time…" Tvrdik's narrative drifted off.

"Oh, I am so sorry." Rel had just remembered that part of Tvrdik's story and regretted her own blunder, "I had forgotten. I didn't mean to open an old wound…"

"No, no. I'm just embarrassed. I guess there must be a part of me that won't let go of those memories."

Neither spoke for a beat, and Jorelial Rey let her mind drift. Then, "Memories can be sweet. There was a young man I fancied once for a little while, when I was about Delphine's age. He was the son of some foreign dignitary who stayed at Theriole one summer. He was tall and dark with smoldering eyes that were always staring at me hungrily. I think I rather liked it. He was so handsome and exotic."

Tvrdik watched her rekindle the sensations of that part of her young life, and felt a pang of bittersweet sympathy for the lonely young girl just

260

emerging into womanhood. He wished that he'd had the opportunity to have known her better back then. She went on.

"That summer there were many balls to celebrate one thing or another – the social events of the season. We danced together, strolled through the gardens, and talked and talked. Later, he sent me a few gifts and some poems he had written just for me. I was besotted with him."

"What happened?"

"Well, at some point I took him to see Tashroth, of course, Tash being the other half of my heart, and the fool ran off in terror. I never heard from him again. I thought I would die of a broken heart."

"Poor, poor Jorelial Rey. What a sweet, sad story. I am so sorry for you."

"Don't be. He would have made a terrible spouse. What was it Tash called him? A vain, supercilious twit, I think? Tash is always right. Still, it hurt for a time. You know, perhaps that is why I found it hard to take Delphine's relationship with Mark seriously. I may have been thinking of what an idiot I was at her age. She is very different from what I was…"

"Mark is a good man."

"I am finding that out."

"I wonder what ever happened to your handsome dignitary's son?"

"Oh, last I heard, he'd married the blonde, buxom daughter of a wealthy landowner with a huge estate, and has three kids already. He's probably fat and boring and opinionated about everything."

They both laughed at that, and as their mirth faded, Rel sighed, "I've never told that story to anyone before, not even Delphine. Promise me it stays between us."

"I promise. And I am glad you told me. I enjoyed hearing it, and getting to know a little more about who you are, Jorelial Rey. Xaarus was right."

"About what?"

"Oh, he said I would find out that we had much more in common than I imagined. I hope that doesn't offend you?"

"Of course not." There was another long silence, not entirely unpleasant, but Rel finally looked up to see Tvrdik drooping, the effort of even this short conversation beginning to take a toll. She sat up straight, "Well, much as I would like to sit here with you all day and reminisce, I am supposed to address my Cabinet on the topic of 'Wizards, Villains, and

Creative Warfare' in less than two hours, and as you so gallantly pointed out, I can hardly appear before them looking like this."

Tvrdik's face fell, "I must go with you. You weren't supposed to have to do that alone..."

"Don't even think of moving an inch out of that bed – you'll undo all the good we worked so hard to achieve. Look, I can handle this. I'll just give them the broad outline, and you can fill in all the details yourself, in person, as soon as you are up to it, agreed?"

"Agreed." He sighed and sank back, knowing he hadn't even the strength to sit up at the moment.

"Right now, your only task is to rest and recover, and get your strength back as quickly as possible. I'd rather limp along without you for a few days, if it means you might feel better faster, and without any setbacks. Rest, enjoy this opportunity; soon enough there will be little time for leisure."

"And here I am in your bed, in your rooms – something else I am taking away from you. That isn't right."

"You just stay right there and don't worry about me. I can arrange to use a spare room for a few nights, and you know I won't be spending much time in it anyway. As soon as the doctor thinks you can be safely moved, we'll see about getting you home. Till then, you can hardly blame me for wanting you close by where I can keep an eye on you. I'll probably come to check in after the meeting, and get your input on how our case is faring so far."

"I will help you in any way I can." His voice was weakening and his eyelids were closing involuntarily. She pulled the blankets up around him, and tucked him in.

"Rest now, friend. Sweeter dreams this time." And as he drifted into slumber, his spectacles still perched on his nose, she set off to prepare herself for the approaching meeting.

It seemed only a heartbeat later, when, having washed up, wolfed down an apple and a fistful of bread and cheese, and dressed for business, Jorelial Rey stood before her Cabinet of closest advisors, lords and Ministers, twelve to be precise, and cleared her throat. Looking from face to eager face, she paused to summon her courage and collect her thoughts. These men were, after all, her support system, not her enemies. *Truth and commitment; truth and commitment*, she repeated over and over in her mind. She took a deep breath, thought, *Daddy, if you could ever help me from wherever you are, now would be a good time,* and then she told them. Pretty much the whole story. There were things she finessed or omitted because she did not feel they needed to know the private details of Tvrdik's emotional journey. In her version, after Xaarus' mysterious disappearance, Tvrdik went off to continue his studies and to practice in distant reaches of the kingdom, until the day that Xaarus' image came to recruit him. She explained how he had made the trip back to speak with her, as per Xaarus' instructions, and how he had accurately predicted everything that had occurred at the High Council, including her election as permanent regent, and Lord Drogue's threats. She told how he had convinced her that a serious struggle over the fate of Eneri Clare was imminent, but that the stakes were even higher than what would happen in their lifetimes alone. She tried to explain Tvrdik's assertion that the only way they could truly triumph was by unconventional means. Up to that point, no one had spoken, interrupted, or commented. But when she tossed out that key piece of information, she heard gasps, and saw the lords shift in their seats and exchange meaningful looks. She went on to tell how she had installed Tvrdik in the old house that had belonged to Xaarus, which he had been restoring with his own hands. Also, how he had been secretly watching over her as an owl, both at the High Council, and at the Coronation. Finally, and with some emotion, she related what they already partly knew – that he had acted quickly to propel her out of harm's way the day before, and been gravely wounded. She told them how she had sat up with him most of the night, fearing he might perish, and realizing the enormous negative impact that could have on all of their futures. Without at least one mage, and one who could contact Xaarus at that, they hadn't a prayer of defeating Drogue either in the conventional or in the more unorthodox manner.

"Tvrdik is an unusual and compelling character, as you will no doubt discover for yourselves. Hearing all of this from me is a poor substitute for our original intention, which was for him to come before you with his own tale, his ideas, his passion, and his absolute commitment to the path that Xaarus, his master, has set his feet on. Let me tell you, that passion is contagious. This very morning, having only just emerged from his own life and death struggle, he was determined to rise from his sickbed and come before you. Of course, I persuaded him that the wiser option was to concentrate on his own recovery. I promised him that I would reveal to you the capsule version today, and give you an opportunity to question him further as soon as he is strong enough. I cannot know how much time we have to prepare for what is coming, but I suspect there is little room for delay. We must all decide on a course of action together, and begin constructing our defenses and our plan of action as soon as possible."

There. She had done it. There was nothing left except to await their reactions. But what greeted her as she finished her narrative was absolute silence. The Ministers were staring at her, speechless and open-mouthed. A wall hanging shifted in a breeze from the open window and banged against the stones. A chair creaked as someone in the audience shifted on it. Otherwise, silence.

"Your thoughts?" She tried to encourage them, standing before them in the awkward pause. Finally, it was Lord Maygrew, so recently her champion, who stood and presumed to speak for the rest.

"Rel, what is this all about, really? You can't seriously expect us to believe this fantastic story, can you? Is this some sort of a test?"

"No, my lord. I swear I have told you the whole truth as I understand it. I admit I was as skeptical as you, at first, and most unhappy with the facts. But, as I began to see things fall out exactly as Tvrdik had predicted, I became convinced."

"Still, all this silliness about time travel and changing the future, and wizards appearing out of nowhere and then disappearing.... You say only this young man can see Xaarus, when no one else can? It's, well, a very pretty fiction, perhaps, but...I mean...you must see how ridiculous it all sounds?"

The Lady Regent's tone of voice sharpened just a notch, "I am surprised at you, Lord Maygrew. You always claimed to be a good friend of Xaarus."

"And so were most of us here, and we miss him sorely. But it has been over a decade now that we have done without magic at court, and we have learned to use our wits and our own two hands to deal with adversity in the *real* world." Rel's eyes narrowed, and she felt her jaw tighten.

The Minister of Justice jumped in with his own concerns, "And, my lady, even if any of this were feasible, which I highly doubt, how do we know this young man isn't just mentally deranged, or part of some nefarious plan of, say, Lord Drogue himself, to leave us defenseless? How do you know he speaks for Xaarus at all? Have *you* seen or heard Xaarus? I had assumed he had been dead for years."

Jorelial Rey had known she would encounter some resistance from the old guard, but the events of the last two days had left her short on patience. She spoke a little more forcefully, taking the room back from the murmuring and private whispers. "Yesterday, you all saw him change forms right before your eyes, and we know what he was doing at the time, so I cannot see how you could attribute any evil intent to the man. When he first came to see me, he presented me with one of Xaarus' old calling card coins. I remembered it well from my childhood – you recall the coins I mean – and I knew there was no way he could have that item if he had not come from Xaarus as he claimed."

A voice from the back of the room called out, "How if he did study with the old man in his youth, and just kept the coin all these years as a memento, but comes back now with his wits turned or on some other agenda, and uses it to give credence to his story?"

There was a general murmuring from the floor. Jorelial felt her face grow hot, and her fingers were twitching in frustration. She had a strong impulse to find the man who had just spoken and shake him hard. But, she knew an angry outburst would not advance her cause. Biting her lower lip, and breathing deeply through her nose, she lifted her voice once more with a veneer of calm. "Gentlemen, gentlemen! I understand that I have given you a great deal to swallow today, much of it difficult and strange. One reason I delayed bringing Tvrdik before you when he first arrived was my own uncertainty about what he was telling me. I wanted to take the time to observe both the circumstances and the man, to test his authenticity before I wasted your time. As I mentioned, circumstances have been proving him right time and again. And, in the two weeks I have been spending time with him, I have never known him to be anything but kind, generous, bright, talented, humble, hard-working, and passionate about succeeding in his mission. If any of you still value the judgment of dragons – and may I remind you that it is impossible to deceive a dragon by any means – I would add that Tashroth, at my instigation, subjected Tvrdik to scrutiny far more intense than anything humans could devise. Tashroth finds him to be without guile, malice, or any deception whatsoever." With that, she felt she had delivered the most incontrovertible evidence.

But there was more mumbling from the assembly in the room, and heads shaking in doubt. Incredulous, she continued, "Look, I have given you the situation as I have learned it. With any luck, in a few days, Tvrdik will be sufficiently recovered from his wound to address you in person, and you may ask your questions of him. You will make your own judgments of his character and intentions at that time. Meanwhile, I beg you all to sit with this information for a while, and to try and keep an open mind. Let time and reflection recommend my policy to you, or not." She paused, closed her eyes, took another breath, and changed the subject. "I wish to commend you all on a memorable and wonderful Coronation yesterday. Every detail seemed perfect, every guest well-pleased, and every tradition beautifully observed. It was a testament to all of your diligence that we have smoothly accomplished this major step, despite those who would seek to sabotage it. Well done. Is there other business that needs to be discussed today?"

Again there was silence, most of the cabinet looking down or away to avoid her direct gaze.

"Right, then. I am sure you could all use time to catch up on your rest, or to visit with friends who are preparing to leave the palace for the journey home. We will reconvene as soon as the mage may safely appear before you, or, of course, if some other emergency finds us before that time. Thank you for being here today, and for all you do."

That was that. Turning her back on the august assemblage, she strode over to the main doors. She briefly considered continuing right through them and away, without another word. But it was as if she felt her father's firm hand on her shoulder, requiring her to stay at the door and give each Minister a personal greeting as they exited. Even if their less than enthusiastic reaction to her news galled her, she could understand their resistance, and it would not do to alienate her own advisors so early in the game. As most of the participants left, they gave her some curt and courteous gesture of deference, faces solemn or troubled, eyes avoiding hers on the way out. *I'd like to be a shadow on the wall to hear this evening's hallway conversations*, she thought.

But, as Minister Boone approached her, she could see he was determined to speak with her, and seemed agitated.

"Minister, is there something you want to discuss? Feel free to speak your mind to me." She urged, striving to sound more gracious than she felt.

"Yes, my lady. Just this: I was impressed at how you handled our prisoner last night. You managed to achieve your desired end in a way I could not have imagined. I can be open-minded to a point, and I can learn new ideas. I even respect your ability to think in creative new directions. But, I can only go so far, and when you come before us and tell me that my soldiers cannot put down an upstart like Drogue, that in a pitched battle the cream of our land will be defeated and the kingdom lost, why, then, you go too far. It is insulting, and outrageous."

"General Boone, I apologize. It is a bitter pill to swallow, for myself as well, and is not intended to reflect poorly on your own genius, nor on the worthiness of your troops. I am but a messenger for those who have seen the outcome. Drogue knows some dark sorcery, he is ruthless, and he operates under no rules of civility. There is no telling what he might bring to bear against us. I am trying to save lives here – please do not take offense. I would not knowingly send your fine warriors to certain death, or how could I ever live with myself? Forewarned is forearmed. I pray you, consider again and do not take any of this as a personal slight." Boone's brows furrowed in confusion. He gave her a quick little nod and hurried away.

Corbin Maygrew stepped up right behind him, taking her hands in his and speaking low, "Rel, I hardly know what to say. Only a week ago, I put you forward as the only candidate I thought stable enough to handle this position, and you are already flying off into territory that causes me grave concern. I know you are tired, overworked – you've been through a personal attack and a great deal of stress. If you are not up to the challenge, say the word, and we can change things…"

"Please stop, Lord Maygrew. A week ago I assured you that I had no desire for this position, but I am stuck with it now, and I promise you, all my faculties are perfectly clear and in good working order. I know that what I have told you is difficult to believe, but do not judge me just yet.

Wait, at least, until you hear from the wizard himself. Search your own heart, your memories of Xaarus, your belief in what is right. Your support and good counsel mean a great deal to me, but, in the end, I must decide what action is for the highest good of all concerned, with or without you." The man stood very straight, clearly taken aback by her passionate words. Indeed, she could hardly believe they had come out of her mouth, and was beginning to wish she could take them back, when all at once he narrowed his eyes, leaned in, and looked her straight in the eye, as if searching for something there.

"There are times, Jorelial Rey, when you sound so like your father that it is almost uncanny." He sighed, "Alright. I will give this some more time, and reserve judgment, as you suggest. But do not disappoint me. Be prepared to present your case well." He squeezed her hands and strode from the room. Jorelial closed her eyes and sighed, feeling that she had just passed a very arduous test that she hadn't even seen coming. Weariness was beginning to overtake her, and she was very glad to be done with the whole business for this day...

"My lady? My Lady Regent?" She opened her eyes to see one last person waiting for her attention, hanging back until all the others had gone. She refocused her eyes. It was Verger, the Minister of Finance. In fact, he had held that post since the current king's grandfather had appointed him to the position decades ago, and he had proved invaluable in it. Quiet, and timid by nature, he rarely ventured an opinion on matters of State, preferring to spend his time with books and figures. He could do wonders with budgets, accounts, and numbers, and could be a brick wall when he deemed it necessary to block what he considered profligate or ill-advised spending. But, otherwise, he tended to let the more outspoken of his colleagues argue policy. And so, his presence here at the end of the line, and his obvious desire to speak with her took Jorelial Rey by surprise.

"Yes, Minister Verger. What can I do for you?"

"I only wanted to say that you shouldn't let them discourage you, or take them too seriously. They have always disliked things that are unfamiliar – things that they do not understand. Some of them will come around in time."

Jorelial was moved. "Thank you, Minister Verger. I appreciate your staying to tell me that. It has been a difficult twenty-four hours, a difficult two weeks. Dare I ask what you yourself think?"

"Lady Rey, I am with you all the way. I believe you were quite bold to share this information as you did, but it is what we all need to hear."

"Why do you feel that way?"

"Xaarus was always a good friend to me. We had many long talks on, oh, so many deep subjects. This all sounds very like him. One thing he always did was to challenge us to stretch our minds further than what was comfortable for us. He was a master of that, he was. But now, we have grown complacent and bored, and we have forgotten how to think outside of ourselves and see a bigger landscape. If Xaarus could, I believe he would reach out even from his grave to shake us up and make us try to imagine more."

"Verger, your friend is not in a grave. He is very much alive, and desperate to get our attention. Xaarus is trying to help us triumph…"

"I begin to believe it, my lady, and if it is so, we would all do well to put our trust in him. I spend my life with books and numbers, long columns of them, endless calculations. Numbers do not lie. They are refreshingly honest and simple. But, when you come to know them better, numbers can be quite magical as well. They dance, they interact, they can be elegant and profound, and lead us to mind-expanding ideas. Lady Rey, all of my life I have sought the truth that lies beneath the surface of things. I do believe you are about to lead us into the most exciting adventure of our lives, something with meaning and nobility. And I will follow wherever it takes us."

She hadn't realized the courage and depth of this quiet, deceptively dull little man, and was so grateful to have found a single, powerful ally, that she almost hugged and kissed him right there. "Sir, your words have salvaged the day for me. Your support means more than I can find words to express." She took his hand, warmly, "Thank you."

He beamed at her, "I look forward to meeting this young wizard of yours. He sounds very likable."

"You shall see him soon, sir, and he will enjoy meeting you as well, I am certain of it. The two of you will understand one another."

"Count on me, my lady, to assist you in any way I can."

She smiled at him with genuine affection, and wrung his hand. "Dear, dear, Verger, I will remember that, believe it." Smiling broadly, he took his leave, Rel staring after him in utter surprise. It must be true, then, the old saying that aid comes from quarters where you would least expect it, and disappointment too. She made a silent vow never again to judge anyone's heart by their outward appearance.

TWENTY

An Alternate Plan

I T WAS AFTER FOUR O'CLOCK when, sagging from lack of sleep and the ebbing of the adrenaline that had bolstered her through the past forty-eight hours, Rel tiptoed back into her chambers to check on Tvrdik. But he was already awake, awaiting her arrival with eagerness. Sitting up in bed, unattended, he sported deep shadows under his eyes, and moved as if all of his muscles were ignoring his instructions. But there was color in his cheek, and the spark was returning to his eye.

"Jorelial Rey – at last!" he greeted her. "How did it go?"

She willed herself over to his bedside, and collapsed into the same chair she had occupied during the long vigil. Her head hung low.

"Not good. I'm afraid your confidence in me as a persuasive communicator was ill-placed."

"Not possible. Tell me."

"Twelve advisors in the Cabinet. I told them everything – your whole story, minus a few of the details I thought you might prefer to remain private…"

"Thank you."

"I told them about what happened to Xaarus, his reappearance and commission to you, along with his reasons. I described how you came here and convinced me, how everything that you said would happen has already begun to materialize, how Tashroth and I came to trust you…"

"Thank you again."

"I was greeted with stunned silence. Lord Maygrew, who virtually handed me the Regency last week, asked me today if I was well enough to handle it, or would I prefer to step down for awhile. He was clearly implying that I had lost my mind. Somehow, I convinced him to reserve judgment until he'd met you in person, but he warned me that he would be difficult to persuade. General Boone was offended to the core at our assessment of his army's chances for victory in any future conflict. Nine others were extremely skeptical, and probably believe I have gone insane."

"That makes eleven…"

"Well, we do have one fervent supporter who claims he will follow us anywhere."

"Who?"

"A great surprise. Verger, my Minister of Finance. It turns out he was a good friend of Xaarus and is a thoughtful and creative soul. He had no trouble embracing our cause."

"Well, he certainly could be an excellent ally to have in our pocket. He holds the purse strings for the entire kingdom, and anything we plan will need his blessing."

"At this rate, I am not even certain that I will be allowed to remain in office to press our case."

"Jorelial Rey, you are now the elected and duly installed Regent of Eneri Clare, and it is each member's sworn duty to back you up and honor your decisions no matter what he thinks personally. Even if you do not heed their counsel."

"Unless I am insane."

"You are not. You know that."

"Ah, but how do I prove it? I told them all to go home and consider with an open mind until I could present you in person, and they could form their own impressions of you."

Tvrdik's mouth was set in a thin line. "I should have been there today. I should have gone with you into that lion's den…"

"No, Tvrdik, don't even think of it. There will be plenty of opportunity for you to speak with them later. And when you go, I want you strong and passionate and filled with confidence, the way I have come to know you. That is what will change their minds, I'm counting on it. So you must let yourself recover for the time being. Rest, and regain your strength. How *are* you feeling, by the way?"

"Tired and sore, and embarrassingly filthy, but otherwise much better, thank you. The doctor has been in to anoint and redress the wound, and seems to feel the worst is behind us."

"If you feel up to it, I'll try to arrange for a bath later. And we must get you some fresh clothes."

He winced, as if it pained him to recall, "Dare I ask the fate of my beautiful silk jacket, Delphine's gift?"

She hung her head and shook it side to side with an exaggerated expression of tragedy, but then her face brightened. "Don't worry, Tvrdik. We'll get you another, and what's left of the original can be put on display in a glass case as a sort of badge of heroism."

"Oh, please, no!"

They laughed, but she grew quickly serious. "Tvrdik, look at you there in that bed, barely back from a near fatal struggle, and yet you always manage to make me laugh, no matter what else is going on. How do you *do* that? I hardly ever laugh."

"Well, that's a shame in itself, Lady, since laughter becomes you so well. But, to tell the truth, as a rule, I share your affliction of too much gravity, and I rather thought it was the other way around. You know – *you*, who often make *me* laugh. Well, whoever is responsible for such a lapse in seriousness," he lowered his voice to feign conspiracy, "I think it is a very good thing."

That drew another small chuckle from her, but soon they settled into a sleepy silence. Tvrdik closed his eyes, and, shifting his position, couldn't help wincing, this time for real. Rel caught the expression, fleeting as it was.

"Do you want something for pain?" she asked.

"No, no," he replied. "It's not so bad most of the time, and I need to be clear to think." He drifted off again. A moment later he opened his eyes and looked straight at her. His face took on a new expression, lit from within by a dawning idea...

"Jorelial Rey, I've been lying here all this time wondering what I could do to help you convince the Cabinet, and what we could say to them to rally their support. Of course, we'll have to keep trying, but it occurs to me now that we may be barking up the wrong tree, so to speak."

Even in their brief acquaintance, she had come to know that look, and what it promised. Fully awake, now, she pressed him, "What are you thinking? Go on…"

"Well, here we are, proposing probably the most unorthodox and unconventional plan of action ever to be conceived, and to whom do we unveil it? Why, the most orthodox and conventional body in the whole kingdom. These are the pillars of society as it *has* been – the old guard. They represent everything the way it has always been done. They cannot *help* being resistant to the new, the maverick, the untried. It is, in fact, their express job to protect the status quo at any cost. There will always be the occasional exception, of course, like our Verger, but for the most part, one could predict that they would defend what has worked for them before." The young mage was sitting forward now, almost trembling with excitement as ideas began to crystallize in his mind. Rel wasn't quite with him yet.

"Tvrdik, that is *not* good news. We can never hope to turn a tide as entrenched as you describe."

"Ah, but there is where we have both overlooked something. In order to accomplish our ends, we will likely need an army – but not the usual sort of army. If we can't rally support from the old guard, we just create a *new* one."

"Just how do we do that? Can you magic them out of little toy soldiers or something?"

"No, no, no! Although I commend you on your creative thinking. No, we go to our friends, those with whom we already have some credibility. Those who believe in us, and those who have a real stake in the shape of the future."

She was beginning to catch his drift, "We reach out, and create our own network – our own force?"

"Precisely."

"Oh, but Tvrdik, the Cabinet is so powerful. They could shut down anything that does not come through the proper channels in a heartbeat."

"They might be able to resist the two of us, indeed, to dismiss us. But they will not so easily be able to dismiss hundreds of us. And maybe, backed by that much momentum, we will either be able to circumvent them, or, better yet, convince them to sign on after all."

"Tvrdik, where ever are we going to get all these supporters you're talking about? Maybe it's *you* who has lost his mind."

"Think, Jorelial Rey. You are more powerful than you know, and very well-connected. We have already enlisted some of the captains…"

"Huh?"

"Mark and Delphine will talk to the whole guild of Bards and Minstrels – creative folk usually detest war and violence. Warlowe has friends among the servants and palace workers. And if magical creatures may be at risk for their very existence in the future Xaarus describes, then we should enlist the aid of all magical creatures. Perhaps you could prevail upon Tashroth to meet with the remaining dragons, and Stewart knows all the talking beasts… Ondine has found a collective of unicorns up the river a bit, and even some local naiads who might listen to her. Perhaps Verger knows of others who remember Xaarus fondly, and might be pleased to join in his cause…and I have Xaarus himself."

Jorelial Rey was staring at the wizard with wide eyes and every muscle taut, scarcely daring to breathe. Finally she found her voice, "Do you really think we can rally all of those to our cause?"

"What have we got to lose? If we can go to the Cabinet with backup like that, with a host of creatures and folks who believe in you, and believe that success is not only possible, but imperative – who will put their lives on the line to see it through – how can the lords and Ministers dismiss you as mad? How can they refuse you anything?"

"It would take some time and hard work, but we just might be able to build a coalition at that!"

"I feel certain it is why Xaarus wanted us to work together, Jorelial Rey. We make a good team, and between the two of us, we have many contacts."

"You have all the brilliant ideas, and I make things happen. A good team indeed."

"To tell the truth, I am hoping the folk we recruit will have a few brilliant ideas of their own, but I do understand that my biggest job in all of this is to come up with a viable list of tools and strategies that we can all use to defend ourselves. I've already begun studying Xaarus' books, and I have a few thoughts."

"And now you see why I called you absolutely indispensible, and why you must stay safe, or all is lost."

"All of this would have come to you eventually," he reassured her.

"I doubt it. But I do think I can accomplish what you have imagined."

"I suppose it is about time for me to contact Xaarus again as well and get his input. I think *now* might qualify as a *moment of great need*." He sank back on the pillows, "The problem is it takes a great deal of energy and concentration to bring him through. Far more than I am capable of mustering at the moment, I am afraid." His face was beginning to look grey again, and his expression somewhat pinched.

"Tvrdik, I want to explore this further, but right now my head is spinning…"

"And mine is aching."

"Here, let me help you get more comfortable." She urged him forward and plumped up the pillows. "You've given me a lot to think about. In fact, I feel sure you've discovered the key to how we move forward from here, but first, you need to sleep. Another day won't matter much at this point. You're starting to fade – I'm afraid I have worn you out."

"No, it's important to me to feel like I'm contributing something. I did come here for a reason, after all." His expression softened as he searched her face, "You should rest, though, too."

"Soon. I just have one or two more errands to take care of. And then maybe I'll see if Tashroth is back from the mountains. I always sleep better beside him."

"Tvrdik chuckled, "I don't doubt it. No one would dare disturb you."

She smiled, "There you go again, making me laugh. Do you need anything? Shall I send for anyone?"

"No, I'm alright. I apologize for drifting already." His eyes were closing. "I take my leave of you, my lady, and hope that I shall be better company on the morrow."

"Fair dreams, Tvrdik," Jorelial Rey stared down a moment at the sleeping figure, then crept out quietly and forced herself to make one more stop before taking her own rest. She padded through the silent, post celebratory halls, to Steward Bargarelle's rooms, and knocked softly on his door. It was dinner time at Theriole, and, though she had no interest in food herself, she hoped she might by some good fortune find him in. She was in luck – the door opened, and Bargarelle himself stood before her, looking startled, "My lady! What are you doing here? You should have sent for me, or had a message delivered…well…please, come in."

She stepped into his office with reassuring gestures, "It's alright. I'll be brief. I was just on my way to the tower, and wanted to touch base with you on a few matters."

"Please, sit down. How is the young wizard, eh?"

Amused, and a little surprised to hear the question, she nodded, "Sleeping now, and better, I think. Thank you for asking. Partly I have come here on his behalf…" She went on to ask if he could arrange for servants to bring Tvrdik a hot bath, a good breakfast, and a fresh night shirt for the morning, and she also made a request regarding a special idea she'd been flirting with for the last few hours – something to surprise and reward the mage for his heroism. Bargarelle, dependable as always, promised all would be taken care of.

"And, dear friend, would it disrupt anything of great importance if I asked you to clear my schedule for tomorrow as well? I haven't gotten much sleep of late, and I could really use a day just to regenerate."

He looked at her with concern, "No, of course, take whatever time you need, my lady. At this point, they can all wait for your pleasure, though I thank you for asking."

"Good. Thank you Bargarelle, and for everything you do to make this place run so smoothly, and my life that much easier. It is truly appreciated."

She rose to go, but he dared to address her once more, "Um, my lady, pardon me, but, uh, may I have a moment more of your time?"

He seemed hesitant, and she was concerned, "Of course. You can talk to me about anything. What is it? Is anything wrong?" She sat once more in the chair he had offered her, and waited for the man to begin.

"Lady Rey, did you truly mean what you said about my work a moment ago?"

"Why, Bargarelle, you are a veritable miracle worker. I haven't a clue what I would do without you."

"You know I have served your family for most of my life – happily – and my aim is to serve you as well to the best of my abilities, for as long as I may. I watched you grow up here, Jorelial Rey, and I feel I know you like a part of my own family…"

"I know, old friend, and I am grateful for your care. Have I neglected or offended you in some way?"

No, no. It's just, well, last evening, when I saw how very close we came to losing you, my heart was in my mouth, both for myself, and for the entire kingdom. I believe the loss would have been staggering."

"That's kind of you to say…"

"You must know that very little gets by my notice in this palace. I have an ear to every stone, so to speak, and I have heard some things about the Cabinet meeting that took place today. Not the details of what was discussed so much, but whispers about your fitness to rule, questions about your mental state. I want you to know that I find it shockingly disloyal that so soon after you risked your life to bring order to this recovering land, they should treat you with such disrespect. Whatever was said at that meeting, I know you have your reasons, and that you are only thinking of everyone's good. I have been hard on you at times, nagging you to make decisions, to get things done, and to stick to schedules. But it is only because I consider it my job to help you to stay organized, and to remind you occasionally of where your attention is most needed. I wish fervently for you to understand that I never mean any disrespect. You may always count on me for anything you need, and I will always be your man. I will support you in any way I can, and I will do my best in anything you ask of me, never doubt it."

Jorelial Rey clasped the older man's hands in her own and spoke to him, eye to eye. "I never have doubted it, and never will. Perhaps I have not expressed to you how fortunate I count myself that I have your remarkable skills to lean on, and your unwavering patience with my weaknesses. Please accept my gratitude now, and my pledge to reward your faithfulness with my absolute trust. In fact, you are right that today has not been my best day, and your words have been a great comfort just when I needed them most. As soon as Tvrdik, the young mage who pushed me from harm's way, recovers some of his strength, we plan to hold a meeting of our own to let our friends know what is going on. I would want you there, of course, and suspect I would also need your help with quite a few details. I will hold you to your promise then."

"Thank you for your confidence, Lady Rey. Consider me your friend always."

"I will, and you will be hearing from me about that briefing very soon. Thank you, again, for everything, Bargarelle."

"My lady." He bowed to her and she rose to leave.

Warmed by that unsolicited vote of confidence, Jorelial Rey summoned her last strength to find her way to the north tower, and climb its steep, curving stairway. She had no idea if Tashroth would be up there, but the place where she usually met him was a comfort to her nevertheless. The sun was just beginning to sink as she emerged on the empty roof, the sky painted in a glorious array of orange and rose. As if on cue, from far away she saw her closest friend winging his way to meet her at their usual place. Standing back to make room for him, she watched him touch down lightly on the rooftop and coil himself comfortably. As soon as it was safe, she ran up and threw her arms around the great, opalescent neck in a desperate embrace. It had been a challenging few days, but comfort and strength flowed freely into her from Tashroth.

"Mark and Delphine?" she queried anxiously.

"They are well, and send fond regards to you. They are enjoying their time at the lake with great delight, and will be fine on their own. Just to be sure, I will check on them again sometime tomorrow. Your address to the Cabinet?"

She sighed, "About as we expected, mostly awful. They all believe I have lost my grip on reality."

"Give them time, little one; it is a great deal for them to digest. The young wizard?"

"We came very close to losing him last night, but thank the heavens he pulled through. He is recovering, but is still very weak. This day has had some bright spots, however. Tvrdik has already come up with an amazing idea, which he somehow found the strength to share. I have so very much to tell you, dearest, only do you suppose it could wait for a little while longer? I am so tired that I can barely put two words in a line. Could we just be together for now?"

"I have all the time in the world, little one," the deep, musical voice lulled her. "Come, sit beside me." The Lady Regent crept into her accustomed nook between the great dragon's forearm and breast, and stroking his warm scales, leaned against his beating heart and fell asleep.

Lord Drogue sat in the big receiving hall of his mountain estate, in the grand chair he thought of as something of a temporary throne. Its hardwood seat galled him now, pressing on the bones of his spare frame, and making him uncomfortable. He shifted his weight, and leaned on the arm of the chair. The hour was late, and he was alone in the oversized room, save for two silent guards and Gargan, his current favorite henchman. Gargan had proved useful on more than one occasion of late, and seemed to understand Drogue. The man never shied away from what was necessary, however distasteful. Power came at a cost. Drogue had long ago reconciled his own conscience to that fact, and remained focused on his goal. But it was not always easy to find others who grasped the concept, who would carry out his wishes without questioning them.

He shifted again, and sighed, "Where is the man? The message was clear. He should be here by now."

"My lord, calm yourself," Gargan rasped. "It has not been so long. He will come."

"There are other matters wanting my attention, Gargan. Am I a servant, to sit waiting at another man's pleasure?"

"My lord, the roads can be treacherous after dark. I am sure…"

A sound of rapid footsteps silenced Gargan, and Drogue rose from his chair, as all eyes turned to the hall's open entryway. A cloaked and hooded figure crossed the long room in long strides, and fell to one knee before the raised dais. His hood fell back, revealing a sun-bronzed and pock-marked face with a bulbous nose, framed by dark curls.

"My lord." The new arrival spoke in a high-pitched tenor, out of character for his appearance. He was out of breath. "My apologies. The roads at night…"

"Yes, yes, I know." Drogue hissed, pacing and making an impatient gesture with his hand. "Do you bring me good news, at least?"

The man swallowed, lifting his head, but not daring to meet his prince's eye. "My lord, the infant pretender and his illegal regent live. Our man came through, as he promised. He had a clear shot. Only, the most…"

he hesitated, swallowed again, "the oddest thing happened. Right before the crowd's eyes, this big bird swooped in, knocked the target down, and took the arrow instead. Then the bird...it...well, it turned into a man right on the steps there. The people are whispering sorcery."

Drogue stopped pacing, his eyebrows raised in surprise. Then his eyes narrowed into slits, as he faced the messenger full on. "Is the bird...the *man* dead?"

"I know not, sire. There was blood everywhere, and screaming. I saw them carry him into the palace. I am sure he was wounded sore."

Drogue exchanged a look with Gargan, "Captain, we must find out more about this mysterious shape-shifter, come out of nowhere. Who is he? Did he survive the attack? What is his purpose at Theriole? Mmmm?" Gargan, a man of few words, nodded. Drogue turned back to his courier, still on one knee. "And our man?"

"They got him, sire. That were another strange thing. It seemed he were sniffed out of the crowd by a big dog. It held him there like it knew what it was doing, until the guards caught up. I ain't never seen anything like it, sire." Drogue's face wrinkled into an expression like someone smelling rotting garbage, and made a sound of disgust. The messenger went on, "By now, that man is in the dungeons, or dead, executed for treason. He could not have pointed a finger at you, my lord. If you recall, we never gave him your name."

Drogue nodded, "And then what did you do?"

The man looked up, meeting Drogue's eyes for the first time. "Why, my lord, it was getting dark. I blended into the crowd and passed the night in town. The next day I went to his house, where I first collected him. It was empty. No sign of his family, stuff just left out like they had run off in a hurry. I searched the place, but there was nothing there of value, and nothing to raise any suspicion of your part in this matter, neither. I questioned the neighbors, but none of them had seen anything, or had any idea where the wife was. There was one goat I cut loose and chased away, and I put the whole place to the torch as soon as the sun was down, my lord. A big blaze it were, too – maybe some of the neighbors' cots might of gone up too, I fear." He chuckled. "I didn't stay to see, wanting to get back here and report to you quick-like, you know. There'll be nothing left there to tell a tale, that's for certain. I made sure of that."

Drogue sighed again and sat down in his uncomfortable chair. "Well, at least I shall be saved the reward money for that particular piece of bungled business."

The man on the ground looked alarmed, "Good my lord, begging your pardon, but I still get my piece, for all my efforts, eh? I did my part, all just as you told me. Fair is fair."

Drogue rolled his eyes, and shot a quick glance to Gargan, who nodded and approached the messenger, as the mountain lord responded, "Yes, yes, you shall have your reward. Although, truth be told, it would have been more to your liking if you had succeeded in your mission, and actually rid me of that cursed child and his aggravating protector."

Gargan had reached the man, and extended him a hand, raising him to his feet. The courier turned his gaze back and forth in confusion, between the man he served and his lackey.

"N-no-one could have known about that blasted bird, my lord, or the dog. That's the truth of it. I done my part, just as you asked, and more."

"Yes, yes," Drogue intoned, soothing, "you certainly did, and I salute you. You have earned your share. Gargan, give the man his reward." And with that, Drogue rose, turned his back, and started past the silent guards, toward the small door behind the throne. Gargan pulled a leather purse bulging with coins out of his breast pocket, tossed it in the air, and caught it again with his left hand, circling the man's shoulders with his strong right arm in a gesture of camaraderie. The man smiled and reached for the purse. Gargan closed his right arm around the man's neck and snapped it. He loosened his grip as the cloaked figure sank to the polished granite floor. Gargan tossed the purse up and caught it again, replacing it in his breast pocket. He motioned for the two guards to come and dispose of the body.

Lord Drogue turned back in the doorway, shrugged, and muttered, "Nothing left there to tell a tale...."

TWENTY-ONE

THE ROAD TO HEALING

BACK AT THERIOLE, THINGS BEGAN to settle into a semblance of normalcy, as if that word were even appropriate for the current situation. But, after a very long sleep, hot baths, fresh clothes, and a good meal, both Tvrdik and Jorelial Rey began to feel human again, even energized. When she stepped in to see him late the next morning, he looked much improved, and happy to see her. She would not be able to stay long, but wanted to check on his progress before tackling the many obligations of her day. He had already tried lobbying to move back to The Cottage, but the doctor had been adamant that he was not to get out of bed, except for necessities, for another two days, and not to even think of travelling any distance for another week or two. Tvrdik sulked at the news, but Rel assured him that she would not be inconvenienced by his presence in her rooms, and in fact thought it better that he be close by while they were brainstorming their next move. She promised to send Stewart and Warlowe back to The Cottage at earliest convenience for more of the medicines that had helped him recover, and for books to keep him occupied now that he was awake, but confined. She put pen and paper near his bed and asked him to make a list of what he would like brought back.

She also remembered to tell him about Praeger, having forgotten all about him during the drama of the first twenty-four hours. Now it was necessary to fill Tvrdik in on her bargain with the accused archer. She had gambled on Tvrdik's ability to see things as she had, and won that bet. Despite his own suffering at Praeger's hands, the wizard was sympathetic to the man's plight, and, of course, wished to see the little girl himself if possible – especially after being told that the palace healers had stabilized her for the moment, but were still at a loss as to what the cause of her distress might be.

Tvrdik found the idea of exacting a personal penalty from the man somewhat distasteful, but Rel reminded him that, while he was recovering both his strength and the use of his arm, he would need a great deal of assistance with everyday activities. Besides, she felt it vital to impose some consequence on Praeger, in order that he might see the real impact of his awful act, and to allow him to feel like he had made some restitution. Tvrdik agreed, and complimented her on her compassion and wise judgment.

Now that the Grand Council meeting and Coronation were past, all the delegates and their families who were visiting from far-flung corners of Eneri Clare were eager to take their leave and begin the journey home. Before departing, however, each wanted a final audience with King Darian and/or his appointed regent. It was important to keep communication lines open, and to strengthen friendships and alliances, especially now. So, Jorelial Rey resigned herself to a heavy schedule for a few days, in order to accommodate all the farewell audiences. Bargarelle, even more sensitive now to her needs, did what he could to keep the interviews fairly brief and on schedule, so that she could have strategically placed breaks, and time for herself at the beginning and end of each day. She was grateful for his extra care of her, and she knew that once the palace emptied out and all her visitors were safely on their way home, there would be at least a brief lull in her public responsibilities. Hopefully, by then, Tvrdik would be well enough to join with her in implementing their plan to rally support.

As she spent time with each group of dignitaries, Rel made a concerted effort to memorize who her subjects were, listen to their individual concerns, and feel out their quality. She had no wish to send folks off in alarm, or to dwell on anything negative, but where appropriate, she would bring up Lord Drogue's recent bad behavior, and try to gauge each person's reaction. In this way, she made a mental list of likely allies and possible adversaries in the event that conflict came. Most of those who came through just wished to pay their respects and swear allegiance to the new monarch, and perhaps to make a good impression in case they were ever in need of the Crown's help in the future. The tantrums of some distant mountain lord barely registered in their consciousness, aside from the entertaining drama that it had provided during their visit to Theriole.

As the infant king was also often present for these interviews, or parts of them, it was a chance for Jorelial Rey to spend some time with him, teaching, modeling behavior, and explaining to him duties he would one day inherit. Even at his tender age, she was amazed at how curious and involved the little boy chose to be, how instinctively gracious he was to those who vied for his attention. There were times when he was just as happy to run around the room, shrieking with delight, or to dig in the mud like a normal four-year-old. But there was also this side to him – a side prematurely serious and quick to learn.

Wherever the two of them were, guards were now posted, standing silent and vigilant nearby. Rel couldn't decide if they made her feel more or less safe, but she had to admit the wisdom of their deployment. She sent a note to General Boone, thanking him for attending to their protection with such diligence, and also for carrying out her instructions regarding Praeger and his family to the letter. She hoped the extra acknowledgement, honest as it was, would serve to diffuse a little of the tension which had arisen between them at the Cabinet meeting. From time to time, in the course of her daily activities, she would run into someone else who had been at that meeting, but no one dared bring it up. It was as if, by avoiding the entire subject, they might be able to chalk the whole experience up to a rather unpleasant collective nightmare, and perhaps it would just go away. Once in a while, someone would inquire into Tvrdik's health, but it was always, "…that young man who saved your life," or, "the youth who was wounded…" There was never any reference to his purpose in coming to court in the first place. Ah, well, she supposed she should be gracious about the expressions of concern, and thankful not to have to engage in any uncomfortable discussion just now.

Meanwhile, Tvrdik, who was spending an increasing amount of time in chairs, reading and studying, had asked if he could take a look at Praeger's little girl. The Palace Physician, newly respectful of the wizard's healing knowledge after watching his own miraculous recuperation, brought the child to Tvrdik's room one afternoon for a consultation.

"Lynette, this is Tvrdik, who knows something about healing. Do you mind if he examines you?" the doctor said, leading her up to the mage's chair. Tvrdik smiled, and held out his good hand in greeting. The little girl smiled back shyly and hesitated, but then came up closer and took the proffered hand. She was thin and drawn and an unhealthy color. Her eyes looked haunted, as she seemed to be in constant pain, which only increased whenever she tried to eat anything. As a result, she was basically starving to death. Quite collegially, and with real concern, the doctor told Tvrdik that they had tried everything they knew to combat digestive distress, with only limited or temporary success. The child would improve and feel more comfortable, only to experience another vicious attack soon after. None of the royal healers had any idea what to do next.

Hanging back in the shadows in abject mortification, Praeger himself accompanied the little girl. The man looked worn and miserable. His shadowed, frightened eyes were fastened on the young wizard, seeming to take in the real hardship his treasonous act had caused an innocent person. Every move Tvrdik made that was stiff or pained seemed to cut him to the quick, and he fidgeted and squirmed as if waiting for his punishment to materialize.

Tvrdik noticed all this, without remarking on it. In his heart he held no malice toward the pitiful man, and his interest just now was on the child's welfare. He smiled at her again and used his hands with great concentration, both to 'feel out' her problem, and to send her healing energy, an awkward task, seeing as how one of his arms was in a sling and heavily bandaged. Somehow he found a position that made it work, talking to her all the while, and asking her questions. She relaxed under his touch and seemed to trust him. At one point, noticing his bandages, she asked what had happened to him, a question that horrified her father. Tvrdik glanced up at the anguished man, and then told the little girl that he had hurt his shoulder, and that they could work on getting stronger together. After a while, he gave her a little kiss on the top of the head and sent her back to her father.

"I can't be one hundred percent certain, but I think your daughter's problem is a severe intolerance to certain foods, which are injuring her inner organs. I did what I could to heal the damage today, and I want to give you some specific herbs she should take every day for a while. I'll have to send for them from Xaarus' stores, but I will get them to you as soon as possible. And then, you must not let her eat anything that is made from cow's milk or grain. No wheat, rye or oats at all."

"But, milk and bread have been the main foods we had to offer her. All the other children grow healthy and strong with these."

"And that explains why she has been so sick. It's alright; you couldn't have guessed – I have only seen or heard of this condition very rarely. Goat's milk and cheese is fine, and potatoes, beans, fruits and vegetables. The Lady Regent wishes to see her well, so you have had a stroke of good fortune there; I am sure she will help you to gain access to the right kinds of foods for Lynette. Stick to this diet, and let me see her again in one week's time. If she has improved, we will know I am correct."

The Palace Physician nodded and clapped him on the back, voicing his appreciation, and suggesting they share a meal some time just to talk about interesting cases, and trade healing secrets. Tvrdik had heard how different the man's attitude had been just a few days before, but was happy to grasp the hand of fellowship offered. As they all left the room, the young mage felt his energy fading again, but he smiled to think he might have done some good.

Five days after the infamous Cabinet meeting, three big things happened: Delphine and Mark returned to the palace, having had their fill of the outdoors, but looking refreshed and happy. Everyone was overjoyed to welcome them back. Jorelial realized how much she had missed her sister's infectious smile during those few days. That same day, the doctor allowed Tvrdik to be moved out of Jorelial Rey's apartments, not to The Cottage, which was still deemed to be too taxing a journey, but to a nearby suite of rooms recently vacated by one of the departing ambassadors. The wizard was frustrated not to be allowed back to The Cottage where he could have his books and remedies to hand, but was deeply relieved to be no longer depriving the Lady Regent of her own quarters.

The third big thing was, that when everyone showed up to help Tvrdik move – Rel, Mark, Delphine, Stewart and Warlowe – there was a further surprise in store for him. In order to mark the occasion, and reward him for his heroic act, Jorelial Rey had arranged for a little presentation right there in her room. There was a medal for Tvrdik and one for Stewart, and a title for Tvrdik. Lady Rey actually took out her ceremonial sword and knighted him, granting him title to a fairly generous portion of the unspoiled lands in the ancient forest surrounding his waterfall and the little house he had built with his own two hands.

"So, now you can officially be called, 'Sir Tvrdik,' and if you ever go back to your cot again, you will at least know the place is yours, and no one will ever be able to order you off that land. The ancient forests have always been under the Crown's protection anyway, so it wasn't such a difficult thing for me to arrange. And I certainly trust you to be the best possible steward of a place so pristine and magical, at least as you describe it. It's just my way of saying 'thank you' for risking life and limb to save the king. And me too."

Everyone applauded, and a few shouted, "Hear, hear!" Stewart woofed loudly, standing proudly erect, tail wagging, his medal hanging around his neck. Tvrdik, sitting in the chair surrounded by his new friends, was nearly speechless.

"I...this...I am overwhelmed by this unexpected gesture, and, my Lady Regent, your extreme generosity. You – all of you – have already done so much while I have been...recovering...that I feel I should be giving *you* gifts instead of the other way around. I don't know what to say."

"Just say, 'thank you', and take the title." One could always count on Delphine's directness in an awkward moment, and everyone laughed.

"There's more." Jorelial Rey announced, "Did you think we were done here? When we Reys do something, we do it big." She gestured for Warlowe to bring forward a large box, which he placed on Tvrdik's lap. The Lady Regent continued, "I spoke to Bargarelle about this only five days ago, and bless him, he delivered this morning. The man is a miracle worker. Well, don't you want to see what's in there?"

Tvrdik sat, staring at the box, blinking repeatedly behind his glasses, brow furrowed in confusion.

"Open it!" shouted everyone, not necessarily in unison.

Carefully, methodically, the young mage untied the strings that held the box closed, and lifted off the top. Inside were three brand new, beautifully crafted and detailed full-length robes, one in deep violet, one a rich slate-grey, and one a deep blue, always a flattering color for him. These were sewn from the finest soft wool, and were almost floor length, with big, full sleeves. They were, in fact, the kind of garment that only a wizard would wear; a potent symbol of his respected standing in the community.

Tvrdik ran his fingers tenderly over the soft folds of cloth, his face lowered so that no one could see it. There was an interminable silence, during which everyone in the room held their breath. As usual, Delphine was too excited for patience, "Well, are you pleased?" she nearly exploded with glee.

Very softly, without lifting his head, Tvrdik spoke, "I – I can't accept these. They are so fine, and such a thoughtful gift, but I haven't earned them yet. They mean something important, and I haven't – I mean, I'm not..."

Jorelial Rey interrupted brusquely, "The rest of us think you are. You're the only wizard any of us know, Tvrdik, and you've been pretty impressive so far. I have kept you in the shadows too long, and I think it's high time that you stepped up and donned the mantle of your calling, literally and figuratively."

Warlowe cleared his throat to get her attention.

"Oh, and the tools as well," Rel added. With that, Warlowe reached into a shadowy corner, where no one had looked, and pulled out Tvrdik's oaken staff. He brought it forward and offered it to its rightful owner.

"I hope it was alright, me touching it and all. Stewart and I brought it out from the house. We figured if you weren't able to go out there and be near your things, then we would bring the important ones to you."

Delphine chimed in again, "So, now you will be Sir Tvrdik, court Wizard in residence! What do you think?"

The pale young man neither moved nor responded, probably due to the lump in his throat. But, Jorelial Rey wasn't taking any chances, "Don't try to argue with me either. I'll just hide all the rest of your clothing, and you'll have to wear these." she nodded toward the box, standing with arms crossed over her chest and one eyebrow raised.

After an excruciating moment more, Tvrdik finally lifted his head to meet the anxious stares of all his friends. His own eyes were shining, and his voice firm as he said, "I *will* wear them, with great pride, and with gratitude for the generosity and confidence you all have shown me today. And I will spend every day of my life working to be the person you imagine me to be, worthy of these honors, and of your friendship. There are no words, except, 'thank you,' from my heart." He took the staff from Warlowe, caressing its smooth, polished curves, and a cheer went up around the room. The Lady Regent strode over to the hallway and motioned to someone outside.

"What now?" exclaimed Tvrdik, "There can't be more."

Rel laughed, "Calm down – we have to at least finish with a little celebration." She held the door wide, and several of the palace staff brought in trays of cold cider and sandwiches, and an entire tray piled high with the little custard pastries that Tvrdik was so fond of. Sounds of approval filled the room, and, and while Delphine moved the box of robes and the staff out of the way, Tvrdik reached for one of the little tarts, and took a generous bite.

"Ummmm!" he sighed ecstatically, "Are you all sure I didn't die after all, and this is the afterlife of my wildest dreams?" That got the laughter going, as food and drink made the rounds.

While the festivities continued, Stewart stole a moment with Tvrdik to report that he had intercepted Ondine one day at The Cottage as she was paying a visit, and had told her all that had transpired. As could be expected, she was upset at the news, turning colors and asking questions about the state of her 'Lovely Man.' Stewart had assured her that the worst was past, and that her friend was well and truly on the mend, missing her company. That seemed to calm her some, and she had asked to be commended to him. Tvrdik had been feeling guilty for not being in contact with the little water sprite, and thanked Stewart for taking the initiative.

"It might be a while before I can get there myself," he added. "If you happen to run into her again, give her my love, and tell her I am coming along well, and will try to see her as soon as I am able. And one more thing?"

"Yes, I'm listenin'."

"Tell her it is time to contact the unicorns, and find out if they will see me. She will understand."

Stewart's ears stood straight up and he cocked his head to one side in curiosity, but he asked no further questions. "I'll be sure t' deliver those messages should I see her." Tvrdik nodded, satisfied.

After everyone had eaten their fill, Mark and Warlowe assisted the guest of honor out of his chair, and into the adjoining room, where they helped him out of his nightshirt, and into one of his new robes – the blue one. The process was slow and tricky, as they had to guide his wounded arm into the left sleeve, and reposition the sling, sleeve and all. Then they helped him on with the boots he had worn for Delphine's wedding, the only footwear he had at the palace, but thankfully soft and comfortable. While they were busy with that assignment, everyone else scoured the room for any personal possessions Tvrdik had accumulated during the week: books and remedies, a few items of clothing, not to mention medical supplies, bandages, salves, and herbs for his own healing – and packed them all up in portable parcels. They cleaned away any trash and most of the evidence of their little party, except the drinks they were still enjoying, and tied up the box with the remaining two robes, the title and decorations he had been awarded. As they were finishing up, the door to the other room opened, and Tvrdik emerged, leaning on the great oak staff, and partially supported by his colleagues, but looking every inch the Court Wizard in his fine new robes, which happened to be a very good fit.

There was a hush for a moment as everyone stopped whatever they were doing and stared in admiration. Then the assembled company burst into applause, cheers, and whistles. Tvrdik, a trifle unsteady on his feet, nevertheless smiled, and did a slow turn to give them the total picture.

Tvrdik grinned, "Look! They even have pockets."

"I thought you might need a place to store a certain coin…" Jorelial Rey answered with a wink, handing him the precious coin bearing Xaarus' image, having salvaged it from his tattered wedding garb. Then she lifted high her glass of cider, "After twelve long years we have a wizard at Theriole once again! Things are looking up. Does anyone feel the same surge of hope and excitement that I do?" There were murmurs and nods of agreement.

"Hang on a moment – I wouldn't expect the moon just yet." Tvrdik remarked, feeling just a little pressured.

"It's not that, dear Tvrdik," Delphine explained, "We don't expect you to do everything by yourself. It's what you represent; just knowing there is someone out there facing the darkness, looking all tall and strong and wise and magical inspires the rest of us. It makes us want to stand up and face it too, and maybe even find what's tall or strong or wise or magical about ourselves."

It was beautifully expressed, and the young mage found himself reflecting on how right Xaarus had been to send him here – how starved everyone was for a bit of wonder. He glanced over at Rel, caught her eye, and whispered, "…the beginnings of our army." She nodded, needing no other clarification.

And so, spirits high and fellowship abounding, they half-escorted and half-carried the new Court Wizard through the winding corridors and into his temporary quarters, installing him and his few possessions, laying out medical supplies, along with a few leftover sandwiches and custard pastries over some ice in case he should feel peckish in the middle of the night. The whole event had been such an island of delight in a trying week that no one really wanted to leave. However, it soon became obvious that even the minor exertions of the last few hours had sapped the strength of the guest of honor, who was beginning to look even paler than usual, and to respond to people's questions with a vacant, confused look. Assessing the situation, Delphine organized everyone to help change the patient's clothes again, get him into bed, prop him up comfortably on a heap of pillows, and swaddle him in warm blankets and coverlets. By the time they were all satisfied that everything was accomplished, Tvrdik had already drifted off without saying his farewells.

Delphine took her sister aside, "Does he always fade so quickly? Should we be concerned?"

Rel shrugged, "I think the wound is healing, but after you left the other night the fever almost killed him, and he had lost so much blood. He is a little stronger each day, but his body went through a great deal, and is making a slow comeback. It is a delicate balance: we need him whole as soon as possible, but I don't want to push too hard and risk a setback. Besides, he already pushes himself harder than anyone."

"I didn't know. Now that I am here, maybe I can help out some. I'll keep an eye on him for you. You have so many other duties to attend to."

"Would you, Sweet Pea? That would be a great help. And welcome home. I really missed you."

"You were so right about the lake. It's the most gorgeous place on earth, and we promise to keep it a total secret. The time we had there was a memory we'll always cherish." Rel smiled. Delphine added, "And, Rel?"

"Hmmm?"

"This was all so wonderful tonight. You did a good thing for all of us. And especially for Tvrdik."

"No more than he deserved. It could have been me lying there in that bed, or worse. Do you think he was happy with everything?"

"I think you bowled him over. He's not used to anyone making a fuss over him. Give him time to take it all in. You'll see him bloom right before your eyes. I'm certain of it."

"How did you get so wise, little sister?" Rel grinned, and gave Delphine a hug. "Come on. We should all get some rest. You must both be exhausted."

And with warm farewells all around, the little band tiptoed out of Tvrdik's new apartments and retired, each to their own chambers, leaving the young mage to his dreams.

TWENTY-TWO

THE PRAEGERS

OVER THE COURSE OF THE next few days, Mark wanted to spend a little time with his family before they headed back to their mountain estate. Delphine was included in some of their activities, but others she was happy to let him enjoy alone with his parents and sister. After they had left, he had work to return to as well. All of this left the young bride with free time to visit little Darian, and Tvrdik, both of whom were glad of her company. She spent a fair amount of time playing with and reading to the young king, who now thought of her as a surrogate mother.

"When I am king, Delphy," he informed her one day, while not even lifting his eyes from the castle he was building of colored blocks, "I am going to make a decree that no one should ever have to go to bed before they are sleepy. And everyone shall be allowed to trade their vegetables for two desserts, if they so wish."

"You do that, Darian," Delphine giggled, "and you will be the most popular king that Eneri Clare has ever known."

Daily, she paid visits to Tvrdik, where she took it upon herself to escort him on therapeutic walks all around the palace halls, extending the distance they covered a little every day. She also helped him to begin exercising his wounded arm, at the recommendation of the Palace Physician, who suggested it might be time for the damaged muscles to work again. At first it seemed hopeless, the arm unwilling even to straighten or lift once the sling was removed. But Delphine was nothing if not determined, and she had her patient on a regimen of stretching, bending and squeezing exercises twice a day. It was slow and painful work, but after only a few days, they were fairly certain all function would return, with diligent practice. Each day brought improvements in strength and range of motion. Tvrdik truly appreciated Delphine's patient assistance and sunny disposition, even on days he felt frustrated or failed to make much progress.

If she had extra time to spend, he would sit and share ideas with her that he had been culling from Xaarus' books and manuscripts, or concepts he'd been toying with. He found her an apt and intelligent pupil. Somehow, in sharing, he found his own creativity stimulated as well, and their brainstorming was often quite productive. Sometimes, after work, Mark would join them for particularly fertile discussions, which fast became Tvrdik's favorite part of the day.

He was up and about and feeling much stronger the day a soft knock on his door interrupted his efforts to straighten the room. It was Praeger, this time his wife beside him. The woman immediately seized Tvrdik's good hand, and pressed it to her lips.

"Gods bless ye, Master Wizard, sir! Gods bless ye for yer kind and brilliant help fer our daughter. We will never be able t' repay ye for givin' her back t' us. Thank ye. Thank, ye, sir." She was pumping his hand up and down and kissing it fervently. He could barely persuade her to stop blessing and thanking and kissing him long enough to handle introductions and inquire about the little girl.

"Madame Praeger, it's a pleasure to meet you. I am Tvrdik. Is Lynette improved, then?"

Praeger, looking quite a different man now, washed and shaven and in clean clothes, jumped in, "Well, come and see for yerself, sir. Ye'll be right amazed, ye will." He was motioning into the hallway. Tvrdik took a step outside his suite, and saw a little girl in the hall, playing at some game involving a throwing stone, skipping, and happily running about. She appeared to be less emaciated than she had been the week before, and pinker, and more energetic. Laughter had nearly erased the drawn, pinched look of her face, and the hollowness of her eyes. She already looked like a normal child, impossible to keep up with.

Tvrdik smiled with genuine enthusiasm to see such a remarkable change, and squeezed Madame Praeger's plump hand, "Oh, my! Look at her. I am delighted to see how well she is doing."

The mother elaborated, "Not even a week, sir, and it was just as ye said. She takes yer 'erbs, and stays away from the cow's milk and bread, and almost right away the pain stops. She's hungry all the time now, and runnin' about with t' other young'ns. I could hardly believe my eyes."

"And are you having any trouble with the diet I gave you, Mrs. Praeger?" Tvrdik asked.

"Oh, it takes a little extra effort, sir, but I'm pretty handy in the kitchen, I am, and she likes it just fine. A few small changes are a small price t' pay t' see her like this at last, and that's fer certain. Lynette, come here and see the healer, child," her mother called her over. Lynette stopped hopping and looked up. Seeing Tvrdik at the door, she flashed him a cherubic grin, came skipping over, and gave him a pretty curtsey.

"Good day, Master Tvrdik," she looked him over appreciatively, "I am happy to see you looking so well."

"And I, you, my dear." Tvrdik responded, "You see – I told you if we both put our minds to it, we would both be strong in no time."

The little girl laughed brightly, and made a beckoning motion with her index finger. Tvrdik squatted down to her level and the little girl promptly threw her arms around his neck and kissed him on the cheek. "Thank you, Master Wizard, for making me better so I can play with my friends."

Taken a little by surprise, but delighted, Tvrdik gave her a little squeeze with his good arm, and replied, "You're welcome, sweetie, but you really did most of it yourself, you know. Come and see me anytime, alright? Now, off you go – have fun." Lynette skipped away down the hall, and Tvrdik stood up again, "I would advise continuing those herbs a bit longer, and of course the diet will be important for life," he advised. Praeger seemed to be having a whispered conversation with his wife, who then grasped the mage's hand again, invoked another blessing on his head, and scurried off down the hall after her daughter. Praeger himself was left standing alone, hat in hand, staring at Tvrdik and blinking, a sort of apprehensive, lost expression on his face. Tvrdik cocked his head to one side and took the man's measure. "Would you like to come in, sir?" he invited, "You'll forgive me, but I think I will need to sit down again." He turned back into the room, Praeger on his heels, and settled himself in his big, comfortable chair. But before he could offer a second chair to his guest, the man was on the floor before him, down on one knee. Head hung low, and hat in hand, his nervous fingers continually worrying and fraying the brim, Mr. Praeger addressed the mage in a low voice hoarse with emotion.

"Ye're a good soul, sir, a good man. You and the Lady Regent have done so much for our little family. Ye have given me back my life, my livelihood, and above all, my beloved child, whole and happy and like to grow up and have babies of her own. All this, and here am I, deserving of none of it – deserving of naught but yer scorn and hatred, and yer curses for the grave wrong I have done ye. I tell ye now, I was not in my right mind, and I have never regretted anything so much in my life. I have never before knowingly harmed a soul, sir, you must believe me. I will carry to my grave the burden of what I did to ye, who had given me no cause, and who now returns so much good for evil. I canna ask yer forgiveness, but I ask you to believe me that I will do no harm ever again. And, I ask you to accept my service now as payment for the troubles I have caused ye. Use me as you will, sir, in whatever way and for whatever time you deem fit."

Tvrdik was taken aback at the man's heartfelt speech, and moved at his obvious distress. "Praeger, I beg you, get up off of your knees. There is a chair here – sit down and we will talk…"

But the man would not get up. Instead, he groveled lower still, and grabbed hold of Tvrdik's boot, beginning to weep, "No, sir, I dare not look ye in the eye. I am not worthy even to wipe yer boots…"

"Praeger, please! I want nothing of you. This is entirely unnecessary. I am happy to see your daughter thriving, and glad to be of some help. She is a charming, delightful little imp, and deserves a happy life."

"Aye, and her father deserves torture and death for his treachery. When I came with her a week ago and saw ye so pale and pained, and yet so kind, it cut me to the quick to see what I had done, and for what? And still, you struggle, yer shoulder…"

Tvrdik willed all of his strength into his sound right arm, which he used to firmly lift the limp figure from the ground and install him in the chair facing his. "Master Praeger, I beg you to calm yourself and let us speak man to man…there, that's better." Praeger pulled out a large handkerchief and blew his nose with a resonant blast. Tvrdik continued, "Sir, I know your story, and I assure you I bear you no ill will. We were all fortunate that no real lasting harm was done to anyone, so there is room for second chances. See, I am mending, every day a little stronger.

And King Darian and the Lady Regent are well, as is Lynette now, so some good came of the whole episode. All of us make bad decisions – errors in judgment – sometime in our lives. The important thing is to recognize the errors, learn from them, and make repairs where we can. I appreciate your apology, but just looking at you, I can see you have suffered enough, and I am content." As he spoke, Tvrdik thought fleetingly of Benjin and Ailianne, wishing there had been a second chance for them.

Praeger squirmed, "But what may I *do* for ye, sir?"

Tvrdik shrugged, "You don't need to do anything, Praeger. I forgive you. I trust your promise that you will never intentionally hurt another soul. That's enough for me. Go. Be happy."

Praeger's face took on a panic-stricken look. "No, no, sir! You *must* let me serve you. It were part o' my agreement with the Lady Regent. This will never do. She has been most generous t' us, and I swore I would do penance for your losses. You *must* employ me in some way, sir. Please, please do not send me away. I dare not break my word t' the Lady, and truth be told, I would rest much easier in myself if I could find some way to repay you. I am strong and able, and will not shy from any task…"

The man was so pitiful and insistent that it took Tvrdik off guard. Perhaps he had underestimated the importance of giving this haunted man a chance to make amends. Jorelial Rey was truly a wise leader to have understood that instinctively. He paused a moment to think.

"Praeger, have you any skill with gardens?"

The little man blinked, then lit up, "Why, I have worked in small fields and kitchen gardens since I was but a lad. My wife and I always grew a good portion of our own food, and enough to sell a bit on the side. This time of year, I do miss having my hands in the dirt. You know we had to flee our old homestead for fear of that wicked Lord Drogue…"

Tvrdik's eyebrows knitted at that. Another wise move he would not have thought of, but then the man must be bored and restless to boot. "I'll tell you what I was thinking. Do you know where old Master Xaarus used to live, on the riverwalk?"

"Aye, or some idea thereabouts…"

"Well, the Lady Rey had only recently given me permission to stay there, and I had only just fixed up the house, and gotten the garden back in shape when all of this foolery happened. It's a rather large garden: some edibles, but also many medicinal herbs and flowers, important to any healing work I might do. One of my chief regrets is that all this time that I am stuck here at Theriole – on doctor's orders, mind you – the days go by and no one is tending to the garden there. Watering, weeding, harvesting, and the like. Before long, it will be back to wild again, and we will have lost this year's yield. And, of course, even when they do let me out of here, I won't be much use for awhile one-handed..." he made a feeble sort of gesture with his bandaged arm in its sling.

"A terrible shame that would be, sir, with so much important growin' there, and the rain being as sparse as it has been this year..." Praeger was sounding positively enthusiastic.

"Yes, I've been thinking that as well..." Tvrdik sighed.

"Oh, sir, say the word, and I will be down there first thing in the morning with spade and hoe. Give me leave to put the land back to rights."

"It would be a tremendous favor to me, Praeger, an important work indeed. You could check in here as often as you wish, so that I could guide you on which of the less familiar plants are *not* weeds, and on what flowers and leaves should be preserved, dried, etcetera. Could you handle that for me too?"

"I daresay my wife would be right smart at helping with those things, sir. She has a way with preserves..."

"Right, then. It's settled. If you see a big dog hanging around down there, his name is Stewart, and he is a good friend minding the house for me. I am most grateful for your assistance."

At the mention of the dog, Praeger's mouth tightened a bit, remembering their first encounter, but he swallowed and said, "Master Wizard, I am well pleased to have a service to do for ye, and again, for the pain and suffering I have caused ye..."

"Let's hear no more of that. In a while all of that will be a distant memory, but at least my garden will be intact."

"Oh, ye'll be well pleased with it, that ye will, sir. Ye'll see." And, fairly beaming, tattered hat still in hand, he made his way out of the room backward, bobbing up and down all the way. Left alone with his thoughts once more, Tvrdik marveled at how little it sometimes took to make people bloom. Not so long ago, he himself had appeared to be a wild man that folk might have shied away from on the road. And now…well, things were different now, was all. And with that, confident that he had put Xaarus' rich treasure-trove of a garden into capable hands, the young mage decided to take a nap.

TWENTY-THREE

BACK TO THE MASTER

As often as possible, during those days of Tvrdik's recovery, Jorelial Rey stole time to visit with the patient. Sometimes they would have tea, or a bite, served in this case by palace staff without any magic. Tvrdik would share some of his ideas for countering Lord Drogue, both the sophisticated and the simple. Some were new concepts he was studying in Xaarus' dusty volumes, difficult to explain. At times she lost patience – and faith – trying to wrap her mind around the things he was suggesting. She would pace the room, chewing at her fingers, and sometimes would lose her temper in frustration. But Tvrdik was always steady and calm, patient and soft-spoken, unshakeable in his convictions. He was beginning to understand and anticipate her moods, what to ignore and what to seize upon. Sometimes, he would draw diagrams for her to take back to Tashroth, and the dragon would pore over them with her late into the night, finding new ways to explain things, and adding his own ancient and magical perspectives. In their time together, Tvrdik and Rel would also discuss individuals and groups they thought they could approach for support, and planned how, and through whom, they could reach out. Little by little, a skeletal sort of framework emerged – mere possibilities, but enough to give them heart.

At last, a full two weeks after the first disastrous presentation to the Cabinet, they agreed it was time for Tvrdik to introduce himself formally, and address that august body himself. The passing weeks had turned the days warm and longer, and the rhododendron were in full bloom in Theriole's gardens. The flowers of early spring had withered and been replaced by fragrant honeysuckle and roses. Stewart had been by often to visit, relaying wistful messages from Ondine, as well as the news that Praeger had made the cottage gardens a personal mission, working with fervor for hours on end in the various patches, and even straying into a few outdoor repairs on the house, which he judged were needed. Praeger himself had come by every few days for detailed instructions on what to do with the medicinal herbs and flowers ready for harvesting. He seemed energized with his new purpose, and, all in all, happy. Only once had he pulled out a few handfuls of medicinal plants, thinking them weeds, and on discovering his error, was on the way back to deep despair when he saw the mage laughing, and realized the offense was nothing serious.

Tvrdik was feeling much better, his energy and stamina greatly improved. His wound was healing well, and he no longer needed bandages, though the palace healer encouraged him to continue using the sling whenever possible. Delphine had taken him out for walks on the grounds nearby, where he could at least enjoy fresh air and sunshine, and he was progressing in his exercise regimens, achieving more strength and flexibility each day. He was already straining at the bit to move back to Xaarus' Cottage, and was told that as soon as he could easily make the journey, on foot, on his own, he would be allowed to go. Jorelial Rey did not want him to be even that far away while they were working out stratagems, if he were going to be confined there in isolation. There might, however, be some advantage to having a place to meet and discuss things, away from prying palace ears. As the mage got closer to being cleared to move, they had to agree that there was no longer any real reason to delay addressing the Cabinet.

Tvrdik was eager to try his hand at swaying the most powerful figures in the kingdom to his cause, but decided it might be helpful to have a conversation with Xaarus before going into the lions' den. He was a little uncertain of the energy it would take to summon his old teacher, but it seemed as good a time as any to give it a try. Jorelial Rey wanted to be present for the communication, and Tvrdik agreed it would be wise for someone he trusted to be around anyway, in case…well, in case the effort proved too much for him. But then they decided it might be a good idea for Tashroth to be present as well, and so needed to find a big enough, out of the way space. The tower roof was still out of the question for the recovering mage, and nothing inside the palace would accommodate even a dragon's head comfortably. At last, Tvrdik suggested that he was certain he could walk as far as the garden alcove where Mark and Delphine had been married. There were benches to sit on, and it was quite private. If they went early, they would avoid discovery, and still have a little of the warm, early summer sun. So, Jorelial Rey sent out a message to all of the Cabinet that on Monday afternoon they should assemble to meet and question the new Court Wizard. And on Sunday morning, before almost anyone was up, she arrived at the door of Tvrdik's room to help escort him into the garden.

Tash had already planted himself on a stretch of lawn nearby, from whence he could arch his long neck and lower his head into the little guarded corner, as he did at the wedding. The dragon was just as curious as the Lady Regent about what this link over time and space would look like, and was delighted to be included in the proceedings. Tvrdik took his oaken staff along for both physical and magical support, and Rel insisted he take her arm as well. But she was pleasantly surprised that he seemed to stride along without any need of external props, and he only winced once when she accidentally tugged on his arm from an unfortunate angle. Within minutes, they were sitting on stone benches in the quiet, lovely alcove, no one else in sight. The sounds of water burbled in rhythm from the swan fountain, and a windchime leftover from the wedding surrounded them with melody. They both felt that with their first deep breath in that place, the doubts and tensions they carried all melted away. It was a magical spot, and a good choice for the morning's endeavor.

Tvrdik sat square on the bench, spine erect, and feet planted solidly apart, holding his staff upright before him with both hands. One end rested firmly on the cobblestones, and he leaned into it, lightly touching its polished gnarls to his forehead. Breathing deeply, eyes closed, he concentrated on all of his memories of Xaarus: the old man's kind, lined face, the roughness of his homespun robes, the scent of sage and lavender. Almost like waking gently from a dream, Tvrdik realized that the image he was looking at had already passed from the remembered to the real, and he felt embraced by a wave of love and deep concern.

"Oh, my dear boy," the image said, "I have taken from your mind the history of the last few weeks and I am so sorry for all that you have endured. This was something I could not have foreseen, and when I think of how close we came to losing you…"

Tvrdik smiled his crooked smile, "You could not have foreseen my foolish, gallant impulse, is that it, Master?"

"I didn't mean it quite like that, boy. You did a brave and wonderful thing, but I am glad that you are still here to tell the tale. My compliments on your skilled use of my healing potions, and also on the compassionate treatment of your attacker – a most creative way to cultivate the new attitude we have talked about so much."

"Well, *that*, Master, was all the Lady Regent. It was she who was wise enough to see his true nature, and treat him kindly. I daresay the man is firmly in our camp, now, forever."

"Well done. You see, there is very little that cannot be healed with enough love and understanding."

"Yes, Master."

"What is he saying, Tvrdik? What about me?" Hearing her name, Jorelial Rey had jumped up from her bench, excited and frustrated to be privy to only half of a conversation.

"He commends you on how you handled Praeger; it impressed him." That brought a proud grin to her face. Imagine, a personal nod from Xaarus himself!

"Jorelial Rey." It was Tashroth's low, musical voice over her shoulder.

"Shhh. Not now, Tash. He has to concentrate."

"No, Jorelial Rey. Listen to me. I can see Xaarus. I can hear him."

"What?" She hadn't meant to shout as she turned abruptly to face the green dragon. This was all too much for Tvrdik, who also started, straightened, and turned to stare at Tashroth in disbelief. The connection was broken.

"I said, I could see and hear the Master as plainly as I see the two of you."

"But, how is that possible?" Tvrdik was incredulous, "The link is only in my mind."

"I am not entirely certain, but as you recall, I have been inside your mind, which is, if I may say so, unusually open. It is not difficult for me to find the frequency again. It is also rumored that dragons have some ancient facility with time and dimensional travel. Our consciousness is not as locked into this plane of existence as yours..."

Rel frowned. "Well, I'm not sure I grasp any of that, but it certainly makes me feel a bit left out here."

"On the other hand," Tvrdik reminded her, "here, at last, is your validation of the reality of my claims: independent confirmation from the most trustworthy source on earth. We should have thought of trying this long ago."

"I admit I am somewhat surprised myself," Tash answered, "but it is very good to see Master Xaarus alive and well, wherever he may be."

"I told you," Tvrdik said.

Rel interrupted them, "But now, what do we do? There was still so much we had to ask him, and we have lost him."

"I will have to try and re-establish the link. I'm not sure I can, but I can try."

"Now that I am aware of what it feels like, I think I can help you to hold it steady, mage. Go ahead when you are ready."

Tvrdik glanced at both of them and then repositioned himself on the bench, eyes closed, head touching the upright staff. He began to recreate his sensory memories. In a moment, his old teacher stood before him once more. A slight rumble issued from the dragon's throat in acknowledgement. Xaarus spoke first, "What happened, son? I lost you for a few moments."

"Apologies, Master. I am here with the Lady Jorelial Rey, and the dragon Tashroth, who says he can plainly see and hear you through this link. Hearing this news startled me, and I could not hold my focus."

Xaarus' eyebrows lifted, but he was nodding in a very familiar gesture. "Interesting. Dragons *are* rumored to have some ability in transcending time..."

"Tashroth pointed that out as well, and also reminded me that he is familiar with my mind, having earlier searched it for deception."

"Ah. Also interesting."

"Can you see him as well, Master?" There was a pause, during which everyone held their breath and concentrated.

"No. I'm afraid I am only tuned into you, my dear boy, but it is a comfort to know that your claims can be backed up by another source.

Greetings to you, mighty Tashroth. What a pleasure to be in your distinguished presence once again!"

"And to you, Master Wizard. Your long absence is much lamented among my people as well as among humans."

"He returns your greetings," Tvrdik relayed.

"Well, this may be useful information later, but I fear our time may be limited. How can I help you, boy?"

"Master, while I was still compromised by my injury, the Lady Rey went before her Council of Ministers and closest advisors, and attempted to explain my true identity, your predicament, and the plan we hope to implement against Lord Drogue. She was met with doubt, resistance, and even the accusation that she might be unstable."

"Tell him about Verger." Rel whispered, tugging at his sleeve.

"Oh, yes. The Lady Rey wishes me to tell you that our only firm support from that body came from Minister Verger, who recognized your hand in it right away."

"My dear friend Verger. I could always count on him." Xaarus smiled reflectively, "Do give him my warmest regards…"

"I will do that, sir, but the issue at hand is that I am now recovered sufficiently to address the Cabinet myself. This is scheduled for tomorrow, and I do not know how I might succeed in convincing them to adopt our strategy any better than Lady Rey did. We were hoping you might have some suggestions. You have been most helpful on such matters before." Tvrdik was referencing his first encounter with the Regent. Xaarus appeared to be thinking. When he finally spoke, he seemed to be continuing the process out loud.

"I know most of these men. They are good men, and generally wise. But they are cautious and aging, very attached to traditions and methods that are tried and true. They need to be unstuck, even shaken up. Nothing as simple as a coin will help you this time, Tvrdik. As I counseled you before, be yourself. Be honest and open. Let your passion and enthusiasm shine through – it can be infectious. Be patient with them. Answer their questions – give them the proof they want. And, if they are still resistant, summon me again in their presence."

"But they will not be able to see or hear you…"

"We may still be able to conjure a few surprises that will turn heads. I will be ready. Seek me when you need me, and go with confidence."

"Master, I have been studying your books and parchments, and have begun to assemble many ideas for our defense. But your input is vital to our success. I am so new at all of this."

"One thing at a time, son. Let us approach the hurdle of the Cabinet first. There will be time for all the rest, and I will most certainly be with you many times as you craft your plans. I can already feel you on all the right roads, though, boy. Hold fast. I am proud of you...." The image was fading again.

"Master, must you go so soon?"

"Tomorrow..." and the word echoed into oblivion, as Tvrdik felt himself falling, falling into a blackness, a void with no end, no beginning. Cold, silent, dizzying. He thought he heard someone shouting, calling his name, but the sound was so very far away, and he could see no-one. He was drowning in darkness, and it seemed of no use to struggle any longer, so he just allowed the current to take him, deeper, deeper, nowhere, nothing...

He opened his eyes to see the face of Jorelial Rey, puckered with concern, just beneath his. She was down on one knee on the hard cobblestones, and her hands were holding him upright on the bench where he still sat, gripping his oaken staff but slumped over limply.

"Tvrdik! Tvrdik, come back to us. Come on – wake up." She was trying to support and shake him at the same time, without much success. As she jostled his left arm, a twinge of pain brought him fully back to his senses, and he sat upright. "Ow!" He yelped.

"Oh, thank the gods. I was beginning to think we'd lost you again."

"What are you doing down there, Jorelial Rey?" Tvrdik frowned, trying to move his hands from their position on the wizard's staff and finding his fingers surprisingly unresponsive.

Rel sprang up to sit on the bench beside him, still keeping a steadying hand on his shoulder. Tvrdik could see Tashroth's huge face behind her, staring at him with as much concern as a dragon face could register. The Lady Regent explained, "You said something like, 'Master, don't go...', and then your head fell forward and you just started sliding off the bench. I shouted and called and grabbed you to keep you from falling, but I couldn't rouse you. Even Tash roared, but you were gone..."

"How long?"

"I don't know. It seemed like forever. Minutes, I guess. Maybe five minutes. But that's a long time to be unconscious, isn't it?"

Tvrdik pried one of his hands off the staff and used it to straighten his glasses, then wiggled the fingers to bring back their circulation.

"I felt my consciousness following after Xaarus, but ending up in this big, vast nowhere, all dark and silent. I felt like I was falling, but I couldn't see any ceiling or floor, or light, or way out, so I just relaxed and gave up. Next thing you know I was back here and you were shaking me."

"I tried to hold you here, but your link with him was stronger, and I lost the touch of your mind. I *am* sorry." It was Tashroth who spoke, still sounding worried.

Rel asked, "How do you feel now? Are you alright?"

Tvrdik shifted on the stone seat, and switched hands, wiggling the fingers of his left hand now. "I-I think so. It just takes a great deal of energy to speak to him over such a long distance. I expect I'm just not quite back to myself yet, and I might have pushed it a little and just blacked out is all."

Rel shot him a skeptical look, then hit him hard across the good arm.

"Hey!"

"Well, don't do it again. Do you realize my heart almost stopped? I don't even think you were breathing all that time." She paused, calming herself with deep breaths. Then, "Listen, you have no idea how frustrating it is to stand out here and hear half a conversation directed at nobody I can see. What did he say?"

"What? Who?"

"Xaarus!" she was losing patience now, "What did Xaarus tell you to do about the Cabinet?"

"Oh. Well, he told me to be truthful, and patient, and enthusiastic, and answer all of their questions – not much new there – and he said that if they continued to be difficult, we should summon him back again in the presence of the Cabinet members, and he would communicate a few things that might make them sit up and take notice."

Jorelial Rey looked as if she were about to explode. "Really? That was his suggestion? Oh, fine. Just perfect."

"What's wrong?"

"Nothing's wrong. Only I can't let you to do that, and now we are back to square one."

"What do you mean, you can't let me do that? You can't *stop* me. Xaarus told me to use the link in front of the Cabinet."

"Tvrdik, look what just happened. Look at yourself. How can we take another risk like that again so soon? What if you get stuck somewhere in between and I can't *ever* wake you?"

"Jorelial Rey, I'm alright. Just a little tired is all, and we had to do it twice, remember?"

They glared at each other in silence for a moment, when Tvrdik, noticing the dark circles under her eyes, and the anxious look behind the flaring temper, softened. "Look, I'm sorry if I gave you another scare today, but I'm fine now, really. I'm not all that fragile. I came here with a job to do, and instead I feel like a millstone around everyone's neck. Let me do what I came to do...please?" She tipped her head, birdlike, one eyebrow raised as if assessing the truth of his words, but made no verbal response. He went on.

"If it happens again, we are right in the palace, with every resource available. And a little melodrama can only help our cause, eh?" Usually his attempts at humor could shift her mood, but she wasn't buying today.

She remained staring at him intently for another moment, lips pressed tightly together, then closed her eyes, and let out a long sigh, "You're right. I can't tell you what to do – or rather, I can, but I don't want to. And I don't have any other wonderful ideas. If bringing Xaarus into the meeting is what it takes, and you're willing, I won't stop you. Just try to be careful, will you?"

Tvrdik smiled, "Relax. I'll go to bed early tonight and eat my vegetables. Besides, he told me he'd be standing by, but only to use him as a last resort. Maybe it won't even come up."

She rolled her eyes heavenward, "You don't know this bunch."

Tashroth, who had been watching their debate with curiosity and interest, moved his face closer to hers, and purred, "Remember to tell them I also see the old wizard. Some might find that an argument of note."

"Yes, Tash, don't worry. I will use every line of reasoning at my disposal, believe me." The dragon nuzzled her once in a supportive gesture, and lifted his great head high, surveying the gardens. "Yes, Tash. It must be full morning now, and people are up and about. As usual, I have a full schedule ahead of me. I suppose it is time to go back. I will come to you tonight on the tower, dearest. Thank you for your help today."

Tashroth nuzzled her again tenderly, "Be well, be strong today. I will await you later." He swung his head over to Tvrdik, closer than the young mage was expecting, and spoke low, "Mage, I will seek your thoughts tomorrow and help you strengthen the link if I am able. I am certain you will use it."

"Very good." Tvrdik responded, his voice breaking like an adolescent. He cleared his throat and tried again, willing himself to just breathe and be comfortable with the dragon at that proximity, "I appreciate anything you can do, Lord Tashroth. Thank you for your help."

Without additional courtesies, the great green dragon swung his head up, extended his wings, gathered his weight, and sprang into the air. Circling once, he vanished in the distance among the drifting clouds. Rel and Tvrdik watched until long after the dragon was only a tiny dot in the far-off blue, and then the wizard, who was still seated on the stone bench, said, "Well, then," grasped his staff firmly in his right hand, and stood up. And almost immediately began to sink down as his vision went gray and his knees buckled. She was under him in an instant, supporting his weight from the other side, steadying him with the help of the oaken staff.

"Stood up too fast," he reassured, "Just a little lightheaded. Probably past time for breakfast, hmmmm?" The wave of faintness had passed, but he did feel inordinately tired.

"Can you walk?" Rel asked without inflection.

"Yes, of course." But truth be told, he was grateful for her supportive presence at his elbow as they made their slow way back to Theriole. If he were honest with himself, he felt like someone had turned a tap and siphoned all the life-force out of him. He really did hope breakfast would help. Jorelial Rey offered no further word of conversation all the way back, and once they were inside, escorted him back to his quarters. All efficiency, she suggested that she arrange for food to be sent to him there. He thanked her and opened the door to go in, concerned that he had displeased her, or somehow added to her burdens. But then she turned back, touched her hand to his shoulder, and spoke just one word, "Rest." He nodded, and she hurried off to begin her own day.

Tvrdik leaned his staff on a corner wall and sat down on the bed. He wanted to be at his best on the morrow. He would convince no-one of his fitness to engineer an entire kingdom's defense if he appeared weak or unwell. What had gone wrong this morning? Even given the fact that he wasn't quite recovered from his injuries and the fever, the brief visit with Xaarus he had conjured this morning should not have left him so debilitated. If he could only focus and think it through, perhaps he could figure out how to prevent the same thing from happening again. But, he was so tired. Just then, a knock on the door alerted him to the arrival of breakfast. He wasn't very hungry after all. But, hopeful that some nourishment might help to restore his depleted energy, he rose to let the servant in. The rest of Theriole might be just beginning their day's activities, but after breakfast, he fully intended to do exactly as Jorelial Rey had suggested, and rest. An hour later, when Delphine arrived to help him with his exercises, she found the wizard fast asleep.

TWENTY-FOUR

THE CABINET

THE NEXT DAY, AN HOUR before the Cabinet was to assemble, Jorelial Rey returned to Tvrdik's door. She had received a message earlier that, if it were at all possible to arrange, he would appreciate a moment with her to compare notes. She was already dressed, in the formal garb of her position: a tailored tunic of deep blue with matching leggings and black riding boots. Her dark hair was plaited down her back in a single thick braid, and the silver circlet of her Regency was planted firmly on her brow. Sick with apprehension, she stood outside Tvrdik's door. It was a good idea for them to meet and get their strategy straight before facing the skeptics, but after the events of the day before, she dreaded that more bad news awaited her on the other side of that door.

It would not do to cancel the meeting at this late hour, but Tvrdik could do more damage to their cause if he appeared ill. She had long ago learned the hard way that most men in positions of authority only respected strength in their leaders: vitality, decisiveness, passion, and strength. Over the years, she had learned how to either cultivate or pretend to those qualities when necessary, as a single moment of perceived weakness could be used against you again and again.

She need not have worried. Before she could even knock, the door opened, and there stood Tvrdik as she had not seen him in weeks. Tall, bathed, clad in his best violet robes, his pale gold hair like an aura around his smiling and relaxed face. He was peering at her in surprise through the golden spectacles on which he relied.

"Ah, there you are. I thought I sensed someone at the door. Come in, come in. I don't imagine we have much time..." Amazed, she followed him into the room, and he closed the door behind them, motioning her to a nearby comfortable chair. Swallowing, she sat, following him with her eyes as he sat himself in the other chair opposite her and leaned forward toward her. He wasn't even wearing the sling today.

"You look, well...wonderful. No sling today?" she asked.

"Ah, well, it aches a bit sometimes, but I don't really need it, and I thought, today..."

"And how do you feel?"

"Much better, thank you. I took your advice and slept through most of yesterday, and then I had a really good breakfast this morning, and was thinking and thinking about what happened..."

"You mean, in the garden?"

"Yes, that's why I wanted to see you now. I think I have it figured out."

"You think you have *what* figured out?" She was mystified, but he could not contain his excitement, and plunged ahead.

"Why I had such a bad reaction. It wasn't just that I was still recovering. I mean, that was a part of it, of course. I'm not entirely back to myself yet. But I knew there had to be something else; it was all too strange and extreme. And I thought and thought, and just couldn't understand it until suddenly it all came clear: Tashroth!"

"Tashroth?" The man still wasn't making any sense.

"Yes, you see, it was the first time I opened the link with Tashroth present, and he got in there through my mind, and strengthened and held it open with his own energy. When Xaarus pulled back, I really wasn't ready to end our conversation, so I hung onto him, and in essence, followed after him. But not just my thoughts this time, you see; my entire consciousness went through the link that Tashroth was making stronger and wider. Somewhere in there, Xaarus disconnected the link, and your dragon lost me, and I was just stranded in the void between times, unable to find my way back over what might have been a really long distance. You were right to be concerned, as I could have been trapped there forever. It was you who pulled me back. You wouldn't give up, and you kept calling my name until I found you, thank goodness."

Rel blinked, speechless.

"I kept wondering why I was so exhausted all day after that, and then I remembered the weeks when Xaarus was here, training me, and how much effort it took for him to stay in this time. Toward the end, he would have moments when he was so weary, he would just collapse, or even disappear for a time. I'm not at all sure how this works, but I think the two experiences are somehow linked. With Tashroth's help, I was close to doing some time travel myself yesterday, with only my physical body left behind. And because I wasn't at my full strength, and I am not at all used to focusing so much power, I ended up useless for the rest of the day. All of this is really hard on Xaarus, too, but he is so much more powerful and experienced than I am. Anyway, I don't claim to understand it very well right now – I know I'm just scratching the surface. And I'm thinking sometime in the future this information might become useful, or clearer, or something…but, what I really wanted to tell you is that now that I know what was going on, it doesn't have to happen again."

"You mean you can link with Xaarus safely?"

"I think so. Tashroth told me he would be helping again today, which, trust me, is an advantage that I would not want to give up. But, I think I have devised a sort of psychic energy shielding that will protect me from drifting out of this time frame. And when it is time for the link to be severed, I know enough now to pull back and break contact. I'm sure it will work. It should be fine. And, look! I'm fine too – I just needed to regenerate. No need for you to waste any more worry on me."

Despite her impatience with his longwinded explanation, it was beginning to dawn on her what he was trying to tell her. "This *is* good news. And I can see for myself how well you seem today. You appear to be almost back to your usual, energetic, exasperating self. Oh, Tvrdik, what a relief."

"I thought you'd be pleased. I didn't want you to spend another moment anxious that something could go wrong. You already have enough on your mind."

"I can't say I understand much of what you just told me, but if you are confident that *you* know what you are talking about, and can work with it, then I trust you. Since I am here now, why don't we take this opportunity to go over the main points we want to touch on today?"

"Excellent idea. Fill me in on how the meeting will begin."

A little more than an hour later, the Lady Regent was standing before her Cabinet, nervous, but poised – the very picture of a confident leader. She took a moment to notice the faces before her. Minister Verger was sitting with Bargarelle (to whom she had sent a special invitation), both looking up at her with happy anticipation. Ministers Boone and Alanquist were close to the front, their expressions not at all so open. There was Lord Maygrew, her one-time champion, sitting back with arms crossed over his chest, curiosity flickering across his bearded face. Near him sat some of his closer friends, lords from the nearby valley provinces, only slightly less influential. There were lesser ministers too, of agriculture, public works, and so forth. She certainly had their attention, but not their faith. The room was silent. Time to make a start.

"Gentlemen, thank you for coming here this afternoon, when I am sure you would rather be out enjoying this beautiful day. We have much to celebrate besides the lovely weather, the pressures of the Grand Council and Coronation being behind us now. King Darian is crowned, and is progressing in his education. He attended audiences this last week with departing dignitaries, and you would be proud of the grace and understanding he showed beyond his years. I am certain he sent most of our visitors home, enchanted by his charm. Almost all have departed by now, and Theriole can settle back into some semblance of normalcy. Peace reigns, the sun shines, crops bud, everything is established in its proper order, and under normal circumstances we should all be relieved to fall back into the lives we know, and the leisure we enjoy. But, my lords, these are not normal circumstances. Two weeks ago, I informed you that there was trouble brewing in our land. You all had a taste of it at the Grand Council meeting, and later after the Coronation, where an attempt was made on my life. We might hope that these were isolated, unpleasant instances that will fade into memory and bear little lasting import. I told you then that I knew they would not. I also told you how I knew we were facing a more serious threat, and what I intended to do about it. Many of you were understandably skeptical, and I promised to present to you, as soon as possible, my main source of information and a valuable advisor on these matters. I would like to take the opportunity now to introduce you all to our new Court Wizard, heir and protégé to the great Xaarus, Tvrdik."

There was a round of polite applause as Tvrdik made his entrance from outside the room. If he was anxious, it did not show, nor was there any hint of the young victim who had nearly perished in delirium only two weeks earlier. Jorelial Rey couldn't help smiling at the tall, lean, serious young man in mage's robes, carrying a great staff of oak and amethyst, who immediately commanded the attention of everyone present as he crossed the room. Standing before them, he seemed to send down roots into the earth, and hold his head up among the stars. His eyes, behind their ubiquitous spectacles, were eyes that had seen visions, yet seemed to pierce each man's heart as he met their gaze head on. There was something of Xaarus about him, but something uniquely Tvrdik too, in the lanky grace and crooked smile. She was thinking of the scruffy, intense youth decked in carry-sacks who had first pushed his way into the Hall of Audience, despite her objections. The man before her now was the same at core, yet much had changed. This was no journeyman at his master's knee. She glanced out at Verger and Bargarelle, looking as if they were about to burst with excitement. Even Lord Maygrew sat up in his chair, and leaned forward. There was a wizard in the room, and he had their attention.

"Everything the Lady Jorelial Rey has told you is true. My name is Tvrdik. Some of you might know my face, though I was but a boy the last time we met. For six years, I lived here among you and studied my craft under Master Wizard Xaarus. He was teacher and mentor to me, and I daresay more father than my own flesh and blood ever was. I am a quiet sort of man, and when he vanished all those years ago, I decided the life of the Court was not for me. I went away to pursue a life of study and contemplation, which suited me well for nearly twelve years. And happily would I have stayed in my solitude, had I not been approached some weeks ago by my old master, Xaarus himself. How is this possible? You have already heard the particulars of what happened to Xaarus during these last years, and how he managed, at great pains, to return over immense stretches of time and space, to find me. Our reunion was too brief, and now Xaarus, alive and well, remains trapped in exile in a far off future. He would be standing here before you himself if it were possible by any means.

"Believe me sirs, after twelve years, no one was more amazed than me to see him standing before me, but I know my master. His story of travelling through time is challenging to even the most credulous among us. But, in the weeks I spent with him and since, so many proofs have emerged for which I can find no other reasonable explanation. Xaarus, from the future, knew to tell me of the tragic deaths of King Darian and his queen, and that of Lord Gareth Rey, when I had heard naught about these events. He urged me to come to court and seek out the Lady Rey with his warnings about what was to come, and predicted that she would listen. He told me that she would surely be acclaimed permanent regent, but that a certain power-hungry lord, Drogue by name, would resent her election and cause a great disturbance at the Grand Council meeting. And he has foreseen the likelihood of what we shall yet face: the greatest challenge of our lifetime.

"But he also showed me how our actions in this time could shape the future for many generations to come, and even affect the character of the time in which he now finds himself, and beyond. I, too, resisted believing these wild tales at first, until I came here and found everything falling out exactly as he had presented it to me. With each new event that fulfilled his prophecies, I became more committed to his plan for our collective salvation. I can see no other possible road. Those of you who knew Xaarus, summon your memories of him now, and ask yourself if you ever knew him to be anything but wise, straightforward, compassionate, and singularly uninterested in wealth, power, or personal gain."

Tvrdik, who held everyone mesmerized, even though he used no magic and spoke in moderate tones, paused here to survey the faces of those who sat before him. It was clear many in his audience were doing as he had bid them – remembering, searching for a reason to doubt what they were being told, and finding none. When he continued, it was even more quietly, drawing them in. "Xaarus convinced me to return here and offer myself in his stead, in service to my kingdom. He took pains to complete my magical education, and to establish a link whereby I may be in contact with him from time to time, to access his wise counsel. A storm is coming, my friends, a very dangerous one. Your old friend is heartsick that he cannot be here to help shepherd us through it safely. Thus, he has sent me to be his mouthpiece and his proxy. I do not pretend that I am his equal, but I have made a commitment to serve with everything I am and have, for as long as I am needed. Xaarus' dearest hope is that all of us will throw our lot in together, and with our combined talents, we will find a way to triumph over Lord Drogue and his forces, over whatever may divide us, and even over the tides of time. I understand your reluctance to trust your fate to a stranger who comes into your midst with an implausible story. But, I beg you to weigh my words with your minds and your hearts. Consider if I could have any reason at all to stand before you and invent such a tale. Question me. Ask for whatever proof you need. I stand ready to answer anything that is within my ability and knowledge."

Here he ended, lowered his head and stepped back a few feet, as if to clear space for someone else. Jorelial Rey picked up the cue.

"The floor is now open for discussion and questions. Our new mage is at your disposal."

There was a pause. Lord Maygrew gathered himself and stood for recognition.

"It is a pleasure to meet you formally at last, young mage. We owe you a great debt of gratitude for your vigilance and swift action on the day of young Darian's coronation. I was present, and saw you put yourself in great peril in order to save the king, the Lady Regent, and all of us from Lord Drogue's treachery. Were it not for your courage, I'm sure we would be assembled here today to discuss very different matters indeed."

That was gracious of Maygrew, Rel thought, *the kind of thing I would expect of him.* Tvrdik blushed and smiled his disarming crooked smile. "Xaarus is committed to young Darian's eventual succession. And to Jorelial Rey as his chosen regent. Part of my task here is to help protect them from danger, but I am young and still learning. Perhaps, next time, I will find a less painful way to accomplish that goal."

A chuckle circulated throughout the group. It was difficult not to like this earnest, self-effacing young man. That was part of what Jorelial Rey was counting on.

Maygrew went on, "I trust then, that you are well? Recovered from your recent ordeal?"

"On the mend, sir, on the mend and well enough. And that, largely due to the tireless ministrations of my friends at Theriole, and the capable staff of physicians you employ here." *And that,* Rel thought, *is gracious of Tvrdik.*

One of the other lords interjected from his seat, "Are you well, enough, Sir Mage, to give us a little sample of your magical skills? It's been a long time since we were treated to any wizardry here." There were exclamations of agreement all around. Tvrdik had expected this, and reached first for the simplest demonstration. Snow began falling in the chamber – first a few flakes, then clumps, then a veritable blizzard. Every face in the room was turned upward as the cold flakes fell on eyelashes and lips. Several men and women rose to brush off their expensive outfits. A dusting began to accumulate on the parquet floor. Then, in an instant, it was all gone. No trace remained, no moisture in anyone's hair or clothing. Another voice rang out, goading, "Nice trick, but is that *all* you can do?" Now that was annoying, and downright rude. In a flash, a giant bear stood upright where the wizard had been. Easily topping seven feet, it snaked its great head back and forth, and batted the air with its huge paws which sported sharp, curved claws the size of carving knives. The bear shambled out into the midst of the assembly and roared, its giant teeth a bit too close to one hapless minister for comfort. The terrified man shrank back, hands thrown in front of his face. And then, the bear vanished, and Tvrdik stood there, rearranging his robes and adjusting his glasses.

"Sorry about that. I may have gotten a little carried away." Out of the corner of his eye, he caught a glimpse of Bargarelle fanning Verger, who had turned green and slumped against him, drawing his breath in gasps. Tvrdik was torn between sympathy, and an inexplicable urge to giggle at the ridiculous spectacle. He turned his attention elsewhere. He would apologize later to their friends.

Lord Maygrew acted again as spokesman for the group, "I think we get your point, mage. You have some skill with illusion. But how will this avail us against Lord Drogue, should he launch a serious attack?"

"Illusion can be a powerful deterrent, if it is convincing and unexpected," he glanced back at Verger, and at the unfortunate lord at whom he had roared, still trembling and white in his seat. "It is possible to turn an attacker's own fears, his weaknesses, or his lusts against him to trip him up without spilling a drop of blood, or putting our own citizenry in mortal danger. But, illusion is not the only weapon at our disposal. Wizards also study to have access to powerful universal energy forces. They must be used judiciously because they can affect the very fabric of the Universe. They can heal or destroy, depending on intention. Human qualities like faith, love, determination, and truth, can also prove powerful forces in holding back evil, which is inherently flawed because it cannot hold community, but turns on itself."

Boone had been growing restless, and now he had heard enough. He sprang to his feet, "Wizard, you do not lack for pretty words, and high-minded ideas, but what can they *do* to protect us? It has been my task for decades to look after the security of this realm, and I have kept the peace by maintaining a strong, dependable force of good men, devoted to their country's protection. They are fearless, skilled in all manner of weaponry and strategy. They are well-trained and responsive to command. And any one of them would give his life to defend his king or his homeland from usurpers. *There*, sir, is your deterrent. Anyone foolish enough to move against us knows he is up against a daunting warrior band, and if he does not hold his own life cheaply, he will think twice. The courage of our warriors has been celebrated in story and song for centuries. They took this land, secured it in the first times, and have kept it safe for generations. Why, now, if there is an imminent, credible threat, would we throw away what has always worked for us, in favor of some other ridiculous, untried remedy?" His words were passionate, and they posed an honest question that needed answering, as it would be on every man's mind.

Tvrdik thought a moment, and spoke in quiet, measured tones. They had to lean in and focus to hear him. "I thank you, Minister Boone, for your very important question, and for the excellence of your forces in keeping us safe and peaceful thus far. They are indeed worthy of respect and honor. But there are two important reasons why Xaarus and I are advocating a different path. One is philosophical, and the other practical. I will give you the philosophical first. The reality is that war of any kind is never as straightforward as we like to imagine it. If war comes now, we will not have started it. We will only be responding to a threat, defending our peaceful way of life, as we have every right to do. But violence has a way of overflowing its borders. Wherever there is war, there is loss and destruction. Young men die, or are maimed, unable to care for themselves and their families. Old folks go without support in their last years, widows and orphans abound. Crops are burned, fertile lands ruined, and herds slaughtered, buildings and property destroyed, water fouled. Poverty and disease follow close behind. Cultural treasures and historic landmarks are decimated or destroyed, and the impulse for creativity and study is buried under the harsh struggle for survival in a ruined landscape. Even if the day is won, and peace is regained, endless resources must be poured into rebuilding and re-establishing a renewed economy. Fear and suspicion become a way of life; neighbor competes with neighbor for scarce resources, and those who are perceived as different, in any way, are reviled unfairly. It has always been so. War has no winners. But Xaarus, from the future, has seen that unless someone here and now breaks the cycle and stands up for something different, more and more irrevocable damage will be done. There will be shorter and shorter periods of recovery between conflicts, and everything I just described will become a miserable way of life instead of just a temporary slump. This is what we will bequeath to our descendants, unthinkable and unbearable. We may still have the power to turn the tide in a more positive direction. Left to our children to address, it may be too late."

Tvrdik's remarks were met with an uncomfortable silence. He could tell they were somehow struggling to reconcile the truths they could not deny in his words with their reverence for military might. Boone was scowling. Tvrdik went on.

"The second reason I recommend an alternate response is, as I said, practical. It is that Xaarus has seen our future in the matrix of potential time lines, from the other side, and we do not triumph. That is, adopting traditional methods of defense, in pitched battle, army to army, we cannot win."

Boone exploded, "That is ridiculous. There is no way he could know that. We are talking about the Royal Guard here, and an upstart border lord."

"It is no reflection on the worthiness, preparedness, or courage of your troops, Minister Boone. Lord Drogue is an unscrupulous and ambitious adversary. He will find ways to raise a substantial force, and follow no rules of civility or fairness. He is even a student of dark sorcery, as near as I can tell, and would not hesitate to use it, if he thought it would work to his advantage. I am talking about destructive forces that I have been trained carefully to steer clear of. I can combat them to some extent, but I am not yet certain how much he knows. As for Xaarus' reports, I cannot tell why our best efforts are fated to fail us, but I do know that Drogue's ascendancy, and his ugly tyrannical rule are a large factor in hastening the downward spiral into endless violence and despair which I have already described. It is so in almost every timeline that Xaarus examined. Simply put, we lose."

"Couldn't we use Xaarus' advance knowledge of the future to change it in our favor? To, say, help us to surprise Drogue, or escape some plotted ambush?" This came from one of Maygrew's friends seated near him.

"A fair question, but I do not believe any of that would change the bigger picture, or the inevitable outcome. In trying to trace back the timelines, it appears that Xaarus cannot see the fine details so much as the larger trends – not enough to really help us move by move. In any timeline he followed through, he could not find for us a military triumph. Men like Drogue only lust after personal power, and thrive on chaos and destruction. It is second nature to him. We cannot beat him on his own terms. Instead we must keep him off balance with the values we know and embrace – those that are second nature to us."

"I have never heard such a load of rubbish in my life," cried Boone. "This is madness. What does any of it mean?"

Tvrdik was quick to counter, "Gentlemen, we have an unprecedented luxury. If you were about to engage in a great enterprise that you knew would be costly in both lives and resources, but you had advance knowledge that you would nevertheless fail, would you not pause to reconsider the wisdom of your undertaking? Would you not do your best to re-allocate those resources and lives so that they would not be wasted in a futile effort? To do otherwise would be foolhardy."

"And if we do nothing against Drogue, we also fail, and we lose the kingdom. At least if we fight, history will not say that we stood idly by and allowed the usurper to take what he wanted unchallenged." Boone was purple. Tvrdik kept his voice calm and steady.

"What we are proposing is in no way inaction, nor helpless surrender. What I am asking you to do is to take the same courage and discipline and skill in which you and your men excel, and add it to the special talents and creative intelligence of everyone in this room to come up with new and fresh ways of frustrating Drogue in his attempt to steal the crown. Ways that, if possible, do not revolve around who has the bigger fist or the most brutal attitude. Ways in which we certainly have the potential to win the day and drive him clear out of the kingdom. Surely, if we believe in the virtues of intelligence, creativity, truth, unity, and the power of right, we must believe they are strong enough virtues to win the day without being backed up by swords…" He paused here for the response he knew would not come. They were confused and conflicted. He did not blame them, and actually counted it a good beginning to at least shake the certainty in some minds that he was dead wrong or insane. He swallowed and went on.

"I have promised to dedicate every ounce of magical skill and knowledge I possess to protecting this kingdom and helping it find a tenable road to victory. And though we do not have Xaarus here with us in the flesh, we will have the benefit of his wise counsel, his hindsight from the future, and his creative thought to help us."

Minister Alanquist, without moving a muscle, weighed in for the first time, "You keep claiming to speak to Xaarus. But there is no proof you have any contact whatever with him. You say you are in touch, and it is he who has sent you on this fool's mission. But how do we know that any of that is true? For all we know, you could be some madman, leading us to our doom. I see no Xaarus, nor hear any directives from him. Can you prove to us that you are, in fact, Xaarus' messenger?"

There were many shouts from the floor in agreement with this sentiment. Tvrdik exchanged a meaningful look with Jorelial Rey. They both knew what was coming next. Someone called out, "If Xaarus came to recruit and train you for a time, why can we not use magic to fetch him back here and help us sort out this mess?"

"I wish I knew how to do that, believe me. Time travel is an extremely delicate matter that no one has yet properly managed. Xaarus, for all his experience and brilliance, and his long study on the subject, botched his first try at it and got himself trapped. My knowledge of the subject at this time is so much less than his that there is no hope of my finding a way to retrieve him any time soon. Xaarus wanted to alert us to the dangers he saw, but knew the best he could manage would be a brief sojourn out of his cage. He judged the time would best be spent preparing a surrogate who could be with you in the flesh, and join forces with you for the long-term. It took every ounce of strength he had to accomplish that goal – to that I can attest. He will not be able to make that trip again in the foreseeable future. But what we do have is a sort of communication link between us over the centuries through which he can advise and guide us. It has already proved invaluable."

During this explanation, Lord Maygrew seemed to be conversing privately with three or four other lords who were leaning in to him and whispering with great agitation. Now, he raised a hand to silence them, and again put himself forward as spokesman.

"Mage, could you summon Xaarus now, here, before the assembled Cabinet?"

"I can. He even predicted that you might ask me to do so, and stands ready on the other side. I must warn you that you will not be able to see or hear him, but you may question him and learn his responses through me."

One of the lords became agitated again, "How can we trust that? It is still just taking his word for it."

"Xaarus will find a way to let you know it is himself with whom you speak."

Jorelial Rey jumped in, "I must inform you that we have recently discovered that Tashroth can also see and hear Xaarus when the link is forged through Tvrdik's mind. It was a surprise to all of us, but a definite confirmation that something more is happening here than one man's imaginings —unless any of you doubt the word of a dragon…?" There were mutterings all around at that.

Maygrew stepped forward, "We understand the limitations you outline. If you are willing, please proceed."

Tvrdik nodded. He was beginning to close his eyes to concentrate when he heard Jorelial Rey's voice, "Psst, Tvrdik! Don't forget the shielding." He nodded again to her and centered himself, right hand holding his staff firmly and fingers of the left in the pocket of his robe closed around the coin with Xaarus' face on it. He focused his attention on all his memories of the Master Wizard. Meantime, Jorelial Rey was sending out a mental message to her dragon companion, "Alright, Tash. It's beginning now. Lend us your help."

There was no sound or motion from anyone present. The assembled lords and ministers stared at the young mage, barely breathing for fear of disrupting his process. Tvrdik's sensations were beginning to be familiar. The sensory memories, then the actual feel of an additional powerful presence on the edges of his mind as Tashroth came on line, and finally the perception that Xaarus stood before him, as real as anyone in the room.

"How is it going, son?"

"About as well as could be expected. Most of them consider me a madman inventing an unbelievable tale."

"Speak what I tell you to say, my boy, and I will do what I can to support you."

"Go on, Master."

During this brief interchange, what everyone in the room saw was a tall, serious young man in robes having an animated conversation with an invisible partner, or else with thin air. They could hear Tvrdik speaking just under his breath, pausing as if listening, and then speaking again. None of this did anything to dispel the notion of possible madness. But then the young wizard turned his attention outward, to them, and began to stroll around the room.

"Xaarus is here, and sends hearty greetings to all of his old friends in this room, from whom he has been parted for too long." As Tvrdik passed Verger, he looked down and continued, "A special warm embrace to both Minister Verger and Steward Bargarelle, whose friendship and hospitality he says he always treasured." The two men smiled at each other and at the mage. As he walked about, between statements, his eyes seemed to refocus inward, as if he were listening to some private music or instruction. Jorelial Rey considered that either he was hearing Xaarus and repeating what he was told, or he was doing a pretty remarkable job of acting the part.

"My master wishes to apologize for his untimely departure from Theriole, and his unintended long absence. He deeply regrets that haste and over-confidence caused him to make an error which has held him in exile. He takes full responsibility for leaving you all without his help and support during this most challenging of times. Such was never his intention. He says, in order to help make amends for being so far away at the crucial moment, he sends his apprentice, in whom he has absolute confidence, and bids you treat him with respect, and heed him well. He will speak to you with honesty, and serve you tirelessly..." Tvrdik's eyes focused outward again as he turned a most interesting shade of pink, "I suppose he means me." he interjected.

Xaarus said, "*Repeat what I tell you, boy. Please refrain from editorial comment.*"

"Yes, sir." Tvrdik responded, to no one visible.

One of the lords whose name he did not know stood and gestured toward him in disgust, "Well, of course, a make-believe Xaarus would say these things, wouldn't he now. 'Sorry I can't be there…please attend to my messenger.' This proves nothing. We are wasting our time here."

"Xaarus asks how your rashes have been, since he has not been around to treat them, Lord Leonti? As he last remembers, they had cleared up well, but he wonders if you still have any of the salve he gave you for that condition?"

The man turned white and stared at Tvrdik." I – I don't believe we have been introduced, mage. How do you know my name? And how would you know about my…about *that*. That was a private matter…I told no one."

"Well, how *are* they?"

"Excruciating, to be honest. The palace physicians do not seem to be as adept in their treatment, nor can they reproduce whatever it was he gave me that was working so well. Why am I talking to you about these personal matters? It is a trick. Xaarus must have told you these things years ago, and you recall."

"Sir, I did not even know your name until this moment, and Xaarus is assuring you that, as a matter of ethics, he never divulged to his students the identities of any of his patients, even if he might have used their ailments as subjects of study. He only breaks confidentiality now to prove that it is indeed himself to whom you are speaking. And by the way, if you see me later about that…uh…*uncomfortable* condition, I believe I can help you." Lord Leonti turned purple and sat down, his lips pressed together. There were a few muffled titters from the other Cabinet members.

Tvrdik then turned to the Minister of Justice, "*Master Alanquist, do you still keep your first wife's jewels and dowry locked up in a special safe so that your second wife will not know of their existence?*" A communal gasp went up from the floor, as Alanquist slid a little lower in his chair. "*And, Lord Morrisey, did I not once accurately tell you where to search for a very valuable ring that had been lost since your father's death?*" The man looked down at his jeweled hand.

At this, Lord Maygrew stood to address the mage once more. He cleared his throat, and seemed uncertain how to begin. "I-uh-if-uh-if I do indeed have the privilege of addressing my old friend, Xaarus, then I want to welcome you with all my heart. Could you, would you satisfy me with some item of personal knowledge you might have of me, as you have for these others? Be gentle. I have, up till now, enjoyed some measure of respect here."

This elicited a few chuckles from about the room. Tvrdik smiled. "He tells the story of how the two of you and Gareth Rey once stayed up all night in a pub discussing philosophy and the meaning of existence, and how you implored him to come home with you at dawn and tell your wife that he had detained you on essential royal business." A much larger laugh went up from the assembled lords and ladies. Corbin Maygrew looked incredulous, and then, his round face broke out in a smile, "I admit I recall the incident well, and divulged it to no one else but Gareth Rey. I doubt he would have told his daughter, though I suppose it is possible…"

"Xaarus says that your wife was pregnant at the time with your only daughter, and that in her unusual moodiness, she told you that had it not been for Xaarus' earnest testimony, she might have had you strung up on a pole by your private parts for causing her to lose a night's sleep with worry." Another laugh erupted from the floor.

Maygrew winced, "Ouch! I asked you to be gentle. Well, that part I am sure would not have been relayed to young Jorelial, and is absolutely accurate. I am convinced, old friend. It is good to see you – or hear you – or at least, hear *from* you, and to know that you are indeed alive and well. Those were good times. I hope we may recapture them one day, though Gareth's absence will be profoundly felt."

"He says, *Truly, I pray someday we may sit together in that pub and raise a glass to his memory. I am greatly saddened by his death.*" There was a general murmur around the room at that. Tvrdik stole a glance at Jorelial Rey, who was sitting in a shadowed corner with her head lowered.

Corbin Maygrew went on, "As strange as it may seem to us, Xaarus, I am now persuaded that I speak to you through this young mage. I have seen his quality; he put his own life at risk to save the Lady Regent from harm. I acknowledge that I am impressed with his foreknowledge of her election to the regency, and of the emergence of Lord Drogue, someone whom most of us have held of little account until his recent antics turned a spotlight on him. I am inclined to trust the judgment of the Lady Rey and her dragon companion. But you cannot expect me to comprehend all of this business about time travel, and following time lines, and our changing the nature of the future. It gives me a headache merely to contemplate. I admit there may be circumstances my simple brain cannot grasp. But, when it all comes down to a directive to leave ourselves wide open and vulnerable to a dangerous foe, without the protection of warriors or weapons, cannons or ships, but only of philosophy, you cannot expect me to readily agree to such a plan. Or any of us, for that matter…"

> *"Oh, Corbin, but I do expect you to agree, because I have never before led you astray, never advised you unwisely, never spoken to you falsely. I should think that I have enough credit with each and every one of you here to ask your trust and support, even on this strategy, as illogical as it may seem, as terrifying and uncertain. Because you all know I have always been committed to Eneri Clare and its leadership, its peace, its safety, and its folk. You know in your heart that I would never willfully cause it to be exposed to harm. And Corbin, you should agree because, by now, in your distinguished career, you will have learned that great achievement usually comes along with great risk. Finally, I expect you to agree because I know your heart, Corbin, and the hearts of all here present. You all serve in this Cabinet because you also love this kingdom, and you would each give anything and everything you have to see it safe, peaceful, and prosperous. All I am asking you to sacrifice are your old, rigid beliefs, your doubts and fears, and to open yourselves to a new way of thinking. It is quite a gamble, yes, and the stakes are high, but the rewards are far greater than you can imagine. I leave you to ponder all of this now. I must sever the connection. This is the longest we have ever attempted to hold this link, and it does wear on both of us. My friends, I have missed you and embrace you all in imagination until our next encounter. Be good to my messenger…"*

TWENTY-FIVE

FROM CHAOS TO COMPROMISE

JORELIAL REY'S EYES WERE FIXED on Tvrdik the moment Xaarus said he would break the connection. As the Master's last words seemed to drift away, even though they were spoken with Tvrdik's voice, she saw the younger mage close his eyes and relax his jaw. His head fell forward, and he began to sway on his feet, still gripping his oaken staff. Sensing what was happening, she sent a quick mental message to the dragon, wherever he was, "Tash, pull out. It's over." The instant her thought was complete, she leapt from her seat, dashed over to the mage and shouted, "Tvrdik, let go. Come back; let Xaarus go. Someone bring a chair quickly..." There was no mistaking the urgency and command in her voice. One of the younger lords jumped up and carried his chair over to where Tvrdik still stood, just in time for the Lady Rey to grasp Tvrdik's arm and guide him down onto it. He opened his eyes then and looked up at her, "Thank you. I thought I was well prepared, but at that moment we were so united, so intertwined, that I almost forgot. It is such a strong impulse to want to follow him."

"Are you alright?"

"I think so. Very glad for the chair, though." He nodded in acknowledgement to the young lord who had delivered it.

Thirteen lords and ministers were watching this brief exchange in alarm, some even standing to see if they could deduce what the problem was. Jorelial Rey paid them no heed until she was certain that Tvrdik had emerged from the link unscathed.

Finally, Corbin Maygrew cleared his throat, "My lady, is the mage well?"

She glanced back at Tvrdik, who nodded, and gave her a wave of his hand. "Yes, my lord, he is fine. Sometimes, as Xaarus mentioned, holding this connection over such great time and distance can be draining on one's strength. He may need a moment to recover." She stood before them now and spread her arms wide, "What say all of you now?"

There was a silence in answer so profound and tangible, it seemed to be siphoning all the air from the room. People loosened their collars, shifted in their seats, and turned their eyes to the floor. Minister Verger, glancing about the room, summoned his courage, and rose from his seat. His voice was not deep or strong, but it rang with conviction, "I know not by what miracles we are put back in touch this day with our old friend Xaarus, but I, at least, am satisfied that we have indeed been in his presence and heard his wishes for us. In the past, when I have been fool enough to act contrary to Xaarus' good counsel, I have in all cases regretted my willfulness and error. Therefore, no matter how unusual and daring his instructions for us now seem, I am ready to throw my support behind them, and to place all the resources of the palace treasury at the disposal of those who will implement his will." It might have been the bravest thing the man had ever done. Every eye was on him, and beads of sweat stood out on his forehead. Would he stand alone? Slowly, Bargarelle rose beside him.

"I am not a regular member of this assembly," he stated, "but what authority and resources I have as Steward of Theriole, this seat of our government, I offer the Lady Regent."

Jorelial Rey, moved by their nerve, walked over and stood beside the two, regarding the rest of the assembly with a look of challenge. One other lord and one lady quietly rose and crossed to join the little band. With a gusty sigh, the sour-faced old Alanquist uncoiled his lanky frame and stepped over to join the Lady Rey and her supporters, arms folded across his breast. Tvrdik took this as his cue, and, leaning on his staff a bit, he raised himself from the seat they had provided for him, and made his way over to stand beside Jorelial.

For a tense moment, the groups on either side of the room glared at one another, and then Corbin Maygrew, always one to speak his mind, broke the stalemate. "Now, wait just a minute, here. I, too, am a loyal supporter of the king and of his regent. Dragonsbreath! I am the one who put her up for the job, you'll recall. But you've given us an awful lot to digest this afternoon. I am a simple man. Alright, I'll stretch a bit and admit I might have spoken to Xaarus today. I like the young mage. Personally, I don't think there's a malicious or deceitful impulse in him, nor do I think he is mad. Something *is* going on here that is beyond the limits of our everyday experience, though I'm a flying pig if I know exactly what it is. I am convinced that Drogue is a dangerous adversary, and that we may be on the verge of a war. If so, I will be very glad indeed to have a real wizard at court again to help us. But I have been around a little longer than some of you, and have seen many things. And this notion that, if it comes down to it and we are threatened, we may not even defend ourselves in any way that is familiar to us – *that* makes me very uncomfortable. Xaarus or no, I am not certain that I can commit to it as our only course of action. There may be good reasons for it, and what you are talking about doing might indeed work. I just can't put all my faith in it right now without a backup plan."

At this, Minister Boone rose as well. He looked positively agonized, and were there tears in his eyes? "Gods forgive me, I have sworn an oath to serve King Darian and the Lady Regent faithfully, and to obey her commands. But I have also sworn an oath to protect and secure our kingdom and its citizenry in peace and in war. And I only know how to do that the way I was trained, as our forefathers have always protected us. How do I reconcile these sacred oaths? How do I tell my warriors that the day they have worked and prepared for all of their lives has finally come, but that their services will not be required? How can I stand idly by and just allow some bloody usurper to march in unchallenged and take the throne?"

His impassioned cry seemed to stir something in the entire assembly, and everyone began to talk at once. In the blink of an eye, order dissolved, hands were gesticulating wildly, fingers pointing, voices rising. In the midst of this descent into chaos, Jorelial Rey saw everything with a new clarity. Stepping to the center of the room, in her most commanding and compelling voice of authority, she shouted, "Stop! All of you, now! Just stop!" The noise ceased as all attention turned to her. "Lord Maygrew, as usual, you are right. We are going about this all wrong, and it is my fault. I apologize. We are not enemies here. There are no enemies in this room.

For the first time in memory, a real enemy is barking at our door, and look at us, tearing each other apart. Xaarus said it; every one of us is here because we love this kingdom, we are loyal subjects of our king, and we all want the same outcome for the future. We are only in disagreement about how best to achieve it. Now, if everyone could go back and find his or her seat, and we could restore some order, perhaps we might all take a deep breath and start over."

At first, no one moved a muscle. But then, without a word, people began shuffling back to their seats. Someone brought in an extra chair for Tvrdik, and smiled at him as he gratefully accepted the seat and the gesture. In a few moments, the Cabinet members were all in their places, expectant faces turned to their leader, Jorelial Rey, who stood in an impatient posture before them.

"Now, I want to thank Lord Maygrew for reminding me that information I have been wrestling with in my own mind for over a month is new to all of you. As difficult a time as I have had believing and comprehending it, I can hardly expect your struggle to be easier. My goals for today were to acquaint you with the intelligence that has come to me thus far, the counsel I have received on it, and in what direction I am leaning in terms of action. I appreciate the support of those who already see things as I do. I had hoped to persuade some of you to go home and consider my arguments as you come to your own conclusions. I wished to introduce you in person to some of the figures who play an important role in the drama unfolding before us. But, I am bound to listen to those of you who still have reservations. That is why I am blessed to have a Cabinet to turn to, a collection of the wisest, most experienced, and knowledgeable minds in Eneri Clare, established to help guide me to the best decisions of which I am capable. It was my dearest hope today to convince you, but never my purpose to ignore your objections. It was certainly not my intention to alienate and torment a man of as much integrity and loyalty as General Boone. My apologies, sir. Your remarks are appropriate, your questions fair, and I have heard them. Lord Maygrew, you have been most generous in allowing that what I have brought you this day is at least plausible, and I do understand your reservations. Is there anyone else at this time who feels they have not been well-represented in this room? Who still needs to be heard?" No one twitched. No one spoke out.

"Right, then. Having heard reasonable debate on the subject, and having shared all that I know, and considered all of my options, I am prepared to offer a compromise position."

Tvrdik's eyebrows shot up, and he leaned forward, whispering, "Jorelial Rey, what are you doing?"

"Trust me," she shot back, and he held his tongue.

"First," she continued, "I still hold out hope that Drogue will reconsider his treasonous plans, and that what we fear is coming will never happen. However, judging from Xaarus' record thus far, we may not be so lucky. If he is planning an attack, I hope and believe I am correct that time is on our side. We know much more than he thinks we do, and it should take him several months at least to levy, equip, and train enough forces for a credible offensive. During this interval, what is key to our own preparations will be intelligence. We must know what he is doing, and how far along he is at any given moment. I can ask Tashroth to speak with the other dragons regularly for news of what they see and hear. But most of what we know will be coming from your organization, Minister Boone. As I know you have already begun to set up a network, I willingly leave that arm of our defense in your capable hands. I will expect regular reports, yes?"

"Yes, my lady." Boone seemed heartened by this public vote of confidence.

"As to further preparations, here is my proposal. Tvrdik and I have already been discussing the necessity of raising a force against Lord Drogue. But, we admit that the sort of resistance we are proposing would require a very different sort of force from any that, say, you would be training, General Boone. What I would suggest is that we each take six weeks to raise and train an army to do battle with the usurper as if ours were the only defense assigned to meet him. I would authorize, within reason, the resources of the palace treasury to supply and equip both groups during that time. My thought is that you, General Boone, would be able to begin immediate training for possible attack, as you would normally do, and the kingdom would have a safety net of our finest warriors, ready to meet the enemy in the traditional way. That should also satisfy those of you who at present only feel safe protected by sword and bow. Meanwhile, Tvrdik and Xaarus and I, and our adherents, get to experiment in recruiting, equipping, and training a force prepared to repel the enemy without bloodshed. If, in six weeks, we cannot prove to you that ours is the superior and more viable way to preserve Eneri Clare, or is at least as effective as yours, then I will turn the matter of defense entirely over to General Boone, to handle as he sees fit. If we manage to impress all of you with our competence, then I have the right to stand down or absorb all our traditional forces, and face Drogue with mine. I am counting on you all to be fair and even-minded in your judgment, and to spend that time contemplating the possible consequences that Xaarus has laid out for us today."

Noticing the horrified expression frozen on Minister Verger's face, she went on, "I realize this will be an expensive way to move forward, but I can see no other road which is fair to everyone present, and guaranteed to give us *two* layers of defense against our common enemy. Minister Boone, will you take my challenge?" She stood looking straight at the man, hands on hips.

After a moment's consideration he nodded slowly, "Aye. We will."

"Minister Verger, will you agree to my terms, and make appropriate allocations available?"

Verger swallowed hard, "Yes, my lady."

"Good. Lord Maygrew, will you consent to head a committee to evaluate the results of our little experiment?"

He was still standing, and was presently shaking his head slowly back and forth in amusement, a spark in his eyes, "Willingly, my lady. I can see my confidence in you as a fair, if somewhat *creative* leader was well placed. It is a good solution."

"In that case, can we take a formal vote here and now to accept or reject my proposal?"'

Bargarelle stood, "All in favor, signify by saying 'aye.'" The room rang with voices assenting.

"All opposed, say, 'nay.'"

There was no sound.

"The 'ayes' carry the day. Lady Jorelial Rey's compromise proposal is unanimously passed." Bargarelle resumed his seat.

Jorelial Rey smiled and let her gaze travel the room, meeting as many eyes as she could. "Right, then. Six weeks from tomorrow we will assemble for demonstrations of our accomplishments, and judgment of how we proceed from there. The gods grant that we are not called to battle before that time."

Tvrdik's eyes were as round as saucers. He had tried to get her attention in vain. Too late. It was already done. "Are you insane?" he whispered loudly, but she made a gesture with her hand to hush him, and went on.

"There may well be cause for us all to meet sooner and often, if Boone's intelligence provides us with matters of importance to discuss. For now, I am indebted to all of you for your time, talent, patience, and commitment to the greater good. Together, one way or another, we will preserve Eneri Clare, and see it happy, prosperous, and safe from alarms once again."

So swiftly had the last few decisions been made that there was a pause, as Cabinet members glanced around the room at one another, wondering if their business had indeed been concluded so neatly. After a moment, there were a few shouts of, "Hear, hear!" from the floor, and the general mood seemed much improved over what it had been only a few moments before.

Corbin Maygrew spoke again, "I think I speak for all in commending the Lady Regent for her even-handedness and skill in brokering an acceptable solution to our dilemma. I would also welcome our new Court Wizard to Theriole. It will be an adjustment to have a wizard at court again, but be welcome among us, Master Tvrdik...did I get it right?"

"Close enough, sir, and I am eager to be of service to any of you in whatever way I may." There were a few more affirmations from the floor, and then the Lady Regent called out, "Meeting adjourned, ladies and gentlemen – go out and enjoy the rest of this beautiful day."

In the confusion that followed, as Cabinet members rose and collected their belongings to leave, Tvrdik was the first to reach her. "Jorelial Rey, have you lost your mind? Six weeks? How can we have an army to show them in six weeks? How can I demonstrate anything, assuming there will be anyone to teach, or anything reliable to teach them?"

"Calm down, Tvrdik. Where is your usual confidence? We can do this. And it was necessary. Xaarus was right...and you were right. These are good men. They mean well, and we want them on our side. But we are asking them to take a huge leap of faith in a direction that is not natural. It is up to us to persuade them – to show them what's possible so that they can *believe* in what we are proposing. Otherwise, it will never work."

"But, what if they choose the other way in the end? Then we've failed."

"Tvrdik, I am not one jot less committed to the cause. We just need to give them a chance to catch up to us. Heavens help us, it falls to us to be irresistible…and so we must be."

"But, *six weeks?*"

"Tvrdik, six weeks ago, you were still in your ancient forest, and we had not yet met. Look how much has happened since then! I took a chance that we even have that much time before Drogue makes his next move. We always knew that time was short. I have just made it a little more concrete, is all, so we know our first deadline." She put her hand on his shoulder, "A little luck, a little magic, and a bit of a miracle, and we can pull it off." She smiled at him. At that moment, Minister Boone interrupted and bowed to her, "My lady, we will not fail you."

"Of that I am sure." He bowed again and walked away, but before she could say another word, Corbin Maygrew was at her side, his arm around her slim shoulders, "Rel, my dear, just when I thought we were headed for disaster, you come up with something like this: a brilliant way to invest everyone in the process, even when we disagree. You are, my girl, absolutely born to this job, and you have my vote again and again for it."

"Ah, my lord, I am not sure whether to thank you or curse you." They both laughed, and Maygrew continued.

"I am not making light, of course, of our situation. I want you to know you did an excellent job presenting your case today. I am at least partly behind you. But I am an old dog, and need a little more time and evidence. I feel better with Boone on top of his game, and I look forward to what you can teach me about these other possibilities. Jorelial Rey, your father would be proud." He gave her a squeeze and removed his arm from her shoulders, extending his hand next to Tvrdik. "A pleasure, young man. Most impressive work today. I look forward to getting to know you better." Smiling and shaking his head, he turned and strode away.

The room was emptying, a few of those gathered hanging about in conversation, or making their way toward the door. Jorelial Rey scanned the room and came back to Tvrdik, lowering her voice, "Do you see? Where Maygrew goes, they will all go. We have to court them and win them fairly. Today was a good start. You really got their attention."

"Well, that was Xaarus, and he could always charm water from a stone…"

"No, no! Xaarus backed you up, but I'm talking about before that, Tvrdik. About you. You were positively glowing. How are you feeling, anyway?"

"A little tired, but nothing unusual for a long day. I'm fine."

"Good. Are you hungry?"

"Famished, now that you mention it."

"Well, then, what are we waiting for? We have to keep our strength up. Tomorrow will be another busy day. Assuming the palace healers agree, I think we should move you back to The Cottage. We will need a headquarters…"

"Yes, my lady." She slipped her arm carefully through his injured one, while he carried the great oak staff in his right hand, and, arm in arm, they made their way out of the room.

"The bear was a nice touch," she commented, as they strolled toward the kitchens.

He chuckled, "I honestly don't know *what* came over me. Did I frighten you?"

"Frighten me? Don't be silly."

"Not even a little?"

"Well, maybe…a little."

TWENTY-SIX

COMING HOME

In the morning, Tvrdik packed up everything he had accumulated at the palace, which, with all that he had sent for over the past two weeks, had grown into quite a substantial collection. The Palace Physician paid him a call, checked him over, pronounced him well on the way to a complete recovery, made him promise to continue the exercises for his arm and hand, and released him to go home. The two shook hands, and Tvrdik thanked him again for his efforts during the crisis. The man demurred, but repeated his suggestion that they should share an ale sometime and discuss their profession. Tvrdik agreed. Then, on a whim, he asked if the man happened to be free that very afternoon for a gathering on another subject entirely. The wizard explained that he did not wish to divulge too much, but that a number of key people were being invited to discuss a matter of great importance. The physician seemed flattered and intrigued, promising that he would clear his schedule to be there.

The Lady Rey insisted on ferrying him back to The Cottage on Tashroth, who was only too happy to be of service. Tvrdik tried to lobby for the footpath, but she would have none of it, instructing him to save his strength for more important things. He found it impossible to communicate to her how challenging – no, terrifying – he still found dragonflight. But he knew better than to resist, once she had made up her mind. Mark and Delphine offered to gather his belongings in a little wheeled cart, and walk them over. They arrived at his suite midmorning, positively bouncing with excitement at his 'release from prison,' as they called it. While Mark packed up the cart, Delphine accompanied her new friend on one last stroll about the palace gardens, and caught him more than once stopping to glance back at the huge structure. At one such moment, she gave him a gentle shove, "What are you thinking?" He hung his head.

"Oh, well, I've been so eager to leave, and now I think I will miss this place. It's funny, considering the circumstances, but, you know, I've led a rather... solitary... life. My memories of this time at Theriole will always be of my first real friends, and a feeling of home."

"I shall miss having you right next door, any time of the day or night. But, it's not like you are losing any of us, Tvrdik. You're not going far, and we'll all be coming to visit you at your place now. You'll see. It's only the beginning. You never even got the chance to settle in at The Cottage and make it feel like home. In a few weeks, it will be like you've always lived there." Tvrdik's mind wandered for a moment to a time when he had indeed lived there. His face clouded. Delphine could not help but notice the sudden change. "Have I said something wrong?"

Instantly he was back with her, smiling down at her, "No, my friend. I was just remembering things from a very long time ago, things best left forgotten. We have so much to do in the next few weeks; there will be no time for brooding over the past. You will come this afternoon? And Mark? I'm counting on you to be there."

"We wouldn't miss this for anything in the world. Of course we'll be there." They stood together in the sunshine for a few minutes, breathing in the fragrant spring air, watching birds fly back and forth to their nests with food for their little ones. Now and then a little beak would be visible over the edge of twigs, or a scrawny, damp head. So much of the world seemed beautiful and fresh today, as the two friends shared their mutual sense of wonder without a word passing between them. A shadow passing overhead broke the spell, and they both looked up to see Tashroth coming in for a landing on the broad palace lawns.

"Time to go," Delphine muttered. "I'll bet Mark is ready and wondering what's keeping us..."

Tvrdik nodded. Then, on an impulse, he turned to her, took her face in both of his hands, and kissed her forehead gently. She blushed as he released her, but they were both smiling as they turned back toward the palace. They made their way to the great stone steps of Theriole, in front of which Mark was indeed waiting, along with Tashroth and Jorelial Rey. Tvrdik's things were stowed neatly in the little cart, and Rel was already seated on the dragon's neck, ready to give him a hand up to the seat behind.

"Should I go in and check one more time? Is that everything?" the wizard stalled.

Mark shrugged. "I'm sure I got everything. Checked several times. And anyway, you're only going down the riverwalk if we forget anything." Tvrdik shook Mark's hand and thanked him, winked at Delphine, and made a small reverence to Tashroth in greeting. There was no use delaying any longer.

"Come on, Tvrdik!" Rel shouted down, "I'll give you a boost." Tvrdik edged up close to Tash's left forearm, and reached up his uninjured hand, which Jorelial Rey clasped. Glad of her support, he clambered up over the huge forearm and swung one leg over the central spine, settling himself between bony ridges, and casting about for something to hold onto. The thought crossed his mind that he was grateful he had worn his tunic and leggings today, and not his robes, which might have been somewhat awkward in this position. Before he had left that thought, Tash's great muscles gathered and rippled in one great leap upward, and as the huge wings beat down, they were airborne. Tvrdik's stomach dropped earthward and then rose into his throat as he looked down to see the ground and his friends spinning crazily away from him when the dragon banked to head upriver. *I will never get used to this*, he thought, but dared not speak aloud.

"Isn't it a glorious day for flying?" Rel remarked, and when Tvrdik tried to respond, "Oh, glorious!" his voice cracked.

Since he closed his eyes for the descent, and for most of his ungraceful dismount, it was a complete surprise when he opened them to a regular reception committee. Stewart was there to greet him of course, barking and dancing about. And the entire Praeger family was there to welcome him. The adults seemed so peaceful and happy, he almost didn't recognize them. But Lynette he knew, even though she had changed in appearance most of all. Rel came down beside him, and Tash settled himself on a wide place in the riverwalk just beside the front gate.

"Come in, come in, and welcome home, Master Tvrdik," Mrs. Praeger cooed, while Lynette ran forward to take his hand and pull him through the gate. Stewart and Praeger seemed to have come to some sort of peace with one another. He noticed they still gave one another respectful space, but did not seem to harbor any animosity.

As he came through the gate, he noticed how smoothly it opened and shut, without the old creak he had not gotten around to fixing, and when he looked up at Xaarus' gardens, he was amazed to see lush, colorful, orderly rows of herbs, flowers and vegetables growing in happy profusion, not a weed or an insect blot in sight. The neat plots were surrounded with stones, and divided with posts and string. Speechless, he let his eye wander upward to the house. He had left it in decent condition, but now he noticed details such as the broken shutters, sagging gutters and cracked sills had all been fixed. There were curtains in the windows. Smoke was streaming from the front chimney, though the day was warm, and his nostrils were greeted with the unmistakable aroma of fresh-baked bread. Tvrdik looked at Mrs. Praeger in amazement, a question on his face. "It's made from potato flour, sir – we find it serves well enough. I hope you like it. There's also a nice hot lentil stew with spinach and potatoes, all ready for you, and some early strawberries." Stewart wagged his tail and barked once. Tvrdik stood staring at everyone in shock, "You – you did all this?"

"A great wizard deserves a proper homecoming. We wanted ye to feel comfortable. I hope we did not overstep?"

"No, no, it's wonderful. I just wasn't expecting such a …surprise!" He turned for support to Jorelial Rey, who was standing behind him, wearing a smug smile. "Did *you* know all this was going on?"

"Not me." she chuckled, "But it seems entirely appropriate – a great wizard does indeed deserve a proper homecoming."

Praeger himself took a step toward the mage, frayed hat in hand again, which made Tvrdik apprehensive about what might be coming next. "Master," the little man began, "we didna mean to put everythin' on ye the moment ye arrived, but since ye asked, well, we have a thought to discuss wi' ye, and perhaps ye might just hear us out and put it in yer mind for considerin' later?"

"Go ahead…"

Mrs. Praeger picked up the thread, "Well, we were thinkin' as how ye'd be fair busy wi' weighty matters now – entertainin' important visitors, doin' healin' work, and attendin' to study and other magical matters and such – why, ye won' be havin' time to take proper care o' yerself. And ye shouldna be wastin' yer time on work like gardenin, fixin' things, cookin,' and washin' up. We were thinkin' how ye might need people to do all those things for ye…"

Praeger jumped in, "And after all that's happened, ye know…my heart just isna in the bow and arrow business anymore. Canna much see the good o' creatin' things that only bring death and sufferin', if ye take my meanin'. This last two weeks, workin' in the earth, and doin' odd jobs here, I feel really good. Always did like workin' wi' my hands, sir, and now it was for buildin' and growin' things." He nodded toward his wife, "Maihre here loves takin' care o' folk, and keepin' a nice, orderly house. Lynette is that wild about ye, and we will always be indebted to ye for makin' her well…"

Again Mrs. Praeger took over, "…and seein' as how ye have that whole wing in the back there that no one's been in fer years, we thought perhaps ye wouldna mind if we fixed it up ourselves? It could be a right comfortable little space for a small family. And then we could stay on and look after ye, proper-like; cook and clean and tend to the garden and the walk in winter…"

Finally they paused for air, but by then Tvrdik's head was spinning. In his mind, he saw a picture of the old dorm, all of Benjin's and Ailianne's things still lying about where they had fallen, covered in dust. Did he have a right to reclaim, to violate that space and its ghosts? And how could he justify having servants when he was of modest background, and used to doing for himself? Mistaking his silence for disapproval, the Praegers glanced at each other in dismay. Praeger broke the silence, "Ye don' need to answer right away, sir. We just thought ye might do us the kindness of thinkin' about it. I wouldna blame ye if ye still weren't comfortable sharin' house wi' the likes o' me, but if ye come inside and have a look around, ye can see a sample of our work. I know a trick or two for fixin' things, and Maihre here is quite a good cook."

Lynette, with his hand still in hers, looked up at him and smiled, "I helped, too. I put flowers on all the tables."

Tvrdik hastened to correct their misunderstanding, "Oh, no, no! Please don't be offended. It's a most generous, wonderful offer. It's just that, well, I've never had…um…*staff* before. Always did things for myself. Plus, I was wondering if the back rooms were even mine to use…"

At this remark, Jorelial Rey, who had been listening with great interest, stepped in and grasped his arm, "Of course they are. I told you to take over the whole house if you could make it livable, and as far as I am concerned, it's yours. Remember, Xaarus told you to use it with his blessing as well." Then she leaned in and for his ears only, she whispered, "Let the past go, Tvrdik. They aren't coming back. It's time we all moved on." Startled, he pulled back and stared at her hard. She nodded, then continued aloud, "You know, the Praegers do make good sense. You are going to be awfully busy, especially over the next *six weeks*, and it would befit your new stature at court to have someone to delegate the chores to. As Court Wizard, you will be receiving a regular stipend from the Crown to cover your expenses. In return, I shall expect you to be on call if necessary seven days a week, twenty-four hours a day. If we stand down from high alert sometime in the future, then those points could be renegotiated." He looked at her quizzically, thinking they both knew he would always be at her beck and call at any hour. But, seeing the twinkle in her eye, he just said, "Oh, yes, that sounds reasonable…"

"And you could choose to pay the Praegers a fair wage out of that stipend, or if you prefer, I could make an arrangement directly with Minister Verger. I do think it is an excellent idea, and suits everyone's purposes."

Still not quite able to process so much at once, he turned back to the family, "You're sure this is what you want?" Praeger and his family nearly tripped over each other to assure him, "Oh, yes, sir."

"Ye'd be doing us a great favor, sir."

"…an honor, indeed, sir."

Tvrdik turned to Stewart next, "What do you say, friend? This house has become almost as much yours as mine over the last few weeks."

Stewart clearly enjoyed being consulted on such weighty matters, "Fine, fine. Bring them on. The more the merrier, I say. Splendid idea. Woof."

"Alright then, I have only one other condition – Praeger?"

Praeger looked nervous, not knowing what to expect, "What would that be, sir?"

"You will let me work with you in the garden from time to time, won't you? I think I'd go mad if I didn't have my hands in the earth at least once in a while – for therapy, you understand?" Tvrdik winked.

Praeger's face broke into a broad grin, "Why, yes, sir. I think we could turn a blind eye to that, sir. Anytime ye want, sir." He was worrying his poor hat again, Tvrdik noticed, but this time with joyful energy.

"Good. We can work out the details later, if that is agreeable to you both, but since you seem determined, you are herewith hired, with my gratitude. You can begin working on the back rooms as soon as you like. I'll even help. Shall we shake on it?" Praeger eyed the hand extended toward him as if it were a fish flying through the air, but Tvrdik held it out firmly before him until at last, gingerly, he grasped it with his own and they shook hands to seal the deal.

"Mrs. Praeger," Tvrdik was beginning to regain some of his normal good spirits, "this feels like cause for a celebration. How much of that lentil stew did you say we had?"

She beamed, "Enough for a few guests, and I hope they are hungry."

At that moment, Mark and Delphine appeared at the gate, pulling the cart full of Tvrdik's books, clothing and medicines. "You're all still standing outside?" Delphine called, "And we took our time, too."

Tvrdik cocked his head at Mrs. Praeger, who chuckled with delight. "Bring them all in, Master Wizard. It is a homecoming, after all; a right grand celebration. I'll see if I can't scare up a bit of meat for the doggie as well." Stewart stood very straight and raised an eyebrow, uncertain if he should be more insulted at being called 'the doggie', or excited about the prospect of meat. Tvrdik looked back at Tashroth, who nodded to him, benediction-like, and the rest of the party made their way inside, laughing, and commenting on the delicious scents that greeted them at the door. Inside, Mr. and Mrs. Praeger began scurrying about to lay a table for eight, including Stewart and themselves, as Tvrdik had made it clear that he expected them to join in the meal, not simply serve. Stewart stayed close by them, ostensibly to help, but most likely to look out for his own best interests.

Lynette guided the other four about the house in a little tour. Xaarus' old bachelor's house had never looked so homey and inviting. Lynette had put fresh flowers in vases on all the tables. There were curtains and throw rugs in every room in bright but tasteful colors. The kitchen and pantry were well-stocked, and Tvrdik even noticed several jars of preserves from recent harvest, just as he had instructed Praeger from his palace room. The bedroom would rival any at Theriole for comfort and coziness. There was a new coverlet and decorative touches all over the room; a chest for clothing at the foot of the bed, painted with flowers, and a few pictures of landscapes on the walls, one even including a waterfall. Even the fireside corner of the library where Tvrdik had enjoyed reading sported a new lamp, an oval braided rug, and a small handmade quilt that one could either sit on for extra comfort or wrap up in on a chilly evening. All the fireplaces had wood and kindling neatly stacked nearby, and the whole place had a warm, inviting feel to it that he never remembered from years before. The floors were scrubbed spotless, and every room was dusted. When Lynette reached the door to Xaarus' old laboratory, she leaned in as if sharing a secret.

"Mama says we must never go in or touch anything in there. She says it is where a wizard does his most special magical work, and it would not do to disturb anything."

"That's true, Lynette, and very good advice indeed, though I am sure it would be alright if I brought you in sometime to show you things." Lynette, eyes wide, looking solemn, nodded. Tvrdik was beginning to decide that he really liked the Praegers, and looking about, he realized just how hard they must have worked to accomplish so very much in so short a time. He leaned toward Rel, "Look at this place! Here was a man you might have had imprisoned or executed for treason. However did you know?"

She shook her head, "Good instincts, I guess. Are you happy with the way it is turning out?"

"I am ecstatic. You took a leap of faith, and I get the benefits. Quite a homecoming indeed. I shall have to pinch myself to be sure it won't all vanish by tomorrow."

"Oh, I think you can count on everything staying just as it is for some time to come." She smiled.

"You'll have to help me figure out how much to pay them. I've no experience with that sort of thing."

"I'll have Verger work up a budget and a contract. He'll know."

During this conversation, Mark and Delphine had taken it upon themselves to unpack Tvrdik's things and put them away in places they thought sensible, and Lynette had vanished for a few moments. Now she came skipping back with a message, "Master Wizard, Mama says just for today we are short several chairs, and three bowls for lunch, and wonders if you had any ideas?"

Tvrdik nodded and bent low to the little girl's level, "Go tell your Daddy there are benches in the classroom in the back wing that he can pull out and use for seats. And then, go out to the yard and see if you can find me three very big rocks."

"Rocks?"

"Yes, rocks. They need to be big, so you might have to bring them in one at a time, alright? Don't hurt yourself. Just do one at a time and put them on the table, and come get me when you are done. Can you do that?"

"I think so. But, on the table? Mama won't like that."

"Tell her I said it was alright. Go along now." Lynette dashed away with the boundless energy of youth, mission in hand.

"Oh, she's absolutely charmed by you," Rel remarked.

"You think so?" Tvrdik smoothed his hair and straightened his glasses in a mock gesture of self-appreciation, but he was blushing. "Well, at that age, their affections are so very fickle. Tomorrow it will be another tall, handsome fellow, and I'll be out with the trash." They laughed.

"What are you going to do with rocks, anyway?"

"You'll see. We'd better go and find her." They worked their way back to the big communal dining area, where Lynette was just placing the last of three rather large, heavy stones on the dining table, her mother scowling at her from the hearth, where she stirred a giant pot. The woman's eyes met Tvrdik's, and she threw up her hands and scurried off into the kitchen. The little girl was struggling to boost the flattish rock onto the tabletop, but she managed the task by adding some rather well-executed grunts. Tvrdik examined her work, "Oh, these will do just fine. You follow instructions very well." She gave him a little curtsey in response. "Now, stand right back there, and watch carefully..." Lynette stood very still and fastened her eyes on the table. Tvrdik gripped his staff, closed his eyes and visualized, concentrating on detail. Then, with a wave of his left hand over the stones, he mumbled something unintelligible. Before their eyes, three

346

rocks reformed themselves into sturdy, earthenware bowls that matched almost exactly the others that had already been placed on the table. Lynette blinked and shook her head, but bowls still sat there where stones had been a moment before. She gasped.

"How did you...? You just....Oh!"

The wizard laughed at her amazement, and then made a worried face, "Oops! I forgot something." He laid his hand over one of the bowls, and when he drew it away, it had changed: painted white with little figures of pink flowers and blue bunnies all around the outside edge, and letters deep in the bowl that spelled out L-Y-N-E-T-T-E. It was lovely.

"Oooooh," cried the little girl, clapping her hands, "is that one for me?"

"Of course, because you are special. Can you read, Lynette?"

"Not always, but I know what my name looks like. See, there, L-Y-..."

"Never mind. In this house, you will learn to read. I will teach you myself, yes?"

"Oh, yes, please."

"Would you take these bowls in to your Mom, Lynette, and ask her if she needs anything else?" She was still staring at them with saucer-round eyes, almost afraid to touch them. Tvrdik laughed to see the awed expression on her face. "Go ahead. They won't bite." He turned away, back to Jorelial Rey, who was standing behind him with exactly the same expression. "What?" he chuckled, "Did you want a bunny bowl too, my lady?"

"I just can't get over how casually you do these remarkable things."

"It's a simple trick, really, but useful. Nice to know this hand still works." He flexed the fingers of his left hand a few times, "They won't stay in that form forever, but they will be fine for today. Eventually, I shall have to get her a *real* bowl like that, or she'll be terribly disappointed."

"You're very good with her."

"I suppose I'm a bit of an overgrown child myself. It's ironic, since in my youth I was far too serious." A loud scraping sound interrupted them, and Mark hurried to help Praeger drag the heavy classroom benches in from the closed off section beyond the kitchen.

"Could use a good dustin', but they'll do," Praeger wheezed, "Och, they are that heavy.""

"Oh, yes. I spent a lot of time on this very seat in my schooldays, and we were often shoving them around the room for different vantage points. I am familiar with their heft."

No sooner did they place all the chairs and benches around the table, when Mrs. Praeger called out, "Lunch, everyone!" She didn't have to invite twice. Delphine and Mark, Tvrdik and Rel, Stewart and the three Praegers converged around the big table, passing bowls, cups, spoons and knives, and sorting out seating. There was a huge pot of the lentil stew, which Mrs. Praeger ladled out generously. Then, trays of warm potato bread, fresh butter, and goat cheese, pitchers of milk and apple cider, and a large bowl of sliced strawberries. Stewart got a special plate made for him, which included pieces of cheese and some sort of cooked fowl. Being a tall dog, he preferred to eat standing up, his bowl placed on the edge of one of the benches, just at the perfect level for him. Everyone else helped themselves to the bounty before them, and enjoyed a peaceful hour of good food, good company, good conversation, and laughter. Compliments abounded for Mrs. Praeger's cooking. Tvrdik marveled that all of this was happening in *his* home, and he harbored a secret wish that such fellowship would be a regular occurrence here. In his heart, he blessed the house, the food, the Praegers, his friends, and was grateful.

Meanwhile, while his mind was thus wandering, and his attention was turned inwards, Mrs. Praeger kept glancing at him sideways and whispering to the other guests at the table. Soon, everyone was lifting their stew bowls to examine them top and bottom, comparing them to their neighbors'. Mark quipped, raising his voice, "Well, I suppose I'd better hurry up and eat my stew before the dish turns back into a rock, and I end up wearing it." This startled Tvrdik from his reverie. He turned beet red and, with utter seriousness, exclaimed, "Well, I think they should last a little longer than that!" The entire company roared with laughter, in which, as soon as he realized he was being teased, Tvrdik joined them. Everyone started shoving their bowls around the table, trading and switching them and guessing who would end up with a rock, while Lynette clutched her painted one in her tiny fingers crying, "Mine is bee-yoo-tee-ful." Sporadic eruptions of laughter continued around the table until everyone's face was wet with tears, stomachs ached and all were spent. And then, out of the breathless silence, someone said, "Could you pass the strawberries, please?" and started the howling all over again.

And so, the meal passed in fun and fellowship until everyone present was well-fed, sleepy, and glowing with a sense of well-being. They offered to help Mrs. Praeger clean up, and insisted, even over her objections. They let her give the orders though, in the kitchen for which she had so recently assumed responsibility. It became obvious that her sense of propriety was confounded that the Lady Regent of the entire kingdom, her younger sister and brother-in-law, and the Court Wizard should all be washing dishes and wiping up crumbs right along side of her, and she made it clear that she would allow that sort of nonsense only this once. In the midst of all this, Tvrdik remembered that that he had already invited perhaps a dozen guests to the house for an important meeting that very afternoon. He took Mrs. Praeger aside to inform her, apologizing for the late notice. If the weather held, he explained, his intention was to assemble on the back lawns, so that Tashroth could attend. The only things he wished to request was that benches and chairs be moved out there, and perhaps, if there were any more cider or tea to serve the visitors so that they might feel comfortable. He also wanted to invite her and her husband to the meeting, if they could make some provision for Lynette, since a matter of great importance would be discussed that he thought they should be privy to. Her eyebrows rose at that last part, but she seemed unfazed by the idea of more company, and replied that he was not to worry one jot about surprising her with this immediate request for hospitality. She had known what she was getting into when she proposed the idea of running his household, and wanted him to feel free to have people in whenever it suited him. She assured him that her husband could attend the meeting, and would fill her in on all the details later, while she and Lynette would make sure the guests had everything they needed.

"Don't trouble yerself, Master Wizard. 'Tis an honor for us to make yer days that much easier."

"Thank you, Mrs. Praeger. You are a treasure." He kissed her lightly on the cheek and she waved him out of the kitchen, blushing.

With many hands, all the lunch things were clean and put away in record time. They were just wiping down the last of the counters when a strange sound drifted in through the open windows. Everyone stopped what they were doing, and heads tilted to better catch the remarkable strains. It seemed to be some sort of music – distant, but sweet, exotic, and wild – like nothing most of them had ever heard before. Stewart figured it out first, barked once, and ran out the backdoor, across the lawns to the river bank. In a flash, Tvrdik had the same realization and followed close behind. Mark and Delphine, Rel and all the Praegers stumbled after them, mystified. What they all saw in the slow-moving waters appeared to be a small, blue girl with curly hair, surrounded by a number of grayish-green creatures, all floating about and singing. The lyrics were in some ancient, liquid tongue that none of them comprehended, but the sweet little voices, all blended in perfect harmony, were enchanting. Ondine was leading a rather large contingent of her city cousins in a special performance to welcome Tvrdik home. Stewart and the humans paused at the river's edge, letting the unearthly music wash over them, mesmerized by its strangeness and sheer lovliness. Mark was particularly attentive, head cocked and eyebrows tented on his furrowed forehead as if he were attempting to commit the entire experience to memory. Lynette and Delphine merely stood together in wonder, grinning in delight. And then, with a heart-wrenching crescendo, the music ceased. There followed a respectful, tangible silence where no one dared stir, breathe, or even blink. Seconds passed, and then Tvrdik squatted down on the bank to be closer to his serenaders. In an explosion of spray, the little blue girl leapt from the water and planted a wet kiss, *smack* on the wizard's nose, turned a summersault in the air, and dove head first back into the water. A moment later she emerged, all smiles.

Tvrdik was dabbing at his dripping face with the edges of his sleeves, and laughing, "Oh, my girl, how I've missed you and your wicked antics!"

"Miss you too, Lovely Man." Several of Tvrdik's guests to whom that appellation was new exchanged glances. "Seventeen days. Seventeen days we wait for you to come and visit with us. Very worried about you. You are well now, Lovely Man?"

Delphine giggled and Tvrdik whispered aside to her, "It's a long story. I keep trying, but I can't get her to stop calling me that." He turned back to Ondine, "Yes, thank you, mostly well. I would have come out sooner if there was any way, but it took me a long time to recover."

"So happy you are better now. We hear you are coming home to live in house; Ondine teaches all her friends special song to welcome you. You like it?"

"It was beautiful. You all did a wonderful job. What a thoughtful, rare, homecoming gift! Will you sing again?"

She grinned, and, alone this time, began to trill something that sounded like, 'Welcome home, Lovely Man...' Tvrdik cleared his throat and raised a hand, "Alright, love. I appreciate it, but we have company. Thank you, dear naiads, for your concert. It is good to be in your company again."

The little grey-green nymphs giggled shyly and spun around in various directions. Tvrdik went on, "You are all welcome here at this house any time you like, and I will be glad to see you. In fact, Ondine, we are holding a meeting of friends to talk about our plan of action right here in about two hours. Can I count on you to attend?"

"Today? Very good, Lovely Man. I will take the others home and come back later. Time we begin our work, yes?"

"Yes, Ondine. What a joy to see you, and thank you, all of you, from my heart." Remembering what they enjoyed, he conjured a ring of flame in the shape of a heart just above them. A host of tiny 'oohs' and 'ahs' filled the air, along with a few from bigger companions behind him. The heart faded to smoke, which drifted away in the river breeze. Ondine waved to everyone, and then sent up a gigantic splash aimed at Tvrdik. She was near doubled over in laughter as he stood there drowned, spluttering, shaking his arms up and down, and mopping his brow with a damp sleeve.

"Master Wizard!" exclaimed Mrs. Praeger, horrified.

"It's alright, Mrs. Praeger. She means it as a sign of affection."

"Lovely Man, where is your hurt?" Ondine called.

"Here, my left shoulder and arm." He pointed with his other hand. There was a moment when the little imp seemed to be concentrating, bobbing up and down in one place in the water. Suddenly, everyone began to notice a very large patch of the brackish water turning clear, and shining with a shimmering blue light, flecked with silver. A few of the onlookers gasped audibly, but no one said a word. Ondine addressed her friend, nodding toward his left side.

"You put that hand in water, here," she insisted, "feel better." Tvrdik rolled up his left sleeve as best he could, and reached his hand into the shining patch, submerging it past the wrist. Immediately, he felt a surge of energy, a sort of cool-heat sensation shooting through his hand and pulsing up his arm. He closed his eyes as the healing energy spread up toward his wound, through that shoulder, and from there, throughout his entire being. So powerful and ecstatic was the feeling that he wished it could go on forever. But after a few moments, the pulsing energy stopped, leaving in its wake an aura of strength, warmth, and well-being. Tvrdik opened his eyes to see Ondine's broad grin.

"You feel better now. Heal faster – you see. Old magic we do here... we know one thing or two." And she giggled.

"Thanks again, dear heart," muttered the mage, moving his fingers and arm about cautiously, but feeling their new flexibility and strength. "Once again, I am in your debt."

"Farewell, all. I come back later and see you again." And shepherding her city cousins into some sort of formation, she led them into the depths and away. Everyone stood on the shore blinking for a moment. There truly was no sign now in the slow-moving, silty flow that anything unusual had just occurred. Stewart barked, wagged his tail, and remarked, "I always find those wee girlies charmin'"

Mrs. Praeger, ever the pragmatist, seemed to come to life at that, "Let me fetch ye a towel, sir. Ye'll catch yer death standing about here soakin' wet."

"Thank you, Mrs. Praeger, but it is a fair, warm day. I'm sure I feel quite well."

"Nevertheless..." and she hustled back into the house, closely followed by her daughter, who had finally found her voice. "Mamma, did you see them? Faeries? They were real, mamma....and did you hear the beautiful song?"

The rest of the group turned from the river bank with some reluctance, and followed back to the house, exchanging hushed remarks with one another, as if they had been standing in a holy place. Upon entering the house, Tvrdik was handed a soft towel and began scrubbing at his damp face and hair.

"Ye should get out of those wet clothes as well, sir." Mrs. Praeger exhorted.

"Nonsense." he reassured her, "They aren't so bad. I'll dry in the sun." He raised his voice and addressed the whole assembly, who were all gathered around rather uncertainly. "You've all made this day a real occasion for me, and you are all welcome in this place, my *home*, any time, day or night. As for today, we have almost two hours until the others arrive and we address serious matters. That's not enough time for you all to leave and return, or to be busy about other things. I hope you will consider staying, and making yourselves comfortable here. The house and grounds are at your disposal. A little calculated relaxation can be a very salutary thing."

"Hear, hear!" Mark said, and Delphine smiled up at him with adoration. They patted Tvrdik on the shoulder and stepped out to walk in the bright sunshine among the fragrant, blooming trees. Stewart found a sunny corner and curled up for a nap, which was exactly what Tashroth was doing in the front yard. Lynette was off to play, as imaginative children do, and the Praegers took their leave and busied themselves about various preparations for the upcoming meeting. Rel turned to Tvrdik and asked, "What about you? Big things ahead. Would you like to rest for awhile?"

He shook his head, "No, I feel strangely energized. Must be something in the water here." He winked at her and she grinned. "I have an idea," he offered. "Are you interested in a short walk? There's a special place on the riverwalk I could share with you. It's sort of a little personal sanctuary I've relied on since childhood, and it isn't far from here. Would you like to see? It would do us both good to stretch our legs after that meal..."

"Are you sure you want to show me? It's your own secret place..."

"I have a feeling there will be times ahead when you will also be grateful for a little hideaway. Let's go. You'll like it. Mrs. Praeger, the Lady Regent and I are out and about for a little while. Be back soon," he called, taking Rel's arm and escorting her through the front gate to the riverwalk. She reached up to pat the snoring Tashroth as they passed by. He immediately opened one eye and winked at her. Tvrdik released Rel's arm, "I guess it *is* true what they say about slipping by a sleeping dragon..."

"Oh, there isn't much that gets by him, awake or asleep."

They strolled up the path, warm sunshine, fragrant air, and birdsong lifting their spirits, and filling them with a temporary peace. Idle conversation seemed extraneous, but at last, Rel ventured, "Ondine is adorable. She seems very fond of you."

"When I decided to return here, she really was my first friend and companion. She insisted on coming along, although I tried to discourage her. She was giving up what for her was a paradise, in order to learn more of the wider world. Now she's finding all the faded naiads in the waters hereabouts and re-educating them in their own traditions and lore. Quite a remarkable creature."

Rel's eyes twinkled with mischief, though she assumed a serious expression to ask, "Why does she call you that...you know...."

He blushed and chuckled, "Gosh, that is so embarrassing. I told you it was a long story."

"Do tell."

"I think I mentioned when I was wandering in despair all those years ago, and came to the waterfall where she lived, I found it so heartbreakingly beautiful that I decided to end my life right there. So, I took off all my clothes, climbed up to the top of the cliff, and jumped. Except I only managed to knock myself out, and woke up bruised and sore quite some time after. I never knew what had really happened, but took it as a sign that I was to go on living. Well, I only just learned that she had been there right at that moment, and saw what I was doing. She believed I was just trying to go for a swim, but had miscalculated the danger. Apparently it was she who saved my life, somehow pulling me out of the pool so that I would not drown. All those years she never revealed herself to me – not until I was ready to leave for good. Now I find that she has been watching me, and watching *over* me for the entire time. She made me her personal project, although I can't think why. Really, I was more of a disruption to her world than anything. I was the first human she had encountered. I suppose she was intrigued, and curious..."

"Or found something in you to care about."

He glanced at her, "Perhaps..."

"And it seems that she liked what she saw..." It was all she could do to keep from dissolving in laughter.

Tvrdik blushed again, a state that his pale complexion succumbed to with some regularity, "Well, that, and the fact that she can't pronounce my name – thinks it is ridiculous."

"If it comes to that, why, then, I should be calling you 'Lovely Man' as well."

He started, "Pardon?"

"The name, silly. It really is a challenge to get right."

"Oh." He replied awkwardly, "Yours is like music." She hadn't expected that, nor had he expected to say it out loud.

"Thank you." She looked away.

"Here it is." Tvrdik raised his voice and pointed out the small gap in the bushes ahead. "Let me hold that branch back, and you go ahead through – that's it – I'm right behind you…" He guided her through the thick foliage, and in a moment they both stood in the sheltered arbor where the flat rock sloped gently down toward clear rushing waters.

"Oooo! This is beautiful." Jorelial Rey turned in place, taking in the whole picture. Tvrdik lowered himself onto the rock, warmed with sunshine that was filtering down through birch leaves, and stretched out his legs.

"I don't think anyone knows about this little place. You can't see it from the riverwalk, and most folks don't take the time to explore off the path. I discovered it by accident when I was around thirteen, and used to come here quite often to study, or dream, or just be alone. It hasn't changed much at all since then, though I confess I thought everything much larger in my youth. Later in summer there will be berries, too." He leaned back on his good hand, and turned his face up to the sky, listening to the rush of water, the rustle of leaves, the rhythmic creak of branches, and the twitter of birds overhead. Rel sat down beside him, her arms around her shins and her chin resting on her knees. It was a childlike pose, but she felt like a girl here. This place had the air of a sanctuary, insulated from the outside world, the pressures of ruling, the demands of court, and the worries she had that their future held danger and uncertainty. Here, there was only nature, and a feeling of timelessness.

"I can see why you like to come here. It's so peaceful."

"It's a good place to disappear for an hour – or an afternoon."

"Hmmmm." They were quiet for a few moments. Rel broke the silence again.

"Were you alone a great deal as a child?"

"Hmmmm, I suppose so. Before Xaarus, I kept to myself a lot. My family thought I was strange, or worse. Afterwards, we spent a lot of time with him, studying, observing, and practicing. It was a grueling schedule he kept us on. But when we had any leisure or private study time, the other two went off together a lot. I was shy, and something of the odd man out. Somehow the time I spent here always brought me back to harmony of a sort. I had my best inspirations here, and some of my happiest times."

"I didn't fit in very well with the other children at court either. I always preferred to tag along with the adults, until they lost patience with my questions and sent me away. I spent a lot of time in my own imagination, but of course, I always had Tashroth. He has always been my best friend, but it's more like he is a part of me. My education was pretty intensive too, and when Delphine was born, I helped take care of her. So, I kept busy."

"Xaarus told me we had a great deal in common."

"Xaarus is a wise man."

"I laughed at him."

"Why? Was it that hard to imagine?"

"Don't be angry. All I could remember was seeing you standing by your father, dressed in expensive clothes, always in important places, and flying around on a dragon with your little nose in the air. I thought your life must be perfect, and that you were insufferably full of yourself."

"Oh!"

"I was an idiot. I was seeing you through the eyes of a child. I am learning to see more deeply, and am glad to learn how superficially I once judged people. I strive now to do better. I hope you will forgive me?"

"If I were honest, I'd have to admit I might have been a bit privileged and conceited back then, so you might not have been entirely mistaken. But it wasn't all my fault. I *was* raised in a sheltered environment. And, I think I also adopted something of a superior attitude in response to being labeled, 'different.' I like to think I've also grown somewhat since those days." She paused to reflect, "I remember noticing you, though. I thought you seemed interesting, if a little strange. You did tend to stand off by yourself a lot even when the three of you were all there with Xaarus. I never saw you smile or laugh."

"I don't think I did much of that back then." His eyes were closed, but a wide smile spread across his face, "I'm making up for lost time now," he said.

They sat in silence then, enjoying the peace and beauty of the place. When it was time to go, Tvrdik rose to his feet with a sigh, "I could stay here all day, but the others will be arriving soon, and we ought to be ready for them." He reached his right hand down to her, which she grasped and sprang to her feet. "It will be here waiting when we need it."

She said, "Thank you for bringing me to this place."

"Don't you think it's nicer sharing a secret with a friend? You are welcome here anytime." He held up a warning finger, "Just don't tell anyone else, or the place will be overrun."

"Agreed." They let their gaze follow the moving waters one last time. "Tvrdik?"

"Hmmm?"

"I'm awfully glad that I don't have to face this particular challenge alone."

"Me, too."

He held the branches back for her, as they both bent to make their way back to the path. It felt like emerging into another world. They headed back to The Cottage at an unhurried pace, not another word exchanged between them, but a bond formed nonetheless.

TWENTY-SEVEN

THE LEGIONS OF LIGHT

Back at The Cottage, Tashroth had shifted his post to the riverbank behind the building, and the Praegers had set up all the chairs and benches they could find on the lawn. The weather seemed likely to hold, and Mark and Delphine were already back from their walk, running about on the lawns with Stewart and Lynette and a brightly colored ball. They waved gaily at the returning mage and regent, but did not interrupt their game. Tvrdik and Rel had just enough time to wash up a bit, straighten their clothing, and run combs through their hair. Tvrdik searched until he found a rather large basin in the house which he filled with water and placed outside for Ondine so that she could be closer to the conversation. He took a moment to run over a few key points in his head, reached for his staff, and went to the front gate, where their guests were just beginning to arrive. In very close succession, Bargarelle, Verger, Warlowe, and the Palace Physician appeared on the Riverwalk, and found their way to the front gate of Xaarus' Cottage.

"Welcome, welcome gentlemen! I see you found us. Thank you for coming. If we are all assembled, I will be happy to show you inside. All the other guests are here already – no, no, you are perfectly on time. Some of them were helping me move back in here this morning. Oh, myself? Much better, thank you for asking. Right this way…"

He led them up the front walk and past the gardens. "With your permission, we'd like to hold this meeting outdoors on the back lawns – you'll see why in a moment. I've arranged some refreshment for you if the sun gets too warm. We can find a shady place, too. If you'll just come 'round the corner here, you'll see chairs set up…" Jorelial Rey was already standing beside Tashroth, and Stewart had trotted over to join them. At the sight of the little cavalcade coming around the corner, Mark and Delphine sent Lynette back to find her mother, and made their way across the lawn to the meeting site. Praeger was coming out the back door of the house, and paused at the sight of so many dignitaries. "That's right, Mr. Praeger, right over here. You are invited, yes, this way. Gentlemen?"

Tvrdik had noticed that his four charges were all huddled at the corner of the house, and had not followed him any further. They were all staring up at Tashroth with some combination of respect and abject terror, never having come in such close contact with a live dragon. Remembering his first encounter, Tvrdik sympathized with them, and attempted to ease their adjustment. "Oh, what am I thinking? I had forgotten that we haven't all met. Gentlemen, I believe you all know our Royal Regent, Lady Jorelial Rey, and this is her oldest friend and companion, Lord Tashroth, of the green dragons." Tashroth, taking his cue, swung his head over to where the four visitors had halted, and purred in his deep voice, "A pleasure to make your acquaintance." Verger looked about to collapse. Tvrdik stifled an involuntary giggle, and hurried back to the quartet, who were still reluctant to move any closer to where Tashroth sat. Throwing a companionable arm about Verger's shoulders, he physically guided the man forward to where the chairs were lined up. "Tashroth, this is Minister Verger, our brilliant High Minister of Finance and Economics, and a great friend of Xaarus." Gently depositing the terrified man in a chair, he went back for Bargarelle. "And this is the Castle Steward for the entire palace complex, Master Bargarelle, who is also acting as personal secretary to your mistress, and keeping her appointment book." Mark and Delphine sat beside the two men Tvrdik had escorted in, attempting to distract their attention from the great green dragon. Tvrdik now grabbed Warlowe and the palace healer each by a hand and led them into the circle. "And here are two good friends of mine from Theriole; this is the royal physician who treated me in my recent misfortune – what is your name, sir? I can't believe I never troubled to learn it."

"Why, it's Andrus, sir, and please feel free to use it."

"Wonderful, Andrus. And this here is Master Warlowe, in fact my very first contact at Theriole, and a staunch friend, who handles all sorts of important tasks at the palace. But I'm sure you all know each other... please pardon my enthusiasm. And for those of you who have not yet had the pleasure, I would also like to present Stewart, a descendent of the great Angus, companion to Xaarus himself."

"Welcome, friends." Stewart remarked graciously, eliciting an expression of wonder from those who were not yet aware of his ability to talk.

"You all know Madame Delphine, sister to the Lady Rey, and her husband, Mark, a talented bard and teacher of music. And just arriving is Master Praeger. He and his family have just agreed to act as staff for this place, and help me with the chores and grounds. We had a sample today of his wife's delicious cooking. Which reminds me, Minister Verger, I would appreciate a word at your leisure concerning arrangements for their salaries." Verger sat with his mouth open in surprise, but after a glance exchanged with the Lady Regent, he gave Tvrdik a curt nod.

Jorelial Rey had been standing near Tashroth, watching the mage bustle about, handling all the introductions. She could not conceal her obvious amusement at his antics, his nervous running commentary, and his attempts to make everyone feel comfortable. This was a very different Tvrdik from the shy, quiet youngster he had just described to her. Or, maybe, his rambling was just another reflection of the lonely misfit seeking desperately to belong.

"Ah!" exclaimed the young wizard, "There remains but one member of our company yet absent, and I believe I hear her arriving now." He snatched up the large basin he had set out and disappeared down a bank by the river's edge. When he returned, he was climbing the short, slippery slope with some difficulty, both hands holding the basin, now heavy with river water, and something else.... Tvrdik managed to carry the basin over to where his guests were arranging their seats, and then set it down as gently as he could. Flexing and massaging his left arm, which had just been asked to do more than it should have, he addressed the group.

"Ladies and gentlemen, we are privileged today to be joined in our discussion by a genuine water sprite. I would like to introduce my dear friend Ondine, who has travelled with me all the way from the pristine fountains of the ancient forests in order to be a part of the work we will do here today. Ondine?" A blue head popped up from the basin's edge and flashed a dazzling smile at the assembled visitors. Then a tiny blue hand waved once before the entire apparition vanished once more into the water. Those present who had not yet met Ondine were staring open-mouthed at the tub, as if they dared not assume anyone else had just seen what they had. Tvrdik laughed, "Yes, there really is a blue naiad in that tub – she's a bit shy this afternoon, but I'm sure we will all have occasion to make her further acquaintance later. I believe I see Mrs. Praeger approaching with some cold cider and biscuits. Ah, Mrs. Praeger, thank you so much for your thoughtfulness. We were just getting started, and this is much appreciated. Help yourselves, please." Mark and Delphine leapt from their chairs, stepping forward to help lighten the woman's load. They began to pass around the wooden cups and plates of cookies, pouring from two large, chilled pitchers. The afternoon was getting on, but the sun was still warm, and a cool drink did seem to be exactly what was called for. Both Tashroth and Ondine politely declined anything, while Stewart chose a biscuit to nibble. Everyone else indulged with gusto.

"Mrs. Praeger, will you stay?" Tvrdik asked.

"I daresay there's a few things needin' my attention inside. You folk go on about yer business, and I'll have my man fill me in later."

"Very well, then, thank you."

Jorelial Rey cast an eye over the unusual group they had called together; twelve, counting herself and Tvrdik. Twelve! The ironic symbolism of that number was not lost on her – that they should randomly invite all the personalities they knew who might be in sympathy with their plan, and by chance come up with the same number of members as were in the Royal Cabinet – well, it was beyond eerie. Also interesting was that, after a bit of shuffling, the benches and chairs had wound up in a roughly circular formation. Instead of standing before a room filled with skeptical lords and ministers, Jorelial and Tvrdik were now sitting as part of the group. The variety of levels of wealth, social standing, gender, even species represented in this group was also remarkable. And yet, all claimed an equal position in this ring. It might seem like a random occurrence, but she could not help wondering if indeed things had fallen out according to some master plan of the Universe. While she was thus lost in thought, Tvrdik began the conversation.

"My friends, how I wish I was only inviting you this day to come celebrate my arrival in my new home and to enjoy some hospitality. But there is far more serious business that demands our immediate attention. Each of you is here for a special reason, because we believe we know something of your hearts, and feel you have something unique to contribute. Some of you already know the gist of what is going on, so I ask you to bear with us while we explain from the beginning for the benefit of those who have not yet heard…"

So, there on the lawn, behind Xaarus' old house, the young mage and the newly installed regent told the story yet again. Gracefully, spontaneously, back and forth they passed the thread, this time as if they were sharing the details of a recent event with a close friend. Those they had invited listened with interest, attentive to every detail. Once Andrus asked a question, and Rel did her best to answer it. Delphine grasped Mark's hand and unconsciously worried his fingers with hers. Tashroth's huge tail gave an involuntary swish back and forth from time to time. Stewart's ears twitched. Praeger refused to meet anyone's eyes, but kept his head lowered while he listened. In quiet moments, one could hear Ondine glide gently back and forth in the water, and her small, serious face was often visible over the rim of her basin. Warlowe leaned forward, completely engaged. Verger and Bargarelle exchanged meaningful looks throughout the narrative. When Tvrdik and Rel had finally arrived at the part about the Cabinet's challenge, and their unorthodox plan to assemble a completely separate army and train them in non-violent resistance, no one uttered a sound.

Tvrdik paused a moment, and then explained further, "You see, we cannot cede the kingdom to a monster like Drogue. We cannot allow our own people to stand defenseless in harm's way, but according to Xaarus', we also cannot win by resisting him with weapons in combat. So, our job would be to disarm, confuse, confound, seduce, discourage, co-opt, and thwart Drogue's forces until they just give up and abandon their intention to subdue us. We can try to discredit and embarrass Drogue in the eyes of his followers, so that his support falls away. All of this we must do by any means possible – trickery, cleverness, persuasion, magic, anything we can think of *except* by intentionally shedding blood or harming them. A daunting and untried task to be sure, but I believe it to be possible – no, more than possible – inevitable."

"As do I." added Jorelial Rey.

"And I." Tashroth rumbled.

In the silence that ensued, Rel and Tvrdik both steeled themselves for the usual arguments, objections, and expressions of shock and dismay. The first words came from Andrus, the healer, completely new to any of this, and someone they expected to be skeptical.

"Alright then. How do we begin?"

Tvrdik blinked, "Excuse me?"

"You have me convinced. I pursued this profession because I wanted to make people whole and well, and alleviate suffering. I have no desire to be called upon to patch up countless young soldiers wounded in senseless battles, or to face hopeless epidemics of disease spreading through a war-ravaged countryside. I am at your service. But what do I *do* next?"

Tvrdik's face broke into a broad grin as it dawned on him what had just happened. He leapt from his seat, and crossed to the palace healer, grasping the man's right hand in his own and pumping it up and down with enthusiasm. "Thank you, Andrus, thank you. I knew I was right to invite you today..."

Warlowe was next, "You know my loyalty to the king and his regent, to preserving the kingdom and the peace of the realm. I would follow the Lady Jorelial Rey nearly into hell, and I have always respected Xaarus. What you are proposing frightens me, but so do the alternatives. Somehow I feel strangely excited at the prospect of being a part of something this new and bold. I wish to speak with my family, but if you believe this will work, I am at your disposal."

"Well, I've already told you my heart," Verger exclaimed, "Whatever plan Xaarus engineers, I support all the way. I trust him."

"And I cast my lot with the family Rey, wherever they lead." Bargarelle stated unequivocally.

"I will call the dragons to assemble and relate all of this to them. Apparently our very future existence turns on the events we will soon face. There may be something we can contribute." Tashroth offered.

Mark rose, a fire within him kindled, "And I will speak to all the bards and minstrels, harpers, artists, writers and archivists that I can find. There is a network; Nyree will help. Almost all of us reject violence as a way to achieve any lasting good – we are all creators, not destroyers. I pledge to bring you the bards." Delphine stood up beside her new husband and added, "I do not know where my true talents lie, but since the two, no, *three* (she glanced at Tvrdik) most important people in my life believe in this cause, I embrace it wholeheartedly, and give whatever I have and am to it."

"Delphine, what you have to give is boundless. Thank you for your faith in us – in me." Rel spoke sincerely.

"I have the ear of all the magical and talkin' beasts," Stewart stood in his most handsome, noble posture to address the group, "We are already few, and forced to be cautious. I have no desire to allow a future where there is not even a dim memory of us. Xaarus is a legend in my family, and we stand with him. Not to mention, I have grown fond of young Master Tvrdik here, and trust his instincts. I will bring the talkin' beasts on board."

"And I tell my cousins and sisters of water," a small voice piped from the basin, "All naiads will help. We are of old magic; have more powers than you know. Maybe talk to trees too. Dryads very strong in old magic. Tomorrow, I take you to unicorns, Lovely Man. They will listen to wizard."

"That's the spirit!" Tvrdik was becoming more excited by the moment. What a different response this was from the staid skeptics in the counsel room. "We are all captains in this enterprise. If each of us can begin by spreading the word among the communities with which we are connected, and can convince even a small portion of those we address to come on board, then we will be a force to be reckoned with in no time."

Andrus nodded, "I will rally the healers, herbalists, and midwives. We are all sworn to preserve and repair, not to harm. And I will ponder if there might be ways to fight back with our knowledge of botanicals and diseases."

"This is what I mean. Creative thinking. Ideas. Faith that there actually *are* ways to succeed." Tvrdik was exuberant.

A small movement from one chair in the circle drew every eye. It was Praeger, squirming somewhat uncomfortably in his seat. Now he realized that all the attention was on him, waiting for his comment, the only one left unexpressed. It was Jorelial Rey who prompted him at last, "Mr. Praeger, what say you? Do you think we are all mad?"

"No, no! Oh, no, my lady, that is the farthest thing from my mind. I have only been sittin' here wonderin' how a plain man, such as myself, finds himself in such powerful company, and what ye all think I could possibly contribute of any value. I am a simple man. I know little of magic or kingdoms or great causes – only that I have seen great miracles, restorin' my daughter to health, and changin' the fortunes of my whole family, near overnight. And, I have seen only suffering, fear, and misery come from an act of bold violence. I have no stomach for the latter any longer. There is no good in it, no matter what we are told by those who hold power in this world. I can tell ye from experience that this Drogue, that calls himself a 'Prince', he is a dangerous man, and greatly to be feared. I have been in his presence, and there is about him a quality that chilled me to my bones. It will be no child's play to defeat him. Even so, I have no wish to harm him myself – only to stop him from taking what is not his. As for you, Mistress Regent, and Master Mage, I owe you my life and my service, and think highly of yer wisdom. Whatever a man such as me has to offer, I give freely."

Tvrdik put an arm around the wiry man's rounded shoulders, "Master Praeger, everything you have just said is precisely why you *should* have a seat here, and your wife as well. Your experience has strengthened your convictions. You have lived the contrast between the fruits of war and peace. And, you have met, however briefly, our adversary, and know his mettle. You have credibility, and are a perfect spokesman for us with the real people of this realm – the farmers and herders and merchants and craft folk. Will you take our message? We cannot succeed without the good will of the people."

"I suppose we still have a few friends in the town and country at that, and I will pass the word, gladly."

"Good. Then we are all in agreement. Time is short. Speak to whoever you can, and see what support there is for such a plan. We meet again one week from today with as many other representatives as you can persuade to come. Thank you all for your confidence and your faith. You cannot know how much you have lifted my hopes today. Each of you will be a leader in a completely new and untried endeavor, a new force for good. Together we will push back the darkness that threatens us now, and that to come..."

Delphine chimed in, "Oooooh! That's good. We need a name, a slogan with which to rally people and inspire them. 'Push back the darkness' is good. That would make us, what? Soldiers of Light? Armies of Light?"

"Legions of Light," Mark pronounced, and shrugged at the approbation he saw in the faces of all present, and at their excited exclamations. "Just a little alliteration..." he mumbled, while Delphine squeezed the hand of her poet.

"Right then," Jorelial Rey summed up, "the first meeting of the Legions of Light is officially adjourned. We leave this place with a name, a vision, a timetable, and work to do. Before a week has passed, everyone in the kingdom will know our name and our purpose, and will deem it an honor to come and sign on. May every benevolent being of the universe smile on our endeavors, and guide us to victory."

"Victory!" shouted everyone else, whipped into a froth of excitement and hope.

As the guests took their leave to find their own homes and supper, the sun was sinking toward the horizon, a giant ball of fiery red. There was much handshaking and enthusiastic back-thumping, words of encouragement and compliment, and a tangible sense that something important and remarkable had begun. Tvrdik returned Ondine to the river, settling on a plan to meet on the following day. The Praegers set about moving the chairs and benches back to their normal places, cleared the trays and cups, straightened up the place, and begged leave to go back with the others to Theriole, where they would spend their nights until they could properly refit the back rooms of The Cottage for their purposes. Tvrdik thanked them for all of their efforts, told them he looked forward to a long and mutually beneficial association, and added that he would look into the details of their salaries on the morrow. Mr. Praeger stopped him in mid-sentence, "Master Wizard, sir, it is kind of ye to be thinkin' of our needs just now with so many things pressin'. But there is no need to hurry about it. The way I see it, I still owe ye labor and service for no pay at all."

Tvrdik replied, "You have already more than paid me back, Praeger, believe me. We will come to an arrangement that is fair, never fear."

They left along with Warlowe, Andrus, Verger, and Bargarelle, while the fading light still showed the path home, Lynette, half-asleep, toddling along beside her mother. Mark and Delphine followed close behind, Delphine giving Tvrdik an enthusiastic hug on her way out.

"Oh, Tvrdik, I knew you'd be lucky for us. We are going to change the world."

Tvrdik smiled as she pulled away. Realizing how very tired he felt, he quipped, "Very likely, my friend, only perhaps not tonight, alright?" and winked at her. Mark shook his hand, and the couple headed off under the colorful twilight sky. Jorelial Rey was the last to approach. "Would you like to stay for supper?" he offered, "I think Mrs. Praeger has left me something simple, and I am sure there is enough to share."

She shook her head. "Thank you, but I must get back to the palace. There will be so much there awaiting my attention before I can go to sleep, and I think I really will sleep tonight."

"I was just thinking the same thing. I felt so energized all day, but now, I feel like all the sap has been drained out of me."

"It was certainly a full and rewarding day, but more than you are used to taking on all at once since your injury. You must be exhausted. Are you in pain?"

"No, I'm fine. Just tired. But hopeful, and excited, for the first time in a long while."

She smiled, "You did it, Tvrdik. You got things started. It begins."

"We did it," he insisted. "It is your faith in the idea that gives it any credibility whatever."

"Too early for congratulations, I think. Still a great deal to be done."

"Yes, but look how far we have come." He walked her over to where the great green dragon awaited, and watched as she climbed to her accustomed perch. "Lord Tashroth, your presence at my home honors it, and your participation in our endeavor gives me hope for its success."

"Mage, I will do what I can. I find the idea both intriguing and appealing, and I have always held Xaarus in high esteem. Be well. I will return soon."

Tvrdik bowed to him and waved to Rel as they prepared to take off, then backed up and watched the duo circle once in the air and head off toward Theriole. Weary now, and alone in the big house for the first time, he wandered to the kitchen to see what Mrs. Praeger had left him for supper. It was then that he realized Stewart was by his side, following along to the kitchen.

"Will you be staying the night, then, my friend?"

"If it is not an imposition. I've grown rather accustomed to it, guardin' the place while ye were indisposed, and such…"

"You are most welcome. Your presence already makes me feel safer, and more at home. Can I fix a place for you by the fire, perhaps?"

"I have all I need, thank ye. It is quite cozy here."

"Share a bite with me before retiring, then?"

"I thought ye'd never ask."

Mrs. Praeger was treating her caretaking duties very seriously, he noted, as she had left out a variety of items, marked with little notes, for the two of them. There was more of the fresh bread, a rather generous wedge of cheese and fresh butter, a bowl of nuts and a few more strawberries. The tea things were set up, and there were some small sweet cakes as well with which to end the day. The two companions bustled about fixing themselves plates and getting the tea started. They ate at leisure at the kitchen table, conversing about the day's events. When they couldn't eat or drink another mouthful, Tvrdik conjured a little magical help with the dishes and tidying up, and bid Stewart a fond good night, as the dog circled and settled down on a rug before the hearth in the sitting room. Despite the warm weather, the Praeger's had lit the fire there before leaving, against the evening's chill breeze. Burning low and steady, it made the whole room seem warm and drowsy.

In the big bedroom that had once belonged to Xaarus, Tvrdik found the fire just smoldering enough to take the chill from the stone room, now hung with tapestries on three walls. The sconces were lit, the covers turned down on the bed, and a few books from his studies at the palace were placed by the bedside to be returned to as his fancy dictated. There was a small tray also on the bedside table, holding a cup and a pitcher of clear water. Tvrdik had felt a little sheepish about sleeping this first night in his master's bedroom. But Mrs. Praeger had spared no effort to make him feel truly at home. His stomach filled, his cheeks warm, his body weary, and his mind swimming with memories and ideas, he undressed, tended to his evening ablutions, and crawled into the big feather bed, glad of its soft embrace. Wrapping himself in the thick quilt, deciding he had not even the energy to read, he mentally doused the lights and lay in the dark, a smile on his pale face, until sleep carried him off.

TWENTY-EIGHT

MEETING THE UNICORNS

Tvrdik's dreams that night, however, were dark and disturbing. There were battlefields and combat, running and being chased. There was fear, and hiding, and the face of Xaarus, oversized, floating in the air, desperately trying to tell him something again and again. But, for whatever reason, he either could not hear or could not comprehend what his mentor was trying to communicate. At the last – and this part seemed somehow different from the rest, clearer and more real, perhaps – there was an image of Delphine, terrified and crying out for help, being pulled away, while someone who might have been Mark, reached out for her and fell short…

That was when Tvrdik woke up, breathing hard and sweating. Relieved that he had been, after all, dreaming, and counting it a result of the previous day's stresses, he resolved to face the new day with a fresh spirit. Looking out of the window, he was surprised to see that he had slept through a good part of the morning already. He could see that Mr. Praeger was out in the garden weeding, and the aromas that greeted his nostrils told him that Mrs. Praeger had also been busy. He washed and dressed quickly and straightened the bedclothes, emerging from the inner chambers into the heart of the house, still a bit tousled.

"Good morning, sir." Mrs. Praeger greeted him cheerfully, "I hope we didn't disturb ye. After yesterday's doins, and ye not bein' up to yer full strength yet, ye must have fair needed a good sleep."

"I suppose so. I don't think I was quite used to the bed, either, but I feel well enough."

"Well, ye just sit yerself down there, and I'll get yer breakfast. Eggs today, sir?"

He frowned, "Mrs. Praeger, I appreciate everything you are doing, but I feel silly being waited on like this. You honestly don't have to do this for every meal and every part of my day."

"Nonsense. I enjoy taking care of ye, sir. And it's the least we can do to repay yer kindness. Trust me, yer days will be filled soon enough with tasks of import, and ye'll be glad of a little help here and there with the small things."

"I suppose you are right, but I don't wish to take for granted…"

"Just sit right here and have yer tea, sir. There. Nice and hot. Honey? Will ye have one egg or two?"

He sighed and allowed her to wait on him, and in very short order, was glad he did. "Mrs. Praeger, our relationship is just beginning, and already I am grateful I dress in wizard's robes that will not show how much my waistline is expanding."

"Well, I'm that glad ye are enjoying yer meals, sir. It pains me to see a young man in his prime so rail thin, if ye'll pardon me mentioning it, sir."

"That's perfectly fine, but if you keep feeding me, I shall have to learn to employ some discipline not to travel too far in the other direction."

She beamed, and begged a word with him. Would it be alright, she wanted to know, if they began work in earnest today on renovating the back dormitories for their family's use? It would be so much easier to take care of him properly once they did not have to travel back and forth to the palace every night. Tvrdik hesitated a moment as a sudden picture flashed across his mind of his classmates' belongings lying about just as they had been left. He was afraid that he could not deal with going through them all by himself, but Rel was right. No one was coming back to claim them, and the space was too precious to waste. He instructed Mrs. Praeger to commandeer one of the larger trunks, and to put in it everything that looked like someone's personal property – clothing, books, mementos, jewelry, grooming items. Anything of general use they could keep for themselves, but the rest was to be packed away in a corner until he had the stomach to sort through it. Then they could tackle the place and rebuild or rearrange it to their heart's content. If there were ever to be a school for wizards again, he did not expect it would convene there anyway. He excused himself a moment, went back to rummage through his things in the bedroom, and came back with a fat handful of letters of credit for local merchants, which had been issued to him by Jorelial Rey and the Crown treasury. These he held out to Mrs. Praeger.

"Sir?" she stared at them uncertainly.

"These were given to me for the repair and restoration of this house by order of the Lady Regent herself. I would say the back rooms qualify as part of the project. Anything you need or want to make them fresh or weatherproof, or comfortable – any construction supplies, or gardening items, or any furnishings you need, you just go to these merchants and the Crown pays for it all."

"But, sir, we weren't expecting…"

"The Lady Regent promised to set your family back on its feet, and also commanded me to put this cottage in shape. I'd say that entitles you to this assistance on two counts. I'll even help you with the labor myself after you've emptied the place out."

"Sir, we never meant to ask you…"

"If and when I have time on my hands, a little physical labor will be good for me. I'm actually pretty good with my hands. You'll see. We'll have you moved in back there in no time. Where is everyone, anyway?"

She took the vouchers from him and accepted the change of subject. "My man is out doin' some work in the garden, and Lynette is gatherin' wildflowers for the house. She takes her time and wanders about, that one – quite an imagination, and a knack for bein' distracted." She sighed in the long-suffering way of a parent, but was smiling as well.

"And Master Stewart?"

"Goodness me, I almost forgot. He was up and out early. He told me to let ye know he was off for a few days to gather the talkin' beasts and fill them in on your plan for the new army. He said he'd have them in tow for ye within the week, gods willing."

"Did your husband explain to you everything that was discussed yesterday, Mrs. Praeger?"

"Yes, he did, Master Wizard."

"And?"

"Oh, I'm all for it. We mothers think it's time for someone to step up and change how things are done. Now, I have no son, as yet, but if I did,

I would certainly not have him out riskin' his neck on some battlefield far from home, for some tiff he knows naught of between lordlings. No, sir. Besides, we stand with ye, sir. We think ye can do anything ye set yer mind to, sir, and that's a fact."

Tvrdik blushed. "Well. Thanks for that vote of confidence, and for your wise insight, Mrs. Praeger. Would you be willing to talk to any of the other mothers you are still in touch with who might have similar feelings, and see if you can get them interested in participating? We are definitely an equal opportunity army."

"Excuse me?"

"I mean we hope to train men, women, beasts, sprites, dragons – anyone who believes in what we are doing, regardless of gender, species, or station in life."

"Oh. Then, yes sir, I most definitely will pass the word."

"Thank you, Mrs. Praeger. Can I help you clean up?"

"Not at all, sir. Ye just go about yer wizard's business now. Go on, shoo!"

Tvrdik was not entirely sure yet what his 'wizard's business' might be, so he meandered out to the yard to see what Praeger might be up to.

"Good morning, sir. Beautiful day, isn't it?'

"Why yes, it is."

"Looks like we're goin' to have a fair good crop o' beans and squashes, sir. They're doin' fine. All the herbs are really thrivin', too. Just look at the lavender and sage."

"Much of that is due to your hard work, you know. Anything you or your family need from the garden, Praeger, feel free to help yourself."

"Thank ye, sir. That's most generous o' ye."

"Can I help you with anything here?"

"No, sir. Just about done here for today, sir. Nature has a way o' largely taking care of itself. Seems a good time to go and take stock o' those rooms. I should be getting' to work on them right away."

"Oh....yes." Tvrdik was a little disappointed and at loose ends, wondering how he should occupy his day.

"Master Wizard, sir?" Praeger was addressing him again, hesitating a bit.

"Unmmm?"

"Well, I was wonderin', sir, seein' as how ye did such a fine job with my daughter, and as ye're feelin' better, do ye think it might be a good time to start seein' folks now?"

"Seeing folks?"

"Ye're a gifted healer, sir, that ye are. And I have a lot o' friends back in the old neighborhood with pains and sickness, complaints and such, who are wantin' to be looked at by ye. Some of them have been askin' after ye for a good while now, after they'd seen what ye had done for my little Lynette. I told them, 'Wait,' says I, 'wait till he feels a bit stronger, and is up to it.' Did I do right?"

"That was very considerate of you, Praeger, and yes, I am doing better. But are there no healers where you lived?"

"No good ones to speak of, sir. A country witch here and there who can deal with yer everyday toothache or croup, and a few studied sorts as charge more than we folk can afford. Some of the friends I mentioned haven't got much to pay ye, sir, but they'll gladly give ye a pail of milk or a good chicken for your trouble, such as they can spare, and ye with yer good heart and all…. Ye know so much, sir, and I've never seen anyone do what ye did with yer hands."

"I just don't want to infringe on someone else's livelihood, that's all. Of course, I'd be happy to see anybody you want to recommend, Praeger. It seems I'm being paid by the Crown anyway, so I might as well make myself useful. I can't promise to fix everything, but we do have quite a good stock of salves and potions here. Tell them to come around anytime I am here, and I'll be glad to do what I can."

"Thank ye, sir. Ye're a good soul, sir…" He took his leave, and headed toward the house, whistling happily. Tvrdik hardly had the time to consider what he had just gotten himself into when he heard the click of his front gate, and turned to see Mark and Delphine just arrived.

"Good morning, Sir Wizard," the girl called cheerfully, "Did you sleep well in your own house?"

Seeing Delphine's lovely face brought back the memory of his nightmares, and he frowned, "Well, I did sleep long, but I had the strangest dreams – not very restful."

"Takes some time to get used to a new bed," Mark offered.

"I'm sure that's it. In any case, welcome friends. What am I thinking, keeping you standing out here? Can I get you anything? Some refreshment?"

"No, it's alright. Mark is just leaving, and wanted to stop by on the way out."

"Leaving?" Only then did he notice that the bard was draped in carry-sacks; his harp and overnight gear, presumably.

"Yes, I was able to cover myself for my engagements all week, and wanted to lose no time in going to see Nyree. She will listen to our plan, I am certain of it, and has the authority to call together all the members of our guild if she sees reason. But she rarely leaves her home these days... I must go and seek her out."

"That will be wonderful, Mark. Is it very far?"

"Not very. A day's journey, perhaps, on foot. I won't be away long. You will look after my bride, though, won't you? I'd feel better knowing she was under someone's wing, times being what they are..."

"Mark!" Delphine protested.

"Of course, Mark. It will be my pleasure. Don't worry. But wouldn't you rather go with him, Delphine?"

"Not a chance. Rel is beside herself already, since Tashroth also left this morning to go and rally all the dragons. He travels faster than Mark, but has great distances to cover, and many stops to make. He might be gone the entire week, and though my sister realizes the necessity of this trip, she is always at sixes and sevens when they are separated for any length of time. She would just explode, if I were to go as well."

"And she could not go with Tashroth?"

"She is the regent, remember? She can't be spared just now, with so many things to attend to on a daily basis. And she should not leave the king alone, either. Besides, Tash needs the flexibility to speak with other dragons without a human present. Many of the others are not as well-disposed toward people as he has been. They are still cautious and suspicious in the presence of humans."

"I see. Please tell her that she is welcome here any time she has a moment to herself. We can talk strategy, or just visit. Both of you. My home is your home. Mark, do you need anything? Provisions, equipment, ideas for how you will present our case to the Guild?"

"No, thank you, Tvrdik. I think I am all set, and I am sure I can explain everything properly to Nyree. She is an old friend, a mentor, and, I feel certain, a likely ally. She can take it from there. I should be on my way. The sun is already high, and I have miles to cover before nightfall."

"Alright, then. Safe travels and good fortune. Come back to us soon with good news." The two men shook hands, and then Tvrdik backed away while Mark and Delphine kissed goodbye. An odd twinge went through him, seeing their closeness, but he dismissed it. Mark backed through the gate, burdened with his packs, and started up the Riverwalk, waving to them as he rounded the first bend and disappeared.

"Delphine, will you stay awhile?" Tvrdik invited.

"I will," she lifted her chin in defiance of gloom, "and the first thing we had better do is get back to your exercises."

"What?" exclaimed the mage.

"Come on. That arm will never be back to normal if we don't keep them up. And don't try to tell me you have been doing them on your own, because I won't believe it."

He hung his head in guilty admission, and allowed her to escort him back to the house, where she started him on his regimen of stretching and strengthening moves. He was surprised to see that he was stiff, and had lost some ground since their last session.

"You see," Delphine scolded, "you *do* need me. I apologize for falling down on the job. I promise to come over often and remedy that."

"Do." he replied, and they both laughed, though Tvrdik was also wincing as they worked on retraining his injured muscles.

"Why is the place so quiet?" Delphine asked.

"Hmmm…Stewart has also gone on his pilgrimage to round up all the talking animals for our cause. Lynette is out, I think, picking wildflowers for the tables, and should be back presently. Mr. and Mrs. Praeger are in the back assessing the work required to convert the dormitories for their use…"

"Oh."

While they were hard at work, and Delphine was a taskmaster that day, Lynette did come in with arms full of flowers to place around the house, and Mrs. Praeger, discovering that there was company, insisted on bringing them tea. After they had finished the exercises and were enjoying their tea, they chatted about one thing and another, and Delphine wandered into asking many questions about the healer's art. Tvrdik was happy to answer her inquiries, but since her interest did not wane, he felt inspired to say to her, "You know, you really have a knack for this sort of thing – a wonderful mind and a real way with people – not to mention that tough streak that won't let anyone get away with whatever is not good for them." He cocked an eyebrow and rotated his left shoulder a few times by way of illustration. "If you were interested in learning something of the healer's art, I could teach you a few things. I know it isn't your first love, but some skill could come in handy. You never know."

Delphine was exuberant. "I would *love* that. Would you really teach me? I've always been drawn to medicine, but here, it's considered more of a man's profession."

"Nonsense! One should follow where one's talents and inclinations lead. Are you finished with your tea? I'll give you a sample today. Come out with me to the garden." She followed him out to the front garden where all the herbs grew in ordered profusion. Tvrdik took her around the large plot, showing her each precious plant, explaining how to recognize it, and what its medicinal properties were. With each, he made her repeat back to him the plant's name, its description, and uses. There were quite a few different species to deal with in Xaarus' garden, so it was predictable that after an hour or so, Delphine finally laughed and called out, "No more, stop! My head is swimming. It can take in nothing else."

"Oh, sorry. This is a sort of a passion of mine, and I'm afraid I get a bit carried away."

"Don't apologize. I loved it. I've learned so much today, and, despite appearances, I really think a lot of it is sticking. I just need a break."

"Well, that's enough for today. Come back anytime you want another lesson. In fact, Praeger asked me today if I would be willing to do some work on the town and farm folk hereabouts. If people start to show up, you could learn a lot in person on real cases. I could use an assistant...at least while Mark is away."

"That sounds like a fine opportunity. I would love to see you in action close up, and to help out in any way I can. You must let me know if you start to get patients."

377

"I will. Good gracious, what time is it? I had almost forgotten, I am supposed to meet with Ondine to go and see the Unicorns. Do you want to come?"

"Ooooh, I'd love to, but I'd better be getting back to the palace. Rel and Darian will be wondering where I've gotten to."

"Well, say hello from me, and don't be a stranger."

"And good luck to you. It's all beginning to come together, isn't it, Tvrdik?"

"More quickly than I might have hoped. We still have a ways to go…"

"One step at a time. It will happen. I can feel it."

"I hope I can trust your intuition. Will you be alright going back by yourself? Mark would never forgive me if I let something happen to you…"

"Don't be silly. It's a beautiful day. A walk in the gardens is good for me."

"I give you your leave, then, Delphine. I will see you soon."

"Thanks for the tea - and the lessons. I promise I will practice what I learned. Goodbye." She let herself out the gate onto the Riverwalk and hurried back toward the gardens and the palace.

The Praegers had already gone to the market for supplies, so Tvrdik just left them a note, grasped his staff, closed and blessed the front door, and dashed through the gate himself, in the opposite direction, headed for his special sanctuary, where he was to meet Ondine. In only a few minutes, he was pushing through the brush, and emerging on the familiar flat rock. Throwing a pebble in the river, and whistling their special little crooked tune, he waited. In a breath, the sparkling blue figure appeared from beneath the moving stream, a petulant frown on her freckled, ageless face.

"Hurry, Lovely Man. Long journey. We may come late – not see them." She took off, moving upstream, while he followed along as best he could along the riverbank, keeping her little blue curls in sight. Sometimes, it was a bit of a scramble through brush, thorns, and steep muddy slopes along the bank. But eventually, the river began widening, winding out of the wood and through green, grassy fields, dotted with wildflowers here and there. An occasional farm or cottage popped up on either side, but Tvrdik cast a spell of invisibility over himself and Ondine, so as not to waste time explaining himself to anyone they should run into along the way. Farmhouses began to appear with more frequency, and then they were crossing through the city, bustling with people, shopping, selling, and plying all manner of trades. Maintaining their focus, the invisible travelers moved with purpose, emerging from the city limits in record time. Residences and streets yielded to more farmland, and farmland gave way to green, rolling hills peppered with isolated copses of trees, and low bushes. It was beautiful country, and a mystery why people had not yet bent this area to their use. Perhaps they somehow sensed the faerie quality it seemed to radiate, and gave it a wide berth out of respect, or superstition.

Tvrdik lifted the invisibility charm, as Ondine slowed her pace. He hugged the riverbank now, so as not to lose her. Together they rounded a bend, defined by a dense arbor, and found themselves peering into a large, grassy area almost entirely surrounded by trees, where light and shadow played chasing games across the landscape, and the stillness was broken only by the buzzing of an occasional bee, or the flutter of butterfly wings. It was a magical place, hidden from the casual eye, removed from the main road, which at this point had left the river's side. The Maygrew ran all along one side of the clearing, and was lost in the trees on the far side. But the naiad and mage halted at this spot and exchanged a meaningful glance. Ondine pointed, though she needn't have, for there, clustered at the other end of this little protected clearing, stood the entire herd. Unperturbed, they grazed or stood dreaming, tails swishing. They gathered in pairs and trios to share gossip or quiet companionship. Some were perfectly white, some black as onyx, some dappled gray. Smaller than horses they were, slender, but sturdy, perfectly proportioned with flowing manes. Their cloven hooves pawed at the grass, and a shimmer of opalescent light seemed to emanate from them. And their horns spiraled from broad foreheads in polished, delicate bone, ending in wickedly sharp points; one would not want to be at the business end of those! It was impossible to keep from staring at them. Tvrdik realized he had been holding his breath as he took in the remarkable sight, and now he consciously released it in a gusty sigh, uttering the single word, "Glorious." Ondine shook her head and put a finger to her lips, but it was too late. Across the field, they saw one of the largest unicorns, white with a yellow-gold mane, lift his head and turn to look right at them. They had been discovered.

The magnificent beast came trotting up to them across the green field, his expression unreadable. Tvrdik did not move, or flinch, or utter a sound, but kept his posture open and non-threatening. One hand was low on his staff and the other palm out, fingers unclenched. Ondine bobbed gently in the blue-green water, but her attention was fixed on the approaching unicorn. It stopped a few yards from them, and seemed to be sizing them up. In a light, but authoritative voice, it addressed them formally, "I am Wynne, leader of this herd. Who are you, and why do you trespass on our sanctuary?"

Tvrdik did not move a muscle and kept steady eye-contact with the beast, "I am called Tvrdik, and my companion there is Ondine, a water sprite. We have come here to seek you out, hoping to speak with you on matters of some importance."

The unicorn tilted its head, "Speak now."

So much for hospitality, Tvrdik thought. He tried to craft his argument concisely, "There is danger coming to this place about which you should know..."

"What danger?"

"Are you aware of the kingdom in which your land lies, and of those who rule it from the palace downstream?"

"We pay little attention to the affairs of men, but... yes, we are aware."

"Those who now reign are honorable folk, who have always attempted to be fair and respectful of your rights..."

"That is a matter of opinion, but go on."

"There is an upstart northern lord, from out of the hills, who desires to rule this kingdom himself. He is cruel and devious, and will use any means to accomplish his purpose – force, treachery, general destruction and mayhem. Everyone will suffer."

The unicorn frowned. Several others in the distance had ceased cropping grass and were looking on in interest.

Tvrdik swallowed and continued, "There is a faction in the government who wish to defend the kingdom from this man in traditional ways, with armies and weapons. I represent another faction who would rather turn the usurpers back, but without bloodshed."

"How is that possible?'

"We wish to use every other tool at our disposal – magic, cleverness, creativity, persuasion. But not to mortally harm anyone if we can help it.

We have a source which has warned us that if we respond to the threat with violence, we will fail, and endanger our very future."

"This 'source'…how can they know such a thing? Is it divination?"

"Of a sort. He has travelled to the future and seen what it may be."

"Is that possible?"

"Not usually. He is mage, and sought to learn the true nature of time. His explorations came at a very high price, but he was able to send us this warning."

The unicorn's eyes narrowed, "You do not speak truth. There are no more mages. Not for years."

"I speak of one who was thought to have vanished years ago. His name is Xaarus."

"You know Xaarus?" Wynne took a step closer. Several of the other unicorns trotted up to join their leader, eager to hear the rest of the conversation. "Xaarus was a great friend to us. We held him in high esteem, while he lived and walked among us."

"He lives still, and sends greetings," Tvrdik seized the opportunity to press his case. "But he sought, years ago, to travel to the future, and now cannot find a way back. I am now his hands, and feet, and voice here. He can communicate his wishes through me."

Wynne made a snuffling, scoffing sound, "Why you, boy?"

"I am also mage. I am his pupil and apprentice."

There was a good deal of neighing and nickering at that revelation. Neither Tvrdik, nor Ondine had yet dared so much as to shift an inch, several sharp horns pointed straight at them. Wynne now took yet another step toward them and addressed the young wizard from an uncomfortably close position. His voice was low and intense, "Can you prove to me that you are mage, or that you speak for Xaarus the wise?"

Beads of sweat collected on Tvrdik's brow, "I may be able to prove later, to your satisfaction that I have messages from the master, but I can certainly show you right now that I am mage." No sooner had the words left his mouth, but he banged his staff on the ground and a wall of flame sprang up between himself and the beasts. They cried out and started backwards. Immediately, he made the flames vanish.

"I am so sorry," Tvrdik said, "I did not mean to alarm you. I was trying to think of something dramatic and impressive, and I over-reached." He rapped the staff again on the ground, and suddenly thousands of rose petals were floating down from the sky, pink and mauve and burgundy, fragrant and delicate, drifting down on all of them and blanketing the ground. Ondine giggled.

"It is enough!" Wynne called out, and the petals disappeared. "We are satisfied that you have some skill. What do you want of us?"

Tvrdik paused, and then, his voice quietly infused with passion, he answered, "Join us. We are many and diverse: magical beasts, sprites, dragons, all of whom have much to lose if the kingdom topples. And there are many humans of good will who have also embraced our cause – bards, healers, lords and simple folk alike, and the Lady Regent herself. Our ranks are growing, but if we are to triumph over the usurper without the usual weapons of war, we need all the help we can muster. We need every mind and heart and able-bodied being who believes as we do that right should triumph over might, and that ideas are more powerful than swords and arrows."

Wynne tossed his head and seemed to relax a tiny bit, "Well spoken, mage. And yet, what have we to do with this quarrel? We have great reason to be suspicious of mankind. Experience has taught us to stay out of the affairs of men, to keep ourselves isolated and safe while the tides of politics and war cycle by. This policy has insured our survival for thousands of years. Why should we change our ways now, young mage?"

"You may choose to continue to hide, and to ignore this latest threat. I would not blame you. But I tell you, this time, if the kingdom falls to the tyrant Drogue, you will never be safe. The land will be ravaged, fear and suspicion will reign. Violence will run rampant, and those who cherish peace and brotherhood will be silenced. It is certain that, within a generation, the whole race of unicorns will be lost forever, perished, or else fled to other worlds."

"An extreme scenario, which serves your purpose in the telling, and yet, I sense that you believe it." There was a pause, while Wynne appeared to be considering. Then, "Shar! Come forward," the leader commanded, calling to one of his fellows who had remained at the far end of the field with his back turned on them all. Shar was black, and sturdy-looking. He slowly raised his head at the summons, turned and approached. But something seemed wrong. What was first noticeable was his gait as he came forward, slow and halting, one front leg partly lame and bearing the angry white mark of an old wound. As he came closer, Tvrdik saw something even more devastating – this unicorn's horn had been broken off mere inches from his brow, leaving only a jagged, useless stump. The creature's eyes reflected his embarrassment and misery at the loss. He stood, head low, awaiting his sovereign's bidding. Wynne continued to address the mage, "A unicorn's horn is his birthright, his identity, the source of much of his personal magic. Once broken or lost, it cannot be regenerated, and we mourn deeply. It is as if a part of our soul has been taken from us.

"There are others who covet our magic, regardless of the price. Humans did this to Shar, years ago, lusting after the gold his horn would bring them. They nearly killed him. Most of his wounds have now healed, but there is a part of him that can never be whole. Do you now understand why we shun the company of men, and are reluctant to join with you in common cause?"

Tvrdik, watching the wounded unicorn's face throughout Wynne's speech, was almost moved to tears. He addressed Shar directly, "I am greatly saddened at the extent of your suffering, sir, and outraged that it should have been caused by some of my race. It is inadequate, I know, but I must apologize for the misdeeds of the immature, and beg your forgiveness. I want to assure you both, as well, that all of mankind is not motivated by lust and greed alone. Please believe me that there are many more good souls who are kind and respectful of their world, and of those with whom they share it. Do not, I beg you, judge us all by the actions of a few." He looked down again at the animal's scars. "Ah, but do my eyes deceive me, or is that the work of Xaarus?" For a moment, Wynne's expression changed, and he seemed to lose his studied mask of indifference.

"Indeed, it was your master who saved Shar's life and healed the wounds he could. How did you know?"

"I recognize his handiwork, the pattern of stitching on that wound. It is how he taught us. I have one very like it across my knee, acquired in a childhood fall. It is as I have told you. Xaarus was likely heartbroken at your distress. He represents the best of us, and I have always striven to be like him." There was another pause, as the unicorns exchanged glances, considering all that had just occurred. "I understand your caution," Tvrdik continued, "I did come here today partly because I need your help to succeed. But also partly because, whatever you decide, you need to be informed, that you may take whatever precautions you deem necessary. It is only right."

Wynne blinked, and turned to Ondine, who had kept uncharacteristically silent during the entire exchange, "And you, sprite? You are old magic. Why do you travel with this one?"

She was trembling, but faced the beast head on and replied, "He is mage. Watch him very long time. Know him well. He is good, Lovely Man. Ondine trusts this one. Wynne can trust too." Tvrdik's heart melted to hear her frank assessment of him – he would have to thank her in private later. But for the moment, there seemed to be a brief convocation among all the nearest unicorns, with much head-tossing, nickering and neighing.

At last, Wynne turned his head sideways, pointing the mortally dangerous horn away from Tvrdik's heart, fixed the mage with one large, liquid eye, and said, "Enter in peace. We will hear more of this plan to engage the tyrant Drogue." It was all he could do to make his feet shift beneath him, but, heartened by his success thus far, the young wizard gathered himself and entered the sacred grove, ready to tell the rest of his story to the unicorns.

It was well after dark when Tvrdik arrived back home, and he was leaning rather heavily on his staff. But his heart was light, since he was fairly certain he had persuaded the unicorns to participate in his growing army. Ondine had seemed pleased and excited at how well the meeting had gone, when he left her off at their special place. There had been hours of serious conversation that afternoon, and at last, Wynne had at least committed to attending an assembly at the end of the week, where it was hoped there would be representatives from all of the other groups the wizard's comrades had gone to solicit.

As he crossed the threshold of The Cottage he called home, Tvrdik had to admit he was bone tired. But, considering that only two days before, his friends would not let him walk the short distance from the palace, he thought he was doing fairly well. This was the weariness of a day well spent, as opposed to that absolute lack of vitality he associated with his long recovery. It occurred to him that spending time with magical creatures, such as Ondine, and the unicorns, had been an energizing experience for him. Still, a soft pillow and a good night's sleep would be most welcome tonight. He closed the front door behind him, and surrendered his trusty oaken staff to the corner. With a thought, he lit the lamps in the parlor, and only then realized he had not eaten anything at all since breakfast. Stumbling into the dining room and lighting the wall lamps there, he grinned to see the tray of cold supper that Mrs. Praeger had already laid out for him. That woman truly was a gift.

Tvrdik reflected to himself that it would be easy to become accustomed to this sort of pampering. So many years of doing things for himself, and only a few days to grow fond of being waited on. He shook his head in amusement, and mentally set the kettle to boil for the tea she had already set up for him. For that matter, with Stewart and the Praegers gone, and the sun down, the big old house seemed awfully empty. It surprised him how much that bothered him. Again, years of perfectly comfortable solitude, and only a few weeks to grow accustomed to company. Well, for tonight, he would have to be content with his own thoughts while he enjoyed a bite. And in a short while, at any rate, he expected to be fast asleep. He wondered how the Praegers had fared in their re-organization of the dormitory space, but he pushed that thought away when it began to drag at unpleasant memories, and instead re-focused on his encounter with the unicorns. How noble and beautiful they were!

TWENTY-NINE

TVRDIK THE HEALER

While Tvrdik was on his way to meet the unicorns, back at Theriole, Jorelial Rey had been spending some long-overdue quality time with young King Darian, when she received some bad news. General Boone requested her presence in his office. Once there, she was presented with reports from his most reliable intelligence officers, recently returned from reconnaissance. It seemed that Lord Drogue was indeed in the process of assembling an army, and it was already growing to alarming proportions. Far off in his mountain stronghold, he thought himself safe from prying eyes, so the fact that Boone's spies were as capable as they were was indeed a coup. But they brought back confirmation that two or three other mountain lords, as she suspected, had thrown their lot in with Drogue in exchange for promised lands and favors. He had also made overtures to several overseas kingdoms which were supposed to be either allied with the Crown or neutral, but which were at least entertaining his emissaries, and considering their offers. Boone's agents reported that it looked like mercenaries, malcontents, and the down–and-out were flocking to him from across the kingdom, and he was beginning to equip and train several thousand foot soldiers for his cause. Worst of all, and most surprising, Drogue, though a mountain lord, was assembling ships, repairing and fitting them for battle. Was he planning a two-pronged attack, then, and how soon would all of this be ready for action?

The news was grim, and made her feel quite behind schedule in shoring up their defenses. But, it was certainly better to know what to prepare for, rather than being taken off guard. Boone assured her that he was busy training the Crown's standing army, even as they spoke, drilling them in all manner of skill and strategy. Jorelial Rey restated her hope to avoid armed conflict all together, but conceded that she did feel safer, knowing he was diligently preparing for the worst. She thanked the special agents for their service, and gave each a small purse of gold as a reward for their dangerous and vital work. After they had taken their leave, the Lady Regent and her Defense Minister remained to discuss precautions that seemed prudent, such as checking the sea wall that protected the castle on the cliffside, for weaknesses. It also seemed wise to shore up their own small navy in case Drogue should attempt an attack by sea. Lastly, any merchandising and recreational activities that had, over the years, crept down to the beaches and along the riverbank must be pulled back behind the protective wall. And all of this should be done without divulging too much information that might alarm the public, or cause a panic. She would choose her own moment to let the citizenry know they were at war.

Taking her leave of General Boone, she immediately went to take a look at the sea wall herself. This was a part of the palace she did not otherwise frequent. Tashroth's absence at this critical time weighed on her, even though he would only be gone a matter of days. When she finally did allow herself to seek sleep, she found her muscles tense and her thoughts racing, so that she could not surrender to its comforts until far into the night. She prayed that Tvrdik and the others were having good fortune recruiting for their alternative army, and that Tvrdik was busy coming up with a long list of brilliant strategies for them to employ.

Tvrdik woke from a sound sleep the next morning and came out of his room to Mrs. Praeger's bright smile, the scent of something delicious, and her cryptic comment, "Best eat a good, big breakfast, Master Wizard. Ye have a busy day ahead." Confused, and not entirely awake, he smiled back and said, "Excuse me?" In response, while she bustled about straightening things, she nodded her head toward the nearest window. Tvrdik adjusted his glasses, glanced out where she had indicated…and blinked, now fully awake, at the sight of an endless line of people standing in his front yard, snaking back to the gate, and presumably onto the riverwalk. None of them looked wealthy, but otherwise, there were all sorts: men and women, children, adults, and aged folks. They waited patiently – standing, sitting, balanced on crutches, leaning on friends, lying in stretchers. Every one of them carried some homespun offering for the healer – a wheel of cheese, loaves of bread, pails of milk or of potatoes, a pole of fish, or a live chicken...

"Gods!" he muttered under his breath at the sight that would not vanish, glasses or no. Alarmed, but without taking his eyes from the bizarre scene, he called out, "Mrs. Praeger, where did all these people come from, and what do they want?"

Without even slowing a beat in her labors, she called back, "Oh, my man told a few folk yesterday that ye were willin' to take a look at what ails them, and they must've brought their friends. Everyone has heard of our Lynette's recovery. Ye're already a fair miracle worker by reputation," she chuckled, and continued. "These are simple folk who don't have much, but they've all brought something to trade, sir, have no worry for that. And all that food will come in right handy, that it will. Now, never you mind. Sit yerself down and take yer breakfast, sir, and you take yer time. They'll wait for ye, they will." She tugged him away from the window, and settled him down at the dining table, where breakfast was already laid out. Tvrdik took a deep breath, counted to ten, took off his glasses to wipe off the smudges, and with enforced calm, cleared his throat to speak, "Mrs. Praeger, thank you for the lovely supper you left for me last night, and for this sumptuous breakfast. And when it is convenient, could you tell your husband that I'd like to see him for just a moment, please?"

His voice shot up in pitch on the last few words, as the magnitude of what he was facing flooded over him. He picked at the delicious breakfast, barely paying any attention to what he was chewing. His thoughts reeling, he wondered how he could ever manage to apply his talents to such a vast army of patients in one day. He had always considered himself rather good at this particular aspect of the wizard's craft, but this was well beyond anything that had ever been asked of him before, and he doubted that he was up to it. Yet, glancing out the dreaded window once more, his heart went out to them. He could see in those faces their hope and faith, and in some cases, their pain. Some of these folks were really suffering. How long had it been since any of them had been able to find any help? He remembered what Praeger had looked like when he had first met him, and what he had been willing to do for just a chance at helping his family. And besides, what better way was there to win friends and allies among the common folk for their cause, than to help ease their pain? Perhaps this was what Praeger had had in mind all along, and this was the little man's special contribution to the Legions of Light. *Except I have to do all the work,* Tvrdik thought. *What if there are people here who are so ill that I cannot help them? They'll hate me. I'm not a miracle worker, after all.*

Now, then, Tvrdik, the other side of his mind responded, *you signed on to be a healer, so then be a healer. You've been lying around long enough – time to make yourself useful.*

"Did ye want to speak with me, sir?" Praeger's voice interrupted his reverie, and he looked up to see the man's curious face.

"Sit," he commanded, which Praeger did, somewhat taken aback. In a low voice, the wizard addressed him, "Praeger, just what is this?'

"What is what, sir?"

"Why, all those people waiting out there."

"Well, sir, ye said I could give the word for folks to come for healing."

"I said you could tell a few friends. I never expected *this.*"

Praeger smiled mischievously, "Word spreads quickly in the villages, sir, and there truly is a need. And people are curious, sir, to see for themselves if there really is a wizard once again in this house – it's been a long time. Good way to meet yer neighbors, sir, and make some friends, if I do say so." He winked. There it was…this man was more clever than he appeared.

"But what if I can't help all of them? This could backfire, you know."

Praeger was still smiling, like the cat that knew where its master's lunch had gotten to, "Aw, ye'll do just fine, sir, I'm that certain of it."

"But…so many!"

"It's early, sir, and Lynette will stand by to help ye with fetchin' and carryin' and all. Glad ye enjoyed yer breakfast, sir," he cocked his head toward the collection of empty plates. Tvrdik raised one eyebrow in surprise, wishing that he remembered eating any of it. Praeger went on, "All right if I take my leave, sir? Full day ahead for me as well, sir, workin' on the back rooms…"

"Yes, yes, go ahead. Thank you." He waved the amused man away and rose from the table, glancing out the window again. *Alright,* he thought, *what's done is done, and nothing for it but to dive right in and do my best.* He pulled back his hair with a tie, adjusted the belt of his robe, went into the parlor and arranged the two comfortable chairs in a sort of doctor/patient arrangement, with the low table beside his seat. In one quick circuit around the house, he gathered a number of the most useful potions, salves, elixirs, and medicines that Xaarus had on his shelves, and lined them all up on the table. Then he added some fresh herbs, bandages, knives, small cloths for washing, and a basin of warm water from the kettle over the hearth. Eyeing it all, and deciding it would do for the moment, he sat himself in the 'healer's' chair, and called for his young assistant.

"Lynette, your father said you might be willing to help me out with a bit of doctoring today, is that right?"

"At your service, Master Wizard." And she did a little curtsey.

"Alright, then. Your assistance is most welcome. As you can see, we have a *lot* of patients to treat today. You tell me when you are tired and need a break, yes?"

"I can do it. Just tell me what to do."

He adjusted his position in the comfortable chair and sighed, "Are you ready? Good. Lynette, will you please show our first patient in…"

The healer/mage sat there all that day, and long after the sun had gone down. He saw thirty-two people and several animals, giving each his full attention, and the best care and advice he knew to give. Lynette ushered patients in and out, gathering up their hopeful offerings for the growing pile in the kitchen, and ran for supplies and medicines as Tvrdik instructed her. She was willing and hard-working, and mature for her age, but a child after all. Thankfully, Delphine happened by for a visit after the first hour and a half, sized up the situation, rolled up her sleeves, and dived in as assistant for the remainder of the marathon. She took over anything to do with fetching, mixing or pouring medicines, explaining instructions, or writing them down, and with any hands-on assistance the mage required in handling patients. Lynette only had to take charge of escorting patients in and out, and collecting the various payments. Even so, Mrs. Praeger came out to spell her every now and then and give the little girl a rest. She was working on the back rooms with her husband, but checked often on her daughter, and insisted that Tvrdik and Delphine also take breaks now and again. Not that they ever stopped for long – a quick cup of tea or a sandwich hastily consumed – but even those brief pauses helped them to address the next patient with renewed energy. In the course of that single day, Tvrdik saw rashes, earaches, toothaches, stomach aches, broken limbs and sprains, strains and wounds that would not heal. There were cases of croup and asthma, burns and warts, babies that cried constantly and aged patriarchs who were thin and bent. Some complaints were fairly trivial, and Tvrdik could tell that the main motivation for the person's presence there was simple curiosity – the desire to see the new wizard close-up, as Praeger had remarked. He tried to be patient and pleasant, and give them something of a show for their efforts.

Others he saw had far more serious complaints, coming in for treatment not a moment too soon. He was glad of the opportunity to help those folks regain their health, and felt he was doing some real good. Thank the heavens there were no pox, no plagues, no contagious diseases in the mix, but a few of the most aged or very ill presented him with the unpleasant task of telling their families that there was very little he could do to restore them. In most of these cases, however, everyone seemed to understand that he was doing the best he could to make their loved ones more comfortable, and to take away any suffering.

There were the heart-touching, memorable cases: the little boy who brought in his beloved cat, and explained tearfully that it had been run over accidentally by the family cart, and had broken a leg. Tvrdik set the leg with great solemnity, applied some salve against infection, and gave the boy very detailed instructions on the care of his best friend, telling him to come back in a week's time. Both the boy and his charge left feeling much better. There were the two friends who carried a third companion for miles on a stretcher to see the healer, since the man was too sick to make the journey on his own. There was the young husband who fussed over his pregnant wife with such concern and attentiveness one would have thought her made of fine porcelain. With such variety, the day was never dull, and the people were all good, honest, plain folk who treated him with great deference, but seemed to bloom at his natural kindness and good humor. Tvrdik took their gifts and offerings out of respect for their dignity, though he would have seen them for nothing. Much of what they brought was actually very useful to a new homeowner, and seemed a fair exchange. In some cases, however, where he sensed that the gift was a hardship or truly beyond the means of the client, he would only accept a small portion of what was offered, and sent them home with the rest.

Delphine had an intensive initiation to the healer's art, learning by watching, listening, and assisting in the diagnosis and treatment of countless conditions. In one day, they decimated Xaarus' stock of elixirs, salves, balms, tinctures, medicines, and dried herbs so completely that Tvrdik resolved to take inventory of everything left, and to get to work his first free day on making or purchasing more of whatever was depleted.

They were all so busy that time sped by unnoticed, and no one had a moment to feel weary until the very last customer limped away down the garden path and disappeared through the gate. Realizing that he had reached the end of the endless line at last, the young mage leaned back in his chair, closed his eyes for a moment, let his arms fall limply at his sides, and allowed a wave of exhaustion to break over him.

"I don't think I can move a muscle more," he sighed.

"Ye'll have to move a few just a bit further if ye'll be wantin' any supper," came Mrs. Praeger's genial quip. And, standing with a monumental effort, Tvrdik replied, "Well, if it is made by yourself, dear Mrs. Praeger, it might be almost worth it. I do think I might cheat a little though,"

"Cheat?" asked Delphine, brows furrowed.

"Under ordinary circumstances, the possession of magic is no excuse for laziness, but I do think this qualifies as one of those extraordinary occasions where I can be forgiven…" He waved his hand, and all the bottles, boxes, tins, jars, and bandage rolls that were piled high all over the parlor began to sort themselves back to the cupboards and shelves where they belonged. Any used materials gathered themselves up and headed to the dustbin, and kitchen items like knives and basins floated right past Mrs. Praeger's nose, into their original home. Mrs. Praeger shook her head, round-eyed, marveling, "I dinna think I will ever get used to seein' things like *that* happenin' all around the place."

Delphine giggled, "In this house, I'm afraid you are going to have to." And they all headed into the dining room, where Mr. Praeger awaited them already. Hot bowls of leftover lentil stew and warm buttered bread already were set on the table, the kettle was heating for tea, and there was a surprise! Delphine had brought a treat from the palace that in the press of the day's activities, had been forgotten: a box of the little custardy tarts that Tvrdik so loved, enough for everyone to have one, and the wizard, two. Lynette had already eaten and had fallen asleep in a chair.

"Poor little thing." Tvrdik remarked, "She was such a great help today, and we wore her out."

"Ach, she'll be fine." Mrs. Praeger replied, "It's the most fun she's ever had

"How are the renovations coming?" Tvrdik asked, as he gratefully tore a hunk of bread from the loaf.

Praeger was happy to report, "I don't think ye'd even recognize the place, sir, it's that changed already. And coming along it is indeed – should be ready for us to move in, in just a few days."

"That quickly? I must say, I am amazed at your progress, but glad to hear it. It will make life so much easier for all of you."

Mrs. Praeger jumped in, "Oh, never ye mind about that, sir, we do alright. 'Twill be a blessin', though, to be right here with ye all the time. Master Wizard...?" She glanced at her husband, and went on, "what would ye like us to do with that trunk o' personal things we collected back there?"

Tvrdik paused before answering her question. "Those are just things that belonged to myself and my schoolmates many years ago. I doubt we'll any of us be needing them again, but I am not sure I...uh...have the time to go through them all just now to decide what might be useful. I appreciate your taking the trouble to pack them up, but I suppose they are in your way. Hmmm. I know. We can store them in the laboratory for awhile. I'm sure there is a space behind something where we could put them, out of the way. Perhaps you could do that, Praeger, any time you wish...I'll help you navigate the laboratory."

Praeger nodded while Mrs. Praeger stared at the mage with an expression of concern. Catching her glance, Tvrdik thought, *she knows. She knows that this is not an easy subject for me.*

"Oh!" Delphine cried, interrupting the awkward silence, "I never got to tell you the news from the palace..."

"Go ahead, Delphine." Tvrdik was grateful for the change of topic, and eager to hear about whatever might be going on.

"Well, General Boone's intelligence agents came back yesterday with a lot of bad news. Seems that Lord Drogue has been quite busy this past month assembling troops, forging alliances with neighbors, and sending out overtures to foreign lands for assistance. It's unclear when he'll be ready to launch his attack, but it is coming, and not too far off. The worst news was that he is equipping ships, we assume to lay siege to Theriole from the ocean side."

"Ships? A mountain lord?"

"They saw them. He has them lined up in the river being refitted. He must think it's an easy way to take us off guard. Luckily, Boone's agents are thorough and resourceful."

Tvrdik was now wide awake and had turned pale, "There's so much yet to do; we've barely begun."

The Praegers looked grim. "Sir," Praeger offered, "I'm wi' ye, whatever it takes to stop that evil man. And there'll be others linin' up to help us as well, believe you me."

"I pray you are right, Praeger. It's time for me to work seriously on my magic, but you do yours as well. We'll need every hand possible, and if this morning was any indication of your gift, I'm glad you are on our side now."

Praeger turned red, remembering, with some embarrassment, when he was not.

Delphine continued, "Rel is beside herself, with Tashroth gone and all. She spent the day yesterday inspecting the sea wall and the gates, and trying to convince the shopkeepers and recreation booths that have spilled over outside those defenses to pull back, without causing a general panic."

"Challenging."

"She would very much like to see you, to hear your ideas for defense, considering this new information. Perhaps you could walk the perimeter, and take a look as well. She told me she wouldn't be able to get away to come here just now."

"Of course, I am at her service. I was planning to spend the morning tomorrow taking inventory of our medicines, and getting the process of restocking started. Some of them require several steps to make, so it would be wise to get them going. I'll go over to the palace in the afternoon, and we can brainstorm, and take a look around. I had some ideas I wanted to run by Verger, Bargarelle, and a few specialists over there as well." He looked around at the grim faces before him, and sighed, "It seems that there are to be no more leisurely days. Mr. Praeger, will I be able to attend to all that I have mentioned on the morrow, or will there be a second wave of patients awaiting my attention?"

Praeger's eyes twinkled, "I doubt it very much, sir. I let it be known ye'd be seein' folk one day a week, except for emergencies, and appointments ye gave out yerself, sir."

Tvrdik smiled, "Why, Praeger, you clever fox! That's perfect. However did you come up with such an idea?" Praeger smiled, delighted with the wizard's reaction, but it was his wife who responded.

"Someone has to take charge o' yer calendar, Master Wizard, to make sure ye have all the time ye need for yer many wizardly tasks. You folk have too much on yer minds to be orderly in these things, if ye don't mind my saying so."

Tvrdik laughed outright, "No, I don't mind at all. I'm lucky if I even know what day of the week it is most times. Bless you both for taking me in hand." There was a pause as exhaustion and the gravity of the last conversation settled over all of them. But then Tvrdik shook himself and looked up at Mrs. Praeger with pale eyes pleading, "Is it time for the custardy thingies yet?"

"Well, have ye finished yer stew, lad?" Everyone laughed, as dessert was passed around. Soon, pleasantly sated, and weary beyond words, having cleaned and tidied the kitchen, and having received his guests' assurances that they would all be fine on the short walk back to Theriole, Tvrdik fashioned a magical glow-ball for them, to light their way. He bid them all goodnight, closed the front door, stumbled to his room, and fell into bed.

The sun was high when Tvrdik arrived at the palace the next day, carrying a sheaf of papers under one arm. It didn't take him long to find Warlowe, who greeted him warmly and went off to inform Jorelial Rey. Not five minutes later, she came sweeping down the hall with a purposeful stride. She had a sort of pinched, grim look about her, and yet, he noticed, there was always something in her that seemed to shine whenever she was contending with a particularly difficult problem. He could not help staring at her with a kind of helpless admiration as she approached…and then, without even breaking stride, swept right by him, calling back, "Come on, then. Where have you been? I've been waiting for you." He fell in step behind her as they hastened who knew where.

"Sorry. I had a great deal to do this morning, and I wanted to come to you with some ideas. I do have a few things to show you..."

"Well, now that you are here, I want you to see exactly what we have to deal with." He followed at her breakneck pace to the sea-side of the complex, up several flights of stairs, down a hall, into a tower, and up and around on the spiraling staircase, to a high battlement overlooking the castle's rear face. There she made an abrupt stop, and pointed down.

"Take a look," she commanded, "You can see pretty well from here."

He could see ocean waves lapping at a sandy beach below. To the right, beneath them, the huge, sprawling palace backed right up against sheer stone cliffs, with a tall, broad wall running along as close to the edge as was prudent. To the left, the land sloped downward toward the Maygrew Delta. The sea wall followed along the ocean's edge until, at the convergence of river and sea, a long, flat beach stretched away to the south. Several boatyards, fishing docks and port slips stood lined up as one's gaze moved away from the palace proper. Just beyond the docks pitched a small collection of larger ships. He presumed them to be the Royal Navy, moored in a protected harbor on the other side of the Maygrew. Directly below them and slightly to the left, where the sand sloped gently down to sea level, there was a great gate in the sea wall that stood wide open. Something about its position suggested that it had not been shut in many years. There were shops and outbuildings lining the wall, on both sides of the gate. But what concerned the Lady Regent now was that the beach *outside* of the wall looked like a fair. There were dozens of colorful tents, booths, recreation areas for swimming and fishing, sunbathing or shopping. There was a small stage where jugglers and minstrels performed, and puppet shows were held. Everything looked as though it had started out portable, but had somehow, over time, grown roots in the sandy shore. Years of peace and prosperity had given the people a sort of sense of invulnerability which was now threatened.

Tvrdik sized up the situation in a flash, "We shall have to tell them soon enough that the nation is at war. It shouldn't be such an impossible task to bring everything in behind the wall."

"We could cause a general panic, perhaps without need. I don't have to tell you, it would be best if Drogue's ships never got anywhere near Theriole, but if they break through our defenses out there, I have to have every possible protection in place. Right now, I'm not even sure that massive gate will close anymore, or if we'll have to build a bulkhead to close the gap in its place. I can't even find out until those people are all off the playground. I'm thinking of telling them we need to clear the area for repairs and renovations, which isn't altogether false…"

Tvrdik caught her eye and held it steadily, "Jorelial Rey, we have little time, and are in need of recruiting people for our cause. Your citizens are not fools. They will guess that something is not right. Trust them, and tell them the truth."

She sighed and lowered her gaze, "You are right, I suppose. Tash would have said the same thing if he were here. It's not that I don't trust them. I just want to protect them as long as I can from this terrifying disruption of their daily routines."

"Your job *is* to protect them, starting with giving them information. Knowledge is a tool they can use to protect themselves."

She looked up at him, "How did you get so smart? I suppose you are right, but there's more. Our distant forefathers were not entirely fools when it came to defensive planning. They chose to build on this spot for the sheer cliffs on that side. They are almost impossible to scale. But, they put in another powerful deterrent as well. Look straight down, and to the right there, about halfway down. Do you see those shadows, at intervals there?" Tvrdik was dizzy and nauseous, looking straight down from their perch, and he found it hard to concentrate on anything but the prospect of hurtling headlong toward the rocky shore. But he tried to calm his irrational fears, and to look where Rel was indicating. There they were, some sort of square-ish shadows directly beneath them, running off in both directions, evenly spaced.

"Those are special windows, for archers, giant pots of boiling oil, and oversized crossbows capable of propelling flaming bolts over long distances. Strategically, they are a traditional defense against enemy ships, or anyone trying to scale the castle walls. Of course, right now, the alcoves and the equipment in them are in terrible disrepair, no one having had a use for them in decades. General Boone is firmly bent on restoring and manning them. It is certainly common sense, if we are indeed facing a hostile force from the sea. But none of those strategies fit with our 'Legions of Light' agenda. So, if we want to head Boone off and save valuable resources, we have to come up with a convincing alternate plan, and quickly. Furthermore, it has to work, or we will have handed the kingdom over to its enemies without any real resistance."

"Jorelial Rey, we always knew our plan would be put to some practical test sooner or later…I'll grant you this is sooner, but of course it has to work! Xaarus never intended for us all to stand idle while the palace and the kingdom slip out of our grasp. I will summon him later and ask his guidance on this matter, but let me see what comes to mind in the moment…I'm all for pulling everyone in behind the sea wall for protection; that makes sense. And I have no problem with setting up some 'uncomfortable' greetings for anyone that might chance to get in through the back door. But it would be better to try and insure that no invading force ever got that far to begin with." Tvrdik pursed his lips in thought, "You know, the water sprites are more powerful in their element than you can imagine. Perhaps Ondine could gather all her nearby relations and stir up the river and the sea. And Tashroth and a few of the dragons – gods grant that he brings them – could be poised on the battlements to harry the enemy. I know *I* would find that daunting." He had backed away from the wall's edge and laid down his sheaf of papers, pacing, considering. His hands painted the pictures of his ideas in the air before them with great animation, as the creative wheels turned in his brain. And then, he stopped midstride, put a hand to his mouth as if to stifle a gasp, and turned to the Lady Regent, eyes wide. "Wait!" he said.

"What?"

"I just remembered something that flashed through my mind the very first time I walked in the gardens here, and turned back to look up at Theriole. I was thinking how vulnerable it looked, and then I wondered… well, I thought…oh, I'm not sure I could actually do it, but it would be worth a try…"

"Whatever are you talking about?"

"Well, that day, when I was walking, I wondered if I could cast an illusion big enough to hide the entire palace. I've never tried anything that big, and it would take some practice, but in theory, it could work."

"I still don't understand."

"Well, when I don't wish to be seen, I can make myself seem invisible, and I've done it for Ondine, too. It's not a matter of making anything go away, but of superimposing an illusion of something else over the real thing so that the observer is diverted or confused. It is a relatively easy trick to cover just myself, but, theoretically, it should be possible to generate a large enough illusion to hide the entire palace, and make the enemy fleet think they are hopelessly lost, until they finally just give up and go home."

"This is beginning to sound interesting. Can you do it?"

"It would take a lot of personal energy to hold a vision that vast. It might be easier if a few friends who understood what was happening could just sit with me and add their strength and their intention...?"

"Done. I hope you've been practicing?"

"I will now. If parts of Theriole wink out before your eyes in the next few days, you'll know why. On a happier note," he pulled back from the frightening edge, and sat down on a stone bench installed once upon a time for guards at the battlements. He patted the space beside him, encouraging her to sit as well, "...on a happier note, two days ago, Ondine took me to meet an entire herd of unicorns. They were...awe-inspiring; they took my breath away. It was difficult at first to get them to even listen to me, they are so wary of humans. But, like everyone else, it seems they have good memories of Xaarus. Once they heard me out, they were intrigued by our ideas, and quite interested in keeping the likes of Drogue out of power. They have agreed to come to our assembly of the Legion. In a few days we'll be hearing from Tashroth on the dragons, Mark will be bringing word of the bards, Stewart from the talking animals, Andrus, the healers, and so forth. Assuming we get at least some positive responses all around, we will need a larger field in which to meet than The Cottage's back yard. Any suggestions?"

She considered a moment, "Why, yes! The gaming fields are quite large. There are arena seats set up all around for those watching the contests, and we can set up a platform for you in the center if you're going to be doing the speaking. The acoustics are naturally good."

"Perfect. Will you arrange that? I think we may have a contingent of local folk as well. Praeger arranged for me to make a few friends yesterday, doing healing work. Did Delphine tell you? We saw close to two score patients in one day, including animals. I don't know what I would have done if your sister had not decided to stop by. She has real talent in the healing arts, you know, and she's eager to learn."

"That doesn't surprise me. She is always taking care of everyone, despite the fact that she is technically the baby here."

"She has a very big heart, as well as a sharp mind."

"Yes. How are the Praegers working out?"

"I'm not accustomed to being waited on, but I will tell you, I *could* get used to it. They have been a godsend these past few days. I credit them with doing half my thinking for me."

"And who is doing the other half?" Rel couldn't resist such an opening, and a hint of a smile played across her face.

"Very funny." Tvrdik was relieved to see her beginning to relax a bit.

She turned and looked him up and down, as if only just noticing his actual presence beside her, "And you are well? I mean you are feeling alright?"

"Yes, quite fit, thank you. I think I might have gotten an extra boost in my recovery from Ondine and the unicorns."

"Well, you've made me feel better in any case. Hopeful. And like I have concrete assignments to tackle. I'm sorry if I seemed a little on edge. I am always anxious when Tashroth is absent."

"Understandable. He'll be back soon. But, speaking of concrete assignments, I do have a few other ideas I wanted to take out for a spin." He brandished the papers he'd been clutching. "I told you I wanted to have something to bring you. One thought, I need to run by Minister Verger, if he's available, as it will most clearly impact his department. The other is a design I drew up for a possible weapon I've been thinking about."

"A weapon?"

"Relax, it is not meant to kill or maim. It is something infinitely more powerful. But, I was hoping to have a prototype made that I could work with and adjust a little. At the moment, it is really only in the imagined stage. If the first one worked, we would need to somehow manufacture hundreds, so I thought I'd better begin the process right away. Who would I need to talk to for having something crafted?"

She was intrigued, "Well, Verger again, just to have the funds released, and then, the palace Armory, I would think. You could go over your designs with the Master Craftsman there, Hancock. He's very talented, and quick. What does it look like? What does it do?" She was peering over his shoulder now, trying to get a glimpse of the drawings as he pulled them just out of view.

"I'll explain it later. I need to know if it's even feasible first," he blushed.

"I'll take you there, and introduce you. Stay to supper?"

"Thank you kindly, I'd love to. Although, I daresay Mrs. Praeger might box my ears if I don't show up at home…"

Jorelial Rey chuckled, "I'll send a page over there and let them know you are detained for the evening. There is still much we should discuss; more brainstorming to do. I want to hear *all* your ideas."

He stood and bowed to her, "I am at your service, my lady. Do but command me." His face was serious, but his eyes twinkled with mischief behind the gleaming spectacles. She rose as well.

"Fine. I command you to escort me down from these battlements; I think it is going to rain."

"Yes, my lady." And he offered her his right arm as they headed toward the circular stone staircase that would take them back to the bustling heart of Theriole.

THIRTY

THE LEGION ASSEMBLES

THE DAYS THAT FOLLOWED WERE a blur of activity. Jorelial Rey decided Tvrdik was right about letting the public know what was going on. She issued a statement, which was read before the main palace doors, and sent out with heralds to be posted all over the kingdom. It stated that Lord Drogue, he who some had seen behaving obnoxiously at the Grand Council, and who already had been responsible for an assassination attempt at the young king's coronation, was now known to be mustering troops for an attack on the capitol, with the intention of usurping the Crown. All regional lords should prepare their defenses, and stand by to assemble the troop levies due the Crown in wartime. All loyal subjects not otherwise attached in service should also consider coming to the capitol to offer their support. And, for their own protection, subjects must cooperate with the edicts of the Crown in pulling back to defensive positions. The message stressed that the authorities had the situation well in hand, and that it was not a time for fear and panic to take hold, but rather for each citizen to stand tall against tyranny and oppression, and so forth. It would take time for the word to travel to all the far-flung corners of the land, and she was well aware that this move would also alert Drogue that they knew some of his plans. But it could not be helped, as it was high time things were out in the open.

What this allowed her was a mandate to start pulling shops and services back behind the sea wall. Folks grumbled, but, for the most part, knowing what was behind the inconvenience, they complied. Unfortunately, no amount of effort would move the great, ancient gates back into the closed position – not men, horses, nor oxen in any configuration. So work began, building a temporary connecting wall to close the opening where the gates stood wide open to the sea. General Boone was happy to be in an active mode at last, and busied himself ordering a refitting of his ships and a restoration of the palace defenses, while recruiting, equipping, and training troops for the imminent conflict. The Lady Regent was uncomfortable that some of these preparations worked at cross-purposes with how she intended to meet Drogue, but according to their agreement, she had to give him the authority to mount a traditional defense, at least, pending the outcome of their contest with the Legions of Light. Minister Verger was near to tearing his sparse hair out over all the unusual expenses piling on at once, but the kingdom was coming off of several years of great prosperity. That, coupled with his talent for thrift and fiscal oversight insured that he coffers were stretched, but far from bare.

Tvrdik balanced his time between replenishing his store of healing supplies, studying, practicing, and treating the occasional patient – mostly either emergencies or scheduled rechecks. Delphine visited frequently, and assisted with some of the herbal work, insisting as well that they fit in his arm exercises from time to time. He resisted, overwhelmed with things to do, but had to admit that his shoulder felt better when he did them. Otherwise, he was back to his old levels of stamina and vitality, and not a moment too soon, since the days were long and left him little leisure.

Hancock, the Master Craftsman, examined his design with great interest, and after several imperfect attempts, provided him with the template he needed in order to create his secret weapon. There was magic to add to it, and field-testing to insure it would do what he intended. In addition, he practiced his skills at creating illusion, expanding the size, clarity and duration of what he was capable of covering, step by incremental step. He spoke to Ondine, who understood quickly what he was asking of her, and her compatriots of the waters. She was delighted to be asked to play an active role in the defense of Theriole. She sped off to collect all the willing participants she could muster from her underwater family, and would presumably take charge of devising the details of their strategy.

Next, Tvrdik summoned Xaarus for a short consult, as promised, careful not to risk any personal consequences from the contact. He filled his old master in on all of their activities since the Council meeting, and on Drogue's alleged actions. Xaarus listened to Tvrdik's defensive ideas with approval, added a few suggestions for improving them, and proposed several additional ideas of his own. He was always encouraging, and offered his own help to hold the illusion of invisibility over the palace, should it become necessary to implement. Xaarus thought that the two of them, together with Tashroth, if the dragon was willing, could link their minds and create a powerful and effective field that would do the job. Tvrdik came away from that contact feeling heartened and energized.

One by one, the Captains of the Legions of Light returned with news of their recruiting efforts. Tashroth was first, flying in just three days after Rel and Tvrdik had examined the sea wall from the battlements. With him were a blue, a white, and a black dragon, representatives of the various clans. Jorelial was relieved to see him, and even more delighted to hear the news he brought. Tash had flown far and wide, gathering all the known remaining clans. Warriors by nature, some of the noble beasts were skeptical of this new way to combat enemies. Others had eschewed the frustrating affairs of men for centuries, and were reluctant to become involved now. However, none were eager to see a man like Drogue gain a foothold in their world. And all were concerned about the grim fate of dragon kind predicted if the wrong side triumphed. Since dragons enjoy extremely long life spans, they tend not to think of time in the same way humans do. So, it did not seem at all strange to them to be considering the ramifications of their actions now in the context of the grand arc of history. In addition, Tashroth himself was a well-respected figure among his peers, as was Xaarus. The support of both of these larger than life figures for the plan carried great weight. In the end, much like the unicorns, the dragons elected to send representation to hear more. Tashroth felt certain that those that accompanied him back were more than favorably disposed, and that Tvrdik would not find it difficult to win them over. It was a magnificent sight in the glorious early summer sunset, to look up from the road and see not one, but four turrets of the great castle crowned with dark dragon silhouettes framed against the gold, orange, and deep pink of the sky. It filled one with wonder, and made one feel safe, beneath their watchful eyes and shining wings.

Soon after Tashroth's return, Stewart arrived with many friends in tow. There were horses, mules, goats, bears, wolves, raccoons, mice, dogs, cats, geese, swans, songbirds, crows, sheep, several fish, and a turtle. These were the talking beasts of the realm, and they were entirely committed to the work of the Legion. Tvrdik enjoyed meeting them all, and found them to be charming company, as well as enthusiastic partners. Andrus sent word that all the healers he spoke with were firmly on board. Warlowe and Bargarelle were drumming up support inside the palace among both the working classes and the privileged.

Last of all, a full week after he had departed, Mark returned, along with Nyree, whose advanced age necessitated a slower pace of travel. Accompanying them were Morelle, and a whole delegation of harpers, bards, and minstrels. Nyree, as Mark had predicted, abhorred violence and destruction, and had wept with joy that she had lived to see a ruler who actually wanted her help in beating back the forces of darkness with creativity and the power of Light. That such a thing could happen raised her spirits and her energy to such a level that she rose from her bed, dressed herself in travel clothes, and insisted that she accompany Mark on the long trip back to Theriole, to be part of the planning. But first she had sent out a message to the four corners of the kingdom, encouraging every member of the guild to come and offer their unique gifts in this most noble of all causes. The Lady Regent and the young wizard welcomed her as an honored guest, befitting her age and status. But neither could conceal the deep emotions they felt at the strength of her commitment. That this frail, ethereal being, almost a legend throughout Eneri Clare, would embrace their cause so completely moved them beyond words, and strengthened their resolve to succeed at any cost.

There was no turning back now. Support and momentum were building, but there remained the task of persuading those that remained skeptical of the merits of what they were proposing. The assembly of the expanded Legions of Light was set for the playing fields, three days after Mark and Nyree arrived, eleven days after their first, tentative meeting in Tvrdik's backyard, and two days after Tvrdik's second healing day. With half as many patients, some of whom were returning for follow-up care, the second healing day was more manageable, and less demanding than the first had been. Delphine had generously offered to continue acting as Tvrdik's assistant, which would further her education in the most practical way possible. And this time they were prepared, both materially and psychologically, for what they would encounter, so things moved along smoothly. Tvrdik found that he was getting better acquainted with the villagers, and growing to like them. This made him even more determined to keep the kingdom out of the hands of Lord Drogue, knowing the suffering the common folk would endure under such a self-absorbed, egotistical sociopath.

In the days between Tvrdik's installation in The Cottage, and the upcoming assembly, the Praegers made themselves more and more indispensible in his life. The more tasks for which he became responsible, the less time he had for the simple requirements of running a household, and the more grateful he was to have someone cooking, cleaning, and ordering his life for him. The grounds and garden were kept in good order, and the harvesting done, along with any repairs and improvements the house still needed. Just a week after Tvrdik settled in, the Praeger family was able to move into the back annex where the school and dormitories had once been. It was not a huge space, but, as they all shared a kitchen and dining area, it was comfortable enough for their needs. Once they were all set up, they invited him to come back and visit, and see what they had done. It was unrecognizable as the space he remembered, a fact for which he was most grateful. The Praegers had reconfigured the very layout of the rooms in the annex, and using the credit vouchers he had turned over to them, they had furnished and decorated the whole place in a very simple but cozy style. Mrs. Praeger's touch was evident, as every area was colorful, comfortable, practical, and attractive.

He complimented their hard work with sincere enthusiasm, and offered a blessing on the newly refurbished place – on all who would live there or come to visit. They were very pleased with that gesture. He went on to let them know how vital their assistance was becoming. Admitting that he didn't know how he would ever manage without them, he thanked them for all the responsibilities they had taken on. Lynette gave him a spontaneous hug, and Mrs. Praeger cried and said he was a joy to be around, and how much better all of their lives were, now that they had attached themselves to him. She hoped it would be a long and mutually beneficial arrangement. Mr. Praeger took him aside privately, and stated that a day did not go by that he didn't regret having caused the wizard so much suffering. But, since that fateful day proved the moment their lives all turned around for the better, he couldn't help but see the blessing in it. He wanted Tvrdik to know that he would work as hard as he was able, until Tvrdik could also see the sequence of events as a blessing, too. Tvrdik smiled, shook the man's hand and looked him in the eye, "Sir, if you work here, let it be for love, or friendship, or wages, but your debt is long since paid. I already see how richly my life has been blessed by you and your family. Think no more of the past – we have much to do to plan for the future." They shook hands, and Tvrdik left the family to enjoy their new quarters, thinking as he walked away about how much good can sometimes come from unexpected places.

The day of the assembly arrived at last, warm and cloudless, with a slight breeze that kept it from seeming oppressive. The gaming fields were large, their edges ringed and defined by tall shade trees. Tiered wooden bleachers, designed to accommodate large audiences, rose high above the fields on three sides. The meeting was called for mid-day, which meant Tvrdik could be well-rested, enjoy a hearty breakfast, bathe, and dress in his favorite violet robes. The blue and grey had been getting quite a lot of wear of late, as he began to take on the mantle of Court Wizard. But the violet he saved for occasions of note, and today would certainly qualify. He rehearsed the most important points of his speech in his mind as he walked from the palace, until he felt satisfied that he was ready to tell his story to a new audience. In one hand he carried his oaken staff, and in the other a prototype of his 'secret weapon,' which he had been working on with the Master Craftsman.

At the same time, at Theriole, Jorelial Rey forced herself to eat, brushed and braided her long, dark hair, dressed in dark leggings and a long, ornate tunic in a striking orange color. She donned the official pendant of her office, and the jeweled circlet which symbolized her authority, along with both the ring of the royal seal, and an amethyst ring which was a favorite of hers; a gift from her father. Most of the burden of speech today would fall upon the young wizard, but, as his plan's most powerful supporter, she wanted to appear the confident and charismatic leader she wasn't always sure that she was. Casting a last appraising look in the glass with a sigh, she left her rooms, and the palace. Tashroth was busy entertaining the visiting dragon emissaries, so she decided she might as well walk. It was not far, and the exercise would clear her mind. On the way, she worked at pushing from her mind the doubts and worries that had a habit of slipping in amongst her thoughts. In their place, she tried to hold a vision of power, success, and solidarity. The Legions of Light *would* come into being, and were certain to triumph on their own terms.

Rel and Tvrdik arrived at almost the same moment, climbing up onto the raised dais that had been erected for this occasion. Chairs stood there for each of them, and without any greeting or preliminary conversation, they sat and began to compare notes on how they thought they could order the afternoon's proceedings. The mage proudly showed off his new piece of equipment, explaining his intentions for its use. Jorelial Rey had many questions....and so it was that, deep in conversation, they did not heed the arrival of their audience – the silent, precise landing of four dragons, who settled themselves behind the dais in an impressive row; the entire herd of unicorns, including Shar with his broken horn; the troupe of assorted talking animals led by the faithful Stewart; Nyree on the arm of Morelle, with a rather large contingent of bards; Andrus and a group of healers; Minister Verger, Steward Bargarelle, Warlowe, and a steady stream of folk from the palace, some dressed in rich clothing, while others filed in wearing aprons, caps, uniforms, and other evidence of their worker's status.

Mark and Delphine had earlier gone to the river behind The Cottage and collected Ondine, along with a few of her feistier compatriots, and placed them in a special pool which had been arranged on the field especially for the naiads. They had then gone back to Theriole and were now arriving with King Darian and his nanny in tow. Just behind them walked the Praeger family, followed by a veritable crowd of citizens from the city, and its nearby farms and villages. Many had already been Tvrdik's patients, and had brought their friends and families.

It was Delphine mounting the dais with the little king that finally snagged Jorelial Rey's attention: spotting Darian clutching her sister's hand gave her a start. She rose and made a small bow to the boy, "Good day to you, Your Majesty." Then, aside to her sister, "Delphine, is this wise? Is he safe out here?"

"Relax, Rel. There are four dragons lined up just behind us – how much safer could he be? Mark and I thought he was old enough to be aware of all that is being done on his behalf, and of all the people willing to risk their lives in order to insure his future. Someday, when they are singing ballads about this day, perhaps he will remember."

Tvrdik scrambled to his feet and bowed low, "Your Majesty."

Darian let go of Delphine's hand and took a step closer to the mage, his pudgy face puckered in a frown, "Are you a *real* wizard?"

"Yes, Your Majesty. I am *your* wizard."

Darian's fingers reached out to touch the smooth staff that Tvrdik held fast, "I should very much like to see some magic. I have only heard tell of it."

Tvrdik met the boy's eyes and saw in them the eager curiosity of a child, as well as the shadow of the heavy responsibility this child carried. He felt a pang of sympathy wring his heart for this boy, who could not enjoy the carefree days of a shopkeeper's son. "Your Grace, we are about to begin now, but at your leisure, I shall be glad to come to you and demonstrate a few of my magical skills."

"Very well." The boy seemed disappointed. Tvrdik smiled, reached out behind the king's ear, and brought out a little live newt, which he handed carefully to Darian. The child's eyes were huge with amazement. "You must be gentle with him, Your Grace, and always have your nanny check behind your ears before you go out." Darian nodded and backed away toward Delphine and his nanny, cradling the little amphibian gingerly in his hands, an expression of awe on his face. He turned and ran toward Delphine, to show her his treasure, but then stopped and turned back to the mage, addressing him in his piping voice, "Thank you for helping us, Master Wizard, with our coming war. We are most happy to have you on *our* side!"

Tvrdik smiled and bowed again, "I am ever at your service, Your Majesty. Do not worry. We will prevail." The little boy nodded, and hurried back to Delphine, who conducted him to his seat, while his entire attention turned to the little creature in his hands. Tvrdik looked up to see Jorelial Rey gazing at him with a peculiar expression. He raised his eyebrows in response, and shrugged. But the interchange had pulled them from their insular focus on the dais. Both of them now turned to look up and out at the field for the first time.

"Holy…!" Jorelial Rey could not even finish her exclamation, no words being sufficient for the wave of astonishment she felt as she took in the scene before her eyes. Tvrdik fell back in his chair with his mouth open. He pulled off his spectacles, wiped them on his sash, replaced them on his nose, and continued to stare, no sound at all finding its way past the lump in his throat. Technically, it was still some minutes before mid-day, but what they were looking at was already much bigger than anything they might have anticipated. Hundreds and hundreds of eager faces were turned towards them. Most of the seats were filled, and more folk were still streaming in through a gap in the trees. Dragons, beasts, magical creatures, sprites in the pool, men, women, children, elderly people all assembled together on the green field, and birds circling overhead. It was an audience they could only have imagined in their dreams, and eerily quiet, as almost everyone present practically held their breath in anticipation and respect for the gravity of the matter at hand. All that could be heard across the vast field was the creaking of tree branches in the wind, the swish of an occasional tail, a splash now and then, or a stray cough. An almost mystical tension gripped the place and everyone in it. It was as if everyone knew they were present at a world-shaking event, and did not wish to sully the moment with ordinary conversation. Sparks could almost be seen and tasted in the charged summer air.

Still speechless, Tvrdik reached over and gripped Jorelial Rey's hand, squeezing it hard. She turned to meet his eyes and saw a tear sliding down his pale cheek. For a moment they could only communicate with their eyes. Then, Tvrdik gave a ragged little laugh, turned away, and said, "Praeger warned me that word spreads like wildfire in these villages. The man knows whereof he speaks."

"Are you nervous?" she asked. He shook his head, wiping his eyes beneath the glasses with the back of his hand.

"I have never in my life felt more connected to my destiny than at this moment, Jorelial Rey. I feel energized, and alive, and blessed beyond measure."

"Just tell them like you've told it before. You are what they all came to hear." Tvrdik nodded, and she continued, "When it is time, I will introduce you…" He nodded again, and stole a glance over at Delphine, who was positively beaming at him as if her face would break, Darian playing intently with his new pet in her lap. Somehow, he knew not when, he had been transformed over a few short weeks, from an obscure, uncombed hermit, to a figure of importance – a leader. This was the moment then, when all eyes were on him, and he either convinced them to follow him down the dangerous uncharted road where he was about to lead, or not. Yet, he felt peaceful, certain, confident, as if some force he could not name buoyed him up in his endeavor. He was ready.

The stream of arrivals slowed and finally halted. Latecomers searched for seats; some sat on the grass with the animals. It was time. Jorelial Rey stood up. Tvrdik quickly wove an enchantment to amplify their voices, so that everyone present would hear every word clearly without having to strain at all. All eyes were on the Lady Regent, as she began.

"Friends, citizens, loyal subjects of the Crown, welcome! Honored guests: dragons, unicorns, magical beasts and nymphs of the waters, a hearty welcome to you as well, and thank you all for coming here on this beautiful day. Most of you know me. I am Jorelial Rey, of the honorable family Rey, and I am the appointed Regent of this kingdom of Eneri Clare, on behalf of King Darian III." She indicated the little blond boy on her sister's lap, who smiled and waved on cue, and a cheer went up from the crowd. "We all have been blessed to live in a kingdom that has long prospered in peace, and has tried to offer its citizens fairness and opportunity. But, in recent times we have wept together over tragedy after tragedy. First came the unexplained disappearance of Xaarus, perhaps the last known wizard in all the world, and beloved by all. Then, we faced the untimely death of my own father, Gareth Rey, a great man, whose good counsel and compassion were well known throughout the kingdom. And worst of all, the terrible loss of our king and queen, still in the bloom of youth, leaving us with an infant in the royal seat. With the election of a permanent regent, and a Coronation, we have striven to take back our destiny, and to shape it into a vision for the future….a future all of us can be proud of.

"But friends, there is at least one among us who does not share that vision. Lord Drogue, till now a respected member of our community, desires a future where he alone is ruler over all. He would have power, and wealth, and personal gratification of his every whim, at the expense of law and order, and at the sacrifice of the good of every other citizen in this realm. What he could not win by craft and seduction, he is determined to take with might and violence. He does not care if, in the process, he destroys lives, lands, and institutions, until little of value will even remain to be ruled. We have no intention of allowing this petty tyrant to triumph in his illegal and immoral designs, nor of letting him destroy what it took centuries to build. We say to him, "We have a King, a legitimate heir to the throne, and we have elected a government that will bring us securely to the time of his reign, and we do *not* bow to bullies and usurpers."

A deafening roar went up from the stands, and, inspired, Delphine stood up and held little Darian high, so that he could be seen by nearly everyone present. The beautiful little boy responded with a cheerful wave, and the crowds erupted with spontaneous shouts and applause. Even the dragons, unicorns, and sprites were caught up in the emotion of the moment, splashing, pawing, tossing heads, and swishing tails. Delphine resumed her seat, the laughing child returned safely to her lap, as Jorelial Rey lifted her hands for silence.

"If there is one thing, however, which I have learned in my brief months as regent, it is that nothing is ever as it seems to be. It turns out that putting a stop to Drogue's ambitions is not only essential to preserving our way of life *now*, but also key to what may occur generations in the future. The very fate of some of the races represented here today, and the quality of life in our future may depend entirely on our actions today. *And*, there is a complication – a catch, if you will. The question is, how do we best go about turning back the tyrant? What methods do we use? The answer is so surprising that we are uncertain of finding enough companions to join us in our fight. We come to you today to make our case, in the hopes that many of you will see its wisdom and choose to throw your lot in with us. But there is only one man who can truly explain to you what that entails and why; the one man who convinced me, who brought me information about what was to come, which I scarce believed, but which has all come true thus far. He will speak to you now, and will tell you a story so amazing, so incredible, that you will doubt that it could ever have happened. And yet, I am now certain that all of it is true. After you hear his story, there will be a call to action, but to action such as you have never before imagined. We ask you simply to hear with open minds and open hearts. Judge, then, for yourself, without pressure or fear, whether it is right for you to be a part of our movement. It is my great privilege now to introduce to you all our new Court Wizard – mage, healer, student and apprentice of Xaarus the wise, Tvrdik!"

As she finished and gestured to him grandly, there was a small measure of applause and cheering from those who already knew him. Tvrdik rose from his seat, steadying himself with his tall oaken staff, and strode forward on the dais. He looked around at all the faces before him, faces eagerly awaiting his remarks, curious to learn who he was and what all the mystery was about. He turned back for a moment to Jorelial Rey, who smiled and nodded to him, and something she had said just moments ago flashed through his mind, "Just tell them like you've told it before. Tell them your story...you are what they all came to hear." Turning to face the assembled crowds of men, women, and creatures, he began.

"Long ago, a mighty wizard made his home in a peaceful kingdom, where he was respected and beloved by all who knew him, and even by many in far-off lands whose lives had been touched by his good works. Despairing that he might be the very last of his kind, he searched far and wide, and found three young people with talent for the mage's profession, two boys and a girl. He took them into his home and cared for them, and taught and trained them in the wizardly arts..."

So he opened, and continued in this manner, telling the story – his story – as if it were a bedtime tale. And there he had them. From the very first sentence they were his, listening with rapt attention to all the wondrous twists and turns, impossible occurrences, and magical synchronicities. They listened because it was a good story, and because they wanted to know what would happen next. Certainly, the simple truth needed no further embellishment to hold an audience, so rich it was in plot. And, as he rehearsed the major events yet one more time, they seemed so far off that even he doubted whether he had ever actually lived them. But the story had no ending, as they were all about to write the next chapter together. Every soul in the arena was leaning forward to catch every word. No one could hear a falling leaf in the breathless stillness that permeated the air. He took them through almost all of his adventures up to that point, and when he had brought them right to the present, and their fears of imminent attack, he was able to do something more this time. He was able to show and describe for them exactly what he had in mind for resisting Lord Drogue's armies. He spoke of many ideas he had been mulling over for weeks in his mind. He transmuted items before their very eyes. He made the entire dais and its occupants go invisible to the audience's eyes for minutes, and then allowed it to reappear. Finally, he was able to publically unveil for the first time his prototype weapon, demonstrating for the entire assembly how it could theoretically function. By the general chorus of 'oohs' and 'ahhs' coming from every part of the field, he was heartened that his presentation might have been enough to rally support to their cause.

Tvrdik explained that he would personally help to train anyone who committed themselves to becoming a part of the resistance force, a force they were calling the Legions of Light, because it was created to push back the threat of darkness, not with more instruments of darkness, but with light, and love, and hope, and truth…and perhaps a clever trick or two. Anyone who joined, however, would know the risks involved, which were real and substantial, and would have to sign an oath that they promised not to intentionally harm another living being no matter what the circumstances. Only then could they together create a powerful enough vision to derail history as Xaarus was experiencing it now, and shift it to an alternate track. He told them all that he knew the level of faith that would take, and that he could give no guarantees except that the Lady Regent, the Lord Tashroth, he himself, and a number of their friends would hold firm to the pledge, and would be right there fighting beside them. He invited any and all input, welcoming any ideas of novel stratagems that could be added to their arsenal. And he ended by pointing to the corners of the field, where Mark and Bargarelle and Verger and Warlowe were already setting up small tables where they would be recording the names of those who wished to sign on today. He blessed all of them and thanked them for coming. Then, with nothing left to say, he turned and walked back to his seat, lowered himself into it and closed his eyes with a sigh.

Silence followed, as the crowd sat riveted. There were no cheers, no polite applause, no expressions of disapproval or acclamation, no rustling, no creaking, no whispering. Tvrdik's heart sank in those moments, as he sat wondering if he had failed in a colossal way. He had frightened or confused them, overwhelmed them with too much information. Perhaps they could not find it in themselves to believe such an outrageous tale, or to embrace such a patently dangerous and untried path. For endless seconds he held his breath, while there was no reaction from the crowd. Then, tentatively, a lone voice began to chant in rhythm, "Le-gions-of-Light! Le-gions-of-Light!" Two or three more added their voices, then twenty, then whole sections took up the phrase. And then, like a gigantic wave cresting before the shore, the whole field was chanting, in unison, stomping on the wooden grandstands, carried away in the deafening din, "Le-gions-of-Light! Le-gions-of-Light!" From behind him came the trumpet-calls of four dragons bellowing their excitement. There were whinnies and the sound of pawing hooves, barks, caws, mewling, and all manner of barely controlled chaos.

Opening his eyes and breathing at last, Tvrdik looked around to see the entire arena fiercely united in purpose, Delphine and Jorelial Rey smiling at him with ecstatic pride, and little King Darian staring at him with wide eyes. The Lady Regent took his free hand and rose from her seat, lifting him up alongside her by sheer will. She led him back to the front of the dais, as the chanting intensified, and then, on impulse, she punched her fist high in the air in a gesture of triumph and solidarity. Taking the cue, Tvrdik raised his staff as if it were light as straw, and held it horizontally over his head, the weapon of the future. The crowd broke into spontaneous cheers at seeing the Lady Regent and the Court Wizard bound together in determination and courage. Still shouting and cheering, they all began pouring from the seats to line up at the four tables, ready to sign on as legionnaires. As the noise died down and individuals and families began to talk among themselves, Tvrdik and Rel looked at the long lines of eager, excited warriors snaking all around the field. All four of their recruiters were struggling to record names as quickly as their pens could move. They looked back at each other, and without a word, fell into a joyous, spontaneous embrace.

"We did it!" Rel shouted over the din, "Look at this. The Legions of Light is a reality. I can hardly believe it." She pulled back and regarded him sidewise for an instant, "You didn't, um, cheat, did you?"

"Cheat?" he bellowed back, "what do you mean?"

"You know, like, put a spell on everyone here, or something...?"

Tvrdik grinned broadly, "My dear Lady Regent, there hasn't been a wizard since the dawn of time who could have used magic to do...this!" He indicated the field with a gesture of incredulity.

"Why, then, you've done it with your sheer charm and eloquence, sir."

He laughed, "*We* did it, Jorelial Rey, just as we dreamed." His face fell a little, "But will it be enough? Now the real work will begin..."

"You're up to it, Tvrdik. I saw what you did up there, what you have in mind. It's brilliant."

"It's only a beginning, Jorelial Rey. Only a beginning."

She smiled at him and squeezed his hand harder, "Ah, but such a beginning!"

Their attention was drawn to one side, where the entire herd of unicorns had trotted over to the dragons, and were enjoying a spirited conversation. Ondine and the naiads, nearby, were splashing about with great animation, adding their two cents worth.

"Now *there's* a sight you don't see every day." Tvrdik remarked, his crooked smile lighting up his pale face. Something caught his eye, then – a movement more deliberate than the milling crowds, and before he could grasp what he was seeing, a running figure approached the dais, and leapt up onto the platform, directly in front of the Lady Regent. Startled, she stepped back, while the wizard instinctively stepped in front of her, shielding her from potential danger. She shot him an aggravated look. "What?" he said, and, shaking his head, stepped aside. The runner had approached unnoticed amidst all the activity on the field, but on closer inspection, they recognized him as a page from Theriole, now bent over double and very out of breath.

"My-my-La-dy..." he gasped, "I-am-sent to-to find you. General-General Boone..." he was gradually regaining his wind. Jorelial Rey came in close to him. Delphine was right behind her, the infant king still clinging to her hand, and Tvrdik beside them, poised for action if the need arose. The Lady Regent reached for the panting page's shoulder, "What, lad? What is it?"

The young man looked up at her, eyebrows drawn together, "Ships, ma'am. Ships. Three of them sighted coming toward the harbor."

"How long ago?"

"I set out to find you as soon as we spotted them. General Boone's orders, Ma'am."

"Good work, lad. Here is a little something for your effort. Go and sit down over there a moment and catch your breath." Jorelial Rey turned to her sister and Tvrdik, "Gods, how could this happen now, just in our moment of triumph? It's too soon. We aren't ready."

Tvrdik put his hand on her shoulder, "Stay calm, Jorelial Rey. We don't know what this is yet, and if it is what we fear, we will make ourselves ready."

"I need to find out, but there's no sense disrupting the good that is going on here. There will be time to sound the alarm once I know for sure what we are dealing with. Delphine, can you take Darian back to the palace as quickly as possible?"

"Of course, Rel. Come on, sweet boy...how would you like a lovely piece of raisin cake?" And she hustled him off toward the palace, the little boy, newt gently cradled in one hand, still staring with fascination at Tvrdik over her shoulder. Jorelial Rey snapped into action.

"Tvrdik, you're with me. Page, follow when you can. We might have need of your services again."

"Yes, Mistress." He bowed his head to her, but she was already running toward Theriole, betting that with all the activity on the field, nobody would notice their precipitous departure.

Tvrdik, trying to run while carrying his seven foot oaken staff, was hard pressed to keep up with her, several paces behind all the way. Luckily, the distance to the palace was not great, and they were crossing the courtyard before the main entrance in mere minutes. Jorelial Rey took the great marble stairs by twos, while Tvrdik, desperate for air, hobbled up one at a time. But at the top of the stairs, General Boone himself pushed open the massive wooden doors and met them with news.

"Slow down. It's alright, my lady, sir mage," he nodded a quick acknowledgement. "They are not Drogue's ships. It is not the enemy. There are three ships clearly flying the flag of Euligia. That nation is among our closest allies."

"Euligia? I was not told to expect visitors from abroad. What could they want? Their timing could not be worse – we are not prepared to entertain dignitaries."

Boone continued, "I am sorry to have alarmed you unnecessarily, but we weren't sure until they got closer and raised their colors. The harbor master is mooring the vessels now. I suspect that whoever is in charge will want an immediate audience with you."

"Alright, then. General Boone, please send word that I will see the delegation from Euligia in the Hall of Audience, as soon as they have disembarked. Will you please keep an eye on the sea wall for me, just in case? And thank you for your vigilance…you were absolutely correct to summon us immediately. Tvrdik, would you accompany me, please?" She swept off toward the Hall of Audience, leaving General Boone in mid-bow, and Tvrdik once again struggling to keep up with her punishing pace.

"Slow down, will you! We aren't under attack, as far as we know, and their party couldn't possibly be ashore yet…."

She dropped back a bit and adopted a more reasonable stride. "Sorry. I'm still in emergency mode, and in the habit of dashing everywhere. Better?"

"Yes, much. Thank you," Tvrdik responded, coming up alongside her. As the Hall of Audience came into view, he quipped, "Ah, sweet memories…"

"Don't be funny. We still don't know why they are here. It could be bad news."

Wryly, he responded, "Yes, you never know *who* might turn up in the Hall of Audience…"

Jorelial Rey's telltale eyebrow raised at that, and she made some indistinct noise deep in her throat, but pushed on. When they entered the room, Tvrdik laid his staff across the big table, and wearily folded his tall frame into one of the chairs. Jorelial Rey stepped up to the raised platform, and paced back and forth in her accustomed manner before the throne.

"Why are they here now? What could they want? Why just show up with no advance notice? Maybe they've joined forces with Lord Drogue. Do I even remember the name of Euligia's king? It's…it's Polis – yes, that's right. King Polis, and we have a robust trade with them. That's as much as I know."

"Jorelial Rey, relax. All will be made clear soon enough. Look on the bright side: you're already dressed up for a state occasion – and may I say, in stunning fashion."

"Tvrdik!"

"Just trying to help. Divert your thoughts a bit. You know…"

"Well, it isn't working. Just be quiet, and *be* there, alright?"

He shrugged, somewhat amused. A loud creak drew their attention to the massive doors, where somehow, miraculously, Warlowe stood, calmly executing his accustomed duties. He must have noticed them leaving the gaming fields and followed them back to Theriole, sensing that his official services might be immediately required. Warlowe cleared his throat, and stood at attention, "The noble delegation from Euligia, our fair sister kingdom across the waters."

Jorelial Rey stared at him meaningfully. It was an ambiguous introduction that gave her nothing to work with. But Warlowe shrugged almost imperceptibly, and rolled his eyes upward. Apparently, this was how the visitors directed he introduce them. The Lady Rey hastened to collect herself, smoothed her tunic, and patted down an unruly lock of hair. As ready as she could be, she then positioned herself before the throne, gesturing that their guests should enter. Warlowe stood aside, and in marched four armed youthful standard bearers. Close behind them entered a slim figure, dressed completely in armor. It was a very dark, steely blue, burnished to a high polish, with decoration suggesting a person of lineage – a Prince, perhaps, or a very high-born noble. The helmet obscured almost all of the visitor's face, so it was hard to tell much of anything there. Perplexed and hedging, Jorelial Rey greeted the stranger formally, "Welcome, guests! Please do not let our lack of preparedness diminish in your eyes the estimation of our love for our dear Euligian friends. We had no forewarning of your arrival."

"No, indeed. We did not take the time to announce our sudden voyage, nor do we take offense at our welcome. Likewise, we beg you, do not let this warlike garb tempt you to think we mean you harm. On the contrary, we come to you as to one of our closest friends, near and dear to our heart, Lady Jorelial Rey."

The voice was rich and melodious, and sounded rather young. It spoke in a peculiar accent which sounded vaguely familiar. It gnawed at the corners of Jorelial's memory, but she could not place it. She was also struck that the person seemed to recognize her.

"You know me then?"

"Very well, and know of your recent election as regent and ruler of this fair kingdom. A wise and happy choice, in my opinion. I also knew your father well, a kind and a very great man. Word of his untimely passing reached us, and my kingdom mourned deeply along with yours. News of the terrible sea accident which took your monarch and his bride also touched and troubled us deeply. We regret that we were unable to send an envoy with our support and condolences until now."

Jorelial Rey cocked her head to the side, intrigued. Tvrdik had risen quietly from his chair, palmed his staff, and faded over to one side in shadow, also examining the visitor, searching for clues.

"I thank you sincerely for your kind expressions of sympathy, and for your apparent interest in the events of our realm…"

"I spent some time here in my youth, and have eagerly followed your progress since. It is a place for which I will always harbor a special fondness."

That got Tvrdik's attention, it being a line he had used himself on his own return to court. It tripped an alarm in his mind, as he wondered what the rest of the story was….

The Lady Regent went on, trying to hold on to whatever semblance of grace she could, despite her confusion. "I am afraid, good sir, that you have me at a disadvantage. Might I also know to whom I am speaking? You are safe here, and may at least remove your helmet without fear."

"My apologies." The figure reached up and removed the helmet, and a long, full, rippling cascade of strawberry-colored hair fell down below the visitor's waist. The face it framed was handsome – light and freckled, with fine features, startling large green eyes, and the subtle lines of middle age. So, the mysterious Prince was a woman. Tvrdik took a step forward, adjusting his glasses. Jorelial Rey could not stifle an initial gasp of surprise, but recovered her composure, glanced at the mage, and motioned him out of the shadows.

"My apologies as well. I neglected to introduce you to Tvrdik, my most trusted advisor, and our new Court Wizard."

Tvrdik, surprised and warmed by that introduction, bowed graciously, "Lady."

"Court Wizard?" the stranger seemed shaken. "I was not aware there were any more wizards. I knew Xaarus when I was last here, and was saddened to learn of his disappearance."

"I was for several years a pupil of Xaarus, and have also recently returned to court from abroad, my lady." On an impulse, he waved his hand and pulled a lovely bouquet of fragrant blooms from the air and handed it to her. Jorelial's eyebrow shot up again. The stranger smiled.

"How charming! Xaarus might have done something very like that. You are indeed his student."

Tvrdik turned quite red, a little dashed at not having been particularly original, and a little flattered. Something about that face seemed familiar, and was also a little mind-addling. He felt a bit like an awkward child under its lovely gaze. The Lady Regent interrupted, a bit louder than necessary.

"Since you say you have spent time here, and know me, I am embarrassed to confess that I do not know who you are, Lady. I apologize if I should recognize you – your face is very familiar to me in a distant sort of way. The cares of the last few months may have clouded my brain..."

"It is not your fault, nor unexpected, considering the last we saw of each other you were but a child of ten, I think..." The stranger lowered her eyes, as if remembering a great sadness, and then looked Jorelial Rey full in the face. Slowly, gradually, the Lady Regent's eyes grew large in shock and recognition.

"Brendelle," she gasped, almost in a whisper.

"The same."

There was a pause, in which Tvrdik looked from one to the other in confusion. What had just happened? Seeing his question, Jorelial Rey sank onto the throne, and with great deliberation, said, "Tvrdik, I would like you to meet the Lady Brendelle of Euligia. Delphine's mother."

THIRTY-ONE

BRENDELLE

In a flash, it was clear to Tvrdik why the face of the stranger had seemed so familiar – there was so much of Delphine in it. With the mystery of the visitor's identity solved, all of them realized that they had more than a few minutes of catching up to do, and that the woman was standing before them in full armor. Jorelial Rey summoned Warlowe, dismissed the standard-bearers, and asked for him to escort them to the kitchens for something to eat. Once there, he was also to arrange for refreshments to be sent back to the Hall of Audience, and leave word for General Boone that the company aboard the Euligian ships were to be invited ashore and made comfortable. Lastly, he was to find Mark, at any cost, either in the palace, or back at the gaming field, and ask him to report to them at his earliest convenience. Warlowe bowed and took his leave, tasks firmly in hand.

Next, Tvrdik and the Lady Regent set about helping their guest to divest herself of her heavy breastplate, arm- and leg- protectors.

"We assumed that war was imminent, according to our information, and came to support you in your fight to preserve the Crown. I have brought you two entire regiments, fully equipped and trained, and three ships dedicated against Drogue." She spoke his name as if the word itself tasted bitter on her lips. "We did not know how we would find the situation on our arrival, and so we prepared for a battle already in progress. Also, I must confess…I did think the armor would mask my identity while I gauged what welcome I might receive here…" She was talking as they worked to untie and pull pieces of heavy metal from her trim figure.

422

"Well, you succeeded in that, at least," the Lady Rey answered, "You had me completely mystified. And, thank the gods, there is no need yet to leap into a pitched battle, though you might not be far off the mark. We were frantic ourselves for awhile, mistaking your vessels for Drogue's warships."

"Sorry. I judged speed to be more important at the moment than courtesy."

"Of course. The moment we saw your flags, we knew, although we weren't sure of your purpose, and certainly had no idea you were…well, you! I am relieved to hear that you sail on our side."

She stood before them now, an attractive woman approaching forty, in plain leggings and a belted tunic. And of course, that cloud of unmistakable hair. She narrowed her green eyes at them, "How could you think otherwise?"

"How, exactly, should I be certain?" Jorelial's cultivated veneer of calm and patience was beginning to crack. "Let me ask you this, then. Why now? Sixteen, seventeen years you disappear; we see nothing of you, hear not a word…you leave that beautiful little girl abandoned and wondering what she had done to deserve such a fate. And then *today* you reappear like the heroic savior in a storybook, and expect that all is forgiven?" She paused, attempting to regain her composure. Her next words were barely audible, "Father was devastated. He was consumed with loneliness."

"I am here now because my baby is in danger, the land that was once my home is being threatened, and a valuable ally is under siege. And now that I have some real resources at my disposal, I could not stand idly by, and watch people I care about be harmed without helping."

"People you care about? Who might they be, Brendelle? And how would we know that? Where have you been all these years?"

"Do you think it has been easy for me, so far away from my only child, and never being able to see her sweet face, or hold her, or speak to her, or even to apologize? Do you think I did not die a little death at every milestone in her brief life that I could not share with her? That I could not be there to see her fall in love for the first time? Do you think it did not hurt to know I was not even invited to my own child's wedding?"

"I don't know what to think." The two women were shouting at each other passionately now. But Tvrdik was standing by, listening for more substance, and when he found it, he jumped in.

"You knew about the wedding? Almost no one knew about the wedding. How did *you?*" He stepped closer to Brendelle as he posed his question. There was a pause. She met his piercing gaze for a moment, then looked at her feet, and answered quietly.

"I – I have been following her life all along. I knew everything that happened to her. The wedding was the hardest."

"How?"

"I have my sources. Someone at court who took pity on me when I was a young girl here, so miserable and lost. He has written to me every week for seventeen long years without fail, so that I might in some measure be able to share my daughter's life. I owe him a great deal and promised to keep his secret."

Jorelial Rey and Tvrdik looked at one another, and simultaneously uttered, "Bargarelle."

The Lady Brendelle's eyes went wide with terror, "How did you…? I never…"

"Relax," the Lady Rey said, "it just sounds like something he would do, the old dear. You didn't give him away."

"Ladies," Tvrdik seized the moment, "now that we are all a little calmer, could we sit down, perhaps?" He indicated the table and chairs where he had first sat down with Jorelial Rey on what seemed a very distant night. Now she shot him a look of fire.

"Don't be flip, Tvrdik. You weren't here. You didn't live the anguish of that time."

Chastened, he lowered his head. "I apologize. I meant no disrespect."

They let him help them into chairs, nevertheless, and all of them were silent for a moment. A knock on the door signaled the welcome arrival of servants with trays of food: fruit and cheese and wine, with a variety of pastries, both sweet and savory. A tense silence persisted while the servants laid everything out and tiptoed back through the heavy wooden doors. Tvrdik poured wine. Jorelial Rey finally broke the silence.

"I had to raise her, you know."

"I know."

"Father did the best he could, and there were nannies, of course, but when she needed a mother, she came to me. I was barely more than a child myself. It wasn't easy or fair."

"I know. And I was so sorry to do that to you. I never wanted to hurt you, Rel. You were one of the few people who was always kind to me, and about whom I cared deeply, though you might not remember it that way. But, from everything I have heard, you did a wonderful job. She was very lucky to have someone in her life who loved her that much. Lord knows I wish I had."

Jorelial Rey, having now completely lost the veneer of the Lady Regent, was staring at Brendelle, open-mouthed, as if she were seeing her for the first time as a human being, and not simply as the objective source of so much youthful heartache. Tvrdik took the opportunity to jump into the conversation. Offering a glass of wine to the Lady Brendelle, he smiled, "You would be so proud of your daughter today, my lady. She is a most remarkable young woman – beautiful, talented, sharp as a knife's edge, with a glorious singing voice and a way with children, and- well- with everyone. I am teaching her lessons in the healing arts, and she is picking it up like she was born to it. She was one of the first to embrace me as a friend when I came to court a stranger. She has an amazing heart."

"I am counting on it. And thank you for that, sir."

Rel seemed to resurrect from her stupor, "I still don't understand why you left. Things would have gotten better. Father loved you. I could have helped you. You barely gave us a chance." She was almost in tears now. Tvrdik touched her shoulder gently, and handed her a glass of wine.

"No, Rel, things would never have gotten better. I don't expect you to forgive me for the terrible thing I did, but I do want you to better understand. Now that you are a woman, perhaps you can put yourself in my position a little. I was so young and naïve. I was barely older than Delphine is now, but, oh, so much less self-aware. My father practically sold me into this marriage for political reasons, and I went along with it out of duty and ignorance. Besides, everyone in my life, including my mother, kept telling me what a great honor it would be, how fortunate I was to be chosen, and what a great thing it would be for my family and my country. No one was asking my opinion. At the time, it seemed a wonderful adventure; I felt as if I had won a prize.

But, I hadn't realized what it would be like to sail across an endless sea to a strange world, leaving behind my land, my family and friends, my language, my culture – everything that I knew and loved. This place seemed like a strange and unfriendly new world. Everywhere I went, people made fun of my accent and my strange ways, and many were cold to me. I could not find friends, and the more miserable I became, of course, the harder it was to attract any. Your father was a good man, Rel. He was kind and generous, and oh, so patient with me. In his own way, I suppose he loved me. But you know it was your mother who was the true love of his life. No one could ever replace her in his heart. I could sense that too, and knew I would never be cherished the way every woman dreams she might be. He tried, but I suspect he was pushed into this marriage on his side as well. He was lonely, and wanted more children, and I was beautiful and young, and a good alliance for the Crown. But there was such an age difference, we had so little in common. He did not know how to talk with a teenager. I became miserable and lonely and unhappy, and that unhappiness affected my health. So, I was ill a great deal and kept to my chambers. All of this just contributed to my problems and made them worse; I was more disliked and talked about, more lonely and homesick, and so forth. When I found I was pregnant, I panicked. I was so distraught over the idea of raising a child when I could not even care for myself that I almost ended my life *and* the babe's."

Tvrdik looked up at her and felt a deep pang of pain and compassion, knowing well what it felt like to be in such despair that it seems impossible or pointless to go on. They had a lot in common, he and Brendelle, and both of them had survived to recreate themselves. His heart swelled with sympathy as he heard her story. He stole a glance at Rel, but her head was lowered, and her face remained in shadow. Delphine's mother went on.

"I decided, however, that since Gareth had been so kind to me, I owed him at least the child he wanted so badly. I knew he had the resources to raise it with or without me, and, I thought, the moment I am quit of it, I will go home. I will bear my shame and the scorn of my family. I will humble myself, and beg for my supper if need be, but I will at least be home, where life is familiar and comprehensible. And that is what I did."

Tvrdik glanced sideways at Jorelial Rey once more, not wanting her to feel like she was being observed in this moment of very private and personal reckoning. Were those tears he thought he saw glistening in the corners of her eyes? It took her a few beats to be able to respond.

"I-I still don't understand why you disappeared so completely...why you never could visit, or send word, or a birthday greeting or *anything* to tell her you still cared."

"Ah, that, my dear, was your father's doing. You did not know that we were in communication after I left. As I said, he was a wise and a kind man. He understood how unsuited I was at the time for marriage, or motherhood, or statecraft, or just about anything." A bitter laugh escaped her lips, "He agreed to annul our marriage, and give me my freedom. But he wanted Delphine. He wanted her to be raised a Rey, and he wanted to insure against any future reconsideration of my right to take her away from him. The price for my freedom was my written and sworn agreement that I would cede all rights to the child to him, and would seek no further contact with her – stay out of her life. I think he believed it was for the best not to complicate things for her, not to create divided loyalties. I was ill-equipped at the time even to consider raising a child, and I agreed, feeling she would be better off with the power and wealth of the Rey family to support her, than she would be with me anyway. What I had not counted on was how much I would miss her and long for her over the years, despite myself. And that, because of my difficult pregnancy and delivery, that Delphine would be the only child I was ever able to bear."

"I never knew that Father had done that. I blamed you for never coming back. What happened to you then?"

"Well, as I expected, my family were shamed and embarrassed by the whole episode, and were disappointed in me. I kept to myself a great deal. I was depressed and lost. Being home did not prove the balm I had hoped for my wounded spirit. My father tried to arrange another marriage for me to get me off his hands. It was then that I woke up and realized that so many of my woes had come from being helpless and malleable, and letting other people run my life, and I thought of you."

"Of *me*?"

"Yes. You might not believe this, but during the whole time I was living in your kingdom, besides your father, I remember only three people who were kind to me. Xaarus was one. I did not know him well, but he came to me as a healer, and always had a sunny word and a fatherly embrace for me. I loved him dearly and always felt at home with him. He got me through that pregnancy. Then there was Bargarelle, brusque and officious, but so sweet beneath. He took pity on a poor young girl so far from home, and tried to make sure I had a little toy or a delicacy from home now and then. He even got me a little dog, who was my constant companion while it lived. After I left, I grew to rely on Bargarelle for word of Delphine, and of life at Theriole, and he has never failed me in all these years.

"The third person was you, Jorelial Rey. Motherless though you were, and serious and thoughtful beyond your years, still you welcomed me from the beginning without reservations, spent time with me, and sat talking with me as an equal. You asked me questions about my homeland, about the world outside of Eneri Clare, about my thoughts. You asked my opinions. No one had ever done that before – asked what I thought. I never forgot that and I blessed you for it. You don't remember, do you?"

"Perhaps. But, then, we could have been friends…why wasn't that enough for you to stay?"

"I was young, and overwhelmed, and you had many other things filling your days. I knew you would grow to be someone of importance. You were remarkable, even as a child: smart, fearless, independent, curious, riding around on that dragon that scared everyone else off. You even introduced me once, do you remember? I was petrified, but I tried to be gracious for your sake. Tashroth tolerated me, I think. Anyway, you were such a different sort of girl than I had been, and when I was back home, reviewing my life, I vowed that if I was to continue living at all, I was going to be more like you. I was never again going to let men, or expediency, or politics, push me into things I did not wish to do. You were my inspiration. I began to re-invent myself around what I remembered of you. I put aside my flowing dresses, and took to wearing leggings and tunics. I walked and exercised to gain strength. I stole down to the stables, and bribed the hands there to teach me to ride, and when I was expert at that, I batted my eyes at some young courtier and got him to teach me archery and fencing, and a host of other skills. When my father found out, he was horrified, but he threw up his hands in despair and gave up. I refused the matches he tried to arrange for me, and instead rode, and walked, and read, and studied.

Though I was still young and attractive, most of the men at court gave me a wide berth, seeing me as odd, headstrong, unmanageable. But I was healthier and happier than I had ever been in my life – independent, strong, informed, in charge of my own destiny. Quite the change from the pale and cowering Brendelle you must remember, no? There is not so much more to tell. Five years later, I caught the eye of our king's most valued advisor, a lord of considerable wealth, with land, men, and resources at his command. He was ten years my senior, but had never had leisure to marry. He is a good man, intelligent, funny, and something of a maverick himself. He liked me exactly as I was, and cared nothing for my history or damaged reputation. We walked and talked together, came to know and respect, and yes, love one another, and we were married the following spring. My lord has never denied me anything I asked, and even took it in stride when we found out that I could no longer conceive. It was a great sorrow to us at first, but he has adopted his sister's son, a worthy lad, as heir, and we enjoy our lives together. I owe much of my happiness to you, Jorelial Rey, and I have always wanted to embrace you and thank you for showing me a different path."

"I – I did nothing. I was only being myself growing up, very unlike the other children, I grant. But that was just who I am. I cannot take credit. I am glad for you that you found some peace and joy in your life, truly. I am sorry that it was not here, with us. I know my father missed you in his way. Perhaps, if you had been older at the time...?"

"Perhaps. Even so, I grieved bitterly to hear of his death. It was such an untimely and unfair blow to the both of you, and to the entire kingdom."

"Thank you for that."

"And, when I heard war was coming, and my child was in danger, and Gareth gone, I could no longer resist trying to do what I could to help. My husband could not be spared from Euligia's court, but willingly granted me ships and men to come support you. King Polis also adds his blessing to the venture, ever an ally to the rightful heir on the throne of Clare. I have in my wallet letters from him to that effect, which I will deliver to you later."

"I must remember to thank him. How did you hear of our predicament? From Bargarelle?"

"In part, but also seasoned with word on the street from dragons, heralds, bards, and Drogue's own messages attempting to seduce us to his side – messages we of course disdained. It was not difficult to piece things together. I acted as quickly as I could."

"And we are grateful for your generosity and support. In truth, we could use all the help we can muster against this stubborn, evil man. But, there are some wrinkles on this side of which you are not yet aware. In good time, we will fill you in on what has been occurring here, and you may judge for yourself whether you and your company are still willing to join our cause."

"Oh? I can't imagine anything so shocking that it could deter me from my intention…"

"Make no promises until you hear all…" Rel raised a hand to defer further conversation on the subject, and exchanged a look with Tvrdik. At that moment, there was a knock on the great door, and Warlowe poked his head in.

"My lady, Mark is here, awaiting your pleasure."

Jorelial Rey rose from her chair, "Please send him right in."

Mark swept in with great excitement, still radiant from the rally at the gaming fields. Without stopping to take in the whole picture before him, he began to address them, "Tvrdik, Lady Rey, you won't believe the lists we have gathered. There are almost eight hundred names we have taken down for the Legions, beasts and sprites included. Oh, and Tvrdik, I have brought your prototype back to the palace for you. You left it unattended on the dais. Why did you both disappear in your moment of triumph?...Oh!" He stopped in his tracks as the Lady Brendelle rose from the table. "Oh, I am so sorry! I had no idea you were entertaining visitors. Please, pardon, my lady." He bowed courteously to the stranger, and as he straightened, his eyes suddenly grew very wide, then narrowed as his eyebrows furrowed in concentration, regarding the face before him. He turned to the Lady Regent as if to ask a question, but no words formed. Jorelial Rey, a reluctant smile pulling at the corner of her mouth at his confusion, moved quickly to his side, took his arm and escorted him up to the stranger.

Softly, she said, "Mark, it is wonderful news indeed about the Legions, but we have summoned you here on an entirely different matter. I would like to present to you the Lady Brendelle of Euligia. She has just arrived here with three ships, and two full regiments come to our aid." Mark looked confounded, turning from face to face, and searching for a clue as to why this required his presence.

"Why, that's wonderful. A generous show of support indeed, and much appreciated, I am sure..."

It was all Rel could do to keep from giggling at Mark's obvious plight, but she could not bear to torture him any longer. Softly, in his ear, she continued, still holding his arm, "Mark. The Lady Brendelle is also Delphine's natural mother."

Mark seemed at first not to process the news. "Ah....Oh! Delphine's...? Oh! You mean...? Goodness – this is a surprise." Tvrdik had to put his hand over his mouth to keep from laughing aloud, as Mark, in an attempt to collect himself, dropped the parchment he was holding with the legion's registry, bent to retrieve it, missed, went for it again and tried to replace it under his arm, apologizing the entire time. The Lady Brendelle stood by, graciously waiting, sizing him up, and likely deciding, as all of them had, that he was most disarming. Finally, Mark cleared his throat, "I am Mark, Lady Brendelle, a bard here – in the palace – and also Delphine's ... um ... husband." He glanced about, possibly looking for support from the others. They nodded. "I am pleased and honored to meet you, my lady. If there is anything I may do to make your stay more comfortable, I hope you will call on me." He took her hand and pressed it to his lips with a little bow. Tvrdik stifled another giggle. It was a very gallant gesture.

The Lady Brendelle, retrieving her hand, seemed pleased, "Mark, it is I who am fortunate to meet you at last. By all accounts, you are the man who makes my daughter's heart sing, and I am grateful for her good fortune."

Mark, usually so composed, stammered, "I-I...you...m-m-my lady, you have no worries on that account, as I cherish Delphine with my life, and will always strive with every fiber of my being to take care of her, and make her happy."

"I can well believe it, sir." She turned away and sat again at the table, smiling.

Jorelial Rey pulled Mark to one side, "Mark, I called you here to help us. Delphine has neither seen nor heard from this Lady her entire life. We did not even know if she lived until today. Meeting her in the flesh might be something of a shock. There might be all sorts of deep feelings that she isn't even in touch with. She might be angry or upset, or she might even refuse to come..."

"Delphine? Our Delphine? But you know she has the biggest heart in the world."

"I know, but, even so, she WAS abandoned. It's hard to tell what her heart will do. Somehow, I thought you might be the man to break it to her gently, prepare her a little, feel her out..."

Mark nodded, "I understand. I will go right away."

"If she will come, bring her here, while we are all present to support her. If she would rather not, send me word, yes?"

"Yes, my lady. I will do my best." He bowed to her, then to the others, and hurried out the door. Rel turned to Brendelle. "I thought it best to let Mark tell her first. I'm sure you'd like to see her, but it's hard to guess what her initial reaction will be to your sudden re-appearance. I've never heard her say a harsh or judgmental word about anyone in all of our years together, but I wouldn't want to vouch for her feelings in this matter. I told him to sound her out, and bring her here straightaway if she were willing. We should know soon."

"Thank you. You have been, again, most kind. Jorelial Rey, do you think, at least, that it is possible we might be friends? One day...?"

Rel considered a moment, and offered a sort of half-smile, "It is an old and deep wound, Brendelle. But hearing your story now makes it very difficult to keep harboring the old grudges. We have both aired our grievances, and they are in the past now. I have no real issue with you, and I am grateful for your offer to help. I suppose, then, the answer is, given a little time for us to come to know one another, yes, it is possible.'" She offered her hand across the table, and Lady Brendelle looked up with a new expression on her face, as if years of care had just fallen away, and the light of hope, or gratitude, or healing, could shine through. She reached up, smiled a wide and generous smile, and grasped Rel's proffered hand, as their eyes met, for the first time as peers.

Tvrdik, looking on, found himself confronting many emotions; he felt proud of Jorelial Rey for letting go of her old anger and hurt, and finding compassion in her heart for the lonely, confused young woman who had done a desperate thing many years ago. He felt incredible respect for the Lady Brendelle, in how she had evolved, and he hoped that Delphine could also find it in her heart to forgive and welcome her estranged mother. He

432

saw many parallels in Brendelle's story with his own journey, and wished to get to know her better. There was much they had in common.

The three of them sat silently for a few moments, picking at the food that had been brought to them, and sipping the wine. Brendelle ventured, "So, what are these so-called 'wrinkles' in your defense plan? If you have an unconventional strategy, I am sure I would be excited to hear it."

Tvrdik laughed, "Oh, it's unconventional, alright, but you need to hear the whole story in order to understand at all, and we are all tired now. I promise to find time to bring you up to date sometime tomorrow. Will that serve? I assure you, you will not find my tale dull."

"You have intrigued me. I will look forward to learning more with eager anticipation." And she flashed him an almost flirtatious smile, quite reminiscent of Delphine's, causing him to turn pinker than usual.

Even though they were all awaiting a knock on the great wooden door, they all jumped when it came, and then exchanged anxious glances. Warlowe took a step in, cleared his throat and announced formally in his best baritone, "The Lady Delphine..." But he had gotten only halfway through the pronouncement when the Lady herself pushed past him and into the room.

"Rel, is it true?" she called, breathless.

Mark entered right behind her, "She ran all the way here, my lady. I didn't even have a chance to get her to talk to me." The Lady Brendelle rose, and stepped away from the table. Delphine, still running toward them, stopped in midstride when she saw the woman with the cascading torrent of auburn hair. Absolutely still, the two women stood and stared at each other across the room, open-mouthed. Equally disconcerting was this moment for everyone else present, as they shifted their gaze back and forth between the two women, so remarkably alike, and yet so different. No one dared speak, or even breathe. Time seemed to grind to a halt, waiting for Delphine to reveal her heart. And then, she ventured into the void. Delphine took a single step toward the strange foreign woman who looked so much like her, she tilted her head slightly to one side, an expression of wonder on her lovely face, and murmured, "Mother?"

Brendelle, living the moment she had dreamed of for so many years, could not speak. Tears welling up in her large, green eyes, she tried to smile at her beautiful daughter, nodded several times, and with amazing courage, held her arms out wide. Rel, Tvrdik, Mark, and Warlowe stood frozen for one eternal second, wondering what Delphine would do. What she did, of course, was to run across the floor, sobbing, "Mother, mother." She threw herself unreservedly into the waiting arms of Brendelle. The embrace that followed brought a lump to everyone's throat. Time resumed its accustomed motion, and those in the room found themselves breathing again. Rel reached for Tvrdik's hand and took hold of it, as he had done hers on the field earlier that same day. Could it possibly be the same day? Both were speechless. Warlowe, a wide grin replacing his usually controlled features, faded back to his post on the other side of the grand doors, which he carefully shut behind him. Mark kept shaking his head, muttering, "That's my Delphine. I knew it. I told you. She only knows how to love." He was watching the miraculous reunion with a broad smile, letting the stray tears that escaped his brown eyes fall where they may.

Delphine, of course, being Delphine, with all her usual natural exuberance, wanted to know everything and hear everything and tell and share everything all at once. But, having assured her sister that there would be time in the coming days for getting acquainted, Jorelial Rey insisted they go and find Bargarelle, and have him assign suitable quarters to the Lady Brendelle. So, stopping to ask Warlowe to arrange for the lady's armor to be collected and delivered to her rooms later, Rel led the little procession through Theriole's courtyards and halls to the Steward's offices – the hub and heart of the palace. She knocked on the door, which was, at the moment, closed. An exasperated voice called out, "Yes, what is it?"

"It is your Lady Regent, sir." Jorelial responded in her best mock indignant voice.

The door opened almost instantly, Bargarelle sputtering apologies, "Oh, my lady, I am so sorry. I was not expecting your visit, and what with being out on the gaming fields all day, I am so behind in my work…"

Jorelial Rey smiled at him, "Sir, I have brought an old friend who wishes to see you."

The little man looked positively mystified until she stepped aside, revealing Brendelle. It took him no time at all to recognize her, and his face transformed. Almost in a whisper, he breathed, "Oh, dear lady, is it you? How can you be here? When did you arrive?"

She smiled at his astonished expression, "However can I repay you for all your years of kindness, my old friend. It is so good to see you once again." And she stepped up close to the Steward and threw her arms about him. Not certain what the appropriate response should be, especially in front of the Regent, Bargarelle stood stiffly in her embrace for a moment. But then his reserve melted, and he returned her hug with obvious enthusiasm. Stepping back, he sized her up more thoroughly, "Lady Brendelle, what have you done with yourself? You look so different, and so wonderful! Welcome...welcome back."

Jorelial Rey stepped in. "Steward, the lady Brendelle has come from Euligia, with three ships, and two fully equipped companies to add to our defensive force."

"Oh...Oh, my!...but, does she know?"

"Not yet," Tvrdik interrupted, as Brendelle's eyebrows pulled together in an unspoken question. "It will be my task and privilege, tomorrow, to fill her in and persuade her to our cause." Brendelle shrugged, deducing that her curiosity would not be satisfied until the next day.

"But for tonight," Rel continued, "Do you think we could find a suitable space for our guest to lay her head?"

"Oh, yes, of course, my lady. Right away. You have all taken me by surprise is all. Let's see..." He consulted a master list on his ubiquitous clipboard, and pushed out between them to lead the way. Before long, they were installing the visitor in a lovely suite on the first floor, appropriate to her rank and station. Bargarelle assured Brendelle that he would have her trunk brought her from shipboard, and her armor delivered to her presently, and that he would see to proper accommodations for her ship's personnel and troops. He then let her know that dinner would be served very soon, if she would like to freshen up and attend. Delphine offered to lend her a more formal outfit until her clothing arrived, and, after a moment's hesitation, Brendelle agreed. Mark excused himself in order to prepare to play at dinner that evening. Delphine and her newly rediscovered mother went off to play with fashions, chatting merrily together as if they had known each other all their lives. Bargarelle, bubbling over with delight at Brendelle's return, bustled out to make all the arrangements he had promised. Tvrdik and Rel were left standing by themselves in the hallway before Brendelle's quarters, uncertain as to what to do next.

"Some day, eh?" the wizard ventured.

"Feels more like several." the Lady Regent replied. "A day we will surely remember, though. Did Mark say that eight hundred people signed the roster for the Legion?"

"I think so. I can hardly take it in, a miracle of that magnitude. We shall have to begin training right away, though."

"Yes. We shall have to take some time tomorrow to organize a plan for the next few weeks. Our deadline with Boone is looming, but we can't even be certain that will be in time for Drogue."

"Right." Tvrdik responded. There was another uncomfortable pause. Then, Rel looked up at him with what he thought was a very vulnerable expression, and spoke her mind.

"I could be jealous, you know. I was the one who was there for her, growing up. I nursed her when she was ill, when her little heart, or her arm was broken. I had to say good-bye to a second mother too, but I had to think about what Delphine needed." She looked down at the floor, "It's hard to stay angry with Brendelle. I suppose I can see it all from her point of view now, and I suppose she has suffered enough. But I can't help feeling a little twinge of hurt that she can waltz back in here after nearly two decades and be welcomed with open arms. No questions, no explanations, no period of adjustment or recriminations. Just take right over as Delphine's mom, as if she had just stepped out for a moment to see what the weather was like." Her voice had become increasingly agitated and higher in pitch, as she had gone on speaking. Tvrdik laid his arm gently around her shoulders and began conducting her slowly down the hall.

"Jorelial Rey, you know your sister. She simply cannot hate, or stay angry for long. It's her nature. When I had to confess to her weeks ago who I really was, and that I had been deceiving her, she treated me exactly the same way, with forgiveness and genuine affection. I was certainly glad of it then. Listen, Brendelle's arrival is all very new and exciting and wonderful for her today. But, trust me on this, no one will ever take your place in her heart or in her life, Jorelial Rey. You are her sister, her mother, her inspiration, and her best friend, and you will always be the one she turns to when she is overjoyed, or heartbroken. It will always be you."

Her shoulders relaxed tangibly under his touch. "Thanks. I really needed to hear that. Stay to dinner?"

"I thought you'd never ask. Yes, please."

She chuckled, "However did you get to be so smart?"

He frowned, "Oh, years of solitude and contemplation…"

"Now, how would that teach you to be so good with people?"

"People? Oh, I couldn't tell you a thing about people. Now, I do know a thing or two about trees and sparrows and squirrels and bears and stars and clouds…" He dissolved in laughter as she pummeled his good arm, and they made their leisurely way toward the dining hall, following the trail of wonderful aromas that always advertised dinner at Theriole.

THIRTY-TWO

UNDER SIEGE

The next few weeks were a whirlwind of activity for everyone. True to his promise, Tvrdik made time to fill the Lady Brendelle in on his story, the plan of action they had committed to as a result, and all about the Legions of Light. When he had related everything there was to tell, she sat biting her lip and contemplating her options. After careful consideration, she told them that she admired their courage in acting on their beliefs, and would be honored to be a part of their campaign. She was happy to dedicate herself and the three ships she had brought along. But, as for her men, she felt it was only fair to put it to them individually, as they would be asked to participate in something quite different from what they had signed on for. She promised to relate the situation as persuasively as she was able, and let each man decide for himself whether he would be comfortable fighting with the Legion under their terms.

Delphine spent as much time as possible with her mother, catching up, showing her around, getting to know her. Mark joined them when he could, and Brendelle seemed to enjoy his company at those times. But his time was divided between his duties as a court musician, Nyree's guild meetings, and trainings with the Legion. Of course, Delphine and Brendelle were also at the trainings.

Tvrdik and Jorelial Rey would hold them on the gaming fields every day except his healing day, which continued to present him with a steady stream of patients. There were also meetings of the various Captains, where suggestions and ideas were broached, complaints and questions aired, and strategies practiced. When a new tool or technique passed these meetings with universal support, it was brought to the field to be taught to the rank and file. Tvrdik's 'secret weapon' had been perfected and cleared for mass production by the palace armory, and he was impatient for the arrival of the finished product in order to demonstrate its uses. Meanwhile, he taught some defensive techniques that Jorelial Rey had brought to the table, demonstrated things he could do as a mage to support them (which was good practice for him as well), and had each group run maneuvers that were specific to their peculiar skills – bards, beasts, healers and so forth. Each day it seemed there were more participants, as word spread and interest grew, until the gaming fields could scarce contain their activities. The unicorns and talking beasts set up a temporary camp somewhere in Theriole's gardens, in order to be readily available. The three visiting dragons, having made up their minds as to the wisdom of Tvrdik's approach, left to rally the rest of their kin, who were scattered across the kingdom. Tashroth was thus freed to support Jorelial Rey, and to appear as an encouraging presence during the practice sessions.

Evenings, Tvrdik went through Xaarus' library for anything that might prove useful. He read, studied, and tried out new skills that were unfamiliar to him. Twice, he summoned Xaarus for suggestions, clarifications, and explanations. These contacts, although brief, were quite helpful, Xaarus sharing his ideas, and offering input on those that had come from others. When he could steal an hour, the young mage would arrange to meet with Ondine as well, who was running a sort of training camp of her own underwater. She understood the vital part her unit played in the line of first defense against Drogue's ships. In a new bit of good news, she informed Tvrdik that, with the unicorns' help, she had worked out a way to contact some of the few remaining dryads, or tree spirits. These were very supportive of the non-violent approach, and agreed to spread the word among trees, in case they could be of possible assistance. Tvrdik was delighted and gratified to hear of this new addition to their forces, despite the fact that dryads were less mobile than the rest of their company.

The Lady Jorelial Rey divided her time between her duties at Theriole, time with Darian, brainstorming meetings, and field practice with the Legion. At the palace, she often crossed paths with Minister Boone, who assured her that his own forces were in readiness for any circumstance.

However, he did not seem terribly interested in what was going on out on the gaming fields. The sea wall had been shored up, the space at the gate closed, and ships were outfitted for battle if the need arose. No further intelligence of Drogue's activities had come in, but everything was at high alert, should information reach him that an attack was imminent.

Lord Corbin Maygrew also sought her out a time or two in the palace halls, or at mealtimes. Still on the fence as to how he felt the looming threat should be addressed, he was gratified at General Boone's reports, but asked the Lady Regent all sorts of serious questions about the Legions of Light, listening to her responses with great interest. He, at least, was paying attention, and recognized a grassroots movement when he saw it. Lord Alanquist, the Minister of Justice, aged as he was, was already out on the field with Verger and Bargarelle, practicing maneuvers. There were still many powerful lords and ladies, however, who were extremely skeptical of the value of this rag-tag bunch of peasants, beasts, and assorted oddball characters playing games in the field every day. Some thought that entirely too much time, money, and energy was being wasted on the venture. Still, there had been an agreement, and the time of reckoning would come soon enough.

These were hectic weeks, filled with hard work, mental challenges, and more tasks than there were hours to accomplish them. Days were long and sleep was in short supply. Everyone understood that the clock was ticking on a grave situation. The stakes were high, every day counted, and no one complained.

And so it was that nearly a month flew by in this manner, Tvrdik and Jorelial Rey becoming accustomed to the punishing schedule they kept, the Praegers making themselves ever more indispensable at the old Cottage, and everyone else throwing themselves whole-heartedly into preparing for the advent of war. After the first week, visible progress was made, as they began to organize their tool chest of strategies. By the end of the third week, the Legions of Light had swelled greatly in numbers, and were operating like a well-oiled machine on many of the maneuvers they had been taught.

Then, one bright summer day, not long before the date set for the formal trials, something happened that changed everything. It was just before mid-day when the great bells in the tallest tower of Theriole began to sound. Horns blasted from the parapets, summoning everyone in earshot to attention. It was the signal they had awaited, and dreaded. The real danger had arrived too soon. Out on the fields, mid-maneuver, Tvrdik and the regent exchanged a grave, horrified look, and began running for the palace. Tvrdik clutched his staff sideways, in both hands. Others who held vital positions were only steps behind them, while the rest of the Legion had been trained to remain assembled in the field until word could be sent to direct their next move. Jorelial Rey, glancing back, saw them hasten into a close, tight formation, just as they had rehearsed. Twelve dragons, recently arrived to assist, ringed the rest in a close circle, facing outward. Tashroth had been tagged as messenger, along with a few of the fastest talking birds and beasts. These were already headed for the lawns in front of Theriole, ready to receive briefings and deliver them as needed.

Jorelial Rey arrived at the palace well before Tvrdik and the others. Before she could even pause to catch her breath, she was escorted to General Boone's office, but was ill-prepared for the awful news that greeted her there.

"You did *what*?" she shouted at him in disbelief. Beside the grim-faced Minister of Defense was a young man in uniform, or what was left of a uniform, really. It was scorched, torn and filthy, as were his face and hair. He stood wearily in place, helmet held under one arm, trying to keep from swaying with exhaustion and wincing in pain. There were bleeding gashes marking his cheek and arm. "Send for a healer!" the Lady Regent shouted into the hall, and then, without missing a beat, addressed Boone once more, "How could you *do* such a thing without consulting me?"

Boone was frowning, defiant, "I judged it to be our best plan of defense. Stop them in their tracks while they were still miles off shore. Keep them from coming anywhere near the palace. It is a good strategy. It makes sense, my lady." Apparently, one of the talking birds who had been sent out as a scout had spotted thirteen enemy ships, flying Drogue's colors, some way out to sea that morning. Thinking to engage them in the open sea, where he could surprise and defeat them, Boone did not hesitate to send out nine of the kingdom's swiftest ships, including one of Lady Brendelle's. He had been confident of their success in routing this attack before it came any closer. He had underestimated Drogue.

441

"Why was I not immediately informed of the danger? I might have counseled you against engaging him directly."

Boone's eyes were lowered, but his voice crackled with tension, "My lady, I am the Minister of Defense. It is my job, my responsibility to see to the protection of these lands. You gave me the authority to prepare for war. You were otherwise occupied. I saw no reason to waste precious time waiting for permission to do my job, or to disturb you with details…"

"Disturb me with details? I am the duly elected acting ruler here, Minister! Would you have treated your king thus, had he been present?"

"My lady, King Darian was well versed in the art and science of warcraft. He had experience in…"

"Stop right there, Boone, before I order your immediate suspension from office. I do not know if this is about my youth, my gender, or my involvement with the Legions of Light, but, by all that is sacred, if you cannot afford me the respect properly due to your monarch, then you cannot continue in this office." Her face was turning a shadowy purple, and sparks were shooting from her dark eyes.

Boone met her eyes, his own blazing with frustration, his voice tight, "My lady, you must know I hold you in the highest regard, but this is war. I have made no secret of the fact that I consider your ideas on defense to be, well, naïve, to come right to it. I thought you would be governed by my counsel in this arena. I am only trying to do my job."

Jorelial Rey closed her eyes, and quickly counted to ten. In a more controlled voice, she asked, "And how well have you done it, Minister? Have you destroyed the enemy on your own initiative, and now bring me back the gift of victory? Can we all live now, secure in our peaceful, unthreatened kingdom? Should I thank you personally for proving to me once and for all the solid merits of your system, sir? Hmmmm?"

Boone was speechless, but a look of pain twisted his grizzled face. Jorelial Rey immediately regretted the cutting edge of her sarcasm, but the man had to understand his error. She turned to the tattered young man, who still stood at attention as a healer began attending to his wounds.

"What happened, Captain?"

"My lady, we sailed out to the enemy fleet, and prepared to engage. They were strangely quiet, so we pulled right up alongside. Then they hurled some sort of green flame at us. It seemed to come from nowhere, and clung to the decks, the sails, the masts. Water was useless to quench it. I gave the order for our ships to turn and put distance between ourselves and the enemy. But it was too late for three of our ships. They were utterly consumed and went down."

"Casualties?"

"We were able to pull almost every man from the burning ships to other decks." He hung his head, and a sound like a sob escaped from deep in his throat. "There was one who did not make it, ma'am."

She stepped closer and touched his shoulder, "Tell me, who?"

"Captain Virian, my lady. I…he…he went down with his ship."

"Jorelial Rey started backward from the hapless Captain and gasped, "Virian, did you say?"

"Yes, ma'am."

Virian, the young officer who had brought Delphine back to her. In a flash of memory she recalled their conversation, the handsome smile, the playful wink – and a young bride and brand new baby! Who would tell them, explain to them that Daddy would not be coming home? Her stomach flipped and her face screwed itself up into an anguished grimace. When she could open her eyes, she fixed them first on Boone, and then on the young Captain. "How?" she asked.

"My lady, he would not leave the ship until all his men were off. We had rigged a plank connecting the two decks, his and mine, and he was handing them off to me. Just as his turn came, the plank caught fire and fell, and the two ships started to drift apart. I threw him a rope, but the distance was growing and his deck was burning. He held up a hand and waved me away. Then he…he…winked at me. And then there were only flames and smoke and water." The young man was overcome with his memories, and at a gesture from the Lady Regent, the healer eased him into a nearby chair. Rel put her hand over her face and forced back the tears she knew were on the verge of breaking through. She cleared her throat, "I will go personally to speak with Captain Virian's family. My father knew them, and I owe him that. They will be well taken care of, and he will be awarded the highest citation for bravery. What other damage?"

The young Captain replied, "There were a number of injuries and terrible burns. And of course, the loss of three ships. The others are seaworthy, ma'am."

The healer, finishing up with some bandages, added, "These burns are unusual, my lady, resistant to the salves I usually use. They look odd, and, I imagine, are quite painful."

"Yes, sir," winced the young Captain, struggling to maintain his composure. "I am ashamed to admit, we turned tail as soon as we got hit with the strange fire. There was no further action from the enemy. It was as if they just…let us go. No doubt they thought we would limp home and terrify everyone with our story."

"Well," the Regent replied, seething, "limp home you have, and not a moment too soon. Terrify us, you shall not. You did the right thing, Captain. I commend you for saving the lives of so many men, and what resources you could."

"Ma'am" the young man bowed his head, fighting pain and shame. The healer nodded, and helped him to his feet, and out the door.

As soon as they were out of earshot, Rel whirled on her Defense Minister. "Do you see, General, that you have squandered three valuable, fully equipped and provisioned ships, lost a fine officer with a bright future and a young family, and endangered many other lives. And all for what? To prove a point? The enemy fleet is unharmed and headed right this way, while we stand here discussing things. Tvrdik!" she called toward the door.

"Here, my lady." he had been waiting for her just outside in the hall.

"Tvrdik, Drogue's ships are headed this way. Thirteen. They are using some sort of very potent sorcerer's fire. We don't have much time. This is it. Are you ready?"

"As ready as I'll ever be, my lady."

"Thank you." It was more than a courtesy she was expressing with those words. She turned back to Boone. "General, I would be sore tempted to relieve you of your command after what you have done, except for the fact that I still need you. And despite everything, I still think you are the best man for the job. But, listen well. From here on in, you will follow my orders exactly, to the letter. You will not initiate any major actions on your own, without clearing them with me first, unless I am cold and dead. You will do all this despite any personal opinions you might entertain on whatever you are asked to do. Is that clear?"

"Very clear, my lady."

"And can you assure me that I can expect your cooperation in this, Minister Boone?"

"You will have it, my lady."

"Good. Then, please tell me if there is any word of an attack from the landward side."

"None, my lady. I believe Drogue is confident that he is taking us by surprise. He is sure he can conquer Theriole from the sea, with little resistance."

"Well, he has misjudged us by a long shot, then. He'll not have this kingdom without a fight. Alright, then, General: I want you to send riders and heralds out immediately, with the message that we are under attack, and everyone in the near vicinity should close shop and either shutter themselves in their homes, or come within Theriole's walls for sanctuary. Pull everyone who does business just outside the walls within – their beasts too – and have all the main gates shut as soon as possible, with guards posted. Get everyone from the beach back behind the sea wall, and deploy your men all around the perimeter of the palace. Position the greatest concentration high up on the parapets, and along the seashore, the sea wall, and the delta. They are to keep their eyes peeled, and be prepared for combat *in case* our first line of defense fails, and Drogue's men should break through, or storm the walls. Set up buckets and basins of sand against the sorcerers' fire in the event they try to use it again on the new section of wall we just built where the gate stood. Your troops are to stay put, alert and ready, awaiting my command, is that clear?"

"Yes, my lady."

"Oh, and it is imperative that we impose a strict noise curfew within the palace walls. We need as close to silence as we can get – no talking aloud, beasts and babes as muffled as possible – I cannot stress the importance of this enough."

"But, my lady, we *must* sail out to stop those ships. You would let them right in at our back door. We will be sitting ducks."

"Not on my watch, sir. I have something else in mind. Will you work with me, or be replaced?"

Boone bowed "I am yours to command, my lady, and pray the gods that you know indeed what you are doing." He hastened past her to carry out the tasks she had set him.

"Well done, Jorelial Rey." Tvrdik spoke near her ear, "We will triumph, do not fear."

"I hope so, Tvrdik. My neck is already stretched out about as far as it could be. What do we do now?"

"Show me how to get to that center alcove up there in the sea wall, where we were before. Then ask Tashroth to come and sit in one of the adjoining ones – it's big enough for him to be comfortable, and I'll need his strength to help hold my focus. Tell Delphine to find Ondine and signal her that the time is now – that enemy ships approach from the sea. Send the birds back to the gaming fields with word about what is going on; the Legions will be anxious, and awaiting news. Ask the healers, the unicorns, and the dragons to come here and assist, and everyone else to barricade themselves in, either at home or inside Theriole's walls. They should be safe in the city, and the outlying farms. We aren't going to let anyone past these buildings. I am hoping they will not even make landfall. But tell the Legions to be prepared for further alerts, wherever they are. Let's see...I think that's it."

"Bless you, Tvrdik. You're sure we can do this?"

"No time for doubts now. If we all pull together, I believe we can."

"That will have to be good enough. Let's get started."

On the way out of Boone's offices, they met Delphine, Mark, and Bargarelle, all awaiting instructions. They were each given assignments from Tvrdik's list, and hurried off. Jorelial Rey conducted the mage through a series of little-used halls and passageways at the back of the palace, and in a short while they emerged in the center alcove, rusty cauldrons and a giant crossbow in disrepair filling some of the space. Tvrdik strode through all the ancient equipment to the ledge overlooking the beach, the delta, and the sea. Far in the distance, a sharp eye could make out dark spots that could be ships – the approaching enemy. The day was fair, the sea blue-green and calm. They could already see civilians crowding in behind the walls, and Boone's soldiers taking up positions to secure the perimeter. Tvrdik stretched, rolled his shoulders and head a few times, then planted his feet in a wide comfortable stance, and his trusty oak staff firmly on the stone floor.

"This will do just fine," he said, "I'll have to begin right away, before they see us clearly. Tell Tash to jump in as soon as he can. I'll know when he comes in."

"Do you need anything?"

"I have all I need." He looked down at her white face, eyebrows knitted in concern, and smiled, "I'll be fine. I've been practicing." Then, in answer to her unspoken question, he added, "I will give you my very best, as I always promised you. And you will handle the rest like someone born to lead. See in your mind what you wish to transpire, Jorelial Rey. Believe it...trust it...create it. All of these are very powerful. It will be enough."

"Gods willing, I will see you on the other side of this, and we will toast our success!"

"Count on it." He smiled again, and she nodded and disappeared back through the old weaponry and out the door. Tvrdik shook out his muscles one more time, took up his stance in the opening, gripped his staff, closed his eyes and concentrated on his breathing...

<hr />

Out at sea, thirteen warships sailed in formation, approaching the spot where the River Maygrew flowed into Mother Ocean, the beating heart of Eneri Clare. Lord Drogue was not on any of them. Not fond of sea travel himself, he had sent his new fleet off under the command of one of his loyal supporters, a neighboring lord named Neritz. Neritz's family had some long-standing, unsatisfied quarrel with the Crown which went back several generations. He admired Drogue's pro-active philosophies of self-advancement, and was happy to attach himself to a man he believed would, in all likelihood, win the entire game. He assumed the rewards for his service would be great once Drogue was triumphant. Neritz had some experience in seafaring and battle command, having travelled and hired abroad in his youth. And Drogue's dabbling in sorcery had equipped the ships with green mage-fire. Lord Drogue was certain that the ancient, disused defenses of the palace on the ocean side, would be no match for the double thrust of a disciplined assault and mage-fire on the sea wall. It would be all over in a day, and he could ride in to take possession of his prize in glory.

At this moment, Neritz stood on the bow of the swiftly moving flagship with a spyglass, scanning the horizon. Encouraged by the complete rout of the Crown's naval forces that sailed out to meet them earlier, he was now daydreaming with excitement of the glorious battle he imagined awaited him. He grinned, invigorated by thoughts of his own daring feats – the smells of blood, sweat, and burning wood; the symphony of cries and groans and clashing steel playing in his ears; the cavalcade of colorful action unfolding before his eyes; the gratifying moment of the foe's surrender, and the thrilling rush of victory! It would all be so easy, almost too easy. He almost hoped they put up a better fight than they had this morning – it would make winning all the sweeter. Neritz was jarred from this flight of fantasy by the arrival on deck of General Gargan, who he knew to be one of Lord Drogue's closest adjuncts. Gargan was a rough sort, entirely un-imaginative – a man of few dreams and fewer words.

"How long, now?" the raspy bass broke into Neritz's reverie.

"Oh, I didn't hear you come up. I haven't yet spotted Theriole in the glass, nor have I heard from the crow's nest, but on our present course, it should be any time now. On these fair seas with a good tailwind, we are closing the gap as though on wings."

"I am not in the mood for poetry, Neritz. I just want to know what to tell the men; they are restless."

"Tell them to channel their frustrations into their sword arms, as they will soon have ample opportunity to express themselves."

Tvrdik stood erect, still as a marble statue, eyes closed, face lifted to the sea breeze, pale hair cascading in waves to his shoulder blades, right hand gripping the mighty staff of oak. He had been standing like that without so much as a twitch for the better part of two hours, lost in deep concentration. He had taken off his glasses and put them in his pocket for safekeeping, as it was his inner vision he needed most now. Without them, the planes of his face seemed sharper, more mature, and, at this moment, oddly translucent. In fact, all around him there was a sort of shimmer one could not so much see, as perceive. It was more like a ripple, or a disturbance in the air, if you looked with narrowed eyes. In the mage's mind was a vivid picture of endless sea, gray and cold, disturbed here and there by wicked rocks that seemed to jut sharply out of nowhere at intervals. The restless waters crashed upon them, and swirled around them in dangerous eddies, while dense white mists flowed over and around the perilous stones, obscuring and revealing them by turns. Despite the presence of those jagged monoliths, there was no evidence of a beach or landfall anywhere at all as far as the eye could see.

Jorelial Rey had made sure Tashroth was comfortably installed the next alcove over from Tvrdik, and waited there until the dragon's eyes began to glow and pulse, indicating his mental connection with the mage. She had then gone back to check on the wizard, quietly slipping in so as not to disturb his focus. Watching him settle deeper and deeper into a trancelike state, she marveled at his discipline, his stillness, the semblance of light radiating from him. And then, for a brief moment, she could have sworn he was joined there by another robed figure: tall, white-haired and bearded, with a distinctive profile. She blinked in bewilderment, and the figure was gone, but she was always certain thereafter that, in that moment, she had actually seen Xaarus come to lend his powerful support in their time of need.

Neritz stood on the bridge of his flagship clutching the spyglass to his breast, and staring nervously at the mist-shrouded rocks ahead. He was flanked by the ship's navigator and another veteran seaman, one of whom played with a sextant, and the other with an awkward pile of rolled charts. "This is ridiculous!" he shouted, voice taut, "We should have been there an hour ago. An entire delta, an entire kingdom just doesn't disappear. You must have made an error back a ways."

The navigator was sullen, "No mistake, sir. I been doin' this all my life, and I done the calculations eighteen times. Take a look up there at the sun, sir; even you would have to admit it cannot change its daily course."

Neritz threw him a threatening look, "Well, then, your instruments must be flawed…"

"Sir, this is the third sextant we have tried, and the other ships are doin' the same with no different results. I don't know how this happened, but I know by every measure, we are right where we are supposed to be."

Neritz scowled, "Well, what is this place then? It appears treacherous, and yet you say nothing like it appears on any of your maps or charts?"

The man with the charts was fumbling with uncooperative rolled parchments, "Sir, I have been poring over these charts for the last hour, and have found nothing on them about a place like this. We should've had a smooth run right up to the beaches and the seawall of Theriole. It's huge. We should see it rising up on the horizon just in front of us. For the life of me, I can't understand what this is."

Neritz was beginning to panic, beads of sweat breaking out on his brow as he peered through the spyglass once more in all directions. He took his frustration out on the hapless men beside him. "You two are worse than useless. The day is getting away from us and we are clearly lost. Send word to the other ships: hard to starboard and follow. We must have missed the entrance to the harbor by some error, and I'm not about to take his lordship's new fleet into that treacherous mess ahead. Go on, don't stand about...you have your orders."

Jorelial Rey busied herself flitting from post to post, checking on every detail of everyone's well-being. The entire palace and inner courtyards were packed with men and beasts: nobles, servants, merchants, farmers, all together. All stood or sat, waiting quietly as they had been instructed, some carrying swords or pitchforks in the event of a breech. Boone's soldiers lined all the perimeters and kept careful watch both for intruders and on the crowds within. Despite the uncertainty and endless waiting, for the most part everyone was well-behaved, and attentive to instructions. Soldiers also lined the beach, and stood on all the ramparts and parapets of the sea wall, poised for action, eyes on the enemy ships out in the harbor. The entire herd of unicorns was down on the beachhead, standing in a tight semi-circle, and organizing some action involving their horns on which the Lady Regent was not fully clear. Out of respect, she allowed them to carry out their portion of the plan undisturbed, and instructed anyone on the beach to give them all the room and assistance they needed. Dragons of every size and color perched in high places on parapets, turrets, and towers, watching from these elevated vantage points, and seeming to listen for some predetermined signal. A white dragon, poised on the highest tower, seemed to be the focus of their attention, while her gaze was held fast by the little drama unfolding in the shining waters before them. For that matter, every creature with even a partial view was fixed on the events transpiring just before the sea wall.

Three hours ago, lookouts had spotted thirteen warships approaching on the horizon. Closer and closer they had come, their dark banners unfurled in the light breeze, close enough for those with spyglasses to discern ship's names on their sterns, and figures on their decks. At the palace, every nerve thrummed, every muscle tightened, adrenaline flowed, and hands closed on weapons with firm resolve. Then, without explanation, the entire black fleet had halted in its progress, and just sat immobile for a time, bobbing on the waves. And then, led by their flagship, all thirteen began to sail off to the left, and from there, in a wide circle. They seemed to sail in aimless patterns, uncertain of their goal, making a foray out to one heading, then changing direction abruptly, sojourning out again, then shifting again, until they had made the entire circuit two or three times. Ships broke formation in confusion and sometimes came perilously near one another. No one on the ships hailed or acknowledged Theriole.

On the shore, and on the walls and towers, those observing turned to each other in disbelief. This fleet was behaving as if it were dead lost, within plain sight of its quarry, just meters away. Had everyone gone blind? Were they all drunk, or conflicted, or confounded, or was it some convoluted and incomprehensible plot? What in heaven's name were they doing out there? It was all the folk of Theriole could do to observe the strict order for silence, so eager were they to exclaim to their fellows in amazement at the bizarre show beyond the wall. But observe it they did, on pain of punishment, under the watchful eyes of Boone's troops, and sensing that somehow their very lives depended on their compliance.

Now, over three hours since Jorelial Rey had first given her orders, the attacking ships were again stalled out beyond the sea wall, facing every direction, riding the rise and fall of the waves, but going nowhere. The Lady Regent hastened to check in with Boone, and every captain, to make sure they enforced the rule of silence, and then she climbed the stairs to peer in at Tashroth and Tvrdik in turn. Neither had moved an eyelash since they had begun their exercise, and an almost audible hum seemed to be emanating in a sort of regular pulse from both alcoves. She sent up a silent prayer to whatever gods were listening that they could hold out a little longer, and come away unharmed.

———————————— ❖ ————————————

"I suppose *you* want to be the one who explains to Lord Drogue that we came within striking distance of our quarry, and had to give up because we just couldn't *find* it?" Gargan's face was purple, and his voice strident. " 'My lord, we sailed around in circles for hours where the charts said the palace ought to be, but we just didn't *see* any palace.' Is *that* what you want to tell him, Neritz?"

"Of course not!" Neritz was beginning to look very much the worse for wear. His eyes were wide with terror, his clothing and face were wet with perspiration, and his hair was disheveled from running his hands through it in frustration. He was beginning to think he was losing his mind. "Look, I am as loathe as you are to return to Lord Drogue empty-handed, but what do you suggest I do? I've tried everything I can think of. Nothing makes any sense, and we are no closer than when we started."

Gargan's face twisted, "I'm beginning to suspect some sort of trickery, perhaps even sorcery here. What other explanation could there be? I say, if all the instruments, and all the charts, and all the navigators say there should be a palace dead ahead, then maybe there *is* a palace dead ahead. I say we sail forward."

"Are you insane? Look at those rocks, and the fog and the surf. We'll be dashed to pieces! We haven't any maps to guide us; we won't be able to see a bloody thing in there…that's all we need to add to our report. 'By the way, my lord, we lost several of your brand new ships, gone down with all hands in a rocky patch…' If we venture in there, whatever happens will be on *your* head, Gargan, and *you* can be the one to tell him."

"And if we do nothing else, and turn tail now, the honor will be *yours.*" Gargan smiled an ugly, gap-toothed grin, "It's the only direction we haven't explored – I say we go. Or are you so much a coward?"

Neritz bristled at that, "Very well, but remember I warned you." He gave the order.

———————————— ❖ ————————————

They all saw it at the same moment. After hours of aimless circling and pointless meandering, the invading ships in the harbor all straightened themselves out, regrouped into a proper formation, and began to sail slowly, but in a direct and inexorable line, straight toward them. To her great dismay, Jorelial Rey had to admit that the enemy might just have caught on to their deception. She wasn't sure at what point they would actually be on the other side of the wizard's illusion, or, for that matter, how much longer he could continue to generate it. All along the beach and the parapets, Boone's soldiers began reaching for their weapons and shifting their weight, in case they found themselves confronted with an invading army. The Lady Regent bit her lip. She was about to lose her own private battle for control of the situation. She could send for the Legions of Light, and have reinforcements on the scene quickly, but she would not have Tvrdik to instruct them in what to do. And the safety of Theriole and everyone in it had to come first. Boone would take over defending the castle his way. Drat. It was a maddening position in which to find one's self, and she wasn't at all clear on her next move.

The ships came inching forward, hesitant, and in a strange, lurching pattern, as if testing the waters, or sailing around invisible obstacles. Closer and closer they sailed, certain to break through the illusion at any moment. Just then, a commotion down at the river's mouth drew Jorelial's attention. From her high vantage point, she heard muffled exclamations piercing the enforced silence, and saw people backing away from the riverbank in alarm, exactly where the Maygrew poured into the sea. Some sort of unusual turbulence seemed to be disturbing the delta waters, foaming and swelling, and though she couldn't be entirely sure from this distance, she thought she saw some small blue and grey-green figures leaping and weaving in and out of the spray, bobbing and tumbling at the juncture of river and sea. She stood mesmerized, as, before her eyes, the sea began to push back at the river, pouring its salty treasure into the mouth of the Maygrew. And the river stood its ground and pushed back. Bit by bit, a huge wall of water between river and sea began to rise. Higher and higher it reached, rearing up like the arched neck of a proud stallion. Impossibly tall the wave grew, foam caps beginning to curl with the impulse to move. For a moment the entire phenomenon hung suspended there, mammoth and terrifying, while the entire population of Theriole watched in breathless horror. And then, it all came crashing down.

Neritz stood at the flagship's helm, trying to steer by eye around the rocky projections he feared could be their demise. Swirling, thick mists were not making the task any easier, and he had to move forward at a veritable crawl to be comfortable that he was being cautious enough. The other ships followed behind, holding formation and using his wake, where they could see it, as a guide. Still no visible sign of structures anywhere on the horizon, but then, they could barely see each other in the fog. Neritz had just skirted a nasty-looking group of sharp-edged boulders when he glanced up ahead. He sighed with relief to notice a dense patch of fog drifting off to the side, but when he saw what the lifted mist revealed dead ahead, Neritz turned white and his mouth went dry. "Oh, ye gods..." he could barely whisper, his eyes frozen on the enormous wave which hung poised to fall on his head.

What he had no way of knowing was that the rocks and mists that so terrified him were but figments of Tvrdik's imagination, while the tidal wave stirred up by Ondine and her friends was real. The flagship, and four other ships just behind it, got the worst of the initial fall; tons of water smashed onto their wooden decks, knocking many sailors down, and washing a few overboard. Neritz himself stopped his careening journey over the edge by grasping a metal loop in the floor, meant to guide ropes. Much of the water cascaded below decks and threatened to weigh down and capsize the boats. Soldiers and sailors scrambled in desperation to bail and pump water out of the hold before things reached a critical tipping point. To make matters worse, behind the vanguard of Drogue's attack fleet, the sea reared up in response to the first wave's fall. It carried the rest of the fleet high into the air. Eight ships bobbed about on the giant crest like so many cork stoppers, and then dropped like boulders through the empty void left by the receding wave. One fell broadside, tipping its passengers and crew into the deep, and smashing timbers in its flank beyond all hope of recovery. The other ships, many damaged by water and impact themselves, raced to the rescue of the men floundering in the sea, well aware that they had better be out of the area with all on board at the moment the capsized vessel chose to sink. But, though the giant wave had passed, the sea was still dark and roiling, tossing the boats about willy-nilly and hampering all of their rescue and salvage attempts. There was no wind, no rain, but the little fleet struggled for dear life in the foaming waters as if the storm of the century was upon them. Every ounce of sea-wisdom and experience, every sinew and fiber of the strongest sailors aboard were strained to the utmost as the crews fought for survival.

Neritz dragged himself upright, soaking wet and terrified. The flagship had righted itself and seemed to be intact, due to the quick thinking and hard labor of the crew. Gargan came sliding across the slimy deck, screaming at him in fury, "Forward, man! Take us forward. They are fighting us with sorcery."

Neritz swallowed hard, wiping the salty brine from his eyes. "Are you insane? We have only just barely escaped ruin. I have no desire to drown in this god-forsaken wilderness. I am giving the order to come about."

"Coward!" Gargan screamed over the chaotic noise on deck, then drew back a muscular arm across his chest and lashed out with such power that he knocked Neritz clear off his feet again. Taking control, he urged the flagship, and any others that were still whole enough to follow, forward once again.

Jorelial Rey breathed a silent prayer of thanks to Ondine and her compatriots for coming through in the nick of time, though it was awful to watch the devastation her action had wrought out at sea. Thank heaven, the force of the great wave and the turbulence of the waters now seemed all to be directed outward at the invaders – there was no backlash onto the shores of the kingdom, no damage to the sea wall or the beach before it. She could still catch a glimpse now and then of the tiny naiads leaping and gamboling in and out of the water at the river's mouth, weaving their own special brand of ancient magic. Tvrdik had been right that it was unwise to underestimate the sheer power of the little creatures; she was very glad to have them on her side.

As the Lady Regent scanned the chaos of what had been the enemy fleet, however, she found herself hoping that no one had perished in the great wave the sprites kicked up. Their mandate had been to do no harm, as far as that was possible. But how were they to defend the palace without killing anyone? Especially given that her adversaries would have been ruthless in their own pursuit of conquest. Several of the talking birds had remained near her where she stood on a high parapet, in order to carry messages and instructions. She sent one of them now, with a missive to the white dragon, who seemed to be leading the saurian contingent today in Tashroth's absence. A moment later, a pronounced nod and a shriek in her direction from the pale beast perched on a high turret across the courtyard, told her that the message had been received, and would be acted upon.

But in the next instant, the Lady Regent was looking down in disbelief, to see Drogue's flagship, and two or three others regrouping and attempting to plough forward once more toward Theriole. Had they not had enough? If they did break through the illusion and realized where they were, she felt confident her forces could hold their own against such a compromised force. But they would have to resort to traditional fighting – exactly what they were hoping to avoid. Perhaps her bag of tricks was not yet empty. She shifted her gaze to the beach, where a dozen unicorns had been standing poised in a tight semi-circle, their horns all pointing up to a spot in the center. She saw that Wynne had also seen the approaching ships, and was shaking his head up and down, as if giving some signal. The unicorns all arched their necks, stepped in and lowered their horns until the points met together, and from that convergence exploded a burst of light so bright she had to step back and look away, all the way up on the top of the castle. The brunt of that beam had been aimed well out into the harbor, straight toward the advancing ships.

Gargan crashed to the deck, his hands over his face, shrieking like a wounded boar. All around him on each of the advancing ships, others were howling and writhing in similar distress. Some of the men even lost consciousness, or ran about the decks in confusion. The flash had come out of nowhere, brighter than anything any of them had ever before encountered, and anyone who had been turned in its direction was blinded by its intensity. Neritz, who had been lying face-down on the deck where Gargan had flung him, picked himself up and took in the scene of chaos and destruction around him. All thoughts of conquest and joyful victories fled from the stage of his mind as he simply attempted to calculate his best chance for survival. Everyone else within earshot was standing or lying on the deck, sightless, and whimpering in pain. He couldn't turn the ship around by himself. He stepped over Gargan's hulking form, and staggered over to the helm, still worried about being dashed to bits on the jagged rocks. It was then that an unfamiliar sound drew his eyes upward, a knot of dread forming in the pit of his stomach. Dragons! Huge, angry dragons emerging from the mist – dragons of every size and color, swooping and flapping their enormous wings, breathing flame, and fastening their wicked eyes on him. This new development was one disaster too many for the hapless lord, who fell in a heap on the deck of his battered ship, folded his arms over his head in a pitiful attempt at protection, and sobbed like a baby, shaking and shuddering.

In truth, the dragons were sent to frighten the intruders, rather than to do any actual damage. After centuries of experience, they were all extremely gifted at inspiring fear in those who understood them the least. Six of them played at wheeling and swooping, breathing flames, and uttering hair-raising shrieks, while the other six flew in close to the water, instructed to search the waves and the wreckage for any seamen in distress – those who might be clinging to bits of flotsam, or were struggling to keep their heads above water. They were scooped up, or plucked up, one by one, in the dragons' very sensitive claws, and deposited with care on the decks of the least damaged ships, in daring pass after pass. Many a sailor in Drogue's fleet owed his life that day to a dragon's sharp eye, and many told the stories of their incredible rescues again and again to their grandchildren, for years into the future.

One purple dragon got carried away with his own playfulness. He had taken to grasping the tops of mainmasts in his claws and rocking the ships back and forth while roaring at them, like so many toys in the bathtub. It was a harmless enough prank, and quite terrifying to the men on shipboard. But one mast, already damaged in the tidal wave, snapped off in his claws, and hung poised in the rigging, useless and threatening to fall. Embarrassed, and wanting to seem responsible, the great beast grabbed the broken piece, pulled it up, seared through mainsail and tangled ropes with his fiery breath, and flung the offending splinter far out to sea. That ship might not make it home under its own steam, but at least no one was hurt. The crew however, completely misread the purple dragon's helpful intentions, and ran about the decks screaming, convinced their vessel would be torn apart a piece at a time right out from under them.

"Use the mage-fire on them!" Gargan shouted, having regained his sight just in time for an eyeful.

"How, sir?" a miserable yeoman responded. "All the components are soaking wet, and we have nothing to set it alight."

"Get out of my way." Neritz roared at Gargan, having finally found his backbone. "I've had enough of you. We are leaving this cursed place before we all perish." He barked out orders to those in his crew still standing, and had them relayed by semaphore to the other ships. With a heroic effort, the battered fleet, or what was left of it, turned itself around. Any ship that could sail headed back out to the open sea. Those that were too damaged, but still afloat, were secured by tow ropes to the strongest of the others. Men were posted at all the railings to scour the waters for anyone still floundering overboard, but the dragons had done their work well. There were injuries and scarred psyches, but as far as anyone could tell, no one was lost at sea – a veritable miracle. In shifts, so as not to give themselves away, the dragons broke off their theatrical attacks, and one by one rode the air currents back through the make-believe mists to their various preferred perches at Theriole. By the time the last of them had returned, it was obvious to everyone in a position to be watching that the only intention of the naval force that had come to conquer them, was now to escape the vicinity as soon as possible. A spontaneous cheer erupted from the crowds that had for so long held their tongues – indeed, had barely breathed – while their fate hung in the balance. But Boone's men, mindful of their orders, hushed the joyful eruption mid-shout. The danger might not be entirely past.

Back on Drogue's flagship, Gargan was arguing again, "But, I tell you, I heard it, clear and plain. Voices. From back there. It sounded like hundreds of people cheering for just a moment…"

Neritz narrowed his eyes and looked straight at the sullen big man, "Those must have been the voices of souls trapped in *Hell*, which is where we have been, and what I am very thankful to have only just escaped by a hair's breadth! I will brave Lord Drogue's wrath before I even *think* of going back to that horrible place again, and if I ever even *speak* of putting to sea again for any reason whatever, you will know that it is time for me to be put away, because I shall have *lost my mind!*" He turned his back and strode to the other end of the ship, while the fleet entrusted to his care limped back toward its origin, gray mists closing behind them.

A little while longer the denizens of the palace kept still and watched, as the ships shrank in the distance, and disappeared at last over the horizon, to even the sharpest eye. Looking around for a cue, everyone still waited a maddening interval just to be certain they would not be heard. And then, almost as if the entire company were one body, with one corporate perception of the perfect moment, every soul in Theriole cried out at once – man, woman, child and beast. The cheer that arose was deafening. There were cries of, "Long live the King!" "Hail our Regent!" Even, "Thanks to our wizard!" The dragons lifted up their wings and roared. And both the talking beasts and those who were not so endowed, bellowed, howled, barked, brayed, and neighed themselves senseless. Soldiers beat their swords against their shields. The unicorns sported and frolicked on the beach, tossing their beautiful heads, while all the naiads cavorted and splashed about in the shallows.

Jorelial Rey, sensing that they were now safe for the moment, gave the order for runners to go immediately out into the neighboring fields, the town, and the outlying farms, to carry the word of the enemy's defeat. Then she stood, eyes closed, breathing in the joy and relief that sang through the warm evening air. They had done it. They had won the first round, and on their own terms, just as Xaarus had promised, and Tvrdik had always believed.

Oh, heavens, Tvrdik! And Tash! They would have no way of knowing that the danger was past, and it had been more than six hours since they had locked minds to generate their false landscape. Her eyes flew wide open at the thought, and without an explanation to anyone, turned and dashed up stairways and through dimming corridors, to the level of the large defensive alcoves set in Theriole's sea wall, overlooking the waves.

THIRTY-THREE

THE HERO WIZARD

She went to Tashroth first, as they had all agreed. It seemed safer for Tashroth to pull out of the mind-meld first so that the young mage could surface more gradually. Jorelial Rey raced into the space where the great green dragon crouched, silent and still except for his glowing eyes. She flung herself against his massive chest, where she could feel his beating heart. Reaching up to stroke his familiar face, she called his name, "Tashroth...Tash, we did it! They are gone. Come back to me, Tash. We've won." The enormous eyes stopped their pulsing, and began to clear. Tashroth blinked, made a rumbling noise deep in his throat, and stretched. He half unfolded his wings, shaking out the discomfort of standing long in one position, and extended each front limb in turn, unlocking stiff joints. Bringing his ancient, beloved face back down to hers, he blinked again, and smiled a dragon smile.

"Where do we stand, little one?"

She embraced him with relief, then backed away to speak with him, "We did it, Tash. The illusion held the whole time, and they never saw us. Then Ondine nearly drowned them all, and the unicorns and your dragon friends scared the stuffing out of them. What's left of their fleet has turned tail and fled back to wherever they came from."

"What is that awful noise, then?" he furrowed his brows in concern.

She laughed, "That, my dear, is the sound of celebration. The people in the palace are cheering our success."

"Oh," responded the dragon. "How very undisciplined."

"I think we can forgive them just this once. Are you alright?"

Tashroth stretched again, "I am very well. In fact, I feel quite invigorated. The mage is remarkably gifted – much more powerful than even he suspects."

"So, Tvrdik did well?"

"My dear, Tvrdik did it all. Xaarus and I only loaned him a little extra amplification."

"Ohmygosh! We have left him still standing there. It's been six hours. I have to bring him back…"

"Go, little one. And thank him from me for a most unusual adventure. Now I feel the need to stretch my wings a bit, and find a bite to eat." The great beast nuzzled her once more, edged forward in the alcove, and just walked off the end of the ledge. Jorelial Rey gasped, as she watched the falling giant spread his magnificent wings in the air and climb upwards on a current. Then, she turned on her heel and ran through the hall to the central alcove where the Court Wizard still stood frozen, staff in hand, eyes closed and face lifted to the sea breeze.

She hadn't the slightest idea how to bring him back from his meditation, as they hadn't had time to plan this part in advance. Following her best instincts, she squeezed around in front of him on the ledge, faced him, and began to rub his arms briskly with her hands. "Tvrdik…Tvrdik, it's over," she told him. "You did it. They're gone. You can come back now. Let the illusion go, and come back to us." There was no response. Frowning, she tried shaking him by the shoulders and calling a little more loudly, but the wizard remained lost in concentration.

Now Jorelial Rey was growing concerned. She had expected it to take a little extra effort to rouse the mage, after such a long time in his trance. But she was getting nowhere like this, and had no idea how aggressive she could be without doing any harm. She stroked his hair with her right hand, smoothing its pale, golden, windblown tangles back from his forehead. Still no motion – not even the flicker of an eyelid. She stomped a foot in frustration.

"Tvrdik, wake up. I *command* you to return to the here and now," she shouted as loudly as she could, to no avail. Growing more and more alarmed, running out of ideas, and with nothing to lose, she remembered something she'd heard in a tale, long ago in her childhood. She glanced about to make sure they were alone, came up close to him, put her right hand on his hair, stretched up on tiptoes and kissed Tvrdik right on the lips. She pulled back in haste, as the mage's eyelids fluttered, and then snapped open, while he began to sway on his feet.

Rel grasped his shoulders once more, in an attempt to steady him. Bit by bit, the open eyes which at first seemed trained on some far-off shore, began to focus, and the light of recognition flashed in their depths. The wizard's mouth began to move, but no sound came out. He tried to lick his dry lips, but there was no moisture in his tongue. Why hadn't she thought to bring water along with her? He fastened his gaze on her, and half whispered, half croaked, "Jorelial Rey…safe?"

A broad smile of relief lit her face, as she answered him, "Yes, Tvrdik. Theriole is safe. We are all safe, at least for now. It's all over. The ships have gone, and they never even saw us. You did it, Tvrdik. You fooled them. You can relax now."

The wizard, still frozen in place, closed his eyes at the news, and heaved a deep, emotional sigh. He struggled to speak again. "How long?" he managed to get out.

"Six hours. See, the sun is just going down now." He winced at that. "Are you alright? Can you move?"

He blinked and cleared his throat, "I…I'm a bit stiff," he admitted, slowly regaining the use of his voice. "I can't seem to make my arms and legs move…"

She frowned, "I think we underestimated how hard it is on a physical body to stand absolutely still for six hours. Here, let me help you." She searched through the debris in the alcove, found an old wooden bucket, and overturned it to make a seat. At that moment, Mark, Delphine, and Stewart came rushing in, worried that Tvrdik had not yet made a public appearance in his moment of triumph.

"Is he alright?" Delphine called out.

"I think so," her sister replied, "Just really stiff. He's been in this position such a long time. Come and give me a hand here." They all crowded around him and began rubbing down his shoulders, neck, arms and legs. Someone pried his stiffened fingers off of the sturdy oak staff and moved it to a safe corner. Once they had gotten the circulation going, they supported his weight and urged him over to the bucket where he could sit down. It was a bit of a challenge, as his body went in an instant from entirely rigid to boneless. He kept collapsing, and then struggling to regain control over his limbs, while apologizing over and over for being so much trouble. At last, working together, they got him seated on the overturned bucket, where Stewart proceeded to lick his face all over. Laughing at these attentions, concentrating on taking deep breaths, and closing and opening his fingers to get the blood flowing, Tvrdik slowly came back to himself, and asked for a full account of what had happened.

"Why, Tvrdik, don't you know?" Mark replied, "Everyone down there is waiting for you to appear. It's a regular festival, and they all want a glimpse of the hero of the day – the wizard who foiled Lord Drogue's fleet and saved us all."

The young mage turned his usual shade of red, a very good sign that things were returning to normal. "Tashroth?" he asked, concerned.

Rel put a comforting hand on his shoulder, "He's fine. I woke him up first. He's already flying around looking for supper. He said he felt 'invigorated' and asked me to thank you for a very interesting adventure – whatever *that* means."

"But what…what actually happened out there after I went under?" Mark handed over a water skin he had been carrying, while they all took turns relating the events of the last six hours in dramatic detail.

"I have no idea what they thought they were looking at out there, but it is certain they did not see Theriole. They sailed around in circles for the longest time as if they had no idea where a whole palace had gotten to," Delphine recounted.

"I made up a mock seascape to mask the real one, and I filled it with endless, turbulent waters, curling mists, and jagged outcroppings of rock, with no real shoreline in sight…if they believed it, they must have been really confused as to where they were, and why there was no sign of Theriole. I gave them a true seaman's nightmare." He was shocked to hear of the water-nymphs' slightly over-zealous contribution, though he had been the one to suggest that Ondine had more tricks up her sleeve than anyone suspected. "Casualties?" he asked, thinking of Xaarus' mandate.

Rel replied, "Only the one on our side, which, while tragic, is a miracle in itself. We aren't sure about their side. Some of their ships were damaged or sank, but I think most of the men were rescued from the water. We even helped them do that."

"How…?"

Grinning, she explained to all of them the dragons' clever deception, and their secret rescue mission.

Tvrdik's eyes were shining with excitement, as he said to them, "Do you realize what this means? We did what we said we could do. We proved that we could successfully defend the palace, and everyone in it, without lifting a sword, or shooting a single arrow. We used our imaginations and our special skills, we pulled together as a team, and we turned them back. If we ever had any doubts, and I admit I have, we've laid them to rest this day. Now we have a real precedent to inspire us. It isn't just a theory – we've proven it can be done."

Jorelial Rey, while just as elated at their triumph, felt honor-bound to point out the sobering facts, "I wouldn't celebrate just yet. We've won the day, but the struggle has just begun. And the trouble with this method is that everyone on the other side lives to come back and harry us again tomorrow."

"Well," replied the mage, after a moment's thought, "every day alive is a new day for someone to change his mind. Even Drogue could see reason. And, if not, I think we'll be ready for him."

"The question of the moment is," Delphine interrupted, "do you think you can stand up and walk now? There is a very large crowd of fans down there, awaiting a glimpse of you."

"I am sure you are exaggerating, but I am feeling better now…if you'll just get my staff over there…thank you."

He leaned a little on the staff to get up, but aside from being tired and a bit slow, he demonstrated that he could get around, and was almost back to his usual self. "You know, I think I'm a little hungry."

"You're always hungry," Jorelial Rey teased him, "but, I suppose you've earned your board today. What if we all made an appearance on the walkway above the courtyard, and then we can sneak into the kitchens?"

"Now you are talking good sense," Tvrdik countered, and Stewart barked his approval. "Do you suppose we could arrange to skip maneuvers tomorrow? I would dearly love a good, long sleep."

"You and me both, friend, but the trials are coming up in less than a week, and we can't afford to lose momentum."

"Oh, right. Drat." Tvrdik answered.

They made their way, at an unhurried pace, out of the alcove and into the hallway, staying together in case Tvrdik needed any extra support. To the end of the hallway, down one stairway and up another, through another corridor, and down another stairway they went, finally coming out on a walkway along crenellated exterior walls that rimmed the top of the courtyard. Stepping out in the open air, they could see the space below was still buzzing with people, even as twilight rolled in, despite the fact that word had gone out that it was safe to go home. It soon became evident why. A voice cried out, "There they are! There's our Regent and our Court Wizard." And suddenly, all eyes were on them, fingers pointing and more voices crying out,

"They saved Theriole."

"He saved us all…"

"Long live the King!"

"Long live our Regent!"

"Long live our Court Wizard!"

They heard all of these cheers overlapping each other willy-nilly, and then, out of the random shouting rose a rhythmic chant that started with one voice, and gained power and momentum as more folk joined in. "Tvr-dik, Tvr-dik…" the crowd chanted, over and over.

As the sound grew to a deafening peak, Jorelial Rey leaned in close, having to shout over the din, "Well, someone's become quite the celebrity."

Tvrdik started backward in alarm, but was relieved to see her broad smile. "I don't understand it," he replied, "it's…ridiculous. RrreeeDIculous!" Somehow the word needed repeating. "Why are they doing this?"

"Word spreads quickly around here," Mark observed, "and you may have saved all their lives. You're a hero, old man. Might as well accept it."

Delphine chimed in. "Do something. You'd better acknowledge them before there is a riot," she urged, but she was grinning, ear to ear. Tvrdik looked at each of them in turn, hoping for some clue as to what an appropriate response might look like. But each of his friends smiled and took a step back. With a small shrug, he turned to the assembled citizenry and raised one of his hands high in the air, waving to them. The chanting faded, every eye on the young mage who had just accomplished the impossible. Searching for some word or action to answer their eager expectation, and moved by the wave of affection washing over him, Tvrdik moved the hand he had raised in the air, closed it into a fist, and placed it over his heart, bowing his head in a simple gesture of acknowledgement and gratitude. He could not have chosen better. The crowd went wild, cheering for their latest darling.

"Oh, brother," Jorelial Rey rolled her eyes.

Tvrdik was startled by her reaction, "What? Too much?"

"Well, maybe just a teensy bit theatrical," Delphine giggled.

"Now, where would I have learned theatrical?" the mage queried.

This time it was Stewart who answered, "My friend, did you not study at Xaarus' knee?"

"Oh." said Tvrdik, taking his point.

"Come on," urged Jorelial Rey, "No speeches tonight. Let's get something to eat. The man of the hour needs to keep up his strength." She smiled and waved to the crowd, before leading the little group along the wall, through an archway, and down another long flight of stairs. And now, the others recognized just where they were – on the main floor, headed in the direction of the kitchens.

Before they had taken very many steps further, however, they were intercepted by Lord Corbin Maygrew, accompanied by General Boone. Lord Maygrew, his bearded face beaming, strode up to the little group, and took Jorelial Rey's hands in his. "Rel, that was simply brilliant! You have convinced me that you know indeed what you are doing. You too, Sir Mage. I understand you had quite a part in pulling this off." He disengaged from Jorelial and clapped Tvrdik on the back. "Stunning – " he went on, "a *victory* against that dangerous fleet, with so few casualties, and not a blow exchanged. It's remarkable." General Boone hung back in silence, while Maygrew went on, "I have to admit, I doubted that it could be done. But, with a little magic on our side, and a little ingenuity, why, it is miraculous what can be achieved. Congratulations. You've sold me." He was so effusive in his compliments that they were almost unsure of his sincerity. Jorelial Rey returned his graciousness.

"My lord, I am pleased at your change of heart. You will also have a very good opportunity to preview our other tools and strategies next week, at the trials…"

"Trials? What trials could you mean?" he wrinkled his brow. "After today's humbling lesson for those of us who doubted, and after your amazing triumph against a very real threat, I think we can dispense with any further competition between factions. I am sure you agree that it would just be a waste of our energy and resources at this point. If you still believe it is in all of our best interests to face Lord Drogue as Xaarus directs, then I will support you with all of my heart. Count me a friend, and I believe I can convince the other hold-outs to sign on as well."

"Your opinion carries so much weight on the Council, sir – rightfully so – that I would be in your debt. So, to clarify, we are cancelling the trials?"

"Better to use the time in preparation against our common enemy. You tell me when and where the next drill is to take place, and I will be down on the field to observe, and maybe to try my hand. Sound good?"

"It sounds wonderful." She turned to address the General, "General Boone, are you comfortable with this plan? You do have a right to insist upon what was agreed."

Boone had been fidgeting in Maygrew's shadow, head low, expression unreadable. He answered her now in a barely audible voice, "No, no, my lady. No need to waste time debating now. You have proven your point in a real battle. I see no reason to object. You have the reigns from here on."

"Thank you, Minister. I confess this is a big relief. I did not relish the thought of competing with our own valiant troops. It is good to be a single, unified force once again. Together we will be undefeatable, and we will send Drogue packing."

"Amen to that!" Maygrew exclaimed, and the others mumbled some affirmation in kind. Boone remained silent. Maygrew continued, "Rel, don't forget to send me word when your Legion meets again, and I will come. But now, dear friends, I hope you will excuse me. It has been a very long and emotional day. I want to go home and hug my family, and thank the gods that they are safe and well, and that our home yet stands. Minister Boone, young mage, dear Delphine, Mark, pleasure to see you again. I take my leave." He gave a curt little bow to each as he named them, omitting Stewart, as he had never been formally introduced to the canine. He then swept off toward the main doors, leaving them all blinking. After a moment, Minister Boone stepped nearer to Jorelial and muttered, "My Lady Regent, a moment of your time…?" He looked around at the little group that surrounded her, and cleared his throat, "um…in private, if you would…"

"Of course, Minister. Friends, would you wait for me a little further down the hall? I shouldn't be long." Tvrdik looked her in the eye to be sure she did not need back-up, but a nod from her sent him down the hall with the others, trying not to eavesdrop. At the moment there was no one else in this particular corridor, and as soon as Jorelial Rey's companions had moved off a fair distance, Boone sank to one knee in front of her, his head still lowered.

"My lady, this is very difficult for me, but I was wrong. I am ashamed, and I will understand if you see fit to remove me from my position. I no longer deserve to hold it. My behavior earlier was unjustifiable. I never should have doubted you…"

Jorelial Rey slipped an arm under one of his, and urged him back to his feet.

"True, General, but you should continue to question me. It's what still makes you the best man for the job. I know that I can always count on you to give me your honest assessment of any situation, and your opinion, even if I might not like it. I know that opinion is informed by years of experience and training, well beyond what I can bring to the table. I also know that what I have been asking you to embrace over the past months goes against every fiber of your being, every instinct. I understand your reluctance to accept it without proof, and I respect that. What disappointed me was being left out of your deliberations, dismissed, and even defied. If all my Ministers were to go off and act on their own, without consulting or even informing me, then we would have a problem indeed. Had you spoken to me this morning the moment you sighted those ships, I would have let you know that we had an alternate plan in place for fending them off, and we could have decided together to go with yours or mine. It is likely, in any case, that we could have prevented the loss of those three ships, the injuries your seamen incurred, and the tragic loss of one of our most promising young officers." Her voice caught as she recalled Captain Virian's brave sacrifice.

Boone nodded, "I see that now, my lady. I took you to be weak in warcraft – a foolish assumption – and presumed to go ahead on my own."

"What is more, I was not entirely confident that our plan would work, untried as it was, and I was more than grateful that your men were standing ready at hand in the event that we failed to drive off those ships. Did you think I would have allowed the palace to be overrun by invaders? Do you think so little of me that you doubt my sworn commitment to protect those under my charge?"

"No, my lady."

She was pacing, as was her habit in stressful situations, while Boone stood before her sagging in misery.

"If I put myself in your shoes, General, I can appreciate that what you did seemed a reasonable course of action. But, even if you had come home with a great victory, we would already have been ensnared in the trap Xaarus warns could be fatal for us. We are in a complicated situation, and I need you, General. Nobody knows strategy or deployment better than you. No one can reach into the minds of the enemy as effectively and predict their moves. Please tell me we can make this work, and that I can count on you to be my right hand, but on my terms..."

General Boone straightened up as she spoke, and searched her face, almost incredulous. It was clear that he was expecting dismissal, or a severe reprimand, but her plea for his support surprised and moved him. After a moment of thought, he replied.

"My lady, I am an old dog. I am slow to accept change, and I come to it with great skepticism. But, what I saw today was nothing short of miraculous. I know that most of my men feel the same way. The idea of battle may have its seductions, but the reality of it is far from glamorous. It is to be avoided at all costs, unless there are no alternatives. The consequences are too monstrous. No one wishes to leave his children fatherless, or his wife mourning. No one wants to look into the eyes of a man on the other side, and then end his existence. If you think you have found another way, and that it can be as effective as what happened today, then I am eager to embrace it. This morning, I would not have thought it possible. But tonight? Tonight, I hope. I believe." He hung his head again and went on, "If you can overlook my stubbornness, and the slights I gave you, my Lady, then I am your man, and all the Royal Army is yours to retrain and command."

Abandoning her patina of formality, she fell upon the grizzled veteran with a warm embrace, one that was received with awkward, but grateful enthusiasm. "Oh, thank goodness!" Jorelial Rey exclaimed, "I have missed your good counsel. You have no idea how miserable and exhausting it has been to be at odds with you, General. Anything we are preparing for in the field, there is no question you can make better. Please come to the gaming fields on Friday and take a look at what we are doing. I know you will be on fire with creative ways to work with what you see. As for your men – our men – they must be fully apprised of what they are being asked to undertake. Anyone who is not comfortable with the concept must be released with no recriminations. I will have no one on the field who does not in his heart believe in the wisdom and power of what we are doing."

Boone gave her a low bow, and it was no formality. "My lady, you are indeed a generous and wise leader. I will not again underestimate your ability to take us through these perilous times unscathed. I can think of no one else I would rather serve. Thank you."

"I look forward to working together. Get some rest, and please pass on to your troops my tremendous gratitude for their courage and discipline today."

"Yes, my lady, I will." And he took his leave, hurrying with lighter step down the hallway. Before he was even out of earshot, the others reappeared to surround her, Brendelle having joined them in the interim.

"Look who found us while you were with Boone, Rel," Delphine began, indicating her mother. Brendelle and Jorelial exchanged nods as Delphine went on, "How did it go?"

"Another miracle. He apologized, and agreed to join us in our maneuvers and take charge of some of the training."

"What a relief!" Tvrdik exclaimed. "It's becoming more and more difficult for me to pretend I know anything at all about military maneuvers."

"You can stick to what you know best, and leave the strategizing to the General." Rel agreed.

Mark asked, "But is he really on board with our mandate for harmlessness? Seems like that would come hard for an old soldier like Boone."

"It has, but today really turned him around. His plan failed, ours succeeded, and now he is willing to concede it is possible to make the new way work. I think we can feel confident that he will stay within our boundaries, while giving us the much-needed benefit of his expertise."

"That is wonderful news," Brendelle chimed in. "And by the way, congratulations on a brilliant victory today. I've never seen anything like what happened out there. If this is just a taste of what you intend to do, I am proud to be a part of it."

"Thank you, Brendelle. Your support is most appreciated. But now, I must apologize for the loss of one of your ships. I would not have given the order to send them out, had I been fully apprised of the situation. We will see that you are fully compensated..."

Brendelle shook her head. "Don't even think of it. We came to help in a war, and we knew the risks. I am more relieved that all of my men are safe, thanks to the quick thinking and bold actions of your Captains."

Rel winced, thinking once more of Captain Virian's heroism, but decided that this was not the moment to bring up such a sad subject. She nodded to Brendelle, acknowledging the compliment, and changed the subject. "Join us for supper?"

"Delighted."

As they made their way to the kitchens, Tvrdik asked, "So, the trials are definitely off?"

"It looks like it, if Corbin Maygrew makes good on his promise, and he usually does. A bit of a let-down, I suppose, but also a relief."

"More of a relief." Tvrdik agreed.

"You got your wish, at any rate," Jorelial Rey went on. "I suppose we should all take tomorrow off and recover."

Tvrdik sighed, "I welcome that idea. But, you know, the reason I asked just now is because, I have been thinking about it, and – mind you, I am not certain – but I think that the day of the trials is actually my birthday..."

Delphine gasped, "Tvrdik, why didn't you tell us?"

"Well, it's not something I really kept track of in the woods, but the more I thought about it, the more it came back to me. Something about being back here I suppose; Xaarus always made sure there was some acknowledgement of those things for his protégés. This would be my thirtieth, too."

"Your thirtieth?" Rel exclaimed, "Oh, my! That *is* old. You'll have to start behaving like an adult."

"Very funny. Right about now, I feel more like eighty."

"Well, we will just have to do something special," Delphine insisted.

"No, no, I wasn't hinting. You have all been too generous with me already. I only meant to say that the gods have a way of arranging things – it would have been a fine birthday gift to beat the pants off the opposition, but an even better one that the competition was rendered unnecessary."

"Still," Rel said, "We *will* have to do *something* to mark the day…"

"Well, now I'm sorry I mentioned it. Honestly, I didn't mean…"

"Sir!" interrupted Stewart, speaking up for the first time in what seemed like ages, "If ye dinna mind my sayin', in times as troubled as these, and with the brutal schedules we all ha' been keepin', it seems wise to seize any opportunity that presents itself for a festive moment." There was a silence, as everyone stopped walking and stared at the big dog. Rel was the first to break the silence.

"Well said, Stewart. Truly, words of wisdom. Next Monday, then, no competition. Instead: celebration. Ideas will be entertained by the planning committee – that would be myself, my sister Delphine, and Stewart here." Tvrdik opened his mouth to speak again, but she stopped him short, "Ha! No more arguments. We are celebrating your thirtieth birthday, and that is that."

"I was only going to say you are all welcome to come to my house, perhaps for lunch or dinner, or…"

"…a picnic." Delphine cried, "How perfect! It is so lovely and spacious down there by the water. If the weather holds, we can have a brilliant party outside."

"Details to be sorted later. Sounds wonderful, Sweet Pea. Everyone hold the date." Jorelial Rey closed the subject as she shepherded them down the hallway and into the huge kitchen. It was indeed dinner time at Theriole. By now the courtyard and halls were emptying out, as all those who had taken refuge at the palace that day headed for home, and their own suppers. But the regular denizens of the castle were collecting for the evening meal, usually served at long tables in the largest dining hall. Weary, and unwilling to mingle this evening with any lords, ministers, or citizens who would want her ear for one thing or another, or who might just want to rehash the excitement of the day, Jorelial Rey asked the staff to serve her private party this evening in one of the smaller adjoining dining rooms. Its single table accommodated the six of them, as they took a well-earned hour of relaxation, with good food and companionable conversation. Tvrdik always treasured these communal meals; sitting down to supper with the Reys, Mark, Brendelle and Stewart, he always had the feeling that this was what it might be like to have a family. After the extraordinary demands of the day, and the heady attention he had gotten, there was something very normal and centering about sharing a meal with people who knew you well.

They all ate with good appetites, their spirits bolstered by the tremendous relief and sense of triumph they were all experiencing. Jorelial Rey noticed the mage had no trouble finding his usual gusto for the meal.

"I am happy to see you tackling your supper with such enthusiasm," she remarked, chewing on some dark bread. "I confess, I was a bit worried how you would come out of this long ordeal."

"I was famished," the mage replied. "And my only complaints now seem to be weariness and stiff joints, from standing on stone in the same position for so long. Nothing worse. I think I might be growing used to these wizardly activities, or at least doing better at weathering them. Nice to hear you were concerned, though…" he quipped with his crooked smile, and batted his eyelashes at her.

She remained serious, "It's not funny, Tvrdik. Tash came out feeling refreshed and energized when I woke him. But when I went to rouse you, I got no response. You have no idea how many things I tried – I tapped you and called, and then when none of that worked, I shook you and hollered, and poked you. Nothing. You really gave me quite a fright. If I'd had a bucket of cold water, I'd have thrown it over you, but there wasn't any, and I would lay odds it wouldn't have done any good."

"Really? I had no idea it was so difficult. I must have been in a very deep state, and, of course, we never had the opportunity to discuss a plan. How *did* you manage to wake me?" the mage asked with genuine curiosity. "What finally worked?"

Remembering what she *had* done, Jorelial Rey turned a deep magenta, and lowered her eyes in embarrassment. By now, the rest of the table had abandoned all other conversations, and were riveted on this one.

"Yes, Rel, do tell." Delphine goaded, eyes twinkling with mischief, "However did you manage it?"

"Never you mind. I don't even remember, but I got him back, didn't I?" the Lady Regent squirmed under everyone's questioning eyes, sounding more petulant than she meant to, but wishing more than anything that the moment would pass.

"Wait a moment!" Tvrdik exclaimed, "I have a vague memory – it's all starting to come back to me. I thought I was dreaming, but there I was, staring at ocean and fog and rocks, and then, I had the oddest sensation that someone had ...well...had *kissed* me, and then I was looking at your face. That can't be true, can it?"

"Rel, you *kissed* him awake?" Delphine squealed in delight.

"I was running out of ideas. I remembered something in an old fairy story from our childhood, and it happened to work. I told you, it would have been cold water had there been any..."

"Now, Lady, don't deny it. You took advantage of my helpless state; was that fair?" Tvrdik teased, and everyone at the table was howling with laughter, buoyed by good spirits and good food. Delphine was choking back tears of merriment.

Her sister scowled, mortified, and shot back at the whole crowd, "You all are terrible. Terrible. Next time you can handle things without me." At that moment, she thought she caught a look from Tvrdik, one meant for her alone – a look that held her breathless for an instant, one she couldn't quite read. And then, he was laughing along with the others. Continuing to grumble, she turned her attention fiercely to the remaining food on her plate.

When the meal was done, Tvrdik excused himself to go home for the night. Delphine begged him to stay in the castle. "We could surely find room for you tonight. You must be so tired."

"Thank you, Delphine, but I think a walk in the air will do me good, as will a good sleep in my own bed. Besides, I think I need to stop and see Ondine. No one has thanked her for her part in today's affair. I don't think it should wait until tomorrow."

"But it's dark out now." Mark sounded concerned.

For answer, the mage made a gesture and a ball of soft, glowing light appeared over his head. "I'll be fine," he assured Mark, who grinned a sheepish acknowledgement.

Rel nodded, "It is important. Would you like me to come?"

"No, you have other things to attend to."

"Actually, I did have things I wanted to discuss with Tash tonight… would you please convey my formal appreciation, then, and thank her and her friends from all of us? We are in her debt."

"I will."

"I will walk along home with you, Master," Stewart offered.

"And grateful I am for your good company, friend."

Brendelle chimed in, "I will be retiring too, then, if no one minds. I have some letters to write home; they will be most eager for the news, especially of today's victory."

Mark and Delphine held hands and looked into each other's eyes. It seemed they were ready to withdraw as well. But as they all rose to go their separate ways, Delphine turned back to Tvrdik, "I have no words to tell you how grateful we are, and with what awe it fills me to see you in action. You amaze me, Tvrdik." She finished by kissing him delicately on the cheek, the mage blushing as usual, and then hugging her sister and mother in turn. Rel promised to send word out that the next day would be a day of rest for the Legion members, since the trials had been cancelled, but that maneuvers would resume the following day under the scrutiny of no less than General Boone and Lord Corbin Maygrew. Warm goodnights were exchanged all around, as the friends parted company.

Wishing to avoid more long conversations with anyone tonight, Jorelial Rey took as many back corridors as possible, as she headed for the special turret where she knew Tashroth would be waiting. The emotional demands of the day had been draining, but as night fell, she sent up a silent, heartfelt prayer of gratitude for all of the wonders she had seen. So many things could have gone horribly wrong, which instead had turned in their favor. Disaster had been averted, and her kingdom was once again united in common purpose. She climbed the long, winding staircase to the roof with a somewhat lighter step than of late, and opened the trap-door to the warm, starry night. The great, green dragon was awaiting her as she had hoped, and she stumbled to her accustomed place near his heart and slid down to the floor, leaning on his warm breast. The enormous head on its long neck twisted around to nuzzle her ear and breathe gently on her face. She reached up, eyes closed, and locked her arms around that familiar neck in a loving embrace.

"It's been a good day, Tash. We're all going to sleep in our own beds, and Lord Maygrew and Minister Boone were so impressed with our victory today that they have cancelled the trials next week, and come on board with the Legions of Light. Not bad for a day's work, eh?"

"Good news indeed," the dragon rumbled, "but you are tired, little one."

"And what about you? I was so relieved when you came back unharmed from holding that illusion."

"I told you," his voice smiled, "dragons are used to concentrating for long periods – time has little meaning for us. I was pleased our efforts bore fruit."

"I still can hardly believe it, but it worked like a charm – which of course, it was."

"How is the mage?"

"Oh, he took a little while to come to his senses, but he seems fine now. Another relief. He has gone to thank the little naiad for her part in our success."

"That is good. My dear, do not underestimate his abilities. I feel we have only seen the edges of his true power."

She frowned in thought. "Hmmm. Monday is his thirtieth birthday. He just told us."

"An important milestone."

"We are going to hold a little picnic at The Cottage to celebrate. Will you come?"

"It will be a pleasure. It is a good thing – both the gesture to honor, and the return of celebration – we are all in need of a joyful moment."

"Yes. Stewart said the same thing."

"He is wise for a young canine."

"He comes from a remarkable family, I hear. Tash, I want to send an envoy to Lord Drogue and offer him terms to drop this whole thing. Not that I really expect him to, mind you, but after today...well, maybe once he sees it won't be quite so easy to break us, he might reconsider. It's a long shot, but at the very least, it might give us an idea of what is in his mind."

The dragon considered for a moment, then replied, "It is a wise idea, little one. A great leader is generous and flexible, harbors no grudges, and seeks to avoid unnecessary conflict by any means. You should never cease to hope that your adversary will have a change of heart, nor cease to prepare for the possibility that he does not. But yes, offer him every opportunity, and sound him out at the same time."

"Exactly. Thank you. I want to do it soon, on the heels of his defeat, in case we could stave off any further attacks. And, I was considering who to send. Drogue is subtle and dangerous. I cannot go myself, for obvious reasons, nor will I send anyone key to our operations, nor anyone whose weakness, or nearness to my heart I fear Drogue could use to his advantage. I could not send you, Tash, for that reason. He *knows* how dear to me you are. But..."

"You were thinking it should be a dragon, nevertheless..."

"You read my mind. What gave me away?"

"It makes perfect sense. You need someone who could communicate your message and your offer accurately, have the wisdom to negotiate, and would listen and observe in great detail. A dragon could also go and return quickly..."

"...and I would be less anxious that my envoy would be safe. Lord Drogue wouldn't dare try to harm such an imposing messenger, and if he did I would feel confident that a dragon could take care of itself against anything he could conjure."

"I agree."

"Is there anyone you could recommend for the job? Someone you feel sure of, who might be willing to undertake such a mission?"

"There is Candelinda."

"Who?"

"The white dragon who commanded our saurian forces today."

"Ah, yes. I had not been formally introduced, but she did a magnificent job."

"She is bright and powerful and canny. And she is devoted to our cause. She would be a good choice."

Tashroth's voice seemed to positively purr as he described the qualities of the white dragon. Rel wondered if she was picking up on something rare and unusual.

"Do I detect a note of – hmmm – *admiration* in your voice concerning this Candelinda, Tash?"

"When could I ever hide anything from you, dear one? Let us say that I have my eye on her."

"Good luck. She *is* lovely; that much I noticed. I hope the lady finds you equally impressive. Though if she did not, I would have to seriously question the quality of her wits."

Tashroth rumbled with laughter. Rel frowned.

"But if she is special to you, would you not worry about sending her into danger? I would not wish to upset you like that."

"Drogue is no match for her, little one, no matter what his intention. She can take care of herself, and is eager to help. Shall I send her to see you tomorrow?"

"Make it the next day, if it is all the same to you, Tash. I have declared tomorrow a day of rest and regeneration; we are all in need of it. Do you feel up to a trip to the lake? I could be ready in half an hour, and we could stay most of tomorrow…it feels like we haven't been there in such a long time…"

"I am overjoyed at the suggestion. We have spent too much time apart of late. Go. Run and get your jacket, and some provisions, and we can leave as soon as you return."

"Thank you, dear heart. It will do us both a world of good." She sprang to her feet, feeling newly energized, and dashed to the trap door. "I'll be right back. Don't leave without me."

Tashroth winked one enormous eye at her as she disappeared down the stone stairs.

Tvrdik and Stewart took their time on the river path down to The Cottage, enjoying the occasional cool breeze, the clear, star-spangled sky, and a little friendly conversation. Tvrdik's magic glow-ball hovered over them, lighting their way. The young mage reflected with satisfaction that there was no longer a need to keep such things under cover. When they arrived, they were greeted effusively by the Praegers – Lynette bestowing hugs and kisses on the hero of the day, and Mr. Praeger pumping his hand, congratulating him on the remarkable feat he'd accomplished in chasing off Drogue's fleet. Mrs. Praeger gushed, and insisted that everyone sit down to a berry pie (made special so that Lynette could enjoy it as well), fresh from the oven, juicy and delicious. Even Stewart took a good-sized slice. "I enjoy a bit of a sweet now and then," was all he said when the others stared at him in surprise.

Tvrdik felt a bit like he was walking around in a trance, and all the shining faces full of gratitude, and the words of praise that kept greeting him were all meant for some other person that he'd never met. But he managed to smile and accept the compliments with grace, at least on the surface. And pie was always good. He let them know the good news that the trials had been cancelled, and about Boone and Maygrew coming on board with the philosophy of the Legions of Light. He told them that official activities were cancelled for the next day, and that he fully intended to make use of the time to rest and recuperate, a statement with which Mrs. Praeger agreed.

"Don't ye even stir from yer bed until yer body has a chance to recover, sir. We'll do our best not to disturb ye. Ye can come and get me any time ye've a mind to have a bite to eat. Seems to me, ye've earned at least a day off."

Then, attempting to appear quite casual about it, he mentioned, "Oh, and next Monday, the day the trials were to be held, happens to be my thirtieth birthday. Not a big deal, but the Lady Delphine suggested we might celebrate with a bit of a picnic right here on the grounds, if the weather holds. Would that be convenient, if I asked a few friends over, Mrs....?"

He was interrupted with a squeal of delight from the woman, "Your *birthday*? Oh, my heavens. Isn't that wonderful. Nothin' like a birthday for bringin' folks together. Why, of course, we'll make a really special day of it."

"Please, please, don't go to any trouble. Just a quiet little..."

"Nonsense. Yer thirtieth, did ye say? How exciting! A good old-fashioned birthday celebration would be just what we're all wantin' now. Let's see..."

Stewart turned to the wizard and winked at him. Tvrdik sighed, "Well, you and the Lady Regent, and the Lady Delphine..."

"And me!" interjected the dog, reminding him of the designated committee members.

"...and Stewart can put your heads together and do whatever you will. I'll just keep the day open, shall I, and you let me know where and when my presence is requested."

Mrs. Praeger stopped bustling and looked at him with a frown, not knowing whether to take him seriously. Tvrdik was quick to salvage the moment, "Only kidding. Of course I'll be delighted with anything you all plan. It will be a wonderful day, and many thanks."

After that, the young mage insisted on going out alone to find Ondine, and wouldn't hear of taking any companion, a decision that no one seemed pleased with. He tried to reassure them, "I'll be fine, no worries. I won't be gone long, and I'll have my mage-light." As if to illustrate his point, he pulsed the ball of glowing bright light over his head. "You've all been wonderful, but I need a little solitude to collect my thoughts, and I promised I would thank our naiad friends for all they've done. Everything is fine. You can go to bed without a care, and I'll see you all in the morning. Thank you so much for the delicious pie. You really do spoil me, Mrs. Praeger. Good night."

Still hesitant, the Praegers bid him goodnight, Lynette with a final hug around the neck, and retired to their completed quarters at the back of the house. Stewart came over and licked Tvrdik's face once. "Take good care o' yerself, sir. Ye were a hero today, and we're all that proud o' ye." The dog circled several times on the rug before the massive hearth, and settled down for the night with a gusty sigh. Tvrdik reached for his staff, wanting it at his side always, now, and, adjusting the ball of mage light to a softer level, he headed out into the night, closing the door with care behind him.

There was a moon out, not quite full, but the path was well illuminated, and deserted at this late hour. As much as he craved the company of his new friends, there were times when the breathing-space of solitude seemed essential. After so many hours of intense, disciplined focus on the inner landscape of his mind, the rest of the evening seemed too loud and crowded and chaotic. He was probably just tired, but this walk in the clear night air felt somehow calming and refreshing to him, as he made his way along the riverwalk to his special secret culvert on the bank. He was fairly sure he could summon Ondine there, even at this hour. It was a little difficult finding the way through the bushes in the semi-dark, and a little less appealing to be pushing through shrubbery which might be crawling with nocturnal creatures, but with the help of the moon and mage-light, he found his way through to the flat rock, the gentle ripple of the moving water, the whisper of the trees, and the musical hum of cicadas. Checking the rock to make sure he wouldn't be sitting on anything unpleasant, he lowered himself down, knees drawn up to his chest, and back braced against a boulder. He laid the oak staff down nearby, and reached his long arms around his knees, clasping his hands together. In this childlike pose, he sighed deeply, and tipped his head back to see the stars circling in their dance overhead. Sometimes they seemed to call to him as he watched them with a kind of nameless yearning. Tonight, they seemed to pulse brighter, as if smiling down on him in approval. But, of course, that was but a trick of his imagination.

He lowered his eyes in the soft light and looked around. The place had a certain silvery beauty at night, very different from its daytime charms. He sat for awhile, and just let the feel of its peace wash over him. His mind drifted to other times and places, and he found himself thinking of Xaarus, especially of the brief weeks they had spent together in the ancient wood, completing his education. It had been so good to spend real quality time together, just the two of them, talking and learning and working toward a goal. He felt himself wishing that his old Master could be there with him now through the events to come.

"Oh, but I *am* with you," a voice partly in his head said, and he turned to see Xaarus' distinctive profile. The Master was sitting beside him, as real to him as the stone at his back, or the leaves that brushed his face. Tvrdik turned his gaze back to the river.

"It isn't the same."

"I know. But it *is* something."

"True. I am glad you are here. I wanted to thank you for all you did to help me hold that projection, and to support me today. I know it probably cost you a great deal, working for such a long time from such a great distance."

"I tried to help where I could, son, but to be quite honest, I did very little. You did it all yourself."

"Tashroth helped too, and I am happy to report that we succeeded. We made the entire palace invisible, and we confused and fooled those ships, so that they couldn't find us. And then, with a little organized help from the water nymphs, the unicorns, and the dragons, we harried and worried them until they turned tail and fled back to their own ports without so much as a single blow being exchanged. Did we make a difference, Master?"

"You tell me. How did the Palace Council react?"

"Corbin Maygrew cancelled the trials. He said he was won over by today's stunning success, and would make it his mission to convince anyone who still harbored doubts. General Boone apologized for his skepticism, and promised to help teach the Legions battle strategies."

"Why, then, you made an enormous difference. You have proved what a little ingenuity can accomplish. By the dragon's egg, you have gathered everyone together at last under one standard. A few weeks ago, all of this would have seemed impossible."

"But, will it be enough to tip the balance in the end?"

There was a pause as Xaarus considered. The old wizard sighed, "I can't promise you that yet, but I tell you, Tvrdik, that you have already exceeded all my hopes and expectations. What you did today was like the mother bird creating a diversion to keep her fledglings safe from harm. You thought of it yourself, you executed it with great skill, and you protected all of Theriole, as if it were your own nest. You have proven yourself a fine wizard, my boy. But I must tell you that you won't be able to keep them out of harm's way forever…"

"Why not? Isn't that what I was sent here to do?"

"Tvrdik, this might be difficult for you to understand, but, to really tip the balance and shift the events of the future requires a change in the beliefs and behavior of a large number of people. You have made a spectacular beginning, convincing so many to even entertain a new way of thinking. But, your most challenging moments still lie before you, because the real battle will not be waged against Lord Drogue."

Tvrdik stiffened, "What do you mean?"

"Oh, do not mistake me; Drogue will never back down, and he will engage you. But the more desperate conflict will take place within the individual hearts and minds of each and every one who has agreed to participate in this great, historic experiment."

"I don't understand."

"It is the battle to stay true to one's professed ideals and beliefs – to align with the highest aspects of one's nature, and to resist falling into old patterns of behavior when the circumstances are most grim, the hour darkest, and the cost most high. You may *think* you know what you believe now, but I tell you, even you, Tvrdik, will face temptation, and will have to fight to master it."

"But, if I cannot even be sure of myself, Master, however can you expect me to keep everyone else from betraying their principles? It is an impossible task."

"You lead by example, my son. You must overcome your own weakness, and then, with compassion, remind everyone else of the highest vision they have for themselves, and hold them to it. You will know what to do. I have great faith in you…"

"Well, perhaps you should not have quite so much faith. Why did you not explain *this* to me ages ago? I thought I was striving to defeat Lord Drogue."

"You are fighting to preserve the identity of a kingdom, yes. But also to preserve its soul, and the souls of its people for centuries to come. I could not reveal the nature of the real task at hand earlier, because you would not have understood. But now….I wish I could make it easier on you, boy, but if anyone can succeed, it will be you."

"Master, it is so much to consider…"

"You'll figure it out, and I'll be in and out to help you when I can. By the way, happy birthday!"

"I was right then; the sixteenth, is it? I wasn't sure…"

"Don't you remember, we used to use those dates for astrological studies, and sometimes we had a little celebration? I just wanted you to know I would be thinking of you as you cross this important threshold into a new phase of your life. Stay well, my boy. Hold tight to your vision, as you did today, and know you are never alone…"

At that moment, a cold splash hit Tvrdik square in the face, startling him. And, when he wiped his eyes, Xaarus was gone, bare rock and shimmering air where he had been. But turning his head toward the river, he almost jumped to find himself face to face with the very person he had come to this place to find. "Ondine," he breathed, his nose inches from the little blue face, cocked to one side, lovely eyes narrowed. She was hovering in the air just before him, and then, with a *sploosh*, she dropped back into the water. Tvrdik adjusted the glow-ball a little closer to the spot where she had submerged, and brightened it a bit. The curly blue head reappeared.

"Lovely Man, it is night time. Are you well?"

"I am very well, my girl. I came to find you and thank you for your excellent work today. Everyone at Theriole is talking about how you and your friends saved the day. The Lady Regent sends her most heartfelt gratitude and admiration."

Ondine leapt up, somersaulted and pirouetted in delight. "*You* do a great thing, Lovely Man. I see. Hide everybody good, make nasty ships go home. But they stubborn – keep coming. I watch. Cannot let them pass. I say, 'Naiads, help my friends. Talk to water. Push bad ships back where they come from.' We do well, friend?"

"Oh, Ondine, you did very well. If you had not acted as quickly as you did, they might have found us out after all, and there would have been a terrible battle. Please thank the water for us, will you, and all your friends, too. You were a vital part of our victory today. A lot of important people came over to our side after our success. We proved that, working together, we could achieve our goals without violence. An awful lot of good came out of this day's work."

Ondine was beaming, her blue-silver gleam intensified with pride and joy, her slim form in constant motion. "So happy to help, Lovely Man. Could feel people on ships – dark and scary. I do not like them. Taste bad, like poison. Make them go away, leave us in peace."

Tvrdik leaned forward, "Now, dearest, you know I am certainly not criticizing, and I didn't actually *see* your work, being... well, being occupied elsewhere. But, I was told it might have been a teensy-weensy bit more powerful than we needed. Is that true?"

She frowned, then giggled. "Maybe true. We act fast. We feel angry – put our powers all together; make one really big wave. We are surprised how tall it goes, too."

"I understand. Why, you surprised everyone with your awesome strength today. But, you will be careful the next time, won't you? We didn't intend to drown anyone, and you might have hurt yourselves, or the people in the palace."

She sounded a bit defensive, "We do not hurt palace. We aim at ships. Why you worry about men in ships? Very bad men – come to hurt you. Very stubborn."

"I know. You're right, of course, Ondine. But, we all took a vow to try not to harm anyone, yes? We just wanted to scare them away, and we did, didn't we? Thanks to you, and the dragons, and the unicorns."

"And *you*, Lovely Man. You make powerful magic. I see…okay…we practice smaller wave, not drown bad people. Why you say, 'next time'? They go away."

"Yes, but, my dear, we expect they will be back. Maybe not in ships next time, but we are far from finished. They will return, bigger, stronger, and more clever, and we will have to face them once and for all, and convince them that it is not in their best interests to try and steal this kingdom." Ondine frowned again, and muttered something almost inaudible. Tvrdik asked, "Did you say something, dearest? I couldn't quite make it out…"

She shouted back, "I say, you should have let us drown them. Not come back to bother us."

The wizard's response was patient, as Xaarus' recent words flashed through his mind. "Now, now, I know that would be tempting – after all, we didn't start this whole thing, did we. But it isn't what we agreed to. We frighten them, convince them, harass them, defend ourselves from them as best we can, every way we can, even try to change their minds. But, as much as possible, we try not to kill anyone. Then we would be just like them, understand? And then *we* would be the ones who tasted like poison. We are trying to represent a higher road."

Ondine's pretty face pouted for a moment. Then, she smiled. "You good man, Lovely Man. Good heart. It is why I love you." Tvrdik blushed, but no one really saw in the moonlight. "OK. We not harm anyone. Scare them good, but not kill."

Tvrdik shrugged, "It's possible that what you did today was exactly what was needed. Perhaps those ships never would have turned back if they hadn't been severely compromised. We'll never know for sure, and it's more important right now that we succeeded, and everything turned out alright. Just be careful, alright? I worry about your welfare too."

"Silly man. We fine in water always. Big waves like games for us. No fear. But thank you for worry. I worry for you, too, so long to hold picture. Good magic! Hard work. You fine now?"

He smiled. "Yes, I'm tired, but fine. Thank you, dearest. We should both get some rest now. No work tomorrow. The Lady Regent made it a holiday for us."

"Very good thing, everybody rest and play."

"Oooh! Before I go, next week, six days from now, is my thirtieth birthday. I'm a little embarrassed, but I mentioned it and Delphine wants to have a party – a picnic outside, at The Cottage. Will you come?"

"Your birthday? Ooooh! Wonderful time, Lovely Man. Yes, yes, I come. Bring friends. We sing you a song, make you happy." She spun around and showered him with water. Laughing out loud, he reached for his staff, and let it support him as he got to his feet. He was still stiff and achy.

"I am already so happy, dearest, to have friends like you."

She stopped, mid-splash, "Six days? Is that not the day set for trials to prove our strength to Council?"

"It is indeed, and because of your quick thinking today, they have been deemed unnecessary. The skeptics are joining forces with us already. So, we will be having a picnic instead." That brought forth a whole new round of acrobatics and joyful laughter. Tvrdik brushed himself off, and made ready to go home. "Thank you again for everything, sweet Ondine. Rest well. I will see you soon."

She spun around, leapt straight up, and planted a very wet kiss on his forehead, then turned to dive below the surface and disappear. The mage lingered another moment, sighing as images of everything the day had brought, danced through his mind, waiting to be sorted and filed. But for now, it would all have to wait. He could only focus on one thing – most welcome sleep. He turned, the glow-ball both following and anticipating his movements, pushed his way through the lush bushes, and started down the path for home.

"We sank three of the enemy's ships, my lord." Neritz reminded Drogue, who stared down at him from a formal chair of audience, an expression of disgust contorting his handsome features.

"You *lost* three of *my* ships, Neritz."

"My lord, it was all we could do to escape with our lives. You weren't there. It was as if all the demons in hell had been unleashed upon us. I beg you to consider that I have returned to you the better part of your fleet, only somewhat compromised, and most of the men as well. Even this was something of a miracle."

"And what victory have you brought me that was worth the sacrifice of the rest, sir?" Drogue's voice pierced the trembling Captain like an icicle.

"My lord, we sunk three of their ships. Three ships they will not be able to use to oppose you..."

"And is Theriole delivered into my hand?"

"No, my lord..."

"Do you see a crown on my head, Neritz?"

"My lord?" Neritz was growing uncomfortable, and uncertain. How was he supposed to respond? He blinked and sputtered a few more words, but before he could even form a coherent thought, Drogue had sprung from his seat, and was bearing down on him, his eyes all fire.

"How could it be possible that you could not even *find* an enormous, sprawling edifice that can be seen for miles? How can you face me, and claim you never came upon it?"

"Lord Drogue, we searched for hours in every direction. We took measurements with all the instruments we had and consulted all the maps. I had all the most experienced seamen putting their heads together. It simply wasn't there!"

"They must have used some kind of sorcery to veil it, or to keep you out of range. Can you not recognize a trick when you encounter it, Neritz?"

"We found ourselves surrounded by jagged rocks and dangerous whirlpools, and hampered by evil mists that made it hard to see anything at all..."

"You are an idiot and a coward. You should have braved all of that, and come to the palace."

Neritz was almost in tears. "My lord, I had no wish to lose your brand new ships to the whirlpools."

Drogue lashed out at him, "You lost *three* of them! It seems your cowardice did not, in fact, protect you."

"You can't know, my lord. There were dragons everywhere, and a tidal wave that nearly drowned us all, and some sort of blinding lights that came out of nowhere..."

Drogue stood still and collected himself, sounding now eerily calm. "All that, but no Theriole, even though you sailed right up to where it should have been. Well, I am so sorry, Captain Neritz. You *have* had a difficult time of it. All that drama, and nothing to show for it, hmmm? Poor Neritz. You did your best, I'm sure, but you simply couldn't *see* the palace, is that right?" The dark ruler was pacing the floor very near him, and Neritz was beginning to feel a sense of alarm. What was the man working up to, and what had he been thinking, aligning himself with such a madman? He took a single step back, but there were two large guards firmly planted behind him. Fear squeezed his heart in its cold fist.

"M-m-my lord, wh-what would you have me say?"

"Say, Neritz? Oh, you needn't say anything more. I understand. You tried your hardest, but you could not see Theriole. Obviously, there is some flaw in your vision. We must strive to correct that, my dear man...we must help you to see properly. Guards!"

At that last word, before he could even turn to run, Neritz was held fast by the two burly strangers, one on either side of him. Squirming and struggling in their grip, he pleaded, "My lord, please, no! I am ever your man. I will go back again. I will let nothing deter me, and I will find it this time, trust me..."

"Oh, Neritz, I *do* trust you, and good officers are difficult to come by. I don't blame you entirely. It seems my plans are constantly being spoiled by that infernal wizard, lately come out of the woods. He is a nasty surprise, like the hand of that idiot Xaarus come from the grave to put obstacles in my way. No matter. I shall soon find a remedy for the annoying young mage."

Neritz was whimpering, "Yes, my lord. You must dispose of him, my lord. I can see now that it was some spell that held us off. It was not our fault. Surely you can see that, my lord…"

Drogue sidled up very close to the sweating, pale man, and clucked his tongue with a scolding sound. "Of course I cannot expect your little brain to comprehend such complex mysteries. There, there, I forgive you."

Neritz' knees nearly buckled in relief, "My lord is generous and good."

"Yes, whatever. But, I really think we should do something to help with your vision, so that next time, it will serve you better. And perhaps to remind you that I do not expect my commanders to fail in their assignments. It rankles me beyond words. Guards, take him below and remove his left eye. Mind you, the right one is to remain undamaged. He will need that if he is to be at all useful."

Neritz howled, "No, no, my lord, please! Please, spare me."

Drogue laid his hand gently on the man's cheek and purred, "Don't struggle so. It is unbecoming of an officer. You will come to understand that this is fair, and that I have, in fact, been quite lenient in taking only the one. I am feeling particularly sympathetic, and I wish to reward your good intentions. Be off, now. Let's have it over with. Guards, take him."

They did, though he fought them with all of his remaining strength. It did him no good, and his pitiful screams were heard all the way from the depths of the dungeons out across the courtyard, where many in Drogue's employ paused an instant, and swallowed hard, before going about their tasks.

In his Hall of Audience, Drogue still paced the parquet floor, and considered a new plan aloud, although no one remained in the room to hear him. "I shall have to march on Theriole myself," he mused. "We shall meet them head-on, and when I do, I shall have a little surprise for that meddling wizard."

THIRTY-FOUR

A Good Deed, an Envoy, and a Secret Weapon

It was already well into the next day when Tvrdik began to stir in his bed. The Praegers had tiptoed around, attending to breakfast and chores. Mr. Praeger had then gone out to work in the garden, while the Mrs. went off to the market with Lynette, excited about shopping for a birthday picnic. Stewart went off on some errand or another as well. But the mage allowed his body the luxury of whatever time it needed for rest and regeneration, and it took him up on the offer. His sleep was long, and deep, and dreamless, and when he finally woke, he started his day feeling slow and addled – not at all refreshed. He was grateful for a day that held no particular agenda, as he suspected it might take a while to reclaim his natural rhythm and energy.

He washed, dressed, and stumbled out into the empty house, wondering for a moment where everyone had gone. Sun was streaming in through the windows, and poking his head out to examine the sky, he was surprised at what time of day it was. He realized he was hungry, and looking around, found a generous tray of cold breakfast awaiting him on the kitchen counter. There was fruit juice, but he used a touch of magic to start some tea, thinking it's warmth and herbal fragrance might perk him up a bit. He ate and drank in silence, his mind still unfocused, enjoying the flavors and textures, and the gift of a leisurely day. By the time he had finished eating, cleaned up and put away the breakfast things, he was feeling more himself, and had decided to devote the next few hours to a project he had tossed around in his mind for weeks, but had not had time to tackle. He rifled around a bit in Xaarus' supplies for a few necessary items, and set to work.

Several hours later, as the Praegers were just arriving from their various occupations, he was leaving the house carrying the fruits of his labors. He stopped to assure them that he was feeling much better after his long sleep, and that he would not be gone long. With a cheerful wave, he made his way to the front gate and let himself out onto the path. He headed back toward the palace gardens, searching for a certain isolated corner, not far from the alcove where Delphine had held her wedding. This out-of-the-way meadow of wildflowers, surrounded by tall junipers and blooming rhododendron, was where the unicorn herd had chosen to make camp, in order to be nearer the center of activity. The mage, a small bundle slung over one shoulder, strode along the path, peering now and then between bushes and under limbs to find the place. Finally, when he was beginning to be concerned that he might not find them, he ventured down one last obscure side trail, turned a corner, and there they were.

It was now the hottest part of the afternoon, and they were all relaxing, some on the cool ground in the shade of leafy bushes, others standing about cropping grass, tails swishing back and forth in a lazy rhythm. Clearing his throat to announce his presence, the mage stepped into view. In an instant, all eyes were on him. Wynne, their leader, trotted over to greet him, "Welcome, Sir Mage."

"I do not wish to disturb you, unbidden..."

"Please, come within. It is a pleasure and an honor to have you here among us. Is there something we can do for you?"

Tvrdik walked with Wynne deeper into the sheltered grove, and noticed there was a small fountain in one corner with a marble rim just tall enough for him to sit on. Indicating to Wynne with a gesture that he was headed in that direction, he replied, "Well, first, I came to thank you for your part in yesterday's victory. I apologize that it has taken me so long, but I was recuperating myself. I wish I could have seen it, but by all accounts, what you did was magnificent. The Lady Regent sends her best regards and humble thanks, and she also thought you might like to know that, due to our resounding success, the rest of the Palace Council has had to admit we offer a viable alternative in defeating Lord Drogue. They have all come on board with our plan, and the trials that were to be our proving grounds next week are suspended."

Wynne nickered, "That is wonderful news indeed. Though I confess, I half looked forward to seeing all of their faces when we revealed everything we have been working on."

"That, you will still be able to enjoy. Field-work has been suspended today, as I am sure you have heard by now. But, Lord Maygrew and General Boone are coming tomorrow to take part in our maneuvers. You will be able to watch their reactions to all we have planned. But, they are also seasoned veterans, with valuable ideas of their own to add, no doubt. It is a very good thing to have all of our forces at last united against our common enemy: Drogue."

"True, of course. Sir, we appreciate the respect you show us by coming here yourself to bring this news, and acknowledge our contributions, which were relatively slight, compared to your own. But I sense there might be another reason for your visit?"

"Well…yes, as a matter of fact. Since our Lady Regent decided that today should be used for rest and leisure, I found myself with the extra time to work on an idea I've had in the back of my mind for a while now. I think it's ready – a little thank you gift from me. Or perhaps just another part of my healing work, if you prefer…"

"My dear mage, you have lost me."

"Oh, sorry. I suppose I am rambling on a bit. I was wondering if it would be possible to see Shar?"

"Shar? For what purpose?" Tvrdik took the small bundle he had been carrying, untied the strings and unwrapped what was inside. He put aside a small bottle, some bandages, and two small knives. Then, with great care, he unfolded a bit of cloth that protected the last item. When Wynne saw what it was, he gasped, and looked startled. "Wait here a moment," the unicorn spoke with quiet excitement, and trotted away to a shadowed corner of the meadow. A few moments later, he returned, accompanied by the darker, smaller unicorn to whom Tvrdik had been introduced when he first met the herd. Wynne stood by and watched as the wizard, doing a poor job of concealing his nervousness, addressed Shar.

"Hello, Shar. It is good to see you again. Ever since we first met, I have been thinking a lot about you – well, your injury, to be precise. Among my own people, I do a fair amount of healing, as well as magic – part of the job, you know – and I have been trying to think of a way that maybe I could help you. I'm afraid that no amount of healing skill, nor magic, will grow you a new horn. But, in my years of solitude in the wood, I also became quite good at whittling. I had to make myself bowls and spoons and utensils and other odds and ends." He held up what had been in his lap; a perfectly carved, smooth and symmetrical spiral horn, made of wood, and just the right size for Shar's head. The dark unicorn's eyes widened in amazement.

"Of course, it wouldn't have the same magical powers as your original horn, but wood has special magic of its own. This is made from ash, a strong, pliable wood that shares most of the letters of your name, so perhaps you will find a connection in spirit. I also knew that Xaarus had been doing some work on perfecting some very reliable adhesives, which I hoped would serve to attach it firmly. It might look better than the broken piece, and might help you to feel a little more like yourself. Would you… could I have your permission to try it out?"

Shar turned to glance at Wynne, who gave an almost imperceptible nod. The dark unicorn then lowered his eyes and spoke in a timid voice, "Master Wizard, I would be most grateful if you would see what could be done."

"Very good!" exclaimed Tvrdik, delighted, "If you wouldn't mind stepping over very close…I think this would work best if I could carve out some notches in what's left of your own horn, so we can get a secure fit. Would that be alright? I don't think it should hurt…" Tvrdik continued, step by step, explaining everything he was doing to the beast as he worked. He had thought the process through, but found the actuality, of course, a little more challenging than he had imagined. Still, in the end, he had knit bone and wood together in a snug joint that revealed almost no seam, applied the special adhesive, and wrapped the juncture in a temporary bandage.

Shar gingerly dipped his head, then swung it back and forth in a broad arc, testing the new weight on his face. He stepped near to the fountain where Tvrdik sat, regarding his reflection in the still waters. And then, in a burst of exuberance, he kicked up his heels, tossed his head and gamboled across the meadow. Tvrdik rose and called after him, "Hey, hang on there, Shar! Be careful with that. It probably needs to set overnight before it's strong enough for those maneuvers." Despite the rebuke, he was smiling to see the little unicorn's joyful reaction. Shar calmed a bit, trotted around in a circle, neck arched with pride. "Once it sets, we can take off the bandages, and then, if you like, we can stain it black, or white, or any color you prefer. We can even dip the tip in silver…I didn't know what you might like best…" The mage stood there, anxiously awaiting some word of approval from either of the unicorns. Were they satisfied with his hair-brained scheme? He added, "And, if it doesn't hold, or if it ever breaks, you can just come and find me, and we'll fix it right up, alright?" Shar did not reply, and Tvrdik fidgeted with the bandage roll, his face the very picture of a question mark. Without a word, the dark unicorn trotted up to the young wizard, fixed him with a great black eye shining with emotion, and nuzzled his face. Tvrdik raised a hand to touch the place in wonder, as Shar trotted off to his accustomed corner of the meadow, head held high, making sure this time to nod and greet his fellows on the way. Wynne was staring straight at the mage, his expression unreadable.

"Shar is my kinsman. It has been many years since the …unfortunate incident that took his horn. Over the course of those years, there have been times when we have all wondered at the wisdom of Xaarus' having saved the lad's life. That is how devastating his loss was for him, as it would have been for any of us. But, even Xaarus never thought to try anything like this. Today, I almost do not recognize him. He stands tall, dances with joy, engages with the rest of the herd…one meeting only, and you could feel his pain, did not rest until you came to us with a solution. You truly *are* different, Master Tvrdik, most unique among men."

Tvrdik was embarrassed, "Not so different. There are many who might have sought to help…"

"Not so many, in my experience, who would have taken the trouble to come back here and *do* something. It is a great gift you have brought. You have given him back his life. Mage, you inspire in me emotions for which I hardly know words. I am in your debt."

"No, Wynne. Men were responsible for the problem to begin with. It only seems right that one of us should try to repair the damage."

"Listen to me, mage. I am bigger than many of my fellows. When you have need, in the battle to come, I will be your steed. You will ride on my back against the enemy, on to glory and triumph."

"Wynne, you are a king. It is not necessary for you to offer such a thing. It is payment enough to see Shar happy, and perhaps to earn your trust."

"Master Wizard, I insist. It serves both of us for you to consider my offer."

There was a pause as Tvrdik searched the unicorn's face for clues as to how serious he was. Finally, not wishing to disrespect such a generous gesture, he nodded his head, "Yes, then. I accept your offer. You do me great honor."

"The honor is all mine," the unicorn said, lowering his head. Instinctively, Tvrdik offered his open right hand, and Wynne laid his muzzle gently in it. Tvrdik's hand worked its way around to scratch behind the unicorn's left ear, knowing that such was a privilege reserved for a very few, and that he was living a historic moment. In the distance, Shar seemed to be enjoying conversations with several admiring compatriots. Tvrdik smiled. He packed up his equipment, took his leave with a gracious bow, and made his way between the bushes back out to the main path. The young mage glanced up at the sun, which was now far advanced on its daily journey, but seemed to be returning his broad smile with its warm beams. He enjoyed an unhurried stroll back to Xaarus' Cottage. When he arrived, and couldn't stop smiling, both Stewart and Mrs. Praeger asked what he'd been up to. Tvrdik's response was, "Ah, my old master often used to say, 'a wizard's ways are inscrutable – not to be questioned or understood.'" And, still smiling, he left it at that, his mystified housemates staring after him.

Jorelial Rey arrived from the crater lake late that night, feeling refreshed and renewed. A part of her knew it might be considered irresponsible on her part to absent herself for the entire day, just after an enemy attack on home ground. But her instincts told her she could have these twenty-four hours in peace, without incident, and that she would be a more effective leader if she seized the chance for a retreat.

Upon arriving at Theriole, she immediately sent Tashroth off to ask Candelinda to come for an audience, despite the late hour, with an eye toward a special mission. The two dragons appeared atop the crenellated turret only minutes later. Candelinda was even more beautiful in close-up, her hide glistening with faint, opalescent rainbows, and her dark, expressive eyes framed with long lashes. Jorelial Rey was even more impressed, however, with her intellect, enthusiasm, and willingness to take on responsibility, just as Tash had described. The Lady Rey began by praising the dragons, and Candelinda in particular, for their excellent work during the recent battle. She then went on to describe what she needed in an envoy to Lord Drogue, and asked if Candelinda were interested in the job. The response was a resounding, 'Yes!', and Rel felt confident that here was someone she could trust to communicate with clarity and eloquence, to observe with meticulous detail, and to take care of herself and come back unharmed.

With Tashroth adding his own sage advice, they discussed what the Lady Regent was prepared to offer Drogue, what she wanted in return, which were negotiable points or deal-breakers, and what information it would be useful for Candelinda to glean while she was there. Jorelial Rey was happy to grant this dragon broad powers, representing the Crown. She also warned her about Drogue's rumored congress in dark sorceries, urging her to watch her back at all times.

"Do not forget that this man can smile and seem charming and reasonable when he is really plotting stratagems to serve his own agenda. I myself have been at least somewhat taken in by him until recently. I found him tiresome, but never guessed the depths of his ambition and his evil. Be careful. Be gracious and courteous, and generous if he is willing to be turned from his express intentions. But don't let him get anything from you without concrete proofs of his intentions."

Candelinda raised an eyebrow, very like Jorelial's own habitual gesture, and nodded her understanding of all she had been told. She was eager to be off about her errand at once, which suited the Lady Regent as well. But it was agreed that she should take some time first in surveying the situation around Drogue's compound, and not request a formal audience until she was sure his ships had returned with the news of their defeat. The Mountain Lord might be more open to discussion once he had been knocked down a peg in his own estimation. Jorelial Rey thanked Candelinda, and wished her success. But was it only her imagination, or was there indeed a private glance, a word, a brief touch between the two dragons on Theriole's rooftop, just before the white beauty lifted off and winged away in the distance?

"You were so right about her, Tash." Rel mused, watching the small shape recede into the starry deeps. "She is a perfect choice to entrust with such an important task."

"She will do well, and return to us safely." The deep voice answered her, while dragon eyes remained fixed on the distance.

Rel lowered her eyes and scraped a toe over the old stones beneath her feet, then decided to voice her suspicions. She looked up to meet her beloved companion's gaze, "You know your happiness means everything to me. We've never had any secrets from each other, you and I. And she certainly is the rare one I'd even consider to be worthy of you." Her smile held a touch of mischief, "So, is there anything you'd like to share, Tash?"

Tashroth seemed to be smiling, although a dragon's expressions can be difficult to interpret, "We shall wait, and see. She has my attention, that one. Perhaps..." He spoke dreamily, as if he did not realize the words were sounding outside of his own head. He shifted his focus back to Rel, "I might mention a rumor I heard of a very novel tactic someone used to rouse the young wizard from his trance only yesterday, hmmm?"

Jorelial Rey pulled back, aghast. "He was...I was only...there wasn't any...oooh, I am going to kill Delphine!" she spluttered, but the dragon was chuckling.

"Do not worry, dear one. We will always be joined, you and I. Whatever else comes, for either of us, is a cup overflowing." His tone shifted, as he began to tease her, in his familiar way, "Your concern for me is most touching, Jorelial Rey, but I trust you will *not* be planning any unsolicited interventions on my behalf? You will leave things to me, dear, and to the lady?"

"I, interfere?" she jested back at him, "Why, I wouldn't dream of such a thing. No, no, not a word from me. You can count on it."

"Hmmmm… " he growled, and the two of them smiled, faces pressed together in silent communion.

The next morning was Tvrdik's healing day, but, luckily, the patient load was lighter than usual, and he had seen everyone who was waiting for his attentions by noon. Delphine was still helping him on those days when she could spare the time. But, for the last few weeks, he had also invited Andrus to come and work with him, whenever the physician's duties at the palace allowed. Andrus had long ago abandoned his original posture of egotistical protectionism, and was only too glad to have access to Xaarus' legendary pharmacopeia, and the opportunity to see it in action. He was a great help to Tvrdik, making the busy hours pass swiftly. And he was always overflowing with questions that were both insightful and caring. They worked well together, teaching each other techniques and tools from separate healing traditions.

On this day, the three of them attended to all who came in need in the space of a few hours, stopped for a brief lunch furnished by the reliable Mrs. Praeger, and headed out to the fields, where maneuvers were already beginning. Tvrdik was grateful for the lack of patients today, as, while he felt obligated to make himself available for healings, he did not wish to be absent from the field on the day Corbin Maygrew and General Boone were coming to review the troops. As they approached the crowded gaming fields, the mage was deep in conversation with Andrus and Delphine about a challenging case they had encountered. So, at first he did not notice the change that occurred the moment he stepped on the field. Startled by the uncharacteristic quiet which greeted his ear, he looked up from his conversation to see every individual in the Legions of Light - man, woman, beast and magical creature, many hundreds that day, row upon row – all standing at attention before him, still, silent, eyes fixed on him as if waiting for something. Confused, he looked around for the object of all this attention, and then settled his regard on Delphine, hoping for an explanation. She obliged, "It is a gesture of honor and respect. They have all seen or heard about the remarkable victory you engineered just two days ago. They are recognizing you as a great leader."

"What do I do?" Tvrdik whispered, taken off guard and near panic.

This time Andrus answered, "You must acknowledge the gesture, and release them to continue their work." Tvrdik searched the faces of his companions for more, but they would only smile. He squared his shoulders, took a deep breath, let it out, and stepped onto the field, facing the rows of waiting warriors. His eyes scanned the sea of faces looking to him with trust, and hope. Humbled and overwhelmed, he gripped his wizard's staff for support and sank to one knee, head bowed. The field erupted in cheers. Delphine, looking on, shook her head, thinking his response so charming and unassuming, typical of the gentle man she had come to know over the past few months. It was good to know success hadn't changed him one jot. While Tvrdik wasn't looking, she raised both of her hands high, behind him, and waved at the assembled troops in a gesture she hoped would encourage them to return to their labors. Comprehending, they ceased their shouting and whistling, and turned back to the business of the day. Tvrdik, raising his eyes, saw that practice was resuming, and pulled his long frame up from the ground, using his staff for support. With a sheepish expression, he turned to Andrus and Delphine.

"Do you suppose that was good enough?" he asked.

Delphine grinned, "It was…unexpected – rather original, even. And, it will do nicely." She took his hand and gave it a squeeze. Then, spotting Mark, she moved off with Andrus to find their respective units.

Tvrdik strode out toward the benches on the sidelines, where he could watch what was going on. It wasn't long before he was joined there by Jorelial Rey, followed by a very agitated looking Corbin Maygrew.

"There you are, mage! I've been hoping you would appear. You know, what you folks have done here is remarkable: so many creative ideas from so many sources, and many of them do make a great deal of sense. Boone is already out there with the Lady Brendelle, refining technique, or some such. But, I am most fascinated with this 'secret weapon' of yours. It's quite impressive how you've trained everyone in manipulating it, but I can't for the life of me figure out what it is, or what it is supposed to do. Can you explain it to me?" Maygrew was referring to the giant, polished, shield-like accessories that many of the legionnaires were wielding in their varied maneuvers.

Tvrdik patted the seat beside him, inviting Lord Maygrew to settle there. Jorelial Rey had already climbed to the spot on the mage's other side. She was listening to the conversation, but her eyes were on the field, watching what Boone was doing with the troops there.

"It is really the centerpiece of our campaign, Lord Maygrew," Tvrdik began, "but you haven't seen it in action yet, as its true function can only be released through magic. It will be my task in the coming weeks to infuse every one of those pieces out there with special spells and energetic signatures. I haven't done it yet, as, to be frank, I am not at all sure they can be turned off once activated, and that seemed a little too dangerous for practice."

"You, yourself, must activate each and every one? That seems a daunting task, especially if you get little notice of an assault. There must be thousands of them."

"There are exactly a thousand, to be precise, and at the moment, there is no one else capable of that sort of magical work. But I am sure that once I get the hang of it, it will not take long. I've made myself a prototype, with which I have been working, and I am fairly certain that they will do what they are supposed to do. Although, I will admit that the results are a bit unpredictable…"

"But, what *are* they supposed to do? They look like great, shiny shields. Is there more to it than protection?"

"Well, of course, they have that benefit too. They can be quite effective as a shield against conventional weaponry. They are strong, light and resilient, and we are training the Legions in regular defensive moves with them. But that isn't their primary function."

Lord Maygrew rolled his eyes in frustration. Tvrdik laughed and stood up, gesturing to Praeger, who was not far away. "Hallo! Praeger… Praeger! Would you please bring one of those over here? Yes, that'll do. Just bring it up, thanks." Praeger, deducing what was being asked of him, trotted in from the field and up into the stands. He handed his own 'weapon' over to the mage, and stepped back to watch what was going on. The Lady Rey's curiosity seemed piqued as well, though she already knew Tvrdik's intentions for these tools.

It was, in essence, a very large oval shield: lightweight, gently concave, with a padded handle behind. The surface that would face away from the operator, however, was polished until it shone like a mirror.

"My goodness," Maygrew quipped, "I can see my reflection in that. Hair could use a bit of a comb. Hope you aren't planning to embarrass Drogue's mercenaries to death." He chuckled at his own joke, and Tvrdik smiled.

"Well, not precisely sir, but you are not so far off the mark. Pardon me a moment, and I will demonstrate..." Tvrdik sat, and laid the shield across his lap, mirror side up. He placed his hands on it, closed his eyes, and began muttering some sort of incantation in a language no one could quite make out. In just a moment, as they all looked on in amazement, the entire oval began to glow and pulse a bright sapphire blue, radiating outward from the center where Tvrdik's hands rested. The mage's eyes snapped open, and he lifted his hands, carefully turning the shield over in his lap. "There, now, that one's ready. It is my contention, sir, that our most powerful weapon in the present struggle is truth, plain and simple. Therefore, I have infused this shield with the sapphire blue energetic ray of truth, and placed within its structure the *intention* that it should reveal to anyone who regards themselves in its reflective surface only the very core truth of their being. That could manifest in a number of different ways, but, from what I have learned in my studies, it is very likely to stop just about anyone in his tracks."

Lord Maygrew's eyebrows drew together, "That's a remarkable notion, young man, but a little esoteric. I'm not sure I grasp how such a weapon could interrupt a charging warrior with a spear, or stop an adversary with a sword who is bent on cutting off my head."

"Are *you* willing to put it to the test?"

"Why not. I have nothing to fear."

Jorelial Rey, glancing back and forth between the two men, thought that Tvrdik's expression seemed almost mischievous, as he rose, and said, "Alright then."

Without warning, he flipped the shield over, holding it up so that Lord Maygrew faced full on its reflective blue surface. All the cocky sureness drained from Corbin Maygrew's ruddy face in an instant, and was replaced by a look of surprise. His eyebrows arched upward, and his eyes grew wide. His jaw dropped, and his mouth seemed to be moving, but no words formed. For a heartbeat that seemed an eternity, he looked as though he could not tear his gaze from the vision truth afforded him, even at the cost of his life. And then, he threw his hands up in front of his face, blocking out whatever it was he saw, crying out, "No more, mage, no more! By all that is precious to you, I beg you, lower the shield." Tvrdik did not wait for a second request. He flipped over the shield and laid it on the bench nearby, face down. He then joined Jorelial Rey at Maygrew's side. A crowd of curious onlookers were beginning to gather. Boone was heading in from the field at a run, sensing that something was wrong. The Lady Rey had reached Maygrew first, taking him by one elbow and supporting him to a seat. She leaned in to him, "My lord, do you need assistance? Are you hurt?" Tvrdik was at the other elbow in a flash, concern on his pale features. When Lord Maygrew finally lowered his trembling hands, there were tears streaming down his affable face and soaking his grey-streaked beard.

"Ye gods!" he finally uttered in a hoarse whisper, "Remind me, young mage, never to spar with you again. There is something in you of your master. I never could best him in an argument. Somehow, no matter how clever I thought myself, he always had me come away the fool."

Tvrdik smiled, "You are no fool, sir, but a man of courage to put this tool to the test. I pray that one day, if what you say is true, I may count you as close and cherished a friend as my master always did, and still does."

Jorelial Rey intervened, "My lord Maygrew, are you well?"

Maygrew made an odd sound like an attempt at laughter, through his tears. "I'm sure I will be. Give me a moment."

"But what you saw," she persisted, "was it…was it…*so* horrible?"

"Heavens, no! It was …so very *beautiful*, that I could no longer bear to see it."

"Say again?"

"What I saw was, I think, some version of myself, only perfected, shining, shed of cowardice and petty grudges. No more fear or self-doubt, no meanness of spirit. The vision beckoned to me, and somehow, I was ashamed, deeply ashamed, knowing that this paragon was who I was destined to be if I could but strive a little harder, reach a little further. The experience was so profound, so many emotions and longings, I never wanted it to end, and yet I could not bear it."

Praeger, standing by, could not help exclaiming, "But, milord, it were naught but a few seconds."

Tvrdik smiled, "…and, during those seconds, my lord, could you have sliced anyone's head off, or stuck a spear through them?"

"Good heavens, that would have been the furthest thing from my mind. No, I don't believe it would have been possible."

"And so…"

"I take your point."

Jorelial Rey made sure Lord Maygrew was comfortable on the bench, while Tvrdik went on, "You are a man of character and integrity, my lord, a good man. What you saw was not so far removed from the reality of how you conduct your daily life, and yet the vision held so much power over you. For those who are so much further strayed from the potential of their spirits, who have descended so far into darkness and despair, and have perhaps been violent and deceitful and corrupt, the experience may be far more of a shock. They might, in some cases see themselves as the shriveled, ugly thing they have become, or see the beautiful soul they have corrupted. I believe in most cases, it will be enough to turn our adversaries from their course."

Praeger, listening, gulped hard, an expression of horror on his thin face, perhaps imagining the visions he might encounter on the oval shield. Boone had arrived in time to hear this last discourse as well, and it was his voice, that of experience, which now spoke out, "Master Wizard, even if your theory works for the most part, those few hard cases who remain unaffected can still do a lot of damage…"

"That is why we have plans to attack from many different angles and in many different ways. If one strategy fails, our hope is that another will succeed."

Boone asked, "Won't the warrior who is stopped by this…this truth-mirror simply recover his wits in a little time and rise to fight again?"

Maygrew shook his head, "No, no. I think I can safely testify that confronting that shield is a life-changing experience, the effects of which do not soon wear off." He still looked pale, and his eyes were swollen with weeping and rimmed with dark circles. "In this, at least, it is quite an effective weapon."

"Would not the advancing army just adapt, and learn to cover their faces?" Boone persisted.

"Perhaps, but they have never encountered anything like this before, so we have the element of surprise. Blinded, they won't be very impressive fighters, anyway. And, also, the blue ray has a way of drawing the eyes to its magic. In the most difficult cases, I believe I can set the shield's intention to do more than reflect…but I get ahead of myself there, and will not speak of that just yet."

Maygrew was beginning to regain his color and composure. He put a hand on Tvrdik's shoulder, "You have me convinced, mage. I am almost afraid to ask what other surprises you have up those big sleeves of yours."

He smiled as he spoke, and Tvrdik responded with a good-natured quip, "A few perhaps. But, then, a wizard doesn't have to reveal *everything*, now, does he?"

Maygrew clapped him on the back, "I like you, sir. And I am very glad you are on *our* side. I think you had better get busy activating those shields." He rose, nodded to Jorelial Rey, and took Boone's arm, "Let's get back out there on the field where you can teach these amateurs a thing or two about wielding these blamed things." Boone glanced at Jorelial Rey and also gave her an almost imperceptible nod, but one which meant the world to her, and the two of them went off to join the training exercises. Those who had gathered to watch Lord Maygrew's encounter, and its aftermath, seeing that all was well, drifted back to their activities. Tvrdik yelled, "Hey, Praeger, look sharp!" and tossed the glowing shield. "Yours is fully functional now, man. Be *very* careful with it."

Praeger caught the weapon, but held it as if it were made of boiling lava. "Sir, perhaps, some sort of fabric sleeve, or veil for these'd be prudent? Just a precaution, so we don't go around tormenting one another by accident?"

Joreliel Rey chimed in, "That's a terrific idea, Master Praeger. That way, we can be prepared in time without courting disasters with the activated ones."

Praeger beamed at her, "I'll run and speak to my Maihre about it right away, then, shall I? She's bound to have a good idea on it, and could probably round up some of the older folk and women, them as won't be fightin' on the fields proper, to get them workin' on it."

"You do that, friend." Jorelial agreed, "Tell her to use the palace credit lines to purchase fabric and such, and pay wages."

"Hey, Praeger," Tvrdik added, "Ask her nicely. We already have her working hard on my birthday." He laughed, and Praeger waved in comprehension and hurried off, carrying his own weapon far more gingerly than he had before.

Tvrdik sat down on the bench again. "That *was* a good idea. I have been concerned about having a thousand of these things out wreaking havoc with our own warriors, but Maygrew is right – it's time I started finishing the job."

"That little demonstration was risky, but impressive." Rel said. "I knew what was supposed to happen, but seeing it in front of my eyes was quite another matter."

"I am a little sorry to have put him through that, but it seemed the only way to convince them it wasn't just a useless toy. I was pretty sure it wouldn't do him any real harm…"

"Oh, no. I think, in retrospect, it was a good experience for him, and for others to witness."

"Aha. Would you like to try it out next, then?" Tvrdik goaded.

"Me? No thank you. I would never want to be confronted by any deep truths about myself."

Tvrdik's eyebrows raised, "What an unexpected reaction, Jorelial Rey. I can't imagine what you would be anxious about. I was under the impression that you were a pretty transparent, no-nonsense sort of person…"

Now it was her turn to crook an eyebrow, "You'd be surprised. I am, in truth, very complicated and private."

"Oh!" he quipped, in mock surprise.

"In any case," she sighed, "keep those things away from me, thank you very much. But, changing the subject, Lord Maygrew may seem a gregarious sort, but he does not often give easy compliments. I think he is being genuine about coming to like and respect you."

"I suppose that's a good thing, though he has yet to call me by my name."

"Can you blame him? No one likes to be humiliated in public." They laughed together like old friends, and then, Tvrdik sighed, slapped his thigh, and said, "Well, if you are going out there, why don't you spread it around that our warriors can take turns bringing me their shields for activation. I will do as many as I can today."

"Do you think that's wise? Before we have the covers?"

"I think Maygrew is right, and I had better stop procrastinating and get started, so that we are not caught again unprepared." Jorelial Rey nodded, and headed out to the field. Maneuvers only lasted until mid-afternoon that day, when the summer sun became too oppressive to bear. But the young mage sat on his bench until sundown in deep concentration, and poured the blue light of truth into four hundred and fifty shields that day.

THIRTY FIVE

THE BIRTHDAY PARTY

TVRDIK OPENED HIS EYES RIDICULOUSLY early on his thirtieth birthday, and could not seem to fall back to sleep. The house was quiet; no one was yet stirring. Through the open window, he could just see shapes of things beginning to be distinguishable in the grey dawn, and just hear the songbirds begin their first serenade. He rose, donned some plain work clothes, and let himself out the front door, taking great care not to let any stray sound wake the house's inhabitants. A walk, alone, seemed just the medicine for his restless mind and turbulent heart. He headed toward Theriole for a few minutes, until he found what he was looking for – a side path that wound through the gardens before joining the river road again, a ways past The Cottage.

Adopting an unhurried pace, he filled his lungs with the fresh morning air, fragrant with last lilacs and honeysuckle. Most of the irises were done now, but in patches under shady trees, one or two still stood proud and erect, like purple sentinels. The giant rhododendrons were in full bloom, and some of the roses had opened their delicate buds. Butterflies, bees, and hummingbirds were beginning to collect around the flowering bushes, and he stopped to watch their angular, darting dances with delight. The sun was now pushing over the horizon, and color radiated from all the wonders surrounding him, as first light bathed the whole world. He counted at least eighteen distinct shades of green in the gardens this morning. And that was in addition to the fuchsia and magenta, golden yellow, deep blood red, lavender, and a whole collection of blues – so many colors painting the day. The path had taken him up a small hill, an island of higher ground crowned with a few well-placed benches. Tvrdik sat down facing the sea, and gasped at the sky-canvas rolled out before him. The invisible artists of the dawn must have been hard at work for hours on this one. Far in the distance, deep teal waters glinted with sun spangles, while hugging the horizon, swirls of rich orange, deep pink, and saffron gold had been brushed across the sky. Feathery violet clouds sailed lazily through the glowing sky. In the opposite direction, he could barely make out inky shapes he knew to be mountains.

Tvrdik drank in the loveliness of the natural world surrounding him, as a rising chorus of birdsong filled his ears. Realizing how much of life's sweetness he had habitually taken for granted, he let his eyes fall at whim on every distinct marvel of this lovely day. Softly, he uttered his own inadequate prayer, "Bless this day, and accept my profound gratitude for this timely reminder that life is good. Odd, isn't it, that now, with danger and an uncertain future ahead, I have at last discovered how very much I cherish my life. Oh, Spirit, in whose hand rests all of our destinies, if it be possible to grant your humble servant more time – more days to savor your rich gifts – I would be grateful. And I would promise never again to let such blessings go by unnoticed and unappreciated."

He sat for a moment longer on the bench, breathing in the pure, fresh air. As the sun began to climb higher, and the brilliant colors of the sky all turned to cerulean blue, he stood, stretched, and headed back toward The Cottage. He took his time, and all along the way, his heightened senses seemed to magnify every small detail. It was as if each perfect thread in the tapestry before him glowed and pulsed with an inner light, and knew its unique place in the grand plan of all-that-is. Arriving wide-eyed at his own front door, he uttered the familiar words, "Bless this house," and meant it, from the bottom of his heart.

The house was still quiet, but now because everyone had wakened and gone out about their various tasks. On the dining table was a small plate of bread and fruit, and a note from Mrs. Praeger that read, "Save yer appetite for the party." Tvrdik chuckled, thinking how novel it was for Mrs. Praeger to encourage him *not* to eat. She must have quite a feast planned for the party. The *party*, he mused, sitting down to his fruit and bread. He had tried to convince the committee not to expand it into a state affair – just a few friends, and a picnic outdoors by the river, he had begged, and he thought he could trust them to comply. It was looking like the weather would cooperate as well, and he was beginning to feel excited, anticipating the festivities.

Those were still many hours away, however. For the moment, he finished his breakfast, washed, dried, and put away the dishes, so they would not be in Mrs. Praeger's way when she returned. Then he went back to his chambers and set about the business of preparing for a special occasion. He bathed, shaved, washed his hair, and decided on the blue robes, which were clean and light enough for a warm, sunny day. He ran an approving eye over himself in the glass; his face scrubbed and clean-shaven, his pale golden locks swept back from his temples, and the blue of his fresh robe bringing out the unusual color of his eyes, behind their ubiquitous spectacles… "Well, that's about as good as it is likely to get," he remarked, to no one in particular, and shrugged. But, it was still early, and no one was home. Looking for a pleasant way to pass the time, he stepped into Xaarus' great library, combed the shelves until he saw something that caught his attention, and settled into the big comfortable chair for a few hours of stimulating reading.

Three pages later, he was fast asleep in the chair.

He was running through a field, warm sunshine caressing his shoulders and the back of his neck, green grass and many-colored wildflowers springing up around his bare feet. He looked down to see his leggings worn and patched, and short for the gangly, thin legs of a growing fourteen-year-old. He was running as fast as he could, but ahead, he could see Benjin and Ailianne, together as usual, unwilling to wait for him. He saw them halt in their tracks and turn to face him, his heart almost stopping to see her as she looked then, flowing golden hair and lovely face, intelligent eyes free of care, free of fear. Then he realized that the two of them were pointing at him and laughing, making fun of the boy who couldn't quite keep up. Ailianne's laughter rang out like little tuned bells, so beautiful – and so cold. He called out to her, and tried to go toward them, but he found he could not move. His feet had disappeared in the long, green grass, and had become rooted, reaching deep into the fertile earth below.

He stretched out his arms to where his schoolmates had stood, but they had vanished, and now his arms were stiffening, and sprouting branches, shoots, and buds. From his head, more limbs snaked and stretched upward to the sky. With a tree's inner rhythm, and a dreamer's perspective, he watched the seasons roll by in endless parade – bud to leaf, flower to fruit, ripe fruits plucked and enjoyed by passers-by, leaves turning color and becoming brittle, then falling away into piles below, swirling about his face as windy gusts spun them up and away. Snow falling through skeletal limbs, drifting into dunes below, then melting in spring's pale sunshine. Birds lighting on his branches, and pouring out their hearts in song. Life coursing up from the earth through his veins, and flowing upward through his outstretched limbs. The entire cycle again and again, over and over in fast motion, until he saw Xaarus come along, bright and happy and whole. The Master plucked one of his fruits, as the seasons ceased their spinning progress, and bit into it.

"Mmmmm. This is delicious, boy," the old wizard said, "But, you still have not half fulfilled your destiny." Xaarus waved a shining wand at him, and at once, where he thought his shoulder blades should be, something new sprang forth, and began to grow and unfold. Wings, pale golden and feathered, massive and eager to try the currents of the air. His tree form melted away, as his feet were released from their bondage, and he soared upward, great wings beating the air. He wheeled and looped and dove and climbed upward with glee, reveling in his newfound liberty, and the feeling of sun on his feathered limbs. Xaarus was laughing, and waved at him from below. Then, in a flash of light, he was a large, white owl, hovering in the air, and when he turned his sharp gaze toward anything on the ground, he could see right through whatever it was, to the very core of its being, down to the tiny molecules and atoms that danced and trembled to the music of the spheres, and shone with living lights. The white owl cried out with a piercing shriek, and pumped its mighty muscles, coasting closer to earth. It stretched its great wings wide, but one was caught on something, would not respond, and was flapping about wildly...

Tvrdik's consciousness surfaced to the odd sensation that his left arm was shaking around all by itself. Confounded by this phenomenon, he opened his eyes to see Stewart tugging and worrying at one blue sleeve, which the dog held firmly in his mouth. The arm just went along for the ride. It fell limply to the wizard's side as the dog let go his hold, and the hapless book fell from Tvrdik's lap to the floor with a resounding thud. Stewart sat down.

"A very happy birthday, sir," he offered. "I am that sorry to wake ye, but it's gettin' on with the day, and yer guests are already startin' to arrive. We thought ye'd want to greet them."

The mage stared at him sleepily for half a moment, blinked, then sat bolt upright. "Oh, my goodness! The guests? My party. How long have I been dreaming?"

"I could not tell ye, sir. We all arrived home to find ye dozin' in the chair here, and did not wish to disturb ye until now."

"Goodness, what a dream I had! But where is the day going? Of course, we should go and welcome everyone. Thank you, Stewart." He stood, rubbed his eyes, then set about smoothing out his wrinkled robes and tousled hair with his hands. Placing his glasses squarely on his nose, he stood before Stewart. "How do I look?" he asked, with a great deal of uncertainty.

"Like a man about t' be the center of attention." Stewart was a born diplomat. "Off wi' ye, now. Mrs. Praeger has quite the feast comin' along, and Lady Delphine has arrived with a sack full of plans for the day."

"Oh, my." said Tvrdik, with a touch of alarm, and followed Stewart out of the room. The moment they entered the hallway, his nose was greeted with a variety of delicious aromas coming from the kitchen, and he could already hear laughter and conversation drifting in from the parlor. Any hint of trepidation melted away, and a wave of happy anticipation washed over him. What delightful promise this day held!

And the promise was more than fulfilled. All of Tvrdik's newfound friends were there, and a few extra guests to boot. Stewart and the Praeger family were all in attendance, being his housemates, along with Jorelial Rey and Tashroth. Candelinda was still away on her assignment. Mark and Delphine had brought Nyree along as a special treat, and had also hired a small consort for music and dancing later on the lawn. Bargarelle came, and Brendelle; Verger, with his charming wife Sallia, and Warlowe and his wife Danelli. Andrus was there, and Ondine showed up around back with some of her naiad friends, spending time in the river and in various basins and tubs throughout the day.

The food began appearing almost at once…and kept coming in waves for the duration of the gathering. There was green salad, cabbage salad, potato salad, and bean salad, all made with ingredients fresh from the garden. There were seven different cheeses, soft and hard. There were sweet breads and savory breads, puddings, and a hot summer squash and onion pie that was scrumptious. There was fresh fruit, preserved fruit, dried fruit, and candied fruit. And later on, of course, there was a very special birthday cake, and a whole tray of the little custard tarts that Tvrdik loved so much.

"You know, after the great naval standoff at Theriole," Bargarelle remarked, "the Palace Chef heard how fond you are of these little pastries, and has taken to calling them Wizard Wheels, after you." That bit of information turned the mage a deep red, and brought on a great burst of hilarity from all present, as various guests made suggestions for alternate names, such as Tvrdik's tarts, or mage-muffins. Unfortunately, all of these appellations seemed to have double meanings that had the entire company rolling on the grass in paroxysms of laughter, until Tvrdik scowled at them all in mock disapproval.

There was fresh milk and aged cider, cold tea, and a seemingly endless stream of wines. Tvrdik had been avoiding fermented beverages for a very long time, as they did not mix well with magical concentration. But he decided to make an exception for this special day's festive occasion, and most everyone partook liberally throughout the day.

There were games. Delphine had taken it upon herself to arrive with a list of competitions testing skill, speed, intelligence, and luck, so that there would never be any opportunity for boredom during the celebration. With a basketful of silly prizes and her usual charm, she wheedled, cajoled, threatened, bargained, and seduced the guests into participating, but, in the end, everyone entered into the various contests in the spirit of fun and playfulness. No one could best Stewart for speed and agility, or Bargarelle for memory and knowledge of trivia. But there were other events that required cooperation, or steadiness, or balance – like walking from point A to point B with an egg balanced on your outstretched downturned hand – where unexpected heroes emerged. There was quite enough glory to spread around. Except that the birthday boy himself grew frustrated with losing badly in every category, and began to use magic to cheat, right out in the open. In response, Tashroth stepped in and plucked up Jorelial Rey by the collar, stretching out his long neck to deposit her a few feet ahead of Tvrdik in his magical winged boots. This elicited loud protests from the other participants, shouts that changed quickly into uproarious laughter, leaving everyone breathless and spent.

There were, of course, gifts. Tvrdik was overwhelmed at their variety and generosity. There were scented candles, and journals of finely tooled leather, pens, and colored inks. There were belts, and tunics, and a knitted wool scarf. Lynette offered him a handmade pottery mug which she had helped to make herself, all painted with bright flowers and smiling suns. The mage wondered if she could see what a priceless treasure it was to him. Andrus presented him with a rare and fascinating old text on contagious diseases and their treatment, a thoughtful and personal gift. Brendelle's gift was a good-sized jar of an exotic spice from her own country, one she said was among her favorites. Mr. and Mrs. Praeger had constructed him a special wooden chair that actually rocked back and forth when you sat in it —very calming. When they had found the time to construct such a piece confounded him entirely. Ondine and her compatriots brought in a great bundle of a certain type of seaweed plant which he had once told her was very useful in creating healing balms. They had located a source, and took pains to gather it themselves. It would be most useful, and Tvrdik was both impressed and grateful.

From Jorelial Rey and Tashroth, there was a floor-length, dark, heavy woolen cloak; hooded and embroidered in silver thread with sun, moon and stars – a wizard's symbols. It was beautiful, the workmanship fine, and would be useful for the cold months, for which he owned no suitable garments. Tvrdik was moved at the thoughtful choice. As he opened his last gifts, Stewart was rolling around upside-down on the grass, enjoying a thorough back-scratching, Ondine was leaping in and out of the water, ecstatically splashing anyone who came near, Lynette was running in circles, fully intent on a small pinwheel he had given her to play with, and a contingent of his guests were forcibly settling Mrs. Praeger in a chair, insisting on serving *her*, after her continuous ministrations all day. They assured her that they would take charge of bringing in the birthday cake. The sun was hanging low on the horizon, marking the approach of evening, and it seemed a perfect time to acknowledge the odd twists of fortune which had brought his life to this place in only a few months.

Here he was, surrounded by friends who were generous, loving, creative and playful, even in the face of imminent danger, who seemed to genuinely enjoy his company. He had work and purpose. He had hope of helping to accomplish their shared goals. He cast an eye again on the mountain of gifts before him, and back out again on the busy assortment of companions scattered about on the lawn, and smiled, realizing that this day had truly been as much about lifting their spirits as it had been about him. Delphine and Stewart had been right; for this one day, at least, dark thoughts were pushed aside, as everyone threw themselves with whole hearts into celebration.

As the oversized birthday cake, decorated in fresh raspberries, was wheeled in by Brendelle and Sallia, Mark, Delphine, and Nyree presented their birthday gift – a ballad Mark had written to immortalize the turning back of Drogue's navy from Theriole. It was quite a robust and catchy piece, Mark having quite the gift for tune-crafting, and after a number of detailed, poetically- rendered, and suitably embellished verses, everyone present was joining in the chorus:

> *He held the vision in his mind*
> *That what they sought, they would not find.*
> *They wandered aimless, as if blind,*
> *And left their hopes and pride behind.*
> *All Hail, Tvrdik the victor!*
> *The wizard who carried the day –*
> *He sent them in tatters away.*

With each verse the company grew louder, more confident, and more raucous in their performance, the sweet voices of Nyree and Delphine and Mark rising like rays of golden sunshine above the merry noise of the crowd. Only Tvrdik was silent, eyes closed, torn between tremendous pride, and a feeling of horror, to be so singled out in song. Truly, it seemed as though they were singing about someone else – a mythical hero in some dim and distant past. When the last chorus had finished, all eyes turned toward the young mage for his reaction. Embarrassed, Tvrdik stuttered, "It's…it's really quite a wonderful song…very beautiful, indeed, but…but, don't you think that some of the tale might be just a bit, well…somewhat… exaggerated?"

Even the staid Nyree burst into laughter at that, along with everyone else. Delphine exclaimed, "Silly, it's *supposed* to be a little…um…*enhanced* for the sake of the ballad. It's called, 'poetic license.' Anyway, I don't think Mark changed much…we were there, don't forget."

"So, how does it feel to be immortalized in song?" needled Bargarelle.

Tvrdik frowned, "Like you are all talking about somebody else." There was more laughter, and then someone shouted, "Speech! Speech. Let the birthday boy make a speech." And the chant was taken up by everyone present until Tvrdik held up his hands for silence.

"My dear friends," he began, "and I do not pronounce those words lightly – up until this time in my life I do not think I ever really knew what friendship was. Anyway, I am glad to have provided an occasion for such delight, such fun and festivity in each other's company. All of us have been burdened of late with heavy responsibilities and the threat of imminent danger. It warms my heart, in the midst of all that, to share a day like today, and see smiles all around. Stewart and Delphine, you were so right to remind me how healing a celebration like this could be, and I feel sure its glow will lighten the days ahead, as we recommit ourselves to our work.

"Many thanks to all of you for coming and making my birthday such a memorable occasion, especially to the members of the planning committee who managed to organize the whole thing in only a few days. And a special thank you should go to Mrs. Praeger for her tireless efforts at keeping us all well-fed and happy." Here there was hearty applause. "But, more than all of this, I want to thank all of you more than I can express for taking me in, a penniless stranger, and making me a part of your family. I look down at this assortment of thoughtful, meaningful, and generous gifts, and I am overwhelmed. I don't really know what I have done to deserve any of this, but I do know that I have never felt so loved or valued in my entire life. This is, indeed, the happiest birthday I have ever experienced, and that is due to all of you. So, from the depths of my heart, I can only say, *thank you.*"

There was an awkward silence as the guests lowered their eyes and shuffled feet, moved by the mage's words, but uncertain of an appropriate response, until some wise soul chanted, "Cake! Cake! Bring out the cake."

There was laughter all around, and one by one, the entire company began to take up the chant. Sallia and Brendelle cut and served cake to each guest, while some still restrained Mrs. Praeger from rushing to the task herself. She had outdone herself on this delicious creation. And there was more wine for the guests as well. After they had all had their fill, the little consort Nyree had brought along tuned up, and there was dancing for an hour on the lawn. But not the stuffy court dances popular at palace affairs. Rather, they played the earthy, traditional jigs and line dances favored by the ordinary folk in village and countryside. Even Tvrdik, isolated as he had been, remembered some of the steps from his youth, and with Delphine's patient encouragement, did not embarrass himself any more than the rest. It was an atmosphere of non-judgment and abandon, folks circling and skipping and laughing until they were all breathless and exhausted. By that time, it was becoming difficult to see in the deepening shadows, and a number of the guests offered warm salutations and farewells, and headed off to the palace or their homes. Tvrdik thanked each departing friend with a warm, personal embrace. Ondine christened him one last time with an affectionate splash, and a wet kiss on the cheek, before sailing off downriver. Then, while Mark, Delphine, and Brendelle lingered to help the Praegers straighten up and put things away, he found himself sitting in the parlor, sharing a last glass of wine with Jorelial Rey.

They sat in companionable silence for awhile, aware they were both a little tipsy, and Tvrdik unable to keep from smiling – a sort of broad, silly smile that reflected his whole mood. At last, he broke the silence.

"Dear, *dear* Jorelial Rey, I want to thank you for the beautiful cloak. It is a most practical and generous gift."

"You're welcome. It occurred to me that you didn't have a proper wrap for the winter. It can get awfully cold, here, you know, when the wind blows off the ocean..."

"Still, you are expressing a lot of optimism with that gift, are you not?"

She wrinkled her brow, "How do you mean?"

"You are assuming I shall be here to use it when the cold months arrive."

"Here, there, anywhere you like...use it in good health."

"No, I mean you are assuming I shall *survive* to use it."

She was taken aback, "Now, why in heaven's name would you say a fool thing like that at the end of a near-perfect day? Why would you even *think* something like that? It's a fine time now for doubts about our likelihood of success..."

His eyes drifted to the floor, "I have no doubts about our success. I have only been thinking that we can't expect to walk away without some losses..."

"Have you seen something, then? Do you know something about the future that you haven't shared? Did Xaarus tell you something?"

"No, nothing like that. I was never very good at that particular component of the wizard's art anyway, and I haven't talked to Xaarus since we fended off Drogue's ships. I don't know. Maybe it's the wine, or the strange dream I had this morning that seemed so full of obscure messages I couldn't quite grasp. Maybe it's instinct, or a natural inclination to melancholy, but I've been thinking a lot lately about how different my life is now – how blessed I am to have a purpose, and friendship, and a place in this community. I was sent here on a mission, and sometimes I think that when we have accomplished our goals, life will have no further use for me. If any of us perish in the battle, it should be me, as I will be content to have experienced more than I ever dreamed possible."

She shook her head foggily, "Tvrdik, you're talking nonsense. I have no intention of losing *anyone* in this conflict, let alone the one person who understands all of our offensive strategies. Don't be in such a hurry to lay down your life for the cause; you'll serve it a lot better alive and in one piece."

He sighed, "You're right, of course, but even so, I just want to tell you that if this birthday, my thirtieth, were to be my last..."

She put up a hand, "Tvrdik, stop."

"No, just hear me out. If it *were* to be my last, I would go happy and content because of these last few months. I want you to know that coming to know you...and your sister, and all the wonderful people you have brought into my life, has enriched it beyond anything I could have imagined. I can't thank you enough."

"Now, you really will have to stop talking, or you will have me going down that road too, and *that*, my friend, is simply *not* a good idea."

There was an extended pause while they both sipped at their wine, and then Tvrdik mumbled, half to himself, "I should have liked to have seen my waterfall one more time, though. I'd love to have taken you there and showed it to you. It is… so very beautiful."

The tone of her response was impatient, tight, "Well, as far as I'm concerned, the sooner we get this whole business over with, the better. This waiting is agony. I would like to get the job done, defeat Drogue, and save the kingdom once and for all so you can go back to your little hut in the woods, and play with your waterfall to your heart's content, and I can get back to some semblance of a normal life. Then, everything can go back to the way it was before you showed up and turned it all upside down."

The moment the words came out of her mouth, she realized what she had said, and instantly hoped that perhaps she had only thought them. She looked up to the certain proof that she had indeed spoken them aloud, to her everlasting regret. Tvrdik's silly smile seemed frozen eerily on his face while his eyes flashed pain from the wound she had just inflicted. Then, before her eyes, in seconds, she saw him shift – his relaxed, open, vulnerable manner retreated behind layers of cold, heavy armor. It was as if she saw the breath of winter move over him from waist to crown, and gradually freeze every part of him, until his eyes grew guarded and unreadable in his expressionless face. She leapt to repair the damage.

"Tvrdik.…Tvrdik, I'm sorry! I didn't mean anything by that. Of course you are very dear to me…none of this was your fault, anyway. It's just the wine talking…and…and just that so much has changed since you came. Sometimes, I wish I could go back to a simpler time, when I wasn't Lady Regent, and responsible for a zillion important things, wondering if there isn't someone lurking around every corner trying to kill me." This last tumbled out all in a rush.

His voice was cold, "I quite understand. I don't blame you. I suppose it would seem that I have brought nothing but bad news and crisis into your life. I wish the circumstances could have been different…"

"Tvrdik, don't let anything I said upset you. I should never have had so much wine."

"Don't worry, my lady. Very soon now, we will be confronting the challenge that has been set for us, and before you know it, godswilling, I will be able to return to the woods you have so kindly deeded to me, and you can resume the life you remember as normal." He spoke softly, weighing each word, carefully delivering them in a cordial, formal tone, but his entire body was trembling with contained emotion. His guarded eyes revealed nothing. He rose from his chair without warning, and put his glass down. "If my lady will excuse me, it has been a very long day, and I fear I have also overindulged a bit. I find I am suddenly very tired. I trust you will not mind if I take my leave. You know the way home?"

"Tvrdik, don't be like this…please listen to me. I was just being childish. Come on, don't let it spoil the whole day." She was on her feet, tugging on his sleeve in desperation. He turned back to her and softened a bit, but the expression she saw break through his reserve was just sad and weary.

"Please go, Jorelial Rey. I think I let myself wander into territory a bit too familiar, and you were just speaking your heart. There's nothing else to discuss. I'm tired now and need to sleep. Tomorrow we'll be fine."

But she could see that they would *not* be fine at all. They would be cordial and efficient, and work together and get the job done, alright, but they would never be fine. "Please, Tvrdik, I beg of you, don't go like this. Don't go…"

At that moment, a deafening sound of rushing air drowned out anything else she might have said, as both of their heads snapped around to face the front door. A moment later they were standing in the doorway looking out at a new arrival on the front lawn. Candelinda had returned from her mission.

THIRTY-SIX

THE UNRAVELING

Tashroth was by Candelinda's side in an instant, nuzzling her and assessing her condition. Other than weariness from her long flight, she seemed to be whole and unharmed. Tvrdik seized a torch from the wall sconce, and he and the Lady Rey ran out to greet the returning messenger. Mark, Delphine, and Brendelle were close behind. Tvrdik held the light high, as Jorelial Rey addressed the white dragon, "Greetings, Candelinda, and welcome back. Are you well?"

"I am well, my lady, and eager to report."

"Good girl. Were you in any way ill-treated or threatened?"

"No, my lady. I was received as a distinguished guest, and treated with some hospitality. At no time was I overtly threatened or ill-used. However, my instinct was that this was largely because it suited Drogue's purpose of the moment, that I should serve as *his* messenger."

"Meaning?"

"He is preparing for war, my lady, by land, and has assembled a formidable invasion force. He did not hesitate to show me much of his army and equipment, holding back a few surprises for later, I am sure. His intent, I assume, was to impress me with his superior power in the hopes that I would come back and frighten you all into surrendering your claim to the throne."

"Is that what you are doing now?'

"By no means, my lady. I only relay the unpleasant facts. We will face a large and well-equipped foe, and it will not be long before they are at

520

our doorstep. By my observations, those who follow him are unlikely to follow codes of honor, or to be easily dissuaded from their intent by any appeal to a higher sense of right. We will have to double our forces and our efforts in probably less than a month to be ready to face him with any hope for victory."

"Dragonsbreath…" muttered the regent, while Tvrdik closed his eyes and sighed.

Candelinda went on, "Drogue is cocky and overconfident, however. He underestimates us by every measure, and has little intelligence of what we are practicing. We have the element of surprise and justice on our side; I believe we can defeat him."

"Did he speak of the rout of his ships?"

"He sneered at his own commanders, called them 'incompetent children,' and congratulated us on our use of a 'neat parlor trick' to confuse them – his words, my lady."

"Yes, I understand. And all of my offers extended for a peaceful resolution?"

"He allowed me to communicate them, my lady, but gave them no serious consideration. He is fixed on his own ascension to the throne - nothing less - and is expecting it to be as easy as plucking a ripe apple from an unguarded tree. As I said, he does not really listen or observe, and may be surprised at the resistance he encounters."

"Candelinda, friend, you have done well, and I am grateful and relieved at your safe return. You must be tired. Can we get you anything?"

"I am happy to be of service, my lady. Rest is all I require now, and I will take it with your permission, and come to you tomorrow with further details of all that I saw and heard."

"Very well. Tash, go with her, please, and see her needs are taken care of. I will walk back to Theriole. I need to clear my head."

"Is that wise, dearest?" Tashroth's deep voice inquired.

Delphine was quick to reassure him, "Don't worry, Tash. We'll all go together; she'll be alright."

He nodded, gave a gentle nuzzle to Jorelial Rey's hair, another to Candelinda, and the two of them rose into the air with a power and grace that left those on the ground staring after them open-mouthed. The two dragons banked in synchronized flight, circled once, and receded into the starry sky in the direction of the palace. A fat sickle moon hung low in the sky, having only just appeared above the horizon. The Praegers had finished tidying up the house and grounds, and put Lynette to bed, and had joined the small company on the lawn watching the dragons fly off. It was a few moments before Jorelial Rey broke the silence.

"I would suggest we all try to get a good night's sleep now; starting tomorrow, there will be very little rest for any of us." Her eyes were still fixed on the far-off point where the dragons had disappeared, but they were seeing things to come.

Tvrdik was also still looking off in the distance. "So. It has come," he murmured, all at once very sober.

"Not yet, but soon. Now it is certain. There is so much more to be done, and so little time."

Delphine was next, "I know you will say this isn't like me," she said, "but I'm feeling a cold chill run down my spine. I think I'm frightened."

"Good!" retorted her mother, "We should all be frightened of men like Drogue, and know what we must face. And then, we must stand up against them anyway. Fear will push us to work harder, prepare better. Courage will give us the strength."

Mark pulled Delphine closer, his long arm circling her shoulder, and lifted his chin in defiance, "We will be ready for them."

"Yes, we will," Tvrdik nodded.

There was another long pause.

Without warning, Jorelial Rey grasped the mage's sleeve and looked up at him with eyes that pleaded, "Tvrdik...what I said before..." He looked down at her, and seeing her vulnerability at that moment, he had an almost irresistible urge to gather her into his arms and assure her that everything was going to be alright. But she was the Lady Regent, and he had been burned already this evening. He stood immobile. The moment passed.

"Let it go," he told her. "There are far more pressing issues that demand our attention now. It is no matter." Jorelial Rey bowed her head.

Delphine stepped in and hugged the wizard. "Happy birthday, Tvrdik, and many, many more to my dear, dear lucky charm."

He hugged her back, incapable of resisting that dependably generous heart, "Thank you for everything, sweet girl. You made it very special."

As they parted, Mark reached out to shake his hand, "Many happy returns, sir."

"Agh! Please don't call me 'sir'. Thank you for the song, Mark. I am honored."

Mark smiled broadly. Brendelle kissed the mage on both cheeks, looked him in the eye, and whispered to him, "Youth, you know, is over-rated, confusing, and painful. It gets better from here on. You'll see." She winked at him, and to his surprise, he nodded to her with the hope and certainty that she, of all people, knew what she was talking about.

Now it was Jorelial Rey's turn to bid him farewell. She was standing a few feet away, uncertain as to what to do. Tvrdik straightened up and gave her a little formal bow, "Deepest thanks, my lady, for all you did to make this a memorable day. And for your very generous and thoughtful gift."

The Lady Regent stood for a moment regarding his face, as if searching for something. Then, she inclined her head in his direction. "My pleasure, mage. I am happy you enjoyed it all. It was the least we could do for such an auspicious occasion. We will be hearing Candelinda's detailed report tomorrow after lunch. We would appreciate your official presence at her interview."

"Of course, my lady. At your service." And he bowed again.

Delphine's brow wrinkled at this public display of formality, "Rel?" she queried.

"Let's go home, Delphine. I'm…I'm tired." Delphine, still puzzled, glanced back and forth between her sister and the mage, but Jorelial took her arm, and headed for the gate. The little party of four let themselves through onto the riverwalk, and disappeared into the night.

Tvrdik turned to the Praegers, "What can I possibly say to thank the two of you for this day? I will never forget it. Every day I bless the heavens for sending you both into my life."

Mr. Praeger shook his head, "Whether ye'll have us or no, I fear ye are stuck with us now; we are for ye, thick and thin."

Tvrdik put an arm around each of them and hugged them close.

"Goodnight, Sir."

"Goodnight, friends," Tvrdik replied, and watched them retire to their quarters in the rear of the house. Only Stewart remained. "My good companion," Tvrdik stroked his furry head, "it was a lucky hour when I met you as well." Stewart's eyes closed while he enjoyed the mage's touch. Then he licked Tvrdik's hand and said, "A very happy birthday to ye, sir, and many more years to celebrate. I am proud to be a friend to ye, and ready to fight beside ye if there is need."

"You have always been there for me, Stewart."

"Would ye mind if I slept outdoors tonight, Master Wizard? There's a fair cool breeze in the yard, and the house feels stuffy to me after so much eatin' and drinkin'."

"Of course, wherever you are comfortable, friend. I will be chasing after dreams myself in a few moments. There will be much to do tomorrow, so sleep well." Stewart padded out toward the garden, while Tvrdik took the torch back into the house, and shut the door behind him.

And now, night fully upon him, Tvrdik stood once more alone in the big house. He made his way to Xaarus' old bedroom and sat down on the edge of the bed, rehearsing in his mind some of the highlights of the day. So many wonderful people gathering to help him celebrate, and all the effort and thoughtfulness they had put into the planning, the food, and the gifts. So many well-wishes, along with all the music, laughter, and good fellowship spun about in his brain. But, then, even as he was beginning to feel valued, like he belonged somewhere at last, Jorelial Rey, of all people, as much as tells him outright that she can't wait to be rid of him, so that she might return to her former normal life.

All right. That wasn't precisely accurate. But he had come to think of her as something more than just his partner in a grand enterprise. They had saved each other's lives, laughed and joked together, shared intimate details of their awkward youths, their hopes and dreams, private sorrows. He had begun to see her as a kind of kindred spirit – a lone wolf reaching out for some connection. She was, in fact, his best friend. He had learned to cope with the thornier side of her personality: her impatience and occasional barbed tongue. He had admired her as a courageous and charismatic leader, well-suited to the role she had inherited. He adored her keen intelligence, her dry wit and unerring sense of right, and underneath it all, her vulnerability and good heart. He well understood how difficult it had been for her to assume so much responsibility during a time of danger and uncertainty. It was a lot for her slight shoulders to carry. Of course there might be times when one might want to just run away and return to a simpler, unburdened time. She could have confided that to him as a friend, and he would have listened, even sympathized. But instead, she had lashed out at him as if he were the source of all her woes. If all he was to her was a symbol of the moment when things changed for the worse – a jinx, a harbinger of bad news, a constant reminder of how unpleasant everything was, well, then, he had misjudged their relationship indeed. That made him feel foolish, and exposed. How could he have so misread their time together, thinking they were growing closer? He should never have forgotten her superior rank and position, which put her far out of his league.

And why did any of this matter, anyway? He knew they would continue to work well together. They knew how to do that. They respected one another's skills, and were both committed to the Legions of Light, and to securing the kingdom for its rightful heir. With a war so nearly upon them, wasn't that all that was important now? And why could he not end this day warmed by the hundreds of loving, affirming gestures, and happy moments he had enjoyed, instead of perturbed by one enigmatic person's single petulant outburst? Tvrdik sighed, and began to undress for sleep, although he doubted it would come to give him peace anytime soon.

At Theriole, in her own bed, a somewhat unusual occurrence stemming from Tashroth's involvement with Candelinda this night, Jorelial Rey was tossing and turning. Weary beyond exhaustion, she should have fallen asleep as soon as she laid her head on the pillow. Certainly, worries over Candelinda's report and the looming reality of imminent battle disturbed her rest. It assaulted her mind with a thousand questions, a thousand more tasks to address, and preparations to initiate. This was to be expected. But, what surprised her was that every few moments, her rebellious brain would replay that brief, but awful conversation in the parlor with Tvrdik. Not the lovely events of the day – the feast, the sunshine, the playfulness and celebration, the laughter that buoyed everyone up all afternoon. No. Only the last five minutes, which had spoiled everything. Each time she went over the scenario in her head, she tried to stop herself from letting the ugly words tumble from her mouth unchecked. But, there was no return. They had been said, and heard, and they cut like a knife. Tvrdik had been so happy before she ruined it all with her childish remark. She had tried to explain, tried to tell him that it was only what one little disgruntled part of her felt, that she knew events would have turned as they had regardless of his arrival, and that he had only come to help her face them.

Oh, why couldn't she have chosen to communicate the *other* truths that were equally clear to her: that she never could have made it this far, or confronted the struggle ahead without him; that she found it strangely new and refreshing to have had a human friend in whom to confide; that she had truly enjoyed their playful banter, their sharing of depths of themselves long hidden, even their easy working relationship. In so many ways, life was much better for her since the young mage had come along. And yet, she had as much as told him that she couldn't wait for him to go back where he came from, or worse, that she wished she had never met him. A fine thing to say to a friend on his birthday! *Sometimes, I just can't stand myself,* she thought, then sighed and turned over again. *But why am I so stuck on this? With so many life-and-death issues to consider, and so much at stake, why am I obsessing over one unfortunate conversation? And why do I care what he thinks, anyway?* Clear as starshine through her window, the answer came back to her, *because I do care what he thinks. I care about him far more than I am ready to admit.*

Candelinda gave her report the following day in the Hall of Audience, in front of the Lady Regent, the Court Wizard, Brendelle, Verger, Lord Corbin Maygrew, and General Boone. Smaller than Tashroth, she could just fit her head through one of the side windows while everyone else sat inside. Warlowe manned the door, as always. Tvrdik and Jorelial Rey maintained their cordial, but awkward formality with each other, as neither wished to be the first to re-open a painful subject. This approach was probably a mistake. The longer their awkwardness went on, the more firmly it became locked in. Those who knew them well could not help but notice the sudden chill, but felt it was not their place to question, especially with other matters of great importance on the table.

Candelinda let them know that Drogue boasted of having up to ten thousand troops at his disposal – a harrowing figure, to say the least. He might have exaggerated somewhat for effect, but not by a lot. The mountain lord had proudly showed her exercises in progress, and with a shrewd eye, she had noted the composition of his armies. Some seemed to be foreign mercenaries, lured by gold or the promise of land. Some were conscripted farmers and peasants from Drogue's own realm and some of the neighboring ones. These were not seasoned warriors, and were probably paid, coerced, bullied, or seduced into service, along the lines of Praeger's story. A small portion of his force were the original standing armies of the mountain states, and there was a contingent of magical creatures…

"Magical creatures?" Tvrdik exploded, "They fight for their own doom! If Drogue is victorious, it will seal the fate of *all* magical creatures; they will eventually cease to exist."

"*We* may know that, with the benefit of Xaarus' hindsight, but *they* do not." Candelinda responded calmly, "It is a sad thing, but many of us are just as gullible and easily turned by greed or glamour as humans are. In any event, he has a small company of mountain gnomes, perhaps half-dozen or so griffins to fly for him, and some of the winged horses. Among them is Valour, one of the most powerful and respected among them."

There was a silence, everyone's eyebrows knitted together in thoughtful frowns. Jorelial Rey shook her head as if to clear it, and ventured to comment first, "Alright. So he has numbers. But with this intelligence of his obvious intentions, coupled with the news of his recent naval attack, I feel sure we can drum up more recruits from the countryside. It is time to send out a royal decree to all parts of the kingdom calling for volunteers. There's a lot of positive sentiment out there for King Darian on the heels of his coronation. Many regional lords saw Drogue's behavior at the Grand Council, and will not be surprised. The catch, of course, is getting them all on board with the philosophy of the Legions of Light; I will not impose it on any who are unwilling. But for those who will join us and embrace our methods, we still have time to equip and train them."

Tvrdik jumped in, "Those of Drogue's soldiers that are bound to him by promise of wealth or by intimidation, perhaps we can seduce or sabotage away from him with our own hijinks. At the very least, they will be confused. With all the dragons on our side, we still have some advantage, and we have the assistance of the water sprites and the trees…."

Candelinda added, "It is always possible that some of the magical creatures have not heard both sides of the story, and might yet be persuaded that changing sides would be in their own best interests. With your permission, my lady, I will try to arrange a quiet meeting with the winged horses and griffins. Not sure we would have much luck with the gnomes. They can be stubborn and greedy."

"We'll have to rely on the blue shields for them, and for the rest. But do what you can with diplomacy." Jorelial Rey was pacing now, hands clasped behind her back and forehead down, as she always did while brainstorming. "What say you, General?" Boone had looked as though he wanted to add something, but was reluctant to interrupt. Now, he cleared his throat.

"I wish to remind Lady Rey that numbers are of far less consequence than strategy and wise preparation in a pitched battle. A key factor now is for us to control where the major battle will be fought, and to have all our surprises in place before he arrives."

"How do we do that?" Brendelle spoke for the first time.

Candelinda interjected, "I told you, Drogue is conceited and over-confident. He believes he will beat you any day of the week, under any circumstances. We could deploy almost anywhere we choose and expect him to come and meet us. If we wait too long, however, he will beat us to the punch."

Boone jumped back in, "That's my precise point. We do know a little of how his mind works. He will want to march straight for Theriole, having failed to take it by sea. Eliminating the true King...and yourself, my lady.... will be his prime objective, and seeing himself crowned and enthroned at the palace will be a close second. These being his goals, he will not care how much chaos and devastation he might cause in the surrounding farms and villages. That is flawed thinking on his part, since all the infrastructure he would destroy would be his to repair, should he win..."

"Heavens forbid!" Lord Maygrew shouted, horrified at the suggestion. But General Boone continued, energized to be allowed to hold forth at last on one subject in which he excelled.

"Yes, yes. I apologize for my digression, but we must understand his thinking. As we are a professed people of peace, he will expect us to hide behind the castle's defensive fortifications, and force him to lay siege. He is confident of succeeding at that, even if it is long and destructive. He will not expect us to be courageous enough to ride out and meet his forces in pitched battle somewhere on an open field."

"And why would we do *that?*" Maygrew asked.

"That, sir, is *exactly* what we *must* do. It is what we have been training to do. We must not let him get anywhere near the palace at all. We must protect the king…as well as everything in the surrounding area that Drogue would put to the torch. It is for us to plant ourselves on his way where he cannot avoid us, and force a pitched battle, winner take all."

"Will he take the bait?" the Lady Regent asked.

"Drogue is proud. He will not care where he meets us. He will expect to run roughshod over us and continue on to Theriole unimpeded. But our strategy will be to choose our location wisely – a place where we are removed from civilian activities that could be a worry, where we are somewhat hemmed in, but cannot be backed into a corner, where the trees and the waters are easily available to do their part, and there is room for our aerial forces to maneuver. An ideal spot would also have some sort of elevated positions where our generals could observe and direct the game. In a place like that, we would be ready for him. We could have every advantage set up in advance and a few surprise snares he could not begin to imagine. Only as a last resort, if things did not go in our favor, we could still fall back to the castle fortifications."

Tvrdik smiled, "General Boone, you are a genius. *This* is what I meant when I suggested that intellect should triumph over brute force."

The Lady Regent was also excited, "Welcome back, General. There is indeed a reason you are Minister of Defense."

"Thank you, my lady, but it is my job to understand these things…"

There was a bit of a commotion at the door. Warlowe seemed to be arguing with someone in low tones that gradually became too intrusive to ignore. Every head turned toward the entrance, to see Mark standing there, Warlowe trying to urge him back. The Lady Regent held up a hand and called out, "It's alright, Warlowe." She strode over to the doorway.

"Mark, what are you doing here? Is anything wrong?"

Mark stood tall and met her gaze. "No, my lady. I hope you will forgive my presumption. I realize that under normal circumstances, a bard would not be privy to what goes on in these chambers. But, as a founding member of the Legions of Light, I felt I should have some idea of our adversary's strengths. I'm afraid I was listening at the window and heard all that General Boone said about a perfect site for the battle. I believe I could be of some service here."

Corbin Maygrew rolled his eyes and made a helpless gesture of frustration, but Boone said, "In what way, lad?" At this point, Jorelial Rey gestured for Mark to enter the room, Warlowe relaxed and shrugged, and Mark approached the General.

"Sir, I am a mountain boy, born and raised. I know well the terrain that Lord Drogue, and his forces, would have to traverse to get here. And, I believe I know a place very like what you were describing. I think it might suit our purposes."

"Go on, boy."

"It is a pleasant valley, larger than it seems at first glance, just this side of the mountains, in the foothills. It is uninhabited at this time of year, carpeted in meadow and wildflowers, and rimmed on three sides with rocky escarpments where one can look down and take in the bigger picture below. These heights are accessible by goat path. We often pasture our flocks in this place. The river runs right through the valley, along the rock face on one side. But there are also wooded areas and copses of trees scattered about."

Everyone present exchanged glances, eyebrows raised. Boone grasped Mark's arm, "Young bard, are you free tomorrow to take me on a little tour of this promising place?"

"I will arrange to be free."

"We can ride out at first light."

Jorelial Rey shook her head, "Might I suggest that Tashroth could take you? It would be quicker and easier. Mark, could you find the place by air?"

"Of course, but wouldn't a dragon arouse suspicion?"

Candelinda replied, "Drogue will have no reason to turn his eyes in that direction. But I will go along, if it please my lady. To any stray glance, it will look like two hungry dragons hunting game in a likely spot."

"Go, with my blessing, Candelinda. All of you report back to me on your return. Thank you, Mark, for your...most helpful intrusion."

Mark bowed to her with a smile and Tvrdik winked at him. Candelinda caught the gesture and added, "One thing the great Lord Drogue does not have in his service is a real Wizard. He fancies himself to be somewhat versed in the black arts, and enjoys showing off his conversance with magic. But it is, for all I can tell, superficial and sloppy. In this, my friends, we are obviously at a clear advantage," and she swung her great head around to regard Tvrdik with an enormous, unblinking eye. The mage, both startled and flattered, felt his face redden as he bowed to her.

"You are most kind, Candelinda, and you all know I will do everything in my power to stop this usurper in his tracks – everything short of inflicting deliberate harm on him or any of his followers. I know we can beat him without becoming like him."

Corbin Maygrew put a hand on Tvrdik's shoulder, "I hope you are right, Master Wizard. I have great confidence in you, and lord knows I have experienced your talents firsthand. But there is much riding on these shoulders, lad. Our lives, our hopes, our futures all depend in large part on your gifts, and on your being right about all this."

Tvrdik paused a moment, feeling the weight of that assertion. "Lord Maygrew," he responded at last, "I know I am right about our methods, because I have been told by my Master, and because I feel its certainty in the very core of my being. With Xaarus guiding us, you will have not one, but *two* wizards at your service until the matter is settled. But when, and I say, *when* we triumph, it will not be his or my triumph alone, but that of so many gifted and dedicated folks that will win the day – all of us here and yourself included. The beauty of our plan is that we all play a part in its success."

Bravo, thought Jorelial Rey, but then moved on to another concern, "I want to go back to what you said a moment ago, General Boone, about the king. You said Drogue's first goal was to eliminate his competition, the rightful heir to the throne."

"Yes, he would need to do that in order to insure the succession for himself and his heirs."

"So, shouldn't we be going to greater lengths to protect His Majesty? What if, heaven forbid, Drogue were to break through our lines and make it to Theriole with even a small contingent? The king would be left vulnerable. We could lose the very jewel we fight for."

"Go on..."

"We might assume Darian is safest behind the castle walls, but perhaps there is a better solution."

"Do you have something in mind?" Corbin Maygrew frowned.

"I propose we allow Drogue to continue to *believe* the king still resides at Theriole, while we have actually spirited him away to a secret location. Somewhere Drogue would never think of looking. That way there is one piece of his nefarious plan that remains out of reach, and one source of anxiety removed from our shoulders."

Maygrew considered, "It is a very good idea, but where would you send him? Where would be the least obvious place for Drogue to look?"

The Lady Rey wrinkled her brow, "I'm not sure. Any ideas?"

Lady Brendelle spoke up, "One of my ships could take him immediately to Euligia. He would be safe and most welcome there."

The Regent shook her head, "A kind offer, lady, but you will forgive me if I balk at trusting our last royal scion to the sea after recent events. Besides, fleeing the kingdom altogether could be taken as a symbolic abdication."

Tvrdik suggested, "What about your secret lake retreat? It is very sheltered, and only accessible by air…"

Jorelial Rey seemed to consider, then sighed again, "There is no infrastructure there for his comfort and care, and no easy escape if he is discovered."

"Xaarus Cottage?" Tvrdik offered, but then he challenged the idea himself, "I suppose Drogue would certainly know to search there, and even with magic, Theriole would be better defended."

"What about your little hut in the woods? Nobody knows about that…" the Lady Regent continued to brainstorm. The confused looks that came from everyone else in the room supported her assertion of the place's remoteness.

"Oh, I don't know," Tvrdik responded, his nose wrinkling in distaste, "it's awfully small and very rustic…"

"Let me think on it. I'll try to come up with something soon. Any other business or discussion?"

No one spoke.

"Very well. Good work, everyone. I think we each know our individual tasks for the moment. Meeting adjourned. Oh, wait! General Boone, how long do you think we have – best guess?"

The grizzled veteran stroked his beard, "Well, the hottest days of summer are not the best times to force march a large army. But, Drogue won't be able to afford supporting a force like that for long, and he'll lose his peasants and farmers at harvest time. So, I'd say three weeks, a month at the outside."

A sober silence.

The Lady Regent finally spoke again, "My friends, every day counts. Every hour. Pour your best into everything you do now, and may the heavens help us. Tvrdik, this afternoon we need to convene a brief meeting of all the Captains in our Legion to inform them of all that was discussed here. May we do that at The Cottage?"

"Of course, my lady. I will see to it right away." She nodded, and everyone turned to take up their appointed tasks. Candelinda pulled her great white head back through the window, as the others filed through the big oak doors, nodding at Warlowe as they passed.

"Warlowe," the Lady Regent called, "You are dismissed from your duties here. Would you go and round up the others?"

"Yes, my lady."

She turned back to Tvrdik, who was last to leave. "I'll see you, then, at The Cottage in two hours?"

He nodded, paused, thought better of saying anything, and pressed past her into the hallway. Jorelial Rey looked after him, sighed, and went off to find Tashroth.

THIRTY-SEVEN

PREPARING FOR BATTLE

In the weeks that followed Candelinda's return, activity around the palace soared to a new level of intensity. Messengers were sent out all over the kingdom warning of the imminent threat of war, and recruiting volunteers for the defensive force. Many provincials were moved to join up, and had to be outfitted, equipped, briefed on the new philosophy, and, if they were willing to embrace it, trained.

A fair number of would-be soldiers backed away in shock at the prospect of facing Drogue's army without any traditional weapons, and Jorelial Rey insisted that no one should be coerced into service if they were not comfortable with the non-violent imperative. But, a surprising percentage of the newcomers were excited about becoming a part of something ground-breaking. If they stayed long enough to witness a demonstration of what the Legions had been practicing, they were usually won over. There was also a contingent who weren't exactly thrilled with the new directives, but were loyal patriots, and were willing to do whatever was asked of them in support of the rightful ruler of Eneri Clare. The result was that the Legions of Light did in fact double its numbers in a scant few weeks, to about seven thousand strong. Original members were now busy training small groups of newcomers in every planned maneuver, and assigning them to special task forces according to their talents. Tvrdik occupied himself activating all the blue shields, and fitting them with the cloth covers Mrs. Praeger and her team were turning out. These sleeves proved an effective accessory, designed for quick and easy removal, and folding up, small and light, when not in use.

Tvrdik also reviewed every other strategy, tactic, and idea they had come up with since the formation of the Legions. He assessed their usefulness, rethought and refined the best, and made sure the appropriate arm of the Legion was well-prepared to implement each. In this endeavor, he consulted at great length with both Xaarus and General Boone. Brendelle, Stewart, Andrus, and Nyree, all commanding specialized units, also spent time with him poring over details. Xaarus was pushing himself hard to remain accessible during this crucial period. The old wizard understood from a unique perspective just how much was at stake in this war, and was beginning have deep regrets at not being able to be physically present for the events to come. Tvrdik felt his Master's solid confidence in him at every contact. But they both had moments of secret doubt that it might all be more than a little overwhelming for one fairly green mage and an army of inexperienced idealists. Tvrdik could sense the unexpressed hint of concern in Xaarus mind.

"Master," he blurted out one day, "I know the odds against us are formidable, but you, yourself, sent me on this mission. Do you now have doubts that it can be done? That...that I...that all of us together can achieve a victory?"

"No, no, son. That isn't it. You must know how proud I am of you. But, now that this battle with Lord Drogue is no longer merely an abstract, I am wracked with guilt about sending all of you into the storm without being there myself to protect you. In some ways, this is really my fight, and I have forced it on you."

"This is a fight that belongs to all of us, and would have come to the kingdom in any case. You have gone to extraordinary lengths to help prepare us, to give us every advantage from your perspective, to pass along your warnings and your good counsel. It has cost you a good deal to keep re-initiating this link, I know it has. I cannot imagine how we would have fared without it. It would have been wonderful to have you standing here beside me in the flesh, directing things with a sure hand, as in bygone days. But, since we haven't yet figured out how to do that, I am grateful for the assistance you are giving us."

"I know. But, even from the future, I can give you no guarantees. There are only likelihoods and probabilities. For all of my skill and foreknowledge, I am operating on faith quite as much as you are. Faith and hope."

"Faith and hope are powerful allies, Master. You taught me that. You always said that we must do our utmost to prepare, and to strive, and then we must rely on faith and hope to carry us the last lap. That philosophy has brought me a great distance already, and I can hold fast to it in the face of nearly anything, so long as I know you are still behind me."

"My dear boy, trust me when I tell you that I can imagine no one to whom I would more willingly entrust this task. You have grown to be a fine wizard, Tvrdik, and have exceeded my expectations in every way. I am honored to have been your teacher. I also think we have a good plan, here – one that will take Lord Drogue in his arrogance quite by surprise."

"Good, then. We will turn him around and around until he does not know which direction is up, and then chase him all the way back to the caves of his forefathers if need be. And, if the gods be willing, someday you and I will sit with a tankard of ale, and reminisce about the glorious battle we once fought together with neither sword, nor bow, nor pike, and we will sigh that things have become as dull as they will be then."

There was a twinkle in the old mage's voice as he murmured, "Tvrdik, you amaze me. So be it, then. Now, go back to the bards – let us discuss once again how they may best be used..."

With General Boone, the young mage would explain every detail of whatever plans he had discussed with Xaarus. He wanted the veteran warrior to comprehend and approve every tool they had in their war chest, and to feel confident teaching them to his own soldiers. Boone needed to be able to lead the Legions of Light into battle himself, knowing what tricks he had at his disposal. Often, the General would suggest a refinement to what Tvrdik brought. Usually his ideas were genuine improvements, which Tvrdik acknowledged with appreciation. Boone never dismissed any of the mage's strategies out of hand. He had learned that most things Tvrdik proposed held power and merit. In this way, the two former adversaries grew in respect and admiration for one another, and began to see themselves as colleagues working toward the same goals.

Meanwhile, the Lady Jorelial Rey was also tackling her crowded days like a whirlwind. She worked with the Council and the Royal Guard to shore up all the fortifications that protected Theriole, signing work orders, requisitions, and budgetary releases. She visited all the training camps on a regular basis. She hoped these visits might boost morale a bit, while she took note of particularly talented individuals she might need to finger for future service. Following Candelinda's suggestion, she sent Stewart, Wynne, and Shar on a covert mission to try to talk some sense into the magical creatures now committed to Lord Drogue. It was a long shot, but any advance blow they could deal him would help. She had decided that sending dragons would be too conspicuous, and so asked Wynne to represent her in this matter. When he introduced her to Shar, and explained how Tvrdik had ministered to the dark unicorn, she enthusiastically agreed that he would be the perfect ambassador for the good intentions of their side. The unicorns had an ancient bond with the winged horses in any case, and could slip in and out of the remote mountain area where the creatures lived, without attracting notice.

This had been the first that Jorelial Rey had heard of Shar's new horn, and she marveled at its beautiful delicacy, and the way it seemed to change the unicorn's entire personality. She was reminded again of the mage's cleverness, humility, and above all, his great kindness. Deeply she wished she could make him understand how much she regretted her thoughtless remark, longed to return to the easy rapport they had once shared. But there was no time for sentiment now. Fortune willing, they would survive to straighten it all out when the fighting was over.

General Boone and Mark flew off as promised in search of a perfect spot for the two armies to meet, and Mark delivered. Boone was ecstatic about the site they selected. It had every advantage they could have wished for. There was a long, broad valley between two tall, rocky ridges. The river ran through it, flanking one of the steep canyon walls, and there were copses of trees scattered among large expanses of meadow. The whole area was unpopulated, now that goatherds and shepherds were gathering in their flocks closer to home. This meant there would be no danger of causing disruption to civilian life. Best of all, Lord Drogue's forces would have to march straight through on their way to the delta, if they were to avoid the much more arduous and time-consuming mountain passes. Many trips were made to this heaven-sent place, called by the locals, the Valley of the Yechtze. Maps were made, strategies adapted to the terrain, and measurements paced off. It was decided where various companies would be deployed on the Legion's side of the valley, where the best vantage points were up on top for dragons and generals, and where additional forces might be hidden. Ondine was taken to explore that stretch of the river, and Tvrdik and Tashroth began a dialogue with the trees there, who, as promised, seemed to be well-disposed toward their cause.

Little by little, a plan emerged. As soon as word came that Lord Drogue was on the move, they would march the Legions' full force to Yechtze, and make camp at the mouth of the valley. There, they would set their traps and wait for Drogue to arrive, forcing him to meet them in pitched battle at this contained location. The hope was that they would be able to push him back with his tail between his legs, without letting him ever get near Theriole. In the event any of the enemy forces did push through, and made for the palace, several regiments of the Elite Royal Guard, and one of Brendelle's companies, would be in place to defend it, and would be authorized to use lethal force as a last resort. The Lady Regent agonized over this decision, but she thought it important to communicate that if all else failed, she had no intention of allowing the kingdom to fall to such as Drogue without using every option available. And in any case, the king would not be there.

Time seemed to evaporate before their eyes, as no one knew the exact moment that the mountain lord would make his move. It felt like they were all racing to beat an unknown deadline, and each new day that they had to complete another list of tasks seemed a priceless gift in which they rejoiced.

One sunny afternoon, several weeks after Candelinda's return from her reconnaissance trip, the Lady Jorelial Rey summoned Mark and Delphine to meet her in the Hall of Audience. Something about the invitation seemed more official than was usual between them, and filled the couple with a sense of unease.

When they arrived, Warlowe was nowhere to be seen, but the great, heavy door stood ajar. Beyond, they could see Jorelial Rey seated at the oversized table, her head in her hands. Mark and Delphine exchanged a look of alarm, and Mark took his wife's hand, clearing his throat loudly. The Lady Regent looked up to see them hesitating in the doorway, and sprang from her chair to greet them.

"Mark, Delphine! Come in, come in. I'm glad you're here. Can you manage to get that door closed? I don't want us to be disturbed. That's it.

Let's all go and sit down. At the table, there. I'm afraid I have nothing to offer you – I didn't think ahead. Are you hungry? Should I have something sent?"

"Rel, we're fine. We just had lunch. What's all this about?" The couple settled themselves at the table and leaned forward, their attention fixed on Delphine's sister. Jorelial Rey took a deep, centering breath, and let it out through pursed lips. For a moment, a tense silence hung over them all, and then Rel began.

"Do you remember, Mark, when you broke into the meeting here for Candelinda's report?"

"Yes, of course. I know it was not proper protocol, and perhaps I could have handled it better, but…"

"No, no, it's fine. You were right to come in. The intelligence you brought was priceless. It's not a problem."

"Then, what?"

"Do you recall that after you told us about Yechtze, there was a whole other conversation about spiriting King Darian away somewhere that Drogue would not think to look for him?"

"Yes, I remember. There were several suggestions of places, but none seemed perfect, and you said you would give it some thought…"

"Have you found a place?" Delphine asked.

"Well, Sweet Pea, I thought I had. There were a lot of possibilities that we looked at, but every one of them had some sort of problem attached. And if it was not a better solution than just leaving him guarded at Theriole, it wasn't worth doing. I was beginning to give up on the plan, and then Master Alanquist came forward last week to tell me that he had a lovely country estate, miles from here, off in the lowlands, away from any conflict. His wife would be happy to welcome little Darian as a guest, and no one would be the wiser, so we started preparations."

Mark and Delphine exchanged a confused glance. Mark spoke.

"That's wonderful. It sounds…"

"It burned down."

"What?" Mark yelped. Delphine made an involuntary shocked sound.

"The whole house. Early this morning. To the ground. Lady Alanquist and the children got out safely, thank the gods, but some of the servants were injured. Master Alanquist is on his way there now to collect his family and bring them all to Theriole. He is devastated. The house had been in his family for generations."

"Was it….an accident?"

"We think so. We hope so. We are still clinging to the notion that Lord Drogue expects His Majesty to be holed up at the palace. I would not like to think word of our plan got out. I suppose it is possible someone might have tried to get to Alanquist simply because he is a major player in our government, and cannot stand Drogue. Or there might have been a more personal vendetta…or a random spark. Just bad timing."

The Lady Regent closed her eyes and shook her head. Delphine saw how weary her sister looked, and reached out a hand to cover Rel's.

"What a terrible blow for poor Master Alanquist. Thank heavens his family is unharmed. Bad luck that Darian can't go there. But, Rel, is there some special reason why you are telling us?"

Jorelial Rey leapt from her chair and began to pace back and forth, in her accustomed manner.

"Delphy, we are just about out of time, and I am out of options. All morning, I have been tormented by the thought that my first duty is to protect the king, and I feel it in my bones that at Theriole, he could be easy prey. I searched every memory and compartment in my brain, looking for another possibility, but nothing seemed right…"

"Rel…"

"And then…" Jorelial Rey turned to look straight at them, one hand raised in a gesture of breakthrough, "…I did have one other idea. It's crazy, and risky, but the more I thought about it, the more it seemed like maybe it could work."

"Go on…" Mark urged.

"Mark, are your parents still at home on their estate?"

Mark's mouth went dry, and the hairs on the back of his neck stood up, but he managed to answer. "Well, yes. I was going to tell you they wanted to come and join the Legions, but they had to wait until the last of the newborn lambs were old enough to be left on their own. I was going to ask if Nelrose could stay at the palace. She's too young to fight."

"Mark, what do you think your parents would say if I asked them to stay at home and harbor His Majesty for a time?"

Mark paused to allow the thought to land with some coherence in his mind. "I...I don't know. Of course they would want to help in any way they could. And Mom and Nelrose just adore children..."

"But their place is in the mountains, not far from..." Delphine interjected.

"I know." Jorelial Rey interrupted, a wild look in her eyes, "Practically right under his nose, and yet, not on the route his armies would be taking to get here. It's against reason, I know. Not without risk. We'd certainly be exposing your family to additional danger."

Mark stood up, his turn now to pace, Delphine watching him with concern.

"But there is danger everywhere now, and they were coming to join the battle in any case," he said. "My lady, my family is loyal to His Majesty and yourself. I could not presume to speak for them, but I feel sure they would welcome this chance to assist their king."

"I thought as much, Mark. And I am also quite certain that despite Lord Drogue deploying spies of his own, he has little interest in my sister's new husband, the bard, or in the young man's roots. In short, I would never dream of conceiving such a plan if I thought he had made the first connection between anyone at court, and a simple gentleman sheep farmer off in a corner of a nearby district. He would have no reason to even suspect. Dressed in homespun, Darian could be just another cousin's child come for a visit."

Mark began to catch her fever, "It's genius," he muttered, "so close and so not worthy of notice. Hidden almost in plain sight. Why, he would be as safe as a fox cub in the autumn leaves!"

"Exactly."

Delphine remained unconvinced. "But what if something did go wrong? What if he were discovered? They are not trained warriors. Who would protect them?"

Rel met her sister's eyes, "Well, that's why I would be sending the two of you along as well."

"What?" Delphine cried.

"What?" Mark echoed, and sat down.

"Yes, didn't I mention that?"

"Rel, you can't! You wouldn't. We are founding members of the Legions of Light. We have been training and practicing for months to stand beside you in this battle. You can't just take us out now. It isn't fair."

Jorelial Rey sat down at the table again, took her sister's hands in her own, and smiled at her.

"Oh, Sweet Pea, I thought you might react like this. I understand. I do. We've all been working so hard to face the day of reckoning, together. You two have been invaluable in creating even a chance for us. What you have contributed cannot be measured. I know you think that I am now trying to pluck you out of harm's way, and, truth be told, I wouldn't be your big sister if that thought hadn't crossed my mind. But that's not what this is about. Think about it. Darian knows and loves you. His Nanny is going to fight with the Legions. He is being uprooted and sent to an unfamiliar place. I cannot entrust his care to a stranger, or even to a friend whose heart I do not entirely know. And both of you have proven your mettle in a crisis, and have trained to confront the enemy if the need arises. If not to you, to whom can I hand over this most important of all tasks, and breathe easy that it will be done?"

Delphine's face seemed to change before their eyes, from uncertainty, to petulance, to the determined, courageous face of one who knows her duty. She narrowed her eyes at Rel, and asked one more question.

"Lord Drogue does know I am your sister. If he follows my movements, will I not endanger the others by being there?"

Jorelial Rey frowned and considered. "We will have to take great care in getting all of you to the estate – disguise you both, cover your hair, figure out an approach from another corner of the kingdom, and travel by night if need be. For all intents and purposes, you will be a young family visiting relatives in another county. If it is all right with you, I should like to send Lynette with you as well. Her parents will be so busy with their duties, and she will have no one to watch over her. She is a bid-able child, and no trouble. A young couple and their two children off to visit their extended family…"

Delphine looked at Mark, and Mark circled her shoulders with his long arm. They searched one another's eyes, and smiled. Mark leaned over to kiss her on the forehead, then released her and rose from his chair. "My lady, I will go and send a message right away to my family, detailing this plan. You should have your answer in three day's time. Rest assured, Delphine and I are honored to be chosen for this vital task, and we will do everything in our power to insure that your confidence in us is well placed." He made a little bow, and waited to be dismissed.

"I already know that, Mark, and I am grateful beyond words that you are willing to help shoulder the burden. Go and send that message. Come to me as soon as you hear. I will breathe easier when everything is in place. Thank you."

Mark nodded to her, cocked his head to the side and exchanged a wordless glance with his bride, turned on his heel, and hurried from the room. Delphine turned back to her sister and took her hand once more.

"This will work, Rel. You are a brilliant leader, and you have come up with the best plan possible."

Rel sighed, "I hope so. It makes a difference that I know who will be there to watch out for him. There is no human in the world that I trust more than you…"

Delphine giggled a bit at that reference, but then grew serious, "It will be hard to be far from you when the battle is raging. I had intended to be right by your side. I'll be frantic not knowing what is happening on the field."

"We can send some of the talking birds back and forth as messengers. They are too small to be much noticed, and will be happy for the employment."

Delphine nodded, and then raised her face to lock eyes with her sister, "Rel, could I ask you something personal?"

"Of course. What is it?"

"Umm…did something happen between you and Tvrdik? The two of you seem so… so, well, *strained* with each other, ever since his birthday."

Jorelial Rey's face turned a peculiar shade of magenta, and her eyes dipped to the floor in embarrassment. "It's nothing, really. Just a little misunderstanding. He'll get over it. Nothing that would affect our ability to work together."

"Well, yes, of course you can work together. But, oh, Rel, he's like a member of our family. I'd feel a whole lot better if the two of you could find a way to patch things up before…before we run out of time. You're making the rest of us so uncomfortable."

"I didn't realize it was that noticeable. Alright, yes, Sweet Pea, I promise I'll do what I can."

"Do you want me to talk to him?"

"No, no. I think it had better be me. Thanks anyway." Delphine's face was full of questions, but she gave a quick little nod, rose from her chair, and followed after her husband. Left alone in the big hall once again, Jorelial Rey sank down on the dais and let her head fall into her hands. It had been an exhausting, emotional day, but at least she was on her way to accomplishing one important task. At that moment, having sent Delphine away, Tashroth off somewhere going over campaign plans with Candelinda and the other dragons, and Tvrdik behaving all distant and guarded, she felt the acute loneliness of authority. A passing wave of emotion, no doubt, but one that drained her of what little was left of her energy. She really should approach Tvrdik, and try to clear the air. Delphine was, as usual, right about that. Perhaps there would be time tomorrow, or the next day. Sighing, she felt herself drift into oblivion, letting go of the myriad cares that fought for her mind like vultures tearing at carrion. Sitting there at the oversized table, hands over her eyes, she fell asleep.

She had no idea how many minutes, or hours, passed when she found herself swimming back to consciousness, and opened her eyes to the vision of Warlowe's concerned face. He was shaking her gently, and when she tried to shift to attention, she found her back and limbs were stiff and achy, complaining about their awkward position and the cold, hard floor.

"Lady Rey…Lady Rey…are you alright?"

"Yes. Yes…fine," she said, stretching each painful arm and leg in turn, "I just dozed off for a moment. What is it, Warlowe? Something wrong?"

"I'm sorry to disturb you, Ma'am, but we have been looking all over for you. Stewart and the unicorns have returned."

Now she was fully awake, and scrambling to her feet. "News?"

"I couldn't tell. They are waiting to see you right outside…"

"Light a few torches, will you, Warlowe. It's getting dark already. Then send them right in."

"Very good, Ma'am." He set about coaxing the wall torches to flame, while she shook out her aching legs, smoothed her garments and disheveled hair, then climbed up to the big throne on the dais and sat down, ready to receive the travelers.

She needn't have worried about how she might look for the interview, as their own appearance left a lot to be desired. They had insisted on seeing her before rest, or food, or a bath, and were all three weary, muddy, and unkempt. Concerned for their well-being, after one glance, Jorelial Rey ordered Warlowe to look after their comfort, and he assured her that preparations were already being made, but that they wished first to deliver their report.

It seemed they had tried for days to maneuver, wheedle, or beg an independent meeting with some of the magical creatures in Drogue's employ, without his knowledge or involvement. They had sadly failed in this endeavor, as security was much tighter than they had imagined, and as they had arrived during a flurry of activity that forced them to go to extreme lengths to stay safe and out of sight. It had taken them awhile to interpret what was going on around them, but once they understood, they gave up their mission, and set out for home at a grueling pace, stopping for nothing on the way.

It was the news which everyone awaited, and dreaded. Lord Drogue's army was on the move.

No matter how prepared they had tried to be, there were still too many tasks left to accomplish in a shrinking pool of hours. It took only two days by talking bird to receive an answer from Mark's family. They were overjoyed to be asked to serve in a way they understood well. They were also relieved and grateful that their beloved son and new daughter-in-law would be safe under their roof for the actual battle. They were a little dismayed to be entertaining their Sovereign in what they characterized as their 'very humble dwelling,' which was actually quite sprawling and comfortable. They did love children, though, and wanting to contribute in some manner to the cause, they were eager to accept.

So, as quickly as the answer was received, Mark, Delphine, King Darian, and Lynette packed a few needful things, and dressed in simple clothing. In the chill of dawn, they assembled in the courtyard in front of the palace. Tvrdik, Rel, and the Praegers were on hand to see the little party off on their adventure. The plan was for Tashroth and one of the blue dragons to fly their four passengers to a village six miles east of Mark's family estate. From there, the dragons would do a little hunting so as to appear unremarkable, while Mark was to purchase a horse and two mules, in order to make the rest of the journey the way any ordinary family might travel. It was hoped that by means of this small subterfuge, the travelers would escape Drogue's attention, while arriving at their destination as swiftly as possible.

Darian's eyes went wide when he saw Tashroth and the blue dragon awaiting them in the courtyard. "Are we going to ride on a dragon?" he piped.

"Yes, we are," Delphine smiled at the little boy. "You aren't frightened, are you?"

"Gosh, no!" he retorted. "When I am king, I shall ride dragonback at all times."

Tvrdik chuckled, "Easy there, sport. There aren't many dragons out there who take kindly to being ridden."

The king made a sour face. Tashroth swung his enormous head around to face the little boy, uncomfortably close. Darian's eyebrows raised, but he did not flinch. The dragon's voice was deep and solemn, his warm breath smelling a bit like amber and charcoal, "I shall be very happy to carry His Majesty always, whenever there is need," he promised. The king nodded, awed by the giant beast, but pretending royal control. When he thought no one was looking, he turned and stuck his tongue out at Tvrdik with a terrible grimace. The wizard threw his hands in the air, while everyone else tried to hide their laughter.

But it was time to go. Tearful hugs and desperate wishes for an easy journey and a safe stay were hastily exchanged, and the four passengers climbed onto the backs of the patient dragons. Bags and carry-sacks full of personal items and provisions were handed up to them, and settled neatly between the neck ridges of their steeds. Delphine and the children waved merrily as they rose into the air, and the forlorn little group in the courtyard waved back, calling out farewells. Mrs. Praeger dissolved in sobs and sniffles the moment the dragons faded from view, comforted by her very dejected-looking husband. It was all Tvrdik and Rel could do to keep from falling apart as well.

They had little time to grieve the absent, however, as the full complement of the Legions of Light had to be assembled for the march to the Yechtze. Tvrdik had activated the last of the sapphire blue shields, and all were fitted with Mrs. Praeger's protective covers. Various other tools, provisions, water, and medical supplies all had to be collected and readied for transport. Ondine was informed to take her small naiad regiment upriver to the appointed place, and to speak to the dryads – the local trees – as soon as she arrived. The unicorns and talking beasts were sent ahead as scouts, while the dragons took the rear as a protective escort for the slow-moving and vulnerable army. Instructions were given to the Royal Guard who would stay behind to defend Theriole, and all who remained within because they were too old, too young, or too infirm to fight. All of these were gathered together in the most secure corner of the gigantic complex, along with many from the villages and farms nearby who felt in need of more protection than their simple cots and houses afforded.

The Legion travelled in regiments, reflecting more or less its various components: Nyree and her bards, Andrus with the physician/healers, Boone's trained professionals, and Brendelle with her own forces from Euligia. Verger had his own small unit, and a dozen medium-sized catapults that moved at a maddeningly slow pace. There were some cavalry, and the vast majority of volunteers, many carrying Tvrdik's blue shields, and the rest equipped with more traditional ones, marched on foot under Rel's command. Most had been outfitted with some sort of light armor and helmets, protection from the more traditional weaponry Drogue's army would be using. The Regent rode Tashroth, overhead, circling and swooping and urging them on, while scanning the terrain ahead for any danger. Their constant presence in the sky served as a beacon of inspiration to those below who knew they were marching into the riskiest and most important encounter of their lives. With the exception of a scant few – some of the foreigners, and a handful of Boone's warriors – none of them had ever been present at an actual battle before, and the conversations en route were full of imaginings and fears. Besides anxiety however, there was also great excitement and eagerness, as each recruit longed to prove his or her mettle.

Tvrdik had elected to make the trip in his owl form, strongly preferring *not* to ride dragonback. His clothing and spectacles morphed into unusual markings on the pale bird's feathers, and around the eyes. And, he had figured out a way to include his all-important staff in the transmutation.

After a bit of practice, he found he could shrink the tall staff into a small twig which he could carry with him in his talons. It made his already awkward landings even bumpier, but it solved the practical problem of having his most important piece of equipment with him at all times. The troops below had somehow heard of his penchant for turning into an owl, and, just as they took pleasure in waving to Jorelial Rey on Tashroth, the foot soldiers of the Legion would also count it a good omen to catch a glimpse of him winging and wheeling above their heads. They would point and exclaim, and shout and wave to him, and he would circle and cry in his owl's voice, doing his part to boost morale, and foster the spirit of adventure.

In his mind, he was rehearsing scores of useful spells over and over again, spells he might need on the field. He keenly felt the pressure of knowing that so much of their success would depend on his personal work out there. Mistakes were not an option. Hesitations or memory lapses could result in disastrous consequences. It was all quite sobering. In his wizard form, he kept the coin bearing Xaarus' face in the pocket of his robe. If there arose a moment of great need, he thought it would help him concentrate on his old Master enough to request his assistance. He knew that in some incomprehensible way, though he was centuries ahead of them, Xaarus would be holding his breath, awaiting news of what transpired at the Yechtze. Somehow, their success – or failure – would determine the entire character of the world in which Xaarus found himself.

One of the dragons, the same blue who had obliged with carrying Mark and Delphine to the mountains, flew ahead and circled back to report Drogue's forces advancing at a moderate, but unflagging pace. Rel pushed her people hard to keep them going. She wanted them to arrive at the chosen site well ahead of the enemy, in order for them to be deployed and well-rested before they would be engaged. Much of their hope for success rested on their control of timing and space when the two forces came together, and there was not much room for errors or nasty surprises. The Valley of the Yechtze was about halfway to Drogue's castle stronghold, but the road there was on easier terrain than he would have to traverse on his way. Even so, it took them the better part of two full days' march, with only brief rest periods, and a short night's sleep, to arrive at the site and pitch camp. They did, however, get there well ahead of Lord Drogue's army. As they set about unloading supplies and equipment before the darkness descended, they were reunited with the unicorns and talking beasts, the naiads and dryads. The advance scouts reported that Drogue was still at least a day away, but that soon enough, his intelligence would likely inform him of what was awaiting him in the valley. He would be surprised, but would know that he faced a traditional pitched battle with King Darian's supporters. There was little chance this change of plans would deter him from advancing. They would have to prepare for battle.

Jorelial Rey, as promised, sent one of the talking crows to Mark's family home, in order to let Delphine know that they had reached the Yechtze and were settling in, that they anticipated action, but that nothing had happened yet. The bird, Jarrod by name, was also to find out how things were sorting out at the house, and if Delphine needed anything. Jarrod knew the terrain, and was delighted and proud to be of special service to the Lady Regent. He made a most formal reverence to Lady Rey when he heard his assignment, then rose up and flapped off to the east as the sun was setting.

Weary as the defenders were, they immediately set up camp, took in the lay of the land, reviewed strategies and maneuvers, and rehearsed details. As the sun set, a generous evening meal was prepared for all at the campfires. Folks sat and lingered a while in quiet thought or conversation, but everyone retired early, adrenaline battling with exhaustion for the prize of sleep. Sentries were posted through the night and the following day, as Drogue's forces arrived and seemed to be establishing themselves at the other end of the valley. But the opposition seemed to be in no hurry to make a move, and it was not the place of the Legion to offer the first hostilities. They characterized themselves as 'Defenders of the Crown,' after all, and could not justify picking a fight unless they were well and truly challenged. Drogue was a patient and canny adversary. He would take his time, set down roots, size them up, and make them nervous and restless.

Even now, reluctant to admit that battle was inevitable, the Lady Rey considered another possibility: maybe, just maybe, she thought, Lord Drogue, who had previously been a distinguished member of the Grand Council, was out there reconsidering his options. What if there was even the remotest possibility that some agreement could still be reached without resorting to a fight? Even after his ill-conceived grab for power, and his attack on Theriole by sea, she might be willing to spare his life and allow him to keep some limited authority in his own region. Or perhaps he would accept banishment, and take his inflated ambitions somewhere else far away. She knew it was naïve, but almost anything would be worth averting bloodshed – anything but the ceding of the crown. Even Drogue had to see that an all-out pitched battle would be disastrous for everyone. She dared not expect much, but felt it prudent to offer one last chance for reconciliation. It was a responsible leader's obligation to try every avenue of resolution before resorting to war. So, she sent Candelinda to Drogue's camp, under a white flag of truce, requesting a personal interview.

He received the dragon, in his own cordial, but unpleasant way, and invited the Lady Regent and two seconds to his cliff top perch. Tashroth was going, of course, and she decided she wanted Tvrdik with her as well. He had always been her best backup before – an extra pair of discerning eyes and ears, and a proven protector, if things went awry. General Boone and Corbin Maygrew were horrified at her decision to meet the enemy herself. They did not trust Drogue, and failed to see why she would put her own safety in jeopardy, just when her leadership would be so vital. But she assured them that she would be fine with Tashroth and the wizard in tow, and that one more attempt at a peaceful solution, no matter how improbable, was the responsible course of action. She convinced them that it must be her who confronted the usurper, or whoever went would not have the credibility to negotiate. In the end, they had to admit that her arguments were unassailable, and, under protest, they let the small party go, remaining poised for action should the other side try anything dishonorable.

The trio arrived in Drogue's camp, and were ushered to a high plateau where he had set himself up in a large, throne-like chair. Jorelial Rey had prepared a speech attempting to appeal to the lord's better and more reasonable nature, but it was obvious from the start that his eye was fixed on the throne at any cost. It appeared that he took her request for a parley as a sign of weakness, perhaps an admission that her cause was hopeless in the face of his superior might. He did make one serious offer, which involved sparing little Darian's life and sending the infant away to some distant country estate under guard. Then he would arrange to marry her, as he did have a certain admiration for her youth, her passion, and her demonstrated capacity to move the citizenry. He would be delighted to have her stand beside him, and they would rule Eneri Clare together. There was an edge of lasciviousness in Drogue's proposal that he made no attempt to conceal, an implication which revolted her, shocked Tvrdik, and incensed Tashroth so, that he stepped forward with a bellow to rip the man's head off then and there. This might have been a tempting end to all of their problems, had they not known what Xaarus had told them of the future. At any rate, Lady Rey ordered Tashroth to back off, and, realizing her mission to be hopeless against such supreme arrogance, she leapt upon the dragon's back, pulled Tvrdik up behind, and urged her mount off of a nearby ledge, back to their base camp as fast as his wings could beat. They would have no compunction now in meeting Drogue's forces head-on with all they had.

And so, the next morning, well before dawn, Lady Jorelial Rey bid the Legions of Light assemble in the valley, ready to move at sunrise. She herself perched with Tashroth above the field, on a high bluff, from where she could survey the entire theater, while Tvrdik made rounds to see that all was in place for the coming confrontation. Each of them struggled with doubts, fears, and regrets concerning what they were about to begin, but this was not a moment to reveal any frailty to the brave souls who would take this field, without traditional weapons, against Drogue's brutal warriors. It was no longer time for contemplation, or conversation, but for action.

Jorelial Rey swallowed hard and settled herself securely just behind the last vertebra of Tash's long neck. A small shadow overhead caught her attention – a white owl, circling closer, and closer, and then shooting past her ear to crash into a nearby bush in a jumble of feathers and dust. She blinked, and now was looking at a tall, pale, bespectacled young man, brushing off his deep grey robes with one hand, while his other hand gripped a crystal-topped staff. Tvrdik looked up to meet her gaze, and made her a little solemn bow.

"My lady. All is in readiness, awaiting your order."

"All is well?"

"Spirits are high, everything in place. We are about as ready as we will ever be."

"And so, here we are at last, just as you said we would be."

"Xaarus said." He corrected her.

"Will we meet again on the far side of this day, and raise a glass to our victory, Tvrdik?"

"I pray it will be so. I believe it will be so."

Tashroth's deep voice interrupted, "Lord Drogue's army comes on. It is time." He had been searching the silvered horizon with his sharp dragon's eyes. Jorelial Rey fastened a leather helmet over her dark, braided tresses. "Thank you Tash. I am ready. Fly well, dear friend. While we are together, I do not fear anything."

"We will always be together, dearest, and today, we will triumph together."

Tvrdik had averted his eyes during this mostly private and emotional exchange, but now he felt her gaze on him, and looked up to meet it. She spoke, "Our place is with the vanguard, Tvrdik – Tashroth's and mine. Will you join us there, or will you be working your charms from here?"

"Here is a good place to begin. Godspeed to you."

"And to you." She gave him a curt nod, and began to turn away.

"Jorelial Rey!" Tvrdik called out to her, "Thank you."

She turned back to him, her eyebrows tweaked in question, "For what?"

"For believing in me. For making all of this happen."

"Don't mention it." With a grim smile, she motioned the dragon to the ledge, then seemed to think again, and turned back, "Tvrdik?"

"Yes, my lady?"

Jorelial Rey frowned. There were so many things she wanted to tell him, but time had run out. "Stay out of trouble, will you? You're the only wizard we have right now, and the only one who knows how everything we planned works."

He bowed low, a cryptic expression on his pale, bespectacled face – a face that all at once felt very familiar and dear to her. "I'll do my best, my lady," he said. For the briefest of moments their eyes locked, and all the armor fell away, all the veils of pride and formality and self-preservation, and they saw, each into the other's heart. Then it was gone, carried away on a breeze, as the first rays of the rising sun reached over the distant hills, illuminating the valley below. The dawn revealed the Legions of Light – thousands of friends, subjects, supporters and colleagues waiting in perfect formation for a sign. Jorelial Rey sighed, turned and spurred Tashroth toward the cliff's edge. The great, green dragon swung his head back around and gave the young wizard one last rumbled acknowledgement, before stepping into the air beside the cliff, and catching himself on a thermal with his huge outstretched wings. Tvrdik stood, watching them circle once, then wheel up and away toward the front lines of their army, which awaited them in the half-light at the mouth of the Yechtze. "So. It begins. Godspeed, Jorelial Rey. Godspeed," he breathed after them as the dragon-shaped patch dwindled smaller and smaller on the shining horizon.

A flash of gold from the rising sun blinded him for a moment, and in the same instant, a blood-curdling roar from far below pulled his gaze from the sky and made the skin on his neck crawl. It was the horrible sound of thousands of frenzied, faceless monsters bent on tearing the Crown's army to bits.

THIRTY-EIGHT

IT BEGINS

DROGUE'S ARMY WAS ON THE move. A dark sea of soldiers flowed into the valley with inexorable rhythm. Howling and roaring their rage, they approached the midpoint of the Yechtze, closer and closer, while the Legions of Light stood in formation and held their ground. Every jaw was clenched, every hand twitched, every unblinking eye peered into the near distant grey for a glimpse of the adversary. Five or six dragons circled overhead, sensing their moment approaching. Only one had a rider.

As the dark forces crossed the midpoint of the valley, that rider lowered her arm swiftly in a pre-arranged signal. A high, clear, unearthly sound pierced the dawn. Rising over the enemy's shouts, its haunting line carried across the whole of the valley. Down a wistful scale it went and twisted around into a melody of such longing, it tore at the heartstrings of anyone with ears to hear. There were no words, but the undiluted emotion in every note spoke to the deepest anguish of human experience. For a moment, everything went still, as the voice of Nyree rose and fell in other-worldly arcs of song. The vanguard of Drogue's force ceased their measured march, faltered, and halted in confusion, staring about at one another for an explanation. Then, the bardic veteran strummed a chord on her harp, and launched her wordless ribbon of sound once more, pure and clear. Other voices joined her, high and low and in between, adding their poignant beauty in the most exquisite harmony. Several of Drogues warriors dropped their weapons and put their hands to their eyes. Louder, and with more confidence, the singing rang out, harps and drums supporting the sound of trained voices, as more of Drogue's army halted in confusion.

Tvrdik, looking on from the high ridge above, cast a spell of protection over the entire company of harpers and bards, brave souls who were now in the forefront of their company. He made it a self-generating invisible shield, which could not render them entirely immune to harm, but would help deflect a good deal of what might come at them for a time. He caught a motion out of the corner of his eye, and turned his attention to the right, to a place well behind the faltering front lines. It was an all too familiar gesture: archers – hundreds of them. Lord Drogue was on the ground, galloping back and forth alongside them, urging them to draw back their bows and fire. Only a second later and hundreds of lethal shafts had left their bowstrings, arcing up and ready to rain destruction on the vulnerable Legions. But, Tvrdik had already waved his hand and muttered a few words, and before the arrows could even crest and turn toward their intended marks, they all turned into geese, honking and flapping, and continuing their trajectory up and away.

A deafening cheer broke out from the defenders as they waved their arms and shields high. Drogue' stupefied archers could only afford to be dumbstruck for a moment before their master, spurring his mount furiously along the lines, roared at them to fire once again. Another rain of arrows rose into the air, and transformed themselves into geese. This time, in an irony Tvrdik could not have planned, almost the entire flock decided to void their bowels over the archers who had released them into the wide blue sky. The results splattered on the upturned, befuddled faces which were watching the magical transformation. Chuckling to himself as more cheering and singing and drumming rang out from the defending army, Tvrdik raised his staff, and set the intention that all arrows should become geese and fly off without inflicting harm. That spell should serve for awhile at least, and disarm one of Drogue's attack forces. But now, he noticed the foot soldiers in the vanguard regaining their composure, and beginning to advance on the Legions of Light.

Jorelial Rey circled over on Tashroth once again, dropped low, and signaled for a second time with her right arm. At that gesture, Verger echoed the signal to his special unit, lined up behind the bards with a collection of catapults. Cords were cut and the siege engines sprang into action, showering the fields with, of all things, buckets of gold coins! These were no illusion, but completely real, a fact that nearly gave the frugal Verger a heart attack. But, the Lady Regent had decided if they did not wish to create and court new enemies for the future, their peace offering had better remain what it purported to be, instead of changing back to a clod of earth or stone. As hoped, when the rain of gold coins fell clinking down on their heads, many of Drogue's warriors – the poor, the desperate, the disenchanted and the plain greedy dropped their weapons in distraction and began scrambling about on the ground for their share of the loot. Hundreds of the first company gathered up all they could hold, and simply ran from the field. As these deserters scattered in all directions, searching for a safe egress from the valley, some of them ran headlong into their fellows, who were still advancing to what they thought was the fight.

From Tvrdik's high vantage point, it looked as if the entire forefront of Drogue's fighting force was roiling about in every direction, wrestling with itself, having totally forgotten their original purpose. Men were dropping to their knees to retrieve the coins as Verger's catapults continued to shower the field at regular intervals. Tripping and colliding with one another, possessed with raw lust and desire, the soon began fighting with each other over the spoils. The Legions of Light stood fast, waiting in formation, Nyree's bards still singing and drumming and playing their harps and horns. Drogue's army began choking and wrestling one another to the ground, clonking their fellows on the head and twisting arms backward. With great difficulty, a determined few seasoned warriors, loyal to Drogue, or else more focused on their original purpose, broke from the melee and rushed upon the front lines of the defenders. Rel and Tvrdik both caught the motion at the same moment; at a gesture from her, the ordinary shields went up to form a near- impenetrable wall. At a gesture from him, the attackers found themselves lashing out with loaves of fresh-baked bread instead of swords, beating on shields with sausages instead of cudgels, and stabbing with cheeses on the ends of their once bladed pikes. Now these were, in fact, illusions, but such good ones in every sensory detail, that the half-starved rank and file of Drogue's army again rushed upon their fellows to wrestle away a portion of the bounty.

It then occurred to the young wizard that perhaps he ought to make some effort to protect Drogue's squabbling warriors from truly harming one another, and he began to systematically turn all the weapons on the field to food items, regiment by regiment. It was a rare and comical sight to see acres of foot soldiers scrabbling on the ground for gold and provender, smashing each other over the head and pummeling one another across the shoulders with bread and cheese and summer sausage. As one would expect at the tail end of summer, all of this sweaty activity coupled with pungent, appetizing, food odors attracted a swarm of flies to the scene, further contributing to the chaos at hand. Men flailed about everywhere, trying to shoo the biting vermin away from their cheese-covered heads.

The bards' unflagging stream of music, and the noise from the trenches almost, but not quite, drowned out the high-pitched, hysterical screaming from Lord Drogue himself. Tvrdik could see him on the edges of the fray, mounted on Valour, half on the ground, half in the air, the magnificent ebony steed rearing up and galloping aloft in pointless acrobatics, while his rider shouted useless orders at the forces who had lost interest in him. The valley was narrow, and his vast army was, for the moment, impotent – trapped behind the scrabbling front lines. Drogue at length realized that trying to restore order to the vanguard was futile. Tvrdik observed him flying back to a grassy knoll on which his cavalry waited – hundreds of experienced riders on powerful mounts, awaiting their part in the battle. Tvrdik saw Drogue talk to the cavalry commander, pointing and gesticulating. An argument seemed to ensue. It appeared that the commander was questioning the wisdom of Drogue's orders, but in the end, shaking his head, he relayed the orders to his men, and waved them forward. Drogue, it seemed, had commanded them to ride along the riverbank in a narrow column, circumvent the trouble at the front, and attack the Legion from an oblique angle. It was a strategy that would make any decent cavalry commander nervous, as his forces would be strung out in a long, narrow ribbon. But despite that disadvantage, it could take the defenders off guard and inflict a great deal of damage. Tvrdik and General Boone had foreseen such a move, however, and were prepared for it. Tvrdik raised his staff high, and with a thought, crowned it with a vibrant orange flame, pouring as much intensity into it as he could, until he was sure Jorelial Rey had caught sight of it. When he saw her reign Tashroth back and wheel away toward the river bank at a clip, he brought the staff down and extinguished the torch. Tashroth hovered close to the river, stretching his long neck down toward the waters, and then the dragon glided along the treetops of a wooded patch nearby before turning back to the defenders' end of the valley.

The only corridor left to Drogue's cavalry would take them straight through that wooded patch, and then, as it cleared, right along the river on the approach to their waiting foe. Tvrdik saw the anxious commander, on a fidgeting horse, line his men up four abreast, and then give the order to charge. Yard by yard, the horse company gained momentum, as they found their rhythm, gauging their space with care. They passed alongside the archers, who were still trying to coax their bows into shooting anything but live geese, and beside row upon row of brawling foot soldiers in disarray. When they came upon the woods to their right, they were at a full gallop, and so focused on not running into the mess of men and sausages to their left, that they never saw the trees pull back in preparation. They had no advance warning that hundreds of supple birches and leafy young oaks were about to slingshot their leafy tops over in front of them as they came on at full tilt. Nor did they expect scores of sturdy elms to twist their solid branches out into the path at the last moment. In fact, there was no possibility that fully half of Drogue's cavalry could have reigned up in time to avoid being swept clean out of their saddles by tree branches that had not been before them only a moment earlier. Scores of men flew through the air or bounced about, clinging to branches for dear life. Their riderless horses, spooked and without room to flee, or anyone to guide them, bolted and ran amok in all directions, mostly straight into the remaining mounted riders. Horses panicked and reared up, in some cases throwing off riders who had not been caught by the trees. Somehow, the quick-thinking commander managed to keep his seat and rally what was left of his company forward. But they had not faced their last obstacle.

As instructed, Ondine, and her little group of naiads had poured their own magical intention into the river right at the spot where it ran past the battlefield. In mere moments, they were able to stir up the waters to a bubbling and churning brew, foaming and swelling until they overflowed their banks, all across the corridor where the horses were approaching, and well into the squabbling troops. The cavalry who made it past the woods intact had only seconds to sigh with relief before they ran smack into a slick of river water and mud. Travelling too fast, the terrified horses shrieked and slid across the muddy ground. Many went down, their riders pitched into the churning mess. Those that kept their footing were slammed into by the next wave of mud-surfing stallions unable to slow their forward momentum. From the cliff top, Tvrdik thought it all looked like a game of toppling dominos in very slow motion. He sent up a prayer that no creature would be injured in the debacle unfolding before his eyes. But he also had to acknowledge that Drogue's army, so far, was being speared on the horns of its own attack. In a few moments, Lord Drogue's impressive cavalry had been reduced to a pile of struggling arms and legs, tails, hooves and manes, tangled and slippery, rolling about on the soaked and muddy riverbank, gasping for air, neighing in discomfort, and desperate to avoid being dragged down, sat upon and smothered.

There was no question that stage one of the battle had been a rousing success for the Legions of Light, who had not yet needed to lift a finger in their own defense. They were jumping up and down and shrieking in delight, waving their hands and banners in triumph. Squinting, Tvrdik could just make out something, or someone, in the waters of the river, leaping and splashing about in glee, and he smiled to think of who that might be. Then he caught a glimpse of Lord Drogue, purple-faced, still mounted on Valour, flying about and shouting to what was left of his army to fall back and regroup. Rendered powerless for the moment, he was filled with fury and frustration that he had not yet struck a blow for his cause, and could not cross the valley to come any closer to his foe. It was proving a daunting task to restore order to his confused forces, even in retreat, and he had already lost hundreds of men and beasts and many more weapons. With persistence, he managed to corral, order, threaten, and cajole his remaining troops back to their end of the valley for a thorough reorganization.

General Rey was also pulling her army back to confer and reconfigure. From a distance, the Legions looked almost giddy with triumph. Tvrdik knew they had performed well against all odds, but that the struggle was far from over. Lord Drogue would not underestimate them again, and that also meant that they had now lost some of the element of surprise. Now they would be facing some of his more ruthless and devious tactics. It would not prove so easy to force their adversary to give up his cherished ambitions, and the drubbing he had just received at their hands would only serve to make him madder, and more determined. At least the Legions of Light still had a trick or two up their sleeves. Tvrdik sighed and decided it was time for him to join the action on the ground. In an instant, he was the white owl, mottled circles around his eyes, twig firmly grasped in his talon, as he flew down to take his place on the valley floor.

There would only be a brief respite, an opportunity for the Legions to regroup and decide on their next stratagem, before Drogue whipped his own people into some kind of attack force. During the pause, the Lady Rey took a moment to send Jarrod the crow back to Mark and Delphine with an account of the first exchange, and of their unequivocal success. She felt it might cheer and relax them to hear good news, and make them feel included in the action. Jarrod, delighted, puffed out his feathers with pride, and flew off to execute his mission. Neither he, nor the Lady Regent noticed the sharp yellow eyes that turned to follow the crow's flight path, the curved beak that clamped shut, and the quick mind that began to piece together a few interesting details…

Almost as an afterthought, Jorelial Rey sent another of the talking birds back to Theriole with the same heartening update. The Royal Guard, and all those who had taken refuge within the sturdy walls, would be grateful to hear the hopeful tidings.

Drogue's forces were already beginning another advance. He had rearranged his companies, and the men and beasts approaching them now looked rough and ruthless. It seemed certain the Legions would not just have to hold their position this time around. As directed, the unicorns arrayed themselves along the forefront of the lines, with the exception of Shar, who had other work to do, and Wynne, who made good on his promise to carry Tvrdik on the field. The proud equine was smaller than an ordinary horse, but the young mage, though tall, was slender, and did not weigh much. Tvrdik and Wynne sat poised to one side where they had a better view of what was going on. Behind the unicorns were arrayed a contingent of Lady Brendelle's warriors, along with General Boone's best, trained soldiers all, carrying long spear-like poles, and ordinary defensive shields. The poles were tipped with non-lethal darts which had been dipped in a potion that Andrus and his physicians had whipped up. This draft, if introduced into the bloodstream in only miniscule amounts, would, with the swiftness of thought, overpower the recipient with irresistible sleepiness for hours. Boone's and Brendelle's warriors had been trained to stay out of harm's way, while pricking or scratching as much exposed skin as they could get near with the envenomed tips – a difficult and dangerous task, but one tailor-made for these brave warriors who were chomping at the bit for action. In this way it was hoped they could reduce the active numbers of their foe by a significant margin. Lady Brendelle had insisted on commanding this unit herself, a move that inspired confidence in the soldiers who were being asked to fight in a way that was unfamiliar to them.

Somewhere in the rear of the camp, a party of physicians and herbalists was busily brewing new batches of the sleeping potion, and preparing a supply of envenomed tips. The remainder of the healers had set up a station to handle the grim possibility of casualties in this second onslaught, something that seemed unavoidable. Some of the bards continued to support their fellows from the sidelines, with fierce drumming and vocal gestures, but the majority had now been reassigned to join a group of women and youths whose task it would be to comb the fields at every safe opportunity, moving any wounded to the healing station, and also collecting and removing all fallen weaponry. This task was an important step not only to deprive the enemy of any means to inflict harm, should any of them awaken while the battle was still joined, but also to remove temptation from the Legion members themselves. It was a real possibility that even those most committed to non-violence as a principle might resort to old instincts when faced with the prospect of death or injury in the actual heat of battle. Better to keep the tools of war out of reach from both armies.

The talking animals had mostly drawn courier duty. Besides those who had been sent on long range missions, Stewart and his compatriots were poised to carry orders back and forth on the field, between sections and commanders. As Tvrdik glanced up he saw the silhouettes of a dozen dragons perched on the high ridge above the valley, awaiting a signal to swoop in and harass the enemy. They all understood that they were constrained as much as possible to harmlessness, but there was no reason they could not have a little fun and turn a few hairs white in the process.

Drogue's re-formed army approached, marching in rhythm and looking grim indeed. Sweat slid down the faces and necks of every

Legionnaire standing to face them. Without warning, the attackers broke into a run, brandishing weapons and yelling obscenities. This time they were determined to break through the defenders' front lines and force a real engagement. But the stalwart unicorns lowered their heads and sent out a flash of white light through their horns that blinded everyone on the field. Once again, Drogue's warriors found themselves knocking into each other in confusion, tripping, falling, stopped in their tracks or flailing out wildly at each other with their weapons. It was another delaying tactic. The unicorns were capable of repeating the maneuver, but without the element of surprise, it would be a less effective tool the next time. Drogue was wiser, and impatient this time. Behind his charging foot soldiers, he had positioned a pair of catapults, hidden until the last moment with camouflage. Tvrdik caught sight of them at the last moment, just in time to see two gigantic boulders, covered in flaming pitch, hurtling toward the tight, ordered lines of the Legion. He raised his staff in an instant and shouted something; the boulders froze mid-air, their flames doused, and then shattered into pieces. Responding to this, Jorelial Rey and Tashroth led several of the largest dragons in to the source of the lethal projectiles, where their strong forelegs lifted the offending machines into the air and flung them far afield, shattering them against the rocky cliffs. They would not be a danger to the Legion again.

But, the damage had already been done. The Lady Regent's impenetrable front lines had scattered in every direction to avoid the falling debris. There were casualties, as dozens were hit by bits of plummeting sharp stone, and had to be taken to the infirmary site. Tvrdik cursed himself for not handling the surprise attack in a less dangerous way, but at least he had stopped the worst from happening. Still, Drogue's army was swarming into the momentary breach created by the catapults, and the battle was finally joined in earnest. Now, it was all chaos and courageous individuals locked in life and death struggles. Tvrdik and Wynne rode back and forth along the edges of the field, trying to turn as many weapons as he could into useless, harmless, everyday objects. He turned pikes to snakes that slithered through the wielder's hands. He super-heated swords and knives so that they burned their owners' hands and were dropped to the ground in a shower of curses and yowls. Cudgels and clubs he turned into bunches of seaweed that slapped harmlessly at the intended victims and clung with slimy stubbornness to those who waved them about. Once more, Drogue deployed his archers, and once more, the arrows racing through the air flew away under their own power. The usurper had to resign himself to the fact that bows and arrows would not avail him on this field. Tvrdik was like a tornado, twisting and waving the staff, operating on instinct, no time for thought, shouting out spells and taking in all that was occurring around him as if it were playing out in slow motion before his eyes.

Meanwhile, the courageous pole brigade threaded through the field, skillfully defending themselves and each other from the blows that were aimed at them, while felling as many of the enemy as possible with their drug-soaked thorns. Luckily, this potion was very fast-acting. Many of the Legion's finest saw their lives flash before their eyes while their adversaries dropped in the middle of a well-aimed thrust or swing, split-seconds away from separating a defender's limb or head from his torso. As they saw how well the tactic worked on the field, however, and found their rhythm, they soon littered the ground in every direction with snoring warriors who never knew what hit them. The harpers, women, and youth went among the pockets of inert bodies, gathering all the weapons they could carry, and removing them to a stockpile well away from the fray, back behind the defenders' lines. If they found anyone wounded, from either side, they helped conduct them off the field and to assistance.

At the river bank, Ondine and company were making any meaningful confrontation impossible, flooding the banks with foaming waters and turning them to a slippery mud-slick of gigantic proportions. Any of Drogue's warriors who thought they could gain ground by edging through the mud found themselves with gallons of water and pelted with a hail of river rocks. Anywhere the trees could reach at the edges of the valley, they also seized the opportunity to swat at the hapless men-at-arms that Drogue kept urging forward. Careful not to deliver any bone-crushing blows, the leafy dryads nevertheless slowed, annoyed, and knocked over a good many of the enemy as they attempted to pass. Several trees suffered wounds for their loyalty, as frustrated soldiers lashed out at their unexpected attackers and hacked away branches.

Up above, Jorelial Rey and Tashroth were wheeling and diving all over the theater of battle. Shouting words of praise and encouragement to the Legionnaires whenever she passed in earshot, she became a beacon of courage, a reminder of restraint, and an inspiration that spurred her troops to feats of which they had not believed themselves capable. In addition, she was now leading the company of dragons over the center of Drogue's force, diving, shrieking, flaming, harrying, and sometimes plucking an unlucky soldier or two up in their talons, to be deposited unharmed on the sidelines later. Though the dragons hurt no one, the terror these maneuvers struck in the hearts of those who were either chosen, or came near to being carried off, often sent them running from the field for good. The unicorns galloped here and there, dodging weapons, poking combatants painfully in the buttocks, and sending out random blinding bursts of light from their magical horns. More than once, an unexpected flash averted some tragedy about to happen. Shar, who could not channel light through the ash wood horn Tvrdik had fitted him with, made himself available for the transport of the wounded from the field to the infirmary.

And there were wounded. As near as Tvrdik could tell, no fatalities. But every time one of the brave Legionnaires fell with a broken bone or a nasty slice, he winced in anguish, feeling personally responsible that some lethal weapon or another had escaped his magical attention with dire results.

The fighting was filling the valley now; all of their tricks and maneuvers had slowed, but not defeated Drogue's army. Even with almost half of his original force defected, asleep, or weaponless, there always seemed to be another wave of ruthless soldiers, consumed with hatred, who were determined to break through the lines of defenders. Tvrdik tried to be everywhere, depriving the savage dogs of their bite in whatever ways he could. Jorelial Rey and the dragons kept up a continuous schedule of assault from above. But more was needed. It was time to reveal their surprise ace. Up soared Tashroth, high above the action, bellowing his harrowing, unearthly call to attention. Every eye turned upward to see General Rey's right arm raised high in the air. When she was sure she had the attention of all her company, near and far, she made an abrupt gesture like punching the air. Another line of Legionnaires stepped forward onto the field, carrying large oval shields before them. Tashroth shrieked again, and in unison, all of Mrs. Praeger's fabric covers slid to the dust, and flashes of bright blue pierced the air.

There was a pause in struggles everywhere on the field as eyes turned toward the flash of glowing blue, some in curiosity and apprehension, and others in knowing expectation and relief. The moment seemed to stretch out in stillness and silence, like a reader closing his eyes to rest them at the turn of a page, or a breath held suspended before the exhalation. And then, line upon line, slow, steady, and inexorable, the shield-bearers began to march forward.

In hindsight, it was a foolish move – in fact, considering the circumstances, it was downright idiotic. But almost no one knew where they were, and with whom. The battle, miles away, was almost sure to have already begun, and would be claiming the attention of anyone who mattered. Darian had been so restless in the house for the past few days. It was the first morning since they had been there that dawned with a promise of relief from the oppressive heat, even if it was a bit overcast. At the time, there seemed no harm in venturing out on the mountain to pick the last of the berries. It gave the young king something to do out in the fresh air, something that had purpose. And later on Lynette and Nelrose could help Mark's mother bake some tarts, and they all could enjoy the fruits of the morning's labors. It was a quiet, lovely morning on the mountainside, despite the clouds. There was a breeze, and there was birdsong, alpine flowers, and a rich harvest.

Chasing the tasty treasures from bush to bush, the infant king wandered off a little further from Delphine's side than was prudent, but she always had him in her sight, and Mark was paying more attention to the both of them than to his own gathering. He was poised, some twenty arm-lengths away, to spring into action if the need arose. Glancing up from the berry bushes every few seconds, he saw the gap between Darian and Delphine continue to widen, and began to think that he should intervene. But he was so mesmerized by their innocent carelessness, their laughter, their seeming obliviousness to the realities of war, or the burdens of royalty. For that moment, they were just a charming young woman and a golden-haired little boy, enjoying a moment of play. His heart swelled to see them like that, and he fell in love with them both in the sheer simplicity of their delight. Not wanting to intrude on such a perfect moment – not wanting to re-introduce them to fear, uncertainty, and heaviness without cause – he hesitated. He held his tongue, held his position. Perhaps if the day had been brighter, one of them might have seen the shadow that fell over them much sooner...

———◦———

Jarrod the crow beat the air with his powerful wings, propelling himself along at a dizzying clip toward his destination. His heart soared, however, at even a greater altitude than his gleaming dark frame. Proud he was, and full of excitement, to be serving the king and the regent as a personal secret messenger. Intoxicated with the good news he was sent to deliver, and confident, since his last mission had proceeded without incident, he was not what one would call 'cautious' with his flight plan. Nor did it occur to him to be on the alert for anyone or anything which might be following him. Singing himself a croaking travel song, which quite engaged his attention along the way, he already had the sprawling ranch house in his sights before he noticed the immense gryphon on his tail. In a heartbeat, he realized what was happening. Alarmed, he made a sharp turn, and tried to seduce the creature into following him to some other place. Cawing and kicking up a fuss, brave Jarrod offered himself up as a decoy to the sharp-eyed, fearsome beast, but it was too late. It had already spotted a much more interesting prey, right out in the open, ripe for the picking. All of Jarrod's desperate maneuvers were ignored as the gryphon smiled; the master would be very pleased at his cleverness.

Jarrod flew to a high branch in a nearby pine and watched in horror, shrieking a frantic alert to the intended victims as the gryphon swooped down...

———◦———

He never knew if it was the uncommon flurry of noise overhead, or the sudden disappearance of even the palest sunlight above him that made Mark's head snap up to see the gryphon approaching with a glint of purpose in its golden eye. Acting on instinct, he sprang from the bushes and began to run. But in an instant, one awful instant, he realized that Darian and Delphine had wandered so far apart that he only had time to reach one or the other. Now, Delphine too had noticed the swift descending danger, and was running too. But, to his horror, the bard saw that she was headed *away* from the little king, who was standing stock still, mesmerized by the great winged creature. *Gods!* Mark thought, *the fool girl is trying to use herself as bait, to draw the beast's notice.* And it looked like it might be working. Recognizing the red-haired sister of the Lady Regent, the gryphon banked and followed her over the meadow. There was still time for Mark to intervene, but he had to decide *now.* Mark, a poet, a bard, a thinker, but not a warrior at heart, was forced into the unenviable position of choosing in that moment whom to save: the helpless king to whom he had pledged his life in fealty, or the woman whom he loved more than life itself. He stumbled. But then, as if in answer to his soul's cry of anguish, he saw Delphine stop running and turn to face him. He heard her shout with all her might, "Mark, the king! Save Darian. To the king, Mark!"

It was as if the angels had trumpeted instructions, and the bard turned toward the frozen little boy, closed the gap between them in a flash, scooped him up in his strong, wiry arms, and headed for the house. Only once did he look back over his shoulder, without missing a step, to see the gryphon's vise-like talons close about the slim waist, and lift Delphine from the ground. She reached a hand out toward him as he thought he heard the words, "I love you," echo on the wind. And then she was gone, the fabled beast winging away on the far-off horizon.

Panting and sobbing, Mark reached the door of his family home, the sanctuary he had always trusted. He handed his small, precious charge over to waiting arms, and fell to his knees on the threshold. His trembling hands covered his tear-streaked face, and his breath wracked his slim frame in waves. But, invisible to those who clustered around him, was his heart, torn to ragged bits.

An eerie silence descended over the battlefield, as the combatants looked up to see what new surprise was about to be introduced by the Crown's forces. Flashes of sapphire blue caught everyone's attention, but as the shield bearers strode forward and spread out, and nothing lethal shot out of the large oval objects, Drogue's troops began to relax and turn back to their more immediate tasks. They shrugged their shoulders, and assumed the new object was simply a new-fangled defensive tool meant to distract and impress. Jorelial Rey was circling overhead on Tashroth, but she stayed near to the block of shield bearers, where she had the best vantage point to see what was about to happen. Tvrdik, still riding up and down the sidelines on Wynne, working at disarming with magic as many of Drogue's warriors as possible, tried to sneak a look between spells. He realized he was holding his breath in anticipation of what their secret weapon would do on a real field. As the fearless shield bearers marched into the thick of the struggle, what the dragonrider and the mage actually saw almost brought a cheer to their lips, and tears to their eyes. The chance they had taken against all odds was working. It was actually working.

The blue shield warriors had been well trained to keep their shields low and defensive, until they had targeted some particular subject. They would then approach as near as they dared, and raise the blue mirrored surface in a sudden gesture, angled so that the intended victim could not help but confront his own reflection. The rest was up to the blue light itself. At first, there were one or two brilliant flashes of blue as the shields were deployed, a few scattered cries of surprise, and pockets of eerie stillness on the field. Within moments, it seemed, blue lights were exploding everywhere, and all over the valley, attackers were disengaging. What each of them saw in the mirrors they confronted cannot be described here, nor indeed known, as each being who gazed into the blue fire had a unique experience, perceiving the deepest truth of his own being. It was the repertory of reactions that was so fascinating to watch. Dozens of hardened mercenaries stopped to stare at their reflections, then made abrupt turns to walk off the field, and out of the Yechtze altogether. There were those who dropped their weapons and fell to their knees, weeping in shame and despair. Some were so crazed by what they saw that they tried to turn their weapons on themselves, while their one-time adversaries from the Legions of Light stepped in to intervene. Some, perhaps, saw potentials in themselves they had never known before, and threw up their hands whooping, and laughing, and dancing playful jigs.

Tvrdik asked Wynne to pull up, and they watched in amazement from a bit of high ground, as the entire field of conflict transformed before their eyes into a theater of the absurd. The shield bearers advanced with grim purpose, training their mirrors on one hapless victim after another.

Those defenders of the Crown who had been in mortal struggle moments before, knew not to look full into any of the blue mirrors, although a few here and there might have been caught by the powerful light of truth, to no lasting harm. The rest took to gathering up all the fallen weapons, backed off the field, and retreated behind their own front lines to watch the spectacle unfold. Even the dragons ceased their harassments, and rose in the air, circling and observing. As if to put a fine point on the wonder of the moment, from somewhere in the crowd of Legionnaires, the soaring, pure, unearthly voice of Nyree rose once more in a haunting arabesque of melody. She was answered quickly by other voices from the bardic company, voices deep, and strong, and somehow sacred. The heart-piercing sound, coupled with the behavior of those who had stared full into the mirrors, unnerved the rest of Drogue's army, so that many turned and fled the field, making signs with their hands to ward off evil spirits. Overhead, Lord Drogue was flying in tight circles on his winged horse, gesticulating and shouting orders until his voice sounded raw, and the veins on his head stood out. But almost no one was listening.

Jorelial Rey closed her eyes for just a moment in satisfaction. The day was not yet over, but the balance had tipped, and once again, they had pushed back the foe with sheer creativity and a touch of magic.

Mark could feel the hands and hear the voices urging him back, trying to comfort him – beloved hands, and voices of his dear family. But not the touch or the sound he longed for most of all. It had not been some horrible nightmare after all – Delphine was gone, and they were all compromised. Somewhere, beneath the noise in his aching head, he knew he had done what was necessary, but at what cost? A big part of him just wanted to lie there and grieve, oblivious to time, without hope, beyond reason. But another voice within told him his work was not done, and he needed to take action. The king must be moved, or they would all be at risk – his parents, his beloved sister, and Lynette, as well as the infant monarch. He had sworn to protect them with his life. Somehow, the Lady Regent must be told. And maybe Delphine could still be saved! Delphine…the thought of his bride brought the pain rushing in all over again, as he began to imagine what awful things could be happening to her. He had to find the strength to pull himself together and take charge.

As he struggled with these thoughts, an unfamiliar voice reached into his despair and tugged at him – a deep voice, baritone, with a rich timbre and cultivated accent.

"Master Bard. Sir, rouse yourself. You must get up. Hurry. Precious time is being wasted." Mark sat up and opened his eyes. He had been lying sprawled across the doorjamb, only minutes since the awful events he could not even name had taken place. As he wiped the tears from his eyes, he noticed in the background his family, Darian in the arms of Nelrose, all looking very drawn and alarmed. But his eyes came to rest on the speaker who had addressed him, very near his face. That rich baritone belonged to a huge grey dire-wolf, who stood regarding him with deep, unblinking, amber eyes. Behind him stood a second, smaller and paler in color, but with as compelling a gaze.

"Who...who are you?" Mark's own voice sounded hoarse and ugly.

"I am Baldezir, and this is my wife, Shekilah. Jarrod the crow came to find us when he saw that trouble had found you. We came as quickly as we could, and are here to help if we may."

"Why would you do that, sir wolf? We are strangers to you, and we are magnets for danger."

Shekilah answered, in a velvety, rich alto, "On your wedding day, it was promised you that the Fellowship of Talking Beasts would look after you and your bride, do you not recall? It was said that we would always be nearby in time of need. We have kept the two of you in our sights ever since, some of us or others, and we are pledged to assist you now. We bear no love for the tyrant Drogue, and are as keen as you to see him defeated in his schemes. And we are all quite fond of the Lady Delphine, and would not allow her to come to harm, if we could do something about it."

"We must act quickly though, or we will be too late," Baldezir insisted.

Mark was on his feet and listening now, his better instincts rallying to the fore. "I am most grateful to both of you for your help, and I am in your debt. But what must we do?"

Baldezir thought, "Your wife is a great prize for Lord Drogue, worth far more to him alive. We hear the battle does not go well for him. It would be my best guess that he will attempt to use her as a hostage, as leverage...

that buys us some time, but how much?" the dire-wolf scanned the rest of the room, "And none of you are safe here anymore…"

Desperation drove Mark to suggest an impossible idea, "Baldezir, forgive me, but do you think you would be able to carry me? Over the hills as far as the battle site? I must get to the Lady Regent to tell her what has happened, and enlist her aid, and that of the dragons. Tvrdik will help us too, with his magic…do you know the Valley of the Yechtze?"

The great beast sized the man up, "You are tall, but slender. You would not be heavier than a deer carcass, or one of my cubs. I can carry you. And I know the way to Yechtze."

Mark turned to Baldezir's companion, "Shekilah, do you know the warren of caves that face the stream about three quarters of a mile west of here? We have sheltered our sheep there sometimes during storms. There are boxwood bushes that nearly conceal the entrance. My father also knows the place…" He could see his father nodding in agreement.

"I have whelped a litter there myself," Shekilah assured him, adding, with a hint of mischief, "Be wary when next you take your sheep there."

"Shekilah, would you be willing to guide the king, Lynette, and my family to those caves? They will not be able to travel as fast as you can, and will require protection, but I don't think they would be discovered once there."

"I agree. Few know of this place, and it cannot be spotted from above. I can get assistance. My brothers and I will escort them safely. I will be back soon; have them ready to go."

"It is a good plan," Baldezir said, and nuzzled his own wife once before sending her off to do as she had promised. Mark's mother sprang into action, gathering up things that might be needful, should they be in exile for any length of time. Mark's father came to him and put a hand on his shoulder.

"My heart aches for you, Mark. How swiftly a beautiful day can turn to a nightmare! You need to go right now. Bring her back safely. Do everything in your power. Don't worry about us. We will be safe in those caves, and your mother and I will watch over Darian. Trust the she-wolf, son. She will do as she promised. Go now."

Father and son regarded each other with great emotion. Mark nodded, and they embraced. The older man turned to assist with the packing, and when Mark saw that all was being handled, he approached Baldezir.

"We must go," the wolf urged.

Mark hesitated, uncertain how to proceed, but Baldezir continued, "Here, take that rope there and tie it around my shoulders and neck, like a harness. Not too tight. There, that's it. Make sure it will hold. Now, lie down flat on my back, face down, and grip the rope tightly with both hands. Press with your knees a bit. Don't worry, you are not heavy for me at all. Settled? Good. Hold on. We are off."

And they were, as Baldezir flew out the door amid cries of "Godspeed," and "Farewell." As they turned away from the house, Mark just caught sight of Shekilah racing in with two other brawny wolves by her side, true to her word. His fears for his family, and the king thus allayed, he buried his face in the coarse fur beneath him, held tightly, and prayed.

Gargan wiped a filthy sleeve across his eyes, but only succeeded in smearing more mud, sweat, and cheese all over his face. He and three of the men assigned to his command had just succeeded in righting one of Drogue's outsized catapults, that had been tipped over by a dragon. But the launch arm was stuck in the upright position, and the rope that would have pulled it back to reset had been singed clear through. Gargan's thoughts were full of blood and frustration. He had expected this battle to be quick and exhilarating, setting them well on the path to establishing Lord Drogue on the throne of Eneri Clare. Instead, the whole exercise had been disastrous. Why couldn't the fool defenders just march out and fight like normal folk, show their mettle? And how *dare* they seem to be succeeding at every lunatic attempt to derail Drogue's forces, superior by every measure? Right about now, he would give a year of his life just to be engaged in a real, adrenaline pumping, manly, dangerous exchange of swordplay, instead of digging a stupid machine out of the mud. He stared at the soldiers awaiting his next order, all burly and able, but dumb as rocks. Shaking his head, he called for a length of rope, and pointed to the top of the catapult, where someone would have to climb up and re-attach it. The rope appeared, but the men hesitated, glancing up in terror at numerous dragons still performing acrobatics in the sky above. Gargan was about to lose his temper, when from out of nowhere, Drogue himself swooped in, on his winged black steed, hovering just over the bedraggled group.

"I thought I told you to get this one up and running! What is taking so long?" the self-styled Prince called down.

"My lord, the field is all mud, and half my men have wandered off – we are doing the best we can!"

Drogue scowled, pulling up hard on Valour's reins, "Gargan, I have told you constantly that the only way to get something done is to do it yourself. Now, get it fixed, and get it moving..."

Gargan, at the end of his own rope, had had just about enough of his master's disrespect and abuse, and was only saved from saying something aloud that he might have regretted later, by the arrival of a gryphon, who positioned himself near to Drogue's ear, and imparted some message to the dark lord. Drogue's entire demeanor seemed to change in a heartbeat. He started in his seat, the expression on his face a curious mix of surprise and glee, wheeled Valour about roughly, and was off to a clifftop in the distance before Gargan could even salute.

But the disgruntled henchman, not about to admit defeat at the hands of the Crown's effete rabble, decided that Drogue did have a point, and began to scramble up the slippery wooden beams to the top of the catapult. Once he had achieved the summit, he positioned himself in the launching bowl and signaled for his men to toss him the rope. It took three tries, but eventually he caught one end and fastened it securely to a metal hasp on the top of the arm. Clearing away any debris that could impede the machine's functioning, and still sitting securely in the launch bowl, he instructed his men to get in line and pull hard on the rope. Hollering for them to put their backs into it, he heard a loud creak, as the springs engaged, and the giant arm began to bend back toward earth. Inch by inch, down and down he travelled, as the heavy catapult was reset. Thinking about what flaming cargo he would load it with against the Crown as soon as it was in position, he was surprised to find himself standing in the bowl as it touched the ground in the fully cocked position.

"Tie it off!" he yelled to his men, who were still holding the rope, muscles rippling with effort.

"Whaaa?" replied one of them, turning to look over his shoulder at his commander.

"Tie it off, you bloody fools!" Gargan hollered, one leg already over the side of the bowl as he began to scramble out.

But at that very moment, a small group of Andrus's healer/spear-carriers, bold to be venturing much further out in the field than some of their compatriots, happened by, and, seeing three of Drogue's warriors whose hands were otherwise occupied, ran up to prick them with their drug-soaked thorns. Gargan saw them approaching as if in slow motion. His eyebrows rose, and he shouted, "No!" Down dropped the soldiers in unison, instantly asleep. "No, no, no..." hollered Gargan, as their grip relaxed on the rope. A deafening note filled the ears of everyone in the vicinity as the rope slipped through open hands and whipped backwards, vibrating as it hung in the air. Released from its leash, up went the powerful catapult arm, hurling its unwilling load with great force, at a steep angle, into the air.

Two of the dragons were just passing over the field, keeping a tight formation, and looking for opportunities below to wreak a little havoc, when the flailing, mud-spattered, spinning ball of flesh that was Gargan, came flying by them, overtaking them and speeding off into the distance. The obscenities he was screaming seemed to emerge from thin air, crescendo and rise in pitch as he soared by, and then fade off with the receding vision of his squirming bulk.

"Now *there's* something you don't see every day!" the pink dragon commented, saurian eyebrows raised, and his companion nodded.

THIRTY-NINE

TVRDIK'S GREATEST CHALLENGE

STILL MOUNTED ON WYNNE, TVRDIK pulled up at the edge of the field, in order to survey the situation and determine where he was most needed. Everywhere he looked, there was evidence that the Legions of Light were making headway. Dragons were aloft, now harrying Drogue's soldiers by dropping bags of kitchen garbage on them. Light warriors were running here and there with blue mirror-shields, wielding them as they saw fit, while their compatriots collected fallen weapons and gathered the wounded. Harpers were still providing a soundtrack to the whole scene with their drumming and stirring melodies. Drogue's forces seemed to be in disarray. Some had already retreated or deserted, and by now, the Lord himself was nowhere to be seen. Best of all, there had been no news of grave casualties on either side. Hope washed over the young mage like a summer rain. *Xaarus, you old badger, I begin to believe you knew what you were doing all along,* he thought, allowing the shadow of a smile to touch his lips for the first time all day.

And then, over all the confused din of the battlefield, clear as a streak of lightning, he heard someone call his name – a light, musical voice that floated over the noise of war, and seemed somehow familiar, as if from some long unused corridor of his mind. He turned toward the sound, and there she was. Alone. Mounted on a dark horse at the top of a little hillock, not thirty yards away. She was clad all in black armor, but her head was uncovered, the long, golden hair streaming behind her in the stormy air. Again he heard her call, "Tvrdik," and she waved a hand to him. His lips formed the word before his throat could utter any sound – just a whisper, "Ailianne." And then, wrenched from the depths of his very soul, a visceral cry, *"Ailianne!"*

He spurred Wynne toward the little hill, while the figure on the horse waited, silent and still, except for the billowing tresses dancing in the wind. At the foot of the knoll, he leapt from the unicorn's back, and ran up the slope in long strides. Arriving at the top, Tvrdik stopped short right in front of the dark steed, and stared up at the impossible vision before his eyes. Words would not form in his mind or on his tongue, and his heart pounded in his chest so that he was sure she would hear it. She broke the silence.

"I've been watching you on the field, Tvrdik. You've learned a few tricks since our schooldays, old friend." She smiled down at him warmly.

"Ailianne," he choked, breathing hard from his ascent, "you…how can you be here in this place? You are…you are…."

"Dead? Oh, Tvrdik, you were always so literal and pedestrian about things." She rolled her eyes skyward and pursed her lovely mouth in an expression of exasperation he recalled all too well. "We are wizards, you and I. What meaning have words like time and space, life and death to us? We can transcend them all. Surely by now you have come to see that?"

He furrowed his brow and cocked his head to one side, watching her, afraid to step closer for fear she might vanish.

She spoke again, "I can see you have become a powerful and gifted mage. But there is so much to which you have not been exposed; so much that old fool Xaarus kept hidden from you. He was jealous of all of us, you know, and only wanted to protect his own position."

Tvrdik took a single step backward at such ugly assertions.

She went on, "Benjin and I were not content to let him limit our power and knowledge to suit his own purposes. We found things out on our own – called in forces, aligned ourselves with primal energies that cannot be contained by a mere mortal. True, we were a little out of our depth, and spent some time resting in a kind of suspension between worlds, as a result of our ignorance. But, we were fortunate that the great Prince Drogue himself has some facility with the ancient arts, and he found a way to wake us from our slumber, and into immortality. We owe him a great debt of gratitude. He is truly a man of vision and decisive action."

Tvrdik took another step back, confused. "Where is Benjin now?" he probed, his voice quivering, "I should very much like to see him again."

She shrugged, "He is not here today. We are free to come and go, and pursue whatever interests us most. But I, I am here to seek you out, old friend. We have missed you...*I* have missed you. We have always belonged together – do you not know that? We are of a kind, the last of our kind. Come with me, and we will all be together again, just like old times." She smiled with dazzling beauty again, and reached a hand down toward him.

Tvrdik stood his ground, and countered, "You must come with *me*, Ailianne, and you will be welcomed with open arms. Your homeland has need of your services. You speak truly that wizards are scarce these days."

She shook her head, "Your world is so limiting, Tvrdik. I could not bear it. Join me now, and you will see Prince Drogue is a man of great imagination, who will appreciate and reward the gifts of one as talented as you. Come with me; I have so much to teach you. I will help you to master time, and death itself. I will share with you the secrets of immortality." Her face shone with a fervor that somehow did not seem altogether salutary.

"I have no interest in immortality," the mage replied. "Ailianne, what has happened to you? Your thoughts are poisoned. Come home, and let me help you."

Her lips pursed in a pretty pout, "I would have thought by now that you would be bored with silly parlor tricks, and would be hungry for real knowledge – longing for something more. You are free now to pursue it, free to explore and experiment in any magic you desire. No rules, no warnings, no limits. How can you turn your back on such boundless liberty, and on access to all the ancient wisdom? *Real* magic. Wake up to who you are, Tvrdik. Wake up and claim your birthright."

He stood stone-still before her, pale eyebrows furrowed and heart pounding. Once more he pleaded with the golden-haired girl, "Ailianne, I have everything I need, everything I can handle right here, right now. I am...I am...overjoyed to see you safe, and alive after all these years. Come home with me. Benjin, too. There is a place of honor here for all of us, I am certain."

He did not see her dismount from the powerful stallion, nor did she walk toward him. Yet now, she was standing on the ground beside him, so close he could feel her breath on his cheek, smell the vague scent of honeysuckle that always clung to her golden hair. Tvrdik fumbled in his pocket, and squeezed the coin he found there hard in his palm, thinking, *Oh, Xaarus, please, please help me! If ever I had need of you, it is now.* But, no Xaarus appeared, no hint of a voice from beyond, no memory of a wise saying to guide him. He was on his own.

"You have doubts," she whispered low to him. "I am real. Go ahead, touch me. Prove to yourself that I am alive." He lifted a trembling hand and stroked the lovely hair. Old pain seared through his being as he laid his palm on her cheek and felt it warm and vibrant to his touch. He dared not look at her face – the pale, pink skin, the sprinkle of charming freckles, the small, upturned nose and dazzling smile – all exactly as he remembered them. She had not aged a day, or changed a wit in twelve years. She was just as beautiful, as intriguing, as fresh as she had been so long ago. She laughed, a soft, musical sound, like a collection of little tuned bells. He had always loved hearing her laugh.

"Satisfied?" she said, baiting him. "Are you still as slow to understand things as you used to be?" She was looking at him in a way he had always dreamed she might. He gazed into her eyes, her lovely, lovely eyes...but something in them disturbed him, frightened him. The wide mouth was smiling, and now she was teasing him again and he thought he must have imagined any darkness. It really was Ailianne after all, alive, in the flesh! She grasped his shoulders, "Tvrdik, listen to me. You loved me once, I know it. You still love me. We could be together, always. I have been waiting for you...waiting so long. You and I are powerful. Together, there is nothing that can stand against us. Join me now, and come away from this world of dullards, and I will show you how to live..."

Her lips were so close now and his hand moved gently down her cheek to trace the line of her perfect jaw, her long, fluid neck. She was gazing at him with longing, and he was snared in her eyes. All around these two figures, chaos raged, but they seemed to be in a bubble of calm, far away from the world, untouched by time, or danger, or urgency. He was falling, falling helpless into her eyes...she was so young, so very beautiful...she hadn't changed at all..."

Tvrdik took her by the shoulders and pushed her firmly away.

"You haven't changed a bit, Ailianne. Why haven't you aged? Twelve long years, years of hard experience and pain that have taken their toll on me, and yet *you* are as fresh and lovely as you were at seventeen. Why are you still so beautiful and untouched, Ailianne? Why are there no marks of life on your face?"

"I told you. We were preserved in a suspended form for much of these years, and now we have learned to triumph over age and decay."

"What sort of life is that, Ailianne? A half-life in the shadows, without grief or pain or experience to shape you, without time to teach you wisdom and compassion? Without real relationships, or the fear of loss? What *are* you, Ailianne?" He was stepping purposefully backwards now, and beginning to shout at her. She looked confused, frightened. In an instant, she appeared back on the horse. The restless animal began to paw the ground, as her glance darted in every direction, looking for someone or something. Was she anxious, sensing failure?

Tvrdik grabbed at the arm of a passing Legionnaire. "Friend," he commanded, "lend me your shield, quickly." Something in his tone admitted to no discussion. The young man gave up the blue shield and kept running.

"No, Tvrdik. Don't do this. Don't throw it all away. I can offer you all you ever dreamed of." The beautiful voice now sounded brittle with desperation.

"What are you afraid of, Ailianne? I have no wish to harm you. I have no weapons, except the truth. A real wizard would never fear truth; it is our greatest ally, our tool." He was addressing her now with a new certainty in his voice and manner.

"No, Tvrdik, no," she begged him, "please, no. You loved me once. I could belong to you forever..."

He held the shield high, and turned the blue light of truth upon her. There was a flash of light as she caught her own reflection in the polished silver, and then a horrific shriek that could never have come from any man or woman or beast on earth – an ear-splitting, bone-shaking, heart-rending, terrifying, endless wail of misery and defeat unlike anything Tvrdik had ever heard, even in his worst nightmares. Before his eyes, the beautiful Ailianne became a skeleton in armor – horrible, as perfect hair, skin, flesh fell away to reveal for just a split second what was not illusion. And then, the entire vision crumbled to a fine, black powder and blew away on the four winds. A riderless horse stood on a windy hilltop, cropping grass and pawing at the ground, no sign, no trace of the mistress it had carried only moments before.

Tvrdik threw the shield down on the ground and stared down at his hands. "Belong to me forever?" he cried aloud, "…and what would I hold in my arms all that time but bitterness and dust? The girl I knew and loved has been dead and gone these twelve long years." He stumbled blindly down the little hill and to the edge of the battlefield, where there was a small copse of trees. Leaning on a sturdy elm for support, he retched in the grass, purging from his being all the horror and disgust and sorrow at what had just happened. Then, pulling off his spectacles with his left hand, he stood there and sobbed, great sobs that wracked his spare frame almost beyond endurance.

He had no idea how many minutes had passed thus, when, having come to some peace, he heard hoof beats approaching. It was Wynne, searching for him.

"Sir!" the unicorn called, "you must mount and ride at once. You are needed. General Rey is down, and our Legions are scattering in alarm. You must bring your healing skills to her now or the day is lost."

Alarmed, and jolted by this news into the present moment, with all its urgent needs, Tvrdik left behind his past once and for all, and swung himself onto the unicorn's back.

Wynne filled him in as they raced across the field to another part of the valley. "The Lady Rey and Tashroth were diving and wheeling across the sky, harrying the enemy, and urging our comrades forward. Without warning, a large stone from one of Drogue's remaining catapults came spinning straight toward them. At the last moment, Tashroth twisted aside to avoid the blow, but that move sent him plummeting at a dizzying angle. It only took an instant for him to regain his equilibrium, but the regent lost her grip, and fell from his back. She landed hard, and is still lying there unconscious. Someone said they heard a *crack* when her head hit the stony ground. They are trying to move her out of the battle zone now, to tend to her injuries, but Tashroth is pacing up and down in front of her, snorting and roaring, and making it impossible for anyone to approach. Word is spreading of the accident, and the bad news is draining all the momentum from our troops on the field. Something has to be done right away to help her, and to restore morale."

As they approached the scene, Tvrdik saw the situation much as Wynne had described it – Lady Rey crumpled on the ground, motionless. She was surrounded at a distance by an assortment of well-meaning colleagues with their hands up in front of their faces, desperate to calm Tashroth, who paced and bellowed and blew fire at them in mindless distress. Tvrdik strode straight up to him and stood his ground.

"Mighty Tashroth, calm yourself," he shouted up, in his most commanding voice, "Let me come to her. I will do what I can to help." Their eyes locked, Tvrdik's determined and honest, Tashroth's flashing, wild. Seconds passed, and the great beast seemed to deflate. His eyes cleared in comprehension, then narrowed to slits as he folded his flailing wings and stepped back. Seizing the opening, Tvrdik ran to where the young leader lay, so still, and knelt beside her. His worst fears were allayed when he saw that she was breathing in a deep and regular rhythm. A quick assessment with his eyes and hands revealed no broken bones, and her neck and spine seemed intact. It was easy to see the mark on her forehead, which was swollen and bruised.

The young mage wasted no time, but scooped her up in his arms, gathered the limp frame to his chest as he rose from his knees, and ran off the battlefield to a more sheltered corner where the river still ran clear. As he laid her down in the muddy grass, Tvrdik thought with surprise how such a huge, powerful personality managed to be contained in the slight, frail body he held in his arms. Ondine appeared from the water, peering over the bank with concern. "Help me, Ondine," the wizard begged, "Whatever healing powers you and your friends have, send them into the waters now. Ondine closed her eyes and concentrated, throwing her arms wide. It wasn't long before the waters around her began to foam and bubble. Ripping off a piece of his sleeve, Tvrdik soaked the cloth in the stream. "Thank you, dear heart," he nodded to the sprite. Then, supporting Rel's head with one arm, he washed her face and head with the cloth, and dripped some of the energy-infused waters into her open mouth. He felt her stir, and she made a faint sound, but she did not open her eyes. Putting aside the soaked cloth, the mage shifted her position a bit so that he could lay both of his hands across her brow. He closed his eyes and concentrated. But, as he focused on his patient's energy field, he could feel Jorelial Rey's life force draining away. He was losing her. Tvrdik broke concentration and looked up at the pale, silent faces all around him, waiting and hoping; at Tashroth, standing quiet and immense just beyond, his enormous eyes fixed with desperate concern on the girl below. Tvrdik thought of all the disastrous consequences that loomed if he could not save her – the Legion failing, the kingdom fallen to Drogue, Xaarus trapped forever in a future of darkness. In that one frozen moment, he realized just how important this small girl was to the hopes and dreams of so many. He looked down at her peaceful, familiar face, dark hair now plastered to her forehead, and something inside of him broke wide open as he understood how much she meant to him as well.

"Come on..." he chided her, renewing his absolute concentration and shifting his hands, "Come on. You can't go. You aren't finished yet. You have work to do." Closing his eyes, he focused every shred of energy at his disposal into his hands, and their ability to heal and restore. He whispered to the still form, "You must come back. Please. I cannot do this alone." A second passed, two, three, an eternity. And then he thought he heard a murmur. He opened his eyes to see hers flutter and open wide, struggling to take in the meaning of what they were seeing. She lifted her head and groaned, letting it fall back on his arm. Tvrdik, with a deep sense of relief, dipped the cloth into Ondine's special water once more, and bathed his patient's face with its coolness. He leaned close to her and spoke in a low voice, "Jorelial Rey, you have had a very bad fall. How do you feel?"

One black eyebrow cocked, "I've been better." Her eyes narrowed, "You look awful! How are you?"

He grinned, "Much the same, thank you."

She raised herself to her elbows, mind beginning to clear, "Tashroth?"

"He is here and just fine. Beside himself with worry for you."

"How do things stand?"

"We hold the field, still, but the day is not over, and news of your injury is causing our people to falter. They must see you alive and well, or all could be lost. Do you think you can walk?"

"Help me up." He supported her weight on an arm, as the two of them tottered to their feet. Tashroth threw his head back and roared, and a great cheer erupted from the growing crowd of bystanders. Over in the stream, Tvrdik caught a vision of Ondine leaping in the waters and clapping her tiny hands in delight. Rel summoned a weak smile and nodded to the well-wishers, waving at them in assurance that she was fine. Runners set off in all directions to spread the good news. Tvrdik let out a long, shaky breath of relief.

"Come on, I'll get you to Tash." With her first step, however, he could feel her weight shift, and see her wince. "What is it?" he whispered.

"My ankle. I must have twisted it in the fall."

"It isn't broken. Likely just sprained. Here, put your arm around my neck...like this...good. How is your head?"

"Alternately spinning and pounding, but I can handle it." They were just about to Tashroth now, and she leaned with gratitude against the great beast's shoulder. The dragon's head swung around to nuzzle her with great tenderness.

"I am so sorry, little one. I was sick with worry that I had lost you. Can you ever forgive my carelessness?"

"Don't be silly, Tash," she patted his nose, "it was my fault for not holding on. You saved us both with that amazing dodge. Without your quick reflexes, we wouldn't be standing here. You know me; it'll take a lot more than a little spill to keep me down."

Tvrdik, knowing how close it had actually come, shot her a cryptic look, but all he said was, "Sit here a moment and let me work on that ankle."

"There is no time. I've been out of the fray already far too long. We can't let them get an edge on us."

"This will just take a moment," he soothed, "and it will help you to feel more like yourself, Jorelial Rey. A little patience with the healer, please, and you'll be back in the saddle in no time." He was directing energy into her injured ankle, strengthening it.

She wrinkled her face, "Why do you always do that? Why do you call me that?"

"What?" he looked up.

"Why do you always use my full given name? It's a lot to say – not many people bother. They call me 'Lady Rey', or 'my lady', or just 'Rel'. It just seems, well...odd."

Tvrdik paused a moment and considered, "Well," he finally answered, "because it is *your* name." He shrugged. "There. That ought to get you through the next few hours. I am sorry I haven't anything on me just now to wrap it with, but later on I will."

He was making some gesture to emphasize the wrapping, when she grabbed both of his hands and held them still, while looking straight into his bespectacled face, "Tvrdik, thank you. I can't begin to imagine what I would do without you." She clambered, a little less spry than usual, up onto the green dragon's back, and waved. Tashroth threw up his head to trumpet his thanks, unfurled his great wings, and they were off skyward again. The young mage was once again left below, scratching his head, "Funny," he muttered, "I was just thinking the very same thing."

Closing his eyes and mopping his brow with what was left of his sleeve, Tvrdik sighed, searching for his inner calm after the events of the last hour. But there was no time for reflection now, as Wynne reminded him with a gentle nudge against his elbow. The wizard mounted and the two companions set off around the battle theater to assess how things were progressing, and discover of what assistance he could be. With Jorelial Rey once more aloft and the Legions of Light newly invigorated, the shield-bearers doing their work all over the field, and Drogue's army appearing to be in tatters, it seemed that things were taking care of themselves for the moment. He decided to pay a visit to the makeshift infirmary where the wounded had been taken. Perhaps he could be of some use there. Sending Wynne off to find the rest of the unicorns, the mage stepped into the circle of tents designated for the wounded.

Most of the healers had retreated there by now, and were busily applying bandages, salves and potions to a variety of cuts, gashes, broken bones, sprains, abrasions, concussions and gouges. Tvrdik looked around to see several score patients sitting or lying on cots, but Andrus and his colleagues seemed to have things well in hand. Tvrdik had supplied them well with a large stock of Xaarus' herbals and remedies, along with detailed notes on how they could best be used. That had supplemented their own medical training enough for them to feel confident handling the wounds of war with much more efficiency than they had dealt with Tvrdik's pierced arm only months before.

The young mage visited every bedside, smiled and praised the patients, assuring them that the Legions were still prevailing in the fight. Each of them seemed heartened, even star-struck by the personal visit, and pride overcame pain with them for many hours thereafter. Tvrdik was surprised and dismayed to find Stewart among the victims. He had been running messages between regiments on the field when a wild, riderless horse from Drogue's cavalry came out of nowhere and trampled him. He had a nasty gash on his forehead, a cracked rib, and a sprained hip. Nothing could dampen the spirits of the big dog, however, and as glad as he was to see his old friend, he was more eager to be back in the fray. Tvrdik took a close look at the wolfhound's injuries, and judged that Andrus had done a fine and thorough job tending to them. He implored Stewart to follow the healer's order to rest for the moment, reminding him that he had already done his duty and then some. Stewart snorted in disappointment, but the mage flung an arm around the big dog's shoulders and squeezed him, looking him straight in the eye and adding, in a low voice, "Please, my friend, take good care of yourself. I am depending on it." That got a half-smile and a raised eyebrow from the canine, as Tvrdik took his leave with a scratch behind the ears. Andrus was soon behind him, and they stepped aside to confer.

"Sorry to keep you waiting," the healer began, "I wanted to finish bandaging that shoulder." He gestured at a patient a few meters away.

"Don't apologize. Everything looks well in hand here, Andrus. I thought perhaps I could be of some assistance, but you have no need of me."

"I wouldn't say that; there were times when we did wish we had the benefits of your skill, but we knew you were busy elsewhere. We made do, and well enough, if I may say so. It's thanks to your efforts that these tents aren't filled with ten times as many casualties."

"Have there been any – I mean – did we…have we lost anyone?" He dreaded Andrus' honest response.

"Miraculously, no. Just what you see – dislocations, abrasions, slices, a few concussions, and some fractures, not to mention several cases of a close encounter with a blue shield. But nothing that won't heal. We've treated a few of the enemy as well…they are contained behind that barrier there. Same thing – nothing critical. I've never seen anything like it."

Tvrdik frowned, "We've been lucky so far, and I am more than relieved to see this, but the day is not yet over. It is not yet time to let down our guard."

"I understand." Andrus made a gesture, indicating the patients, "Do you have any suggestions or recommendations, sir?" Tvrdik put a hand on the Palace Physician's shoulder, "They are fortunate to be in the best of hands, friend. I just dropped in for moral support." Andrus smiled at that vote of confidence, and Tvrdik shook his hand, and headed once more to the front.

He climbed to one of the lower cliffs, from where he had a complete and not too distant view of the field. He arrived just in time to witness a most extraordinary scene unfolding below. Lord Drogue had cleared the field again, and then sent an entire regiment of mountain gnomes, along with his personal guard, marching in formation through the valley straight toward the defenders. They were steely-eyed, well-armed, and more disciplined and determined-looking than some of his earlier representatives. They bore down on the front lines of the Legions of Light in great numbers, bent on destruction. Tvrdik scrambled to raise his staff, searching his memory for a spell that would at least render the weapons of this new and dangerous force less lethal. But, before he could utter a sound, he saw a figure that, from this distance, looked like General Boone, waving a signal. A wall of dazzling bright blue light almost blinded him, even from the valley floor. All of the shield bearers had been lined up to face the new onslaught with a tight, many-layered formation, which they had held until the moment when the advancing foe began their final charge. Then, at General Boone's signal, they had all raised their shields as one, edge to edge, creating one enormous blue mirror that spanned the entire end of the valley. Its first effect was to blind and stagger the opposition, slowing them down and weakening their resolve. But, then, as the first line of the assault opened their eyes and beheld themselves in the great wall of reflective blue light, Drogue's toughest soldiers faltered, dropped weapons, sank to the ground, fled in confusion, or stood stock still. Confused, column after column of warriors arrived at the same place, only to be confronted by the steady mirror-shields, and the visions they showed from which there was no escape. Something about the shields acting in concert seemed to increase their power and range, and the Legionnaires holding them neither faltered nor flinched. Tvrdik's hand in his pocket fingered the coin bearing Xaarus' likeness, as he watched row upon row of Drogue's fierce fighters succumb to the stark and sudden sight of their own inner ugliness…or their true core of beauty.

The wall of brilliant blue stood fast, and the would-be conquerors milled about in disarray on the field weeping, crawling, stumbling, bent over double in pain, or wandering away in madness. A formless howl arose from the valley floor, the like of which had never been heard, a composite of the most primal utterances of hundreds of lost souls rediscovering their wounded inner selves.

Tvrdik was so mesmerized by the haunting sound, and by the bizarre picture unfolding beneath him, that at first he did not notice Tashroth touching down lightly on the ridge nearby, and Jorelial Rey hobbling over to stand by his side. She touched his shoulder without a word, leaning for balance, just as entranced by the spectacle below as he was, and the two of them stood there in silence for a time, watching Lord Drogue's final assault unravel.

"Brilliant maneuver of General Boone's, was it not?" she finally spoke.

"Yes, indeed it was." He responded, not shifting his gaze.

"Brilliant bit of sorcery in the first place, those shields…" she continued.

"I was lucky to stumble across the technique." Tvrdik answered.

"I doubt that luck had very much to do with it," she countered, then looked at him, "Tvrdik, it's over. We did what we set out to do. Look down there…"

She was right, though her tone held no note of triumph in it – only weariness, with an edge of disbelief. Lord Drogue was still flying about on Valour, shaking his fist and shouting, to no avail. His cavalry had foundered, his catapults were in splinters, his sorcery had failed, half his forces deserted, another portion in a drug-induced sleep, and the rest now confronting their own inner demons, and in no shape to rejoin a pitched battle. He was, in essence, out of options.

At that point, one of the gryphons in Drogue's employ appeared at his shoulder, catching his attention, whereupon Valour wheeled in mid-air, front hooves pawing at the empty sky, and horse and rider bolted off into the far end of the valley. She assumed the defeated mountain lord was fleeing from more bad news.

"I suppose I should offer him terms, or request a formal surrender, or some such," she sighed. "Blast! I don't even know how these things work…" she admitted, still staring at the action in the valley below.

"Boone will know." Tvrdik also had his eyes glued to the theater of battle, where the Legionnaires were beginning to cheer and hug one another in triumph. "I went down to the healer's tents," he added, absently, "There were no…we didn't…no one was killed."

She sighed, "I was dreading the question."

They both stood there for a moment, battered and weary, somewhat dazed, but beginning to grasp the reality of their victory. Tash looked on from a few yards away, his great tail swishing back and forth. No one had the energy to speak, or think, or make the next move.

Someone else made it for them. Shar came galloping up the rise, breathless and wild-eyed, "Master! My lady! I have been searching for you everywhere. Someone has arrived in camp with urgent news. He is desperate to speak with you both."

Jorelial Rey was first to regain her demeanor of authority, "Who is he, Shar? What does he want?"

"I'm sure I do not know, but he looks like he has been through something terrible, and he arrived on the back of a…a dire-wolf, my lady."

Jorelial Rey and Tvrdik exchanged a wary look, and came to full attention. "Come on," the Lady Regent ordered, "Tash will take us. Thank you, Shar. We'll see you down there." She helped the dragon-wary mage onto Tashroth's back, and climbed up behind him, favoring her swollen ankle. Up into the air they rose and tipped sideways, banking the turn. Tvrdik closed his eyes and gripped the bony ridge in front of him until his knuckles were white. Down they swooped, to the place where Lord Corbin Maygrew was standing just beside the wall of blue. But, well before they landed, Jorelial Rey recognized the tall, bedraggled figure standing with stooped shoulders between Corbin Maygrew and a very large wolf.

FORTY

WHAT FRESH HELL?

"MARK!" SHE SHOUTED, SCRAMBLING OFF of Tashroth's back before he could find a clear place to touch the ground, people scurrying in every direction to make way.

"Mark." she yelled again, dropping to the dirt and limping toward him, despite the searing pain in her damaged ankle.

"Hey, be careful," Tvrdik called after her, "you'll undo all the good we did on that leg...," but then he, too, recognized the identity of the newcomer, and was sliding down Tash's side right behind her.

The young bard was scraped and filthy, and trembling from head to foot, but had refused any assistance until he had spoken to them. Corbin Maygrew was propping him up while he fought to catch his breath. Reaching his side, Jorelial Rey looked him over, sizing up the details, and then, grasping both of his arms, tried to make eye contact with the distraught man.

"Mark," her voice was low and measured, "What happened? Where is Delphine? Darian?"

Mark choked back a sob, but he got the words of his story out, "Lady Rey, we were discovered. One of Drogue's gryphons followed your messenger to us and saw us out picking berries. I-I was several yards away when he appeared. I could only save one of them. He took Delphine." His voice broke on her name.

"His Highness?"

"Safe. I grabbed him in time and ran with him. Baldezir here and his family were watching over us, and his wife has conducted my family, the king, and Lynette to a secret place of safety that only shepherds know. But the gryphon flew off with your sister…I couldn't get to both of them. She…she ran off in the other direction to draw the creature away from Darian. She shouted at me to save the king. Oh gods!" He put his hands over his face and sobbed in earnest now. Jorelial Rey let go of the bard, wincing now with the pain of this news. Gears were turning in her mind.

"You did the right thing, Mark. As awful as this is, you had little choice. You protected the king, just as I charged you to do." She turned to the wolf, who was sitting erect beside Mark, panting from the exertions of their difficult journey. "Baldezir, is it?"

"Yes, my lady."

Mark composed himself again and interrupted, "He carried me all the way here at a breakneck pace in order to find you…"

Rel nodded, "Sir, our entire kingdom is grateful for your extraordinary service at this critical hour. No matter what happens, I will see you knighted for your courage when this is over."

Baldezir made a small bow and fixed his great yellow eyes on her, "Lady, my people are more than happy to do our part in thwarting men like Drogue. But I thank you for your kind acknowledgement."

The Lady Regent waved her arm. "Someone bring water and meat here!" she called. A few unoccupied legionnaires claimed the assignment, and scurried away toward the camp. Tvrdik stepped in and pulled Mark into his long arms, enfolding him with all the compassion and comfort of a brother, while grasping for some inspiration that might help Delphine. Delphine…sweet Delphine – his first real friend in this place. They couldn't just leave her to the tyrant.

Mark was grateful for the support, still trembling with emotion. But he straightened and spoke again, determined to set some action in motion, "Baldezir thinks he will not harm her until he can find some way to use her as a bargaining chip, since things have not gone well for him here on the field. We may yet have a chance to rescue her, but every moment is precious."

Jorelial Rey was pacing. Hobbling, but pacing nevertheless.

"That man is capable of anything – we mustn't underestimate him. But, I agree that she is probably still alive. I will go to him and see what he wants in exchange for her safe return."

Tvrdik's eyes widened, "My lady, you cannot hand over to the foe a victory that was so hard won by our friends this day. You cannot let him terrorize you like that."

"I can offer him myself in exchange..."

"You *cannot*! You are needed here. We will find another way to get her back without that..." This was Lord Maygrew, vehement in siding with Tvrdik, but Rel was becoming more agitated by the moment.

"Then, what *can* we do? How will we find her? We don't even know where she is..."

They did not have to wait to find out. Almost as Lady Rey spoke the words, a sound caught all of their attention. It came from overhead – a strident shriek something like a horse's neigh, only tinged with a whiff of madness. Lord Drogue was back, circling over them on a dark winged horse – Valour. Muscular black wings beat the air in rhythm, while the horse's powerful frame reared up from an invisible floor and struck at the clouds with his forelegs. Drogue moved with confidence in his seat on the beast. He was an experienced horseman who read his mount's every movement with ease. Seated sideways on the saddle in front of him, bound at wrist and ankle and gagged as well, secured on the steed only by Drogue's left arm around her narrow waist, was Delphine. Even from that distance, they could see the expression in her eyes, which flashed both defiance and terror.

Mark stepped out, gripping Tvrdik's arm like a vise. "Delphine!" he called upward. In response, they heard laughter, hard and mirthless, and the voice of Lord Drogue, amplified by a trick of simple sorcery, so that each of them heard every blood-curdling word as if he stood beside them.

"Yes, my young harper, Delphine. Sweet, lovely Delphine. We are having a little tete-a-tete, your *bride* and I. Oh, yes, word has reached me of your recent nuptials. I must congratulate you, you lucky cur. She is most charming company, I must say."

Only Corbin Maygrew's strong arm kept Mark from lunging after his tormentor, a futile gesture in any case.

Every eye on the field was turned upward to a sky now vacant, save for the lone dark rider on his flying steed. All remaining conflicts ceased. The shield bearers lowered their weapons, as did any of Drogue's warriors who were still in play. The sun had begun sinking toward the western horizon and shadows of twilight were slowly creeping over the landscape. Still, the figures of the dark flying horse with its sharp-featured rider and helpless captive stood out in clear relief. Everything had come down to this: all their preparation and efforts, the future of an entire kingdom, against the life of one girl.

"Let her go, Drogue." It was Jorelial Rey's most commanding tone. "She is only a girl. She is no threat to you."

"Ah, my Lady Rey. So nice to see you once again. And to hear you plead so affectingly for your sister – how sweet. But, why would I let her go when she is so very useful to me right now?"

"What do you want for her?" the Lady Regent responded, making a monumental effort to contain her fury. "I will offer myself in exchange for her safety..." The others glared at her, but Drogue just laughed.

"Now that is a very generous gesture, my dear, very generous indeed, but I am afraid I have no use for you. You are far too shrewish for my tastes, my lady. I suspect we would never get along."

"How dare he talk to you like that?" Lord Maygrew rumbled on the ground, and seemed about to shout something threatening. But the Lady Rey touched his hand, and threw him a look that silenced him. She addressed the dark rider again.

"Alright, then. But everyone has his price. You know I want my sister back, unharmed. I know there is something you want. What is it, Drogue? Surely, we can come to an agreement."

Mark was staring upward in horrified silence, unable to move or speak, or even breathe, for fear the slightest error would send his beloved to her doom. Tvrdik kept a firm hand on the young bard's shoulder, while scouring his memory for some magic he could wield that would snatch Delphine from the clutches of her captor. Nothing he could come up with seemed foolproof, and they could afford no fumbled attempts.

Drogue adopted a tone of mock ennui. "Oh, I don't know," he sighed, "I weary of this game. There isn't much you could offer me that I care about..." They all gasped as he spurred Valour higher in the air and leaned

Delphine over his arm, as if to drop her. "Unless, of course, you could tell me where to find little King Darian? Now, that might be a fair trade – one golden-haired little boy for one red-headed sweet maid? I hardly think I'd even be getting the best of that bargain, but I'd be willing to overlook that."

They circled overhead one more time. Jorelial Rey shouted up, "Now, you know I cannot do that, Drogue. We are all sworn to protect our king with our lives. That is not negotiable."

"But it is what I want," he whined.

"What else can I tempt you with?" She was desperate, but kept her voice conversational, with a monumental effort, "Riches? Land? Amnesty, a commission, titles? Name it. If it is in my power, I can make it happen instantly. Surely there is something that will satisfy you?"

He was laughing again, that irritating, skin-crawling laugh. "You just don't get it, my lady, do you. I told you once before that I have everything I need already – save one thing only. I am not interested in your puny favors. I will be king here. That is my price."

Tvrdik could hold his tongue no longer, "Give it up, Drogue. Look around you. Despite your wealth, and power, and skill at intimidation, you have lost the day. You underestimated the power of good folk defending their homeland, and a principle. You are defeated. Your army is broken. You cannot win. You may dispatch Delphine, and me, and all of us here, but you will never be king in Eneri Clare. Let the girl go, and surrender, and it will go far easier for you."

"Ah, it's the famous mage, now, is it? Brave words from someone so young and inexperienced. I have a bone to pick with you, mage. Did you not appreciate the lovely gift I sent to you, my personal selection for you? Did you have to go and destroy her? Was that done like a gentleman? I went to such pains to surprise you – where is the gratitude, I ask you? You, sir, have cut me to the quick."

"What is he talking about?" the Lady Regent snapped.

"Never mind. I'll tell you later." Tvrdik whispered, turning an odd shade of purple.

Drogue went on, "She was a lovely thing. I rather liked her myself. Hmmm, since you were so thoughtless, and broke the plaything I sent to you, perhaps I should show you how it feels, and break yours..." and Drogue seized Delphine by her slender waist, and held her out over the rocky valley floor. She closed her eyes without a sound, but those on the ground watching cried out in terror for her.

Jorelial Rey forced herself to appear unrattled, and tried once more to appeal to Drogue's better nature. There had to be some small remnant of a human being still flickering in the ugly caricature he had become. "Please, *please*," she cried, "my Lord Drogue, do not harm my sister. She has never done you, or anyone else any harm. She is a poet, a singer – not a politician or a warrior. Even you could not be so heartless as to slaughter an innocent for no reason. You have family yourself – friends, perhaps? You can imagine…do not do this just for spite."

At this the dark rider's cackling laughter crescendoed to its highest peak. Something in her earnest plea had quite amused him, as he drew Delphine's slim form back onto the seat in front of him. He seemed to be wiping his eyes with the other hand, as Valour, neighing, hovered in the air.

"Oh, you lot are so entertaining. I confess I have not had this much fun in an age. Poor, deluded children that you are. You *deserve* a child king, yes, you do. You still have no idea at all with whom you are dealing." More laughter and eye-wiping. "Such a heartfelt plea! I don't know whether to laugh or weep. My dear girl, I *never* do things just for spite; I do them to suit my purposes. Master mage, you point out that I underestimated the performance of your raggle-taggle mob on the battlefield. That much, perhaps is true. You were creative, I'll give you that. Clever, too – even downright amusing. I am a bit peeved that it has not been as simple a task as I had imagined, to achieve my goal. But, achieve it I will, make no mistake. And, speaking of underestimating things, you all don't seem to understand that all of the chaos you see on this field, all that has happened today – it makes no difference. I care not for any of this; it is but a chessboard where the game is yours today. But I will take the tournament. I *will be king*, whatever it may cost. I have come too far, done too much, crossed too many lines to be denied my prize now."

Rel was confused, "What do you mean by that? Only months ago, you were a respected member of the court."

This sent him into a whole new fit of merriment. The man was insane. He shifted Delphine to his other arm with a carelessness that elicited gasps from everyone on the ground. "Oh, yes, I played my part well: the disaffected mountain lord so concerned by the idea of a child king, then alienated by being snubbed in the election... Tsk, tsk, tsk, you fools! Do you not know a fine performance when you see it? It was always my intention to have the throne. I have been working at it systematically for years. Now, I am at last so close I can taste it, and nothing will stop me."

"Working at it systematically...?" Jorelial Rey still could not wrap her brain around that statement.

"My goodness, do you think it is an easy thing to arrange for *both* halves of a royal couple to take to the sea together, and then to create a large enough storm to insure that they would never see their home again? It was genius, I tell you. No one suspected a thing. Mother Nature's most brutal trick. A shame that stupid little imp wasn't on board with them."

The group watching from below had swelled in size as many of the Legion's fighters hastened to the scene, wanting to help in some way, and drawn to hear the interchange between Lord Drogue and their own leaders. This last announcement produced a wave of shock and horror that nearly felled some of the company.

"Ye gods..." Corbin Maygrew mumbled, "it's murder – no, *regicide*! How could we have missed it?"

"You see," Drogue went on, quite proud of his achievements, and elated to finally have the opportunity to brag about them to an audience, "I play to people's weaknesses. Yours, my dear, is a ridiculous sentimental attachment to this useless creature here. Darian's was his longing for adventure and fresh experience, while the queen just couldn't bear to be parted from him, even when wisdom dictated it was prudent. Now, in your father's case..."

"My...father...?"

"Why, yes! How could I have gotten anywhere with that old geezer in the way? He was far too powerful, and popular. He had to be eliminated. But a little bird told me he had a penchant for a certain vintage of imported port wine. A little gift I sent him to celebrate his birthday. He was delighted. Soothed himself with it nearly every night for months, especially when he began to feel ill. Never suspected the poison for a moment. And his healers just watching him waste away, helpless and without a clue...so tragic. I suspect Gareth was in a lot of pain toward the end."

Andrus had joined the crowd earlier, but now put his hands over his face in shame, remembering how he himself had sanctioned the glasses of port to soothe and relax his patient, when he could find no other relief, nor effective treatment. How could he not have suspected?

Jorelial Rey, however, had turned white, and was shaking with rage. No more sound could pierce the loud buzzing that was swelling in her ears, and almost all thought was obliterated by a wave of blood-red behind her eyes. Before anyone else realized what was happening, she had dashed forward and taken up from the field one of the latest discarded weapons of Drogue's hapless force – a long spear, with a sharp, jagged head. With near superhuman strength, and without any conscious consideration of consequences, she gripped its shaft, drew it back, and hurled it at the monster on horseback. Straight up and well-aimed, it hurtled toward its intended target.

"Nooooooo!" wailed Mark and Tvrdik in chorus, Mark shouting that Delphine would be endangered, and Tvrdik gesturing with his hand in the air. The spear became a long-necked goose, flying right past Drogue, on the way to some distant lake.

The Lady Regent turned to face Tvrdik, and in her eyes was a look he did not recognize, one that frightened him. "Why did you do that, mage?" she demanded. "It would have hit him."

"Jorelial Rey, you cannot *do* this. Everything we fought for, believed in, struggled to convince the others of…the whole point of it all hangs in the balance. You are the leader, the model for us all. You must not throw it all away like this."

"Stay out of my way, mage. That demon killed my father – killed him with forethought, cruelty, and glee at his suffering. He took away the light of my life, and the hope of the kingdom, and left me with all of this to cope with on my own. And now, he would take my only sister from me as well? I tell you, he is mine. I will face him here and now, and I will see him die in agony or I will perish in the attempt. Now, get out of my way."

Tvrdik grabbed her by the shoulders, "You don't know what you are saying. You've just had an awful shock, and you are not yourself. Please, *please*, Jorelial Rey, think. Stop and think of all you have spent and sacrificed to get this far, all the effort and faith. Trust now, we are so close…let it go."

She struggled out of his grip, and dashed past him to the field again, where she was able to pick up another lethal-looking spear, and was preparing to launch it. Tvrdik dropped his hands in despair. Mark moaned. Drogue taunted.

"Oho! I see the little lady has more spunk than I gave her credit for. So, you are a warrior after all, my lady. You feel rage, and bloodlust, and the desire for revenge, and you are capable of acting on them. I applaud you. *If* I decide to let you live long enough, you might yet mature into a real leader. You have a delicious temper, and a ruthless streak I admire. A little time, and I could teach you how to conduct yourself just like me."

She pulled back the spear, aiming, hesitating, hating his words, hating him, hating herself.

"And that is what you wish, then, dearest? To be like him?" This time it was Tashroth's deep rumble in her ear, his great head beside her, eyes regarding her evenly, warm breath on her shoulder.

"Go away, Tash. I have to kill him."

"And if you can, what would be gained? You have already won the day here. You cannot bring your father back, nor the king, nor the days of your carefree youth. And what will become of your sister if you should strike him down now? Do you even care anymore?"

She hesitated, hot tears of frustration welling in her eyes. She dashed them away and looked up to see that Delphine was now dangling over Valour's flank, high above the ground, Drogue holding only her wrists. "Oh, ye gods! Delphine." she muttered.

"Go on and throw it, missy." Drogue shouted down at her, still relishing his position of power, "Show us what you are made of."

Tashroth whispered low again in her ear, "Do you hear how he goads you? He *wants* you to strike out in rage, to prove that the vision of the Legion is but a wisp of smoke in this world. He wants to hold you up as an example that we are all no better in the end than he is. Dearest, will you give up your soul to him so easily?"

For one single, suspended, eternal moment in time, Jorelial Rey paused long enough to allow the dragon's words into her mind, her heart, her true best self. Then, every muscle taut, the trembling Lady Regent drew back the awful spear...and threw it to the ground. In that moment of decision and surprise, a host of things happened: as Jorelial collapsed against Tashroth's forearm, and the great, green muzzle reached down to comfort her, Tvrdik made a sudden grab for the blue shield mirror of the

Legionnaire nearest him, and with lightning-quick dexterity, he spun it around and flashed it up toward Drogue as the great winged steed came around for one more pass. Drogue dropped his head and looked away, but the blue mirror caught Valour full in the face. The powerful beast stared hard at the uplifted surface, his eyes wide with horror at what he saw, and then he reared, curved his great muscular neck, shrieked and writhed in torment. Lord Drogue's balance was upset, and he lost his tenuous hold on the helpless girl, who plummeted toward earth, hands and feet still bound. With one well-timed leap into the air, Candelinda launched herself at the falling bundle and snatched it out of the sky with her talons. Still well above the ground, she twisted around to soar upwards with her precious cargo, carrying Delphine to a safe space several hundred paces away. There they set down with the grace of a drop of rain on a summer blossom.

The white dragon had been watching, concealed behind a boulder, and in mental contact with Tashroth throughout the entire drama, waiting for a clear opportunity to make her move. Cheers and applause greeted her landing, and Mark was in the forefront of those running across the field to free the Lady Delphine and to thank her rescuer.

Meanwhile, Tvrdik held the blue shield skyward, his arm unwavering, and Valour was twisting and bucking, as if trying to rid himself of a swarm of stinging wasps. Drogue was holding on one-handed to some portion of the horse's tack, gripping it for dear life. At last, the great beast screamed, lost control of his wings, flipped over upside down and began to fall to earth in a dizzying spiral. Proud Valour landed on the dirt with a sickening thud, and lay still. Tvrdik threw down the shield and ran to the place he had come down. Andrus was with him, and a small contingent of others determined to help. Jorelial Rey climbed up on Tashroth, and they followed behind by air. When they all arrived at the site, the elusive Lord Drogue was nowhere to be found. But the Lady Rey had regained enough of her composure to order scouting parties to make haste in searching every inch of the valley.

Mark and Warlowe and the Lady Brendelle were among the first to reach Candelinda and Delphine. They set about freeing her from her bonds and removing the gag.

"Are you hurt? Did he do anything to you?" Mark asked.

She shook her head, "I...I'm alright, I think. There was only time for him to tie me up and put me on the saddle. Just a bit shaky, is all. I'll be fine."

Now that she was free of the ropes, Mark reached to pull her into his arms, but at the last minute, instead, he fell on one knee, bowed his head, and in a hoarse voice that in no way resembled his usual baritone, addressed her, "Delphine, my love, can you ever forgive me for allowing you to be spirited away right before my eyes? I was supposed to be protecting you. I am so, so sorry. I don't deserve..."

"Mark," she interrupted, smiling, tears flowing down her cheeks, "just hold me." And in one move the bedraggled young harper was on his feet wrapping his arms around his bride, rocking her back and forth, and holding her close to his breast as if to fasten her there forever.

She pulled back and stared at him with wide eyes, "The king. Is Darian...?"

"Safe." Mark finished the sentence for her, "Thanks to you, I was able to get him inside, and we have moved everyone from the house to a secret place where Drogue should not be able to find them."

"I am so proud of you," she sighed. "That was heroic."

"If you had not come back to me, it would have been ashes on my tongue to claim it."

"It's alright now, darling. Everything's going to be alright."

They turned to Candelinda, joining the others in congratulating her on her dazzling rescue. Delphine stroked her glowing, opalescent scales, and expressed her gratitude for the white dragon's quick thinking and bravery, which had saved her life. Candelinda smiled with appropriate humility, but Delphine noticed that her eyes were fixed on something – or someone – a few meters away. As she turned to follow the white dragon's gaze, she saw Tashroth at the center of a small crowd, bending over Valour's still frame. "Oooh!" thought Delphine, "I know a secret." and she smiled. A moment later her mother, Brendelle, was embracing her and cooing over her with relief. That was wonderful too, but she realized the face she wanted to see most just now was Rel's. Where was she? Well, there would be time later for emotional reunions. Right now she was content to rest in the arms of her beloved.

Tvrdik's skilled hands were feeling all over the winged horse for broken bones and internal injuries. The great dark steed lay on the ground, breath shallow, tongue lolling from his mouth, eyes rolled up in his head, and his eyelids fluttering. He was surrounded by concerned and anxious faces from both camps. Though he had cast his lot with Drogue, all of the magical creatures and legionnaires retained a grudging respect and admiration for the proud and handsome Valour, descended from a long, distinguished line that could trace its ancestry back to Pegasus. Tvrdik's brow furrowed as he worked. He had used the shield in an effort to rescue Delphine, but had never intended to cause the death of such a magnificent being. No one wanted that.

Valour flinched to be touched in several places. His wings were bent, some feathers broken. It would take some time for him to be sky-worthy again. But Tvrdik could find no broken bones or obvious hemorrhages, remarkable, considering his size, and the height from which he had fallen to earth. Valour's head did not show any bumps or scrapes or signs of concussion, even though he had had the wind knocked out of him and seemed to be unconscious. Tvrdik suspected that the more profound wounds were psychic. He laid hands on the animal's forehead, and concentrated on healing, comforting, regenerating energy, and sweet, warm blankets of unconditional love – like bright sunshine, only glowing in intense gold and pink. From behind him approached the entire company of unicorns, Wynne in the lead, and Shar by his side.

"He comes from a clan that is cousin to ours," Wynne stated. "We wish to help." Tvrdik nodded, keeping his hands and concentration where they were. Soon, all the unicorns had surrounded the patient, each one touching him with the point of a horn. Even Shar joined in, to Tvrdik's delight and surprise. In response to the mage's glance and raised eyebrow, the black unicorn leaned toward him and whispered, "I concentrate on the qualities of ash, as you suggested: strength and flexibility. It serves me well." And he gave Tvrdik an affectionate wink. Soon, all the horns, including Shar's, were glowing brightly, and Tvrdik's hands felt hot. Tashroth, Candelinda, and several of the other dragons added their concentration and healing skills. They stood erect, eyes closed, and a sort of low hum emanating from them that could be felt more than heard. Mark and Delphine stepped up, Rel fumbling for her baby sister's hand, and clasping it tight, and some of the bards, who added their own voices in a wordless harmony with the dragons. All of them surrendered to the pulse that generated from the dragons and unicorns, and let their hands and voices be guided by a force they could not name. Other well-meaning folk dropped to their knees and laid hands on the fallen creature wherever there was room. Most were uncertain what they were doing, but they sent out heartfelt intentions for love and healing.

Minutes passed while the collective efforts of those who joined in, and the sincere prayers of others looking on, bathed Valour in a veritable sea of nurturing and redemption. At length, the horse's eyelids fluttered and opened, and anxious eyes stared out at a collection of concerned faces. The great body shuddered, rocked several times, and rolled up to stand on its own four legs, all the would-be healers scrambling to make room. The rhythmic, mystical sounds ceased and left in their wake a breathless, uncertain silence. Shivering and wild-eyed, his wings drooping and disheveled, Valour stood, his glance darting about in suspicion.

"Steady, boy. There is no need to be afraid. You are among friends." Tvrdik tried to calm him, keeping his voice low and even.

The horse's eyes narrowed, "How may that be, when I recognize some of you as defenders of the Crown?"

Jorelial Rey spoke now, "The battle is ended now, your old master defeated and missing, and none of us here bear you any ill will."

Tvrdik added, "It was never our intention to cause you harm – only to stop Lord Drogue in his dangerous plans."

There was a pause, as Valour scanned the faces surrounding him for the truth of their statements, and then the great beast lowered his fine head and big tears splashed on the ground. "I cannot recall when or how I came to his service, but I have seen in the mirror how far I have wandered from my spirit's true path. I am ashamed. I have betrayed my heritage and destroyed my good name."

Jorelial Rey approached, her face grim but compassionate, "Let the follies of yesterday go. It is possible Drogue used some sort of dark sorcery to press you into his employ. He had most of us fooled on a good many matters up until now. If it is your purpose to make peace with us, all else is forgotten, and we are pleased to welcome you home."

Valour looked at her with his large eyes, an expression in them something like wonder. Then he flung back his head, once again taking on the haunted look of one chased by old demons, and asked, "The girl...?"

Delphine shouldered her way quickly into the space before the creature, offering her warmest smile, "I am here, unharmed, and I do not in any way hold you accountable for my misadventure." Valour snorted, pawed the ground, and swept his head around to meet the eyes of each unicorn, each bard, each dragon, and every person who stood there offering him healing, forgiveness, and friendship. The battered wings stretched and straightened and the powerful neck arched, as he stood handsome, tall, and prouder than he had in many months. Then he tossed his head up and down, whinnied, and addressed the company surrounding him.

"For the great honor you do me, your generosity and kindness, and for the gifts of my life, and my dignity, I am in your debt. I would consider it a privilege from this day forward to serve King Darian and his court with all that I have to offer."

Jorelial Rey reached out her right hand, which bore the official royal ring, and Valour kissed it in token of his offer and its acceptance. A great cheer went up from all assembled on that field. Hats were thrown in the air. Comrades hugged, and laughed, and shouted in joy. But a moment later, that happy noise was quashed by those on the edge of the circle who had seen something else approaching. A hushed intensity spread through the crowd as four young soldiers staggered into the center, half dragging, half escorting none other than Lord Drogue.

The young captain who seemed to be heading the party came before the Lady Rey to make his report. He saluted her, "My lady, this one had evaded all the sentries and would have sneaked off through the woods if one of the trees had not caught him. Pummeled him good, too. We thought you would want him brought to you at once." He ended with a nervous glance up at the large face of Valour, still standing beside the Lady Regent, and at the even larger face of Tashroth, which swung in closely to see what miscreant had been captured. Drogue stood straight and arrogant in their grasp, hands tied behind his back, a condescending sneer on his fine-boned face. His black, expensive clothes were torn. There were twigs in his dark hair, and a rather nasty bruise on his forehead where the tree had struck him.

Jorelial Rey stared at the man who had terrorized them all only moments before. She searched her feelings and found traces of pity, revulsion, disgust.... But, welling up from her gorge and drowning all the other emotions was a violent, overwhelming urge to cause this man pain; to make him suffer, as he had made so many others suffer. She could feel Tashroth's eyes on her. For that matter, pretty much all eyes were on her. She pushed down the angry impulse, regarding him instead with an icy cold stare.

"So, we meet again, my lord," she murmured.

He lifted his proud chin, "You had better go ahead and kill me now, Jorelial Rey, because you will live to regret any other choice you make. As long as I am alive, I will fight you. I will plot, manipulate, scheme, and harass you until the crown I desire sits on my head. Nothing will stand in my way, and no one will be safe. All that you care for will be at risk, and you will live in fear of what I will do next. Best to behave like a true leader now and get it over with." His stare was unflinching. But when she drew her sword – an emblem of state, but sharp, nevertheless – and held the point to his pale throat, she saw fear leap into his black eyes. There was a collective gasp, and then silence. She pressed the blade to his Adam's apple so hard that a thin red line began to appear on his skin. Mercilessly, she held his gaze, and saw the terror creep in to his mocking, careless expression. Then, with as precipitous a motion as she had made to draw it, she withdrew the sword and sheathed it.

"Sir, it seems I am, in fact, *not at all* like you," she spat out and turned from him, considering what to do with him. Tvrdik, relieved and proud of her, waved at a nearby legionnaire who had one of the blue shields by her side. Catching her attention, he motioned for her to bring it over. Thanking her with a curt nod, he took the shield, closed his eyes, turned it upward and laid one hand on its face. With the other hand, he grasped his wizard's staff, and set it firmly on the ground, feeling the energy surge up through its core at his summons. As everyone watched, the mage muttered some words in an ancient tongue, and then intoned, "Master of the Blue Light of Truth, I here set my intention that this receptacle of your power not only reveal the inner truth of the one who looks upon it, but that it send him back to the exact time and place where he became divided from his better nature, and turned down the darker path of hatred and despair. I ask this in the name of the forces that direct and create our journeys here, and for the highest good of all." He opened his eyes and seized the shield's handle, making a move to deploy it, and then stopped. With great ceremony, he offered it instead to the Lady Jorelial Rey.

"My Lady Regent, Jorelial Rey, I believe this is *your* privilege?" Their eyes met for a moment, and she reached out to take the shield from him. "Ladies and gentlemen, creatures of all sorts, cover your eyes!" he shouted. Valour whinnied, as the Lady Regent lifted the blue mirror shield, and twisted it to catch Drogue square in the face. There was a split second where his eyes went wide in abject terror, and he strained against the firm grip of his captors and the bonds that held his hands fast. Then, there was an explosion of bright sapphire blue that lit the twilight like a summer noon, and blinded all who were near enough to perceive it, even with closed or averted eyes. Jorelial Rey threw the shield to the ground, her hand still trembling with its power. When the glare diminished and it seemed safe to lift her eyes, the shield lay before her, cracked, blackened, and smoking – destroyed. But there was no sign of Lord Drogue. Fearing that he might have escaped, his captors cast about in a panic for some clue to his whereabouts – and nearly stepped on a small child sitting on the ground at their feet, crying in misery.

He was perhaps two or three, thin and frail-looking, and pale-skinned, with wisps of dark hair framing his pinched face. He sat swathed in an oversized black shirt, trying to reach out his arms to some invisible object of desire. Everyone's eyes were on the lost child by now, and standing in shock, they all heard the boy call out in heart-rending despair, "Mama! Mama, where are you? Why don't you come? Mama, it's dark here. I'm cold. I'm hungry. Mamaaaa…" The word dissolved into a pitiful wail that could have cracked the hardest heart. The little boy put his fists to his eyes and continued to weep and call out.

"Is that…?" Jorelial Rey whispered in amazement.

Tvrdik nodded, "I asked that he be sent back to the turning point, the moment that caused him to choose the road we know he took. Small wonder he was so set on being the center of everyone's attention, not to mention trying to insure that his primal needs would always be met, once and for all."

"But, will he stay like that?"

"He is starting again from that place. He will grow up again and become someone, the same or different, depending on his experience from here on. But, he is no threat to anyone now."

"I…I didn't know you could do this."

Tvrdik leaned in closer, "To be frank, I didn't either. I thought it might be worth a try. Pretty amazing, eh?"

She pulled back and regarded the mage with horror, "Well, that was taking a pretty big chance, wasn't it? Now what do we do with him?"

There was a pause as everyone stared at the unfortunate infant, still sobbing his heart out. Delphine, unable to bear the child's suffering any more, stepped forward and lifted the boy into her arms, where he burrowed his head in her breast and clung to her. One hand supporting him and one on his little head, she bounced him and spoke to him in soothing tones, "There, there, little one, dry your tears. You know, Mark and I could raise him."

"Delphine!" Mark cried out, sideswiped.

"Delphine," her sister warned, "he murdered our father. He just tried to kill you as well. How can you even consider such a thing?"

Delphine pulled back, frowning, "That Drogue is gone. This is a whole new human being – a helpless child. All he needs is a fresh start to help him become something other than what he was. There is nothing that cannot be transformed with enough love."

Another voice broke the standoff between the two sisters. It was Lady Brendelle, pulling off her helmet, and stepping up to her daughter with great tenderness, "No, Delphine, dearest. I am so proud of your great heart. But your sister is right. Even if this child is innocent now, he will always remind the two of you of grief and loss you have both borne at his hands. Besides, you are so young, and newly married. You should enjoy time with your husband, chase your dreams, enjoy your youth, and someday, when the time is right, you will have children of your own together." Mark was blushing, but relieved.

Delphine wrinkled her lovely brow, still holding the baby Drogue against her breast, "But then, what…?"

Brendelle smiled a wistful smile, "Darling, I believe it is *my* destiny to raise this child – a second chance for both of us, so to speak, from some kind hand in the heavens. When I had my one chance to raise a child,

I ran away. I abandoned you. Thank the gods someone stepped in and helped you grow into the woman you are, so beautiful inside and out." She turned to Jorelial Rey and met her gaze, "For that, I will always be grateful. But I am punished for my mistake by being childless all these years. This little boy was also abandoned, and did not have such good fortune as my Delphine, I imagine. His need for love and attention turned sour and made him a monster. Now, he can start over, and perhaps, as you say, with enough love, walk a new path. We belong together, he and I. Perhaps we can help to heal each other." She looked down at the dark child who had stopped crying and fallen asleep in Delphine's arms. "I will take him across the sea to my own country, where no one knows his history. My husband will be thrilled to have a son, and we will shower him with affection and opportunity, and teach him what is right. From henceforth his name will no longer be Drogue, but Drake, and he will be my son."

Tvrdik cocked an eyebrow at her, "Are you sure, my lady? There is no guarantee he will not turn out bad again, despite your best efforts…"

"No more than there is any guarantee with any child of one's own birthing. I will take that risk. Delphine, my dear, you have such a beautiful heart, but I must believe this is our miracle – his and mine." She held out her arms, and after only the slightest hesitation, Delphine handed the child over to her mother, with a smile and a blessing. As Brendelle shifted the sleeping bundle against her own heart, the little boy, without waking, sighed deeply, and murmured, "Mama…" Brendelle gasped and looked up, speechless, tears in her eyes, and everyone present smiled back at her, knowing that at the end of this long, frightening, exhausting, amazing, magical day, they had all, in the end, been present for a true miracle.

FORTY-ONE

AFTERMATH

As word spread that Lord Drogue had vanished into thin air, his army evaporated. Neighboring lords who had supported him with troops or supplies, or even captained regiments for him, lost their nerve and slunk back to their own estates, hoping that their treachery would not be called to account. In this case, it seemed obvious enough that with the head cut off, the rest of the rebellion would wither, and the Lady Regent saw no reason to take any punitive action other than keeping an eye on the malcontents. She hoped that her leniency in this matter would serve to draw the renegades closer in gratitude. It helped also that there would be no fatalities, on either side of the battle, to provoke personal vendettas. In any case, time would tell.

Among the rank and file, those who were lucky enough to collect gold from the field were already gone to celebrate their good fortune. The foreigners headed for home, or went searching for another war elsewhere in the wide world – one this time that wouldn't hold so many surprises, and would be closer to what they were accustomed to. The mountain gnomes sighed and headed back to the hills, to their normal, secluded lives, working the earth for gems and metals, quite relieved to be done with all the politics and unpleasantness, which they did not care for in the slightest. Valour helped to reunite any of the magical beasts who had fought for Drogue with their ancient cousins on the other side. Talks occurred, and bridges were built, especially when it was revealed what Drogue's plan would have meant, in the long run, for all magical creatures. The gryphons, including the one who had snatched Delphine, were surrounded by dragons, given a stern talking to, and sent off somewhat shame-facedly, but nonetheless forgiven.

Those that had been frightened almost to death by dragons, or enchanted by the blue mirrors wandered off, and for the most part turned fresh pages in their lives. Some despaired and fell into ruin, but many went about trying to erase their past misdeeds by doing service to others. There were none whose lives were not changed in some measureable way forever. Any whom Drogue had blackmailed, pressured, enchanted, or deceived into his service, now free of whatever bondage held them in thrall, were out celebrating their newfound independence. Scores of these began showing up, hat in hand, at the Legion's campsite, begging amnesty, and seeking to bend the knee to the rightful king. Jorelial Rey and her counselors did their best to welcome all comers, and to assure them that every effort would be made to find them useful employment upon the Legions' return home. Verger, calculating the financial ramifications of such promises, all but tore the last of his hair out. But the Lady Rey managed to calm him with her word that they would soon sit down together and work it all out, and reminded him what the cost of a prolonged war might have been in comparison.

Boone, Maygrew, and Bargarelle congratulated each other on a brilliant campaign, well waged, and admitted to Tvrdik and Jorelial Rey that their eyes had been opened to the benefits of this new way of responding to threats. They all wanted to continue planning for a standing Legion, and for developing a peacetime training regime. The Lady Regent and the wizard responded with sincere gratitude for their eventual faith, commitment, and expertise, without which there would have been no victory.

Jorelial Rey wished to keep Mark and Delphine close by her side, but she asked Baldezir if, after a suitable rest period, he might be willing to return to his wife and family with the message of the battle's ending, and to help them liberate and escort the humans in their charge back to Mark's family estate, where they could now wait in comfortable safety until it could be arranged to take Lynette and Darian home. Baldezir was more than happy to undertake the mission, and the Lady Regent repeated her intention to call him to the palace, knight him, and grant him lands carved from Drogue's own holdings. These lands would be declared safe zones for all wolves, talking or not. Baldezir was moved by her generosity, and thanked her on behalf of himself and all his clan. The Lady Regent reminded him that no words or favors could ever thank him enough for the major role he played in saving her sister, and perhaps the king as well. The great dire-wolf trotted off with his head held high.

Messengers were sent to Theriole with the joyful news of victory. Among them was Jarrod the crow, who had returned to camp frantic and miserable at the near tragedy his carelessness had caused. It was Tashroth who took the time to soothe him, assuring him that no one held him responsible for Delphine's misfortune, especially since it had all worked out well in the end. The dragon added that every great warrior at some time or other had learned from mistakes and grown from them. Jarrod acknowledged both the gentle reprimand, and the confidence in that remark, and was comforted.

Several Legionaires who normally worked in the palace stables went about rounding up any horses from Drogue's cavalry who were wandering about, riderless and frightened. Shar, seeing what they were up to, lent his presence and voice to calm the muddy, confused beasts, and shepherd them to a still-grassy area where their needs and injuries were seen to by compassionate, knowledgeable folk.

Andrus reported that all the wounded were doing well, and on the road to recovery, remarkable as that might seem. He then became very solemn, and offered his deepest regrets to the Lady Jorelial Rey and to Delphine that he had been so helpless and blind during their father's illness. In hindsight, foul play seemed an obvious possibility, which, at the time, had never occurred to him. He told them that he would never forgive himself for failing that great man, and them. "I brought him that port myself every night. It seemed to soothe his pain..." The man's voice broke at the memory.

In answer, Delphine threw her arms around him, and Jorelial Rey said that it was Drogue, not he, who deserved their wrath – old Drogue, who no longer existed. The would-be usurper had all of them, including their wise and clear-eyed father, so fooled and manipulated, that no one could blame the doctor for not realizing what was going on. They assured him that they both knew that he had done everything he could think of to help

Gareth, and they begged him to forgive himself for not discovering the poison. They already had.

Tvrdik summoned some glow-balls to light his way in the deepening shadows, and went to the river for a joyful reunion with Ondine, who couldn't resist a pirouette and a splash or two at the sight of him. He thanked her for the important part she and her compatriots had played in winning the day, and when he inquired, was assured that she and all the naiads had emerged well and unharmed. He also shared his deep appreciation for her help in pulling Jorelial Rey out of the darkness that almost claimed her. "I don't know what would have happened this day if we had lost her, Ondine, and I wasn't able to bring her back on my own."

Ondine beamed, "We work together, always, Lovely Man. I tell you at waterfall, I can help – you need me. See, I show you how you need me for great adventure. We send nasty folk away, make things right again."

"That's right, dearest. It was my lucky day indeed when you insisted on joining me on my travels. I couldn't have accomplished any of this without you. We are great partners… and great friends." She splashed him just a little, and then leapt up to kiss him on the cheek. He laughed, taken by surprise, and then shared her ebullient company for a time, rediscovering the deep feelings of delight she always stirred in him. Then, excusing himself, he walked the edges of the wood, thanking and blessing the trees for joining their cause, doing such a wonderful job of derailing the enemy's assaults, and, in the end, of capturing Drogue. A whisper of leaves and a gentle swaying of branches welcomed his acknowledgements.

It was almost midnight when he approached the central campfire, where Jorelial Rey, Mark, Delphine, Stewart, Warlowe, Verger, Bargarelle, Boone, Maygrew, Andrus, and the Praegers were bustling about trying to put together some semblance of a meal from the supplies on hand. There had not been much sleeping or attention to eating for days. They were all beyond exhaustion, but wide awake, unwilling to let go of the day – its accomplishments, and its feelings of camaraderie, of confidence, and of vindication. Now, at last, they allowed themselves the luxury of feeling their weariness and hunger, but it felt good to be all together.

"Where have you been? We missed you." Delphine asked brightly, not in the slightest changed by her frightening experience.

"Thank you, my friend. I was out talking to the naiads and dryads, thanking them for their part. They are all well, and very proud of what we pulled off today. They send their love. Where is Lady Brendelle?"

"Oh, she begged leave to retire early and attend to the baby-uh-the child...Drake. You know. I suppose her life will be quite different now."

"Children will do that, I hear." Tvrdik smiled.

"Are you hungry?" Rel asked.

"Yes, famished. But there is something I think I need to do first. Don't you all think it seems incomplete to enjoy this victory without letting Xaarus know? Aren't you all just dying to see if we changed anything – the future, I mean – if we accomplished anything bigger than the here and now? And don't you think we should let him know what happened here?"

Everyone was staring at him. Bargarelle smiled and answered for the whole lot, "Well, young man, *yes*, to all of it. But you are our only link to the great wizard, and we didn't want to push you, figuring you must be tired, and that there would be time enough for most things tomorrow."

"I am weary, I suppose, but I think I owe Xaarus, and all of you, at least a brief contact. With my energy this low, I could use Tashroth's help. Where is he?"

Jorelial Rey put something hot in her mouth and shrugged, "Last I saw, he was going off somewhere with Candelinda."

Delphine giggled, "I think those two have something going on."

Rel frowned, "If I have to share him with someone, I'm very glad it's a girl as remarkable as she is. How could I *not* be crazy about her? Especially after she pulled off that brilliant rescue and brought you back to me, Sweet Pea." The two sisters smiled at one another across the campfire.

Tvrdik tried to redirect the conversation, "I hate to disturb him, but I think it's important, and it shouldn't take long..."

"I'll call him," Rel agreed, still eating. Someone handed Tvrdik a plate, which he received with appreciation while the Lady Regent concentrated on sending a mental message to her saurian companion. Tvrdik had only begun to sample some of the simple fare he'd been given before they were all aware of the familiar sensation, and noise, of giant wings. Tashroth and Candelinda both soared into range, and landed with precision in a nearby space. Tash's great, green head swung into view in the firelight, a sight that startled more than one of the friends sitting there.

"What is it, dear one?" Tash's patient voice rumbled.

"We are sorry to bother you now, Tash, but Tvrdik thinks we need to contact Xaarus right away, and I think he's right. He is afraid his energy is too low for a meaningful contact without your help. Are you up to it?"

"Of course. A very good idea. We can begin anytime." The head withdrew, and she knew he was arranging himself in a comfortable position, and setting his concentration on holding the energetic space for Tvrdik, amplifying his mind's outreach. Tvrdik put his plate aside and seated himself on a stump near the fire where he too could be somewhat comfortable. He handed his staff to Mark to hold, and, placing his hands on his knees, closed his eyes, knowing he was surrounded and supported by his friends. Before casting after Xaarus, he teased, "If you all concentrate, perhaps some of you might even catch a glimpse of him." And then, he set his mind on some of his most vivid memories of his old teacher: the familiar voice, a peculiar scent, the touch of his long, bony fingers, the ageless, twinkling eyes...

"Oh, my boy, my boy...you did it! You did it."

"Master, is that you?" Tvrdik opened his eyes, and Xaarus stood solidly before them. Tvrdik could not recall a time when his mentor had last looked so young, so joyful and light-hearted. He was beaming, his eyes were shining, and he moved about as if he would break into a dance at any moment.

"Of course it is, son. I am so proud of you, and of all the rest, that I cannot contain myself. I knew you could do it. I *knew* you were the right man for the job. I *knew* it, even when you weren't so sure, my boy, but you are quite a wizard – *quite...a...wizard*, if I do say it myself. And now, you've done it."

"Uh...yes. We defeated Lord Drogue, and we did it just as you showed us, no lives taken, none lost that we know of. Even Drogue, twisted as he was, managed to get a second chance. But, however did you know?"

"Lord Drogue? Ah, yes, Drogue. Yes, yes. You've saved the kingdom, defended the king, and managed to prevent a war of great destruction. I imagine all of those things mean a great deal to those of you there right now, and they were well done. You have every right to be proud. *But*, I am talking about the bigger picture, lad. You changed history! You have shifted the timeline, just as we had hoped. Oh, my boy, we were *so* right that your moment in time was indeed the turning point for everything that was to follow. I knew you had succeeded, because, in an instant, everything was different here in the future. Well, not different, so much. But *different*, if you know what I mean. Before, the place felt gray, miserable – dying, in fact. Now, it vibrates with *life*, with energy, with hope, my boy. The magic is back, the people are happy. The extraordinary is accepted as ordinary... oh, the changes are subtle, but so very, very deep. I have faith now that life and love and creativity will go on from here, robust and healthy. If I must remain here, at least I can be content to do so now. I cannot express to all of you the magnitude of what you have done. Your courage and resourcefulness, your willingness to take a leap of faith have changed the course of everything."

Tvrdik could not conceive of how to respond to such amazing news. "Wait, Master. I want to take a moment to relate to everyone here the basics of what you are telling me." And he repeated as best he could to the assembled company around the campfire all that the elder wizard had described. They sat listening, wide-eyed and open-mouthed at the remarkable reach of their actions that day. Of course, they had all hoped that Xaarus' plan would have the desired impact on what would come after them, but to hear that such an instant, profound, positive transformation had taken place was...was...well, more than any of them could have wrapped their minds around.

Candelinda asked, "Find out if there are magical creatures and talking animals now in his time." Tvrdik relayed the query and the response, "He says he is pretty sure yes, though most of them have settled in remote areas and keep a low profile. But people talk of them as if they encounter them on occasion, without amazement. And he swears he heard a woman having a two-way conversation an hour ago with her cat, and no one even batted an eyelash in surprise."

Mark spoke up, "Is it possible we might have done some irreparable harm by changing the timeline, even with the best of intentions and results that appear to be positive?"

"Ask if there wasn't a sudden huge increase in the goose population!" Jorelial Rey quipped, her mouth full of bread and cheese.

Tvrdik frowned, and then paused to listen, "He says that *Mark's* is a very astute question, and one he had long considered. But the truth is that we did not set out on purpose to change the timeline to suit our own desires. What we did was to make better choices in the present, which came from a place of love and compassion, rather than the usual fear and defensiveness. We always intended that things would unfold for the highest good of all involved, and the results, at least right away, seem nothing but exciting and positive. He doesn't believe anything but good could come from such an approach."

Now Tvrdik's focus came back to his own time, "Master, we are overjoyed by your news, but we will need time to understand and absorb all that it means. It has been a long and very eventful day on this side, and I am not sure how long I can continue to hold this link even with Tashroth's assistance. In the interest of efficiency, can you enter my mind and scan my memories of recent events, so that you will be up to date on all that has occurred here?"

"That sounds prudent, son, and of course, I am eager to know of it all. Wait a moment." The image of Xaarus closed its eyes this time, and Tvrdik concentrated on his own detailed memories of the day they had all just come through, all the events of the battlefield and beyond. With Tashroth strengthening the connection between the two men, it proved a quick and simple operation. When Xaarus opened his eyes again, however, they were welling up with tears. "My, my, you lot have been through quite a day there, haven't you. How I wish I could have been there to assist you and share some of the burden."

"Did you get it all, Master?" Tvrdik asked.

"I think so, son. But you can fill in the details later on when you are rested. I hope you will not stop contacting me because these matters are done with. I am still an exile missing home, you know...I can only say that all of you rose to this occasion with true greatness of spirit, and you have reason to be very, very proud of how you have conducted yourselves, and what you have accomplished under the most fearful circumstances. Most of all, lad, my heart swells with pride for you. You have made your old master's heart sing."

Tvrdik then lowered his voice, although there was no possibility he would not be overheard by the others, "Master, did you see...was it there about...about what happened with Ailianne?"

Xaarus let loose a long, heavy sigh, and chose his response with care. "Yes, my boy, I saw. It was like a knife through my own heart as well." There was a pause. Tvrdik needed more, "Master, please help me to understand…"

"Tvrdik, it pains me to believe that some part of her, maybe of Benjin too, has been trapped all this time, and may have been re-animated by Lord Drogue's dark sorceries. But whatever part that was, whatever you encountered, was not the Ailianne we both loved and remembered. You were correct in asserting that our Ailianne perished long ago. We cannot have her back, son, though it breaks both of our hearts to admit it. I would like to think I would have been strong enough to resist that illusion, as you did, Tvrdik, but I am not so sure I would have succeeded. You passed a very difficult test, my boy, and that makes you a true master."

"I tried to call on you then, to help me understand what I was facing, but nothing happened. Why did you not appear?"

"I'm not sure, but I assume you were too emotionally overwrought in the moment to focus on our link. I am sorry. But, in the end, you handled a most difficult encounter with great wisdom, and without my help."

"It could have gone either way…"

"No. I don't think so. Your heart is too pure. Remember, all you did was to hold up the Light of Truth; the real Ailianne would not have been harmed by the confrontation. What you revealed was so corrupt and unholy that it could not even survive seeing the truth of itself. It was like a thing of smoke and foulness, cobbled together and masked with a pleasing illusion. That was Drogue's targeted plan to defeat you, and get you out of his way. Had you not seen through her seductions, we would have lost you too, my boy, forever. And *that*, I could not have borne. I have to admit, Drogue had a few more tricks up his sleeve than I gave him credit for. But thankfully, all that is over now."

"Yes, Drogue will not be bothering us anymore…at least in the state we remember him."

"And that, too, son, was sheer, magnificent inspiration."

"We never could have defeated him or his forces without all of your good counsel and help, sir."

"Tvrdik, how I wish I could come through this channel in the flesh to clap you on the back. Rest assured I will continue working to find a way to do it, too. If it takes the rest of my days, I will never cease trying to come home."

"I wish it with all of my heart. But I am tiring, and must disengage. For now, goodnight, Master."

"Be well. Rest content in what you have done. Speak to me again soon…" The vision of Xaarus began to blur around the edges and recede. Tvrdik looked up at Jorelial Rey, "Now, take both of my hands, and ask Tashroth to disengage…" She did not need a second prompting. Tashroth dropped his part of the connection, and as Tvrdik closed his eyes and began to sway, she squeezed his hands hard and pulled on them. Tvrdik blinked, looked around a bit dazed, and then down at his hands, still clasped in the lady's. As they both registered the sensation of touch between them, Rel dropped the hands as if they were hot coals from the fire, and then covered her embarrassment by asking, "Are you alright?"

"Fine. Just tired like the rest of you. We are getting rather good at this, though." In the darkness, it was impossible to tell if either of them was blushing.

"Well," Delphine stood and stretched, wincing to feel her muscles growing stiff and sore, "my brain is done trying to take in the marvel after marvel which we have been a party to this day. I almost wonder if the morning will dawn and prove that all of it has been just a dream…"

Mark broke in, "Parts of it a nightmare, at that."

She smiled at him, "I think I will have to discover the truth tomorrow. I'm for bed, now."

"I'll go with you," Mark stood and threw a protective arm around the slim waist as they turned to find the tent allocated for them. It was well past the middle of the night, and Jorelial Rey called out to them, "Sleep as long as you wish, Delphy, and all of you. You have more than earned it, and we will handle at leisure all that needs doing, and then find our way home."

One by one, the rest took their leave of the Lady Regent, with a smile, a touch, an embrace for her or for the wizard, a look of wonder on their weary, dazed faces. Then off they went to find their tents. Tvrdik did not make a move to leave. Tash asked if he were needed for any further business, and Rel rubbed her cheek on his green muzzle and said, "No, dearest. I think I am a little too wound up to go to sleep just now, but you go ahead…I'll be alright. The striking green dragon breathed on his charge with great tenderness, then caught the wizard's eye for a meaningful moment. With a respectful nod, he turned and strolled off into the shadows, Candelinda by his side. Rel looked after them, amused, "They are really growing quite attached to one another," she commented.

"You don't mind?" Tvrdik asked.

Playing with a stick in the fire, she shrugged, keeping her eyes on the flames. "No. I've had him to myself for so long, and a part of him will always be mine. But, he deserves some happiness, some companionship of his own kind."

"It is good of you to feel that way."

"Of course." They were alone at the fire now, and the camp was silent, save for distant sentries dutifully calling the hours. "Tvrdik?"

"Hmmm?"

"I remember what you had told me about…about Ailianne, and then just now, I heard you talking to Xaarus about her. What happened today?"

He weighed telling her, but he needed to talk to someone about it. "I…I met her on the battlefield. She was mounted, and in armor, and fighting for Lord Drogue. But otherwise, she was exactly as I remembered her."

Rel's eyes went wide, "Did she…attack you?"

"No. She said she had been freed from some sort of awful limbo by Drogue's sorceries, and that if I went away with her, she would teach me the secrets of unlimited power and eternal life…and that she would…she would…be with me."

"Gods, what did you do?"

"I turned a truth shield on her, and she crumbled away to dust and bones before my eyes. It was not really Ailianne, or at least not the Ailianne I cherished."

"How horrible. How did you know?"

"I told you, she was *exactly* as I remembered her. She hadn't aged or changed a bit in all these years. Plus, she should have known that I never had any interest at all in limitless power or eternal life."

The fact that he pointedly left out the third offer was not lost on Jorelial Rey, but she chose a sympathetic response. "I am so sorry. What an awful thing to have to go through. More evidence of Drogue's absolute wickedness. Somehow he knew what to use to get to you, and I am grateful you could not be bought, or fooled. I never would have doubted that, anyway. But, after...after...however were you able to come back to the field after such a terrible trauma?"

Tvrdik answered matter-of-factly, "Wynne came running up to tell me you had fallen. You needed me."

"Oh." She paused to digest that information. There was a long silence as they each gazed into the crackling flames, following the thread of their own thoughts.

Tvrdik spoke first, "I wanted to tell you...about that spear.... I'm sorry I intervened. It was presumptuous of me. You had a perfect right to want him dead just then."

"No. You were right. It was hearing about my father, you know. He died so young, and suffered so. All for nothing – to satisfy that horrible man's ambition. I was so angry I couldn't control myself. But we took an oath, and convinced all the others to take it too – no violence. If I had broken it in front of everyone, the consequences would have been grave. I would not have been able to lead or command any more, and I could not have lived with myself. You weren't going to let that happen, and I appreciate it."

"In the end, you made your own decision."

"Well, Tashroth pulled me back from the brink too, but...I did, didn't I!"

He nodded, "Congratulations. That was a pretty steep initiation. I'm proud of you."

"Thanks."

The fire was dying down and a few logs crackled and popped. The night was a bit chilly for summer, and the warm flames had been a welcome comfort. Now, she shivered and stood up, "Tvrdik?"

"Hmmm?"

"I think I have to sleep now..."

"You should. It has been a long day, and there will be more on your plate tomorrow."

"What about you?"

"I will go soon. I am just sitting here realizing that my work here is almost done. We have, by some miracle, accomplished all that I laid at your doorstep months ago. I am happy, I suppose, but right now, I feel sort of ...numb." He was sitting gazing at the fading flames, cleaning the lenses of his glasses over and over again. She stood there looking at him, knowing that this was an opportunity. She wanted to tell him so many things: how she had come to rely on him, how she had begun to think of them as a team, how she could never imagine going back to a life where he didn't exist. But, there was a lump in her throat that stopped all of those things from pouring out. And, then, she did not want them to be said when she was at her weariest and most vulnerable, perhaps for fear they would not be taken with any seriousness.

She said, "Get some rest. Tomorrow, things will seem clearer. You'll feel better then. Goodnight." And she walked away.

The next day began at a slow pace, as folk took the time to recuperate from the stresses of the past week. There was much to do. The wounded needed to be tended, and there seemed a constant parade of former enemy combatants arriving to surrender and pledge fealty. There were plans to be made regarding packing everything up for the journey home, and, of course, everyone had to be fed. Soon the camp was bustling with activity, even if its inhabitants seemed a bit dreamlike in their motions. The realization that the danger was truly past, and that, after months of anxiety and intense preparation, it was all over and they had indeed triumphed, was sinking into everyone's consciousness a layer at a time. As they went about their chores, you might see someone standing still, staring into space, or breaking into a smile and exclaiming out loud for no immediate reason. Friends and colleagues clapped each other on the back as they passed. Women embraced and wept in relief. Bit by bit, the tense, wary, pinched look of a people facing battle, tyranny, and death fell away, transformed into an expression of gratitude and wonder. Thus, the day unfolded like a long and languorous sunrise, ending in glorious colors and bone-drenching, joyful warmth. As the ice of fear melted, laughter, song, and random whistling could be heard. Lighter hearts and a spring in the step returned to the Legions of Light, one corner at a time, until, at last, they had spread everywhere in great, open-hearted abundance. It was a beautiful day.

It was well into the afternoon when Tvrdik, heading toward the healer's tents, heard a familiar voice behind him calling his name. Turning, he saw

Jorelial Rey hobbling through the busy crowd to catch up with him, and he paused to see what the matter might be.

"Tvrdik, I am so glad I found you. I've been trying to track you down for an hour."

"Sorry. I had no idea. You know you are supposed to stay off of that ankle."

She scowled at him, "Yes, I know, but there's so much to do, and I had to come and find you myself, at any rate. Tashroth wants a word with both of us, and he wanted me to keep it between us for the moment."

The mage frowned and cocked his head to one side, "Do you know what it's about?"

"Not a clue. I am just the messenger, but I could tell he was excited... must be something important. He's waiting for us now."

"Well, I suppose what I was doing can wait. Lead on. Let's hear what the old boy has to say."

"I wouldn't call him that to his face," she suggested, pointing him back in the direction from which she had come.

"No, indeed. Wasn't planning on it," he quipped, striding along beside her. Noticing a slight grimace on her face with each step, he added, "Hey, slow down. Can't I at least offer you an arm to lean on? You can't keep pushing it like that or it will never heal. Let me at least be a physician, and a gentleman."

She stopped, scowling again, "Whole thing's more of an annoyance, you know. Nothing serious." But she took his arm, nevertheless, and slowed to a stately limp.

"Where are we going, anyway?" Tvrdik asked.

"Up there, on that ridge. Do you see them?" She pointed off to a ridge overlooking the valley, where the silhouettes of three dragons were just visible against the deep blue sky.

"Hmmm," he said, "that's a bit far. What's the use of being a wizard, if you can't give a little assist to a friend? Hold on tight..." And in the space of a single breath, the tall mage was replaced by the white owl he favored, only in a version much larger than usual. Spreading its oversized talons, the great bird grasped Jorelial Rey by the collar of her General's coat, and lifted her off of the ground.

"Hey!" she called out, startled, waggling her dangling arms and legs in protest.

Stop struggling…you're already a handful, came a voice within her mind. *Think of it as payback for all the delightful dragon rides you have treated me to.* His sarcasm made her laugh despite herself. Besides, it was exhilarating to see the ground spinning away below her.

I'm a bit worried about the landing, she thought back at him, *As I recall, it isn't your strong suit.*

Thanks for the vote of confidence, she heard the wry comment in her head. *Don't worry. I'll hand you off to Tashroth.*

Travelling by this means, the trip to the ridge where the dragons awaited them was brief indeed, and, true to his word, the giant white owl that was Tvrdik transferred its precious cargo to Tashroth, who gripped her in his claw, and deposited her with great delicacy on the grass before them. By contrast, Tvrdik's owl landed with his usual somersault and pratfall, picking himself up off the skid-scarred ground, once more a wizard, brushing himself off, and setting his spectacles on straight.

"Darn. You would think I could get that to be a little less bumpy by now," he muttered.

"What a wonderful way to keep a low profile for the secret meeting." Rel's voice oozed sarcasm.

"Oh, pish tush. They're all used to me flying about at whim by now. No one will have even noticed. And think of the wear and tear we've saved on that ankle. Not to mention saving time…" He was interrupted by a rather loud and unusual sound. It took a moment to identify it as the sound of a dragon clearing its throat.

"If the two of you are quite finished," came the deep rumble of Tashroth's familiar voice. He seemed to be taking on the role of spokesperson. "Thank you both for coming. You already know Candelinda, and this…" he motioned toward a purplish dragon on his left, "…is my esteemed colleague and friend, Danoral." There were nods of greeting all around. Tashroth went on, "We called you here, because we had an idea which we wished to present for your consideration, but we did not want word of it to spread about the camp. We are not yet sure if it would be possible…or practical…or safe…"

Tvrdik and Rel looked at one another, all at once quite serious. "Go ahead, Tash," Rel urged, "we're listening."

"Hmmm. How to begin. Well, you know that I have always told you that my age was irrelevant, since dragons have some facility in moving through and manipulating time?" She nodded. Tvrdik's brows furrowed. Tashroth went on, "We are a very ancient breed of creature, and not altogether bound by the laws and limitations that hold later races to the space-time continuum. Generally, we choose to live within those laws because it creates a more satisfying experience of life, and allows us to relate to the other beings on this planet. But we can stretch them, on occasion…"

"Yes, I remember you saying that…" Rel was all attention, a little impatient for the point of this dissertation on dragon lore. Tashroth continued.

"Do you also recall how I discovered the nature of this mage's mindlink across the centuries with Master Xaarus, quite by accident? How I realized that I could see the image of Xaarus through Tvrdik's mind, and how I could use my telepathic powers to stabilize, and even amplify this connection between them? And we have used that fortuitous ability on several occasions to assist Master Tvrdik in contacting his mentor, and in holding the connection steady, yes?"

"Yes," the two humans answered in concert, then glared at one another.

"Well, last night, Candelinda was watching how we accomplished this feat with great fascination, feeling out our bond to see if it could be added to. We talked about it afterward. Well, it was her idea. But we still weren't certain it was actually possible, so we brought in Danoral here, who also thought it might work. In any case, we brought the idea this morning before the entire company of dragons. There was a great deal of discussion this way and that, but the consensus was that it was definitely worth a try, and they are all willing to stay and participate if you are."

Tashroth finished, and gazed at them as if expecting a reaction. Tvrdik and Rel stared at the dragon, speechless. Tashroth seemed impatient for their response, "Well, do you wish to attempt it, or not?"

Tvrdik spoke first, treading with caution, "With all due respect, sir, we have been listening with care to everything you have said, and we still don't have any idea what it is you are talking about."

Rel chimed in, "Yes, Tash – what exactly is it you are all going to attempt?"

Tashroth rolled his giant eyes, "Why, bringing Xaarus home, of course!"

Now Tvrdik was listening in earnest, cold chills climbing his spine, and gooseflesh crawling on his forearms. "Did you say, *bringing Xaarus home?* Here, to this place, and in his own time? Do you mean, in the flesh?"

"Of course. But, it is not something that has ever been done before. We do not know for sure what the consequences could be..."

At this point, Candelinda stepped in, "Dearest...(Rel's eyebrows lifted at the endearment), let me try to explain it to them. You see, Xaarus managed to catapult himself into the future, and even to stretch back here for a brief time when he came to train you, sir mage, as I understand it. But his physical form is anchored in that future time, and he has been unable to summon enough energy to leap back here for good and all. Still, he forged a powerful connection to his home time and place through this remarkable mind link with you, Tvrdik. By now, this thoroughfare between you is well worn, and familiar. You see each other and converse with ease, creating a strong bridge over the centuries. Tashroth says that when he adds his own concentration to the link, it becomes even stronger, easier to access, and to hold steady. The picture of Xaarus grows clearer and more of him comes through the link. Tashroth said that we even almost lost you once as well, as your consciousness tried to follow after your Master."

"That is so, my lady, but I dread thinking of how that episode might have ended had my friends not pulled me back in time."

"True," the white dragon responded, "because the corridor still was not wide enough for your whole essence to go through in safety."

Rel asked, wide-eyed, "What are you proposing?"

Tashroth picked up the thread of the idea then, "If I can strengthen the connection between the wizards, then what if Candelinda joined her mind to the link as well? And then Danoral here linked in, and one by one, all the dragons here added their own concentration to strengthening and widening the passage through your mind, to that moment of time where Xaarus is? Master Tvrdik's link would sort of act like a kind of ...guidepost, for us to find him. And then, with our ability to somewhat circumvent time, one of us might be able to travel to him, while the others hold the corridor open, just long enough to fetch him back here. I am not exactly sure how or why it would work, but somehow, all of the dragons who have heard the idea seem to intuit that it *would* work."

Danoral spoke for the first time, his voice rather heady and buoyant for a mature dragon. "Yes, we dragons agreed that the combined mental power of all of us joined would be enough to accomplish amazing things. We all respect and admire Xaarus, and would like to give it a try, with your permission…" He was looking straight at Tvrdik.

"With my permission? Heavens, there is nothing in this entire world that I want more than to bring Xaarus back here where he belongs. If I could play some part in it, I think my life would be complete. In fact, I can't believe you are coming up with this plan *now*, after all we have all been through. If it were possible for him to come home all along, and he might have been here to help us…"

Tashroth frowned, "Immaterial. Things happen at the times they are meant to, young mage. Dragons can be very solitary creatures. It simply did not occur to us until now that our cooperation as a group might, and I stress the word, *might*, achieve this good result."

Tvrdik sighed, "I apologize, sir. You have me so excited that I want it done yesterday. Of course I am all for this inspired plan, which you have all devised. And grateful for your willingness to participate in implementing it. I say, the sooner the better. Why would you need to ask my permission?"

Tashroth and Candelinda exchanged a meaningful look, and then the white dragon addressed the wizard in a grim tone, "Because our only real concern, besides failure, is the danger all of this might pose to you, sir mage. You see, your mental link is the only pathway we have to Xaarus. We would all have to go *through* you. Your mind would have to hold the joined forces of a dozen dragon minds, all at once, all trying to open and expand a passage that was never meant to be there in the first place. That is the only way Xaarus could be located, and come through. We are not sure how accustomed you are to such mental discipline, how strong your mind is. You could be injured, or even killed. You could be left mentally broken, mindless. Failing in our purpose would be the least of our worries."

Jorelial Rey looked back and forth between Tvrdik and the dragons in a panic, "Well then, we cannot do it. It's too dangerous. The plan will have to be refined. Or he'll have to work up to it. You can't risk anything happening to Tvrdik."

Tash swung his great head around to her, "Little one, the time can only be now, and the choice only his. It is not an easy matter to assemble this many dragons together in one place. Such a phenomenon has not happened for centuries, and may never happen again. Also, the link between Xaarus and Tvrdik is very strong now. The necessity to work together toward their shared goals forged it, and it may fade over time as their purpose vanishes. If it is to be done, it should be done soon."

"But you said so much could go wrong. Tvrdik is the *last* wizard!

"We but disclose all the possibilities. We have no memory of any similar event. We wish the mage to agree or not in full understanding of what he might face. But, of course, we have every intention of doing all that is in our power to help and protect him during the process."

Tvrdik held up a hand, "I understand, and you are correct that this is the moment, and the decision is mine. And I say every, and any, risk is worth the slightest hope that we may succeed in this mission. Think what a treasure it would be to restore Xaarus to his rightful place in a kingdom that still needs him. I am ready any time – as soon as possible."

"But, Tvrdik..." Rel seemed to be pleading, but he stopped her from going on with a look.

"Jorelial Rey, I wasted so much of my life mourning, hiding, denying the truth of my being. Xaarus brought me out of my self-imposed exile by giving me purpose, and in so doing, he restored me to the land of the living. These past few months have held for me a lifetime of excitement, of adventure, of new friends, of hopes, and fears, and accomplishments I never thought myself capable of. But I always held before my eyes like a beacon the certainty that I had been given this second chance in order to achieve a purpose. That purpose was threefold: to defeat Lord Drogue and insure the proper succession to the throne; to convince you and your court that we could do it without violence, so that we could change the quality of the future for our descendants; and lastly, to find a way to bring my beloved Master and friend home for good. By some miracle, we have managed to complete the first two tasks, and I would gladly have spent my whole life searching for a way to accomplish the third. But, as my mind is not gifted in the same way as Xaarus', it is probable that I would have failed. These good dragons have offered another road, and I will give my life in the attempt if it means I can complete my mission. I would then count my existence to have been of some worth. Please don't try to stop me from doing what it is my destiny to do, Jorelial Rey. I beg you."

He fixed his pale, intense eyes on her, waiting, while she glared at him, lips pressed together in frustration. At last she said, "Could you at least assure me that you would prefer *not* to 'give your life in the attempt' if the job can be done without your going out in a blaze of selfless glory?"

There was a silence, as they locked gazes. And then, he laughed; first, a small chuckle, but one that bloomed into a big, hearty laugh that quite dissolved the tension that had crackled between them a moment before. Eyes twinkling, he grabbed both of her arms, looked her square in the eye, and answered, "Yes, my friend. I promise I will do everything in my power to make this happen, and live to rejoice in it. All right?" She nodded, swept away by his enthusiasm. He turned to the triumvirate of dragons, "When can we begin?"

Tashroth spoke for them, "There is more discussion we need to determine our part in this."

Jorelial Rey added, "May I also suggest that we might better address all this at Theriole, where we are at home, with resources available to us, and we can better control the conditions?"

"Agreed," nodded Tvrdik.

"Agreed," Tash vouched for the dragons. "Make what study and preparations you think wise, and we will be in frequent communication. Perhaps it would be wise to keep this plan a secret from any but your most trusted inner circle. We do not wish to raise hopes that might yet be disappointed. But, if it is in any way heartening to you, mage, I believe we will succeed."

Tvrdik's eyes were shining, "As do I, friend. As do I."

FORTY-TWO

DOUBTS AND MISGIVINGS

JORELIAL REY SAT ON HER stool atop the north tower waiting for Tashroth to arrive with the last details. The sun was well on its way to meeting the horizon, and most of the color had gone from the landscape below. A breeze stirred up white peaks and rolling breakers on the shore below, and blew wisps of unruly hair, that would not stay braided, into her face. As the sun withdrew, she wished she had brought a jacket, feeling the chill of evening approach. Two weeks had passed since the great battle in the Valley of the Yechtze, which had been re-christened the Valley of Miracles, and the triumphant army had come home. King Darian was back at the palace, as were Mark and Delphine, and of course, little Lynette. There had been victory celebrations at Theriole, cheering crowds to welcome the Legions of Light on their return, and a parade through the streets of town to honor the brave heroes who saved the kingdom from an evil usurper.

The Lady Regent and the golden-haired mage were treated like new deities in the pantheon of heaven – feted and honored at every turn, common folk crowding up for a chance to glimpse, or even touch them, in the flesh. Petals were strewn on the paths they travelled, and chains of late flowers laid around their necks. It was all very heady and gratifying, but in the end, more exhausting than exhilarating. They were weary from the long months of stress, and even less interested in celebrations because their minds were already consumed with their next project: the proposed rescue of Xaarus from the future.

Out of necessity, they had shared news of the dragons' plan with their closest family and friends: Delphine and Mark, Stewart, Bargarelle, Warlowe, Verger, Andrus (in case his services might be needed), Ondine, and the Praegers. But the general public could not know the grave thoughts and serious considerations that filled the minds of their anointed heroes so soon after their great triumph.

Of course, there were also a host of matters of state to be addressed as well – the regular business of running a kingdom coupled with the aftermath of a major campaign. Verger seemed on the edge of nervous exhaustion tallying up expenditures, budgets, and spoils, while Bargarelle turned his attentions to whipping Theriole back into the finely-honed machine it had been before all the excitement. General Boone set about absorbing those fighters from both sides who wished to make a career in the Crown Military, into a small standing army, and rewriting his training briefs to better reflect the philosophies of the Legions of Light. There would be no going back to the old assumptions and the old ways. And a new focus on diplomacy would help to insure that most conflicts never reached the stage that this one did. Nevertheless, the remaining inventory of activated blue light shields were re-covered with reverence in Mrs. Praeger's cloth sleeves, and locked away in the palace armory against future need.

Jorelial Rey had to deal with a number of important royal decisions: the disposition of Lord Drogue's titles and lands, awards to the brave and deserving, disciplines for the rebellious. There were several knighthoods to confer, among them one for Baldezir the wolf. She made good on her promise to rope off a parcel of good wooded land as a safe haven for his clan. Another piece of Drogue's territories adjoined Mark's family estate, and she annexed these to their holdings to honor their service. It was mostly earmarked by his parents as additional acreage for Mark's dream of a school.

There were honors conferred on Ondine, Wynne, Shar, Nyree, Andrus, Candelinda, Stewart, and Lady Brendelle. The Lady Regent offered to knight Warlowe, and to grant him and his family lands, but while he accepted the commendation, and a small purse to make his family secure, he begged to continue in his position at Theriole where he felt he could serve best. There was no argument from Lady Rey. A similar offer to advance the Praegers' state for their contributions was met with horror and embarrassment by both Mr. and Mrs. Praeger. Both of them insisted they could be no happier than right where they were, as personal aides to the last wizard of Eneri Clare. Mrs. Praeger so enjoyed feeling needed – indeed, how would Tvrdik ever get by without her to run his household, and especially to *feed* the slender young man? And Mr. Praeger opined as he still had a debt to the young wizard to pay off, and would hear nothing to the contrary.

The Lady Regent did insist on knighting Mark, and brushed aside his protest that such a move might be considered nepotism. She pointed out that his daring rescue of the infant king, while they were in mortal danger, deserved recognition. Delphine was delighted, and Mark's parents were beside themselves, although he assured everyone it would not change his plans for the future, nor his current occupation, even a little bit. Drogue had no surviving family, and in the end, she dissolved his fiefdom, and distributed the unaccounted-for lands and holdings as fairly as she could among his neighbors who had been supportive of the king.

Lady Brendelle had been homesick, and eager to bring her new adopted son home to meet her husband. With the loving care she lavished on him, little Drake already seemed like nothing so much as a normal, happy child – if a bit on the frail, shy side. If one week could create such a remarkable transformation, there seemed hope that an entire childhood with loving parents might indeed ensure that he would grow into a very different person. One week after their return to Theriole, Brendelle, her warriors and sailors, and her son Drake set sail for Euligia. There were tearful farewells, kisses, and long embraces, and promises all around to stay in close touch and visit often. And then, the mother Delphine had found for the first time only weeks before, was gone from their sight once again. But this time, not from their hearts.

Tvrdik, when not pressed to appear in public, had thrown himself into reading and studying on any subject that might facilitate the process of bringing Xaarus back. Books on dragons and their legendary abilities, on mind training, on time theory...he devoured whatever portions seemed pertinent, and practiced whatever disciplines they suggested, with diligence. At earliest convenience, he contacted Xaarus himself once again, and informed him with great enthusiasm about their plan to bring him back. Xaarus was intrigued, but at first cautious. As he considered further, he became excited about their prospects for success. But, soon enough, the old wizard arrived at a deep concern for Tvrdik's welfare.

"There is no doubt that if it were possible for the dragons to bring me home in safety, I would leap at the chance," he said. "I would like nothing better than to be back at my little cottage, among my friends, living out the rest of my days in peace, and perhaps some usefulness. But I would not attempt such a thing if it meant risk to you, lad. It wouldn't be right."

"You are a very great wizard, Master, and you are needed here. I will assume the risks. I count them as well worth it."

"I am old, son, and I did this to myself. I will not let you play the martyr for me. There must be another way."

"Master, the risks we speak of are only *possible* ones, and the dragons and I will do our best to minimize them. We must seize this opportunity while we can; we do not know when another one this promising will come. You have done so much for me, Master. Please, let me do this for you."

In the end, Xaarus was persuaded that this could be his last, best chance at returning to the time and place he called home. He saw that Tvrdik was determined to make the attempt despite every argument he could think of to dissuade him. And so, he set about doing his own research, hoping to discover some additional piece of the puzzle that might make the process safer, surer, or easier.

And now, in the chill, late summer twilight, Jorelial Rey sat with a restless heart, and awaited word of the last details of their plan: day, time, place, procedure. The dragons were all eager to be off to their own respective territories by now, and this thing must take place very soon, or else be abandoned. A noise behind her caught her attention, and she rose and spun around to see the trap-door which accessed her rooftop perch spring open. Her momentary stress at someone's invasion of her sanctuary was relieved on seeing the thick, auburn waves on the head that poked through the square opening: Delphine.

"Rel, I know you like to come up here sometimes and hide, and I hated to disturb you, but it's getting cold, and I thought I might bring your jacket."

"You're an angel. I was just thinking I could use it. Come on up. Tashroth isn't back yet, and I could use some company. My own thoughts are driving me crazy."

Delphine clambered out of the stairwell, closed the door behind her, and came over to sit on the stool. Her sister wrestled with the jacket, and then paced over to a crenellated rampart, gazing out into the dimming sky.

"Something you want to talk about?" the younger girl asked.

Rel sighed, "I suppose it wouldn't hurt to talk. Delphy, you know I have grave reservations about this rescue…"

"But, why? You loved Xaarus. It's so exciting to think that he is alive and well, and that they might be able to bring him back. Wouldn't it be wonderful to have *two* wizards at court?"

"I'm afraid we could end up with *no* wizards after this crazy scheme. I…I did love Xaarus, but I made my peace a very long time ago with his absence in our lives. The other one I don't think I could bear to lose." This last she spoke so softly that Delphine almost missed it. Almost.

The younger girl jumped up and embraced her sister from behind, "Tashroth won't let anything happen to Tvrdik, Rel. He'll be fine, whether they succeed or not."

"Tashroth said it was very dangerous, and that they would all try to protect him, but that there were no guarantees." The proud Lady Regent seemed to be on the verge of tears. Delphine was astounded at her pragmatic sister's uncharacteristic display of emotion.

"Rel, there is risk in all of life…there are never any guarantees. Tvrdik is excited about this. He *wants* to do it. You mustn't make it harder for him…"

Jorelial Rey snapped at her, through the tears streaming down her face in earnest now. "Why not? That idiot makes everything hard for himself, *and* for everyone else. He won't listen to anyone, and the fool has convinced himself that he is supposed to be a hero, or a martyr, or some such. He doesn't even seem to care if he lives or dies, so long as he gets to chase his precious destiny…"

Delphine, wide-eyed with surprise, still spoke in soothing tones, "But you *do* care if he lives or dies?"

"Yes, blast it. Though, if you tell him that, I'll break your arms."

"I wouldn't dream of it." Delphine fought to keep a serious expression on her face, when a broad smile at her sister's obvious deep feelings was wrestling to get out. She focused on the very real uncertainties of the project. "You know how I feel about Tvrdik. I adore him. He's like the big brother I never had. I would be crushed if anything happened to him. But somehow, I feel certain that he will pull this off, and be just fine. He's stronger than you give him credit for."

"I know. But, what if the dragons are right? What if we got all the way through the war in one piece, and then he insists on doing this fool rescue, and…and…" she could not even speak her fears.

"But, why are *you* so concerned, Rel? Honestly, I didn't even think you were getting along these last weeks. You know, after you nursed him back to health from that arrow wound, I thought it was wonderful how you two were getting to be such great friends – the both of you being such loners and all. But, for the last month or so, you've been downright icy with each other."

At that, Jorelial Rey, General, ruler of an entire kingdom – the smart, savvy, fearless leader of men, collapsed onto her stool, covered her face with her hands and dissolved into abject sobs. Now there was nothing funny in her sister's distress. Delphine was alarmed.

"It was me. It was all my fault," Rel wailed. "I never could figure out how to fix it, and things just got worse and worse."

"Calm down, and tell me what happened."

"It was at his birthday party. It was such a fine day, and at the end we were sitting by the fire talking about personal things, and we'd both had a good deal of wine, and I…I said that I couldn't wait for this whole awful business to be over so things could go back to normal again, like before he showed up and turned the whole world upside down!"

"Oh, Rel, you didn't!"

"Well, I didn't *mean* it like that…I just wanted all the problems to go away, all the responsibility. I didn't really mean they were his fault…"

"But, he assumed you meant you couldn't wait for him to go back where he came from and leave you alone."

"I tried to apologize. I tried to explain, but then everything happened, and we had work to do. There was no time to talk about such things. He's been cordial and professional to me ever since –even saved my life *again* on the battlefield, and we got the job done, didn't we? But now, he won't look at me, or talk to me. Not like before. And now he's determined to do this fool thing…he could be broken or *killed*, and I've never even had the chance to tell him…"

Delphine stood back from her sister, her eyes twinkling with mischief, "Why, Jorelial Rey, you're in love with him!"

"Don't be silly."

"No, no. Don't try to deny it. That's what this is all about…you're in love with the man, and you're afraid you'll lose him before he even knows. Oh, Rel, I couldn't be happier for you. I knew you two would be perfect for each other – I just *knew* it."

"How can you be so cruel to me, Delphy? I swear, I don't know what love is. I mean, I loved Papa, and you, and Tashroth, of course, but men? I never had any luck at all with men. And then, this scrawny, pale-haired, bespectacled stranger comes along and involves me in the most terrifying and difficult adventure of my life, and he is gentle, and kind, and funny, and compassionate. He listens. He makes me laugh. He cares what I think, how I feel. He isn't even afraid of Tashroth. I didn't plan to love him, but, oh, Delphine, it's like he's my other half. I never felt so easy with anyone before…at least until I opened my idiot mouth! I didn't even know how lonely I was until I got used to having him around all the time…," she started to cry all over again. "And what would I ever do without him? I can't go back to that solitary place again, I can't. Why won't he see what he's doing to me?"

"Well, why haven't you told him?"

"I don't even have a clue that he could ever think of me like that. He's been so distant. I'm sure he hates me."

Delphine laughed – but not with meanness – and surrounded her older sister, who was shorter and slighter than her, in a warm, loving embrace.

"There, there. Put your head on my shoulder, that's it. Don't forget I've been there. Don't you think I went through some of this myself with Mark? Don't you know we are always the last to see the obvious? The rest of us have known for ages how Tvrdik feels about you – the way he stares after you when you leave a room, that look of pure admiration on his face when you speak, the way he seeks out your company at every turn, and is always the last to leave so that he can have his time alone with you… he's like your guardian angel. Heavens, he's already saved your life twice, maybe three times. How could you not know how much he cares?"

The sobs were abating, replaced by shallow breaths and shaky sentences.

"But, then, why hasn't he said something, done something...been clear?"

Delphine pushed her away far enough to look her square in the eye.

"Rel, first of all, you as much as told him to go away. And besides, think who you are – the absolute monarch of a whole kingdom! He probably assumes you are so far out of his reach..."

There was a pause, and now Jorelial Rey's eyes widened with the dawning of a new insight, "I – I never thought of that."

Delphine swung an arm around her shoulders. "Look, you must tell him how you feel as soon as you can. Trust me, you'll get a pleasant surprise. Take a risk. It can't be scarier than facing horrible Lord Drogue and his army." She giggled, and then whispered, "Don't worry – he'll be alright. I feel certain nothing bad will happen. I can't explain it, but I feel it as sure as we are standing here together."

Rel wiped her eyes and stood taller, to hide her embarrassment, "Thanks, Sweet Pea. You really are awfully wise."

Delphine smiled, "I know. I learned from the best. See, here comes Tashroth now. I'd better go."

"No, stay. He's just going to go over the details of the plan with me I'd just as soon you heard it all too."

"Alright." Delphine kissed her sister on the cheek, brushed a stray hair out of Rel's eyes, and they stood, arms around each other's waists, waiting for Tashroth to touch down.

———— ● ————

Earlier that day, Tvrdik had been sitting on the flat rock at his special place by the river, alone with his thoughts. He had found himself restless with too much study, and almost before he knew it, his feet were headed down the path to the secret alcove where he had always found peace and clarity. Ondine had met him there, and they had shared a happy, playful visit. There weren't many flowers or berries left as summer drew to a close, but the leafy green canopy and the sounds of the river running by, along with the cool breezes, and soft kiss of sunshine still created the feel of a small piece of paradise on earth. Ondine was her usual irrepressible self, but now that much of their work here had been done, Tvrdik promised her that soon he would take her back to her beloved waterfall in the depths of the ancient forests. He knew she was enjoying her adventure in the wider world, but that she was beginning to miss her sisters, and the familiar surroundings of home. My, would she have some tales to tell them, upon her return, of the great events in the outside provinces, and of the vital part she herself played in making history. Tvrdik and Ondine laughed to imagine it, but she grew serious then for long enough to caution him about this new experiment, involving time and dragons. She wished him to be, *oh, so careful*, as she was counting on him to come out of the experience unscathed, and ready to take her home. After a while, she whipped up a good splash, as was her habit, blew him an affectionate kiss, and was on her merry way again.

Much as he delighted in her company, Tvrdik had come to this place today hoping for solitude, and perhaps some relief from his own thoughts. He was excited that, any day now, he would participate in an action which had a good chance of bringing his beloved teacher and mentor back from exile after almost thirteen years. It was a bold plan, and he felt confident that he could hold up his end, and that it had a better than average shot at succeeding. Everyone seemed concerned with the potential risks to him, but those didn't bother him. He was consumed with giving this one last gift to Xaarus, and perhaps he had been feeling a little reckless of late as well.

The truth was, that since they had been successful in defeating Lord Drogue, and in shifting the timeline to the future as well, he had been feeling a little adrift. He had been persuaded to come back to court to accomplish those particular, impossible tasks, and now that they were completed, he wasn't sure he had a reason to stay, or indeed what his life purpose was. Yes, he was changed. He'd set down some roots, made friends, done some healing, some good. But he was pretty sure that, at this point, the healing, the friends, the restoration of normalcy at court, would all carry on quite well without him. If he could bring back Xaarus, and restore him to his old position as Court Wizard, then things would have come full circle. His mission would be complete, and everything would be once again back in its proper, normal place. Then he, Tvrdik, would be somewhat extraneous, and he could go back to his cozy, hand-hewn stone dwelling in the ancient wood, to live out the rest of his days in peace and privacy. He missed that life sometimes, the simplicity of it, the deep connection with Nature and her rhythms, the absence of complicated relationships and uncomfortable emotions. Besides, that's what Jorelial Rey said she wanted, wasn't it? For things to go back to the way they were? And, he agreed, everyone would be happier. The sooner, the better.

And, if by some chance something went wrong in this attempt to save Xaarus, it didn't matter anyway, as he would have, at least, the good work he had done to show for his thirty years. And he would have made the ultimate sacrifice in a worthwhile endeavor. It would also save him the trouble of trying to figure out what to do next.

And yet, as he reclined on the river-smoothed rock, and felt the sun playing on his face, something in his thinking seemed somehow wrong, flawed. Something was missing from the equation, but what? Searching his memory, he kept lighting on moments that had transpired over the past few months – joyful moments, meaningful moments, moments where he seemed to understand that the true essence of life came from relationship. Not thoughts. Not even deeds. Not study or achievement, or even heroic sacrifice. The moments he would recall most from this time involved smiles and laughter, tears, shared meals, events celebrating friendship, griefs borne together, memories, wounds, hopes, dreams, fears. And so many of the moments he was sitting here reliving had one thing in common – Jorelial Rey. Aww. Why must his thoughts always circle back to her, her eyes, her voice, her gestures, the scent of her hair, his desperate panic when he thought she might slip away into death's cold grasp. She was so much a part of him now that there was no line of thought, no memory, that didn't lead to her. He loved her. That much was clear. He had almost known it since their first encounter in the Hall of Audience that fateful night, and the feeling had only grown and deepened with prolonged exposure. But she had made her own feelings clear. Oh, she liked and respected him as a colleague. She relied on him as a partner in achieving peace and security in the kingdom. She saw him as important to the health and well-being of the nation. After all, he was a wizard – the *last* wizard anybody knew of, unless they could indeed bring back Xaarus. They had worked well together, and she had been friendly and made him feel valuable. But, green, naïve soul that he was, he had mistaken that for something else. When he thought about it now, it seemed positively ridiculous that the acting ruler of a vast and powerful kingdom, princes and dignitaries courting her, could have any interest in a vagabond like himself. What had he been thinking?

And now, she would not need him for anything at all, once Xaarus was returned to his proper place. And, loving her as he did, knowing the sentiment was not returned, it was too painful to stay around and be reminded of a dream that could never be. So, there it was – as it had been before – you get involved with people, and you always come away with pain. This was a difficult paradox for one with such innate sensitivity as Tvrdik. His nature was always compassion. He could not help approaching everyone, and every situation, with honesty, and a wide-open heart. Too often, his reward had been disappointment and hurt. Better to go back to the ancient forest, alone again, where expectation and reality were better matched. Trees were more steady and predictable than human beings.

As that thought crossed his mind, a small twig from the tree under which he reclined snapped off under the weight of a bird, and fell, leaves and all, down through the array of branches and onto Tvrdik's upturned face. Spluttering, and scrambling to clear the unexpected debris away, the mage sat up, blinking in surprise. Then his eyes narrowed. "Very funny," he muttered, and rose to make his way back to The Cottage.

FORTY-THREE

RESCUE ATTEMPT

THE RESCUE OF XAARUS WAS set for two days later, at dawn, in the most secret place they could think of: Jorelial Rey's hidden lakeside retreat. Only this time, it would not be a vacation spot. It seemed a logical choice. It was quiet there, and unpeopled, conducive to concentration, room enough for all the dragons, and close enough to Theriole in an emergency. They would not be disturbed there, and they would not have to explain what was going on to any curious bystanders. They all agreed that it would be unwise to allow word of Xaarus' possible return to leak, in case they were unsuccessful. If they pulled it off, his unheralded reappearance would be a happy surprise.

Since anything and anyone essential for the operation had to be transported by air, it was also agreed that the list of attendees for the event would be kept short. There were an even dozen dragons, and the human list included Tvrdik, of course, and Jorelial Rey, Mark and Delphine as family and support, Warlowe to help with odds and ends, and Andrus, in case of medical need. The others who knew about the project, were to await news back at home, keep silent, and send good thoughts. Stewart was quite disappointed at being left behind, but was not so keen on riding dragon-back, in any case. He understood that there was little he could do to help with the actual process anyway, and that he could send moral support just as easily from The Cottage.

Those who were going intended to be well-rested and at their best for the event, but excitement and jitters chased away any hope of sleep the night before. The early hour was chosen for its peace and coolness, and the relative mental acuity with which most people - and dragons - began their days. The actual process would not take long at all, they guessed, and they had discussed and rehearsed the plan over and over so that each participant knew his or her part well. Xaarus had been living in the future, in what he described as a large city, but in order to minimize the risk of interference from bystanders on his end, and for him to be recognizable to Danoral, who would be making the pick-up, he had arranged to take a small dinghy out into the middle of the harbor at dawn, and wait there, apart from everyone and everything else. Danoral was the dragon with the most experience and facility in time-hopping. Dragons, like people, had individual special aptitudes, and he emerged as the logical candidate for the actual physical retrieval. Once Tvrdik had summoned his usual mind-link with Xaarus, Tashroth would be the first to join on, as he had done so many times before, stabilizing and amplifying the link. Candelinda would come into the mix next, with the other dragons adding the power of their minds one by one.

Beside participants who needed to be transported by dragonback, there were also chairs, cushions, blankets, medical supplies, lamps, and other equipment to be packed, secured, and air-lifted. The dragons did not seem to mind a little mule duty, in this case.

And so it was, in the chill, pitch-black hours before any inkling of morning whispered in the breeze, Tvrdik found himself once again on Tashroth, behind Jorelial Rey, soaring through the star-dappled skies. For once, he was so enchanted by the beauty around him, and the emotional rush of flight, that he forgot to be afraid. Jorelial Rey spoke in his ear, over the roar of beating wings.

"Are you nervous?"

He answered with shining eyes, and a sincere smile, "No. Why should I be? We are on our way to do something wonderful." No other words passed between them.

Arriving at their destination, dragon after dragon found a space to land, using their remarkable night vision, and the business of unpacking and setting up began. Lamps were lit, and Mark and Delphine built a campfire on the lakeshore with extra wood they had collected for that purpose on their honeymoon. Rel and Warlowe untied and pulled down the chairs, and arranged them on the sandy shore as had been pre-determined, not far from the fire. The extra cushions and blankets they dragged up in a nearby pile in case they should be needed for comfort or warmth. Andrus took charge of the medical supplies, and a small folding cot, which he set up in a convenient alcove between some rocks near to the center of the action. In case of a problem with either Tvrdik, or Xaarus, the idea was for him to be standing by, prepared with whatever might be needed.

Tvrdik swept his gaze over the vast, pristine lake, just becoming visible in the first hints of dawn. "You were so right about this place, Jorelial Rey," he called. "It is indeed magnificent."

"You haven't even seen the half of it," she called back from behind a pile of cushions. "Sometime, I'll fly you over and *really* show you around…" But her offer drifted off unfinished, as she found herself fighting off the thought that such a thing might never happen.

When all the preparations were complete, the young wizard took his place in the center chair, leaning against its high back, facing away from the water. He wore a loose, comfortable robe, unbelted, his powerful staff in his right hand, and his left fishing the old coin bearing Xaarus' image out of a pocket. Delphine and Mark sat down in chairs on either side of him, each laying a hand on one of his forearms. If Tvrdik sensed at any moment that he was in the slightest trouble, or he wished to discontinue for any reason, he was to move his hand or his arm so that they would know to call for help. They would also be in a good position to use the leverage of physical contact to pull him back from the brink to reality. They were to do that, in any case, at the end, if the process succeeded. Cushions were stuffed under Tvrdik's arms, as well as behind his head and at the small of his back, to keep him comfortable and relaxed for the duration of the exercise.

"I feel like a salmon packed for shipping," he quipped, a slight edge of hysteria to his good humor. "Is this necessary?"

"We don't know how long you'll have to sit there in the same position," Delphine answered, fluffing one of the pillows. "Just relax, and let us make you comfortable."

Jorelial Rey would sit in a chair facing him, watching him at all times, and also keeping an eye out over the lake, which was where Danoral would be making his exit and re-entry. Andrus and Warlowe watched from a few paces away, ready to step in if need arose. And now, eleven dragons, of various sizes, ages, and colors, began to arrange themselves in a ring surrounding the odd little scene. Tash took his place right behind Tvrdik, in the closest and most supportive role. His mind would be the first to join with Tvrdik's consciousness, and the last to pull out. Candelinda stood at Tashroth's right, as near to him as practical. A rust-colored creature called Morenwood stepped in beside her, and so on, dragon after dragon placing themselves beside their fellows, until the full circle was complete. Danoral remained by himself, facing the lake and the sunrise, poised to execute his peculiar function at the appointed moment. When the circle of dragons unfolded their wings even just a little bit, it was like being in an enclosed shelter made of vibrant, living tissue. One felt cocooned in safety, warmth, and power.

Jorelial Rey took her seat, and Tvrdik reached forward and handed her his glasses for safekeeping.

"Please look after these. You know what they mean to me."

She slid them with care into a pocket, and nodded, leaning in close to him.

"The sun is just coming up. Are you ready?"

"As ready as I'll ever be."

"You can still change your mind, you know. No one would think any less of you."

"I'll see you on the other side."

"Don't wait to signal us if you feel the slightest bit uncomfortable…"

"Alright! Let's just get on with it."

Tashroth's deep voice coached now, "Master mage, you will forge the link as usual, and I will lend my assistance, as we have done before. Candelinda will then add her mind to the link. Once you are comfortable with that, each of the others will join at intervals, stretching and opening and strengthening a corridor through time, one layer at a time, right to where your mind tells us Xaarus is waiting. At any time, you may tell us to stop, if the experience becomes too much for you, and we will reverse the process. As soon as Danoral feels he has a clear fix on your teacher, he will attempt to dive in and fetch him back. In and out, precise and quick. It may take only a few of us to create a safe corridor, but we anticipate needing the minds of all of us present to accomplish our goal. If we succeed, once

Danoral and Xaarus are safely through the corridor, we intend to disengage one mind at a time, to bring you back in gentle stages. Is this clear?"

"Thanks, Tashroth. Very clear. We've been through it a hundred times."

"Patience, mage. No harm in making sure we all know what we are doing. Fine, then. Whenever you are ready."

"Wait!" cried Jorelial Rey, and all eyes were on her, as she fumbled for something of worth to say which might delay things further. She glanced at Delphine, her eyes pleading. Delphine returned her look with sympathy, but there was nothing at all to say now that made any sense. Rel swallowed, and muttered, "Good luck, Tvrdik." Everyone nodded and echoed the words, voicing their support. Tvrdik closed his eyes and fingered the small coin, imagining Xaarus in his mind – the expression in his eyes, the timbre of his voice, the grace with which he moved...

"I am here, son," the familiar voice seemed to say aloud. "I'm going to keep talking to you as much as possible throughout this experience in order to keep us both focused on our connection, yes?"

"Yes, Master. It is good to see you again."

"And you as well, my boy. With any luck at all, very soon we will see each other in the flesh for the first time in a long, long while."

"That will be wonderful, indeed."

"Ah, and here is Tashroth come in with us. I recognize that familiar *boost* in the transmission."

"When Tashroth joins us, I always hear you better, and your image seems to be more solid, less...translucent, if that is the word. Also, I always feel like I can relax some, as if a weight is lifted from my shoulders."

"He is providing some of the energy that helps us connect, so that we both needn't work quite as hard. But, mind you do not relax too much today. We need you to have all your wits about you."

"Don't worry. I'm paying attention. I don't wish to miss a moment of this adventure. Whoa, I think that must be Candelinda joining on. Now, *that's* a different feeling. It's as if we are standing in the same room talking, but I feel sort of euphoric. Light as a feather...." Tvrdik giggled. Candelinda had indeed come aboard, and things were moving along. Those who were outside observing had had various levels of experience with the phenomenon of this mind link between wizards, and were not all comfortable with what they were watching. It was like a strange, disjointed performance where half the characters and half the dialogue were missing. Tvrdik's eyes were open, and he seemed very alert, but stared at a point in space where there was nothing to see. Since they could only hear his part of the conversation, it seemed as if he kept up a running dialogue with the air. Not all of what he said made sense to them, but they listened, nevertheless, for signs of potential danger. So far, what they had heard was a bit odd, but the mage seemed fine. A third, and then a fourth dragon added their consciousness to the joined minds.

"Oooooh! This is amazing. There are all sorts of remarkable visions spinning by. So many colors. So much knowledge and wisdom. Centuries of records. And flashes of scenes – blood and fire and ice and stars and wind and motion…I-I can't make sense out of it all. My mind is reeling."

"Now, Tvrdik, I know it is tempting, and I know you are curious by nature," Xaarus soothed, "but don't go wandering around in the dragons' minds, alright? You wouldn't want to get lost there. They can be very convoluted. Focus. You are pointing them to me, remember? So, stay with me, boy. Here, take my hand…"

"Oops, no, Xaarus, they're panicking. That was our signal for trouble, and I've moved my hand now. False alarm, everyone. Xaarus asked me to take his hand, and I must have flinched. I'm fine. Keep going…"

A fifth dragon came into the mix. Delphine, who had jumped when the fingers on her side had suddenly twitched and reached, appeared shaken. The coin bearing Xaarus' likeness had fallen to the ground. She searched and picked it up, folding it back into the mage's left hand and cupping it in her own. "Tvrdik, this is Delphine. Can you hear me too? Can you hear any of us? We're all right beside you. Can you see us anymore?"

"I can heeear you, from a veeery looong way off, but I can't see yooooooou. No. I am too big, you see. I am so very, very enormous, and you are so very small. I can't find you. I'm glad you're there, but you have no idea how huge I am. I can step from star to star. I am stretched across the sky…" The sixth dragon had taken his place in the group consciousness. They were only halfway there. "Wait a moment, Xaarus is calling me again – I can see him."

"Tvrdik, Tvrdik! Look at me. We are still linked, and you need to focus on me, lad. This is all about finding the way to me. Now, listen carefully.

You don't have to move your physical body. You don't have to lift a finger at all. Just imagine your energetic self, standing right here in your mind's eye, just as you see I am, and I am thinking that my hand should reach out to you. Can you will your energetic hand to reach out and clasp mine, son? There, that's it. That's right. Can you feel me beside you now?"

"Yes, I can. Master, can you not see all of these wonders? Do you not feel all of this as I do?"

"Not with the same intensity as you. Partly as I am older and more experienced with disciplining my thoughts. But mostly because everything is coming from your side; your mind is the doorway. You are the conduit, so you are the one who must contain everything. It is a lot to ask, I know. Do you understand? Are you all right? Do you still wish to go on?"

"Yes, yes, of course. I couldn't be better. I am amazing! I know so many things. There is no possible way I will remember all of this later with my own tiny brain. Someone should be out there taking all of this down before I forget it all."

The seventh dragon came into the link, and Tvrdik began to cry. It was abrupt, and heart-wrenching. Jorelial Rey, who had been sitting very close, observing every detail, and trying to hold her tongue as the experiment proceeded, could do so no longer.

"Tvrdik, what's the matter? Are you in pain?" she shouted out in alarm.

He didn't actually acknowledge her question, but gave an answer nevertheless.

"It's all so very beautiful. So wise and beautiful, I can't bear it. There is light everywhere, and color everywhere, and music everywhere, and all in such perfect order. Everything sings and dances and makes sense. Even the smallest of the small – the gnat, even – is down there working out his assigned purpose. It is too much to conceive, too pure, too beautiful…" He continued to weep.

The Lady Rey's eyebrows furrowed as she shouted to Danoral, "I don't know how much more of this he can take. We're only just past halfway. Do we need all of them?"

Danoral shouted back to her, "I think so, to be safe. I have a vague target here – the beginnings of a window, but I'll need more. It would not do if I was to be trapped over there on the other side, or worse, somewhere else."

The eighth dragon linked in, and Tvrdik cried out, "Master, where are you?" But, he had stopped sobbing.

Jorelial Rey asked, "Perhaps we should speed the process up a bit and be done with it, then…?"

Danoral answered, "They're trying to give him time to adjust to each layer. They are being cautious."

"Well, they might be adjusting him clean out of his wits!"

"Don't panic, lady. So far, all of this is quite in line with what we would expect. His mind is just being stretched a little."

"Dragons," thought Jorelial Rey, with an edge of annoyance, and a flash of pain in her own head, like a pinch, told her that Tashroth's connection with *her* was still very much functioning, despite his being otherwise occupied. She sat back down in her chair, pressed her lips together, watched, and waited. The ninth dragon linked.

"Master, where are you? Are you still there?"

"I'm right here, lad. Can you see me? Yes? Good. Now, focus. Concentrate. Look into my eyes. Use that staff of yours to ground yourself. It's only the two of us here, sitting and talking. Just two old friends. Tell me about all the improvements you've made to my old Cottage. I want to hear all about it."

"Oh, it's lovely. We didn't change much at all. Well, except the school….there isn't a school anymore, so the Praegers re-invented that whole space for their family to live in. They have the most delightful little girl, Lynette. Lynette is her name. And Mr. Praeger has the front garden in tip-top form. He loves to work in the dirt. He has all the medicinal plants growing apart from the food plants and the flowers…" There was a pause, and his mood seemed to change again, "But all of them are gone now, aren't they. All of them were dead and ashes years and years ago. Gone and blown away. Lynette, and the Praegers, and Stewart, and the flowers, and The Cottage…all gone." Tvrdik's grip on the oaken staff loosened, and it fell to the ground with a muffled thud, narrowly missing Jorelial Rey's head on the way down. She and Mark, who was holding Tvridk's arm on that side, glanced over to where it lay, but no one dared move to retrieve it. Meanwhile, Xaarus was diligently trying to recapture the young mage's attention.

"No, no, Tvrdik. Hang onto me, but don't come to me here. Don't try to follow me. It's all right. Stay where you are, and I will come to you, yes?"

"He's getting clearer," Danoral shouted.

Xaarus must have heard that, as his next words were, "It can't be soon enough for me. This blasted boat is pitching up and down in the most nauseating fashion, and there are beginning to be people up and about."

"Master, what is it like there? Shall I come and visit with you now?" He sounded positively childlike. Delphine and Mark were gripping his arms now with all their might, trying to keep him in the chair. His entire body was shaking now as if it were full of pressurized steam that must be vented somehow or explode. Warlowe and Andrus ran up to help and hold him in the chair. Andrus tried to take his pulse, but could not get him to hold his arm still.

"No, Tvrdik, stay where you are. Don't come here. I'm coming to you. Focus on the sound of my voice in your mind. It's all there is now. Just my voice. Let everything else go."

The tenth dragon came on board. Tvrdik stood up, with little effort, and a sense of purpose, despite four strong pairs of hands trying to hold him down. Jorelial Rey sprang up and stepped forward, reaching up to take his face in both of her hands, and smoothing his hair back from a perspiration-drenched brow. His eyes stared through her, seemed frightened.

"Master, I was wrong. It is too difficult to hold it all. I have failed you. I am so sorry. I am spreading myself out on the wind…I am losing myself. I have no name. I am a part of all that is, but I don't know who I am. I-I've forgotten my name…"

"Tvrdik! It's Tvrdik." Jorelial Rey shouted at him, knowing he could not hear her.

"You are Tvrdik, dear boy, and you are one with all that is, but you are still you. Hang on just a little longer, I think we are almost there…"

The eleventh and last dragon joined the group lending its powerful concentration to locating Xaarus through Tvrdik's stretched, bedazzled mind, and opening a doorway in the shifting planes of time for Danoral to travel through.

"No. No. It's too much. I don't think I can hang on any longer. There is nothing left of me. I am tired of struggling. So tired. I think I'll just drift away now…" his voice sounded colorless and empty as the trembling ceased, and all the muscles of his body went limp at once. His friends caught the dead weight, and eased him back into the chair, scrambling for cushions.

"Don't go yet, Tvrdik," Xaarus coached, his tone firm. "Just hold onto the sound of my voice a little longer, do you hear me? I am your master, and I *order* you to hang onto the sound of my voice..." The eyelids closed, but flickered, revealing the whites behind them.

"Got him!" Danoral cried. "I have a clear fix; I'm going in." And the purple dragon launched himself from the beach, up into the space of air above the lake, circled once, silhouetted against the golden disc of the rising sun, and – vanished.

———— ⊗ ————

No one else was at the rail. Most of the early, savvy travelers were within the ferry's warm cabin, dozing on benches, or enjoying a hot cup of coffee. The woman, and her companion, George, were enjoying the fresh air and early sunshine. She sighed, gazing out at a lone, small vessel containing a single vague figure, tossing on the waters in the distance. As the two friends stood watching, a huge purple dragon appeared without warning in the sky over the little boat, back-winging to hold himself suspended there. The old man they had wondered about stood, with some difficulty, in the dinghy, stretched his arms straight upward toward the dragon, and waited while the beast dropped low enough for his front talons to be in reach. The man grabbed one of the dragon's claws with both hands, and the great purple beast lifted him clear up out of the boat, circled once, and appeared to vanish into thin air, dangling passenger and all. The little boat bobbed, aimless and lonely, on the gentle waves.

The woman and George stared wide-eyed, not daring to move or speak until well after the odd spectacle had ended. At last, she cleared her throat, "Well, I'll be! You – you saw that, didn't you? I'm not hallucinating?"

"I saw it. Pretty amazing."

"Wow! It really pays to get up out of bed early now and then. What a treat that was."

"Too bad nobody else was looking. They'll never believe us."

"We'll know what we saw, George. You and I. I'll bet we'll still be telling this story years from now. You know, I've never seen a dragon before – that was one, wasn't it?"

"I've never seen one either, but I think so, yes."

"It's pretty rare to catch them all the way down here…I'd always heard they holed up in the mountains, or places where there are still some big tracts of old forest."

"Yes, but I seem to recall some news reports that there have been more and more sightings this year all over the place. Seems they are enjoying some sort of resurgence of late."

"Well, whatever the reason, it's our lucky day. You don't run into things like that all the time. Wonder who that old guy was? You don't think the dragon was going to eat him, or anything like that…?"

"Naw…seems almost like he was waiting for it. Bizarre, is what it is. Maybe there will be something on the news about it. Publicity stunt or some such, maybe for a new movie?"

"Sounds right. I'll be sure and check."

"I wonder how they do that popping in and out thing? It's very cool. I'd like to be able to do that."

"Well, anyway, that was very exciting, but now I am getting cold, and I think I would like a cup of coffee after all. Want me to see if the snack bar has any of those excellent milk bone things you liked?"

"That sounds perfect. I am feeling a bit peckish."

And the woman gathered George, her Pomeranian companion, into her arms and turned away from the railing toward the staircase into the ship's warm cabin, reflecting on the special bit of magic that had begun her day. The empty dinghy drifted further away, unnoticed by most.

Jorelial Rey leaned this way and that to get a better view. She was struggling with Tvrdik, and trying to see around Tashroth's great bulk. But, no. Danoral was nowhere to be seen. Her heart sank…had it all been for naught? A moment later, there was a small disturbance in the sky, like radiant heat waves that distort the air. Then, an odd, spiral-shaped cloud appeared that expanded before her eyes. With a flash of light, from out of its center sprang the dragon-transporter himself. And dangling from his front talons was another figure, a man. They had done it!

Andrus was signaling that Tvrdik's heart was racing and erratic, and his eyelids were still fluttering. The dragons, fearing for his life, let go of the time corridor they had built, and began to disengage, one by one, at a much faster pace than they had intended. After the third dragon had pulled out of the collective consciousness, the young mage's eyes flew open in terror, and he let out a howl that startled Mark, Delphine, and Jorelial Rey several paces backward.

"Nooooo! Please, no. I can't go back there. Please don't leave me. Please, please, I'll do anything. Don't make me squeeze back into that small, pitiful body and that puny mind again. I can't...I can't go back there." He was thrashing about, and wailing in agony, genuine fear on his face, and tears rolling down his cheeks. With each dragon's exit, subtle as they tried to be, he winced, and begged them not to make him shrink down any further. He grabbed his head in his hands and howled again with an almost inhuman sound. Once more the coin bearing Xaarus' image fell into the dust. And Tvrdik stood up again, grasping his own head as if it would fall off. Not knowing what was happening, or what to do, Rel, Mark, Delphine, Warlowe and Andrus had all taken another step backward in helpless shock. Rel clapped her hands to her mouth, and found herself biting the skin of her palm, tears of concern and frustration welling up in her own eyes.

At that moment, another tall figure strode through the little group of onlookers, and with a gentle, but firm gesture, pushed them all aside. With confidence and presence, he grasped the young mage's arms and lowered them to his sides. Then, with a father's care, he wrapped the young man in a bear hug, guiding Tvrdik's head onto his shoulder, and speaking to him in a soothing voice.

"There, there, Tvrdik, it's all right now. It's over. Let them go. You can do this yourself. You are sufficient. You are remarkable. Come back to us, son. Come back to yourself where you belong. Everything is going to be all right. Better than all right. You'll see."

Between encouragements, the stranger seemed to be interjecting words in some unknown foreign tongue, and where he stroked Tvrdik's pale, damp hair, the others swore they could see light radiating from his hand. Or perhaps it was a trick of the sunrise.

As the last few dragons, then Candelinda, and finally Tashroth, stepped back, folded their wings, and nodded to Jorelial Rey, signifying that they had disengaged from Tvrdik's mind, the young man seemed to grow calmer in his comforter's arms. No one else stirred, or dared to make a sound. Tashroth had broken the last of the link, but the pair in the center of the circle seemed to be swaying in their embrace for an eternity longer. At last, the stranger's arms loosened, and he held Tvrdik at arm's length and regarded him with a heart-warming smile. Tvrdik, drained, but himself again, looked back at the hooked nose, the twinkling eyes, the great bush of snow white hair…

"Master, if it is finished, then why are you still here, in my mind?"

Xaarus' smile broadened, "Because I am not in your mind, dear boy. I am standing right here beside you on solid ground. You did it. You brought me home."

Tvrdik's eyes widened, and a single wordless sob escaped his lips. He shook his head once, a bit like a dog does after a rainstorm. Then, as it dawned on his consciousness that Xaarus was there in the flesh, his face came alive with joy, and he whispered, "The gods be thanked. Welcome home." And he hugged his mentor with a child's enthusiasm.

Their worst fears alleviated, and the realization of their success beginning to dawn on them, the others rushed up for hugs and handshakes all around. Great shouts and cheers and dragon trumpeting filled the dawn sky with such a cacophony that later they all swore that they had expected their celebration to be heard all the way back at Theriole.

"Sir, my name is Andrus, and I am currently the head Palace Physician. It is an honor to meet you in person, sir."

"Do I know you, Andrus? Forgive me if I have forgotten…" chatted Xaarus, shaking the man's proffered hand.

"No, sir. I came to Theriole after you had already…left. But I have heard so much about you from so many sources that I almost feel as though I know you." Andrus was a bit star struck. Xaarus leaned in very close, "Don't believe everything you hear." He winked at the healer.

Andrus forged on, "I-I wanted to ask your permission to examine you, sir, and make sure that all is well after your...journey. Just a precaution, you understand...part of my function here..."

"Of course, my good man. Examine away. I think you will find everything in good working order. I feel fine. I could sleep for a week, but otherwise, not bad, considering..." Andrus thanked him and went to work, still a bit in awe.

Mark and Delphine and Jorelial Rey were crowded around Tvrdik, congratulating him. Mark was pumping his hand, "You did it! You brought him back from the future. That was incredible."

Delphine intervened, "I may be no physician, but I picked up a thing or two from all of our Thursday healing marathons. Why don't you sit back down and let me check you over? Andrus will be here in a moment. He's going over Xaarus."

Tvrdik managed a faint smile, but still looked somewhat dazed and confused. He allowed himself to be guided back to the chair and ministered to. Warlowe arrived with a skin of cool water, having brought one to Xaarus as well.

"You must be thirsty. It's only water. Will that do, or would you prefer something a little stronger – wine, perhaps?"

"No, water is fine, Warlowe. How kind of you to bring it. I am awfully thirsty; give it here." He took a long draught from the water skin.

Jorelial Rey laid a hand on the young wizard's shoulder, her face unreadable, "I can see you are in very good hands here, so, if no one minds, I would like to go check on Tash and the rest of the dragons. I shouldn't be long."

Tvrdik looked up at her, "No, of course, go ahead. Please thank them for me, especially Tashroth."

"I will, but you'll be doing it yourself soon, I'm sure." She started away, but stopped and turned back to him, "Tvrdik?"

"Hmmm?"

"Well done. I'm...I'm really happy for you." She turned and headed over to Tashroth, Tvrdik following after her with his eyes. As she came to the green dragon, who was in conversation with Danoral and Candelinda, he swung his great head around to welcome her.

"Is he recovering, little one? Is he all right?"

"Andrus will be over in a moment, but he seems well. Quite a bit dazed, but all right. He asked me to thank all of you – for the inspiration, and the brilliant execution too. Xaarus is fine, Danoral. Thank you for your part in this. It will be a real coup to bring Xaarus back to Theriole, alive and well, after all this time. The people will be overjoyed, and will take it as an omen of good fortune for the future. No doubt, it will be. More good news to celebrate, eh? Anyway, we owe all of you dragons a great debt for this. Anything I can give or do for you that is in my power, just ask, and it will be arranged. Tell them, Tash, please."

Tashroth's laughter rumbled out, low and earthy, "Dearest, we are all delighted that our idea bore such joyful fruit. Xaarus is well-loved among our kind, and we rejoice in his return. We are also content that Lord Drogue is no longer a threat to dragonkind and our way of life. Now, each of us may continue to live as he chooses in peace and freedom. In addition, we have all experienced something new and fascinating here today that we will long remember. We have explored, and learned, even about ourselves and our own potentials. These are things that bring our kind great joy. There is no other gift, necessary, little one, but we appreciate your generous impulse."

"Are all of you all right Tash? The dragons suffered no ill effects?"

"No, on the contrary. We are feeling quite exhilarated by the joining and expanding of our consciousness. We are interested in exploring further the power of the collective, and the ancient skills we had almost forgotten. But all of that will wait for another time, as most are eager to take their leave and return to their homes."

"So soon, Tash? May we not tempt them back to Theriole for a while longer? It was wonderful to have so many of your kinsmen and women around."

"Most gracious. Candelinda will stay on awhile, but the others are missing their homelands, and their normal routines. Our work here is done, and they would beg to be released as soon as is convenient."

"Oh, of course, if that is your desire." All of the dragons were focused on her by now, their large, bottomless eyes seeming to search her soul. She addressed the whole group as one, "For all you have done for me, for these two wizards, and for our kingdom and all of its citizens, we are forever in your debt. From henceforth and ever after, the royal flag of Eneri Clare will bear the image of a dragon, without whose generosity we might not now have a free and peaceful kingdom." The dragons exchanged glances and nods, and made sounds of approval. The Lady Regent went on, "On behalf of all, I pledge you eternal friendship and support, and bid you farewell as you return to your homes and families. Be welcome always to come and visit us again any time, or to call upon us for aid in any circumstance." The great, colorful beasts continued snorting and nodding, regarding her with those huge, glowing eyes, and with what she could only guess were something close to smiles. But before any of them could make a move to leave, Xaarus approached the saurian circle, Tvrdik still under his protective wing.

"I beg your pardon if I am interrupting something, my dear, but do you suppose the two of us could have a moment alone with the dragons, to speak with them one last time?"

"I was just leaving. Oh, Tvrdik, I almost forgot to give you these..." She handed him the precious spectacles, which he received with a look of relief, but no words. "Dragons, I wish you safe travels. Tash, Candelinda, will you be near?"

"If you are staying a while, we were thinking of having a bit of a hunt... mind-melding is famishing work." Candelinda offered.

"That's fine. Take your time. We should all rest before going back. Oh! If all the dragons are leaving, how will we get everyone and everything back to Theriole?"

"We will take it in shifts and all will be taken care of. Go and eat and rest. We will return in the afternoon."

"All right, Tash. I'll look forward to your return."

He nuzzled her, and whispered, "Once again, dearest, you have distinguished yourself with the respect you show my kinsmen. You have garnered much goodwill among dragon kind this day. I am proud of you."

Jorelial Rey grinned, "Maybe I learned something at Dad's knee about diplomacy after all." He winked at her, and she turned, heading back to where Mark and Delphine seemed to be waiting for her, while Tvrdik and Xaarus walked among the dragons. Looking back, she saw them deep in conversation, and then, both standing still, silent, eyes closed, faces lifted, as the great beasts also sat in communion together, eyes flashing. A tiny pang of jealousy disturbed her. She was the one who was supposed to have the special, unique bond with dragons, after all. But the thought only lasted a moment, as she watched them take off, one by one, and fly away in every direction, leaving the two wizards alone on the ground, earthbound and sighing. At least she knew Tashroth would always be back for her.

"Rel?" Delphine called, and then came up to meet her. "You know, we did bring along a few provisions just in case. I'll bet we could fix up some bread and cheese and fruit for everyone if you thought it a good idea?"

"It's a very good idea, Sweet Pea. We'll be resting here for a little while before we try to go back. Most of the dragons have gone, now. Tash and Candelinda are off hunting, and will ferry us all back later. So, it's...let me see...just the seven of us. A bite would be most welcome, and maybe even a nap. Besides, I need some time to figure out how to bring a wizard who's been missing and presumed dead for twelve years, back to life."

Sitting around the campfire, enjoying a simple meal, they all spent the time getting to know the real Xaarus, or in some cases, getting re-acquainted. Andrus was dazzled by the charming, witty gentleman, who was equally at home in a musty library, a pub, or a High Court function. Xaarus was legend to him, and he asked a hundred questions, and listened with delight to numerous anecdotes and stories. Warlowe extended the old man a warm greeting, welcoming him back with genuine affection. Xaarus inquired about his family, recalling names and interests, and the two of them indulged in a few happy reminiscences.

"And little Delphine. Last time I saw you, you were a chubby toddler with red curls – always laughing, always bringing home stray cats, or injured birdlings. You were the apple of your father's eye, and now grown up beautiful, and wise, and kind. Take good care of this one, master bard, and thank your lucky stars that she has fastened her affections on you. She had all of our hearts at court almost from the moment she was born." Delphine blushed, and Mark smiled, knowing the truth of the old wizard's words. There was some discussion between them of the Lady Brendelle, her transformation, their reunion, and how highly she had spoken of Xaarus' kindness to her in her darkest hour. Xaarus nodded, pleased, "A little kindness and compassion, my children, they cost us so little. But they may mean the world to the person on the receiving end. In my *long* experience, it is rare that I have seen any heart, or any situation that cannot be transformed with enough love, and enough kindness." Rel and Delphine exchanged a surprised look, remembering that Delphine had used almost those exact words on the battlefield only weeks before, concerning baby Drake. Delphine shivered with the strangeness of it.

At last, Xaarus' keen eye fell upon Rel, who squirmed with discomfort under it, despite the warmth and admiration in that regard. "Jorelial Rey. What an amazing young woman you have grown into. You know, I sent Tvrdik to you on purpose, because I was certain he would find in you the one powerful ally he needed, and I was right. Look at the marvels the two of you have accomplished together in such a short time. Your father – bless his soul and I miss him sorely – would be bursting with pride over you, my dear, as I am over my boy here. He touched Tvrdik's hand, and there was a moment of awkward glances all around between Tvrdik and Rel, Rel and Delphine, Tvrdik and Xaarus, Xaarus and Rel. No one replied, though Jorelial Rey smiled and acknowledged the old man's compliment with a coy bob of her head.

Tvrdik had been silent throughout the long, sociable meal, picking at his bread and cheese, alert to the many conversations, but contributing little to them. No one thought very much of it. They all assumed that he was weary from a sleepless night, and a harrowing ordeal, and needed a little rest to be back to himself again. But now, Xaarus, sensing that he had blundered into some small minefield that he wasn't exactly up to date on, found a way to break the tension. Leaning in to Jorelial Rey, he frowned and said, "What's that?" Flinching, she replied, "What's what?" Xaarus pretended to study her head, "Why, there. Behind your ear...there's something there. What is that?" He reached around behind her left ear as she sat mystified, and pulled out a shining bit of silver, a coin with his own face stamped upon it. On an instinct, Tvrdik reached into his pocket, but his own coin was still safe and sound in its usual place, where Delphine had replaced it after the rescue. The redheaded girl now squealed in delight, and Jorelial Rey melted into easy laughter.

"You remembered! You used to do that to me on every visit, and I never questioned it, even when I was a teenager. I *loved* that trick. Look, Tvrdik. I have my own now." She held it up, beaming, years of cares falling away from her face. Tvrdik responded with an unconvincing half-smile.

Rel's expression shifted to concern for him, "Goodness, you must be beyond exhaustion. What are we thinking? So sorry, Tvrdik. Let's find the hero of the hour a place to lie down for awhile. I could do with a bit of a nap myself. What about the rest of you?"

And so, gathering up the blankets and cushions they had brought, along with the one cot, they all found a place to curl up by the fire, and fell asleep.

FORTY-FOUR

WHAT LOVE CAN TRANSFORM

Tashroth and Candelinda soared in and woke them all not long after midday. They opened their eyes to a brilliant blue sky, tangible sunshine, and white, puffy clouds sailing along on a breeze from over the water. Everyone was a little disoriented by the odd schedule that had them waking with the sun at its zenith. But they were all relieved to see Xaarus actually still with them, flesh and blood, so they knew the events of the early morn were more than just some collective bizarre dream. Jorelial Rey had been half-awake throughout the morning, thinking through her options on what to do next. No one had dared to plan ahead, in case the rescue attempt had failed. But, now, she gathered her small company: the two wizards, two dragons, her sister and brother in law, the physician, and the employee who seemed more like family. She told them all that she had been considering all morning, and would very much like to give both Tvrdik and Xaarus a chance to return to full strength before being thrust into the public eye. She felt they needed rest, and a chance to acclimate to new circumstances before their days were overwhelmed with fans and well-wishers.

"So, I am asking you all to keep this news quiet for just a few days, and I'd like all of you to come back with me to Theriole, where I can better keep you under my wing. I will arrange for suitable quarters there for anyone who doesn't already have them. Then, we'll begin to plan a grand banquet for, say, a week from now, where Xaarus can be formally presented as returned from long exile, and can resume his post as Court Wizard.

Staying at the palace will also give you two mages time to sort out what will happen with The Cottage. I am content to let you decide which of you will live there. There is always a place at Theriole for either of you. After you are presented to the people, Xaarus, I'm afraid you'll be subjected to all sorts of public appearances and functions. I will try to keep things from getting too taxing, but, sir, you have always been well-loved here. Everyone will want a glimpse of you, or a personal moment.

"Not to forget our closest friends, who knew of our purpose here today, and would never forgive me if they did not get to embrace their old friend right away, I will host a small dinner in the private dining room this evening. I would like all of you, and your families to be there, and I will invite Verger, Lord Corbin Maygrew, Bargarelle, and Stewart of course – oh, and Mr. and Mrs. Praeger. I think that covers all the important players. Does this plan meet with everyone's approval?"

There were nods and exclamations of affirmation all around.

"My, my. You *have* learned a thing or two about taking charge of a situation, my dear, haven't you," Xaarus called out in good humor. The Lady Regent searched his face for signs of sarcasm, but found nothing but pride and delight. A broad smile spread across her face, as she replied, "Thank you. It will be wonderful to have you back with us where you belong, dear Xaarus. I think you will find that in the most important ways, very little has changed. Ask for anything you need or desire, and we will be happy to do our utmost to make you feel comfortable, and welcome." There was applause at that, and a few shouts of, "Hear, hear!"

They set about packing the chairs, provisions, and equipment in compact bundles on Tashroth's back, while Candelinda took Mark and Delphine back to Theriole. Their assignment was to assure those who waited for word that Xaarus would indeed be coming, and to start making arrangements for supper that night.

Tashroth carried most of the supplies, along with Warlowe, who was a bit nervous to be sent on a dragonflight alone, but managed, nevertheless. He was to find Bargarelle and enlist the Steward's aid in unloading everything else Tashroth carried, as well as in arranging for rooms. Rel sat by the campfire with Andrus and the two wizards, waiting the next shift of dragon transport, but enjoying the lack of urgency for a change. She realized that a very unfamiliar feeling of peace was beginning to descend on her being, now that all that she had dreaded was done, and all that she had worked for had come to fruition. The only dark spot marring her deep joy was that Tvrdik was still uncommunicative and withdrawn. He hadn't said much of anything, in fact, all day, which was not normal for him. Xaarus was making a point of staying by his side, keeping a watchful eye on the younger wizard. Before they had packed most everything, Andrus asked if he wasn't feeling well, and might he prefer to be strapped into the cot for the return trip? Tvrdik thanked him for his concern, and replied that he was fine, and would be more than able to travel as everyone else would. Whenever anyone tried to engage him in conversation, his answers were polite, but curt, and he offered no more than what was required. When Tashroth returned, Rel went to greet him and voiced her concerns about Tvrdik.

"He does not seem at all himself, Tash. Do you suppose he will recover with rest, or could something have gone more wrong than we thought?"

Tash blinked and felt for the young mage's aura with his mind. "It was a taxing ordeal for anyone to have endured, only hours ago, and at the time there were moments when we were all very concerned for him. But his energy feels whole, now, and strong – in the main, recovered. No, to me, he seems more like a man consumed with his own thoughts."

"But, how can we help him? He is so closed to everyone. This should be his most triumphant day, and yet he seems so...so...detached."

"Let him be, dear one. Many things are changing around him – around all of you – that require adjustment. When he is ready to share his inner world with someone, you will know."

"If you say so, Tash," she sighed, "you are almost never wrong."

They doused the fire with extra care, looked around one last time at the beautiful, pristine lakeshore that held so many important memories. Then Xaarus helped Andrus up onto Candelinda, climbing on after with practiced grace. Jorelial Rey found her accustomed seat on Tashroth, and reached a hand down for Tvrdik, as they had done so many times before. She waited for his accustomed comments on the discomforts of dragonflight, but they never came. Tvrdik spent the trip staring at nothing in particular, preoccupied with his own private musings.

Supper late that afternoon was an occasion of great celebration. Verger, Bargarelle, and Corbin Maygrew were all overwhelmed to be once again in the presence of their old friend. Lord Maygrew shook the proffered hand, an expression of wonder on his face, and murmured, "I never thought I would live to see the day I could do this again, old friend." And then, he pulled the wizard into a bear hug, each thumping the other on the back. The food seemed more delicious and plentiful than usual. There was wine, and laughter, and some tears. Stewart, on the road to recovery from his battle injuries, was introduced to Xaarus as a hero.

"Wait, don't tell me!" Xaarus exclaimed, "Why, you are far too young to be my old, dear companion, Angus."

"Angus was my grandfather, sir, the gods give 'im peace. He spoke o' ye with such high regard, all of my young life, that I had no choice but to resolve never to bond with anyone but a true wizard. Thank the stars, the fates obliged me. When young master Tvrdik came along, why, we just seemed to hit it off. I've lived with him more than not ever since." The dog leaned in toward Xaarus with a conspiratorial tone, "To be frank, sir, the boy needs a bit o' lookin' after." And he winked at Tvrdik, who smiled that wan smile once again, as if he got the joke, but simply could no longer find anything in life amusing.

"Well," replied Xaarus, "he is lucky indeed to have found a protector and companion from such a bloodline as yours. Angus was a faithful friend to me and a wise companion for many years. I missed him sorely while I was...when I was ...away."

"And he missed ye as well, sir, and held out hope o' yer return, until the day he died. He would be so proud to know that I am here for our family, to welcome ye back, in his stead."

"Proud indeed, and with good reason. Good man." Xaarus gave Stewart's forehead an affectionate scratch.

There were plenty of reminiscences, and shocking, naughty stories about times gone by. And, of course, the stories of the recent battle had to be told in great detail, with only a little appropriate exaggeration. Xaarus was a rapt audience. Then, for the benefit of those who had been left behind that morning at Theriole, the tale of that day's dramatic rescue had to be rehearsed, which also generated huge excitement all around the table.

"I suppose I should begin work right away on the "Ballad of Brave Tvrdik, Bold Danoral, and the Dragons Eleven!" laughed Mark, and Xaarus cried, in mock indignation, "Master bard, do you mean to say that *my* name won't figure in the title? I should think I was at least some small part of the story..."

"Suit yourself," Mark teased, "I shall try to work you in, but you realize 'Xaarus' is a very difficult rhyme."

Loud laughter ensued, and Jorelial Rey picked up the thread of the conversation, "You know, Xaarus, I had grave reservations about the dragons' plan to bring you back here. I wasn't sure that it would work, and I didn't think I wanted to risk the well-being of the only other wizard we had. But Tvrdik insisted. He wouldn't take no for an answer, no matter what the risk to himself. He wanted nothing so much as to get you home."

"There, my boy, Tvrdik." Xaarus acknowledged, "Man of the hour. It seems I owe my return to you, and I am grateful beyond words to be here, lad. You've no idea. This whole dinner should be in your honor, son. Everyone, I give you my champion, Tvrdik."

Those at the table rose, raised glasses, and repeated, "To Tvrdik." Tvrdik, still seated, had a sort of pained look on his face, as though he had no idea what the proper response to such silliness could be.

Xaarus tried again, "Well, what say you, my brilliant, brave protégé?"

"He's shy." Delphine shouted, sensing disaster, and trying to help, "Shy, and very modest."

Tvrdik rose to his feet. "Please, everyone, sit down and enjoy the party," he told them. They did, and finding himself still standing, he spoke, at last, in a quiet, calm voice, that was nevertheless firm and clear.

"I only want to say that there is no one who rejoices more at Xaarus' safe return than I. His absence over these last years was a great loss, both to me, and to the entire court and kingdom of Eneri Clare. That I could play some part in his rescue is a source of great happiness to me. And I toast," he raised his glass at last, "to many wonderful years ahead of his wise counsel and compassionate shepherding, as he returns to his rightful post as Court Wizard." Again, Tvrdik raised his glass, and the others followed suit, shouting, "Hear, hear! To Xaarus."

Then, still on his feet, Tvrdik put down his glass and looked straight at the older wizard. In a more intimate tone, he said, "Welcome home, dear master. We have been working to refurbish your old Cottage, and are almost finished with the repairs and renovations. We have kept your library and laboratory exactly as you left it. All is prepared and awaiting your return. If you could just indulge me with a few days to assemble my few possessions and clear out, I'll be on my way."

Mrs. Praeger gasped, and Delphine cried out in dismay, "On your way? But, where? Where are you going?"

Tvrdik shrugged, "Why, back to my own little stone house in the ancient forest, of course. It's been sitting empty for too long. Anyway, it's high time I took Ondine back to her waterfall. I promised her. I confess it will be lovely to see that waterfall once again. You must all come and visit, and take a look some time." He turned his gaze to Jorelial Rey, and smiled his old, familiar, crooked smile, "I even have my own deed to the property, now, thanks to the generosity of our Lady Regent." He made a little bow.

Corbin Maygrew cut in, "But, I don't understand, mage. Things are falling into place here for the first time in years. We have peace and prosperity, and you are much revered for your accomplishments."

Tvrdik responded, his voice even, "My work is done. I was sent here by Xaarus to tackle a special mission. With all of your participation, and with fortune behind us, we have done all we set out to do. Lord Drogue is no longer a threat, Darian sits secure on his rightful throne, well represented by a brilliant and competent regent and a fine council of advisors. We have shifted the timeline and the very quality of life in the future, and we have brought our beloved Master Xaarus home. There is nothing else left for me to do here, so I should take my leave and go home."

Everyone at the table was so shocked by the young mage's surprise announcement that for a moment, they all sat staring at him, unable to summon words, brows furrowed, forks frozen in mid-transport…

"Nooo!" This forceful exclamation came from Jorelial Rey, who, despite how slight she was in frame, stared at him with fire in her eye. "This is no time for you to abandon me. Us. I-I mean - your kingdom has need of you. If you would rather not stay at The Cottage, you can live at Theriole, or in town if you like, or even build yourself a whole new house. But there is no reason for you to go back to being a hermit in the ancient forest."

Tvrdik's voice stayed level, betraying no emotion, "I beg your pardon, my Lady Regent, but I have promised at least to take Ondine home, and I mean to keep my word. I owe her that much. I believe we all do. Besides," and here he sat down and ran his fingers through his pale golden hair,

"Besides, this entire adventure has been...well...rather overwhelming for a hermit like me. Now that the danger is past, I could do with a little peace and quiet for awhile."

Xaarus, who sat beside him at the table, put a hand on the young mage's shoulder, "Son, I've had a very long time to think this over, and I was going to speak to you – all of you – about the matter in any case. I suppose now is as good a time as any..." All ears were on the older wizard, as he cleared his throat, "Tvrdik, I am more proud of you than I could ever express in words. You have proven yourself a fine and capable wizard a thousand times over. Yes, you have managed to accomplish every task that I sent you here to do, and more. But, you know, the doings of a palace, and a kingdom, are a young man's work. I am very old, and weary. All of this knocking around between times has taken a great toll on me. I had thought, if I were ever fortunate enough to get home alive, I would spend the rest of my years in research and contemplation. I don't think I am up to much else, despite your confidence in me, and your kind offer to reinstate me, my Lady Regent. I can't think of any more perfect spot for that sort of quiet life than your little house in the woods, son. It is a beautiful, unspoiled place, and you did a wonderful job of making your own little corner comfortable enough. I quite understand how you could call it home for twelve years. With a few minor improvements, I think I could be quite happy there. As for my Cottage, I'm afraid it is filled with sad memories for me now. I give it to you, with my blessing. Perhaps you can rechristen it with happy ones, eh? Tvrdik, will you take your rightful place here, as Court Wizard, and allow an old man to retire in peace in the ancient wood?"

Tvrdik wrung his hands in confusion. This was unexpected. He swallowed hard, "Master, you know I could never deny you anything you asked of me, but it is you who are Wizard to the Crown. You are needed – your place is here. Everyone is expecting it."

"That may have been so, once, my dear boy. But now, it is high time I passed the baton on to a worthy successor. I will always be near if you need assistance." He clapped his protégé on the back, but the younger man still seemed uncertain, casting about desperately for another approach, another well-seasoned argument.

"Well, then, stay here and start another school. Surely you will not abandon the search for promising candidates?"

"You have a point there, but I was speaking with young Mark here, and his bride, earlier, and I believe they have some interesting plans for you if any potential students of magic do turn up. I think we can leave the school in their capable hands." The young couple smiled, and exchanged an ecstatic look, confirming Xaarus' assertion.

Tvrdik stood again, his eyes darting about in near panic, a little like a cornered mouse, his mouth opening and closing, but no words coming out – no more arguments he could think of to put forth. At this point, Jorelial Rey had heard enough debate. She stood up with an air of determination, stepped forward, took Tvrdik by the arm, pulled him aside, and addressed her guests, "Will you excuse us, everyone, for a few moments? We need to have a little private chat. Perhaps I can make him an offer he can't refuse. Please make yourselves comfortable and have some dessert. I expect we won't be long." At that, she near dragged the hapless mage out of the room and into the gathering twilight, through an archway and around a corner into a deserted area of the palace courtyard. In fact, it was the very alcove where, not so very long ago, a ragged, bespectacled stranger had waited for hours for his first audience with the Lady Regent. Checking that they were alone, she pulled him around to face her, and with hands on hips, and eyes ablaze, she gave him a fair piece of her mind.

"What in heaven's name are you thinking? I have been very patient with you, since I thought you needed time to recover. But first you sulk all day, and then this…this announcement, so unexpected, and so insane! You can't leave, just like that. 'Oh, we're done now…I guess I'll go back to the woods…' How am I supposed to keep everything running here all by myself? You know I never wanted this job, but now I am stuck with it for life, and you know I can't do it alone."

Tvrdik, stunned, confused, and backed up against the wall, adjusted his glasses on his face, "I…I thought this is what you said you wanted. And, anyway, you aren't alone. You have Tashroth, and Mark and Delphine, and Bargarelle, and Warlowe and all the rest. You are a natural born leader. You'll do just fine."

"Dragonsbreath!" she shouted, "We were supposed to be a team, remember? You have the ideas, and I make them happen, wasn't that it?

What happened to that, eh? It isn't fair for you to show up here and stir everything up, and then, just like that, out of the blue, up and disappear again."

"I'm sorry, but I…I…simply cannot stay here any longer. Please, *please*, just let me go…" It was a desperate plea now from somewhere deep within his being.

Jorelial Rey heard it, stopped in her tracks, hung her head and shook it slowly in disbelief. Then she raised it and looked him straight in the bespectacled eye. Crossing the distance between them so that she was standing closer than was comfortable, she lowered her voice to something more intimate, "Tvrdik, can you think of *no* other reason to stay on here, at Theriole?"

He stood there stone still, speechless, gazing down at her proud, upturned face. For a moment, another face appeared before his eyes, a beautiful face from the past, golden hair blowing about in the gentle evening breeze. Perfect features, porcelain skin, lovely blue eyes regarding him, now seeming shallow and dangerous. The sound of far-off laughter like little tuned bells fell on his ear from a time long past, but now rang somehow cold and hollow, even cruel. The vision faded, and in its place was another face, an achingly familiar face – sun-browned skin and a crooked smile, dark arched brows, one raised higher than the other in a sharp question. And, under those brows, the deep brown eyes, brimming over with intelligence and warmth, staring at him, but looking into his soul as if they knew everything they would find there, and embraced it all…real eyes, eyes that spoke volumes, and at this moment seemed to be searching, pleading for something….

And then, in one of those eyes, a single tear eased its way from the corner and began a slow journey down the cheek. Before he even knew what he was doing, Tvrdik had raised a trembling hand, and was tracing with a delicate finger the line of dark hair where it framed that face. His hand was caressing the damp cheek – such a gentle caress, a feather's brush of a touch. And then he was leaning down to kiss away the tear. Somehow his lips moved sideways to find her mouth, her lovely mouth raised to meet his. Eyes closed, he kissed her long, with tenderness and passion.

Tvrdik straightened up in horror, trying to back away, but there was nowhere left for him to go. "Oh gods…" he stammered, "I…I'm so sorry.

I never meant to…I had no right to…" He was pacing, hands fidgeting in abject mortification. But she was laughing now, tears pouring down her face.

"Oh, Tvrdik, you ridiculous man! Why in heaven's name did you wait so long?"

"What?" he froze, fixing her with an incredulous stare, "Why, you are the Lady Jorelial Rey, the most powerful individual in all of Eneri Clare. You are responsible for the entire kingdom. There is no possibility you could ever see *me* as…I mean…we could never…there could *never* be anything…"

"Stop talking," she commanded, stepped to him, took his face in her hands and kissed him on the mouth. When she pulled away, and smiled up at him, he drew her close and circled her slim frame with his long arms, her head resting just on his heart. He leaned his face down to kiss the top of her head, breathing in the sweet scent of lavender and vanilla, like an elixir, and for the first time in his life, he felt every corner of his being release its tension, uncoil. Every old burden, wound or stress, every fear, doubt, and sadness was melting and falling away like so much sand pouring out of an hourglass. All he knew at that moment was the warmth of that embrace, the bliss of being wanted, the joy of dreams fulfilled. He had at last found his way home.

"Bless you, heavens, but what did I ever do to deserve this?" he breathed. "Jorelial Rey, I think I have been in love with you from the first moment I saw you, but I dared not even admit it to myself. Can you understand, that's why I was so desperate to go away – after all we have been through together, I couldn't bear to spend even one more day so close to you, without being able to hold you like this."

He was stroking her hair with such tenderness it renewed her weeping. She whispered, "How could you believe I would ever want to go back to the lonely existence I lived before you came along? I couldn't have gone on without you." Tears fell from his eyes now, too, onto her hair, and he smoothed them away with his hand. She spoke again, "Aren't you wizards supposed to be able to see beneath the surface of things, to read people's thoughts? How could you not know?"

"I guess there are certain things to which we are deaf and blind. And you keep your secrets pretty well guarded, my lady."

She was looking up at him again, "Oh, Tvrdik, how could I ever keep secrets from you? Who knows me as well as you do? Who just allows me to be myself? Nobody makes me laugh like you do, or makes me feel like who I am, is sufficient!"

"You are so much more than sufficient, dear heart, you are magnificent."

"And you wonder why I like having you around."

His grip tightened for a moment, "Will it be all right? I mean, will anyone object?"

"Not that it would matter to me, anyway, but remember I am not of royal blood, and you, my dear, are a person of some fame and distinction now, whether you believe it or not. It will be more than all right. But, I am still regent, and my responsibilities are here. Will you stay, my magical friend, and help me to rule well?"

"Winged horses could not drag me away from you, now that I know you love me. You *do* love me, don't you?" He pulled back a little to look at her face.

"Stop talking," she said again, and kissed him. Then, "You do realize you'll have to share me with a dragon?"

"I have already had the worst of this dragon, and, you will notice, it did not chase me away. I almost think that Tashroth might approve, the crafty old worm."

"I wouldn't call him that to his face."

"I meant it with the utmost respect and affection," he covered, "but, I am afraid, I, too, have a confession." One of her eyebrows arched. He went on, "I think Ondine might have a bit of a crush on me."

Rel laughed out loud, "Well, someone has a rather high opinion of himself, doesn't he now."

He tightened his arms about her, "Tonight, my love, I feel like I could take on anything."

And then, in a grave voice, and with a slight furrow of her brow, she asked, "What about Ailianne?"

"Who?" was his response, just before kissing all her worries away.

Just around the corner, several pairs of eyes were spying on the couple. Delphine giggled, "Look, Mark, his spectacles are all fogged up."

"Delphy, that's terrible. Hush! They'll hear us."

"I can't help it. It's so perfect. I *knew* Tvrdik was lucky for us the moment I met him."

Mrs. Praeger sniffled, a hanky in one hand, dabbing at her eyes. Her husband patted her on the back, in an awkward comforting gesture, "There, there, Maihre. It'll be alright..."

"I can't help meself, I'm that happy for the pale, bony boy!"

Bargarelle was wiping his eyes with his sleeve as well, with Minister Verger's arm around his shoulders. Warlowe joined them, a broad smile on his face, while Corbin Maygrew stood with his hands on his hips. "Well, I'll be..." he chuckled, not knowing exactly how to finish the sentence. Andrus scratched his head, and looked down in embarrassment.

"I was so hoping this would happen," Xaarus murmured, grinning ear to ear. "After all, I *did* foresee it, but you never can tell with people. Free will, you know, and they can be so dense, so stubborn. Well, what do you say, Stewart? You could come out to the woods with me and pick up right where your grandsire left off?"

"A great honor, sir, for ye to ask, but if it's all the same to ye, I think I have already found *my* wizard. I have a cousin, though, who might be quite interested in a position, if ye're offerin'. And I also know a very clever turtle, one of us talkers, by the name of Philip ..."

A strange sound drifted down into the courtyard from high above on the north tower. Tvrdik and Rel looked up, along with everyone else, to see a white dragon, close beside a green, peering down from atop the tower, silhouetted in stark relief against the flaming sky of sunset. Again, the strange, dragonish sound trickled down and tickled all of their ears. It was a sound not unlike laughter.

CPSIA information can be obtained
at www.ICGtesting.com
Printed in the USA
LVOW11*1429220217
525090LV00006B/60/P